What you don't know can get you killed.

Construction company owner Scott Holland doesn't go looking for trouble, but he's just stumbled on plenty. The rundown mill he's bought is plagued with mysterious incidents, and his investment partner, heiress Heather Silva, is as stubborn as she is intriguing. Dumped by his ex because of his blue-collar job, Scott is wary of Heather's privileged background. Yet he's drawn to her independence and strength, especially as the "accidents" grow more terrifying.

Determined to succeed without anyone's help—especially her wealthy parents—Heather clashes with Scott again and again. But a grisly discovery in the basement makes them both targets. Someone wants Heather and Scott silenced for good. And as a killer closes in, the only option is to trust each other—or become the next victims…

Visit us at www.kensingtonbooks.com

Books by Kari Lemor

Love On the Line
Wild Card Undercover
Running Target
Fatal Evidence

Published by Kensington Publishing Corporation

Fatal Evidence

Love On the Line

Kari Lemor

LYRICAL PRESS
Kensington Publishing Corp.
www.kensingtonbooks.com

Lyrical Press books are published by
Kensington Publishing Corp. 119 West 40th Street New York, NY 10018

All Kensington titles, imprints, and distributed lines are available at special quantity discounts for bulk purchases for sales promotion, premiums, fund-raising, and educational or institutional use.

To the extent that the image or images on the cover of this book depict a person or persons, such person or persons are merely models, and are not intended to portray any character or characters featured in the book.

Special book excerpts or customized printings can also be created to fit specific needs. For details, write or phone the office of the Kensington Special Sales Manager:
Kensington Publishing Corp.
119 West 40th Street
New York, NY 10018
Attn. Special Sales Department. Phone: 1-800-221-2647.

First Electronic Edition: December 2017
eISBN-13: 978-1-5161-0074-3
eISBN-10: 1-5161-0074-3

First Print Edition: December 2017
ISBN-13: 978-1-5161-0077-4
ISBN-10: 1-5161-0077-8

Printed in the United States of America

To Cheride and Owl, who first talked me into putting words on the page.

Acknowledgments

As always, thanks to my husband and children for supporting me and encouraging this dream. To Kris and Em, for your constant devotion and friendship. You are always there for me to brainstorm and provide support whenever I need it. To the Fab Five, for everlasting motivation and honest feedback. To Martin, for believing in me and taking a chance on my books. To Amanda, who makes my words shine. To Tom, for all the inside information on police procedure and the ideas to make my characters suffer more. For Paul and the verbal glimpse inside a county jail. And, of course, to my most prized possession, my invaluable CP, MA Grant, who has never let me down when I needed guidance, critique, or just a kick in the pants. Thank you, dear friend. I still don't know what you get from this relationship but I'm glad you're still here.

Chapter 1

"What the hell is she doing here?" Scott Holland muttered as his gaze took in the stunning brunette sauntering across the Connecticut Auction House like she owned the place. Considering her daddy's money, maybe she did.

"Hey, isn't that the heiress to that fancy clothes fortune?" Pete, another contractor here for the auction, was looking for cheap houses to flip. Not him. Scott had his eye on a nice mill building he could renovate into condos and sell for big money.

"Her name's Heather Silva. Her father owns Silvaggio's."

"Yeah, that's it. I've seen her picture in the paper. She looks damn good in those fancy clothes."

Eyeing her slim skirt and fashionable blouse, Scott agreed, but in his opinion, she looked even better without them. Not that he'd share that information with Pete. It had been one night, but the memory still played through his mind of her long, slender limbs tangled with his as he explored all her lush curves and secrets. Why was she here? She sold real estate. She didn't buy it. Representing a client maybe.

Pushing back a strand of caramel-colored hair that had escaped from the twisted bun at her nape, she scanned the room, freezing when she saw him. He lifted an eyebrow then grinned before she could turn away. *Nope, not today, princess. Your snub isn't going to work this time.*

"Think I'll go say hi," he told Pete and pushed away from the wall he'd been holding up.

"How do you know her?" Pete's eyes widened. "She doesn't exactly run in your circles."

"No, but her best friend is married to my cousin Jack. We've known each other for years."

Years that they'd pretended to be together so he could keep an eye on Callie and her son, Jonathan, while Jack was on the run. But Victor Cabrini, the mob boss who'd put a hit out on Jack, was now dead. He couldn't hurt them anymore. There was no reason for Scott and Heather to pretend any longer. They still saw each other because of Jack and Callie, but she'd been avoiding him lately. She must have been slumming it the night they'd been together.

But, hey, sex was sex. He sure wouldn't complain about having that time with her. As he strolled up from behind, her floral perfume filled his nostrils causing more memories to stir, and he had to tamp down his desires. *Yeah, keep convincing yourself it was only sex and that it didn't affect you in any way.*

"Princess, this is a little far from the castle, isn't it?"

Her lips twisted at his gibe but then the two of them had always been a little heavy on the sarcasm. It was part of their pretense for several years.

"Scott." Her prim tone wafted toward him and a hint of a smile found its way to her pretty face. "I didn't expect to see you here."

"It's not like we chat on a regular basis anymore, so no, you wouldn't."

"Are you in the market to buy? Don't people usually hire Holland Construction to work for them?"

"Typically, but I know a good deal when I see one. There's an old mill I want to purchase and renovate."

"A mill?" Her eyes narrowed. "Please tell me it's not the one on Prescott Street in Menatuck by the river?"

Shit. What was her interest?

She trailed a finger down the list of buildings for auction and her tight smile disappeared. "There's only one mill building on the block today."

"And I plan to get it," Scott said, pissed at the thought she might also be bidding. Heather was tenacious when she wanted something. Of course, she'd grown up with a silver spoon in her mouth.

Crossing her arms over her nicely endowed chest, she raised one eyebrow at him. "Can you really afford it?"

He focused his eyes on her face to avoid the memories of her body and what he'd done to it. "Don't think you can scare me off. I want that building."

"So do I. And I'm guessing I might have more funding than you."

She might be right, but no way in hell would he admit it to her. He'd fight her tooth and nail until the end.

"What could you possibly want with an old run-down mill building?"

She cocked her head. "Maybe the same thing you do. To renovate it into something better. That neighborhood hasn't been great in the past, but a few blocks over they totally rejuvenated some of the old buildings and this one has perfect placement."

"Isn't your office in Waterbury?"

"Yes, and it's only a half hour from the building. Not a long drive."

"You're a real estate agent, not a contractor. What do you know about renovating buildings?"

A tinge of doubt entered Heather's eyes and Scott pounced on it. This woman was too freaking confident in most areas.

"You have no experience with structures like this and what they need. Take my word, this won't be the cake-walk you think it is. I've been inside. The work is extensive. Leave this to the people who know what they're doing. If you're real nice to me, maybe I'll list the property with you when I finish with it."

"What are your plans? You've been redoing mostly college dorms and office buildings lately."

Scott slid his hands into his front pockets trying to move away from her tantalizing scent. It was playing havoc with his thought process. "Which still makes me more qualified than you to take on the renovation. I plan to make it into high-end condos."

"That's great, but not the most feasible plan for the area." Shuffling the file in her hands, she peeked inside then shut it again. "Be nice to *me* and maybe I'll contract your company to do the renovations into upscale shops and offices."

Conversation halted in the room as several people stepped up on the podium to begin the auction. When Heather moved to sit in a row near the back, he followed, dropping into a chair next to her. Not the smartest thing if he wanted to focus on the proceedings. His common sense always took a hit when she was near.

"It's not exactly the typical location for Silvaggio's."

Narrowing her eyes, she frowned then faced front and whispered, "I don't plan to put a Silvaggio's in there. That's my father's company, not mine."

The buzzing up front grew louder and Scott moved his focus to the auctioneer. There were several buildings on the auction block today. He didn't want to lose out on his chosen one because he wasn't paying attention.

Heather pushed her shoulders back, ignoring him as the first property was described. He took the opportunity to glance at her peripherally. The updo left her long, slender neck exposed. Imagining his lips skimming along the soft skin was not helping his case. The fact he knew exactly how sweet she tasted, remembered that long hair, loose and tickling his chest, almost made him walk away and let her have the building.

But he wouldn't give in to some spoiled, pampered princess no matter how hot the sex had been. Besides, that night with Heather had been three months ago. He'd put himself out there but no response. When he'd called several times and they'd seen each other at Jack and Callie's wedding and a few other occasions, she'd always brushed him off. Was his blue-collar status that much of a turn off?

"Is Daddy giving you the money to buy this?"

She glared at him but remained silent. He couldn't help but throw that at her. Being the daughter of the man who owned the Silvaggio's empire, Heather probably had some big cash behind her. Must be nice having easy access to that kind of money.

Even though his business was debt-free, it had been a lot of work to convince the bank to loan him the money for his new project. They were taking a risk on him. He'd never tried something like this before. Every project he'd done in the past had been paid for as he went along by whomever he was renovating for. It would take some work as the building hadn't been updated in ages, but he was willing to put in the time and effort. Once it was done, he could turn a tidy profit selling each unit for a hefty fee.

Heather straightened in her chair so Scott snapped to attention. They were starting bids on the mill building. The auctioneer called out an opening bid and it climbed higher much faster than Scott had wanted. Several hands flew up and down. Shit. He'd hoped there weren't too many bidders.

Sitting up straighter, Heather flipped through the papers she had in her lap. More bids were called out and Scott waited. He didn't want to tip them off that he also wanted the property. He'd slip in when they got to final bids.

"Damn, this is higher than I thought." She shifted in her seat and glanced at him. "Why aren't you bidding? I thought you wanted this building."

He clenched his teeth. "I do. I thought it would go for lower than this also. You aren't bidding yet either."

Her mouth turned down at the corners as another bid shot the price up again. Her fingers tapped nervously against the file she held.

"What's the matter? Daddy give you a limit on this? His pockets aren't deep enough for his little girl's whims?"

"Shut up. My father isn't giving me any money. He doesn't even know my plans. It's *my* project and *my* financing."

"You got some banker on a string then? What do you have to do for him?"

The look she threw at him should have left him in ashes.

"Heather, I—"

"Screw you."

His mouth turned into an automatic smirk. "You already did. Must not have been satisfying since it wasn't repeated."

* * * *

Heather's head snapped up at Scott's words. Not satisfying. Hardly what she would have called their one night stand. Too satisfying if she was being honest. So much so that she'd avoided the man if she could. The emotions that had filled her when they'd had sex had been too intense, too needy. She didn't ever want to need someone that badly. Her independence was the most important thing she had.

She ignored what he'd said and focused on the bidding going on in the front of the room. This project would make her father finally see that she could make it on her own, and didn't need the family money. Okay, most of the money for the building was from the trust fund her maternal grandmother set up for her, but she would be the one to arrange for renovations and turn the old mill into something amazing.

"Shit," Scott swore under his breath and his face tightened even more. Anxiety was zapping through her too. This was the only building that was situated in that urban renewal neighborhood. It was almost out of her range. Sounded like it was out of Scott's too.

The price rose again and disappointment flooded her. She couldn't go any higher. Not without some other funding. Where was Scott getting his money? His construction company did well, but she knew he wasn't pulling in millions. Too bad they couldn't pool their money.

Pool their money? What the hell. No, that would be crazy. He purposefully egged her on. Taunted her every chance he had. She'd strangle him before they got any of the renovations done. As he shifted, she got a whiff of that manly scent he always exuded. When did the smell of sawdust become an aphrodisiac? *Maybe when you let the man go down on you and he sent you into the stratosphere?* She had to stop her mind from going back there.

His shoulders rose then fell and he clenched his jaw. Was he getting ready to leave? Give up? There had to be a way for them to get this building. She must be crazy to consider working with him.

They *had* managed to get along the last few years when they'd been helping Callie and Jack. But the excuse for them to be together was married, living in suburbia. Could they work with each other now? It would be business, plain and simple.

The price went up and the auctioneer started toward the final countdown. Damn, and double damn. She needed this building, this project. When Scott made to stand, she grabbed his arm pushing him back down.

"What if we went in together? We pool our money and outbid the others?"

His eyebrows went up and he scowled. "You and I work together?"

"We did it for two years. We can do it if we really want this."

"I do want this, but a whole building of offices and stores won't make us as much profit."

If they rented them, in the long run they might. She needed the stores there. It was part of her plan.

"Going once." The voice of the auctioneer rang out like a death knell in her head.

Compromise. You'll both lose if you don't. "Stores on the ground floor, offices on the second. Condos on the third and fourth. Deal?"

Scott paused and Heather wanted to slug him. Now wasn't the time to debate. Opening her file, she showed him her bottom line.

"Going twice."

His eyes flicked back and forth between her and the auctioneer.

She shook his arm. "We can do this. It's the only way we both get what we want."

Throwing his left arm over her shoulder, he raised his right and called out a price above what the others had bid. The auctioneer looked at the men who had been bidding and they both shook their heads.

"Sold to Holland Construction. Please see the clerk outside for details."

"We did it!" Her excitement bubbled over and she jumped up, pulling him along behind her to exit the room.

Her heart raced as she thought about the project. Once they were in the hallway Scott turned and she slipped right into his arms. He'd done this with her.

Leaning into him she pressed her lips to his. He stiffened for a second then his hands slid up her back. Pulled close to his chest, she could feel his heart beating. Fast like hers. The kiss deepened and the memories of touching him this way surfaced and swarmed over her like cicadas. *Too intense.*

Easing away, she looked up. His eyes devoured her like the night they'd had sex. *Shit.* Had she just made the biggest mistake of her life?

Chapter 2

"Thank you," she said as she eased from his grasp.

The crooked smile that always made her stomach twist appeared on his face.

"For the kiss, no problem. Any time. Day or night."

His voice deepened with the word *night*. No, she couldn't go there. Independent. Her goal was to be totally independent. No construction site Romeo could sway her from her mission.

"I mean for the bid and agreeing to work with me."

"Yeah, about that…it would have been nice if we'd had time to discuss it first."

"Did you want me to tell the auctioneer to sit back and wait while we formed a committee, outlined a plan, then got things notarized?"

His chest went in and out with a deep breath. The snug cotton of his shirt clung to it, mesmerizing her.

"You're a Silva. He might have done it for you."

Like a splash of cold water, reality returned. Scott had a stick up his ass about rich people, and hated that she came from a wealthy family. He never missed an opportunity to remind her.

A few more people exited the auction room and they stepped aside to let them pass.

"They might do it for my dad but not for me."

His expression showed his doubt. He reached into his suit coat pocket and pulled out an envelope with a local bank name on it.

"How did you want to go about paying for this? I've got a letter from the bank with the amount I'm pre-approved for. But it's less than what we bid."

"I planned to pay cash."

His eyes rolled up. "Of course you did."

God, he drove her crazy. *Suck it up, sweetheart, you just made a deal with the devil.* Too bad she remembered the heaven it was to be in his arms.

"It's trust fund money I got when I turned twenty-five from my mom's mother. It's been sitting in a bank for two years earning interest. She had faith that I could use it to help my career. That's what I plan to do. With this building renovation."

"What were your thoughts regarding money when you had this collaboration idea?"

She wanted the building and hadn't thought beyond that. Okay, perhaps she'd thought about his lips, how they'd felt skimming along her stomach and lower. Damn, she needed to stop with the memory lane trip. Business. They were here for business.

"It was a split second decision. I didn't have time to calculate percentages and margins."

He raised one eyebrow. "Then may I make a suggestion?"

"By all means." It better not be a sexual one. She might throw away her pride and goals and jump him right here.

"I suggest we use my loan plus your extra to pay for the building. Then we can use the rest of yours for supplies. They won't be cheap. It'll be easier and quicker to pay cash for them than to go through the bank for the funding."

It sounded reasonable. Or was this something that might benefit him more? Nothing jumped out at her, so she nodded her agreement.

They moved to the payment desk and sifted through the pages of documents they needed to finalize the purchase. After the last 'I' was dotted and 'T' was crossed, and both their signatures graced the papers, she let out a sigh. The building was hers. Well, hers and Scott's. Not exactly what she'd planned, but he was an easygoing guy, when he wasn't ragging on her for being rich. They could do this. She hoped.

Throwing his arm around her shoulder, he whispered, "I think this calls for a celebration drink. My treat."

* * * *

What the hell was he thinking suggesting a drink with Xena, Warrior Princess? It was bad enough she'd talked him into a partnership of sorts. She'd want to take over and run the whole show. They probably should bang out a few details regarding their deal. He'd have to call his Army buddy, Drew, to draw up a legal document. Andrew Thayer worked for the Connecticut DA's office, but he helped out his friends with legal stuff when it was needed.

Heather glanced at her gold diamond-studded watch. "It's only three o'clock and you want a drink?"

"It's five o'clock somewhere, and we should talk about this partnership before we go any further with the project."

"I guess. There's a little bistro a few blocks from here that I go to often. We can take my car."

Here she was, taking charge again. He'd need to watch that if he didn't want to get screwed by her. Well, financially. He sure hadn't minded the other screwing. It had been the highlight of the year. Although, technically, it had been the previous year. December. Sadly, it had been the best part of last year too.

"How about I follow you?" *Can't totally give in.*

"Fine," she huffed and turned on her fancy heels. Her hips swayed nicely as she walked away, the slim skirt hugging her form. Hurrying to catch up, he settled in his truck as she revved the engine of her black sports car. The one her daddy had bought her.

At the restaurant, she'd already spoken to the hostess and gotten them a large private booth. Her well-manicured fingers waved at him as he walked in. He slipped in and slid all the way around so he was sitting next to her.

"Are we expecting anyone else?"

She shook her head, sending a few wisps of hair floating around her neck as she scooted a couple inches away.

"Then why do we have a table that seats eight?"

She stared at him with an expression that said *don't question me.* He'd seen that look before on pampered women. "It's a slow time. No one's using it and I wanted some space to spread out."

She reached into her briefcase, pulled out a slim laptop and turned it on. "You're absolutely right that we need to set some ground rules for this project. We should get them written down."

"Ground rules sounds like we're playing a game. This isn't a game for me, princess. If you think it is, I should find the money to pay off your portion of the building."

Her eyes stared daggers at him. "Oh, no, you don't. I want this project as much as you do. Maybe even more."

She started typing and he shifted closer to see what was on the screen. "What, you don't trust me?"

"I just want to check your spelling."

"You're going to check my spelling?" Her eyes held disbelief.

"I do have a college degree."

Her perfectly arched eyebrow rose. In surprise? Snob.

"I do too, and my spelling is fine. Besides, I have spell-check."

When the waiter appeared, he ordered an appetizer and iced tea for both of them. Another surprised look floated his way.

"What? I didn't say it had to be an alcoholic drink. I need to keep my wits when I'm around you." This was true, but for a different reason than not trusting her. He didn't trust himself. A soft floral scent wafted off her hair as he bent closer, sending desire through him and straight to his groin.

"We need to make sure it's a fifty-fifty split for both money spent and profit." Her fingers flew over the keys.

"Agreed. My buddy, Drew, is a lawyer. I'll get him to draw up a document for us."

"The one I met at Jack and Callie's wedding? I'd prefer to have my lawyer do it."

"You don't trust my friends? I'll have you know Drew works for the district attorney's office."

She glanced up from what she was typing then lowered her eyes again. "Then he's probably too busy to help us. I pay my lawyer good money to focus on my needs, exclusively."

"What needs would those be?"

"Get your mind out of the gutter, Holland. Are there any suggestions you have to add to this agreement?"

"Well, if you go by how much we both currently put into it, I guess you could say I own a larger portion of the building."

Her face hardened and he ran his hand down the soft skin of her arm to calm her.

"How about we put your funds into a joint account that we both have access to?"

"You want me to give you access to all my money? Right. Not happening."

"Let me tell you how construction works. When I need supplies, I either have to fill out copious amounts of paperwork then wait for the bank to approve the request, or I pay for it myself and get reimbursed whenever they get around to looking through the forms."

"That won't happen if we use my money to pay for the supplies."

Why had he agreed to this partnership? Stupid mistake. Rich people didn't know how to compromise. "Sure, but I don't want to wait around until after you've gotten your hair and nails done. Delays cost time and money. I have to pay the sub-contractors whether they have the needed materials or not."

Oh, yeah, she had a retort on her lips all ready to zip by him. Taking a deep breath, she started typing again.

"Fine, but we use my bank for the account, and you have to run every purchase by me."

His jaw hardened. "Before I make them?"

"Simply send me a list of what you're buying as soon as you know you need it. Is that more palatable?"

"Sure. Once I get in and take a good look around, I'll know most of what I need. But sometimes things crop up that you aren't expecting."

The waiter appeared with their appetizer but Heather kept her eyes on the computer screen. She tapped a few more times with a flourish then closed the laptop.

"There. I sent you the details of the agreement. Look it over and let me know if there's anything that needs to be adjusted. I'll have my lawyer draw it up, then we can sign it."

Once she stored her computer back in her bag, she pulled the plate of nachos toward her and grabbed one oozing with cheese.

"What kind of shops were you planning on putting in there? Something that sells fancy women's shoes?"

"What do you know about fancy shoes?" Cheese dripped from her finger and Scott had the desire to suck the digit in his mouth and lick it off.

"I know enough."

"Says the man who wears work boots twenty-four seven."

"Hey, I wore dress shoes for Jack and Callie's wedding. And I know what I like in a woman's fancy shoe. The ones you have on right now make your legs look amazing."

Her cheeks turned pink as she shoved another nacho into her mouth. "Let's get back to business."

Opening the file she'd had earlier, she showed him the plans she'd made.

"I was thinking one large store for the central space, then half a dozen smaller ones surrounding it. I'd love to get a nice coffee or sandwich shop in there. Doing so could lure people over to the building, plus anyone working or living there would have a convenient place to eat."

Her ideas were sound and sensible, though he hated to admit it.

"What were you thinking for condos?"

Pulling out his phone, he scrolled through to the preliminary drawings.

"Did you do these?" Her eyebrow rose as she glanced at the pictures.

"Yes, I took a few drafting classes in college. What's wrong with them?"

"Nothing. They're quite good."

"Surprising, huh? Holland Construction was started by my dad and Jack's. My uncle ran it after my dad died. We both inherited the company, but Jack went straight to Quantico when he got his discharge so it fell to me to take over."

Sympathy lit her face, softening her features. "How old were you when your parents died? I know you were raised by Jack's mom and dad."

"I was five. Jack was seven."

"What happened?" Her expression was sincere. "If you want to tell me."

Taking a deep breath, he answered, "Drunk driver. Guy got away with killing my parents with no punishment at all."

"There are strict laws for that. How did he not get charged?"

Scott swallowed, still affected by the memory. "It was twenty-four years ago and the laws weren't as tough. Plus, he was loaded. I'm sure he paid off a few people."

"Not all rich people use their money to buy their way out of trouble."

"No, sometimes they use their money to try and influence people by giving them nice things."

Reaching for the last chip, her watch jingled against the plate. She looked at it, her expression guilty. Who'd given her that little gift and what had it cost her?

The conversation steered toward the renovations again and when the check came, Heather reached for it.

"Using your money to influence me."

Why did he love to tease her all the time?

Glancing at the bill, she tossed it in his direction. "Fine, then you pay. It was your idea to have a drink."

Gathering her bag, she scooted out of the booth as he threw some cash on the table. They exited together and he walked with her.

"I'm perfectly capable of getting to my car on my own."

"I'm trying to be a gentleman. Humor me. It doesn't happen that often."

Thrusting her hand out, she tilted her head. "We should shake on the deal. You want us to spit on it first? Isn't that a guy thing?"

No, spitting on her hand wasn't the first thing on his mind. Her soft skin caressed his rough skin and he pulled her closer.

"We can do better than that. The deal should be sealed with a kiss."

Slipping his hand into her hair, he cupped her face. Her eyes widened. "No, I think a shake is—"

Those eyes drifted closed when he touched his lips to hers. *Addictive.* Damn, he wanted more even though it would be bad for their new partnership.

His tongue skimmed across her lips but her hand pushed at his chest.

"This is a business deal, Scott. We need to keep it that way." Shit, she was right, but her breathing was as ragged as his. *I'm not the only one affected.*

A business deal. Yeah, he needed to keep reminding himself. That sassy mouth certainly wouldn't help. Every time it opened, he wanted to keep it from speaking...by covering it with his own.

Chapter 3

"What's the hold up? You wanted access to my money so you could get started. Why haven't you started?"

Heather placed her hands on her hips, staring at Scott's gorgeous ass in nicely fitting olive Carhartt's as they walked up the stairs inside the mill building. Stopping abruptly, he turned and she plowed into him, her face close to the waistband of those pants. Seeing where her eyes lingered he moved down a step and glared at her.

"Listen, Xena, this is why real estate agents shouldn't try to renovate buildings. Stick with selling them."

"Can we go up to the third floor before we debate our merits?" Staring at the snug gray T-shirt covering his broad chest wouldn't help keep her mind on business. "It might be too tempting to push me down the stairs."

His eyebrow rose as he glanced at the three-inch heels she wore. Okay, not the smartest footwear for construction work but he'd said they made her legs look amazing. Score one for vanity.

Sighing, he walked the rest of the way up and into the center of the large dilapidated space. Looking around her heart fell, fears of failure filling her mind. *No, you can do this. You only need Scott to start doing what he said he'd be doing.*

Straightening her shoulders, she cocked her head. "So, my question?"

His eyes roamed the room, his mind seemingly elsewhere. "There's this little issue of a building permit. You can't start doing any kind of renovations until it's been issued."

"You took the money out of the account for it. Why don't we have it yet?"

Moving closer, perhaps too close, he narrowed his eyes at her. "Did you research at all what's needed for a building renovation of this size?"

"Yes, I did." All right, she could have done more. "I was planning on hiring a contractor and figured they'd walk me through most of the red tape stuff."

Scott slipped his hands into his front pockets and rocked back on the heels of his steel-toed work boots. "Let me take you for a walk then. First, when you apply for the permit, you need to submit three sets of the plans by an architect or engineer."

"But you already had plans drawn up. You showed them to me weeks ago when we decided to do this."

"When *you* decided to do this and dragged me in with you."

"You were dragging yourself in. I only joined the fun."

His crooked smile drove her crazy and his blue eyes grew intense. "The plans I had aren't accurate anymore. Not since you wanted to put retail space on the first floor. The walls are all different, the front windows needed adjusting, plumbing, electric, you name it. Everything is different."

"Yes, I know. We sat together for almost a week getting the details right." And her vibrator had gotten a good workout each night they'd been together. Shit, the man got her lady parts singing.

"I needed to work with my architect, have him draft the official blueprints. It takes a while to draw up plans of this magnitude. I submitted the plans and the application two weeks ago. It can take up to thirty days for the permit to be issued."

Damn, that sounded familiar. Probably read it while she'd been researching the project. "Sorry, I'm just anxious to get these renovations going and finished."

"Did you need this completed by a specific date?"

Kind of. "Not really, but there is a fund-raiser in a few months where I thought I could entice investors or business owners. I can't very well get them interested if the building still looks like this." She waved her hand around the neglected room.

Scott's expression softened and he slung his arm over her shoulder. "It's going to be outstanding, you'll see. It'll take time though. You need to be patient."

Rolling her eyes, she pointed to the pile of rubble in the corner. "Okay, tell me all about the great transformation that will take place."

As they walked through the space, Scott highlighted where each condo would start, end, and how he envisioned the final product. It came to life as his excited voice described the woodwork, cabinetry, and fixtures.

"Let's go upstairs. The fourth floor condos will have cathedral ceilings and we may be able to put a few loft spaces in as well."

As they entered the stairwell, her heel stuck on a loose board and she stumbled. In barely a second, Scott had her in his arms, her feet off the floor.

"What are you doing?" she squealed as he trotted up the stairs, her arms around his neck for balance.

"You're going to kill yourself in these shoes. I'm merely protecting my investment."

He was also copping a feel on the side of her breast. Not that she'd complain. A girl had to get her thrills someplace. Scott Holland was definitely thrilling. The strong arms that held her were the result of years of hard labor. It was like she weighed nothing as his muscled legs jogged up the stairs. At the top floor he didn't put her down, simply gazed at the space.

His eyes lit up and a smile appeared on his face as he looked around. The dimple in his chin stood out against the stubble surrounding it. Too clearly she remembered how that stubble had left marks on her body everywhere it had touched. *Oh, God, stop mooning over the construction guy.* What was wrong with her that she got turned on by the smell of sawdust and manly soap?

"What do you have planned up here? Anything different?" Why the heck was her voice all breathy and soft? Where the hell was her rough exterior? The one that had made Scott start calling her Xena, Warrior Princess to begin with? Not that she'd ever tell him she secretly didn't hate the name. It wasn't great, but it was far better than what some of her other boyfriends had called her. Sugar Tush. Poochypoo, Scooter Pie.

Whoa! Boyfriend? No, he certainly was not her boyfriend or even anything close. *You did sleep with him.* Fine, they'd had sex. Un-freakin-believable sex, but that's all it was. It didn't mean anything, obviously, since they hadn't done it again. *And whose fault was that? He called you, texted a few times, and got blown off.*

Wiggling in his arms, she tried to get down. Get the voices in her head to stop arguing with her was more like it.

"Hold still," he scolded and pulled her tighter to his chest. "Now listen up while I give you the run down on the condos up here."

He walked around the space as if he wasn't carrying a full-grown woman in his arms. Damn impressive. The pectoral muscles beneath her hand weren't too shabby either. Continuing on with his description, he seemed to not even realize she was there. At the windows, he set her down and stood behind her looking out, pointing to certain landmarks in the small mill town that you could see from here.

He *had* been affected by carrying her. The erection digging into her back was evidence enough. Good to know. Not that she wanted anything to happen. They were business partners now. They had to be professional.

"Ready to go?" His gravelly voice sent goose pimples crawling across her arms, and she rubbed them.

"Cold? You should have worn a warmer coat. You've lived in New England all your life. You should know April can be chilly. Plus the heat hasn't been on in this building for years."

"I'm fine," she lied. The cold wasn't getting to her. It was him and his annoyingly sexy presence. She wouldn't tell him though.

"I'll make sure to let you know when the permit comes through. If I don't have it by next week, I'll call and check on it."

"Perfect, but remember I'm in on this too. If you need me to do anything, you only need to ask."

"I will." His sexy smile was back as he glanced up and down her body. "Ready for your ride down."

"You don't have to carry me. I'm fine walking."

"And killing yourself by falling down three flights of stairs. Then where does my funding for this project go?"

"You already have access. You don't need me."

"Stealing from a dead woman, though. That just seems...wrong."

The chuckle escaped before she could stop it. He seriously had a warped sense of humor at times. Moving closer, he placed his hand on her hip.

At her indignant look, he said, "You could always ride piggyback if you don't like me carrying you."

Scanning her slim skirt, she scoffed. "A piggyback ride? In this?"

"You could hike up the skirt then jump on."

"You'd like that, wouldn't you?"

His eyebrows went up and down. "Very much."

Closing her eyes, she sighed then held out her arms. "Fine, come get me, my prince. Rescue me from the dangerous crumbling castle."

Scott sidled closer then ran his hands down her hips. One hand continued down her leg until it slipped under. His other hand caressed her back then he scooped her up in his arms. She wrapped her arms around his neck and held on as he trotted back down three flights of stairs. At the bottom he didn't release her right away. And for some reason she didn't tell him to.

His eyes roamed over her from head to toe and lingered on those heels. Slowly, he allowed her feet to slide to the floor, her body rubbing against his hardness, sending fluttering sensations through her blood stream. As her shoes touched the ground, he leaned in close, his manly smell assaulting her nostrils. Inhaling the scent, she waited for his next words.

His breath drifted across her cheek. "Next time, you should think about wearing a sensible pair of shoes."

* * * *

"What are you doing here?"

Scott looked at Heather as she paused in the doorway of the municipal office. Her usual sexy business attire in place. Slim skirt, high heels, and today she had on a snug-fitting top that caressed her curves and dipped low in the front, allowing him a peek at her cleavage.

Raising one elegantly plucked eyebrow, she replied, "You said you still hadn't heard about the building permit so I decided to come check on it."

Shuffling the extra blueprints into one arm, he planted his hands on his hips. Here she was taking charge again without discussing it with him. "I told you because you wanted to be kept informed. But I also told you I'd be taking care of it. There's no reason for you to miss your weekly tennis game for menial labor."

Her eyes drilled holes in him.

"What? Not tennis today? The nails and hair look great so I figured it wasn't them." He stepped closer, right into her space then glanced down at her skirt. "Waxing."

"I don't..."

It was his turn for the raised eyebrow. He'd been downtown with her and she most certainly did. Had she forgotten what they'd done already? Her cheeks tinged a lovely shade of pink and she took a deep breath.

"Why don't we simply do this together and get it over with? The sooner we get the permit, the sooner the building renovations get started."

"After you." He swept his hand out to indicate she should go in first. He was a gentleman. And he liked to watch her sweet ass in the tight skirt sway from side to side. It was pure poetry.

The young man behind the counter looked up as they walked in and his face lit up. Yeah, Heather had a way of making people take notice. Maybe she could get further than he'd been able to. He'd already spent over an hour on the phone with someone, and they hadn't told him anything about what had happened to the permit application.

"Hi, I'm Heather Silva. My partner and I have been waiting on a building permit, but it seems to have gotten misplaced. Perhaps you could help us."

Scott pulled out his receipt then handed it over. "This is a copy of the application."

The man frowned. "That would have been sent to the Division of Building Codes. It's down a flight in the basement. Room Twenty-Seven. Is there anything else I can help you with?"

His expression said he hoped there was. But it was directed exclusively at Heather.

Moving forward, Scott leaned against the counter. "I talked to someone in that office earlier and they have no record of it ever being there. They said it might still be here."

"I sent everything we got to the appropriate offices. There's nothing here."

Heather leaned over the counter. "Room Twenty-Seven, you said?"

He merely nodded, his eyes slipping lower. Scott grabbed her elbow and muttered a "thanks" as they walked out the door.

"You didn't have to be rude," she said, pulling her arm out of his grasp and marching down the hallway. He whistled, heading in the other direction. Her heels clicked on the linoleum behind him.

At the top of the stairs, he turned and grinned. "Did you want a ride down these? They don't seem to be as rickety as the mill, but I certainly wouldn't want you to fall."

"I think I can manage." She held tight to the banister as she went down, though. He controlled his tongue. There was only so far he could push her. He knew his limit. For now.

They passed several empty offices and at Room Twenty-Seven, Heather gave a soft knock before she turned the knob. A thin man, approximately in his fifties, sat at one of the desks, his glasses resting low on his nose.

"Hi there." She went into action. "We're looking for someone who can help us with some blueprints sent here for a building permit."

The man waved around the room. "We're all about blueprints here. I'm Ted Farmer. What can I do for you?"

"Heather Silva." She extended her slender hand and shook Ted's. "This is my partner, Scott Holland. We sent some drawings here a few weeks ago with an application for a building permit. They seem to have disappeared."

"They'd be listed under Holland Construction," Scott informed him.

Ted scanned down a page in a large book sitting on his desk. He flipped the page and scanned some more. "Nothing with that name in the last month or so. When was the check cashed?"

"It wasn't. Not yet."

Ted's mouth twisted. "Then we must not have gotten them. The check usually gets cashed within a day or two. You sure they came to this office?"

Ted's eyes stayed on Heather, but Scott answered. "I delivered them upstairs myself."

Bending over, Heather placed her hands on the desk in front of Ted. "Do you think you could take a look for them? They might have gotten misplaced." Her voice was soft and sweet. Damn, she knew how to play.

"Sure." Ted took a few minutes sifting through the stacks of plans then turned back and sat down, his eyes on Heather once more. "Sorry. You'll probably need to fill out another application and resubmit the plans."

Pulling the plans from Scott's arms, she placed them on the desk and leaned over Ted. "Can't you put them in your system from down here? We'd greatly appreciate it."

"I really shouldn't."

"Please." Her whisper floated across the desk and Ted visibly swallowed, his eyes skimming her figure. "It's already been three weeks. I hate the thought of waiting another month to get it going."

Scott held back the snort that fought to come out.

"I guess I could, but I'd need the application filled out."

Keeping her body facing Ted, she twisted enough to hold out her hand for the form. Handing it over, Scott stepped back toward the door letting her do her thing. God, he'd never had to stoop so low to get something through. Not that he was doing any of the stooping.

"Here's a copy of the application and here are the plans. When do you think you could get to them? This project has already taken too long."

Her voice was still sugar-coated and Ted was buying every ounce of it. Looking around the desk and the overflowing table behind him, he placed the plans in the bin on his right.

"This is tomorrow's pile. That's the quickest I can get to them. Will that do?"

"Thank you so much for all your help." Reaching out, she patted his arm then stood. "I'll remember this, Ted."

Ted gave a little smile and stared until Heather exited the room. Scott moved back and started down the hall after her.

"Nice moves there."

She rounded on him, her eyes flaring. Looking around the hall, he pulled her into a deserted room and kicked at the door.

"I managed to get the job done." Her voice was low, dangerous.

"Maybe you would have gotten it done even faster if you flashed your tits at him. They're quite prominent and lovely today."

"What an ass."

"I suppose you could have flashed him that too, though he sure did like the view he had."

"Don't be crude. I was simply being nice." If her eyes could shoot flames he'd be cinders.

"You can be nice to *me*." Walking closer, he pressed her against the wall. "Then I'll do things faster."

Her breath hitched. "You're fast enough."

"Too fast? Is that why we haven't repeated the experience? I didn't take enough time with you?"

She avoided his eyes.

"I could have sworn you enjoyed it, but I'm not an expert on women, so what do I know?"

Her breathing increased and he pressed closer, sliding his hand down her hip to the edge of her skirt. The skin beneath his fingers was soft as silk as he skimmed his hand up her leg.

"I can go slower if that's what you want." Feathering his lips over her cheek, he whispered, "I can take all night pleasing you."

Her skirt had traveled up her legs. Had he done that? His hands on the outside of her thighs indicated he had. No complaints from her so far. Shit, he wanted to take her right here against the wall. Grinding his arousal against her, he ran his tongue over her ear.

When his hands reached the lace of her panties she shook her head and inhaled sharply.

"We're in business together. We shouldn't do this."

"Great reason for now, but what about before we formed this partnership? What's your excuse for that time?"

She only stared, her expression unreadable.

Stepping back, he dropped his hands. "I guess everyone's got to slum it once, huh? You tried the blue-collar thing and got it out of your system. Time to move on."

Turning away, she straightened her skirt then adjusted the neckline of her shirt. "Let's go."

Catching up to her on the stairs, he couldn't resist one last jab. "Your friend in there was certainly willing. If you gave him the sign, you could have checked municipal worker off your list too."

He chuckled when she didn't even glance over her shoulder.

Chapter 4

"I cannot believe he did that." Heather stormed through the back door into her best friend's kitchen. Callie sat wiping what looked like peanut butter from the hands of her son, Jonathan.

"Did what? Who?"

Heather took a deep breath and kissed the little boy's head. Moving away so she didn't frighten him, she mumbled, "And I simply stood there and let him. What the hell is wrong with me?"

Lifting the two-year-old down from his chair, Callie scooted him into the living room. "Play with your blocks before you have to take a nap. Make sure I can see you from here."

The dark-haired child, so like his father, shuffled through the archway and settled on the carpet with his toys. Callie cleaned up his lunch then put some water on to boil. "Tea?"

Nodding, Heather sat at the table and clenched her hands on the surface. "I have no control when he's around. I can't be that stupid, can I?"

As her friend got cups and tea bags, Heather let her mind wander to what happened this morning. How had she not punched him in his gorgeous face? *You liked it. Admit it.* No, she hadn't. He was groping her. *And you wanted him to continue. Wanted his hands to slip inside your panties.* Oh, God, she had. It had taken all her control to tell him to stop.

Callie set two cups on the table before she sat in the chair next to her. "You want to tell me about this person who has you all worked up?"

Glancing into the front room, Heather shrugged. "Maybe I shouldn't say anything."

Cocking her head, Callie leaned her elbows on the table. "Really? After three years of carrying around my biggest secret, you're not going to tell me what's bothering *you.*"

Three years of being there whenever Callie needed her. Okay, she might need someone right now. If only to vent and tell her she needed psychiatric help.

"Give."

It would be much easier if Callie wasn't now married to the cousin of her problem. "Scott."

"What about Scott? What did he do that you can't believe, and what did you do that made you stupid?"

"This morning we were trying to get the building permit issued. We've had some problems. I may have...flirted a little to get it done quicker."

A smile appeared on Callie's face. This was why she loved her friend. She never judged and always held her tongue if she had an opinion.

"He made some crude comment about it."

"And that surprises you? Why? You've known Scott for a while now. Sarcasm is a second language to him."

"It's not the crude comment, but the crude action that followed it."

"Crude? As in sexual?"

"Yes, up against the wall. Practically felt me up while I simply stood there."

"You didn't say anything?" Callie's voice held confusion. "Or clock him one?"

Staring into space, she shook her head. "I couldn't."

An unladylike snort burst from her friend's mouth. "Heather Silva, speechless. Oh, I wish I had seen that."

"Laugh all you want. I'm still so damn frustrated."

A grin split Callie's face. "Sexually frustrated?"

Freakin' heat rushed to her face and she looked down.

"Oh, my God. Seriously? You've got a thing for Scott?"

Rolling her eyes, she tried to deny it. "No, not a thing."

"You spent the last few years pretending to be together. Was any of that real? Have you done...you know...it?"

Her cheeks burned and she kept her eyes averted.

"You did. When? Where? I want details."

Damn, she couldn't lie to Callie. They'd been best friends since their early teens. Callie hadn't cared who she was or how much money her family had. She was a true friend. And she'd shown her how to be independent. Not to rely on others like her mother relied on her dad.

"Right after Christmas in Vermont."

"How did I not know this? I was there."

"You were a bit busy with Jack."

Sitting back, Callie patted the tiny bump on her belly. "Yeah, I guess I was a little preoccupied. You know stuff like *that* can lead to stuff like this."

Where did that twinge of envy come from? Heather didn't want to be pregnant. Now or any time soon, though she was thrilled for her friend.

"I'm guessing you remembered protection. Not that I regret this at all. It made me reach inside, find the courage and confidence to get the evidence that put Victor away."

And thank God she had.

"We remembered. It wasn't my first barbecue, thanks."

Callie sipped her tea, hiding her grin behind her cup. "Have you and Scott had many of these barbecues?"

"You and Scott are having a barbecue?" Jack Holland walked through the back door. "Isn't it a little early in the season for that?"

More envy flashed through her as Jack leaned over to kiss his wife. A long, sweet kiss. Why was she envious? She could have guys kissing her if she wanted. Scott would certainly be willing. But where were the ones who held her face and stared deeply into her eyes when they kissed her? Like Jack did with Callie.

Whoa. Wait a sec. That wasn't what she wanted. Independence. That was her current goal. Her biggest desire in life at the moment. She wouldn't find it being dependent on some guy. Perhaps once she had this mill project done and proved to her father she could make it on her own, then she could start looking for a full-time man. Not that she needed one of those for her happiness. But it would be nice to eventually have the comfort of one to come home to.

"Why are you home so early?" Callie asked her husband.

"I was working close by and thought I'd stop in for a quick visit."

The transformation in Callie from a few months ago to now was lovely to see. She finally had the man she loved with her all the time, and they both could be parents to their son and, soon, their new baby.

"Daddy," Jonathan yelled as he spotted his father.

Jack moved to the living room, scooping the child into his arms for a hug.

Leaning closer, Callie whispered, "So tell me about you and Scott."

Keeping her voice low, she said, "There's nothing to tell. We got a little carried away with all the pheromones you two were giving off and had a one-night stand. Nothing's happened since."

"Except him feeling you up today."

The heat in her cheeks crept down her neck. "He caught me by surprise. That's all."

"But you liked the surprise."

"No." The denial came quick and Callie rolled her eyes.

"Right. That's why you're so sexually frustrated."

"No, I just haven't done anything since Scott. Any guy would have gotten me hot and bothered."

"Sure, you keep telling yourself that."

She *would* keep telling herself that. If only to delude herself into thinking there was nothing else to her feelings.

"Calico," Jack interrupted, holding Jonathan in his arms. "He's getting tired."

"It's almost time for his nap."

The grin on Jack's face widened as he moved closer and skimmed his hand down his wife's arm to pat her belly. "I was kind of planning on that when I decided to come home."

A blush covered Callie's cheeks. Jack kissed her then left the room saying, "I'll put him down."

"I think this is my cue to leave," Heather said, standing.

"You don't have to," Callie replied, though her eyes followed the handsome man and boy as they walked toward the stairs.

"Yes, I do. I don't want to be responsible for someone else being frustrated. You guys have fun."

Walking out the door she tried to tamp down the envy that almost overwhelmed her. Damn, her emotions were not coming at a good time.

* * * *

"What do you mean you're recalling the loan?"

Scott's heart beat double time at what his banker, Bill Bradley, had told him.

"I'm sorry, Scott, but my supervisors have gotten some new information that makes them worry you won't pay back the money."

"What information?" Stalking across his office, he pulled out copies of the loan application forms he'd filled out. What could possibly be wrong?

"It seems you defaulted on a loan a number of years back. They must not have caught it initially."

"I've never defaulted on a loan. What are they talking about? Where did they get this information?"

"I'm not sure. I'm simply giving you the message. They want payment back of everything you borrowed."

"I already used it to buy the building." Seriously, what the hell? "You knew that, Bill."

"They want it back within the week and they won't hold it against your credit."

"Hold it against my credit. You're already holding something against my credit apparently. How the hell am I supposed to get that much money in a week? The point was to renovate the building, then sell for a profit."

"I understand there were other bidders for that building. You might try contacting one of them to see if they're still interested."

"What loan are they claiming I defaulted on?" And who was behind giving the bank this so-called new information?

"It says here it was a car loan for a Ford Ranger."

"I haven't owned a Ranger for ten years. I sold that truck."

"Then you must not have paid off the whole loan."

"Of course I did."

"Do you have the forms showing that?"

Did he? It was ten freakin' years ago. That loan was paid off, though; he had no doubt.

"I'll find them and if not I'll contact the bank where I had the loan."

"You'd better do it fast. I've got them on my back to recall the loan. I'm really sorry, Scott. I've appreciated the business you've done with us."

"Apparently not enough. I'll get back to you."

Pressing the disconnect button, Scott fumed, wishing for an old-fashioned phone he could slam down. It might release some of his anger. Another damn problem. This project was cursed. First the bid going too high, then having to form a partnership with Heather. The stupid permit application being lost, and now this. Only three days after finally getting the permit to build.

Slumping down into his desk chair, he pulled at his hair then scrubbed his face. The stubble on his chin reminded him he'd been burning the midnight oil a few too many times in recent weeks. Trying to get the memory of Heather's soft skin out of his mind. No, he shouldn't be thinking of her. She'd shut him down too often. When would he get the message?

Like when her voice didn't go all smoky and her breathing stayed even. She wasn't as unaffected by his nearness and touch as she wanted him to believe. He'd bet every last dollar he had on that. Shit. If he couldn't find the damn loan payoff, he might have to give away every last dollar and then some.

After two hours digging through every file cabinet he had, he finally found the payoff notice. Thank God he'd saved it. What the fuck had happened to make the bank think he'd defaulted? They'd gotten information from somewhere. Where? Or should he say who?

Who would benefit from his losing the building? One of the other bidders? Heather? But they were in a partnership. She still had the building project. Unless she wanted it for herself as she originally had. But she hadn't had enough cash. Had she gotten more funding and tried to sabotage him?

First thing he needed to do was get the bank loan straightened out. Making a few copies of the loan payoff, he stuffed one back in his files and headed out the door. When he got to the bank, Bill couldn't apologize enough after seeing the statement. The banker couldn't tell him where the incorrect information had come from, though.

Now to deal with the possible troublemaker.

Her office was on the fifth floor of a swanky building near downtown Waterbury. Entering the suite, he noted the elegant secretary sitting at an impressive oak desk outside a few closed doors. She looked up, smoothed a strand of her flawless blond bun into place, and smiled.

"Can I help you?"

"I'd like to see Ms. Silva, please."

Scanning the calendar that sat at her elbow, she asked, "Do you have an appointment?"

Obviously he didn't, considering she'd just checked. "No, but she'll see me. Tell her Scott Holland is here, please."

"She asked not to be disturbed. I can take a message and have her get back to you as soon as she's available."

The woman's glance to her right gave away where her boss was. Striding down the short hall, he peeked through a large window into a conference room as heels clicked on the floor behind him. Heather stood inspecting a blueprint. Their project or one of hers?

"I'm sorry, sir, but you can't go down there."

"Apparently, I can." Tapping lightly on the glass part of the door, he pushed it open and strolled in.

"Scott, I wasn't expecting you."

"I'm so sorry, Ms. Silva. I told him you were occupied."

"It's okay, Wendy. This is Mr. Holland, my business partner in the mill building renovation." She threw him a forced smile. "He's welcome here, though it would have been nice to know that he was coming."

Wendy nodded politely and scuttled back to her desk.

"Thanks for calling off guard dog Barbie."

Something was off about Heather's appearance. It took him a second, but when she moved to the side of the table and bent over, he realized she wasn't wearing any shoes.

As she slipped the spiked heels back on her feet, she apologized. "I wasn't expecting anyone to come in."

"Don't bother putting them back on for me." The sight of her bending over in her slim fitting skirt and the long, trim legs emphasized by the heels made his pants get snug. Why couldn't all of him stay mad at her?

"To what do I owe this pleasure?" Her voice reeked of sarcasm.

Leaning against the table, he scanned the papers on it. Yup, the plans for the mill building. Her original ones, or the ones they'd come up with together? Hard to tell, since it was only the first floor plans in view.

"I had a call from my banker earlier today."

Her eyes narrowed and she crossed her arms. "Nothing bad I hope."

Was she playing the part of concerned partner because she already knew what he was about to say, or did she really care?

"They wanted to recall my loan."

Her arms dropped and her eyes opened wide. "What? Why?"

"Something about a defaulted loan from ten years ago."

"You defaulted on a loan? How did that not get picked up by the bank before this? And what does it mean for our partnership?"

"I suppose it could mean that you could buy me out of my half of the building and do it all yourself."

Something flared in her eyes but he couldn't quite decipher what. Greed? Anxiety? Guilt? Euphoria? The typical smugness of a rich girl getting her way.

"What does the bank plan on doing?"

Let her continue swinging, or fill her in? "Nothing now, as I had the documents to prove I hadn't defaulted."

Her brows knit together. "Everything is fine then?"

"Yup."

"Then what was the big rush to tell me? You scared the crap out of me for a minute."

"Did I? Or were you hoping to be able to continue this all on your own?"

Tilting her head she stared at him. "On my own. How would I do that without both of our financing?"

"I didn't know if you managed to coerce some other schmuck into helping fund you."

"Helping fund…" Anger, swift and fierce, descended over her features. "You thought I had something to do with the loan default? Why you arrogant piece of—"

Stepping closer, he backed her against the table, stopping her tirade. "Admit it, you originally wanted to do this solo."

"Of course I did, but now…"

"Now?"

Her jaw tightened and she looked away. Taking a deep breath she returned her gaze. "I understand the project is a lot bigger than I could have handled by myself."

Leaning in, he put his hands on either side of her. "You mean you need me?"

Her eyes focused on his lips, and he wanted nothing more than to connect his to hers.

"Or someone like you. A contractor." She pushed at his chest. He didn't move.

"There's no one like me, warrior princess, not for you." His breath swirled around her ear and she shivered. Damn, he loved having this effect on her. Too bad she wouldn't admit she felt it.

Pushing harder, she managed to slip out of his grasp and move near the window, facing him. Her expression was formidable.

"I can't believe you thought I'd try and sabotage this project. How could you think I'd do something like that?"

Slipping his hands into his front pockets, he rocked back on his feet. "You like things your way. Why not get rid of the guy who keeps questioning everything you do?"

Pushing away from the window, she barreled toward him, her finger pointing at his chest. "Look here, Holland. No, I don't always like having to debate every little screw and nut that you purchase, but we made a bargain and I plan to stick to it. We've known each other for a few years and apparently you still don't trust me. Haven't I proved my loyalty by keeping your cousin's secret all these years?"

His anger deflated. Yes, she had proved her loyalty and faithfulness. To her best friend. No debating that. But she was still a rich woman who liked things her way.

"I'm sorry for doubting you. But it seems this project is being slowed down every step of the way. You don't have some gypsy curse on you, do you?"

"I'll put a gypsy curse on you if you ever act this stupid again. If we're going to make this partnership work, we have to trust and help each other."

"You're right. What are you going to help me with now? Looks like you've been studying the plans."

Walking to the table, she pointed to the blue prints. "I'm making notes on possible locations of outlets and walls depending on who we get in there."

Standing behind her, he checked out what she'd written. Not that he could keep his mind on the plans with her floral scent filling his nostrils. Her shoulders stiffened as he pressed closer.

"Hey," he rubbed his hands down her arms. "I said I was sorry. I'm frustrated at how slow this project is moving and didn't handle this new development well."

At his apology, her body relaxed. That only made it worse as their bodies came in contact, causing his arousal to grow. It never quite diminished when he was near her. One more thing that had him frustrated.

Chapter 5

GO AWAY!

Heather squinted at the graffiti scribbled on the wall of the entryway to the mill building. Pointing to a strange symbol, she looked at Scott.

"What the heck does this mean?" The hairs on the back of her neck stood up.

Glancing around, Scott's face tightened. "That's a symbol the Northside Dragons use to mark their territory."

"The Northside Dragons? We aren't in Hartford, Bridgeport, or even New Haven. This is an old mill town. What would a gang be doing around here?" Her voice rose in pitch. *Stay in control. Don't show fear.*

Shrugging, Scott unlocked the door and stepped into the large open room that now housed stacks of lumber and piles of debris. Seemed work had finally started. Her eyes were drawn to another wall decorated with more writing. A shiver ran through her.

"I didn't think they were, but some gangs have been known to expand their territory if they think it's profitable. We're only twenty minutes outside of Hartford." He held up his phone and snapped a few pictures then got busy texting.

"Are you sending that to the police? We can't afford to have gangs around here messing with our project, or extorting money from the companies we put in here. Totally bad for business."

Sticking his phone back in his pocket, he strolled through the cavernous room. "Do you still need help walking?"

Glaring at him, she shook her head. She'd put sneakers on for this trip, not wanting Scott to have to help her. A tiny part of her resisted and still wanted him to. Wanted his hands on her hips, on her thighs, on her—*Stop.* No hands on her anywhere. *No fun.* That little voice still niggled inside, but she pushed it back. Focus on business.

Following behind him, she took inventory of what had already been accomplished since she'd been here a week ago. Mostly demolition it seemed. As they wandered through the building, Scott filled her in on the reconstruction project.

When his phone pinged, he read the screen then frowned. Moving closer, she touched his arm. The tingling she always got with him near surged through her skin.

"Is that the police? Are they coming to help with this?"

Scott's eyes rolled toward her from where he was still scanning his messages. "I'm not on texting terms with the police. But I do have someone coming to help figure this out."

A frown still marred his face.

"What's wrong? You're scowling. Or is it because of the vandalism?"

Taking a deep breath, he slid his phone back in his pocket. "It's information about some things Jack is implementing at a few other job sites."

"Things you don't want him doing?"

His lips twisted and he stared across the room. "They aren't decisions I would have made."

"Isn't it your company? Tell him to change it all back."

"It's half Jack's company too. Both our fathers started it. I was simply the one running it when Jack was working for the Bureau or on the run. But he has as much right to decide things as I do."

Something in Scott's expression led her to believe he wasn't happy with the joint ownership. Running her hand down his arm, she asked, "Would you have preferred Jack stay in the FBI?"

"God, no. I almost lost him a few times. I don't ever want to go through that again. He's like a brother to me."

"But there is something about your partnership that's troubling you, right?"

Looking down, he searched her face. For what she didn't know. But he must have found it because he lifted his hands to rest on her shoulders.

"Jack's a few years older than me, and was always the best at everything. He played more sports, went to a better college, had a higher rank in the military. And I was living with *his* parents."

"They didn't treat you well?"

"Oh, no, they were fabulous. Don't get me wrong, I was lucky to be living with them. They never made me feel like a burden, but I was well aware that Jack was their son. I was their nephew. I always felt second best. It was my own doing but I still couldn't shake it. I was totally envious of all that Jack had and accomplished."

Remaining silent, she held his hands that had slipped from her shoulders.

"When Jack got in trouble with Cabrini and was on the run, I stepped up to the plate and finally had my chance to shine. I was helping Callie in every day matters. I even gave Jack places to hide and work to earn money to send to his family. Between running the company and being responsible for all of them, I finally felt in charge, like I was doing something better than him."

"And now that Jack is back, able to provide for his family?"

A crooked grin twisted his mouth. "I'm being stupid. Ignore me."

Stepping closer, she leaned toward him. "No, you aren't. You're being human." Closer, not where she should be, but his revelation had made her see a different side to Scott Holland.

"Dude."

The voice at their backs had them whipping apart and turning around. Her stomach dropped. Three young Asian men, dressed in black with red bandannas around their necks crossed the large area. Who the hell were these guys? Gang members? The ones who had warned people away from their territory? Reaching into her purse, she grabbed her pepper spray and held it in front of her.

"Don't even think about coming another step closer," she warned, though her hand shook visibly. Maybe they couldn't see it in the dim lighting. Good thing electrical hadn't been first on the list of things to fix.

Scott's chuckle surprised her. Standing next to her, he lifted his chin at the new arrivals.

"Jian, how you been, man?"

The tallest of the men strode forward and grasped Scott's hand, shaking it hard. What the hell? How did they know each other? If her knowledge of attire and colors was correct, Scott was having a friendly greeting with a gang member.

"Been okay. Trying to keep things quiet, but you know how that goes."

"And Mei, she doing all right? Staying out of trouble?"

Jian, as Scott had called him, grinned. "I got her set up in a private girls' school in Vermont. It's a little boring for her tastes but she likes the freedom to be who she wants to be."

"Not the sister of the Northside Dragons' leader?"

Holy shit. This guy was the leader of the Northside Dragons? Seriously, how did they know each other? What other little tidbits of info did Scott have in his background that she didn't know about?

Jian chuckled then looked around. The other guys with him merely stayed in the background, their eyes sharp. "I saw the symbol when we first came in. That ain't ours. Someone wants to scare you off by using our mark."

"That's what I thought," Scott answered. That's why he hadn't been freaking out like she had when they first got here. "Figured I'd check with the real deal though. Wasn't sure if you had decided to expand your territory to this little town."

"Not yet," Jian answered, his eyes alight. Damn, did that mean he might in the future?

She took a step forward, but Scott slung his arm over her shoulder and held her back. Damn man seemed to have radar as far as her thoughts went. Pulling her along, they walked to where the other graffiti was.

Lifting his finger from the still wet paint, Jian said, "We would have written this in blood. Not cheap paint."

"We've had some trouble since starting this project."

Jian's eyes wandered around the room. "What's the problem and what are your plans for this place?"

Staying tucked behind Scott, she listened as he explained the mill expansion and the issues that had delayed the renovations. While she wanted to give this guy a piece of her mind, it seemed Scott might have it all under control.

"While this is out of our territory, I'd be happy to have a few of my guys keep an eye out. It's not that far and it's nicer scenery than our typical haunts."

"I'd appreciate that."

"I appreciate what you have been doing for me. You got any big jobs coming up soon that might need more men?"

"As a matter of fact, I recently signed a contract for some new projects. Plus this one will need quite a few good workers. But you know what my stipulations are."

Was Scott seriously considering hiring anyone this gang leader sent him? He couldn't be that stupid.

Jian shifted his shoulders. "Yeah, I know what the rules are. So do my guys."

"Send me their names and I'll see what I can do."

Jian mumbled something that sounded like "syeh-syeh" and pulled Scott in for a hug.

"You know if you ever think about getting out of the business, I've got a place for you too. You've got great managerial skills that could be useful to me."

"Perhaps someday," Jian said, smirking, then tilted his head at her. "This your lady? She's fine."

Her mouth wanted to scream "no" but the fear that filled her at the menacing men so close kept her silent. Pulling her to his side, his hand on her hip, Scott replied, "Yeah. And I'd be pissed off if anything happened to her."

The wink from Jian unnerved her as he said, "You got it, man. Duly noted. We'll be in touch."

Scott nodded and they left as stealthily as they'd arrived. She waited a few moments then rounded on him, glaring.

"What?"

He damn well knew what. The grin on his handsome face was too large and smug.

"How the hell are you in that tight with the leader of the Northside Dragons?"

"I did him a favor a few years back," he tossed over his shoulder as he walked to the other side of the room, where the lumber was stacked.

"That must have been some favor." He didn't turn around, forcing her to stare at his tight butt and long lean legs in those damn Carhartts again. Clenching her thighs, she tried to ignore his looks. Why did work clothes get her this turned on? Or was it *him* in work clothes?

"His sister was in a jam. I helped her out."

She narrowed her eyes. "Helped her, huh? I'll bet."

He did turn around now and his jaw clenched. "I found her hiding at one of my construction sites. She'd already been kicked out of a few other places she'd tried to hide in. She was being chased by some guys from a rival gang who were doing initiations by raping little girls. She was only thirteen at the time."

"Oh, my God. Did you call the police?"

"They wouldn't have done anything except turn her loose to be chased down again. I managed to get her in my truck without being seen and once we were in a safe location, she contacted her brother to come get her."

"Now you're best buds?"

"We understand each other. We're both businessmen."

An unladylike snort escaped her. "And you also hire his gang members to work for you? Not here, I hope. I don't want any trouble in that form."

"I only hire those who have quit and are looking to have a real life. Mostly the guys with families, a wife, kids, you know. My stipulations are strict. Jian knows that and he makes sure the guys he sends me know it too."

"People can actually quit a gang?" Hadn't she heard it was difficult to do that?

"Jian's not a bad guy. He honestly wants to help his people, but he also knows that sometimes to keep them safe you have to bend a few rules and get a little dirty."

"And why did you say I was your lady? I'm not. If you think because we slept together that one time—"

"It was to keep you safe." His hands wrapped around her face as he stared into her eyes. "The word will be out within minutes that you are not to be touched by any of their gang members and they will keep you safe at all costs. From other gangs if need be."

"Why?"

"It's their code. I saved one of their members. Now they owe me allegiance and safety."

"I mean, why do I need to be kept safe? I haven't had any problems with gangs."

"Maybe not, but it makes me feel better. And Jian said he'd keep an eye out around here too."

The hands on her face felt good, but she shouldn't enjoy them. It wasn't how their partnership worked. For some reason she didn't tell him to let go.

"If you were friends with this gang for so long, why didn't you ever ask them to kill Victor Cabrini? It would have solved all of Jack and Callie's problems."

His thumbs caressed her cheeks and she smothered a sigh.

"Believe me, I thought of it. But the mob is another whole layer of corruption and protection. They don't mess with that. Not even for me."

Leaning toward his warmth, she said, "Then thank you. It's nice to know I've got people looking out for me. Even if they are on the wrong side of the law."

"You can thank me better than that." The glimmer in his eyes taunted her.

Without her heels, she had a height disadvantage so she stood on her toes, pulling his head down to hers. And as their lips touched it all became better.

* * * *

"Hey, Scott, that shipment of lumber just arrived at the Danbury campus. We should be good to go next week." Jack sauntered into the office as Scott looked up from the paperwork he was ensconced in. As his cousin plopped into the chair behind the new desk, Scott sighed.

"Sounds like you've got everything under control." He tried to hide the annoyance in his voice, but the constant problems with the mill building site were causing him a permanent headache. Today he'd been here at the main office of Holland Construction for too long. He had managers, accountants, and secretaries to handle all the paperwork. He liked to be in the field.

"Everything okay?" Jack asked, his feet propped on the desk.

"It's fine."

"Doesn't sound fine."

"Why did you order the shipment for this week when we don't have the employees available for the job for two more weeks?"

"You sent me those two new guys from your friend, Jian. They seemed capable, so I figured I'd get them started on the preliminary stuff before the rest of the crew arrives."

Silence filled the room like a viscous substance and Jack lowered his legs. "That's not a good thing to get started early?"

"It's fine, Jack. You're half owner and have a right to make any decisions you want."

"But it doesn't sound like it was what you would have done."

"You're running that site, so it's your call."

"I can check with you first if that's what you want."

Running his hands through his hair, Scott swallowed hard. "As half owner you don't need to check anything with me first."

Jack stood, moving closer. "I owe you a lot. My life. Callie and Jonathan's lives and well being. If it weren't for you, I might have been picked off by one of Cabrini's men long ago. I'm simply trying to do my share around here so it doesn't all fall on you. I'm not trying to take over."

"I didn't say you were." Though often lately it felt that way. But he didn't need an argument right now. There was enough on his plate with all the crap being delayed on the mill project. They'd had yet another permit somehow go astray this week, setting the electrical work behind schedule.

"Tell me what you want me to do, Scott. Do you want me gone? The business to yourself? We can do that,"

"No, of course not. I'm thrilled you're around more and don't still have a damn price on your head. I'm simply being stupid. I ran this place by myself for years, and I guess I'm a bit territorial. I built this business into what it is today."

"And you don't want me walking in, taking half of what you made. I get it."

"No, Jack, it's not—"

"No, Scott, listen, if it's easier for you to simply hire me as a foreman, then that's what we'll do. Or I can leave and find other work. I didn't want to be dead weight, but I don't want to usurp any of your authority either. Just tell me what you want."

Lowering his head, he rubbed his eyes with his thumbs and breathed in deep. What did he want?

"This company was left to both of us. We both need to run it. I'm used to doing everything my way but that isn't necessarily the right way. I have to accept that."

Leaning against his desk, Jack folded his arms. "It's worked until now, so why don't I back off?"

"I don't want you to back off, Jack. I want to be partners with you. If I can pull this stick out of my ass then it won't be such a problem when you make choices that differ from what I would have done."

"If we're partners then we can also check with each other. You have far more experience in this business than I do. I'll make it a point to check with you if it's something I'm unsure of."

"Go with your instincts, Jack. You've done a great job so far. Let's do this. You take care of the college dorm contracts and troubleshoot any of the other sites if I'm not around. I'd like to spend a bit more time on the new project with the mill building."

"How's that coming along? Any more problems since the vandalism last week?"

"Another hitch in a permit but it's fixed now. The delays are driving me crazy. It's one of the reasons I've been crabby lately." The other reason for his frustration smelled like a floral arrangement and sent his blood pressure soaring, not to mention made his pants too tight.

"I might be a bit short on patience right now too," Jack admitted. "Jonathan has an ear infection and was up all night. Callie offered to stay up with him but she's exhausted with being pregnant and all. I wouldn't let her. She didn't argue."

What would it be like to have a child and wife you loved enough that you'd stay up all night to help them? Would he ever get the chance to find out? He'd been so busy with his company that dating hadn't been high on his list of priorities. Plus he'd spent the last few years pretending to be with Heather so Victor Cabrini didn't suspect anything. How do you explain that to a date?

"Is everything okay with Callie's pregnancy?"

Shoving his hands into his pockets, Jack stilled. "The doc seems to think so, but she's had some cramping that's making me nervous. She says it's only some early contraction stuff and nothing to worry about, but since I wasn't around for her first pregnancy I didn't see it."

The concern in his cousin's eyes was apparent.

"It would kill me if something happened to this baby, especially if it was because Callie didn't get enough sleep or did too much. I finally have her and Jonathan and I don't ever want to chance anything happening to them again."

"If you need some time off to help her, let me know. We've got other people who can step in."

"She'll be all right." Jack looked like he was trying to convince himself. "I stop in most days at lunch time since I'm in the area and Heather checks on her often too."

"I'm glad that you and Callie finally have the chance to be a family. I'm a bit envious actually. Now. Certainly not for the past few years."

"You should try it sometime, Scott. Not the being-on-the-run part, but the married-to-your-best-friend thing. There's nothing better than having a woman next to you in bed at night and not only for the sex. Though I won't lie and say that isn't great too. But the same woman every day that you love and respect, right by your side, it's amazing."

Thoughts of Heather next to him in bed did things to his blood that didn't need to be happening right now, in his office. But a lady like her would never settle for a blue-collar worker like him. It would never happen.

Chapter 6

"Nice shoes, Ms. Silva."

Goosebumps appeared on the skin of Heather's arms at the low tone whispering behind her. Turning her head, she smiled pleasantly at the man. "Mr. Holland."

Scott stood behind her in a charcoal-gray suit, the one he'd worn to Callie and Jacks wedding a few months ago, and a plum paisley tie. At the wedding he'd worn blue. So he had at least two ties. Good to know.

"That dress is pretty fabulous too."

As his finger slid up the bare skin between her shoulder blades, she cursed her choice of this outfit. The draped fabric on top showed off her toned back while the snug skirt emphasized her lower curves. If she'd known Scott was going to be here she would have gone more for the burlap look. The last thing she needed was to get him even more amorous than usual. It was a public place, though; maybe he'd behave. Smoothing down the silky blue fabric of her skirt, her face heated, almost wishing he wouldn't.

"What brings you here?" For some reason he fit in with the rich and pampered celebrating the opening of the new wing of the Law Library at her alma mater. In his nice clothes, he didn't look like a builder, though she still caught a whiff of sawdust mixed in with the clean soapy scent.

He shoved his hands in his pockets and rocked back on his heels. No steel-toed boots for him today. "Who do you think did the construction?"

"Nicely done. My father donated a sizable chunk of money for this addition so he insisted we all make an appearance."

"Your parents are here? I've never met them." His gaze searched the room.

Did she want to introduce them? They'd both been curious about the man she'd gone into partnership with. Her responses had been vague as she couldn't always read how her parents would respond to things.

"Sweetheart," her father's booming voice sounded behind her. "Speaking with Winston, I finally put together the Holland Construction who did this addition with the Scott Holland who's your new business partner." He thrust his hand out toward Scott.

"Dad, yes, this is Scott who I've told you about. I hadn't realized he was involved in the new wing here."

The men shook hands and eyed each other for a few seconds. Sizing each other up? What was the conclusion?

"Scott, this is my father, Domenic Silva, and my mother"—she indicated the petite blond woman behind him, always behind him—"Nicoletta."

"It's a pleasure to finally meet Heather's parents."

"Winston was telling me what a great job your company did on this project. Good to know Heather's pulled you in to help her with this new scheme she's got going."

"It's not a scheme, Dad, it's a business project."

"Of course it is, sweetheart. Now, Scott, tell me about the plans you've got. I might have some work for your company if I like what I hear."

The two men walked away and her hands clenched. It was her damn idea. Well, Scott had one too, though different from what she wanted. Figures her father only wanted the man's version. When Scott glanced back at her, the conciliatory look he sent made some of the aggravation ease, but only slightly.

"What is your relationship with Scott Holland, dear?" her mother asked, her voice modulated and calm as always.

"He's my business partner."

"That's all? His hand running up your back earlier was a bit friendlier than I would have expected for a business partner."

Damn, she'd seen that. Who else had? She knew lots of people here today. Clients as well as associates of her father.

"I mentioned to you before that his cousin, Jack, is married to Callie, so I've known him casually for a few years. He likes to tease at times, nothing more."

"I hope it's nothing more, dear. While his company did a fabulous job here, he's not in your circle. You need a man who can support you in the way you deserve so you can give up this silly career thing. There are multiple charities and events that I could use help with. I don't know why you insist on actually having an outside job."

"I like what I do, Mom. I have no desire to give it up and depend on some man to provide for me."

"What will you do when you get married? You'll be dependent on a man then."

"I may never get married." Her mother's eyebrows rose so far up she wasn't sure they wouldn't fly off her face. "Not if it means I'll be beholden to some man and have no say in what my life is like."

"Heather, don't be ridiculous. Of course you'll get married. And soon I hope. You know there are several men who have been quite verbal in their interest in you. Encourage one of them."

Interest in her family's money was more like it. No thanks.

"Well, I have no interest in them."

Huffing, her mother shook her head. "Well, at least Charlotte will do as we ask."

Heather only smiled, knowing full well Charlotte wasn't in the market for a man either. Too much fun being free and easy for her younger sister.

"I think I'll go chat with Charlotte about all these men who like us so much." She needed to get away from her mother. She meant well but her exclusivity was frustrating. "We could get a matched set. Would you like that?"

Her mother actually considered it. "The Bredbenner brothers are both single."

Walking off, she snickered. The Bredbenner boys were barely twenty but were filthy rich. She spotted Charlotte near the buffet table and pulled her aside.

"Watch out. Mom's on the marriage warpath again."

Her sister rolled her eyes. "Great. Who's she got picked out for us? And is that hunky partner of yours on the list?"

"Seriously, you think Mom would put a mere contractor, a blue-collar worker, on a list of potential mates for the infamously rich Silva heiresses?"

Charlotte scowled. "Of course not. Everyone on her list will be deathly dull and of the highest quality. Though I've got to say your blue-collar worker looks pretty high quality to me."

Scott was quality. No matter the differences they had, she had to admit he was a good person.

Leaning in closer, Charlotte whispered, "Damn, he is gorgeous. If you aren't doing him, could I have him? Even just for a few days?"

Steam nearly rose from her ears at the thought of anyone else touching Scott. Which was stupid, because she'd vehemently denied being attracted to him. Well, maybe not denied that she was attracted, but denied that she could get involved with him again.

"No." She narrowed her eyes at her sister but didn't give an explanation.

Pouting, Charlotte said, "Fine, but if he has any friends, send them my way. Dad's coming back. I'm out of here."

Her father walked toward her, but Scott was nowhere to be seen.

"I like him. He's got a good head on his shoulders, great business sense, and does a solid job. Plus he's served his country and is a hard worker."

"Glad you approve, Dad." She wouldn't admit how much those words truly meant to her. She'd spent her whole life trying to get him to see she could be much more than her mother was: a beautiful accessory for some wealthy man.

"You'd do well to stick with him, sweetheart."

"As a business partner only though, right? Mom didn't seem to think he fit the bill for anything more."

Pulling her hair like he'd done since she was a little girl, he stepped closer. "Don't let your mother dictate how you run your life. I think Scott Holland would be a good addition to any part of your life that you want him in."

"Thanks, Dad. For now it's simply business."

"Speaking of which, have you given any long-range thoughts to putting all those brains to work for Silvaggios? You know we could use someone with your intelligence and savvy to help run the company."

"I have this new project I'm working on right now. I need to dedicate any extra time I have there. And my real estate business will be handy for when we start selling and leasing."

"How about a Silvaggios there then? I'll make you manager." His grin warmed her heart.

"You don't ever stop, do you? I appreciate all you've taught me. I do. But I want to make my own mark on this world. Not simply profit from the mark you've already made. Can you understand that?"

"I can, sweetheart." Hugging her, he continued, "Can't blame a guy for trying to see his daughter more every day. I am proud of you. You've done a great job and I love you."

"Thanks. I love you too."

"Now if only I could get your sister to get off her skinny ass and do some work."

Glancing across the room, she saw Charlotte looking bored as she chatted with some socialite and her son. Poor girl.

"Encourage her to follow her interests instead of the business."

"Who knows what her interests even are. She's taken all these classes on so many different things. She hasn't actually decided on a major yet. She'd be happy sitting around playing with puppies and kittens all day long if we let her."

Charlotte did have a way with animals. "I can have a talk with her, Dad. But in the end she has to decide where to go."

"I'm glad she has someone there for her. And remember that I'm here for you any time you need me. For anything."

Hugging her dad, she scanned the room. Her mother would want her making the rounds, talking to all the important people. The only person she had any interest in smelled like sawdust and wore work pants better than anyone she knew.

* * * *

"You got something going on with that new partner of yours? She keeps glancing over here like you might disappear." Drew Thayer tilted his head in Heather's direction then looked back at Scott.

"She probably wants to make sure I'm behaving and not embarrassing her. You know those stuck-up socialites, ever so proper."

His Army buddy narrowed his eyes and laughed. "I met her at Jack and Callie's wedding. She hardly seemed like the stuck-up type. I thought you were okay working with her."

"Yeah, she's been fine, I guess. Wouldn't be my first choice for partners though. She's quite bullheaded at times."

A smirk lit Drew's face. "Cause you're so easygoing. Remember the time you had to fly in to get some of the guys after their jeep malfunctioned?"

"Damn insurgents."

"Once the Captain realized it was a trap and you'd all be blown to bits, he ordered you to retreat."

Scott stared at his friend, his jaw clenching at the memory. "I couldn't leave them there. They would have been dead in no time."

"Good thing Nick's as stubborn as you and decided to go along as your gunner."

"Yeah, that man's got an aim better than anyone I know. Took out half of the enemy so I could concentrate on flying in to scoop our guys up."

"Now that's bullheaded."

"Enough," Scott snapped, his eyes crossing the room. "Here she comes. I don't need her hearing old war stories."

He turned and smiled. "Hey, Heather, what was the conclusion? Did I pass muster with your father or is he planning to buy me out of my share?"

Her eyes bore into him. "Surprisingly, he likes you. Not sure how you managed that, but it's a good thing. You don't want to be on my dad's bad side."

"Been there too often, have we?" he teased, then saw her expression falter so he stepped nearer and took her elbow. "Have you met my friend, Andrew Thayer? He was at Jack and Callie's wedding."

Heather shook Drew's hand and nodded. "Of course, I remember him. There were only about twenty people at their wedding."

"I just meant being the maid of honor might have kept you busy doing important things, not socializing."

"How are you, Drew?"

As they exchanged pleasantries, Scott gazed around the large room, noting the crowd who'd come for the event. Not exactly his standard company but Heather seemed to fit right in. Her silky dress had his blood heating up as he imagined slipping the loose top down her arms then having her shimmy out of the snugger skirt. *Down boy. Don't embarrass yourself.*

"I'll see you at Chris and Meg's wedding next weekend, right?" Drew was asking as Scott turned his attention back to the conversation.

"I'll be there. Do you know how big it is? Are they going all out or something simple like Jack's?"

"Last I spoke with Chris, it seemed like it was bigger than he wanted, but he said Meg's parents can't afford much. Are you bringing anyone? I got a *'and guest'* on my invitation."

"Well, Chris and Jack will both have someone, maybe I should look around so I'm not standing by myself."

Drew's eyes drifted toward Heather and he grinned. Yeah, she might be fun. "Want to go to a wedding next weekend in Pennsylvania with me?"

"Why should I?" Her eyes narrowed.

"Because Callie and Jack will be there. And I need a date so I don't look pitiful. It'll be fun. I promise to behave."

"If you behave it won't be any fun," Drew said.

Heather shook her head. "He doesn't know how to behave anyway."

Running his finger down her arm, he sent her the crooked grin that usually worked. "Please."

Rolling her eyes and sighing, she answered, "Fine, I'll go."

Yes, what else could he talk her into? Staying overnight in a hotel? Reenacting their little Christmas chalet scene?

"Do you have a date, Drew?" she asked.

"No. I'm not seeing anyone. Guess I'll have to just look pitiful. Pick someone up at the wedding. Chris said Meg has a few bridesmaids."

Drew wasn't the type to pick up strange women, but he liked to joke that he was.

"My sister's right over there. She might be willing if you ask real nice." Drew's head turned at Heather's direction. "The thin blonde in the beige dress."

The expression on Drew's face indicated that wasn't an option. "She looks like a strong wind would blow her away."

Charlotte was wispy and delicate but if she was anything like her sister, she'd be tough as nails. He'd only met her a few times and hadn't talked to her much.

Sighing, Heather clutched his arm. "Oh, God, my mother is waving me over. If I don't come back in fifteen minutes, send out a rescue party, please."

"Sure, only so I don't lose my investment."

As she strolled across the room, Drew chuckled. "She's very different from her sister. That one looks like she'd make my sugar level go through the roof."

"My temper's going to go through the roof if we don't stop having all these delays in renovations."

"What's up now? I thought you solved the lost permit issue."

Shoving his hands in his pockets he made tight fists to try and relieve some of the stress. "The Historical Society has suddenly developed an interest in the building we bought. It's practically falling down and they haven't cared for years. But I want to develop it and now it's got some sort of historical value."

"You know, I saw Judge Stokinger here tonight. He's a retired judge who went to school with my father. He was the one who gave me the push to apply for my job. I don't know if he helped me get it but he's always been good to me. I can introduce you. He knows everyone on every committee in most of Connecticut. He might have some influence."

"I usually hate asking for favors, but in this case I'll take you up on it. Lead the way."

Following Drew through the room, he scanned the area for Heather. She was smiling brightly at something her mother was saying but it was as fake as some of the Rolex knockoffs he'd seen here today. The man with them only had eyes for her. Couldn't blame the schmuck, but he had no chance with her. Her body language said it all.

"Judge Stokinger, this is a good friend and Army buddy of mine, Scott Holland."

Scott brought his attention away from the sexy woman across the room and back to the man who might help him.

"It's nice to meet you, Your Honor. Drew says nice things about you."

"Scott's company did all the work on this addition," Drew pointed out.

"Congratulations on a job well done. What other work have you done that I might have heard about?" The judge tipped his head and his mop of white hair fell across his eyes. He pushed it away and shook his head.

"Don't let him kid you, Scott," Drew said. "If it was here in Connecticut he's heard about it."

"We've got the contract for the state college systems dorm renovations and I'm working on renovating one of the mill buildings down by the river in Menatuck."

"That big one on Prescott Street?"

At his nod, the judge frowned. "That's a hefty project. Might not even be worth it. That area is in bad shape. Can't imagine you'd get any legitimate businesses to go in there."

"You don't think it has any historical value then?"

"Absolutely not. It's simply an old factory that's been neglected. I wouldn't waste any money in that part of town."

"Actually, sir, it's in an urban renewal district. Many of the surrounding buildings have already been updated. It's getting quite popular."

"I wasn't aware. I've been in Florida the last few years, retired and loving it. I guess I haven't paid as much attention around here as I should."

There was a strange look in the judge's eyes, but he couldn't figure out what.

"You wouldn't happen to know Florina Betts would you? She's the head of the Historical Society around here."

"Of course I know her. Her husband and I used to play tennis together when we were younger. She's here tonight, not that I've spoken with her. She can certainly get on her high horse about some of her causes."

Drew stepped forward. "Do you think you could talk to her about that building for us?"

"Well, I don't know as much as I—"

Florina caught sight of him and he waved her over. "Ms. Betts, you know Judge Stokinger, don't you?"

"Of course I do. Old friends, right Bernie?"

"We were just discussing the mill building down on Prescott Street." Drew stared at the judge waiting for him to jump in. He didn't.

"What was it you were saying about the area, sir?" The prosecutor in him began to come out.

"It's not a great place. Certainly never was in the past."

"What was your opinion on the condition of the building itself?"

He shrugged, his shaggy white hair flopping a bit. "It's rundown."

"And the historical value of the building?" Scott was glad he didn't have to face off against Drew.

"Well, I'm sure there's lots of value being down by the river and being such a large space."

He cleared his throat. "If it's in bad shape, wouldn't renovating it like the other local buildings give it more value, especially if the original design was kept intact?"

Pulling at his collar the judge looked uncomfortable. Of course Florinaa was staring at him with accusatory eyes. She certainly gave him the creeps.

"I honestly don't know about real estate value. I'd probably tear it down if I had the chance. Put up something new."

"Oh, no, not there," Florina objected. "You can't have something modern in that district. Simply can't be done."

Turning to her, Scott asked, "If you don't want it torn down and replaced, and leaving it a mess isn't good for the economy, wouldn't it be best to renovate it into usable space?"

"Hmm, I suppose. I still have to check some of the background on this place. We got a tip that there was some significance in this specific building. If nothing comes of it, then you get to go ahead with your project, Mr. Holland."

He should feel elated that she sort of agreed to let him go forward. But he couldn't help wonder who had given the Historical Society their little tip.

Chapter 7

"Here's to Meg and Chris." Scott lifted his glass to the bride and groom. "May all their future undercover assignments be only under the covers."

"I'll drink to that." Chris Shaunessy took a sip then kissed his new bride full on the lips. Cheers broke out in the room.

Scott was happy to see another of their group in love and full of bliss.

"I should join the FBI and go undercover," he told Nick White, Keith Cho, and Drew, who stood with him near their table as more toasts rang through the room. "Apparently it's the place to meet your soul mate."

"I don't have a soul," Nick muttered under his breath. "Don't think that'll work for me."

"Those Bureau guys sit on their lazy asses all day while we cops do all the hard, dangerous work." Keith Cho chugged his beer. He'd recently lost his partner in a shoot out and his attitude reflected the loss. "No way I'm joining them. The soul mate will have to be put on hold for now."

"I'm not doing much undercover work at the DA's office so I guess I'm out of luck too."

"Hey, Heather offered you her sister and you turned her down," Scott reminded him.

Drew's face was comical. "Can you seriously see me with the tender, pampered princess and her frivolous ways? I'd probably go broke the first week trying to pay for her clothing bill."

"What are you complaining about Fly Boy?" Nick said, using his nickname for Scott from the military. "You actually have a date for this shindig. Unlike the rest of us losers."

"Speak for yourself, Nick," Jack joined in the conversation. "I've got myself the perfect partner."

His eyes turned to watch Callie as she walked back from the rest room with Heather.

"My date is the sister of the pampered princess." Scott sighed. "The princess and the carpenter. Sounds like a freakin' fairy tale. Not happening in my life. Not with my luck."

The ladies approached the table and Jack immediately pulled Callie in close. "Everything okay?"

His wife glared at him though her mouth turned up at the corners. "I only went to the bathroom. You can stop worrying about me."

Jack would never stop worrying about her. His cousin skimmed his hand over Callie's swollen belly. Yeah, Scott would admit to some envy for the man. But they deserved all the joy they could get after what they'd gone through.

"When's the baby due?" Keith asked as dessert was served, wedding cake with fresh strawberries on top.

"Late September," Jack replied, his eyes never leaving his wife. "Only a few weeks after Jonathan turns three."

Drew removed the spoon from his mouth and swallowed. "Is he excited about being a big brother?"

"That and the fact his daddy is always home with us," Callie said. "We'll see how excited he is when she's screaming in the middle of the night."

Nick grinned. "It's a girl. Sweet."

Nick might act tough but inside he was a softy.

Callie shrugged. "Not sure yet, but Jack is positive it is."

"Which means we need more room. The house is only two bedrooms."

Chuckling, Scott took a sip of his beer. "Happen to know anyone who does additions or renovations?"

Jack narrowed his eyes at him. "You've been a bit preoccupied with your new project."

"I can find time to help put on an addition, if that's what you're thinking."

"You could always sell," Heather suggested. "I've got tons of new houses that are gorgeous and walk-in ready. And lots of clients looking for a new place."

"Seriously? Your clients would want to live in Callie's cute little bungalow? Why don't I believe it?" He'd seen her office and most of the pictures of the houses she sold were million dollar places. Not quaint two bedroom deals.

"Not all of my clients are rich, jackass." She scowled, her eyes glaring at him. Great, he could kiss that shared hotel room good-bye unless he buttered her up again.

A soft love song rang from the speakers. He bent over and whispered in her ear, "Can I apologize on the dance floor?"

Air huffed out of her lungs but when he ran his finger along the back of her neck, she shivered and nodded. Taking her hand, he led her to the wooden square in the center of the room. A few dozen people were already swaying to the music, along with the bride and groom.

"I'm a little sensitive about rich people," he said, as he slid his arms around her waist. "You'll need to forgive me if I get a bit snarky regarding them."

"Seriously? Rich people bother you? I never would have guessed." Sarcasm dripped from her tone and her eyes lit up.

Chuckling, he swirled her in a circle then pulled her close again, right up against his body. Not the smartest move as having her near usually ended up with a boner that wouldn't go away. And doing something about it at the wedding reception wasn't likely.

Leaning in, her lips tickled his ear. "Is it because of what happened to your parents?"

"That's one reason."

She tilted her head to the side as her fingers slipped through the hair at the back of his neck. Damn, that felt good.

"One reason? And the other?"

That wasn't something he liked sharing with anyone. Jack knew, but then he'd been around when it had happened. He skimmed one hand up her back while the other moved lower to caress her great ass. Only for a second, since they were out in public, but it was enough to distract her from the question.

"Um, watch where your hands are, Mr. Holland."

"I'm quite aware of where my hands are, Ms. Silva. Quite aware."

"I'm sure you are. Now back to my question that you tried to avoid."

Damn, she was tenacious. "What question? It's warm in here. Would you like a drink?"

"Scott." She stopped swaying and stared straight at him. "You wanted company for this wedding. The least you can do is talk to me."

"We're talking. We should be dancing." Twisting her around, he moved his hips in time with hers to the slow beat.

Sidling up as close to him as possible, she rubbed her chest against his. Now *she* was playing dirty. Or giving him back what he'd been trying. Too bad they couldn't be playing this game in a bed.

"Help me to get to know you better."

As he pressed his groin into her pelvis, he said, "That's what I'm trying to do. Can't you tell?"

Rolling her eyes, she sighed. "Seriously, do you ever think of anything other than sex?"

"Every now and then I think about construction. But I got to be honest with you, I like thinking about sex better. It's way more fun."

"Maybe I wouldn't get so exasperated with you if I knew why you did things. Like putting down rich people. Always assuming I have an ulterior motive for what I'm doing and that it involves money."

"Okay, I might jump to conclusion a bit faster than some but...let's just say that once you've been burned you learn to stop playing with matches."

"And I'm matches?"

Oh, he'd gotten her off the subject again, kind of. Grinning he said, "You're definitely hot and dangerous."

"And the reason you don't like rich people?"

Shit, tenacious didn't even begin to describe her. Taking a deep breath, he danced her to a quieter part of the floor. "Fine. When I was in college I had this girlfriend, Patrice. Her family was wealthy but she never flaunted it much, though she did have the nicest of everything. We were serious for a while. When we graduated I started working for my uncle at the construction company. She didn't like that. I'd gotten a degree in business and she thought I should become some big businessman, not a carpenter with dirt under his nails who smelled like sawdust and wood chips."

Her lips twitched. "I actually like the sawdust smell. But go on. What happened?"

"I started talking about getting more serious, like marriage. She told me flat out she wanted nothing to do with a guy who worked with his hands. She needed someone who would be able to give her everything she'd always gotten from her parents. So she dumped me."

"I'm sorry." Her expression was sincere.

"I'd helped her with a ton of her classes, and apparently came in handy then, but once I didn't follow her plans, it was over. I joined the Army the next week and was deployed within a year."

Heather looked around then pulled them near a wall. "Not all wealthy people are jerks like her, Scott. Giving you up was her loss. You're a great guy. Any woman would be lucky to have you."

"But not you."

Her eyes narrowed. "Why do you say that? We're partners now and we need to keep it that way but"—she shrugged—"in the future things could be different."

Did she mean that? Or was she playing him like Patrice had? Getting what she could for now then ditching him when he wasn't needed any longer?

"Your mother doesn't feel that way."

Her eyes widened. "My mother?"

"Yeah, at the library opening last week, she made it a point to talk to me about your future. She mentioned a few young men who were pursuing you and that you were seriously considering which one would be a better match. That you had your future to think of and it couldn't be with a blue-collar worker with dirt under his fingernails."

"She didn't say that." Her eyes blazed, her grip tightening on his arms.

"I'm sorry, Scott. She had no right. She loves me and means well, but she's never done anything except follow behind my dad. Be the perfect little wife. She lost a baby a few years after she had me then threw herself into organizing his life, household, helping with charities, and being the arm decoration she is."

Losing a child must be as difficult as losing your parents. He knew the hardship first hand. "Does your dad expect that of her? I didn't get the impression from him that he was old fashioned regarding women. He seemed awfully proud of your accomplishments."

Color flooded her cheeks. "He did?"

"Yeah, I mean, he was glad I'm helping you with the mill project, but mostly because I have an extensive background in renovations. But he didn't have any doubt you would have found a way to do it even without me."

Her shoulders dropped as if in relief. "Thanks for sharing that with me. And no, my dad doesn't expect my mom to do all she does. She seems to think it's her job to live only for him. It's one of the reasons I was so desperate to start my own business. I didn't want to be like her, nothing more than a sidekick to a man."

"I don't imagine that will ever happen, Xena. You've got more fire and determination than I've seen in many men. It's one of the things I like about you."

"Anything else you like?" Sliding her hands up his chest, she sighed.

"Lots of things I like. These perfect lips that taste like sin." One tiny touch of his to hers was all he allowed himself.

"These expressive eyes that always tell me exactly where I stand."

"What are they saying at the moment?"

"They're telling me you want another kiss." He hoped that's what they were saying.

"I might. Is that all you like about me?"

"Fishing for compliments now, are we?"

"Maybe. I can return the favor later." Her eyes sparkled with mischief.

"What you like about me? That'll be a short list."

"Longer than you'd think."

He caressed down her cheek and let his finger dip between her breasts. "I like the little noises that come from your mouth when I suck on your nipples." It had only been one night, but the details rolled through his mind like a video.

One of those sounds squeaked through her lips. "You're not playing fair now."

"And the fact those nipples respond nicely to my touch, or my words, like now..."

The silky dress wasn't thick enough to hide the pebbled centers he'd caused. Either that or she was cold. But if his heat level was anything to go by, she wasn't cold.

"I can still see those long legs wrapped around my shoulders and how you—"

"Enough," she rasped out, her voice throaty and low. "You should go back to what my eyes were saying."

"About wanting a kiss?"

"Only a kiss. Nothing more. We're business partners, right? But a kiss isn't going to ruin anything."

"Sure." He was already ruined from thinking about touching and kissing her.

Lowering his head, he feasted on her lips, placing his back to the crowd, hiding her from prying eyes. What he wanted to do was push her up against the wall, wrap her legs around him, and plunge inside her warmth.

"Looks like someone's getting lucky tonight."

Chris Shaunessy's voice came from behind him. Backing away from Heather, he glared at his friend. "Since you just got married, I hope it's you."

Meg grabbed her husband's arm and tugged. "If he keeps saying stupid things and drinking shots with his buddies, it won't be him."

"Come on, sweetie, you know you love me."

Meg's mouth twitched. "Yes, I do, muffin, and I need you sober on our wedding night."

"Muffin?" Scott laughed.

Chris rolled his eyes. "It's a joke from when we were undercover." He looked at his bride. "Keep me away from the Bureau guys if you want me sober. They're brutal."

"We'll go talk to my brothers then," Meg instructed, and led him away. He'd met Meg's brothers. They'd keep Shaunessy in line.

Turning back to Heather, he hoped for more of what they'd been doing, but she had moved away from the wall and was sipping some wine she'd gotten from a nearby waiter.

"Why don't we go back to join Jack and Callie? She doesn't know anyone here either and I'm sure she'd appreciate a friend sitting with her."

He wouldn't point out that Callie's husband was with her. Heather obviously had second thoughts about the kiss. Probably about him. He'd let it go for now.

* * * *

Damn, why'd she go drink all that wine? It made her head woozy and her thoughts muddled. Of course it hadn't helped that Scott kissed her senseless in the reception hall.

"This is your room," he said as he opened the door. Usually she hated a man taking charge but she wasn't sure if she could stay steady enough to insert the key card into the slot. "Thank you."

Holding the wall, she moved inside. The door shut behind her. Now that he was gone she could relax.

"Do you need any help?"

Spinning swiftly, she glared at him. The room twisted too. *Damn.* "I'm fine. I don't need any help from anyone."

"Sure you don't. I'll leave you to get some rest then. I thought we could leave around nine in the morning. Is that too early?"

"Nine. Fine." Great, now she was Dr. Seuss. And the gorgeous man in front of her was staring at her like she was the last morsel of bread in the jail cell. He was a tasty morsel too. His tie had been removed and the top few buttons had been undone on his shirt. A few tufts of dark hair peeked from the opening. She remembered running her fingers through it when they'd been together in Vermont. Running them down his chest, around his...

Oh, yeah, there it was. Her eyes automatically lowered to the tenting in his dress slacks. Mmm, that had been a lovely surprise.

"If you keep staring at me that way, I won't be held accountable for my actions."

"What actions might that be?" Definitely the wine talking.

Walking closer, he didn't leave any space for her to stand. Her back bumped into the wall as he pressed against her.

"Ones that involve you and me with no clothes."

Those actions sounded yummy. Dropping her purse on the floor, she ran her finger down the low neckline of her dress.

"You did ask if I needed help."

"You said you didn't."

"A girl can change her mind, can't she?"

His pelvis ground against hers and she almost melted. God, she wanted him. But she shouldn't have him. Why? Why shouldn't she have him? Her muddled brain refused to cooperate and tell her.

"I think I need help getting out of my clothes." And him out of his.

"Always happy to help there."

She couldn't take her eyes away as he skimmed his hands across her shoulders then slid them under the thin straps of her dress. Pulling them down, he caressed her arms. The skin on his fingers was rough, but she loved the friction it caused, sending shivers up and down her spine.

Her dress top fell around her waist and he licked his lips. Could she get him to lick her as well? Reaching up, she stretched her arms, pushing out her chest.

He trapped her hands there with one of his then lowered his mouth. Yes, this was what she wanted. Oh, damn and double damn, his tongue twirling around her nipples sent her nerves skyrocketing, liquid pooling between her legs.

"Shit, that is amazing. You have quite a talented tongue, Mr. Holland."

His chuckle vibrated against her chest and she shivered. Of course the hand he skimmed up her leg and cupped her ass with might also have been the source.

"You have no idea how much I love touching you," he growled against her nipple.

"As much as I love you touching me, perhaps." Damn, she shouldn't be telling him this, but her tongue didn't seem to have any control. Luckily, his knew exactly what it was doing.

Inching his hand inside her panties, he stroked her sensitive flesh. Sweet Mother of all that was Holy. Heat built up between her legs then moved to the center of her desire. He continued to nibble on her rigid peaks and rub her slicked skin, causing the flames to grow. A moan escaped her lips.

"Oh, my God, I need this so much."

More sensations assaulted her as he pulled her dress down then helped her step out of it. Somehow her panties had disappeared too. Nothing left but her high heels.

"We should remove some of your clothes too. I'm feeling under-dressed."

"I think you've had a bit too much to drink," he whispered against her mouth. "I should get you to bed."

"Only if you come along with me," she said, attempting to pull him along.

He scooped her up in strong arms.

She wrapped hers around his shoulders then allowed her tongue to explore the thick column of his neck. Then she was falling, the mattress soft under her. If only she could get Scott on top of her. He simply sat watching, his eyes intense, hungry.

Scooting over on the bed, she slid her hands under his coat and slipped it off his shoulders.

"We'll put this right here so it doesn't get ruined." Twisting to set his jacket aside, she heard an intake of breath. Her ass was right in line with his face.

"Oh, God, woman, you do tempt me."

"I hope so. It's what I'm trying to do."

"You don't actually mean that. You've been telling me for months we can't have sex."

Why couldn't they have sex? They'd had it before. "It had been amazing."

"Amazing, huh?"

Shit, had she said that aloud? But dammit, it had been good, better than good.

Her hands clenched in the fabric of his suit coat. "I want it to be amazing again, Scott, please. I'm sick of my vibrator. It's nowhere near as efficient as you are."

The laugh behind her made her freeze. Would she be frustrated again tonight? Then he grabbed her hips and pressed his soft lips to the skin on her backside. Oh, Lord in Heaven.

"Yes."

He nibbled and nipped as he skimmed his hands up her legs. Still bent over, she pushed back into him, wanting more. Her breasts swayed from side to side. He reached under, playing with them, his thumbs flicking at her tight nipples.

"Oh, my God, you don't know how much I need this."

"I have an idea. I also think you might regret it tomorrow."

Straightening, she turned around, leaning into him. "Don't even think about stopping without a happy ending."

He pushed her back until she lay sprawled on the bed then he crawled toward her. His eyes shone with a need that surely mirrored her own. Before he reached her, though, he bent his head and kissed up her thigh. Hmm, this was good too. They'd get to him later. His talented tongue got busy again right where she wanted it.

"Yes. God, don't you dare stop."

She rode the wave, flew higher as he licked and stroked her into a frenzy. Crying out, she saw colors spiraled across her vision and soon she was falling, falling into an abyss of sensual pleasure. Her eyes drifted closed as she landed softly on the ground.

"Hope that was happy enough, princess."

"Mmm." Her body was too satiated to move.

Her shoes were slipped off and the comfort of sheets surrounded her then a warm body pressed against her back. Scott's soft voice whispered in her ear, "I have a feeling you won't remember this in the morning," as she slipped into oblivious slumber.

Chapter 8

"Sir, I do think you should go to the hospital. Get yourself checked out."

Scott shook his head at the EMT and waved his hand toward the door. "Just get them there. Make sure they're taken care of."

The two gurneys rolled out behind the emergency crew and he sighed. Damn it. More problems. A supporting wall had collapsed as they'd begun work. It shouldn't have happened. He'd checked the wall thoroughly, made sure it was safe. But something happened and two of his men had gotten hurt.

Rubbing his elbow where he'd been hit with debris, he pulled out his phone, pressed the buttons and put it to his ear.

"Jian, do you have a crew of men who I could hire for a security detail?"

He listened to his friend then gave him the short version of the story. He'd have men here in an hour. It might not be smart using members of a street gang to protect his building, but he trusted them more than anyone he could hire. Something was happening here, he just didn't know what. Jian assured him it had nothing to do with the gangs. He believed him. But what the fuck was it?

"Okay, let's get back to work. We need to find a way to get this beam back up and make this damn wall strong enough so the whole fricking building doesn't fall down on us."

The dozen men working on the first floor grabbed tools and headed toward the wall. Thank God he'd kept the job down here today. Imagine if someone had fallen through from upstairs when this wall went down. As it was his insurance premiums would go through the roof with the injured men.

They got back to work and his aching muscles screamed in protest. Screw them. He'd stay here all night until the building was safe.

An hour later the wall and beam seemed secure. He'd gotten word from the hospital that his men would be fine and were currently being released to family members. Thank God.

"Scott, what happened? Are you all right?" The click of heels warned him who it was.

No, he did not need the warrior princess here today messing with his mind. What they'd done a few weeks ago at the wedding still flashed through his memory too frequently. Luckily, she'd avoided him since then, aside from the occasional text to check on the work site.

"Get out of here, it's not safe."

She looked around, her expression concerned. Yeah, she should be. It was costing them money every time one of these damn screw-ups happened.

"I stopped by to check on progress and someone outside told me what happened. Are you hurt?"

Nailing in a last board, he dismissed the other men then turned to her. "I'm fine."

"You don't look fine. You're covered in dust and scrapes." She pressed a finger to his arm. "Your shirt is torn."

Looking down he noted a rip from his shoulder to his elbow. Blood soaked through the fabric. Shit, it was a new shirt too.

"I'm tougher than I look. Now get the hell out of here. I don't want you in here while we're still doing renovations."

"This is my building too, so don't tell me what to do. Why is it okay for you to be in here but not me?"

"Because I know what I'm doing and I'm not wearing a skirt with three-inch heels."

"Then I'll get myself a pair of work boots and you can't kick me out. What are you going to do now?"

"I'm waiting for a security detail."

"Security? Do you think someone did this on purpose?"

"It's a distinct possibility. Made even stronger by the rash of other shit that's been going down since we took on this project."

"But why would anyone object to us renovating a building? It makes no sense. It'll only add value to the neighborhood."

"Your guess is as good as mine."

"Dude, your task force is here." Jian walked in with two large lethal-looking men.

"Thanks, man. Appreciate the quick response."

"He's providing the security detail?" Heather whispered behind his back.

Grabbing her hand, he walked toward the gang leader. "I'm going to assume you'll want this gig to be off the record."

Jian smiled coyly. "That might be best for all involved. Ms. Silva, nice to see you again."

Her hand tightened in his, but she responded, "You too. Thank you for your help."

"Anything for my man here."

Turning to him, she said, "And now that you have your security detail, I can take you home and clean up some of these cuts."

"I told you I'm fine." The last thing he needed was Heather getting her hands on him.

"Jian"—she addressed the darkly dressed man—"does he look like he's fine to you, or do you think he should get someone to tend to his wounds so they don't get infected?"

A grin lit Jian's face, damn traitor. "I think your woman might be right. Can't have anything getting infected now. Let her take care of you and don't worry. My men will see that nothing gets in here tonight."

Looking around to check out the mess, he sighed. It was late and his muscles were sore. He could use a hot shower.

"You've got my cell. Call me if anything strange happens. Doesn't matter what time."

Jian nodded. After cleaning up and replacing some tools into the toolbox, he escorted Heather down the few stairs to the street level door.

"You seriously trust those guys?" Her eyes weren't accusatory, merely curious. He appreciated that.

"I trust Jian. He trusts them. That's good enough for me. Plus there's nothing inside to steal except some tools and lumber. Not exactly what they deal in."

"I don't even want to know what they deal in."

"Smart girl. It's better not to know. I stay out of it as much as possible."

"Where's your truck parked?" Her eyes scanned the street.

"It's a few blocks over in a lot. We haven't cleared out the back parking lot yet. You don't have to follow me home. I promise I'll go there and clean up. You've probably got important plans for tonight."

"Actually I don't. Charlotte borrowed my car this morning then dropped me off at work. I took a taxi over here from my office."

"How are you getting back home? Not too many taxis in this small town."

She narrowed her eyes and glared, which made him grin.

"I guess I could be persuaded to give you a ride home."

"I'll drive. You're limping."

Was he? He hadn't even noticed, though now that she mentioned it, his leg did throb, plus a few other places.

"I think I'm still capable of driving a vehicle. Thank you."

He was capable of a whole lot more than that. Remembering how she'd practically thrown herself at him after the wedding had his pants growing tight. Her whimpered admission that he was more efficient than her vibrator had worked him up so much it had taken every ounce of control he had and then some not to screw her right against the wall that second. But she'd gotten her rocks off. He'd gotten a sleepless night watching her naked form next to him on the bed.

When they got to his truck, she moved toward the driver's side. Opening the door, he allowed her to get in, a smirk on her face, then slid in after her.

"No, get in the other side. I'm driving," she argued.

"Not in my truck you aren't, princess."

* * * *

Damn, the man was stubborn. Heather pushed over on the worn leather, lifting her skirt to help her get past the stick shift in the middle. Scott scooted in behind her, slamming the door.

"I know you live in the same town as Jack and Callie, but you'll have to give me directions since I've never been there." Turning the key in the ignition, he started the car.

"We're going to your place so I can tend to your wounds."

"I told you I'm fine. I'll take a shower and it'll clean up all the dirt and germs. Unless you were planning on scrubbing my back for me?"

"I'm more concerned about your arm and shoulder. How do you plan to bandage that yourself? It looks like it's still bleeding."

His silence was like a win for her. As he drove, she studied him. Even covered in dust and debris he was still gorgeous. The loose waves of brown hair called out to her to push them off his forehead. The sleeves of his shirt were rolled up, showcasing the muscles of his forearms. Muscles honed to perfection by real work, not some gym equipment. His hands clenched the wheel, indicating his stress level. Because she was here, or the incident at the site?

As he reached down to shift, his bruised and scraped knuckles stood out against his tanned skin. "Does this hurt?" She softly brushed the torn flesh.

"Stings a little. I'll let you kiss them better once we get to my place if you feel the need."

His knuckles weren't all she'd like to kiss. *Partners. You're partners. Business and romance don't always mix well. Remember that.*

Keeping her thoughts to herself, she remained silent the rest of the way. They pulled into an apartment complex and he turned off the truck.

"I've got to warn you I'm not the neatest housekeeper in the world. I don't even remember if I made my bed this morning."

"As I don't plan on using your bed, it's not a problem."

His eyes glowed. "Then why'd you come back with me? Don't tell me my injuries, because I don't think they're all that life threatening."

Why had she insisted? They hadn't seen each other or spoken since the wedding a few weeks ago. The wedding where she'd had way too much to drink.

Scott opened the door on her side then walked beside her up to the front entrance. Her mind couldn't get rid of the images she had of them together. But what was from the wedding and what were her memories of Vermont? They definitely kissed at the reception, but after that it was fuzzy. Scott kissing her against a wall, skimming her dress down her body played vividly in her mind. His head between her legs. Yeah, that was one that kept her awake at night, trying to recall if it had happened, or if it was only her imagination.

But when she'd woken the next morning, he'd been up, showered and dressed already, and hadn't said a word. There'd been no condom wrappers. She'd looked, and she hadn't been sore down there. But she had been naked.

"I usually take the stairs since I only live on the third floor, but we can take the elevator in consideration of your shoes."

"I can do three flights of stairs in these, wise guy. I've been wearing heels practically my whole life. My mother trained me early how to walk in them."

"By all means." He steered her toward a door. At the bottom, he grinned at her and said, "Want to race?"

"Walk in them, funny boy, not run." But by the top of the third flight it was apparent she should have taken the elevator. She'd do it on the way down. Which should be soon since watching his ass all the way up three flights of stairs had sent blood flowing to parts she shouldn't think about right now.

As he unlocked his door, she took in the hallway, then the apartment. Nice. Not too fancy or upscale but certainly clean and homey. One large room housed several areas. Kitchen behind a half wall, dining area in front of it. The living area had a couch, a few comfy chairs, and a large screen television. Of course. If she recalled, Scott was a big sports fan. A few open doors near the furthest wall were most likely bedroom and bath.

"I'm going to jump in the shower and clean all this dust off. Feel free to check the fridge for a drink. I know I've got beer but there should be some juice or soda also." He moved toward one of the doors then paused. "Unless you want to join me."

Damn his cocky grin. And the adorable dimple in his chin that made her want to kiss it.

"As tempting as that is, I'll pass. Come out when you're done. I'll patch you up. Where's your first aid kit?"

"In the bathroom. I'll bring it out when I'm done."

Slipping off her shoes and dropping them on the floor, she waited a few moments after the shower started up then peeked into the other room. His bed had actually been made, though it looked more like he'd simply thrown his comforter over the sheets and smoothed it out. No accessories or designer pillows like she had in her bedroom. A hamper in the corner was full, with several items hanging off the side, like they were trying to escape the smell. Although she hated to admit it, she kind of liked the way he smelled. Earthy and clean even when he'd been working. Unlike so many of the overly cologned men who existed in her circles. Well, her parents' circle. She still got dragged into it often enough, but she'd been trying to slowly extricate herself for years.

The shower stopped so she hustled out of the bedroom and moved to the kitchen. His refrigerator was stocked with food that she never would have imagined for a single guy. Vegetables, meats, cheeses, some condiments she'd never used before. What was she expecting? Beer and pizza boxes? Yeah, kind of.

"Here's my bandages and stuff. It's not exactly hospital grade but it'll have to do."

Lord almighty. Standing there in front of her was a god risen from the sea. Scott, wrapped in only a black towel, as water dripped down his leanly muscled chest into the terry cloth. His hair had been rubbed so it was only damp but the waves stood up, begging to be smoothed down by her hands alone.

"Where do you want me?"

In bed. In the shower. Against the wall. On the kitchen counter. Her mind had too many places she'd like him. Instead she said, "Why don't you sit in one of the chairs?"

Moving to a dining room chair, he settled then handed her the box filled with medical supplies. She took a deep breath as she sifted through it. Mostly to give herself time to adjust to the slick skin in front of her.

"Let me start on the shoulder. It's kind of deep and still bleeding a bit."

He adjusted so she could get at the shoulder then cricked his neck. "I might have gotten hit with some of those bricks a little harder than I thought."

"See, you should have gone to the hospital."

Looking up, he grinned, sending her heart fluttering. Damn heart needed to stay calm.

"But the hospital doesn't have nurses who have as much tenderness and care as you."

Tenderness and care. Like that had ever been her style.

"You're full of horseshit, Holland. Now keep still while I bandage you up."

Her hands tingled as they touched his skin and she tried to be gentle. She didn't have a whole lot of experience with injuries, but it was mostly common sense. When his shoulder was finished she stood in front of him, glancing at the rest of him.

"Looking for something special?" he teased.

"Where else you need tending."

"Hmm, let me think where else it hurts." His eyes lowered to his crotch and she couldn't keep her own eyes from focusing on the bulge under the towel.

"You've got some scrapes on your shin." Let him think that's what she'd been staring at. Lowering herself to kneeling, she dabbed cream on them, studiously avoiding the glimpse of his strong thighs under the towel. She wouldn't even think about what else was under that towel. Not if she wanted to keep her sanity.

Picking up one hand, she rubbed some antiseptic on his battered knuckles. "How did these get banged up?"

"When the wall started coming down I automatically covered my head with my hands. And then a few of the guys were under the building material so I started digging it off them. Probably got scratched up worse then."

Leaning over him, she began to press a cotton swab to some of the cuts on his face. His eyes dipped to the opening of her blouse.

"Looking for something special?" She parroted his earlier words.

"Most definitely. Everything on you is pretty damned special."

Thinking about the last time they'd seen each other, she straightened and took a deep breath. "Um, about the night of the wedding."

His lips pursed. "Yes." Damn, he was enjoying her discomfort.

"Did we...um?"

"Did we what?" He was going to make her say it.

"I mean, I woke up naked, but I didn't see any condoms." A terrifying thought entered her head. "Unless you didn't use any." God, could he have been that irresponsible?

"Calm down, Xena. I didn't use any because we didn't have intercourse. I don't have sex with unconscious women, or women who are rapidly heading in that direction, no matter how much they come onto me."

Relief surged through her. Relief he hadn't done it or that she hadn't missed it?

"I fell asleep?"

"Or passed out. Who knows."

"I'm sorry."

"Sorry that we didn't have sex?"

Those stupid images swirled through her mind again. "Well, I do remember...something."

"What do you remember?" His eyes grew mischievous.

"You...me...and a wall. And that whole naked thing. Mostly images."

"You asked me to help you get ready for bed. You were a little tipsy so I figured I'd better."

"And you put me in bed naked? You didn't think to check for pajamas?"

"You didn't really let me. You had other things on your mind."

Heat crawled up her body, rushing through her cheeks. "There are a few other memories slipping in."

"Like?" He pulled her hips so she stood in the V of his legs. Damn towel was in the way.

His nose nuzzled in the neckline of her blouse causing her nipples to harden. Shit, why was her reaction to him this powerful?

Averting her gaze, she shrugged. "Nothing important."

Flicking open one of her buttons, he whispered, "Like sucking your nipples. Do you remember that?"

God, yes, she did.

"My face in your ass, licking your luxurious skin?"

A tiny noise squeaked from her mouth before she could stifle it. So that hadn't been her imagination.

A few more buttons came undone. She was powerless to stop him, not with the memories of what they'd done, what he'd done, flashing like a porn flick across her vision.

"And the highlight of my night." His hands crept up her thighs, slipping under her skirt to tease the edges of her panties. "My head between your legs. Mmm."

"I'd had too much to drink."

"Yes, you did, but you also insisted on a happy ending. Quite adamant about it. I aim to please."

How could she get herself in such a predicament as to not fully remember that? Or even allow it to happen. Her cheeks burned.

"A gentleman wouldn't have mentioned that."

"You brought up the subject and, let's face it, who ever said I was a gentleman?" He proved this by stroking his tongue up her collarbone then down into her cleavage while his fingers clenched on her ass.

Pushing at his shoulders, she made a half-hearted attempt to move away.

"You're not drunk now," he pointed out. "Or asleep. Care to try again, this time with all your faculties intact?"

"No, I'm not drunk, which means I have more sense about me." She pushed away with more strength and conviction this time.

Sighing, he stood up, his towel dangling low on his narrow hips. Her willpower was slipping.

"Yes, you do. More's the pity. Let me get dressed. I'll make us some dinner."

"You don't have to," she objected. Getting away from him would be the smart thing to do right now.

"Let me repay you for the nursing services. It's the least I can do."

She nodded not sure she had the strength to do anything else. Except watch him walk toward his bedroom, his sculpted back ensuring she couldn't look away. He pulled the towel off before he shut his door. Shivers racked her body at the amazing muscles of his backside. Slumping into the chair he'd vacated, her thoughts went back to what he'd said. About not being a gentleman. Bullshit. Apparently she'd been all over him. She knew her reaction to him and she had no doubt with that much wine in her, she'd done some stupid shit. But aside from pleasuring her, he hadn't done anything for himself. She'd been totally drunk. He could easily have taken advantage of her and he hadn't.

The truth was, in absolutely every way, he was a gentleman. And that just made her want him more.

Chapter 9

"I got confirmation that they poured the cement for the addition foundation," Scott told his cousin as they sat in a local bar having a quick beer before calling it a night.

"Yeah, I stopped by at lunch time and checked."

"You don't trust that I set it up right?" He smirked, knowing full well why his cousin liked to stop at home during the day.

Jack's face flushed. "I promised Callie I'd drop off a gallon of milk so Jonathan would have some for his lunch."

"What did she think of the drawings for the addition?"

"She loved them. Attaching the garage is a favorite of hers, especially for hauling in groceries in the cold weather. She figures the little office you threw in on the first floor will be great to keep all her accounting stuff in so the kids don't get at it."

"Kids. It's still weird to hear you talk about kids."

"Jonathan will be three in a few months." Jack's jaw clenched.

"I know, but for so long you could never mention him in public. It's nice to hear it now."

"You don't have to remind me. There are times I want to shout it from the rooftops."

"And everything's good with Callie and the baby?"

"The doctor says all is great. The little aches and pains she has are perfectly normal. She thinks I'm being overprotective. Maybe I am."

"Listen to the doctor. Now that you aren't on the run, you can actually go to her checkups, right, to assure yourself?"

"Yeah, I loved seeing the ultrasound. Knowing my child is growing inside her. I never got a chance to do anything like that when she carried Jonathan. I hate to admit I still look over my shoulder at times, thinking

Cabrini—or one of his men—is going to jump out at me. I don't know how long it'll take for me to get over that paranoia."

Patting Jack's shoulder, he said, "It hasn't been that long since Cabrini was killed. Give yourself some time, and keep reminding yourself he can't hurt you anymore."

"I remind myself every day."

"How's it going with the job? Are you happy?"

"We had this conversation not too long ago, Scott. I told you I appreciate everything you've done for me. I'm happy working for the company in any capacity you want."

"And you're doing great. I guess I was wondering if you missed the Bureau."

Jack glanced around the bar room. "You know, I thought I loved that lifestyle and would always want it, but after spending three years on the run, I think I've had my fill of cloak-and-dagger for a lifetime. To wake up next to Callie every morning, and be with her every night, it's the most thrilling thing I've ever done."

"You don't miss the challenges of the FBI?"

Jack laughed. "Oh, believe me, trying to deal with a pregnant, hormonal woman and a two-year-old holds its own challenges. Ones far more complex than anything I came up against in the Bureau. But I wouldn't give it up for anything. Callie and Jonathan are my world."

Picking up his mug, Scott took another swig of the cold brew. Envy pricked along his spine. What would it be like to wake up to the same woman day after day? A woman who was everything to you. Not that he'd ever had anyone like that in his life. Memories of Heather in the bed next to him after the wedding flitted through his mind. Shit, he'd wanted to wake her up and finish what they'd started. For some strange reason, he'd been satisfied with simply watching her sleep.

He wouldn't lie and say he hadn't been turned on by her gorgeous naked body or that he hadn't stared at her quite extensively before he turned off the light. The next morning, his hands had itched to touch the perfection, see if she would respond to him like she had the night before. But he'd also spent time inhaling her unique scent and reveling in the warmth of her body pressed to his. His completely clothed body, because he wasn't stupid enough to press naked skin to naked skin.

Even in her sleep, she exuded a confidence and determination he found as beautiful as her outward appearance. As much as he'd wanted to touch her again, he hadn't. He respected the hell out of her. Disrespecting her that way would have been wrong. A cold shower and the thick covers over her was what he'd managed.

As if his cousin could read his thoughts, he asked, "How's the new project with Heather coming along? Any more problems since the wall collapsed?" And Heather had patched him up.

"No, Jian's men seem to have scared off anyone intent on more damage."

"I still can't believe the relationship you have with a gang leader." Jack shook his head. "But more power to you if you can use their strength for your own good. Legally, of course."

"All very legal. Kind of. I'm not actually paying them anything, but Jian knows I've given many of his guys jobs. It's kind of payback for that."

"And your injuries?"

"Did Heather squeal to Callie?"

"She may have mentioned something, but you've still got a few cuts on your face and knuckles."

"I'm fine. Mostly cuts and bruises. Had worse in the sandbox. You know that."

"And the renovations are starting up again?"

"Yeah, though I'm one man short. After the accident one of the crew didn't show up again. He wasn't injured, so I wondered if he'd gotten spooked by the accident. Called him a few times then went to visit. The address he gave was an empty lot and all his other info was fake, right down to his former employer. I should have checked that out better, but I was strapped for more workers for this project and might have skipped a few steps."

"You think he had something to do with the accident?"

"I don't think it was an accident, Jack."

His cousin's eyes narrowed. "Why not? The building's kind of dilapidated."

"I'd checked that wall a few days earlier, and it had some problems that needed fixing but it was stable enough. Now that I think of it, the guy who skipped out had been working in that area earlier in the day and was there before it crumbled. Right as I walked up to it."

"You think he could have been targeting you?"

Shrugging, Scott said, "Me or the project in general. You know how many fuck-ups we've had since we started. I wish I knew what the hell was going on."

"I've still got friends in the Bureau. I could see if anyone would look into it."

"Appreciated, but I don't think I want to go there quite yet. No one has been seriously hurt and each incident could be simple mistakes."

A tone sounded and Jack fished his phone from his pocket. Sliding his finger over the screen he read the message then slid off the stool.

"Gotta go. Callie needs me to pick up some milk before I head home. Supper's almost ready."

"I thought you dropped off some milk at lunch time."

The grin on his cousin's face was huge. "Well, you can never have enough...milk." He threw a few bills on the counter. "I'll catch you later."

Waving to Jack, he turned back to the counter and finished his beer. He didn't have a family waiting for him. Once this mill project was done he should try and take some time for his own social life. It had been a while since he'd dated anyone. Except the pretend dating he'd done with Heather.

Would she want to date him? She'd commented on something like that a little while ago. Once they weren't partners any more. Although if they ended up renting the bottom floors for retail, they'd be in business together for a while.

Throwing more bills on the bar, he moved to slip in between the crowd. A tug on his arm had him turning. A young woman stumbled and fell right into him. He grabbed her wrist and kept her from landing on the floor.

"You all right, miss?"

She reared up, her eyes flashing fire. "Leave me alone. Don't touch me."

"I'm sorry, I was trying to keep you from falling." What the hell was her problem?

Her large bracelet jangled under his hand and she gripped his arm to push away, leaving some long scratches from her painted nails.

"I said don't touch me!" Her shrill voice caught the attention of many of the crowd in the bar, so he dropped his hands and backed away a few steps. She shook her head and the aqua strands in her hair shimmered. Interesting color.

"Is everything all right, miss?" The fear in her eyes had him searching the room for any potential trouble. Aside from people staring at them, mostly at him, thinking he'd done something to her, nothing seemed out of the ordinary.

Turning away with a sharp cry she rushed from the building. People stared at him and he stared right back. Hadn't anyone seen what had actually happened?

Looking down at his arm, he put his hand over the scratches. One more war wound to add to his collection. Too bad he didn't have Heather nearby to mend his injury. As he walked to his truck he wondered what she'd do if he called and asked her to patch him up?

* * * *

"The new front windows look great, Scott."

Scott stared through the new triple panes on the first floor then turned to Heather. "They do, but I'm worried about vandalism. It's the Fourth of July long weekend and who knows what could happen."

"I thought you had people watching the place." She shoved her hands into the back pockets of her slim-fitting jeans and rocked back on her stylish boots. Some might call them work boots, but the fancy plaid fabric around the high cuff was hardly what his men wore. Still better than a tight skirt and heels. Although he certainly liked those too.

"I do, but they aren't here every second or invincible. They need to stay in the background to avoid suspicion. I'll probably pop by a few times over the weekend."

"Aren't you going to Jack and Callie's for the barbecue on Sunday?"

"I am. But I'll still have time to drop by here. I assume you'll be there too."

"Yes, Callie asked me to help her get the house cleaned up and cook some of the food. She can't bend over as easily as she used to."

Jack probably wouldn't let her do much heavy lifting anyway.

"I've instructed the men to board up the windows. We'll keep them that way until we've got the whole place ready. That way no one sees all the tools and materials we have inside and isn't tempted to steal anything."

"I'll defer to your judgment on this one. I don't have any experience in that capacity."

A snippy comment rose on his tongue.

"Scott Holland?"

A middle-aged man and younger woman in dressy casual clothes walked through the door from outside.

"Can I help you? This is a construction site. You shouldn't be here."

Moving closer with Heather at his side, he watched as they took out badges.

"I'm Detective Tabitha Thomas. This is Detective Walter Harmon. We're with the Waterbury Police Department."

Holding out his hand, he said, "I'm Scott Holland, and this is my partner, Heather Silva."

Detective Harmon shook his hand though Thomas stood stiffly with her hands at her side, an envelope in one of them.

Heather looked at him sharply. "Did you file a report on the accident with the police?"

"Yeah, not that I expect anything to come of it, but I wanted it documented since so many things have gone wrong the past few months. But I filed it here in town, not in Waterbury."

"We're not here about an accident report, Mr. Holland. We'd like to ask you a few questions."

"About what?"

"Where were you Wednesday night of this week?" Harmon scribbled on a notepad in front of him.

Wednesday. "I went to a bar in downtown Waterbury after work and had a beer with my cousin. Then I went home."

"The name of the bar?"

"Jake's."

"Can anyone verify your whereabouts after you left the bar?"

Scott shook his head. "I was home by myself."

"Do you know a woman named Carla Findley?"

"No. What does she have to do with me?"

"We'd like your permission to search your vehicle."

"My vehicle? What are you looking for?"

Detective Thomas ran one hand through her dark cropped hair and lifted the envelope. "We do have a search warrant but we were hoping you'd cooperate without it."

"It's parked out back. What is this about?"

"Do you have the keys?" Thomas began to walk to the door so Scott followed, digging the keys from his pocket.

Heather and Harmon came up behind as they went down the few steps to the back lot that they'd finally cleaned up enough to park cars in. Thomas held out her hand for the keys. He held them up but didn't release them yet.

"You still haven't told me what this is about."

Harmon pulled out some latex gloves and slipped them on. "We're working on an assault case."

"And my truck was identified in it?"

Neither one answered, but Harmon took the keys and unlocked the truck then began digging inside. Thomas climbed in the back.

"Scott?" Heather sidled closer, touching his arm.

He didn't have any answers and it didn't look like he was going to get any right now. Hopefully whoever had filed the charges had gotten the wrong vehicle. There were tons of black trucks in the area.

"Do you have a key to this toolbox?" Thomas asked, pointing to his industrial size container that was clamped onto the front of the bed.

"It's on the key chain your partner has."

"Walt, I need that key."

Harmon tossed the key chain to her and she proceeded to open his toolbox then rummaged through his tools.

"What do my tools have to do with what you're looking for? I assume it was a hit and run. Shouldn't you be checking for dents in the fenders and stuff?"

Thomas slammed the toolbox shut and kicked at the tarp crumpled in the corner. Bending over, she looked closer at the material. What the heck was so interesting in there? He'd recently hauled some lumber in, so it couldn't be much more than wood chips and sawdust.

Pulling a plastic bag from inside her coat, she used a corner of the tarp to pick something up. An adjustable wrench. How did that get there? He was meticulous about putting his tools back in the box. He couldn't afford to keep buying new tools if the old ones got wet and rusted.

"I've got something here, Walt."

Thomas jumped out of the back of the truck bed as her partner climbed from the cab. She'd put the wrench in the bag.

"What is so interesting about my wrench? And what the hell is this all about? What assault are we talking about?"

"There's a bit of blood on this and a few hairs stuck in the screw." Thomas's eyes lit up and a smirk split her face.

Blood? And hair? Moving closer he gazed at the evidence bag. A tiny bit of red dotted the metal surface, but the hair was a vivid shade of aqua. Aqua? He glanced down at his arm and the still noticeable scratches. Shit. Another fuck-up, but this one was moved to a whole different level.

"Heather," he mumbled his eyes searching her concerned face. "Do you know a good lawyer?"

Her hand clutched his arm tighter. "What's going on, Scott?"

"I don't know. But I'm beginning to get the feeling all these little inconveniences weren't simply coincidental."

"Sir," Harmon addressed him, "I think you should come down to the station with us. If you feel you need a lawyer, they can meet you there."

"Am I being arrested? Because if so, I want to know what the charges are."

"We merely need you for questioning right now, Mr. Holland. We can provide you with more information once we get to the station. It might be best if you rode with us. We're parked out front. We'll need to impound your vehicle."

What would they do if he refused? The lady cop looked like she was itching to whip out her handcuffs and slap them on him. He hadn't done anything wrong, though. Once he explained it all to them, they'd apologize and let him go, right? Okay, they might not apologize, but he didn't care. As long as everything got cleared up.

"What do you want me to do?" Heather's anxious expression warmed him. "Should I follow you down?"

"No, but you should call Jack and let him know what's happening. Not that I even know. Just tell him."

Lifting his hand, he stroked his fingers down her cheek. "Stay near your phone. I'm hoping this will be over with fast and I'll need a ride back here."

"I'll be waiting."

As he got into the back of the dark-colored Crown Victoria, he liked the idea of Heather waiting for him. Is this how Jack felt when he returned each night to Callie and Jonathan? If it was, it wasn't a bad feeling. Hopefully he'd get a chance to explore it further. With the way his luck had been lately though it was a long shot.

* * * *

The tick of the clock echoed in the still room. Scott ran his hands through his hair again, taking a deep breath as he paced. He'd been escorted here about twenty minutes ago and been told someone would be with him soon. Glancing around the stark room, he wondered if they were watching him behind the mirror. Waiting to see if he'd crack? Like in the cop shows he watched too much of. He'd texted Drew on his way over. Hopefully, his friend could help him figure this out.

He sat in the wooden chair near the table and rested his head in his hands. Since he'd bought the mill building four months ago, too many problems had cropped up. Now this. They hadn't given him any more information, but seeing the aqua-colored hair on the wrench provided him with some of the answers he needed. The crazy lady from the bar a few days ago. Damn, had it been a set-up? Or was she simply spreading more craziness with an assault story?

The door opened and the two detectives walked in. Thomas moved to the wall near the mirror while Harmon sat across from him putting a folder on the table.

"Mr. Holland, sorry it took awhile. We had a few things we needed to process first."

"You want to tell me what this is about?"

The detective pulled out a card and started reading. "You have the right to remain silent. Anything you say can and will be used against you in a court of law. You have the right to an attorney. If you cannot afford an attorney, one will be provided for you."

"Do I need a lawyer here?" Even if Drew did show up, there was no way he could represent him. He worked for the district attorney.

"It's your right. Do you want one here for questioning?"

"I didn't do anything, so why would I need one?"

"I'm simply clarifying. You are agreeing to be questioned without an attorney present?"

Nodding his head, Scott wished he had thought about this a bit more. But he wanted the truth out and this over with. He hadn't done anything.

"You claim you were in a bar called Jake's on Wednesday night at about six PM," Harmon stated.

"Yes, I told you I had one drink with my cousin then went home."

"And you don't know a woman named Carla Findley?"

"No." The blue-haired lady?

"Surveillance tape at Jake's says otherwise," Thomas interrupted, her tone accusatory.

"Is she young with aqua streaks in her hair?"

"Then you do know her?"

"I'd never seen her before that night. And I haven't seen her since. She stumbled into me then threw a tizzy fit when I tried to keep her from falling."

"That made you mad?" Thomas sneered.

"Not mad, no. I was curious why she was having such a fit. She almost looked afraid and I thought someone might be bothering her."

"So you followed her out of the bar?"

"No, I paid my tab and left. I never saw her after that."

Thomas took a few steps closer and leaned on the table. "The wrench we found in your truck says otherwise."

"What exactly is this lady saying I did?" He wasn't sure he wanted to know.

Opening the folder, Harmon picked up a picture, flipping it in his direction. Fuck. The woman's face was barely recognizable. Eyes swollen and red, lip cut and bloody, and bruises dotting her cheeks. Her blue hair was apparent, though.

"Holy shit. I did *not* do this. Aside from the few minutes in the bar I never saw her again."

Harmon tilted his head. "And you have no one who can verify your whereabouts after you left the bar?"

Damn it, no. Why hadn't he gone to Heather's to have her tend to his scratches? She may have kicked him out, but at least he'd have an alibi.

"No, I told you I went home. By myself. I had another few beers and watched the game."

"Do you often drink that much, Mr. Holland?" Thomas asked.

"It was a few beers. I'd only had one at the bar. I certainly wasn't drunk. Not then. And I never touched that lady. She said I did this to her?"

Harmon put the picture back in the file. "She didn't come willingly to the station. Someone reported her passed out a few streets over from Jake's. The hospital called us and we took the report."

Thomas leaned closer. "She said it was some guy she met in a bar who wouldn't take no for an answer. We processed her clothing and jewelry and found your fingerprints on her bracelet. Plus the footage at Jake's showed us your confrontation."

His heart beat faster at the implications of this evidence. "It wasn't a confrontation. I only tried to help her." Taking a deep breath to control his temper, he continued, "My fingerprints are on her bracelet because she almost fell and I grabbed her to keep her steady. If you look at the footage you'll see I didn't do anything to her."

"She seemed awfully upset in the video."

Scott shook his head. "I have no idea why she started flipping out. I didn't do anything except help her up."

"You say you had nothing to do with her assault yet your knuckles are all bruised and cut. Like you hit something a few times. There are bruises on your face too."

"We had an accident on the job site a few days ago. I got them then." He glanced at his hands. Would they believe him? He certainly had witnesses for that.

"Did you see a doctor?"

"No, it wasn't that serious. My partner cleaned them up for me."

"How did you get those scratches on your arm? From the accident too?"

Running his fingers along the healing skin, Scott said, "No, that lady, Carla you said her name was, scratched me when she pulled away."

Thomas narrowed her eyes. "Why would she have to pull away if you weren't hurting her?"

"I thought you people said you looked at the security tape." He was getting worked up and that wasn't good. *Deep breath. Keep it calm.* Like when you were under fire in the sandbox.

"We did."

"Can't you see that I didn't hurt her in any way?"

Harmon shrugged. "There were a few people in the way so we can't see much except Ms. Findley and her reactions. As you said, she looked anxious and afraid."

How could he convince these people he was the good guy? The odds weren't looking too favorable.

"Ms. Findley claims you followed her out of the bar then forced her near your truck parked in a dark lot. You attempted to gain sexual favors from her. When she refused, you started beating on her. She fought back, kicking and punching, but at one point you grabbed the wrench from your vehicle and struck her with it. She said noise from a group of people caught your attention and she was able to get away. She stumbled into the alley and doesn't remember anything until the paramedics showed up."

Heat crawled up Scott's neck and rushed through his blood. What the heck did this chick have against him?

"I don't know why she's saying all this, but I'm telling you I never touched her after the bar."

"But you admit you did touch her in the bar?" Thomas said. "We've got DNA from under her fingernails. Her hair, and I assume her blood, on a wrench found in your vehicle, your fingerprints on her bracelet. Not to mention the video evidence of you having an altercation with her in the bar. That's pretty damning evidence, Mr. Holland. Are you sure you don't want to give us a statement?"

He stayed quiet. Anxiety and rage filled him but screaming at these people sure wasn't the way to convince them he was innocent.

"Have you looked at my background?" he finally said, needing them to know the truth. "I've never been arrested, have no violent tendencies, and run a legal prosperous business. I have no reason to attack this woman."

Harmon flipped through the file in front of him. "It says here you were in Afghanistan for a few years."

"Yes." Where was he going with that information? Didn't service to your country deserve bonus points.

"War can do terrible things to someone's mind. Were you traumatized while over there?" Thomas asked, her lips pursed. "Perhaps there was some sort of flashback and you attacked Ms. Findley, not realizing who she was."

"I wasn't having a flashback and I don't have PTSD." Not that he didn't have nightmares occasionally, but he'd certainly never tell them that. It wasn't relevant.

"You were upset about the recent accident on the job site and decided to take out your frustrations on her when she wouldn't concede to your advances."

"How many times do I have to tell you, I never touched her?" His tone showed his annoyance and he flinched at the anger coming through. *Stay in control. Don't let them get to you.*

Thomas pulled the file closer to her then pushed aside a few of the sheets. Damn, what did they have in there?

"What is your connection to the Northside Dragons?"

Shit, this was getting too hot.

"The street gang?" he stalled. "What do they have to do with this?"

"According to our intelligence, your company has hired quite a few members of the gang."

"I don't hire anyone who is still in a street gang. All my employees have to go through a rigorous training. They stay clean and legal while they're working for me."

"And yet you employ dozens of known former gang members, but only from the Northside Dragons. I'd like to know what your connection is. Why that gang and not another one?"

Did he tell the truth or shrug it off? What would be better for his case?

"I helped out the sister of one of them once and they know I'll give them a fair shake if they want to get out. I have nothing to do with the gang itself."

"Did you assault Ms. Findley as a favor to the Northside Dragons?"

"What? No. I admit to hiring some of their former members but I have no knowledge of any of their dealings." That much was true. He kept his nose out of their business, happily.

"You know, Mr. Holland, this doesn't look good for you." Thomas looked downright smug.

"I don't know what else to say to you to make you understand I had nothing to do with assaulting Ms. Findley. Maybe you should spend some time finding the real culprit instead of harassing me."

"This information"—Thomas pointed to the file still open on the table—"indicates we have found the perpetrator."

Looking at Harmon, Scott hoped to find more sympathy. The detective's face was set and he shook his head.

"I'm afraid we do have enough evidence to charge you with assault and battery. The victim identified your picture plus the wrench and fingerprints."

"Scott Holland, you are under arrest for assault, battery, attempted rape…"

The words melted into the pounding of his heart, so loud he though his head might explode. This shit was real.

"The DNA results from the skin under her fingernails won't be back for a few weeks, but until then we have enough to hold you."

The DNA. That wasn't going to help him at all. He knew damn well what they'd find. The DNA would be his and that might be the final nail in his coffin.

Chapter 10

Heather paced back and forth in front of the police station, her heart beating rapidly. Jack sat on the bench next to her, texting on his phone. Scott had been in there for over three hours. What the hell was going on? Checking her phone again to make sure he hadn't called, she sighed and shoved it back in her jeans pocket.

Two hours ago they'd gone inside asking about Scott, but hadn't gotten any information. They'd been told to wait until he contacted them. No way was she going home when he was sitting inside being questioned. She still didn't know what this was all about. A sexual assault on a woman? No freakin' way. Not Scott Holland. He hadn't taken advantage of her when she'd been naked in bed next to him. And willing. She didn't believe he'd do it to some stranger.

"What is taking them so long?"

Looking up, Jack pocketed his phone then shrugged. "I don't know. I made a few calls to see if I could get some answers. Nothing yet."

"Heather? Jack?"

Turning at the sound, relief settled in when Drew Thayer trotted down the steps of the station.

"Drew. Have you seen Scott? What happened? Is he coming out?" She looked behind him, hoping to see the tousled brown waves and blue eyes heading in her direction. Nothing.

Drew's expression tightened. "I'm not his attorney so I didn't see him, but I got some information. Working for the DA's office has some perks."

"The only thing I know is he was being questioned about some assault on a woman."

"You said they questioned him about Wednesday?" Jack asked. "We had a drink at a bar, but nothing happened while I was there."

Looking back at the building, Drew took her elbow and escorted her to the bench Jack had been sitting on. Jack followed then stood next to Drew, his hands on his hips.

"Apparently there was a woman assaulted Wednesday night. It must have happened after you left, Jack. Witnesses reported they'd had some sort of altercation. Scott's statement said he was simply helping her but the woman claims he came on to her then followed her outside."

"Why would he do that?" Scott certainly didn't need to go running after women.

"He claims he didn't. But the woman was beaten badly and Scott's fingerprints were on her bracelet. They also got the surveillance tape from the bar and have the evidence that she looked scared when he grabbed her."

"Grabbed her?" Jack asked. "Why?"

"I can only tell you what's in the reports. According to the woman, Scott made sexual advances on her then followed her out and assaulted her when she resisted them. She said he started beating on her and even hit her with a wrench."

"The one they found in his truck?" Her lungs dried up. She needed air.

"Yes. It has blood and hair on it. They'll send it to the lab for analysis but the hair had blue tints on it and the woman also has blue highlights in her hair. They also found skin under her fingernails. They sent that off to the lab as well."

"He didn't do it." Her voice shook at the thought that Scott was being accused of something so heinous.

"Of course he didn't," Jack growled in agreement.

"I know. I don't think he did either but he's got scratches on his arm that match fingernail marks and he admitted that she'd scratched him. The DNA will confirm this and that's not good."

"How do we prove it wasn't him?"

"We need to find him a good lawyer."

"You're a good lawyer."

He shook his head and frowned. "I work for the prosecutor's office. I can't defend him."

A strange thought entered her head. "You won't prosecute him, will you?"

"No, I don't work in this district, but I do know the ADA who's been assigned his case. Virginia Dennis. She's usually fair, but she has a stick up her ass about domestic abuse and loves to set examples of men who hurt women. I'm afraid she'll go for the maximum penalty."

Horror filled her, running through her blood. "But it won't get that far, right? I mean, he's innocent. They'll figure that out."

"I hope so." Drew's brows creased. Like he wasn't sure?

"What do you mean, you hope so?" Her voice rose a few octaves. "What about truth, justice, and the American way? The law should protect him."

Clearing his throat, Jack said, "Yeah, that worked well for me, huh?"

"I won't lie and say we always get it right. I don't personally think Scott capable of anything like this. However, the woman was beat hard, and they have a lot of evidence that points to him. Plus she claims it was him. Why would she do that?"

"I don't know. All I can think is it has something to do with all the crap that has happened since we started this building project."

Drew tilted his head. "Yeah, Scott mentioned he's had some problems with it."

"It's making him a little crazy," Jack said.

"What is this woman's name? Have they done any background checks on her?"

"Not really, and I'm not supposed to give you any information. I've already jeopardized my job simply with what we've discussed. I'll keep digging myself, see what I can find on her. I'll have to do it quietly, though. If the ADA finds out I'm linked to Scott and am tampering with the case, it would be bad for both of us."

Jack shuffled quietly. "I'll try to call in a few favors, too."

"What will they do with him now?" The thought of Scott hanging out in jail scared her.

"They formally charged him and have been processing his information. Fingerprints, photos, that type of stuff. He'll be sent to the Hartford Correctional Facility for the weekend and be arraigned on Tuesday."

"They're putting him in jail for the three-day weekend? What about bail?"

"He has to be arraigned first and court is closed for the day. It won't open again until after the holiday. I have a feeling Detective Thomas took her time with the questioning so it would be too late for him to be arraigned today. When I spoke with her she seemed thrilled to get Scott off the streets."

Moisture welled in her eyes and she blinked it back. Sometimes Scott drove her nuts, but she'd never want to see him behind bars. Lowering himself to the bench, Jack hugged her to his shoulder.

"Can I see him before he goes? Bring him something?"

"Like a cake with a file inside?" Drew grinned, though it didn't reach his eyes. He was worried about his friend too. "No, no visitors while he's in lock-up."

Her eyes blurred as she stared at the police station and the squad cars parked in the side lot. People moved in and out. One set of figures caught her attention.

"Is that Scott?" She stood to get a better view.

Jack took her elbow standing too. Drew grabbed her other arm. Had she started to move toward Scott? With his head and shoulders down, he walked between two uniformed officers, his hands cuffed together. They gently pushed him into the back seat of a squad car, shut the door, and got in the front.

Jack's fingers tightened on her arm. "I'll call around and see if I can get in touch with a lawyer for him. With the long weekend, I'm not sure how many would be available. Otherwise he gets a court-appointed lawyer."

"Let me talk to my dad and see what he suggests." She hated asking her dad for favors, but she'd do it for Scott. No expense was too much. "If he doesn't know anyone then I'll call you."

The squad car with Scott inside rolled past them. He sat in the middle, his head facing the window. As their eyes met, his mouth tightened and he looked down.

Running his hand down her arm, Drew said, "Are you all right to get home by yourself?"

"I'll make sure she gets there," Jack offered.

"I'm fine. I don't need either of you worrying about me. Thank you for the information."

Moving toward her car on autopilot, Jack and Drew watching from a distance, her mind roamed to the man who had been hauled away to jail. *He* wasn't fine. What would he be like after three days in the county jail? And what about after? Bail? A hearing? What if the lawyer couldn't prove he hadn't done it?

"No, he's innocent," she stated, and a few people looked curiously at her. They had to prove he was. Although it was supposed to be innocent until proven guilty. Was the evidence they had against him strong enough to convict him?

She took it back. She wasn't fine. Her stomach churned and dread filled her bones at the thought of Scott being sent to prison for something he hadn't done.

* * * *

The lock clicked behind him and Scott flinched.

"Step forward, please." The burly guard indicated the line he had to stand on. Far enough away so he couldn't hurt anyone, but close enough to be subdued if needed? Like that would happen with his hands in cuffs.

"Scott Holland," the police officer who had driven him here said. "Waterbury PD. Sexual assault, battery, and attempted rape."

Flinching at the charges, he kept his temper under control. It sucked being treated like a criminal when he knew he hadn't done anything wrong. Except be in the wrong place at the wrong time. Or it might not have mattered where he'd been. He suspected this whole thing was a set up. Why the hell else would that bitch say he'd beat her? But why was he being set up? It all came back to the renovation project.

And he'd be here until Tuesday morning. More than three days. Fuck. He was supposed to be enjoying the long weekend with his cousin and friends. He'd been hoping to entice Heather to the beach with him. Seeing her in a bathing suit would be a highlight. Not that he hadn't seen her in less. Shit. This sucked.

The guard eyed him up and down then reached behind him for some orange fabric. Oh, yay, just his color.

"Go in there, put these on. Leave your clothes on the bench."

"Um..." He held up his cuffed hands.

"Go inside and put your hands through the door."

Oh, there was a slot in the door. How convenient. Also a nice big window.

"No curtains for privacy," he joked. The guard didn't look amused. Clothes plopped in his arms then he walked inside the small enclosure. After the door closed behind him, he dropped the orange ball of fabric on the bench then stuck his hands through the slot. The cuffs were removed and he rubbed his wrists. They hadn't been that tight but they'd still chafed a bit.

"You can keep on your socks and underwear. Leave the boots on the floor. Bang on the door when you're done."

As quick as he could, he shed his pants and shirt then shrugged into the orange pants and top. The material was lightweight and loose, like scrubs. He took a second to tighten the tie on the pants then turned back toward the door. As soon as he knocked the guard appeared. At least he hadn't been staring at him while he changed.

"Hands through the door."

He complied and the cuffs were replaced. Would he need to wear them the whole freakin' weekend?

"Sit over there." The guard pointed to a bench in the outer room and another guard took his boots for a thorough search of them. Were they expecting to find a weapon?

"Put these back on."

No casual chatter for these guys. Once his boots were on, the guard who'd checked them put his hand out toward the back door. Big and metal, with a window in the middle, it clanked open and they stepped through. It took a few minutes of walking through long hallways then up a set of stairs to finally reach their destination.

"Orientation first."

The room was small with a half dozen chairs on one side. He was pushed into one and his handcuffs were connected to a chain attached to the chair. As if running away were an option.

For the next few hours he was lectured on all the rules of the facility and what to expect. Not that he'd be allowed to roam around at all. Apparently when you were in here simply for "lock-up," the term for the safe keep of people who hadn't been arraigned yet, you were stuck in the cell the whole time. Yeah, he felt so fucking safe.

"Unit six, cell nineteen."

The same guard was back, escorting him through a few more hallways and big metal doors. Each door had to be locked then unlocked as they went through. To keep him safe. Right.

"You're in here. Meals will be delivered twice a day."

"Do I get one tonight?" It had been midafternoon when the detectives had picked him up and he hadn't eaten a big lunch. Although whether his stomach could handle food right now was another question entirely.

"Kitchen's closed. You'll get something tomorrow. There's a sink in there if you need water."

"Thanks." Did he catch the deep sarcasm?

Walking into the tiny seven-by-ten-foot room, Scott sighed. Luxury accommodations. Lots of privacy. At least he didn't have a roommate.

At the sound of the door closing, he turned.

"Hands through here."

Slipping his hands through the slot, he sighed as the cuffs were removed. Apparently, he wouldn't be wearing them all weekend.

"Lights out at ten." The guard left, walking down the corridor, a few comments from other inmates floating on the air. Looking through the lovely shade of orange bars, to match his outfit maybe, he gritted his teeth. Never in his life had he expected to be in a place like this.

Sighing, he turned and examined the cell. Small. Metal slabs jutted out from the right forming bunk beds, their thin mattresses folded together. Hmm, did he want top or bottom? Another small piece of metal came out on the left with a round pedestal-type bench secured to the floor underneath.

Excellent, he had a desk. He could spend the weekend catching up on his correspondence.

The *piece de resistance* was the lovely metal toilet/sink combo in the back corner of the cell. Peeking closer, he saw it was at least somewhat clean. And damned if he didn't need to use it now.

The lights flickered then went out. Must be ten. Not that he'd know since they took his watch. But he hadn't left the police station until after six and they'd lectured to him here for a few hours. At least he'd have a tiny bit of privacy without the glaring lights, although they were still on out in the cell block.

After taking care of business and thoroughly washing his hands and face, he stood there clenching his fists then shaking them. No towel. Deciding on the bottom bunk, he unfolded the mattress, sniffing it. Not the sweet scent of Heather, that's for sure.

Heather. Damn. The look on her face as they'd pulled out of the police station had almost gutted him. She'd looked like someone had kicked her puppy. What had she been doing there? Thank God Jack had been there for her. He'd keep an eye out for the woman. She was Callie's best friend after all. He'd told her he'd call when he was free to go. That plan had gone FUBAR. And wouldn't happen for more than three days.

But would he even be allowed to go free then? Would the evidence be enough to actually convict him? Why hadn't he asked for a lawyer when they'd first brought him in? He certainly needed one now. He'd been told one would review his case and meet him at the arraignment on Tuesday. That was comforting. Probably some pimply-faced recent college grad who'd been last in his class and the only job he could get was standing next to low-life criminals, pretending to defend them.

Sinking onto the thin mattress, he closed his eyes then snapped them open again as a guard strolled by, flipped on the light then peeked in. Sure, he'd get some good sleep tonight with the light streaming in, the constant walking vigil of the guards. The light clicked off as the guard moved to the next cell.

He settled down again and begged his body to relax. His thoughts turned back to Heather. Her silky skin pressed against his in the Vermont chalet. His mouth skimming over her heated body after the wedding. The moans of ecstasy that escaped her throat as he brought her to the edge.

Shit. Now he was rock hard. And he sure wouldn't ask anyone around here to help him fix that. Instead he imagined Heather next to him, snuggled tight to his chest, kind of like she'd done at the hotel. He'd never admit to anyone how much he'd enjoyed having her close. For now, though, it might be the only thing to keep him sane.

* * * *

"Did you get in to see Scott?" Heather rubbed her hands together as she stared intently at Jack.

"No visitors allowed," he answered, his jaw tight.

"Yeah, that's the response I got too." Turning to the counter, she grabbed the plate of cut veggies and moved to the kitchen door.

Drew held it open for her. "When you're in lock-up waiting for arraignment there's no leaving your cell. It's regulations."

"I hate those regulations." Placing the food on the picnic table, she turned, taking a deep breath. Scott should be here. His Army buddies had dropped in and he was missing it. Callie had talked about how much Jack relied on his friends, how close they were. Scott was part of this group.

Callie took the plate Jack held out then arranged it on the table. "Charlotte didn't want to come today, Heather? You did tell her she was invited?"

Sweet Callie, always trying to get her mind off her troubles. "Yes, I told her. She's got plans with some friends but said thanks."

"What's the plan for getting Scott out of this shit storm?" Nick asked, then tipped his bottle of beer, taking a long swallow. The men wanted to stay on the topic of their friend. She couldn't disagree.

"Not much we can do at this point," Keith answered. "It's illegal to interfere with a criminal investigation. He needs a good lawyer."

Unfortunately, due to the holiday weekend they hadn't been able to contact one yet.

"Illegal for you law enforcers." Nick tilted his head at Keith, Drew, and Chris. "But I don't work for the government or answer to any of them."

"Do you really not care about getting arrested—or worse, killed—Nick?" Chris asked, his eyes on his wife, who carried more food to the table.

Nick shrugged. "Need to help my friends. That's more important than myself."

Heather wondered about their friend, Nick. She'd only met him a handful of times but he seemed like a bit of a rebel. Scott never said too much about Afghanistan but had hinted that something had happened to Nick to make him this dark and reckless. Did Scott have trauma in his past too? War was hell on everyone. Would she ever get the chance to ask him?

"Any plans to help your cousin, Jack?" Nick directed his stare across the table.

Setting Jonathan into a high chair, Jack cut up some of the food on the child-size plate. "I've got a call into some friends at the Bureau. They plan to look into this Carla Findley, who Scott supposedly hurt. We'll see what her background is and who she associates with."

"You got the woman's name? Drew wouldn't give it to me." She glared at Drew accusingly.

He looked down at his plate and took a deep breath. "I hated not being able to divulge the information but it could cost my job. If Jack discovered it some other way, that's a different story."

"I can do a little checking myself," Chris offered. "Though I can't dig too deep if she's not on my caseload, but I can run a general background check."

His wife, Meg, placed her hand on his arm. "If you lose your job we can always live on my salary. You know we teachers really rake in the dough."

"Except you don't even start for another few months, sweetie." Chris leaned over to kiss her.

Heather was beginning to like Scott's friends. They were loyal. She hated to admit she was a bit envious of Jack and Callie, Chris and Meg, and how in love they all seemed. At some point in her life she wanted that. It used to be far away, but the more she saw it, the closer it got on her radar.

But for now she had to focus on making sure the mill project stayed on schedule and Scott could get off these ridiculous charges. Carla Findley. Yes, Chris and Jack had people checking her out, but was there anything she could do? Her father certainly had resources. Probably not better than the FBI.

What about street resources? An idea came to her, but she pushed it aside. No, that would never work, plus it was dangerous. But then again… Jian owed Scott a life debt, and it seemed like the man was willing to pay. Would he be able to get more information on this Carla and why she had it out for Scott? How could she get in touch with him? She could hardly stroll into the south side of Hartford asking around for him. From what she understood, there were numerous gangs who hung out in that city. Like the ones trying to rape Jian's little sister. God, talk about evil. No, she couldn't do that.

But she could go check on the building. Scott had planned to do that this weekend at some point. She was co-owner, it was her responsibility to keep things running too. Perhaps some of Jian's men would be there and they could get a message to him. To meet her somewhere.

Scooping some potato salad onto her plate, she listened as the others chatted about a variety of things. She'd hang out here for a few hours and help Callie clean up. But once things calmed down she'd take a visit to the project. It might not be the smartest thing she ever did, but Scott had said being dubbed his lady would keep her safe.

Chapter 11

Scott shifted on the lumpy mattress again and peeked over the edge. Halfway through yesterday he'd gotten a roommate. The man, Billy Chadwick, was in his mid-thirties, but looked like he'd been around a lot longer than that. Apparently he'd been here before if the interaction with the guards was anything to go by.

The foul smell from the toilet drifted up and he tucked his nose into the less than fragrant mattress. He'd happily given up the bottom bunk when Billy had started heaving and crapping on the toilet. No way did he want the man puking over the side of the bunk from the top. Or shitting his pants as he tried to climb down to get to the toilet. The guards didn't care that Billy had some stomach issues.

Right now he should be at Jack's having a cold one and roughhousing with Jonathan. Or shooting the shit with Nick, Keith, Chris, or Drew. Or attempting to get Heather backed into a private corner and messing with her mind. The way she totally messed with his.

"They're gonna come get me," Billy wailed from below, his scratchy tone like fingernails on a chalkboard. He'd been spouting off dire warnings since he'd shown up twenty-four hours ago. "Don't let them take me."

"I think I'd be happy for them to take you right about now," Scott muttered under his breath. Aside from a few stretches, he hadn't slept the last two nights. The first night had been constant lights flickering on and off every half hour while inmates randomly yelled profanities at the guards as they did.

"They'll get you too." Apparently Billy had heard his words. Like he cared what some nutjob ranted about. If someone wanted to take him away from here, he'd welcome it.

"Throw you in a hole. Keep you there with no light or food. All tangled up in your own nightmares."

Scott tried to ignore the rantings, but some of what the man said struck a nerve. There'd been a time he'd been stuck in a hole with no light or food. Afghanistan. It was during the shelling of a village they'd been working to evacuate. The whole damn building had fallen down around him and some other men from his unit. He'd been wedged in between concrete walls, his arm twisted underneath his body, unable to move.

Sitting up, he shook his head and tried to get the images out of his mind. Not that the images were clear. It had been pitch-black for the two days he'd been stuck there. Sound, though. There'd been plenty of sound. More shelling, letting him know his unit wouldn't be able to get to him until it stopped. Groans and screams of others who had also been trapped nearby. More injured than him. Like Todd.

They'd been working together when the shelling started. Todd had pushed him ahead as the rubble rained down. Hadn't mattered. They'd both been caught in the debris, buried under tons of concrete and steel. Civilians had also been trapped, their cries of pain echoing throughout the destroyed walls.

Two days of listening to the sounds of agony and despair and having it slowly stop as each person succumbed to their injuries. That had been almost more painful to hear. Praying these people were simply unconscious but knowing the real possibility of what had happened. He'd managed to get out with a broken arm, a few broken ribs, a slight concussion, and dehydration. Guilt too. Tons and tons of guilt. For living when many others hadn't.

Staring through the bars out into the cell block, he gave thanks that he had that view from this tiny space. He'd found small enclosed areas now sent him into a place he didn't like. Made him feel weak and vulnerable, like he'd been while trapped in the rubble. This room was small, but at least it had the open front. Sure, that wasn't a ridiculous thought. He was somehow thankful for iron bars locking him in. But at least it gave the illusion of being able to get out, breathe.

"Aarrgh." Billy groaned and hefted himself to the toilet again.

Scott tried to block out the sound of the man's distress. The smells from the unit were bad enough without his roommate adding even worse to this small space.

The rustle of fabric preceded a few choice swears.

"They shut the damn water off."

"What?" He twisted on the bunk gazing down to where Billy stood turning the tap. No water flowed and the toilet was full. Good thing he hadn't been able to stomach much of the nasty lunch they'd delivered.

"Why would they shut the water off?"

Billy shook his head as he rocked back and forth. "Bad things happening. They gonna come now. Gonna get us. Get us, get us, get us."

The sound of metal doors being opened and inmates rumbling objections echoed down the cell block. What the hell was going on? For the next hour, cells were opened and curses lit the air. All the while the foul smell of the unflushed toilet churned his stomach, reminding him of some of the places he'd served in.

"All right, we need to search the cell," one of the guards thundered as he slipped the key into their lock and turned.

"Search the cell? What for? We haven't left it since we got here." What were they looking for?

"Got a report of a shank in the unit. Every cell, every inmate has to be searched."

"Every inmate?"

"Shut up," the guard snapped pulling on a pair of rubber gloves. "I don't like doing strip searches any more than you'll like it, but it's regulations."

"Strip search?" Shit, it had been bad enough when they'd patted him down at the police station. "I thought someone in 'safe keep' couldn't be strip searched because we haven't been arraigned yet."

"Not without probable cause, but a shank in the unit is enough reason. Both of you step outside."

Billy scurried past him and stood in the hall while Scott moved behind him. Four more guards stood there surrounding them. Another set of guards did the same thing on the other side of the block. The first guard went in, flipped up the mattresses then looked inside the toilet tank, avoiding the bowl. Yeah, he totally understood that. The contents were vile.

"Okay, Billy, you first. You know the drill. Everything off, one piece at a time, and hand them to me."

Billy walked back inside the cell and pulled off his shirt, throwing it to the guard inside, who then patted it down to examine before he handed it to another guard. Scott turned away, attempting to give the man some privacy. The guards didn't seem to have the same decency, but then it was their job to make sure everything was safe.

"Why do you shut the water off when you do this?" he asked the guard closest to him.

"So you can't flush something down the toilet."

"Like I'd even go within twenty feet of that toilet after he's been using it all day."

The guard's eyebrow rose, his lip curving up. "The cell's only seven-by-ten."

He kept himself from rolling his eyes. It was only a saying.

"All set, Billy. Out in the hall. Your turn, Holland."

Scott walked into the cell, holding his breath from the stench. "What do I do?"

"Stand right there and remove your clothing, one piece at a time. Don't take off the next one until I tell you to."

Reaching for the collar, he pulled the shirt off. When he handed it to the guard, the man turned it inside out then gave it to another guard, who dropped it on the floor near his feet.

"Boots next."

When he started to sit, the guard poked him, shaking his head. Great, he couldn't even sit to remove his boots. He bent, untied them, then passed them over. They'd already checked these when he came in a couple days ago.

"Pants."

The pants dropped and he kicked them in the direction of the guard, who snarled, picking them up to examine them. This wasn't too embarrassing, standing here in his boxer briefs in an open cell with five guards standing around.

"Socks."

The floor was chilly against his bare feet. God knew how many germs were jumping on for a ride right now.

"Shorts."

Swallowing, he pulled them down, tossing them over. Shit, this sucked big time.

"Hands on your head. Open your mouth."

Open his mouth, what the fuck? But he complied and the guard stuck his fingers inside and swept around.

Whistling came from the cells across the hall and his cheeks heated. Great, he had an audience. It might be a good thing he couldn't leave the cell. He had a feeling from the expressions of some of the other inmates, he'd be popular in the shower.

Over the calls of "pretty boy," and "you're mine," Scott said, "The least you could have done was put on a new pair of gloves. Those things were all over Billy's clothes."

The guard growled. "Yeah, life in here sucks. Turn around and bend over with your hands on the bunk."

God, could this get any worse? Hands cupped his junk then swiftly moved away. His clothes were tossed back at him with a gruff, "Get dressed."

All eyes were still focused on him while he slipped into the lovely orange ensemble then was hustled back into the hall. Two more guards went in and did another, more thorough search.

"Found something," one of them called out. The guards in the hall surrounded him and Billy, while the first guard took what looked like a piece of bent metal and held it up.

"Either one of you going to take responsibility for this?"

Shit and fuck. Did he have no luck at all? It had to be Billy's, but the man was three fries short of a Happy Meal. Who knew what he'd do.

"No, no, no," Billy wailed, starting to rock back and forth. "Don't want to go in the hole. No hole for me. No."

"You know the rules, Billy. Is it yours?"

Still rocking back and forth, the man muttered, "No, no, no."

"Yours, Holland?"

"Are you kidding me? Where would I get something like that? And why would I even have it? It's not like I'm allowed to wander around this lovely establishment. It looks a little too big to clean my teeth with."

The first guard sighed, looking like he wanted to slap Scott's fresh mouth. Damn his sarcasm. Too often he forgot to check with his brain if it was an appropriate time.

"Hands out."

Billy thrust his hands in front of him and Scott followed suit. Handcuffs were slapped on then another guard came over with leg irons. Seriously? Leg irons. What the fuck did they think he could do in handcuffs that leg irons would prohibit? These people watched a few too many action flicks. He may have been in the Army, but if they thought he could take on these five guards and the five across the way, all with sticks and bulging muscles, they were sadly mistaken.

After his legs were encased in the metal, they led him and Billy out of the unit into a small hall nearby with several doors. Two of them were opened and they were each ushered inside. No slot for them to remove the restraints on this door. That didn't bode well.

"What is this?" Scott dared ask, as the guard started to close the door.

"Segregation. Regulation for when something is found in a cell."

"It wasn't mine, I swear. I just want to stay quiet and get to my arraignment without any trouble."

The guard shrugged, his face slightly apologetic. "I gotta follow the rules. Doesn't matter what I think. At least you won't have to smell Billy and his mess anymore."

"How long am I in here?"

"Until you get arraigned."

"Will this go against me at my arraignment?"

"Nah, it's just a policy. Enjoy the quiet."

Scott glanced around the small room as the door closed. Was it even smaller than the one he'd come from? No bars on the front making the place seem more open. No windows, except for the one in the heavy door. One bunk and the toilet combo. Nothing else.

Sliding onto the thin mattress on the bunk, he pulled up his legs as best he could and thrust his hands into his hair, the handcuffs clinking. Hair that hadn't been washed or combed in two days. Like the rest of him.

One dim bulb lit the tiny enclosure, casting shadows on the walls. Small. Closed in. Suffocating.

No, he could breathe. He took a few deep breaths to prove to himself that he could. Why was he feeling jittery? He could do this. He only needed to get through another thirty-eight hours and he'd be out of here.

But would he actually be free to go home? Best-case scenario was the police had discovered the truth and the blue-haired chick had come clean. He'd be exonerated and allowed to leave and continue his life.

Worst case? He didn't even want to think of the worst case. Because it involved being labeled a sexual predator, a woman beater, and spending way more time in a place like this than he ever wanted to think about. He'd gotten through the last couple days. It hadn't been great, but he'd certainly managed. But what if he needed to stay here for any length of time? Having strip searches whenever something seemed off. Being ogled by other inmates or surrounded in the shower. He'd heard stories, knew what happened. In a one-on-one fight, he could take care of himself, but if there was a gang, he wouldn't stand much of a chance.

And what of Heather and their project? Something was going on, and putting him in prison wouldn't keep someone from going after Heather if the building was what they wanted. He needed to get out of here to protect her.

Jack would keep an eye out for her. He could count on the other guys to check things out too. But they had their own lives and couldn't be with her all the time. Not like he could. Or wanted to. If anything happened to her because he wasn't around to help her, he'd have even more guilt piled on the shit that already overwhelmed him.

Being alone, not having to listen to Billy ramble and shit, gave him too much time to think. Think about being here permanently. About Heather and how much he wanted to spend more time with her. The verbal sparring they participated in got his brain warmed up, and what it did to his body... *Don't go there.* Or to the memory of her body. Dangerous territory.

Hours later when the lights flickered and went out, Scott finally allowed himself to recline on the bunk and close his eyes. It was a good way to pretend he wasn't in a tight space with a locked door he had no way of opening. The chains on his hands and legs were a bit harder to imagine away. Not that he hadn't fantasized about Heather in handcuffs, but they were both wearing a lot less than his orange prison suit in those dreams.

He kept his mind moving through various mundane tasks he needed to accomplish once he got out. If he kept himself busy with that, perhaps he wouldn't feel the suffocation of being trapped in the rubble again.

* * * *

The streetlamp flickered as Heather walked along the deserted sidewalk. Laughter rang out and cars screeched, carrying over from nearby sections of town, letting her know she wasn't alone. A scream, then silence, had her jumping and glancing into the growing darkness. Taking a deep breath, she continued on, hoping to find some of Jian's men. She needed to speak to him. See if he could shed some light on why this blue-haired bitch thought it was okay to accuse Scott of some nasty stuff.

The streetlamp next to the mill building was out. She made a mental note to ask the town to fix it. Once they had businesses and people living here, they needed it to be a safer environment. She'd only been here during the day or with Scott and had never felt threatened, but now with the shadows falling around the buildings, her skin prickled and the hair on her nape stood up.

"Ooh wee, lookie what we got here."

Spinning at the voice, she found herself flanked by two men. Shit. She couldn't see much of them in the dark, but they were tall and closing in on her. Reaching into her pocket for her pepper spray, she sidestepped one only to bump into three more. Where had they come from?

"What's the matter, rich girl, don't like playing with the poor boys?"

She'd worn her most faded pair of jeans and a plain button-down blouse. How could they tell she was rich? Or did it even matter? Her eyes darted from one to the other, then away to see if anyone else was around.

"I'm not looking for any trouble." Her voice squeaked trying to get through her dry mouth.

"No trouble here, sweet cheeks. We're the fun squad. You'll enjoy being with us."

Doubtful. They didn't have on the black and red the Dragons usually wore. A variety of hoodies and ball caps let her know they weren't part of a gang. Didn't mean they weren't dangerous. She sucked air into her lungs, hoping to help her breathe. Best get the hell away from them. But go where? Inside the mill building? The last thing she wanted was to be trapped in there with these thugs, and they could most likely get in even if she managed to lock the door.

Her stomach dropped as they surrounded her. Shit. Holding out the pepper spray with shaking hands, she gave them one last chance. "I'd like to be alone, thanks."

The spray was ripped out of her fingers. What the hell had she thought they'd do? Whimper at the sight of it then slink off somewhere? Her heart pounded heavily and she jolted as an arm wrapped around her waist. Jerking back against the man behind her, she kicked out at the one in front. Catching him in the stomach, she twisted but another grabbed her leg, causing her to lose her footing. In seconds she was held aloft by three of them and yet another moved closer as she struggled.

"I told you it'd be fun, but you don't believe me." This guy seemed like the ringleader.

Fun, right. One brute holding her from behind and a few clutching her legs. Shit, and double damn. She kicked her feet, squirming. Nothing. Oh, God. Why'd she come by herself? Dumb move. Scott had friends who would have come. Stupid girl. Stupid, stupid, stupid. If her heart beat any faster it might explode.

"But I'm okay doing it the hard way. I kind of like someone who fights back." He flicked his hands away from each other and the thugs pulled her legs apart. Shit, was he going to rape her right here on the street? Sweat trickled down her neck and back.

A scream escaped from her mouth but the guy walking between her legs slapped his hand over her lips stifling the sound. She clamped down on it with her teeth and he pulled it away only to backhand her. Her vision tilted and twirled.

"Tape."

Shit, damn, fuck. Duct tape covered her mouth as she began twisting and struggling harder. It didn't matter. It was like she was caught in a steel trap.

The leader ran one hand down her blouse and used the other to pop the snap on her jeans. "Now let's see these pretty little tits." The buttons of her shirt scattered as he ripped the front open.

"Look boys, I found Victoria's secret. I bet she has other secrets we can find."

Oh, God, oh, God, oh God! This was really happening. Tears streamed down her face as she kicked and squirmed. Her skin crawled as four of them groped her, keeping her from gaining any leverage. The blood rushed from her face and the street swirled around her.

The big fucker's hands grabbed her waistband, tugging, while the man behind her pulled. Her jeans started to lower and there was nothing she could do to stop these bastards. Tightening her muscles, she squeezed her eyes shut, praying for a miracle.

"I'm not sure the lady is willing." The soft voice with a different accent had her eyes popping open.

"Fuck, Dragons. Get out of here, man."

Her body tumbled as the thugs rushed off, but something caught her head before it hit the ground. The tape was gently tugged from her mouth, the taste of glue sour against her lips.

"Are you all right, Ms. Silva?" Footsteps and rustling barely registered as background noise.

Looking up, she saw black clothes, a red bandanna. One of Jian's friends. Thank God. Truly, she'd be back in church tomorrow saying a shitload of novenas with this sacred rescue.

A giggle escaped. What the hell? The world spun and she crumpled into a ball, sobs racking her body. The tremors wouldn't stop. It was her own damn fault for being such an idiot.

Arms held her gently, rubbing her back as a soft voice said, "I am Kang. I met you when you were with Holland."

It took a few moments to rouse from her fetal state. The face nearby looked familiar. He'd been with Jian before. "I remember. Thank you." Another sob escaped and she wiped her hand across her face. The damn thing wouldn't stop shaking. "For helping me."

"You want us to kill these men?" Kang asked, pointing down the street to where several Dragons had the four brutes on their knees, hands on their heads. How had she missed that scuffle? Shit, she'd been out of it. Knives dug into their throats. They were crying now too. Good.

Kill them, yes. She wanted that with every fiber of her being, but that would make her no better than them. "We should let the police take care of them." Damn her trembling voice.

Kang shook his head. "Police will wonder why a lady like you was here alone. Good lawyer will say you wanted them to take you. Better us to take care of them."

"Sure, but can you do it without killing them? Teach them a lesson so they won't do it again." These creeps couldn't be allowed to get away with it.

"Yes, teach them not to mess with Dragon's protected people." Kang lifted his chin and his friends dragged them off down the street.

"Why are you down here without your man? It's a dangerous place alone." Wrapping her arms around her legs, she glanced left and right. Dangerous. Which meant they needed to find a way to clean it up before they finished renovating the building. Another giggle. Sure, keep her mind on something besides the fact she'd almost been gang-raped. A shiver rushed through her. God, she was a mess.

"Scott's in jail. I need Jian's help to find out what's going on. Do you know where he is?"

"Come with me. I will take you to him."

Would her legs even work? Tremors shook her enough that she stumbled as Kang assisted her to her feet. Her blouse fell open and she immediately pulled the sides closed. Holy shit, she couldn't control her twitching muscles. It had been too damn close. Her legs felt like jelly. When she swayed, Kang held her arm and walked her toward a car.

"Here," he said, handing her a black button-down shirt he pulled from the vehicle. It was huge on her but she didn't care as she buttoned it all the way up to her neck, fuck the summer heat. Her pants zipper stuck as she tried to get it up, so she only did up the snap and let the shirt hang over it.

"You must put this on before we go." He handed her a red bandanna and she tilted her head in question.

"You cannot see where we go. It is for your protection. This way you cannot be forced to tell where we are. You do not know."

She looked up and down the street, her heart racing in her chest. Would the thugs come back? Was she safe? Scott trusted these people, but she still wasn't sure.

"You are safe. No one will harm you. I promise."

Nodding, she wrapped the fabric around her eyes, tying it. The car rolled down the street and she sighed at the relief that coursed through her.

"How did you know I was in trouble? Or did you stumble on us while you were watching the building?"

"We have eyes and ears in many places. You are under our protection. I apologize we were not sooner."

"Oh, your timing was freakin' perfect. Don't get me wrong, before they ripped my Dior blouse would have been even better, but you got there before any real harm was done. I am eternally grateful. I guess I now owe you."

"No, you owe us nothing. Men who rape are cowards, not real men."

The car slowed then stopped and she was led from the vehicle still blindfolded. Kang helped her so she didn't trip then she was settled in a comfortable chair. Her nerves still stood on alert and her skin prickled when she felt another presence.

"You may remove the blindfold, Ms. Silva," Jian said, his voice in front of her. "Thank you for agreeing to keep our location a secret."

Pulling the bandana down, she said, "Did I have a choice?"

Jian only smiled. "Kang said Holland is in trouble."

"Yes, I need your help." Her chest was still tight, her muscles tense, but she had to push past her fear to help Scott. She explained what had happened and that the evidence was stacked against him. "Her name is Carla Findley. I don't know why she's claiming Scott did this to her, but he didn't. I know he didn't."

"I will have my people look into it. Could be she is doing this under someone else's command. We will find out. How can I contact you?"

Heather rattled off her phone number, her heart ripping to shreds at the thought of Scott serving jail time for a crime he didn't commit. Jian obviously believed he hadn't done it either because he never even questioned it. Or he didn't care and his debt to Scott was true.

"Kang will bring you back home."

"I have my car near the mill."

"Are you well enough to drive?"

Her stomach still felt like it was going to revolt and her lungs might have collapsed somewhere along the way but she'd pull it all together and be fine. She nodded.

"Then Kang will take you to your vehicle and follow you home. Please, do not argue. Holland would be quite upset if we did not assure your safety."

The thought did make her feel less anxious, which was strange, since typically having a street gang member follow her home would freak her the hell out.

"Thank you, Jian. I can't tell you how grateful I am for this." She reached up to kiss his cheek then picked up the blindfold. "I assume I need this again."

"You are a wise woman, Ms. Silva. Holland is indeed lucky to have you in his life."

As she sat in the car on the way back, she truly hoped she'd be back in Scott's life. And that he'd be able to be in hers.

Chapter 12

"Next case: Scott Holland."

Scott stood and walked over to the table where the other defendants had been standing. He'd been here for over an hour listening to the other people being arraigned. Apparently, it had been a busy weekend for crimes.

The bailiff read out his right to a trial and all the other information. He'd heard the same thing six times already this morning. He understood. When his charges were read, Scott cringed. It sounded horrible. It was horrible. But he hadn't done it.

The judge looked him up and down. A woman. Usually he was more than happy to have a woman doing any kind of job, but it seemed everything was stacked against him now. A female detective, an Assistant DA whose goal was to stop men who hurt women, and now a female judge. He'd bet his life she had some agenda against women beaters too. Not that he was one, or wanted them to get away with it, but shit, couldn't he catch a break?

The ADA read off the evidence against him. Too damned much. He almost believed he'd done it.

"How do you plead, Mr. Holland?" Judge Mary Barlow asked.

He clenched his hands at his side, wishing he'd had something nicer to wear to this hearing. But he hadn't even been allowed time for a shower before he was given back his dirty work clothes and brought to court.

"Not guilty, Your Honor."

She tried to keep her expression neutral but the tightening of her jaw let him know her thoughts on attacking a woman.

After whispering a few things to the court clerk, she looked back up. "Pre-trial conference will be scheduled for two weeks from today, July nineteenth."

"Your Honor," the prosecutor cut in. "We are asking for the defendant not to be released on bail considering the violent nature of the crime and the condition of the victim. You've seen the evidence of her injuries."

No. Fuckin'. Way. How could they do that to him? Spend another two weeks in that facility? This time he'd most likely be able to move around, hanging with the nice boys. Like the ones who'd asked for a date when he'd been dragged past their cells this morning. Shit.

He looked at his lawyer, who was practically shaking at the thought of talking in court. Scott cleared his throat and glared at the kid.

"Um, Your Honor. Mr. Holland has no prior convictions and runs a respectable business in the state. He is not a flight risk. We request he be let out on his own recognizance." Finally, something in his favor. It probably could have been more though. He'd done lots of good things in his life. Where was his list of them all?

The judge scanned the documents on her desk and looked up. "I see that, but prosecution has a good point. Due to the violent nature of the crime bail is set at five hundred thousand dollars."

Five hundred thousand. Holy shit. How the hell would he come up with that kind of money? He certainly had equity in the business, but he'd taken out a huge loan for the renovation project.

"Next case: William Chadwick."

Scott threw Billy a tight smile as he moved away from the table. The court officer who escorted him here led him back out to a waiting area in a private room. A few other men sat there too.

"What happens now?" he asked the officer.

"You stay here until either your bail is posted or the van is ready to bring you back to the correctional facility. There's a phone over in the corner if you want to arrange bail."

Scott nodded, moving into the room. The phone was currently being used. Who would he call anyway? Jack? He and Callie certainly didn't have the money to post bail. Keith was a Boston cop. Cops didn't make big money and his friend sent much of his pay to help his parents. Drew? Would that be a conflict of interest having a prosecutor for the DA's office bail him out? Plus, Drew was still paying off huge law school loans.

Nick? He came from money. Lots of money. But he and his dad were on the outs. Would he be willing to eat some crow to get a loan? Scott wasn't sure he wanted to ask his friend to do that.

That didn't leave him with a whole lot of options. *There's one option you haven't mentioned.* He didn't even want to go there. Heather. Sure, they were partners, but did she believe that he didn't do this? Or was there some niggling doubt in her mind that he had? He'd pushed her a few times with the sexual innuendos. Maybe more than innuendos. Would she think her refusal had set him off to do this to someone else? He stared at the window in the room, wondering if it would be one of the last times he'd get to see outside. Three more guys took their turn on the phone before it was finally his. He moved toward the table to pick up the receiver, still not sure who he'd call.

"Scott Holland."

The clerk waved at him. "You've been released on bail. Here's the form with the dates of your next appearance. You are reminded to stay away from the witness. Please sign here."

"Wait. Bail? Who...?"

Her finger pointed to where he needed to sign, but his eyes skimmed the rest of the document. Heather Silva. God, he could kiss her. Desperately wanted to kiss her.

The pen moved across the form and he looked at the clerk who pointed down the hall. He didn't need to be told twice. Shoving his copy in his pocket, he half-trotted down the corridor. There stood Heather. Gorgeous as ever, her silky hair falling around her shoulders, not pulled back into its proper confines. Her smart business suit showcased her shapely figure and her high heels accentuated those incredible long legs. He could eat her up right here.

"Scott. How are you?"

Pulling her in for a hug, he nodded, not wanting to let her go. "I don't even know how to thank you. That's a hell of a lot of money."

Easing back, she said, "You're worth it. But I'll get it back when they drop these ridiculous charges, so no worries."

"Let's hope they drop the charges," he said, taking her elbow and walking toward the exit. He couldn't get out of here fast enough. "The evidence they have against me is stacked pretty high."

Outside the entrance, she stopped on the top step. "But you didn't do it and we'll prove it. For now we're going to get you home. I'm guessing it's been a hell of a weekend."

"You have no idea." He skimmed his hand along her cheek, noticing a discoloration. One she'd tried to hide with makeup. "What happened here?"

Rolling her eyes, she shrugged. "Stupid me. I walked into something."

Her discomfort was apparent, and he wondered if she was embarrassed or if something more had happened. He was too tired to push the question. The ride was quiet. What was Heather thinking about and what should he say to her? The rhythm of the vehicle lulled him into an almost comatose state. Little sleep, and the constant anxiety of what would happen, had drained him.

"I'll get the money back for you." He finally broke the silence as they pulled up to his apartment complex.

"Scott." She got out of the car and glared at him.

"I will," he broke in before she could argue. "Regardless of what happens. If I get sent to jail, I'll sell my share in the company. But I will get it back to you."

Linking her arm in his, they went inside and used the elevator. He didn't have the strength, emotional or physical, to think about climbing stairs today. Once inside his place, he sagged against the door.

"What can I get you?" Heather cocked her head, her expression concerned.

"I need a shower. Want to scrub off all the scum of the prison cell before I do anything else."

"Go take it then, and I'll throw something together to eat while you're in there."

"Thanks." As he walked past, her lips begged for a kiss. Not in this condition though. "Don't go to any trouble. I can get something later if you need to be somewhere more important."

"Nowhere more important than here, Scott."

His eyes slid to where she bent over to slip off her shoes. Damn, she had a fine ass. He shut the bathroom door firmly and adjusted the water.

His typical shower was only a few minutes, but today he spent much longer. The memories of Billy and the smell of the cell flickered in his mind as he scrubbed harder, allowing the warm water to wash away the images of sitting alone in the segregation cell. At least it hadn't reeked, not as badly as the other one.

Grabbing a towel, he dried off and ran it through his hair to get rid of the excess water. His clothes were in the bedroom, though. Heather hadn't minded him in a towel last week so he slung it low on his hips and opened the door. Although to be truthful, her cheeks had turned pink as her eyes skimmed his bare chest while she cleaned up his cuts.

"I made you an omelet." Her voice rang from the kitchen.

"Just throwing on some pants," he called. Her perfectly-styled head poked out then back in the doorway when she saw him looking in her direction.

Sweatpants were all he had energy for at the moment. He pulled on a pair and then went to sit at the counter where a plate sat ready for him.

"Milk or orange juice?" She looked cute in her bare feet, sticking her head inside the fridge.

"Milk, but I can get it myself. You've already done enough."

Bringing a glass over, she sat on the stool next to him and watched as he dug into the eggs.

"Thank you, again."

"It's what friends do for each other, Scott. And my father gave me the names of a few lawyers who might be available to help you."

"Pick one who can work miracles. Listening to the evidence they have today made *me* almost believe I was guilty."

* * * *

Putting his fork down, Scott ran his hands through his still-damp hair. The hair Heather wanted to slide her fingers through. A few locks fell over his forehead and she brushed them back.

"No one who knows you would ever believe that."

"Not sure those are the people who will be on a jury. Don't they have rules against that stuff?"

"There are already people working on the case. We need to figure out why this lady said you beat her up. And get her to tell who actually did it."

He let out a big sigh and dropped his head into his hands. Only half his meal had been touched. When he looked up his gaze zeroed in on the bruise on her arm. The one the thug trying to rape her had given her. Along with the bruise on her face. Her jacket had concealed it earlier.

"What happened here? Why do you have all these bruises?" His concerned voice was sweet but she couldn't tell him the truth right now. He'd been through enough.

"They all happened at the same time. Me being stupid and clumsy." That was the truth at least. Part of it anyway. "Finish your food and then you should take a nap."

The twinkle in his eyes returned, warming her heart and sending flutters to her stomach. "What, I'm an infant now?"

"Sure, baby," she teased, then said seriously, "You look tired."

"You know those parties in the county jail."

His lips turned up but something flared in his eyes, letting her know it had been anything but fun. Reaching over, she squeezed his hand. He squeezed back then took a few more bites of the omelet.

"Maybe I will sack out for a short time."

"I'll clean up here and let you sleep."

Standing, he took her hand and pulled. "You could join me."

Usually he said those words with such sexual heat, it took her breath away. Today his eyes held desperation. She couldn't have walked away if she tried.

In his room, he slumped on the bed and tugged until she stood between his knees. Wrapping her arms around him, she kneaded at the knots on his shoulders. His head leaned against her, right between her breasts. But he wasn't trying to get into her blouse. She stood there for a while, hoping he was getting the support she was sending.

"Lay back," she said after a few minutes then pushed at his chest. His nicely muscled and bare chest. He complied but didn't let go of her, and she toppled next to him. Twisting, he settled so they were facing each other, side by side.

"Um, you're supposed to be resting."

"I'll rest easier if you're here beside me." His bare foot nudged against hers.

Grinning, she said, "Would you like me to rub your back? Sing you a lullaby?"

"Sure." His lips touched her forehead as he pulled her closer. She began to hum. It certainly wouldn't be relaxing if she sang. Her singing usually sent dogs running away, howling.

His body tensed beside her and she stroked her hands down his torso and back up again then pulled on his neck. Their lips came together then Scott tightened his arms as his kiss grew in strength and intensity.

"God, Heather."

She allowed him in, gasping as his tongue tangled with hers. When he rolled her on her back, she took advantage and skimmed her fingers over the taut muscles of his shoulders then down. Damn, this man was built. Not in a body-builder sort of way, but all lean and sculpted muscles. Done the old-fashioned way, not in a gym.

The kissing continued but Scott never moved his hands. One held her head while the other, at her waist, made sure she stayed where she was. His lips gentled and his face eased back but his forehead stayed touching hers.

"I'm sorry. I was too rough."

Caressing the side of his face, she said, "You didn't hear me complaining. Seems like I was equally as involved."

He closed his eyes and breathed deeply. When he opened them again, gratitude shone in their depths. He kissed her again, this time sweet, and—dare she even say—lovingly. His lips skimmed along hers, his tongue tracing the outline. Watching him was heartbreaking. Like she was the answer to all his problems. Not likely. She was merely a distraction. But she was happy to help him if it meant he could forget everything for a short while.

Pushing him, she adjusted so they faced each other again, their lips still in contact. They felt right, touching, nibbling, nipping, and caressing. His fingers stroking her cheek.

As his eyes fluttered, she moved her lips down his face, snuggling up closer. "Rest."

"Mmm" was all she heard, though his arms encircled her in a steel band. Nothing too tight but he wasn't letting her go anywhere. It was all right, she didn't want to leave where she was. It felt good. Was this how Callie felt when she had Jack next to her in bed every night? It was pretty damned fantastic.

Scott's heart beat under her ear as his breathing evened out. She should wait a few more minutes until he was definitely asleep then sneak out. There was lots of work to do at her office. His nose nestled in her hair and the scent of his natural soap wafted into hers. Work could wait.

The man in her arms needed her at this moment. It hadn't been too often she'd been needed. For her money or her connections, sure. But for the comfort of her presence, maybe Callie, but no one else. It was kind of nice for someone to want her here simply for herself. She wouldn't be giving that up any time soon.

* * * *

"Where's Scott?"

Heather let Jack and Drew into Scott's apartment then closed the door gently behind them.

"He was sleeping a few minutes ago. It must not have been too relaxing in the prison cell."

Jack glanced in the direction of Scott's bedroom. "How's he doing?"

"Hungry and tired," she said, leading the men to sit in the living area. They didn't need to know Scott's sleep had been troubled. Staying beside him for a few hours, she'd needed to whisper in his ear and stroke his face when nightmares had assailed him. She suspected more than the weekend in jail caused them.

"Has something ever happened to him to make him feel trapped?"

Both men turned to look at her, eyes concerned.

"Why do you ask?" Jack leaned forward, his forearms resting on his knees.

"He said something in his sleep." Thrashed in his sleep was more like it. Not that she'd share that right now. Not unless it got worse. But their eyes told her she was right.

"In Afghanistan, Scott was in a village when insurgents started shelling," Drew said. "The building he was in collapsed. He was trapped for a few days. Pretty tight quarters. He told me once it was like being in a coffin." Drew looked away and his jaw tightened.

"We couldn't get in there until the shelling stopped." Jack's face was like granite. Was he remembering how worried he'd been for his cousin?

"How bad was he injured?"

Looking around the room, Drew said, "He made it out. Lots of others didn't. I know that still bothers him."

"Have you gotten any information on the woman who's accusing him of beating her up?"

"I'd like to know that too." Scott's voice behind them was scratchy, like he'd swallowed gravel. From sleep or anxiety?

Settling on the couch next to her, he reached for her hand and squeezed. His smile was grateful. Because she stayed near him as he slept, or something else? Whatever it was, she was more than happy to support him.

"I spoke with Chris and he did some background checking on Ms. Findley," Jack said, leaning back in his chair. His eyes roamed his cousin, his expression one of worry. She checked him out as well. He'd pulled on a T-shirt but still had the sweatpants clinging to his muscular legs. His hair was tousled, like he'd had some wild sex. Didn't she wish that was true. With her, of course.

Shaking her head, she threw off those thoughts. He'd given her plenty of opportunity to be with him. She'd been the one who had pulled away. And right now, he needed her support and comfort, not sex.

"She has no priors and doesn't seem to be mixed up with anything unsavory," Jack continued. "However, her brother is a different story. He's into all sorts of shit. This could have something to do with him."

"I spoke with Judge Stokinger," Drew said. "You met him at the Law Library opening. Asked him if he had any advice, or if he could speak with the judge on the case, put in a good word."

"What'd he say?" Scott asked, his hand tightening on hers again. The fact he hadn't let it go spoke volumes. Scott wasn't the hand-holding type.

Drew's expression wasn't hopeful. "He seemed aware of the evidence and said it was solid. Said he'd check further into the case and if there was anything that could help us, he'd let me know."

"We shouldn't hold our breath, though, right?" Scott sighed and slumped back against the cushions.

Shrugging, Drew said, "He can't do all that much. He's retired now. But I appreciate his efforts. It's more than we could ask for."

Scott nodded. "Tell him I appreciate it. Jack, we should talk about what to do with the company."

"What do you mean, what to do? The company will stay the way it is."

Scott chuckled dryly. "If things don't go well for me, and they look pretty dismal right now, you'll need to take over everything."

Standing, Jack towered over his cousin. "Get that out of your head, now. We still have a few weeks until the pre-trial hearing."

"And it would be even longer until the actual trial," Drew added. "A good lawyer could stretch things out for a while. Give us more time to figure this out."

"Thanks." Scott's crooked grin held no warmth and his eyes narrowed in pain. "I don't understand what the hell is happening. I've been racking my brain, trying to remember if I did something to anyone in this lady's family. I need to do more digging to see if one of my projects affected her somehow. Anything else doesn't make sense."

"Or it's something to do with this mill building," she suggested. "We've had a bitch of a time getting permits through. I'll see if I can dig up the history on it."

"Or check out the other bidders who wanted it," Drew suggested. "This could be a way to get you to sell."

Running his hands through his hair, Scott took a deep breath. "This is an awful lot of trouble to go to just to get a building."

Heather's phone buzzed and she grabbed it from the table. Jian.

Looking at Scott, she slid her hand over the screen to read the text. "Jian has some information he says we should hear. He wants to meet."

"Jian? Has something else happened to the building?" Scott asked.

She shook her head. "No, it's about Carla Findley."

His eyes drilled into her. "How the hell does he know about her?"

"I told him."

"When did you see Jian?"

Heat crawled up her neck. He wouldn't be happy about this. "I went looking for him a few days ago."

"You went..." He held her upper arms, glaring. "What the fuck were you thinking going looking for him? His crowd is dangerous. You could have been killed, or worse." Yeah, she knew what the worse was but she'd never tell Scott about that little incident.

"I know but you said I was under his protection now. And I was fine." And she had been once Jian's men had come to her rescue.

"Jian? You mean the street gang guy?" Drew sat up straighter. "You aren't still hanging around with him, are you?"

"I don't hang around with him. But occasionally I need a favor and he's able to do it for me."

"This won't look good if the cops find out, Scott. It could make your case worse than it already is."

"Too late," Scott replied. "They already know. Probably one of the reasons my bail was so high, even though I'm not a flight risk."

Running her hand down his arm, trying to calm the anger she felt in him, she said, "What do you want me to say to Jian? Did you want to see what information he has?"

Scott shoved his hands through his hair again then rubbed them over his face. "I guess it can't hurt. Tell him I'll meet him at the mill in thirty minutes."

"We'll come too," Drew said, standing beside Jack.

"No." Scott shook them off. "Lawyer and ex-FBI. Not a good match for Jian. His trust only goes so far."

Tapping her fingers on the phone screen, she said, "I'll tell him we'll meet him."

Scott pushed himself off the couch. "You're not coming with me. I don't want you anywhere near these guys."

Standing, she followed him across the room. "You're not going by yourself. I want to help. And don't even try to give me the 'it's too dangerous' lecture. You'll be with me and I know I'm safe with you."

Scott didn't argue, simply entered his room to change his clothes. Strangely enough Heather wasn't worried about meeting with the street gang leader. With Scott, she felt safe. He'd never let anything happen to her. And as much as she hated admitting to needing anyone, for some weird reason, she didn't mind Scott wanting to protect her. It felt kind of nice.

Chapter 13

"I wish I knew what the hell this building has to do with all our problems," Scott grumbled as he and Heather crossed the large room on the first floor. Only a single light dangled overhead, and darkness filled the corners of the room.

Moving closer, she slipped her hand through his arm and hugged it. Was she afraid or simply seeking warmth? The warmth of another person, not heat, since the day was close to ninety degrees and humid. She'd changed from her earlier court clothes into capri pants with a snug T-shirt and sneakers.

"Did anyone do any work in here today?"

"No." He shook his head. "Once I knew what was happening Friday, I had Jack give all the workers another day for the holiday. Figured I'd need to see what my situation would be first. Jack has enough to deal with running the other sites we've got contracts with. He doesn't need this one too. This was supposed to be my baby."

"It still is. Hopefully Jian will have some good news."

"Not sure if it's good, dude, but it's information," Jian said from behind them. The man was total stealth.

"Thanks for helping out. What did you find?"

"This chick, Carla Findley, she owed quite a bit of money to one of the big crime bosses in Hartford."

"Do you know why? One of my FBI friends said she didn't have any brushes with the law."

"No, doesn't mean she can't need money in a hurry. Money she can't get at a bank." Jian shifted from side to side, his eyes alert. Scott didn't see any other members of the gang, but then he probably wouldn't.

"Did you find out what she needed the money for?" Heather asked, her voice strong but respectful. Good girl. She knew how to talk to Jian. He wasn't too happy she'd done it on her own, though.

"Her brother was big into drugs and needed help. Apparently, she sent him to some rehab place. But word is that her debt was paid in full."

"Paid in full? Because she took a beating and pinned it on me?"

"It wasn't from her waitress job, dude."

"Any idea who paid her debt?" Maybe he could find out who was behind this whole mill building fiasco.

"Nah, I can keep digging though. The information I got was that she agreed to do a job for someone but didn't expect what happened to her."

"I need to find out who she did the job for then get her to tell the police it wasn't me." The evidence would send him straight to jail for a long time. Her beating hadn't been a mild one.

"She's too scared to tell the police. They threatened to do worse next time if she said anything."

"Can't Drew get her into protective custody?" Heather suggested. It was a good thought.

Jian laughed. "From the vibes I get, protective custody wouldn't keep her safe. Could be some higher-ups are involved."

"Great, someone in the system has it out for me." Like Jack had FBI agents playing him against a mob boss.

"Or they might have friends in high places."

Turning, he faced the boarded-up windows. They reminded him of the closed-in cell. Something he might have to get used to. Shit.

"So I'm screwed."

"Not so fast, dude. I said the law couldn't protect this chick. I never said we couldn't."

Scott whipped around. "You'd keep this lady safe if she came clean?"

"You kept Mei safe for me. You didn't even know me then and how charming I can be."

Laughing, he held out his hand. "I don't know how I'll repay you."

Jian's grip was strong. "Seems to me we have a nice little give-and-take system going on between us already. This is something I'm giving to you."

If it was someone other than Jian, Scott would be worried about what the man would want in return. So far it hadn't been more than hiring his old street gang members. He was getting to know Jian's character, and the man had honor.

"How do we go about getting Carla to tell the truth to the police?" Heather's hand still clung to his elbow.

"I think Drew could make arrangements to have her talk to the ADA trying the case. Jian, can you contact her, tell her what you have proposed?"

"I've already got my people working out where to put her. I hear she has some good cooking skills so she'd be helpful in a few places. Places no one would ever think to look for her and where she'd have constant eyes on her."

"Great. Let me talk to my friend. See what we can set up. Hopefully they'll go for it. And she'll go for it."

"I'll contact you when I have her agreement."

"No forcing her, man. I don't need even more charges against me."

Jian's lips quirked, his eyes flashing. "What, you don't like all the attention you got in lock up this weekend? Some of the guys inside said you were the belle of the ball and number one on the list for prom date. Especially after the strip search."

"How the hell did you hear about that?"

Jian's laugh echoed through the building. "I got connections everywhere, dude."

"Great. But if you can help me with this, then I guess I don't care what you heard. Let me know as soon as you get anything."

Jian tilted his chin up and waved his hand. "Sure, but you might want to make sure your lady doesn't come looking for me again. Have her use the number I gave her. She could have been in a shitload of trouble if my guys hadn't seen her."

Turning to Heather, he asked, "What happened? You said you were fine."

"Yeah, the four guys who were ripping her clothes off and ready for business thought so too." The gang leader walked out with a shrug.

Turning slowly, heat rushed through his blood, burning him alive. "What the fuck were you thinking? Is that where you got the bruises from?"

"I'm fine," she choked out, backing away. Yeah, she should be scared. He wanted to throttle her for taking that kind of chance. The thought of any other man touching her, hurting her that way, made his blood turn to ice.

Reaching up, he held her shoulders and glared. "Do you have any idea how stupid that was? Nearly getting gang-raped isn't anything to brush off. I can't believe you came down here alone. What could possibly have been going through your head?"

A tear slid down her cheek and her lower lip trembled. Afraid of him, or was she reliving the attack?

"I know it was stupid. And I realize what could have happened. What *almost* happened." Her voice caught on the words. "But I hated the thought of you going to prison. And for something you didn't do. I couldn't let that happen to you. I'm sorry."

Damn. How the fuck could he be mad at her for wanting to help him? Pulling her closer, he pressed his lips to her hair. "I'm glad you're all right. But promise me you won't ever do anything that asinine again." "I promise." She held tight to his waist and he didn't let her go. He was beginning to think he didn't want to let her go. Ever. And if Jian's information was correct, perhaps he wouldn't have to.

* * * *

"Is there a reason we aren't meeting at police headquarters?" Virginia Dennis asked. As the prosecutor for his case, she certainly had a right to know. "This is most unorthodox." She glanced around the park they'd met in.

Scott looked over at Drew, thankful his friend was here to run interference. Lord knew *he* didn't have any clout with the woman who wanted to see him hang. She didn't hide her disdain for him or what she thought he'd done.

"I told you, Virginia, the witness needed to speak with you but is afraid to go to the station."

"Then she should have come to my office. And you"—she pointed at Scott—"shouldn't be anywhere near the witness. I don't know what you're trying to prove here—"

"That the witness lied," Drew broke in. "She's willing to tell you the truth and even sign a statement, but not at police headquarters. She's scared."

"Of the man who beat her. Yes, I'm aware of why she might be frightened."

"I'm not afraid of Mr. Holland," a timid voice came from behind them. Jian stood a few yards behind the blue-haired woman with several of his men scattered beyond that. Her face was still swollen and multi-colored. Shit, someone had done a number on her.

"Miss Findley, why didn't you simply call my office and arrange a meeting?"

Carla looked around, her eyes anxious. "Because I don't know who I can trust."

The prosecutor's eyes narrowed. "I seriously doubt it's this street gang you're with."

"It does seem odd, but I do trust them. I think they have my best interest at hand. They aren't involved in this case or what I was forced to do."

"You mean when Mr. Holland tried to force you into sexual relations?"

Scott cringed but kept his eyes turned away from Carla. He didn't want Virginia to think he was trying to intimidate the witness.

"He didn't do anything to me other than try and keep me from falling. The whole thing was a set-up."

The tension in his body eased out like water rushing down a stream. Would the prosecutor believe her? Or push to get him convicted?

"Are you being coerced to say this?"

Carla shook her head, her eyes lowered.

"You purposefully made us think Mr. Holland attacked you? Why?"

"I borrowed a lot of money for some medical bills. I was having a hard time paying it off. These people approached me and said they'd pay it off if I did them a favor. I didn't realize part of the deal was to have the crap beat out of me. I never would have agreed."

She sent a sideways glance at him and grimaced. "I'm sorry. It was a lousy thing to do. But I was scared what they'd do to me if I couldn't pay back the money."

"Who are these people who wanted Mr. Holland charged?"

Shrugging, Carla said, "I don't know. The guy who approached me said he worked for someone else. Someone willing to pay off my debt. All I had to do was stumble into this guy, make a fuss. I didn't know why. Until they beat me up and the police found me. One of the men who beat me said I needed to say it was the guy from the bar."

Tears slid down her cheeks and her lip trembled. "After what they'd done to me, I didn't dare say anything else."

"Can we speak privately for a minute?" Virginia tilted her head toward a nearby bench.

Drew and Jian nodded while Scott remained silent. The two women strolled away and spent a few minutes conversing. Scott's heart beat faster, wondering if the prosecutor was attempting to get Carla to stick to her original but false story.

When they came back, Virginia chewed her lip then looked at Scott. "Looks like charges will be dropped. I'll need a written statement from you, Ms. Findley. And descriptions of the men who did this to you."

"No, I can't give you any more information. The first guy wore dark glasses and a big hat. The men who attacked me dragged me into a dark alley. I couldn't see what they looked like. And they'd kill me in a second if they knew what I was telling you now."

"We'll keep her safe until you can figure out this mess," Jian said quietly.

Virginia's expression was skeptical. "I'm still curious about this connection you have to Scott Holland."

Jian lifted his head. "A few years back he saved my sister from a gang rape. For that he is considered under our protection. And anyone else who he feels needs it."

"And I think Ms. Findley needs to be protected until we can figure out what the heck is going on," Scott said. "Because something strange has been happening since I bought this mill building to renovate."

"Yes, Andrew mentioned the troubles you've been having. None of them sound harmful, but I want to be kept informed if there's any new information that comes along."

Carla held out an envelope and handed it to Virginia. "This is my statement."

"I'll need contact information for you."

Jian stepped forward. "If you need to contact her, let the lawyer friend know." He indicated Drew. "Scott knows how to get in touch with me and I'll get the word to Ms. Findley."

"I really don't think—"

"No," Carla cut her off. "I don't want you having direct access. It's not that I don't trust you but…"

Virginia tilted her head. "You don't trust too many people right now. I understand. Hopefully we can correct that soon."

Taking a cautious step in Carla's direction, Scott thrust out his hand. "Thank you for coming forward. I know it had to have been hard for you."

"No harder than the weekend you spent in jail. Or for the embarrassment of the accusation and being arrested. I'm sorry for that."

"Doesn't matter." Scott shrugged. "Jian, make sure you keep her safe."

"She will not be harmed. You have my word, dude." He placed his hand on Carla's back and led her away, his men staying on the outskirts of their vicinity.

Looking back at the prosecutor, Scott asked, "What do I need to do now?"

"Nothing. Simply accept my apology for the false arrest. The charges will be dropped. But keep me informed if anything else happens that's even slightly suspicious."

"I will, believe me. Thank you."

Virginia walked off and Scott slumped onto a nearby bench. Drew dropped down next to him.

"How are you doing?"

Shaking his head to clear his mind, he pulled his shoulders back and took a deep breath. "Much better now. Appreciate the help."

"You look like you could use a drink. I'm buying."

Scott snorted. "Having a drink with a friend is what got me into this mess in the first place. Think I'll pass. I've got something else I need to do."

Drew patted his shoulder then took off. As he watched his friend walk away, he thought of what he should do first. Letting Jack and Callie know was right up there. He'd give them a call. But Heather had been instrumental in getting Jian's help. Telling her in person would be better. There were all sorts of ways in which to thank her. He couldn't decide which one would be more pleasant.

* * * *

"Ms. Silva, Mr. Holland is here to see you. Are you available?"

Heather pressed the intercom button on her desk phone. "Of course. Send him in."

Her heart beat in anticipation. Had he met with the prosecutor yet and had the Findley lady told the truth? The anticipation was also at seeing Scott again. For some odd reason, she didn't feel as antagonistic with him lately. Seeing him go through this ordeal could be one reason. She didn't like to see anyone in pain, physical or emotional.

The door opened and he poked his head in, his face neutral.

"Come in." She waved him in then closed the door behind him. "What's going on?"

Moving toward her desk, he leaned against it. She stepped closer, drawn to him and his damn charisma.

"I wanted to thank you," he said, reaching for her hands and running his thumbs over her skin. "For getting in touch with Jian."

"You seemed kind of pissed that I did."

He tightened his hands on hers then pulled her closer. She wouldn't object, though Scott and close proximity made her mind fill with mush.

"That you took a risk like that. I am. It kills me to think you might have been hurt." His eyes closed and his jaw clenched. When he opened them again they drilled into her. "I care about you, Heather. I don't want anything to happen to you." His finger slid down to where the bruise was starting to fade.

"I don't want anything to happen to you either, which is why I went looking for Jian. Was he able to get the woman to rescind her claim?"

His smile lit up the room, the dimple in his chin deepening. "Yeah, we met with the prosecutor and she says all charges will be dropped. Jian's taking care of Carla until we can figure out what the hell is going on."

"Oh, Scott, that's great," she said, propelling herself into his arms. They tightened immediately.

"Any idea how I can thank you properly?" His voice was low and rough.

Running her hands up his chest, she grinned. "Well, there might be a few ways you can do it improperly."

"Do they include my lips and yours?"

"My favorite certainly does."

Her breath hitched as he slid his hand behind her neck then kissed her. Damn, this man heated her up and sent chills through her all at the same time. How was that even possible? He skimmed his tongue over her top lip and she opened for him. Excitement coursed through her veins like a virus. He got inside her blood so easily, but she wasn't sure she wanted a cure. It was more than she'd ever felt with anyone else.

The rough skin of his fingers skimmed up her back. How had her blouse gotten untucked? His addictive lips plundering her mouth had kept her busy while his hands moved in. She didn't have the will to make them stop. Didn't want them to stop.

"You drive me crazy with all the little sounds you make." His voice in her ear snapped her back to earth.

Sounds? What was she doing? This was her office. Her place of business.

A soft knock sounded on the door followed by it opening. Scott twirled her around so she was closer to the desk and hidden from view. Good thing, the first few buttons on her blouse had somehow come undone. She'd almost come undone.

"Ms. Silva, I'm sorry to bother you, but your next appointment is here."

"Thank you, Wendy. Get them settled in the conference room and I'll be there shortly."

The door closed and she sagged against the firm chest in front of her. "I need to straighten up. I must be a mess."

"Not from where I'm standing," he said, his thumb caressing her cheek. "I think you look amazing, as always. Like you've been thoroughly kissed."

Oh, God, she had been. This man didn't do things by half measure. Taking a deep breath, she tried to get herself under control.

"I'm glad you stopped by to share the good news with me. In all the excitement I forgot to tell you I had one of my employees do some digging on who owned the building before us."

"The bank did. That's why it was at auction."

Twisting her hair back into its neat bun, she glared at him. "Yes, but the reason they had it was because the previous owner is in prison and wasn't able to pay the taxes. I've got his name right here." Turning around, she grabbed the slip of paper from her desk. Scott moved right behind her and slid his hands around her waist, his nose nuzzling her neck.

"I'll check it out. Thanks."

"I need to get to my client." It was the last thing she wanted right now, but standing here kissing Scott wouldn't keep her mortgage paid.

"How about I take you to dinner tonight to celebrate my release from prison?" he said as she tucked her top back into her skirt. "We can discuss the project if you feel the need to keep things business between us. Or we can ditch the work conversation and simply enjoy each other's company."

Doing up the buttons on her blouse, he added, "Your call."

How she wanted to enjoy his company and forget all about the crap that had been happening. Throwing caution to the wind, she nodded.

"Sounds nice. I'd like that."

"And I'd like nothing better than to continue what we were doing here, but I know you've got work to do. I'll pick you up at your house around seven. Is that good?"

"Perfect." Standing on her toes, she kissed his cheek and left the room. As she walked past Wendy, the woman blushed then started to apologize.

"I'm so sorry—"

"It's fine, Wendy. Next time use the intercom, though." She couldn't blame her. Mixing pleasure at her place of business had never been an issue before. But Scott had a habit of making her throw out all the rules she'd always lived by.

Chapter 14

"We're here to see Mickey Bogasz," Jack informed the guard at the state penitentiary.

Scott shivered. This is where he could have been sent if the charges against him hadn't been dropped. It still chilled him to the bone when he recalled his weekend in jail. Yes, Afghanistan had been worse, but at least there he'd had his whole unit watching his back. In prison you were on your own.

Their identifications were checked and they were led into a small room with half a dozen tables in it. Guards stood throughout the room. Hopefully this guy could shed some light on why everything had been turning to crap since he'd bought the mill.

"Thanks for arranging this," he said to his cousin as they sat on one side of a table near the corner of the room. "Not sure I'd want to do this solo."

Shrugging, Jack said, "No problem. Luckily I still have some contacts in the field. Lots of them happy to help me out after the shit storm the Bureau put me through."

A guard walked in with a skinny man in his midforties and led him over to the table. "Your visitors. You've got ten minutes."

"Who are you?" Mickey grunted as he checked them out.

"Just want to ask you some questions."

Sitting in the chair opposite them, he snarled, "And why would I want to answer them?"

Jack cleared his throat. "Because I have connections in the Bureau who could make things a bit easier for you if we like what you say." Jack lifted his hand and a fifty dollar bill peeked from underneath.

"Tell me what you'd like then and I'll say it." The greasy hair on the man's head flopped in his eyes and he shook it back. His hand crept along the table but Jack's clamped back over the money.

"You were listed as the owner of a mill building on Prescott Street in Menatuck. What can you tell us about it?" Scott let Jack do the talking. As an agent he had experience questioning people.

The man's face look confused. "I don't own no mill building."

"According to the town records, you purchased the place eighteen years ago."

"Eighteen years ago. How the hell could I have afforded some big building at that age? I was mostly running errands for...a friend."

"What friend would that be?"

"Guess it don't matter now 'cause he's dead. Come to think of it, he might have mentioned putting something in my name. Told me I didn't have to worry about it though."

"Who?"

"Victor Cabrini. He got whacked like six months ago or so."

Jack's eyes darkened. Cabrini was the reason Jack hadn't seen Callie and his son, Jonathan, for over two years. Running with a target on his back had finally ended with Cabrini's death.

"Cabrini owned the building. Do you know what he used it for?"

Mickey shrugged. "Nah, he never told me nothing. But he paid me a few thousand dollars at the time. Wasn't gonna argue with that."

Nodding at the guard, Jack stood. "Thank you for your help."

"Did you like what I said?"

"I'll put in a word and get you a few benefits in here." Jack left the bill on the table and Mickey scooped it up in less than a second.

"Come ask questions any time."

The guard came to take Mickey away. Scott stood also and they left the building. "That makes sense now. Looking at the information Heather got, Mickey has been inside for almost four years and paying taxes this whole time. He only stopped in January."

"Obviously Cabrini was paying the taxes until he died," Jack replied. "I'm going to take a stab in the dark and say the building wasn't being used for anything remotely legal."

Scott laughed. "Really? Did Cabrini have any legal businesses?"

"Actually he had more than you'd think. Some were used as fronts for other things. Tony Pascucci has been busy cleaning many of them up. He would have paid the taxes on the mill if it had been for any profitable legal reason."

"Pascucci? He's the one who killed Victor, right?"

"Saved our lives." Jack moved toward the truck. "I'll pay him a visit. I'm curious now how your troubles came back to Cabrini."

After starting the truck and putting it in gear, Scott maneuvered onto the road. "It must be hard to hear Cabrini's name again."

"He's dead." The gravel in Jack's tone wasn't fooling anyone that it didn't affect him.

"Doesn't get rid of the years you lost because of him."

"No, it doesn't. But I'm trying to get past all that and make every second I have with Callie and Jonathan count." Looking anxiously at him, Jack said, "Don't mention any of this to Callie yet. I don't want her to worry."

"I won't say anything to Callie but I need to let Heather know. I'm not sure she'll keep that information to herself. Callie's her best friend. They don't keep secrets from each other."

Chuckling, Jack said, "Yeah, which brings me to my question of what's been going on with you and Heather? I've heard your name bantered about when the two women think I'm not listening."

"We're business partners who keep running into shit problems."

"And that's it? Because I'm pretty sure I overheard the phrase 'makes my panties drip' a few weeks ago. Unless she's talking about some other guy."

Seriously, Heather thought that of him? God, he hoped it was him.

"By the smirk on your face, I'm thinking you're cool with that."

"Let's just say I wouldn't mind getting in there to check it out." Biting his lip, he tried to get rid of the grin. Jack's next words did it for him.

"Remember she's my wife's best friend. And we owe her a lot. She kept our secret for years and helped Callie more than I can ever repay. I don't want her hurt."

"I'd never hurt her. I care about her too. I know what she's done for you and your family. But she's also a grown woman who can make decisions on her own."

"Fair enough."

They drove in silence for a while, Jack busy on his phone. Getting information on Cabrini's involvement in this whole fiasco?

As he got on the highway, Scott's mind turned to the date he and Heather had gone on a few days ago. Nice, quiet restaurant. She'd worn a sweet little number that got his blood pressure in the danger zone. Her high heels had his head spinning, making her almost as tall as him. Putting her mouth at the same level as his. Dangerous.

He'd even changed out of his work pants and boots and donned a tie. One apparently he'd worn to Callie and Jack's wedding. He only owned a few. Maybe he'd need to purchase a few more. Right? When the hell would he ever wear them?

The conversation had flowed well and the sexual interplay had been there, but only as an undercurrent. He hadn't wanted to push her. It was nice to see her in this different light. Although when he'd dropped her off, they'd sat in her driveway and made out like horny high school kids, fogging up the windows. God, he'd wanted to take her right there in his truck but figured her neighbors might object if his bare ass pressed against the window as he pumped into her. His mind had gone through all sorts of possible scenarios. All of them with him buried deep inside her.

When they'd finally broken apart and he'd walked her up to her door, she'd been quiet. Like she was torn as to whether she should invite him in. Her actions in the truck made him think she'd welcome it, but her wide eyes had seemed confused. He'd let her call the shots. No way was he going to push his way inside and make the decision for her. Though he figured if he'd said even the tiniest word of wanting to come in, she wouldn't have said no.

"Thanks for a great time tonight" had been all she'd managed then kissed him before she slipped inside her door. Standing there for a few moments, he knew it was good she'd made the decision. If it was up to him, he wouldn't have had the control. She was damn potent stuff.

* * * *

"Scott, what are you doing here?"

Scott stood in front of Heather's door, typical work clothes in place. Those damn Carhartts she found so freakin' sexy and the snug T-shirt that showed off his well-honed muscles. It was Sunday. Didn't he take the weekends off?

"I got some information when Jack and I visited the guy who supposedly owned the building before us. I wanted to share it with you."

"I had a friend do a little digging too," she answered, standing back to let him in.

"Are you working today?" he asked, staring at her slim skirt and tailored blouse.

"I had a showing this morning but I'm off for the rest of the day."

"Nice," he commented, looking around the room. Her house was small but quaint and homey. She'd taken time to choose each piece of furniture and knickknack.

"I have to say I'm kind of surprised you live in a house like this. I might have been a little distracted the other night when I dropped you off to notice."

"What did you expect?" She knew what he expected. Some large mansion or penthouse apartment. Sure, her parents had many of those and she'd grown up with all that wealth. The place she'd always felt at home though was Callie's little bungalow. It was warm and inviting.

"Not a Cape style house. But I like it. Makes you seem more real."

"Because I was fake before?" Seriously could he take the stick out of his ass about her being raised in a wealthy family? She thought they'd gotten past that.

"Never fake, no. Sorry, I didn't mean to insult you. You know I have a slight problem in that area. I need to keep working on it. Forgive me."

"Fine, but no more cracks about the rich and famous."

"Why don't you give me a tour while I tell you what I found out?"

"Sure, we can start here in the living room." It was good sized, though nowhere near as large as the area he had. Probably why he seemed surprised. He wouldn't expect that she had smaller living space than he did.

They walked through the doorway into the kitchen. She'd updated it with all the modern conveniences while still keeping it simple. "I was about to throw a frozen pizza in the oven for lunch. Did you want to stay?"

"Stay for lunch?" His eyebrow raised and his lips twisted.

Always the same thing on his mind. It had been on her mind a lot lately too. She wasn't sure what she wanted to do about it, though. With only a simple touch, he set her on fire, yet how could she give up her independence for him? He was the type of guy who wanted to take care of his woman. Take control. Having control over her own life had been her goal for a long time now.

"Yes, lunch. You know, when you eat."

"That'd be nice. To eat here." He would have been more believable if his gaze hadn't wandered down her skirt to the juncture of her thighs. Memories of him dining there seized her and she had to shake her head to rid herself of the images.

"I have two rooms down this hallway," she said breathing deeply, trying to ignore how close he'd come up behind her. "I use one for my home office. The other is for relaxing." She indicated the television, stereo, and comfortable couches within.

"What was the information you got?" he asked, as they moved back toward the living room.

"I had a friend, who's extremely talented with a computer, check out where the payments came from for the taxes on the building. They'd been paid until January but this guy had been in prison for almost four years. That didn't make sense."

"Exactly what I thought too," he said, his gaze wandering over her knickknacks and decorations. What was he thinking? And why did she even care? He was her business partner, nothing more. *Except you want to rip his clothes off and jump on for a ride. And he'd be happy to oblige.*

He hadn't pushed the issue a few days ago on their date, though. She'd wondered about that. Especially since she knew he'd been plenty aroused with their bout of tonsil hockey in the car. Her hand had skimmed over his pants and he'd been hard as a rock. For some reason, though, she hadn't invited him in. God, she'd wanted to. Her girly parts certainly hadn't been happy with her decision. And yet, he hadn't pushed or even tried to seduce his way in. He would have been successful.

"This guy followed the money trail for who had actually paid the taxes. It took a few random turns but he finally came up with an account from which the money was drawn. Can you guess who?"

His grin grew and the dimple stood out in his chin, making her want to kiss it. "I think I can. Our man in prison gave us a name of someone he'd been working for at the time he supposedly bought the building."

"Victor Cabrini," they both said at the same time.

"I can't believe it. How is this man still screwing with our family?" After all he'd done to Callie, the name still gave her chills.

"It is a weird coincidence but I think that's all it is. We were the ones to go after the building. Cabrini had his hand in lots of pies. I'm still trying to figure out what he was doing with this building. The answer to our troubles could be in there somewhere."

"I know he's dead, but did he leave someone who's trying to finish some of his work?"

Stepping closer, Scott pushed a strand of hair off her cheek then rested his hand on her shoulder. "Jack plans to get in contact with Tony Pascucci, Victor's right-hand man. The guy's trying to go legit but he might have some information that'll help us. I plan to go with him once he sets up a meet."

"I wouldn't mind talking to him myself."

"I don't know how smart that'd be. He might be doing things legal now, but he's the one who let Angelo Cabrini die and took out Victor."

There was that protectiveness again. Didn't he realize she could take care of herself? *Like you did when looking for Jian?* Okay, maybe she needed some assistance at times. She still wasn't completely helpless.

"Let me know what you find out. Did you want to finish the grand tour?" His smile told her he did.

"Upstairs I have three rooms." They walked up the stairs and she pointed to the left. "I have a guest room and one I use for exercise. This room on the right is my bedroom."

After he'd peeked into the other rooms he stopped in her doorway. "Am I allowed in this hallowed sanctuary?"

Stopping herself from rolling her eyes, she shrugged. "You're allowed. Don't make yourself too comfortable, though. If you don't mind, I'm going to get out of these work clothes."

"I don't mind at all. Go right ahead."

His look had her holding her breath. Did she want to tempt him? He still stood in the doorway as his gaze roamed the room, taking in her furniture and decor.

"It's not as froufrou as I thought it would be. I like it."

Moving toward her dresser, she pulled her blouse from the waistband of her skirt and started unbuttoning it. As she slipped it off her shoulders, he looked in her direction. He was trying to be polite and not stare but he wasn't being all that successful.

Placing the blouse on the nearby chair, she reached back to unhook her skirt. Damn thing got stuck. Should she ask Scott? God, she wanted him to undress her and rock her world but what did that mean to her independent status? *You can screw the gorgeous hunk and still be independent.* That inner voice never had any control.

"Can you help me with this hook, please?"

Pushing away from the door frame, Scott sauntered over. "Happy to help."

The hook was undone in seconds and the zipper started to lower. She should tell him she was all set and he could leave now but for some reason her vocal chords were frozen.

"Did you need help getting it off too?"

In the mirror his eyes zoomed in on her breasts nearly popping out of her bra. It was demi-cut, lacy, and her nipples barely fit inside. Currently they were hardening. He must be able to see that. If the arousal at her back was anything to go by, he did.

"Are you an expert in undressing women now? Or has that always been a talent?"

The rough skin of his hands skimmed her waist and slid the fabric of her skirt lower. "Well, a guy learns a lot when he's done time on the inside."

Her chuckle escaped and she looked to see if he was offended by it. The grin on his face said he wasn't. His eyes were still focused above her waist while his hands continued to slide her skirt down. It finally dropped, landing on the floor. Scott knelt down, lifting one of her feet then the other to pick up the fabric.

"We wouldn't want this wrinkled. I love the way it hugs all your curves." His voice was so rough and husky it caused goosebumps on her skin. There was no way she could move if she tried. His presence mesmerized her. What would he do next?

After folding the skirt then laying it on the same chair as her blouse, he moved back behind her and slid his hands around her waist then up to cup her breasts. Lowering his head, he kissed up the side of her neck. Shivers ran through her and she tilted her head to one side. God, he could do this all day. With his tongue stroking her skin, he nibbled on the back of her neck.

"I love hearing you moan like that," he whispered near her ear as he bit softly on that too. Sensations began to overwhelm her. Arching her back she pushed into the hands holding her. Pushing the lacy fabric aside, he scooped her from the cups and began kneading her flesh.

"God, Scott," she moaned, to hell with her pride. She wanted him to touch her, stroke her, take control.

"Something you like?"

"Mmm" was all she managed as he pinched her nipples and gently pulled. Grinding her hips against his arousal, she wanted more.

"Now that I'm a bad boy who's been in prison, I'm acceptable. I didn't know you had that naughty side to you, princess. We'll need to explore it some more."

"Yes, please," she begged, wanting him to explore every part of her.

Her bra dropped away. When had he undone that? This desire coursing through her had made her lose all sanity.

"Apparently you've got someone who makes your panties drip," Scott said, his hand lowering down her stomach. "I was wondering if it was me."

Damn, how had he known that? She'd said that to Callie. Had Jack overheard? It didn't matter now.

"Could be." She wouldn't let his head swell too much. Well, not that head anyway. The other one pushed against her back quite prominently.

"Guess I'll have to check for myself," he growled as he slid his hand into her panties. The heat and sensation nearly made her fall over. His free hand held her tight while his capable fingers played in her folds. Holy Mother of God. Her brain exploded from feeling too much.

"Totally dripping. And all for me."

He turned her around and she wanted to cry at the loss of his touch. But he lifted her to sit on the dresser then attached his lips to her erect nipple. The sucking caused her center to clench and more moans to escape from her lips. She clutched at his head keeping it firmly against her chest.

"I could do this all day."

"Please do," she cried wanting nothing more than to have his hands and mouth touching every part of her.

"Are you sure? You didn't want to ruin the business partnership?"

"Screw the business partnership." If she didn't get him inside her soon, she'd explode.

His chuckle brought her back for a second then he picked her up, walking toward the bed. Her legs wrapped around his waist and she held on, pushing his shirt up his torso as he moved.

"Screw the business partner, you mean." He dropped her on the bed and crawled toward her slowly. The predatory look in his eyes should have scared her. It didn't. It excited her more than anything.

Lowering his head toward her middle, he pushed her legs apart. God, yes, please. This is exactly what she pictured every time her vibrator got some use. This was the real deal, though.

He paused halfway up her body then turned his head. No, he couldn't stop now. His eyes narrowed and he took in a deep breath through his nose. When he looked back at her the desire had dimmed. What the hell?

"Do you smell that?"

His testosterone? Sure, it blanketed the air and almost suffocated her.

"It smells like gas. Do you have a gas stove? Did you leave it on?"

Could he be serious about this? "Yes, I have a gas stove but it's not on." Now that he mentioned it, she smelled it too. It was getting stronger. "Can't we check it out later?"

His expression was one of conflict. "There's nothing I'd like better than to have you screaming my name, but I think I better take a look first. You can wait here if you want. The thought of you on this bed, your legs spread open for me, will make me get back here faster."

He backed off the bed then moved toward the door, his face disappointed. His footsteps echoed down the stairway and she ran her hands down her body. Shit, this was bad timing. As she lay there she realized the smell was even worse. Where the hell had it come from?

Getting off the bed, she threw on a tank top and a pair of shorts then trotted down stairs. Scott stood at her cellar door, his expression concerned.

"It's really strong in the basement. I think the best bet is to call the gas company and have them check it out."

As she went to grab her phone, he pulled on her hand and dragged her to the door. "We can call from outside. Safer there."

What did he think would happen? Yeah, the gas smelled bad but it wouldn't poison them in only a few minutes time.

They'd barely cleared the front door when a large bang echoed through the house.

"Run!" Scott yelled, pushing her in front of him.

Heat and flames exploded behind them, the force throwing them across the front lawn. Her back burned from the temperature, and debris rained down upon them. Her house was engulfed in flames. Her beautiful house. Another explosion roared through the air with more debris flying at them. Something hit her in the head and blackness descended.

Chapter 15

Sirens filled the air as Scott shook his head. What the fuck had happened?

"Sir, are you okay?"

Opening his eyes, he saw a small crowd standing near him. Flickering light from enormous flames danced in his vision. The house had exploded.

"Heather," he yelled, attempting to sit up. His head spun but he pulled himself to his knees and looked around.

A few people surrounded her as she lay on her side, unconscious, hair spilling over her face.

Crawling the few feet that separated them, he pushed aside one of the spectators and touched her shoulder. Ashes and red marks covered her bare skin. Scorched holes dotted her top. He had some too.

"Hey, wake up," he called softly to her. "You're stronger than this." Touching her neck, he felt for a pulse. *Please God, let it be there.* Blood pumped through her veins under his thumb. Yes.

Two fire trucks pulled up, the men jumping out, pulling hoses with them. The crowd moved back as they turned on the water then sprayed the house. There wouldn't be anything left. It was too far gone. But he and Heather had gotten out, so nothing else mattered. As long as she was fine.

"How long were we out?" he asked one of the people still nearby, an older woman in a bathrobe and slippers. She seemed quite concerned for Heather.

"About ten minutes. I'm Sadie, I live there." She pointed to the house to the right of Heather's. "I hope she'll be all right. She's such a sweet girl, always helping me when I need it."

"I hope so too," he replied, running his fingers over Heather's cheek.

"Do you live here? Do you know what happened?" The fire chief had come over, one eye on the firefighters and one on them.

"This is her house, Heather Silva. We were inside and smelled gas. We figured we'd call to get it checked once we got outside."

"Good thing you did." He bent then slid his fingers over Heather's wrist. "Paramedics are pulling up now."

Relief surged through him, and he moved only slightly away as they checked her neck then gently turned her over onto her back.

"How is she?" His voice sounded like he'd eaten nails.

"She's got a good size bump on the back of her head." The man glanced around and nodded. "Lots of debris around. Possibly she got hit with something, or had she hit it before you got out?"

"She was fine, but it all happened so fast. I think something in the cellar went first and we hightailed it out of the house."

A soft groan slipped from Heather's lips and Scott reached for her hand. "It's okay, princess. You'll be fine." He hoped that was true.

Her eyes fluttered open and she struggled to sit up. The paramedics helped her, but when she saw the flames behind him, her face crumpled.

He rushed closer then pulled her into his arms as she cried, "My house."

"It's only a house. The most important thing inside got out. You."

Holding her tight made him realize he never wanted anything bad to happen to her again. What the hell had caused this? Just another coincidence? He didn't think so. This time they'd gone too far. Whoever the hell *they* were.

"We'd like to take you to the hospital to get checked out. There are some burns and cuts that need to be cleaned and treated. It wouldn't be a bad idea to make sure nothing's broken. There's a possibility you both have concussions from the blast."

The fire chief asked a few more questions, then they were hustled into an ambulance. They were allowed to ride together, and he held her the whole way. She was quiet except when one of the paramedics asked them questions, making sure they weren't confused or disoriented. Unfortunately, they were led to different rooms in the ER to be examined. He didn't want to be separated from Heather for even a second.

"Mr. Holland?" A woman in a lab coat walked in and pulled over a rolling stool. "Let's see what we've got."

"I'm fine," he insisted, his mind on Heather. "I'm more concerned for my friend who was brought in with me. It took her a little longer to regain consciousness."

"And the fact you were unconscious yourself, even for a few minutes, is enough for me to take a look at you."

Scott sat still while the doctor poked, prodded, and asked questions. The light she shone in his eyes made his headache throb like a bastard, but all he could think about was Heather and how she was.

"Slip off your shirt, please. I'd like to see the skin where you've got holes in your shirt."

He did as asked and the doctor made a few grumbling sounds then stood up. "I think you'll live," she joked, her smile wide. "You've got a few minor burns and cuts. I'll send in a nurse to clean them up. You've also got a possible concussion. Slight, but I'd like to keep you here for observation for a short while. Mostly because you lost consciousness. If everything looks good, we could send you home by dinner time."

"Is that necessary?"

"Humor me," she said. "I'm going to assume your friend will have a similar treatment."

"Could we share a room?" He winked at the doctor and grinned.

Laughing, she answered, "Probably not, but don't give me any more hassle and I might be able to get them near each other. Let me go check on her."

A few minutes later a nurse walked in with a tray holding ointment and bandages. "Your friend, Ms. Silva, is still being treated at the moment. The doctor's recommending a few hours of observation. Most likely she'll be sent upstairs in a short while. She's been asking about you too."

If Heather had time to worry about him then she must not be too bad off. A weight lifted from his shoulders. As the nurse finished with some of the wounds on his back, Jack showed up.

"Scott? Are you all right? I drove past Heather's house on the way here and there's nothing left."

"We got out right before it blew."

"How's Heather? Callie wanted to come, but we couldn't get a sitter this quickly. I told her I'd call as soon as I saw you."

"Heather's still being treated. Guess we're both getting watched for a bit. There's no reason for it. I'm good to go."

Jack glared at him. "You were both almost blown up. Let them keep an eye on you for a while."

An orderly walked in pushing a wheel chair and Scott groaned. "I do not need that. I'm perfectly capable of walking."

"Sorry, sir, hospital regulations." The man maneuvered the chair next to the bed but Scott refused to allow him to help. Even when the room did a little dance and spun around.

"Let me call Callie to tell her I'll be a few hours." Jack pulled out his phone.

"No. I don't need you sitting, watching me. Go home. I'll call you when I need a ride." Hopefully his truck hadn't been damaged too badly, as it'd been farther away from the house. Heather's car had looked totaled under all the flaming debris.

Jack raised an eyebrow and Scott pointed out the door. Jack left and Scott had to sit through the embarrassment of being wheeled down the Emergency Room hall. As they passed another room he heard Heather's voice and put his foot down to stop the chair.

"Mom, Dad, I do not need you hanging around while I rest. You'll be wasting your time and I'll feel like I have to entertain you." You had to love her argument.

"But dear—"

"No, Mom, I'm a big girl. I can handle this. You heard the doctor. I'm fine. It's simply a precaution. I'll call if I need a ride later."

Heather's wheelchair rolled out and her face lit up when she saw him. "You're all right?"

"Same as you, it seems. Observation."

Scott held out his hand and nodded at the orderly who rolled him down the hall. Heather's orderly followed beside them. She now wore a scrub top that snapped up the front. Her shirt must have been more damaged than his.

In the elevator the two orderlies looked at each other and said, "Fifth floor."

"I bribed the doctor to put us close together," Scott told her.

"Bribed or flirted?" She chuckled though her eyes seemed blank somehow. "I saw your doctor was a woman. I'm sure there was a little charm involved."

"Are you saying I'm charming?" God, he would love her to think that. She narrowed her eyes. "You can be. When you want."

Unfortunately their rooms were a few down from each other. The nurse who came in to check on Scott pulled the shades then made him rest in the bed. No sneaking down to see Heather.

After a few hours of being constantly interrupted and checked on, the call was made to let him leave. He strolled down to Heather's room to see the doctor giving her the same instructions for wound care and concussion symptoms. "If any of these things get worse, please come back immediately."

"Jack's on his way to pick me up. Did you want a ride or have you called your parents?"

Her sad expression almost killed him as she nodded. "I'd like to go with you, please."

It was the soft *please* that got to him. His little warrior was nowhere to be seen. Sitting next to her on the bed, he pulled her into his arms. Her head fell onto his shoulder. He simply held her until Jack poked his head in.

Once they were in the truck and driving away, he asked, "Do you want us to drop you at your parents'?"

Her head shook, but she didn't say anything, just stared out the front window as she chewed on her lip.

"You're more than welcome to stay with me." No response from her. It started to worry him.

"Why don't both of you stay at our house tonight?" Jack offered. "That way Callie and I can keep an eye on you, per doctor's orders."

"You don't really have the space for us, and I don't want to displace anyone. We can go to my apartment."

Heather stirred. "They blew up my house." Her voice sounded dead, emotionless.

Pulling her closer to his side, he said, "We'll go to my place, Jack. Thanks."

The ride was quiet and soon Jack pulled up to the parking lot.

"Thanks for coming to get us. Appreciate it. Tell Callie not to worry. I'll make sure Heather is all right."

"Call if you need anything. Anything. We owe the both of you more than we could ever repay."

"No, you don't." He helped Heather slip from the truck and guided her in to the building, then the elevator. Once in his apartment, he pulled her toward his bedroom. He needed to change out of his dirty clothes but he didn't want to leave her alone. The stupor she was in scared him. It was so unlike her.

"Sit here while I clean up a bit. Can I get you something to drink first?"

Shaking her head, she sighed but never looked up. He quickly pulled out some sweatpants and threw them on, discarding his burnt T-shirt. She never stirred, her eyes remaining on a spot on the wall.

Sitting next to her on the bed, he stroked her face and lifted her chin until she looked at him. Despair filled her eyes.

"I know this totally sucks, but we're alive. Nothing else matters right now."

Her face crumpled and her lip trembled as she leaned forward then fell apart in his arms.

* * * *

Her house was gone. They'd almost been killed. Scott's arms around her were comforting, but nothing right now could fill the emptiness

Heather felt deep in her soul. Snuggling closer, she let out everything she'd been trying so hard to hold in since she'd woken up with her house in flames earlier today.

"Shh, it's okay. I'm right here," Scott whispered as his hands gently caressed her back.

It wasn't okay, though. Everything she had was gone.

Tears continued to fall and loud sobs shook her body. Scott's soft words kept her only partially sane, but at least she had someone here to help her through this. If it hadn't been for him smelling the gas, they'd both be dead.

"Thank you," she said, her voice barely audible muffled against his shoulder.

"I'm not doing anything."

"No." She looked up at him. His face was etched in concern. "I mean for getting us out of there. I was totally lost in what we were doing, I didn't even notice until you said something."

"I was in fairly deep too," he replied, lifting his hand to push back a strand of hair from her face. His fingers stroked her cheek and she briefly closed her eyes to enjoy the sensation. "As a builder, the smell of gas is something that signals a big warning for me."

"You saved my life."

The smirk on his face deepened the dimple in his chin. "You know, in some cultures that means I own you now. That could be cool."

She tried to smile but didn't quite succeed. "I certainly don't own anything anymore. Everything I had was in that house." Her voice cracked on the last sentence.

Pulling her closer again, Scott kissed her cheek. "It's all just stuff. You're alive and that's the important thing here."

"I know that. I do," she cried. "But it was all mine. And not simply my possessions. There wasn't anything in that house that wasn't a part of me. Part of who I am. I bought the house with money I earned myself. The furniture, the decorations, everything I bought myself."

Running his fingers through her hair, he simply listened, allowing her to vent.

"I chose the colors for the walls. I shopped for every single knickknack and picture frame. I painstakingly matched and coordinated accessories, picked out furniture according to what I liked. Not what my mother thought would be appropriate or accepted by her friends and society. My dad didn't pay a cent for any of it. I bought it all. Me."

Her heart raced, beating painfully in her chest when she thought of all the time and energy it had taken to get the house exactly the way she wanted. To make it a home. One she felt comfortable in. It hadn't been the showcase her parents had, but it had been something she could be proud of. It had been hers.

The tears wouldn't stop falling. Her head pounded in a terrifying rhythm. From her loss or the concussion? Why couldn't she get herself under control? She never let anyone see her cry. It showed weakness. But Scott wasn't treating her like she was weak. He was simply holding her, letting her mourn a loss. Yes, it was only a place and it held only things, but they'd been her things.

"I had so many personal items from when I was a kid and some pictures. Everything else in there I'd purchased. It signified me, who I am now. It was my house, not one of my parents' that I happened to live in. It was my home. I had made it a home."

Now it was gone. She was homeless. The hollow feeling inside grew and expanded. Were her lungs even working? It was hard to get air in.

"Breathe, princess," Scott encouraged. How had he known? Was he reading her mind, feeling her thoughts?

Despair rushed through her once more as the visions of her house engulfed in flames flickered through her mind. "I just wanted something that was all mine. That my mom or dad didn't have anything to do with. Now it's gone. I have nothing."

"You have me."

Scott cupped her face with his hands, kissing the tip of her nose. He was barely visible with the wetness that clogged her eyes. Wiping his thumb under them, he touched his forehead to hers. "You also have your family and Callie and Jack. You've still got your job, your clients, and lots of friends. It won't matter to any of them what you don't have. You're still you. That's why we all hang around. You're beautiful, special, a unique individual."

His arms slid lower and tightened around her back as he pressed his mouth to hers. The touch of it made everything fade. It was all still there way in the back of her mind, but the slide of his tongue over her top lip helped ease the pain of loss. Grabbing his head, she slid her fingers through his wavy hair and pulled him closer. She needed him to make her forget. To keep her sane and help her cope.

"God, Scott, I need you."

"I'm right here. I'm not going anywhere."

She leaned back and pulled him to lay next to her on the bed. After adjusting them so her head rested on his shoulder, he didn't do anything else. Didn't he want to have sex? Finish what they'd started?

Skimming her hand down his chest, she marveled again at the lean muscles honed from hard labor. Before she reached her goal, he stopped her.

"Right now I think you need to get some rest. We both do. Everything else can wait."

Shifting slightly, he pulled the covers from under them then slid them on top, stopping at their waist.

Concentrating on the warmth of his body so near, her eyes fluttered, beginning to close. The day had been shot to hell, her whole life now in disarray, but with Scott's arms around her and his lips pressed to her hair, it didn't seem to matter.

* * * *

Scott's eyes flew open as he felt the pillow next to him. It usually didn't have anyone there but tonight Heather had been resting next to him. Practically on him. She'd been so distraught though that he hadn't even dared do more than give her a light kiss. The weight of her against him was solid, supportive, and nicer than he'd ever thought it could be. When they'd slept together in Vermont last year, he'd scurried back to his bedroom afterward. Mostly to keep Callie and Jack from knowing what they'd done. It wouldn't have looked good for his young nephew to find Uncle Scott naked in bed with Auntie Heather either. Awkward didn't even cover that scenario.

And as much as he'd like a repeat of that night, it wasn't what Heather needed right now. She'd just lost her house. And they'd both almost been killed. Shit. Once she was feeling better he had to dig a little deeper into what the fuck was going on. For now he should find where she was.

Slipping out of bed, he padded barefoot into the large living area. He tugged up his pajama bottoms, which had slid lower on his hips as he'd slept. Slept better than he'd expected to after almost being killed. Must have been the amazing woman next to him.

A light in the kitchen was on and the clatter of something metallic alerted him to where his missing guest might be. Heather stood by the stove pouring liquid into a mug.

"Hey," he said softly not wanting to startle her. "Couldn't sleep?"

"I slept for a few hours." Her gaze went to the clock on the microwave. Two fifty-seven. Not quite when he typically woke up.

"What do you have in there?" Walking over to the counter, he glanced in the mug. Hot water.

"I figured coffee wasn't what I needed at this time of night, but I couldn't find any tea bags."

"Yeah, sorry. Tea isn't really my thing. Guess I'll have to get some if you stay here."

"Stay here?" Her eyes searched his face, her expression confused and maybe a little hopeful.

"You're certainly welcome to until—"

"I find someplace else to live." She looked around the room and her eyes clouded over. Was she going to start crying again? Surprisingly, he hadn't felt awkward when he'd been comforting her earlier. He usually shied away from out-of-control female emotions. With Heather, he'd simply wanted to ease her grief.

The expression on her face grew fierce, more like the warrior princess he knew. "They blew up my house!" she thundered. "Who the hell are these people who think they can get away with blowing up my house?"

"We'll find them. The police need to get more involved after this incident."

"Incident?" She slammed her hands on the counter then turned around, her eyes holding him in place. "They blew up my damned house."

Pacing back and forth, she fumed. "I'm gonna rip their balls off when I find out who's responsible."

"Calm down, princess." Moving closer, he reached to pat her shoulders.

"Don't tell me to calm down." Slapping his hands away, she continued to shout, "They didn't blow up your house."

"No, but they almost blew me up. I have a right to be pissed too."

Her expression went from furious to horrified. "Oh, my God, they did. And here I've been wrapped up in my own little drama." Slipping her fingers into his hair, she tugged him closer. "If they'd hurt you…"

Before he could console her, she kissed him. Not sweet or gentle or even sexy. Hard and filled with fury. All the pent-up anger that had been simmering under the surface since they'd escaped seemed to rush forward into her lips. Shit, he should push her away but he couldn't. He needed this too. If anything had happened to her, he'd never forgive himself. Thank God he'd decided to stop by. What if he hadn't? Or if he'd stopped by later?

Pulling her off the ground, he turned and pressed her against the fridge. She clung to him as their lips smashed into each other.

"Scott." Her voice held desperation as she dragged her hands down his bare chest, her fingernails scraping lightly over his skin.

"I know. I know." He couldn't get enough of her. Energy surged off her body and into his, sending his nerve endings into a frenzy.

"I need you. Don't leave me." Slipping her hand lower, she skimmed over his arousal. Fuck, she got him harder than ever with barely a touch.

"I'm not going anywhere, princess. I'm right here with you." He grabbed her ass and lifted her up, her legs wrapping around his waist. Shit, was she even wearing underwear? All he felt was skin. Smooth, silky and meant for him. His for the taking.

Against the fridge, though? Looking around, he stumbled to the table. Gentle was how he meant to be, but her hand on his cock sent him into a tailspin he couldn't pull out of. The table hit her back and he ripped at the scrub top she wore, the snaps popping open to expose her to his eyes.

God, she was fabulous. Full, ripe breasts, rising up and down as her lungs expanded with each deep breath. Dark pink nipples standing at attention, begging for his mouth to suck on them. Her caramel-colored hair spread out around her on the table, making his dick twitch even more. His fingers itched to touch. Everywhere.

"Damn, you're beautiful."

He took a step back to truly admire her, but she lifted her feet and caught him by the neck then pulled him back.

"Don't even think about walking away." The desperation in her voice sliced through his heart.

"I couldn't if I tried." Not with her legs up around his ears. He took a few moments to knead those gorgeous tits and pinch the nipples as her legs tightened and she bent her knees, pulling him closer.

"Did you want something, princess?"

"You. Now. And I don't want it gentle."

Holy sweet Heaven on earth. Her panties were barely more than a few strings. He disposed of those easily enough. A slight tug and they lay on the floor, exposing her precious gift to him. He slid one finger inside testing her readiness. Oh, yeah, wet and wild.

"Hold on, Xena, we're going for a ride." He thrust into her and she arched, crying out his name. It took only a second to realize it wasn't from pain. Ecstasy wreathed her face so he shoved in again and again. Grabbing her hips, he held on tight as he moved faster and faster, her feet still up around his ears. This had been a fantasy, having a woman in this position but shit, the reality was better than he'd ever imagined.

The table shook as he continued to plunge into her. He ran his hands up and down her amazing long legs then fingered the tiny nub at the apex of her thighs. She threw out her hands, grabbing the edge of the table near her head.

Moans, loud and strong erupted from her throat as her walls clenched around him. When he fingered her again, they tightened even more. Shivers wracked her body, her eyes squeezed shut, her mouth opening wide.

"You aren't going without me, princess." Slamming into her harder and harder, his own pinnacle was right there. He skimmed his hands over her stunning figure. The texture of her silken skin sent him over the edge. Wrapping his arms around her legs as his body shuddered, he let go and fell. Luckily she was there to catch him.

Barely able to breathe, he finally loosened his hold and said, "God, sorry. When you said rough, I shouldn't have—"

"Yes, you should have," she countered. "It's what I needed." Her face was more relaxed than he'd seen it in weeks. Backing away, he couldn't help but stare at her spread on the table like a feast set out only for him.

"Come on, let's get cleaned up." He scooped her up and she curled into him. Damn, it felt good, but anxiety filled him knowing fighting him tooth and nail was more her thing. She was either too satiated to care or her spirit had been blown out of her with the explosion. Hopefully it was the former.

As he entered the bathroom, he set her on the floor then adjusted the water in the large shower stall. "We'll be careful with the burns on your back."

"It's fine. I need this smoky smell off me. I was too tired earlier to do anything except a quick wash with a face cloth, but now it's got to go."

Stripping their remaining clothes, he stepped in beside her and made sure to keep her back away from the spray. She lifted her head up and allowed the water to run over her face. The shampoo was man stuff but for now it would have to do. The idea of having female smelly soap in his bathroom suddenly appealed to him. Not to use but to signify the presence of a woman in his life. Someone like Heather? Yeah. Because there truly wasn't anyone like her.

Filling his hand with shampoo, he massaged it through her hair and the groan that escaped had him getting hard again. A thought entered his head as what they'd done sunk in.

"Hey," he said, moving to cradle her face in his hands. "I was stupid a few minutes ago."

Her eyes narrowed. "Why? Because you did what I wanted you to."

"No. I forgot protection. I'm sorry, Heather. You had me so worked up I…" Damn, how could he be this dumb?

She touched his arm then smiled. "It's fine. I'm on the pill. I have irregular periods and it helps keep me on schedule."

Her eyes clouded over and she bit her lip. Leaning down he stroked his thumb down her cheek. "What?"

"They were at my house so I don't have them anymore. Don't worry, though. I took one this morning. Well, I guess it's yesterday now. I should be fine. Unless you have cooties I should know about."

Laughing, he kissed her nose. "My love life has been a bit slow in the past year. It's basically been you...and you. No cooties."

The smile she gave him was forced as she rinsed the soap from her hair. He scrubbed himself and washed his own hair as they maneuvered around each other in the stall. Good thing it was huge, though he certainly didn't mind her naked skin brushing against his.

Once they were cleaned up, he shut the water off and grabbed his fluffiest towel to wrap around her. "Turn around so I can dab some of this burn cream on the spots on your back." He tried to be gentle, but there were a few times she winced at his touch.

"I'm sorry."

"No, it's not you." She couldn't hide the sob in her voice. Finishing off her back, he turned her around. The tears in her eyes pulled at something inside him. "I can't seem to get the image of my house exploding out of my mind."

Leaning in, he touched his forehead to hers pushing her hair off her shoulders. "I'll build you a new house, princess. I promise. I'll put in everything you could ever want in a home." Would she want him in it? And where the hell had that thought come from? They were combustible. They'd more than proved it in the kitchen. Though it had been a good combustible. He sure wouldn't mind having a do-over.

She kissed him sweetly, and he held her for a few minutes then eased back.

"Let's get your hair combed out, then you back in bed."

Pulling her into the bedroom, he stood behind her and picked up his brush. In only a few minutes her silky strands drifted smoothly down her back. As he guided her to the bed, she slid her arms around his neck.

"You know that pill is still working. Might as well get some use out of it."

Sliding in next to her, he chuckled. "If that's what you need, it's yours."

"Mine," she whispered as she slid her legs to tangle with his. Her need was apparent, but this time he had more control. And he wanted to take it sweet and slow.

Chapter 16

Heather stretched luxuriously and Scott watched in amazement at the beauty of her limbs. Even with the odd spots of burned skin. After the hard and fast in the kitchen, he'd taken his time to explore every gorgeous inch of her. It had been amazing. As good as the first time in Vermont, maybe even better.

How would she feel now? Earlier she'd been out of her mind with anger and despair. Had that been why she'd been wild and reckless? Or had she finally decided he wasn't such a bad guy after all? They *had* started something before the house blew up.

Damn and fuck. Who the hell had blown up her house? The red tape, accidents, even accusing him of assault had been minor compared to this. Someone had tried to kill them. Or had it only been her and he'd been collateral damage? No way he'd sit around and let someone hurt Heather. She was beginning to mean something to him. Maybe she had for a while but he'd simply been too stupid to notice.

Running his finger over her exposed skin, he wondered if she'd want to continue this relationship. It was a question he'd been asking himself too. Both Jack and Chris were enjoying wedded bliss, making it look easy and exciting. He'd always figured it was something he'd do much later in life. Get his career in shape and enjoy being free before he chained himself to a woman forever.

Stroking Heather's arm, he wondered if she wanted that too. Her independence had always been strong. She took great pride in not relying on anyone else for anything. He wouldn't mind having her lean on him, occasionally.

"Mmm," she hummed and turned onto her back. One eye opened, a smile lighting her face when she saw him. "That's nice. Don't stop."

"Your wish is my command." Lowering the sheet to her waist, he skimmed his lips over her neck to her throat then finally reached the stiff peaks that always made his dick turn to concrete.

"Fulfilling my wishes now, are we?"

"Absolutely."

Her eyes stared at a spot on the ceiling and began to darken. She must be thinking about the house explosion again. Best get her mind on something else.

For the next half hour he did his best to distract her by playing with her body. And she played right back. God, this woman was refreshing, fun, and didn't seem to have any hang-ups about exploring her sexuality.

As he lay replete with her straddling his hips, holding herself up with her hands on his chest, he again thought about forever. He didn't think he'd ever get tired of her sparkling personality and sarcastic wit. It stimulated him.

Her wiggling hips did that too. How the hell did she get him this excited in such a short period of time?

"If you keep doing that, princess, I'll have to flip you over and go for round three."

Her sassy smile twitched. "I think it might be round four."

Shit, she was right. He'd have no energy left if they kept going. It was only…he glanced at the clock…damn, it was after nine. It was a work morning and he'd been hanging out in bed.

"Good thing my boss is an understanding guy," he said, sitting up, licking a path across her shoulder.

Heather chuckled. "My boss is a real bitch, but I think she has a thing for you. Could you get me out of trouble for not being there on time?"

"Sure, I can start right now." Running his hands up her back, he pulled her closer, kissing her soundly. The ringing of the doorbell broke through the passionate haze, and he groaned.

"Don't answer it," she begged, her own hands running over his shoulders then down his back.

That sounded perfect, but after what happened last night with her house, it could be something important.

Scooting out of bed, he lowered her down to the mattress and kissed her lips. "Stay here. I'll deal with whoever it is." Pulling his discarded sleep pants on, he hoped round four wouldn't be too far away.

The bell buzzed again as he walked toward it, a T-shirt in his hands. He'd grabbed it to put it on then realized the front of his pants tented out dramatically. Best use it to hide his condition.

He opened the door to Heather's parents and sister standing there, concern etched all over their faces. Had Heather called them? "Mr. and Mrs. Silva, Charlotte, come in." Now he was glad he had the T-shirt, though the sight of her parents here did plenty to deflate him. "We're assuming Heather is here," Mr. Silva said, his tone filled with both strength and fear.

They all moved into the living room and Heather's mom held her hand to the pearls around her neck. "She never called to say they were releasing her from the hospital."

"We called this morning and they said she'd been discharged," Domenic stated. "With you. Is she here?"

"I'm here, Dad," Heather said, as she walked past the dining set to them. She wore one of his button-down shirts that hung almost to her knees. Nothing else.

"Darling," Mrs. Silva cooed, rushing over to Heather and wrapping her in a hug. "We were worried. Why didn't you call us to come get you?"

"I'm sorry, Mom, Dad." She hugged her father then Charlotte. "Things were crazy and I was more than a little overwhelmed. I let Scott take care of me and handle everything."

"How are you feeling now?" Charlotte asked.

"And why didn't you come home?" Her mother's posture was stiff, her arms crossed tightly over her chest.

Tugging on a button of his shirt, she said, "I'm better. Scott offered to let me stay here since I obviously couldn't go back to my house."

Tears filled her eyes and he wanted to rush over, hold her. Her sister filled in for him.

"I brought you stuff to wear," Charlotte said, holding up a bag she'd brought in with her. It had the Silvaggio's name on it. "Figured you wouldn't have much with you."

"We would have been here sooner except Charlotte insisted on stopping at the downtown store to get you these." A frown appeared as he glanced at his youngest daughter.

Scott searched Heather's face to see if she was embarrassed to be found in his apartment, wearing his shirt. It didn't appear that way.

"Thank you, Char," Heather said, taking the bag from her sister. "I think I'll get dressed if everyone doesn't mind."

"I'll come with you," Charlotte answered, her impish grin directed at her parents.

Great, that left him alone with Heather's parents. From the curious look on Charlotte's face it might be a while before Heather satisfied her sister's questions.

"Can I offer you some coffee, Mr. and Mrs. Silva?"

Heather's dad sighed and nodded. "I'd love some. And please, it's Domenic and Nicoletta."

Moving his hands to indicate they should sit on the couch, Scott shuffled toward the kitchen. The T-shirt was still in his hands so he pulled it over his head and began to make coffee. Looked like round four was being postponed due to interference. Damn.

* * * *

"Thanks for bringing me something to wear," Heather said as they entered Scott's bedroom. "I was wearing a tank and shorts. They're covered in burn holes."

Charlotte glanced around. "A girl's got to have something better to wear than—" She pointed to Scott's shirt that Heather had grabbed when she'd heard her dad's voice. "Although you are totally rocking the boyfriend look."

Plopping on the bed, Heather reached in the bag taking out a sundress, shorts, a few tops, and half a dozen pair of lacy underwear. A pair of strappy flat sandals rested at the bottom of the bag.

"I wasn't sure what you'd be in the mood for so I got a few things."

After pulling the tags off, she slid the panties up her legs then took off Scott's shirt. Charlotte's gasp had her looking over her shoulder to where her sister gaped at her back. The burns. She'd forgotten they were there. Well, she hadn't actually forgotten, but many other things took precedence over a little sting.

"Scott pulled us out in time, but we got hit with the blast. They're minor, though, so don't worry."

Her sister's expression was still one of concern as Heather slipped into the sundress. It was light and airy and didn't cling too much to her damaged skin. Although it certainly was short. Charlotte always did like to show a little leg. Hers were spectacular.

"No bra, huh?" She peeked in the bag again.

"Sorry." Charlotte grinned and looked down at her own small chest. "I never think along those lines."

The sisters weren't that dissimilar in height, but even though Heather was thin, she had some meat on her bones. Charlotte was wisplike and ethereal, almost fragile. A heart condition had kept her from being too physically active. Their parents had basically spoiled her growing up. Even more than Scott thought *she* was spoiled.

"So, how was it?"

Turning, she tilted her head at Charlotte's question. "How was what? Getting my house blown up?"

Charlotte rolled her eyes. "No, sex with the stud out there."

Heat rushed to her face and she turned away to buckle one of the sandals. "Who says we had sex?"

"There's only one bedroom."

"What if Scott was a gentleman and slept on the couch?"

Laughing, Charlotte said, "Please, this room reeks of sex. Don't try and deny it."

"How do you know what sex smells like?" She and Charlotte were close but Heather liked to keep her sex life private. Especially since Charlotte was four years younger than her.

"I'm not a little girl anymore, Heather."

"You're only twenty-three."

Lifting her nose in the air Charlotte sniffed, ignoring Heather's words. "And it's strong. You guys must have done it at least twice, right?"

More heat rose to her face.

"Three times?" Charlotte's voice rose in excitement.

"We were going for four when you got here. Although the first time was in the kitchen."

Charlotte pretended to swoon then fanned her face. "With the color of your face, I'm assuming it was good."

"That's none of your business, little sister. Now we should probably go and rescue Scott from Mom and Dad."

A thoughtful look crossed her sister's face. "Dad will be cross-examining him on his intentions toward you. Mom will be having an apoplectic fit because Scott doesn't have the right breeding and manners."

"Too bad for both of them. It's our lives and we can decide what we want from it."

Charlotte stopped her before she opened the bedroom door. "And what do you want?"

With Scott, she didn't know. That would have to play out in real time. "I want my house back."

"I'm so sorry, sweetness," Charlotte said, as she wrapped her arms around Heather's waist. "I was trying to keep your mind off that."

"I know." She nodded.

Their parents were sitting at the dining table with coffee cups and cinnamon rolls in front of them when they came out of the bedroom. Heather poured a cup, grabbed a piece of pastry, and sat with them. Charlotte nosed around the kitchen.

"Where's Scott?"

Her mother pointed to the bathroom. "He's taking a shower."

The water wasn't running so he must be done. Which meant he'd be coming out any second with a towel wrapped around his gorgeous body. Good thing Charlotte was in the kitchen. Heather had seen how her younger sister ogled him when they first got here and he was bare chested.

The bathroom door opened and Scott came out, fully dressed, a pair of light brown Carhartts paired with a black T-shirt.

"Where—?" she began, tilting her head in question.

"I had clean clothes in the dryer."

His hair had been hastily rubbed with a towel and the waves stood out in a few spots. She wanted to run her fingers through it, push it back into place. Having her parents here prohibited that, for now. Perhaps at some point in the future.

"Have they figured out what caused your house to explode?" her dad asked, setting his coffee cup down on the table.

"Scott and I smelled gas right before it happened. There must have been a leak." How much did she want to tell her parents about what had been happening? They knew there'd been a few paperwork snafus, but she hadn't confided the rest because she didn't want to worry them.

"Whenever you're ready, we can bring you home." Her mother took a dainty sip from her coffee. The large ceramic mug looked out of place in Nicoletta Silva's hand. She was used to fine china or porcelain.

"I need to check in at the office then do some errands." She'd lost everything in that explosion. Where did she even start?

"I can drive you around," Charlotte offered. "You can even stay with me at my apartment if you want."

"It might be better to stay at home. I have lots of people who can help you get things settled."

"I appreciate that, Dad, Charlotte. But I need to do this myself. I'm not sure staying with either of you is the best thing for me."

"You're not thinking of staying in a hotel, dear, are you?" her mother said with disapproval in her eyes. "How would that look if you didn't stay with your family?"

Sneaking a peek at Scott, who kept his face neutral, she took a deep breath. "I think I'll stay with Scott."

All eyes swung to him. His calm demeanor was only disturbed by a tiny twitch of his lips as he said, "You're more than welcome here, Heather."

"I'm not sure you're thinking this through well enough," her father said, disapproval now apparent in his expression. "No offense to Scott, but he's had a nasty brush with the law recently."

"If you're talking about the assault charges, they've been dropped. The woman admitted she lied to the police."

Scott's posture was so stiff he could pass for a mannequin. Why wasn't he defending himself?

"Even so, dear, it simply wouldn't be right."

"That I'm staying with a guy? Please, Mom, this isn't the Victorian era. And I honestly feel safer here with Scott. I wouldn't want any of you to get hurt."

"Why would we get hurt?" her father thundered, his eyes blazing. "Is there something you aren't telling us?"

Sitting up straight, Scott cleared his throat. "We've had some mishaps on this new construction venture. At first we thought they were all coincidence, but between the bogus charges against me and Heather's house, it might be more than that."

"You're saying someone might be trying to kill you? Both of you? Are the police aware of this?"

"The prosecutor who was trying my case is aware someone had it out for me, trying to put me in jail. She wanted us to let her know if anything else questionable happened. I consider this questionable. I was planning to speak with her and the police today. And my cousin, Jack, still has friends in the FBI. He'll be contacting them."

"Hearing this new information, I definitely think you need to stay with us, Heather."

"I don't want to, Dad. I don't want any of you getting hurt because of me."

"Then give up this project. It's not worth getting killed over."

"I agree, but it's too late now," she told her father. "We'll be looking further into what the building was used for and who might want us out. I'm not losing the money I put into the project because I'm scared."

"No money is worth your life."

"Now that I'm involved it may not matter if I stop the project."

"Then I'll get a security guard to be with you."

"With all due respect, sir," Scott started, "I can keep her safe. I've got military training and I know what to look for."

"How safe did you keep her when her house blew up?"

"Dad." She reached over, squeezing her father's hand. "If it wasn't for Scott, I'd be dead right now. He stopped by to check on me. He was the one who smelled the gas and got us out of there. I was ready to wait and call the gas company but he wouldn't even let me get my phone before he grabbed me and ran."

"Which is why you didn't answer when we called," her mother said.

Her father took a deep breath in then exhaled slowly. "I didn't realize. Thank you, Scott, for saving Heather's life. I still don't like the idea of her not being with us but I guess I have to respect her wishes."

Wow, she hadn't expected that from her dad. Was he finally seeing her as more than his little helpless girl?

Looking at Scott, he said, "I'm trusting you to keep her safe. And if you need any of my resources, do not hesitate to ask. Whether it's money, people I know, or simply vehicles or tools, they're yours if you need them."

"Thank you, sir," Scott said. "I promise I'll do everything I can to keep her safe. And find out who's behind this. She's come to mean a lot to me."

Scott had come to mean a lot to her too. But what exactly was she to him? A friend, business partner, lover, more? She wished she knew, not only for him but for herself.

Chapter 17

"Is there anything else you need while we're out?"

Scott looked at the pile of bags sitting in the cab of his truck. They'd been running from place to place trying to get whatever Heather needed to survive for the next week or so. He still couldn't believe she had chosen to stay with him over her parents. Well, he could see why she didn't want to stay with them: she was twenty-seven and had lived on her own for a while. But her sister had also offered.

"I need to stop at the pharmacy and pick up my prescription. The doctor's office said they'd call it in so I could get a refill."

She got in beside him then shut the door. It only took a few minutes to get there and he went inside with her.

"I'm capable of picking up a small bag of pills by myself, Scott."

"I know you are." He guided her inside and to the counter. "Humor me. I told your father I'd keep you safe."

As she waited for the pharmacy tech, he slipped into one of the waiting area chairs then leaned his head back. There hadn't been much sleep for either of them last night. Partly because of the sex, but also because they were so hyped up over the explosion it had been difficult to relax enough to fall asleep. Her behavior toward him today had been warm and friendly. Not that they hadn't had that before, but he wondered if it was simply because she was grateful. It's not what he wanted from her. He wanted it real.

The tech asked Heather a few questions about any allergies and his mind wandered. The pills she was getting were her birth control pills. He'd heard her talking to the doctor's office earlier, letting them know what had happened and why she needed more. Her face had flushed when she'd told them it wasn't only for the irregular cycle.

Kari Lemor

Peeking at her in her cute dress, he pictured what she'd be like if she were pregnant. Round and filled with his child. Shit. The feelings knocked him over like an armored tank. Is this why Jack always had a grin on his face when he looked at Callie? The thought of Heather having his child filled him with emotions he didn't know he had.

Shut it down, soldier. It was too early in their relationship to be considering a baby. But after the past week, with their date, the unbelievable sex, and Heather wanting to stay with him, it certainly wasn't out of the question. Plus they'd known each other for almost three years. They weren't strangers.

Holding a small paper bag, Heather approached and he snapped back to the present.

"I'm ready."

She slid her hand through his arm as they walked back to his truck. "Thanks for running around with me doing errands today. I can't believe my car was totaled with the explosion damage. The insurance company said I could get a rental, so I'll probably do that later today."

Glancing at his watch, he noted the time. "It's already after four. We can do that tomorrow. Why don't we stop at the grocery store and I'll cook you up a great meal tonight? What would you like?"

After tossing her bag in the truck she leaned in close and whispered, "You. That's all I need."

He kissed her then nudged her into the seat, following behind. "That does sound perfect, but I'll need some food for my stomach if I want to keep chauffeuring you all over the place."

"I told you it wasn't necessary to stay with me all day. I can use a cab or you can bring me to the car rental place right now if it's that much of a problem." Just like her to challenge him, yet her tone was hurt as she stared at him.

Shutting the door behind him, he started the truck then wrapped his arm around her shoulder, pulling her near. "It's not a problem. I told you that. It's been fun running around with you, seeing you in action as you get people to snap to it and do your bidding."

Her nose crinkled and he reached up to smooth it out. "Hey, that wasn't a put down. You are an incredible woman who has so much drive and ambition that you almost glow with it. I like basking in that glow."

"Sweet talker. Where'd you learn how to dish out all that bullshit?"

"Had to do that in the Army to get the best choppers and supplies for my men. They appreciated it."

She rolled her eyes. "I appreciate it too."

Laughing, he kissed her again. "Yeah, that sounded sincere."

"No, Scott, I do. I guess I'm still a little shell-shocked about my house being gone." She hadn't mentioned it much today, maybe trying to remove the horrid memory from her mind. The image of her lying on the ground unconscious was one he couldn't seem to shake. It made him go cold inside.

"That's understandable. I'll help you any way I can."

"But you don't need to protect me. I'm a big girl."

Yes, she was, and he wouldn't remind her of the mess she'd made when she went looking for Jian. She'd probably kick him in the balls.

The grocery store was fun. Heather kept pulling out her favorite snacks then tossing them in the cart. He'd hold it up to ask, "Do we really need this?" She'd nod and throw it back in.

"Seriously?" he said, holding up a packet of marshmallows.

Planting her hands on her hips, she responded, "I'll have you know those have multiple uses. To put in hot chocolate."

"It's eighty-five degrees out today."

Her eyes rolled to the ceiling. "You need them for Rice Krispie squares."

He smiled at her. "Are we sending them in for a birthday at school?"

Pursing her lips, she took the bag and placed it back in the cart. "S'mores. You need them to make s'mores."

As he pushed the cart farther down the aisle, he chuckled. "You're worse than Jonathan."

She jumped up and down then grabbed his arm. "Yes, we can stop by Callie and Jack's and make s'mores with them." The jumping stopped and she cocked her head. "This weekend we'll go over. It's a school night for Jonathan."

"I bet he'd like some Rice Krispie squares too," Scott said as he continued down the aisle.

"I'll put one in your lunch box for tomorrow."

"Where am I going tomorrow?"

"Work."

"I'm going wherever you are tomorrow."

"You need to stop this, Scott. We can't be joined at the hip forever. I have clients I need to take care of and show houses to. And you need to get the men working on the renovation project."

"Until we know exactly what's happening, I'm not risking anyone else's life."

"So the men there lose their paycheck?" Her eyes flashed with anger.

He put some milk in the cart and closed the cooler door. "I moved most of those men to one of my other contracts. No one's missing anything."

"But our project is getting behind schedule."

Moving toward the checkout, he stopped and put his hands on her shoulders. "We have to be patient and take our time with this. I don't want to risk any more accidents or incidents. We could end up dead next time. I kind of like being alive, thank you."

"You're right." She leaned against his arm as the cashier rang up their groceries.

"Aren't you going to fight me to pay for these?"

A sheepish smile crossed her face and she bit her lip. "No. I used up all the cash I took out of the bank on all the other things I needed. I can pay you back."

Shaking his head, he laughed. "I think I'll manage."

The trip home and unloading of groceries and all her bags was done in companionable silence with an occasional remark. As she tucked her items in with his, he threw together supper.

"The casserole will be ready in about thirty minutes. Why don't we sit and relax until then?"

"I'm not sure I know how to relax, Scott."

"Then I'll teach you. Come here." He took her hand and led her to the couch, where he got her settled in the crook of his arm.

"I'm sorry if I keep fighting you about everything. I'm used to doing everything on my own. I forget that sometimes I can accept help from others."

"Yes, you can."

"I hate being beholden to anyone, though. I've tried not to accept anything from my parents because I'm afraid my mom will hold it over my head to do something she wants me to do. Like marry some boring banker."

"They're simply trying to protect you. They love you and don't want anything bad to happen to you."

"Like you?" Was she asking if he loved her? Did he?

"I mean that you want to protect me too." Her breath was raspy as she corrected her words. He'd think about the other later.

"Yes, I promised your father. But I'd do it even if he hadn't asked."

"I understand that. But I don't want you to smother me."

"No smothering. Got it."

Her sassy smile got his heart thumping harder than ever. Damn her. "Hmm, I'm taking back that promise not to smother."

"But—"

"We've got a little time. I'm going to use it to smother you with kisses."

Her eyes lit up as she reached for his face. "Well, in that case, go right ahead."

* * * *

"We're here to see Tony Pascucci." Jack's deep baritone made the mocha-skinned beauty at the desk look up and smile.

"Do you have an appointment?"

Shit, had they come all this way only to be turned away? Scott had tons of other things he could be doing today instead of driving down to Jersey to meet with the guy who'd been Victor Cabrini's right-hand man. That included being with Heather and making sure she was fine. Her thick shell of protection had come back strong, and she'd practically kicked him out when he wanted to hang out at her office. She wasn't quite steady after having her house explode last week, though, no matter what she said.

"No," Jack answered, his smile growing. "But he'll see me. Tell him Jack Holland is here."

The woman spoke into her phone softly then nodded her head. "Mr. Pascucci's office is at the end of the hall on your right."

"Do you trust this guy?"

Jack's smile slipped. "No, not really, but he did save Callie and me from Cabrini. And I've had some friends from the Bureau check on him. It seems he's trying to make sure any of the companies that survived the criminal sweep stay legit."

After a quick tap on the door and a call to enter, they walked into a large office where the dark-haired man sat. His expression was pleasant if not a bit surprised. He stood as they walked in farther.

"Holland, this is a nice surprise. Tell me you've decided to take me up on my offer of a job."

Jack shook the man's hand. "No, but I've got something I could use your help with."

"Of course. Have a seat."

After sitting, Jack began, "This is my cousin, Scott. He and a partner recently bought a mill building they planned to renovate. They've had quite a few problems crop up along the way. Victor's name happened to pop up as possibly owning the building previously."

Pascucci looked thoughtful. "Victor owned many properties along the eastern seaboard for a variety of reasons. Where is this one located?"

"Prescott Street in Menatuck, Connecticut," Scott supplied.

"Menatuck. That doesn't ring any bells, but then I wasn't in charge of stuff like that. A lot of the warehouses and mills were used for supplies and stolen goods. Hold on. Let me check something."

As he clicked away on his computer, Jack shot him a curious look. "You still have information on Cabrini's holdings?"

Looking up, Pascucci grinned. "Sure. The Feds took most of the computers and drives that belonged to Victor's companies, but there might have been a few they missed." He winked at them. "Information is a precious commodity, my friend. It's always good to have as much as possible."

A minute later, he tapped the screen. "Yes, Menatuck. Victor used that building for supplies and stolen goods he got from some of the Boston syndicate. Had it under someone else's name so it wasn't traced back to him. Typical practice."

"You have no dealings with that building anymore?" Jack asked.

"No, looks like it was emptied a few years ago."

Scott leaned forward in his chair. "Do you know why anyone would want the renovations of the place stopped? To the point of murder?"

"No." Pascucci shook his head, his lips pursing. "I didn't have anything to do with that building so can't answer much about it. According to this, one of the guys who used to be responsible for the place is still around. In your neck of the woods."

"Do you have a name and address?" Jack asked.

Checking his computer, Pascucci scribbled on a pad of paper, ripped it off, and then handed it to them. Scott took it and stood, thrusting out his hand. "Thanks. Appreciate the information."

Pascucci shook his hand. "I appreciate what your cousin did for me so I could retain some of Victor's companies."

"You saved my life. And that of my wife and baby. It's the least I could do." Jack followed Scott to the door.

"That job offer is still open, Holland," Pascucci called out. Jack nodded, chuckled, and then walked down the hallway with him.

"Where are we going now?" Jack asked as they exited the building.

Glancing at the paper, Scott shook his head. "You don't need to come with me. I've taken up enough of your time today. Thanks for doing this."

Jack grabbed the paper, scanning the words. "New Haven. At least it's kind of on the way home."

Once they were in the company truck and on the highway north, Scott glanced at his cousin. "You don't need to come with me, Jack. I'm a big boy and can handle a few questions."

"I know you are, Scott. But if this guy worked for Cabrini he's more than likely a little slimy. Even the best agents don't approach someone like this without back up."

"Good point."

They continued on in silence, Scott's mind going a mile a minute. Would they get any answers from this guy? Would he be able to tell them why someone wanted this project stopped badly enough they'd blow up Heather's house, with her inside? Had they timed it so Scott would be there too?

The thought of someone wanting him dead scared the crap out of him. Not only because he liked being alive, but because of the potential for others around him to get hurt. Jack, Callie, Jonathan, or any of the people who worked for him.

"How's Heather doing?" Jack's question interrupted his thoughts. "Callie asked her and she brushed it all off. Like almost being blown up was nothing."

"She's had a few meltdowns. Her emotions are ranging from sad and devastated to angry and ready to rip someone's balls off."

Chuckling, Jack said, "Sounds like Heather. And what's up with you two? Do we need to have that talk again about not hurting her?"

"Back off," he snapped then regretted his tone. He sighed. "Sorry, got a lot on my mind. Anyone even suggesting I'd hurt Heather kind of pisses me off. Right now I'm focusing on how to keep her safe."

"You could pull the plug on this renovation project."

"I could but I'm not sure that will solve the problem. It might for us, but whoever we sell the building to will most likely have the same issues. We need to figure out what the fuck is going on. Before someone else takes a potshot at us."

"Agreed. It's why I'm taking time out to go with you today."

The miles flew by with Jack filling him in on the house addition and some of the possible name choices for the new baby.

"Do you know if it's a boy or girl?"

"Callie didn't want to know, so I'm honoring that. The ultrasound was a bit sketchy anyway. Good thing I'm not a tech for that. Head, arms, legs, yeah, but anything else was dubious in my opinion."

"I can't even imagine."

"It's amazing, Scott. You might think about trying this marriage and baby thing."

A laugh escaped and he shrugged. The truth was he had been thinking of it, a lot more than he'd ever done in the past. Did he want to admit it, though? He sure didn't want Callie playing matchmaker.

"The address we got is down here," Jack said as he turned onto a street in a rundown section of New Haven. They got out, checked the apartment, and when there was no answer started asking around. They both had on working clothes, which made them blend in among the casually dressed people of the neighborhood.

"Kenny, sure. He usually hangs out at that bar around the corner during the day. You can probably find him there," one older guy who'd been sitting on the stoop told them. Scott pushed a ten dollar bill into his hand and thanked him. The man quickly shoved it in his pocket, scanning the area.

"Let's go find this guy," Jack said, heading in the direction of the bar.

Once inside, they asked around, and though no one would tell them who he was, many eyes swiveled in the direction of a forty-something guy shooting darts.

"Thanks," Scott said to the bartender as he and Jack left. They didn't go far. The alley next to the building was wide and empty.

"How long you think we'll need to wait until he comes out?" Scott wanted to get back to check on Heather. The images of her crying and falling apart in his arms jabbed deep inside. He wouldn't even go anywhere near the ones of them entwined on the bed, or God help him, the kitchen table. After dinner yesterday they'd spent a long portion of the night exploring every inch of each other.

"Here he is," Jack warned and they flanked the man as he moved on the sidewalk.

"Kenny Jefferson?"

Kenny's eyes narrowed and he frowned. "Who wants to know?"

"Tony Pascucci gave us your name. Said you might be able to help us." Jack threw out the ex-mobster's name. Would it help?

"Tony, huh? I ain't got nothing to help no one."

"All we want is some information. It'll only take a second." Scott didn't want to be hanging around this guy any longer than they needed to.

Kenny attempted to walk around them, but Jack moved closer and Scott maneuvered him farther into the alley.

"You worked for Victor Cabrini for a while."

"Yeah, what of it? The guy got whacked and left me with no job." His eyes darted around the area.

"We were told you worked at the mill building on Prescott Street in Menatuck. What can you tell us about that place?"

"I can't tell you nothing. Get the fuck out of my way." He reached into his pocket and Scott grabbed for his hand then twisted it behind his back. The man held a knife.

"All I'm doing is asking you a few questions. Cabrini's dead, so you don't have to worry about snitching on him. I want to know what the building was used for."

"Yeah, what's in it for me?" Kenny grunted.

Memories of Heather lying still on the ground after her house exploded flashed through his mind. She'd almost been killed.

"How about I don't break your face?" Scott snapped, as he slammed the man into the wall harder. "Is that reason enough to give me a few answers?"

"Okay, man, let up. I'll tell you what you want to know."

Releasing him, Scott allowed him to turn around but hovered right in his face.

"The building was used to hold stolen goods. We used to move them in and out at night."

"What else?"

"I don't know what else."

Scott's hand pushed against the man's throat. "Why would someone be opposed to renovating the building?"

"What the fuck, man, I don't know. Unless there's still stolen shit in there. I...wait, the basement. We were told not to go into the basement."

Easing back on the pressure, Scott asked, "Why? What was in there?" He only remembered debris and empty boxes.

"I don't know. I never went down there. You think I was going to risk getting my ass killed by disobeying Victor Cabrini? I ain't that dumb, man."

He'd have to look more closely at the basement. Stepping back, he crooked his head toward the street. "Thanks for the info."

Jack stepped in front of Kenny, and it almost looked like he handed him something. Then the man took off down the street. Once back in the car, Scott glanced at his cousin.

"What'd you give him?"

Jack shrugged. "Some money. Figured we didn't need someone like him holding a grudge. He may have been harmless enough, but I'm sure he has friends."

"Never thought of that. Guess I'm not cut out for this cloak-and-dagger shit."

Laughing, Jack said, "You seemed to do the tough guy questioning thing well enough."

"This thing with Heather almost getting killed has got me freaked out. I need to find answers."

"You don't have to explain it to me. Trying to keep Callie and Jonathan safe for so many years was about the only thing that kept me going. But you keep saying how Heather almost got killed. You were right there in the explosion too, Scott. Don't forget to watch your own back here."

"I won't. But isn't that what I have you for, cuz?"

They both laughed then got in the truck to head home. At least now he had a place to start in finding the answers to all the crap that had been going down since he and Heather had bought this building. Hopefully once he found them, he could go about setting everything right. Get back into the renovations. He wanted everything back in the right with his relationship with Heather because he knew now that it was something he definitely wished to go forward.

Chapter 18

"Are you sure you don't want the lava stone counter tops?" Scott asked, as they looked through brochures and samples at the building supply store. "They're the newest craze."

"I don't need the newest, just something functional." Heather had to keep smiling and shaking her head whenever he suggested something outrageously priced. Did he think she had the same budget as her parents?

"Functional we can do," he said, moving around the other displays of counters and fixtures. The past week had been trying and great all at the same time. Scott had wanted to stick to her like glue and at times she was more than happy to have him that close. Especially at night, when he'd wrap her in his arms then take her places that made her dreams sweet.

Other times, like today at work, she wanted to slap him silly. He'd been stopping in at lunch, insisting he know her schedule and where she was going and with whom. He'd even become good friends with Wendy so she'd let him know if anything out of the ordinary happened. Wendy had fallen right under his spell. Something about that dimple in his chin went straight to every woman's heart. She wasn't immune.

"I'm getting kind of hungry," she complained a few minutes later as they looked at yet another set of kitchen cabinets. Slipping her hand through his, she peered up at him and swiped her tongue over her bottom lip. As expected, his eyes flared as he leaned down to kiss her. She liked this part of being close to him. In the past week kissing had become a common occurrence.

"Did you want to stop someplace? I'm not exactly dressed for anywhere fancy."

He wore her favorite outfit. The work pants and snug T-shirt. She looked down at her own shorts and tank top and frowned.

"Do I look like I'm dressed for a nice restaurant?"

"Princess, you look good wearing anything." Leaning down, he whispered, "And even better wearing nothing."

"Well, if you bring me home, we can get some food then see about that wearing nothing part."

"Done."

It didn't take long to get home and they both worked side by side to get dinner ready. She stirred the roasted potatoes again and stuck them back in the oven and then went to the balcony to see how the grilled chicken was coming along.

"About fifteen more minutes. I'm cooking it on low so it doesn't blacken." After turning the meat, he slid his arms around her where she stood at the railing.

"Thank you, Scott."

"For the chicken? You marinated it. I'm simply giving it heat."

Leaning back against him she said, "No, for everything you've done this past week. Allowing me to stay here. Sifting through dozens of house plans to help me pick one out. Going with me to all the stores trying to figure out what kind of fixtures and flooring I want even though I know we're nowhere near ready to use them."

"It's been my pleasure having you here. I wouldn't have offered if I didn't mean it."

"Your pleasure, huh? I've gotten some good pleasure from it too." Wiggling her behind against his crotch, she felt him harden.

"You little tease. We don't have enough time right now for anything."

She tipped her head to glance at him. "You said we had fifteen minutes. What's the matter, you aren't up for that kind of challenge?"

"Challenge? I've got to keep an eye on the meat."

"Your balcony is private and it overlooks the back woods."

His hands drifted to her waist then up to caress her breasts through the thin top she wore. Lowering his head, he nipped at her shoulder then nibbled on the back of her neck. Damn, he always knew that one spot that sent shivers down her spine and heat rushing between her legs. Lightly pinching her nipple with one hand, the other slid inside her shorts to tease her. *Holy shit, he knew where to touch.* It didn't take long before her breathing was heavy and she squirmed against him, needing more.

"Challenging enough for you, princess?"

"Oh, God, Scott. Please."

A zipper sounded and air rushed past her ass as he lowered her shorts and fingered her again. His erection pressed against her cheeks and she bent over to rest her head on the railing.

"That's an invitation if I ever saw one," he groaned, then thrust into her from behind. Damn, that was amazing. It hit the most intimate of spots. Then he began to move in and out and her mind exploded with colors and patterns as the intensity began to build. The hands gripping her hips were firm but gentle and his heavy breathing behind her told her he was close too.

As he thrust in and pulled out, he nibbled on her shoulder, biting softly, escalating her desire and need. His touch, his presence was all she'd ever wanted and needed. Why hadn't she seen it earlier?

"Time to let go, your highness," he said, fondling the folds between her legs. She spiraled out of control and pushed against him. He kissed her shoulder then stiffened, still holding her close. After a few moments he eased away, pulling their clothes back in place.

"Let's hope I didn't burn the chicken."

Straightening her top and buttoning her pants, she responded, "For that, I'll give you a pass."

His laugh drifted her way as she headed back in the apartment on wobbly legs. The potatoes needed to be taken out also. Would he give her a pass too if they were overcooked?

Luckily, they weren't. They filled their plates then sat on the balcony in the wicker chairs. Scott had opened a bottle of wine and poured them each a glass.

"I'm not sure I can look at this balcony the same again. I'm getting excited just remembering what we did out here."

After taking a sip of her wine, she blew him a kiss. "You mean we christened the place? You've never done it out here before?"

"I've never done it anywhere in my apartment before. I've only lived here for three years and I told you the last few have been a bit light in the romance department. Before that it was at someone else's place."

He'd never had sex with anyone here before. As she'd lain in bed with him the last few nights, she'd wondered how many women had also shared it with him. She told herself she wasn't jealous. She'd had her share of boyfriends and didn't expect him to be upset about them. But it had kind of bothered her, and she wasn't sure why.

After finishing the meal and cleaning up the dishes, they settled on the couch in the living room and Scott surfed through the channels.

"In the mood for anything particular?"

Shifting closer to him, she shook her head. "No explosions please."

Laughing, he clicked the remote a few more times, settled on a romantic comedy, and then tossed the device on the coffee table. His feet lifted to rest there too and he settled his arm around her shoulder. They'd done this a few times this week, and she found she enjoyed having the company. Her other single friends wanted to go barhopping or clubbing, and Callie had Jonathan to take care of and now Jack. Which usually left her home reading or watching TV alone.

"Did you and Jack meet with that guy who worked for Cabrini?"

"Pascucci, yeah. Yesterday. He confirmed the building had been one of Cabrini's. Said it was used for stolen goods and other supplies. He didn't know why anyone would want to kill for it, though."

Disappointment seeped through her. "So it was a dead end? Damn."

"Actually no, he gave us the name of someone who was responsible for the warehouse for a while. We paid him a visit with a few questions."

"And...?" Scooting on to her knees, she faced him. "You can't stop there."

"What? You don't like a little teasing?"

"You want teasing, do you?" Slipping her hand down to his legs, she skimmed it up and over his now growing arousal.

"You're insatiable. The guy we saw told us the same as Pascucci. It was used for stolen goods. But he also said they were told in no uncertain terms to stay out of the basement."

"The basement? Have you checked it out yet?"

Shrugging, he said, "I took a quick look when we got back yesterday but there's so much debris and trash down there I couldn't see anything out of the ordinary. I didn't want to leave you alone too long."

"Don't you be using me as an excuse. We need to figure out what the hell is going on."

"I agree," he said and pushed her back on the couch his face inches from hers. "So, princess, feel like going dumpster diving with me tomorrow?"

"Hell, yes."

He pressed a kiss to her nose. "It's a date."

Pulling his head closer, she replied, "Oh, Scott, you always take me to the nicest places."

* * * *

"I'm here. Let's go."

Scott turned as Heather entered the first floor of the mill building. Faded jeans and a concert T-shirt hugged her figure while a ratty pair of work boots graced her feet. Damn, she looked cute. Her hair was in two braids that ended right in the middle of her plump breasts. *Get your eyes back in your head and stop staring.*

"Where'd you get the old clothes?" They fit like they'd been molded to her body.

"I still had some stuff at my parents. I think these are from college. I may have put on a pound or two since then." She rubbed her hand over her hip.

They were some damned fine pounds. But they had work to do.

"Did you bring some gloves?"

Her eyes narrowed. "Gloves?"

"Work gloves," he said, pulling his from his back pocket. "A lot of the stuff down there has sharp edges and nails sticking out. Can't ruin your manicure."

As she rolled her eyes, he pulled out another pair of gloves from his other back pocket and smirked. "I have some if you forgot yours."

She grabbed the gloves and turned away, muttering, "Thanks."

"You're welcome." Her backside sure was fine in the snug jeans. It was fine without the jeans too, but for some reason the jeans were turning him on even more. It could be the thought of tugging them off her later. For now they needed to concentrate on finding whatever the hell was in the basement that some asshat didn't want them to find.

Pulling the key from his pocket, he unlocked the door leading downstairs. He flipped on the lights and took her elbow.

"The stairs need some work and the lights have a tendency to flicker. I need to get the electricians on fixing the whole damn electrical system in here."

"Which we can do as soon as we find out who's causing us trouble. And I'm perfectly capable of walking down stairs by myself. I have boots on today if you hadn't noticed."

"Oh, I noticed." And not simply the boots. At the bottom of the stairs she dropped one of the gloves and bent over to pick it up. Hot damn, those jeans were giving him fits.

"What?" She crossed her arms over her chest and glared.

"Nothing. You look good when you're slumming it. That's all."

Shaking her head she walked away...and almost fell over a pile of debris. He grabbed her, pulling her close, then kissed the lips that always had a habit of screaming at him to do just that.

"You need to be careful, princess. Half of the lights down here are out. It's why I brought flashlights."

"Oh, now you tell me. You couldn't have said something before I tripped?"

"Then I wouldn't have had the opportunity to save you. And kiss you."
He pressed his lips to hers again. Her arms crept around his neck and the
kiss continued, long and sweet.

"You've been doing quite a bit of kissing me lately. I think you'd be
sick of it by now."

"Are you kidding me?" Their lips met again, this time more passionately.
"I think you've become an addiction."

Her smile warmed his heart and a few other spots he needed to
ignore right now.

"Do we need to get you a twelve-step program? Some rehab?"

Pulling her in tight and feeling her breasts against his chest was not
the smart thing to do. But he did it anyway.

"The addiction isn't a problem...yet. Now stop distracting me and let's
get down to business." Slapping her butt, he grabbed the flashlights he'd
left on the stairs then walked deeper into the room.

The gasp she let out made him chuckle and he wanted to turn around
and see her outraged expression, but he didn't. It would push her buttons
even more. She followed behind and grabbed his arm.

"Did you bring one of those for me?"

Handing one over, he replied, "Got to take care of my gal."

Her face got all scrunchy, but she simply took the flashlight and turned
away. His princess sure didn't like accepting help from anyone. It was fine,
though, because her independence was one of the things he liked about her.

"Why don't we start in one corner and work our way across the room?
Some of this stuff is big and will need both of us to move it."

"Sounds good."

They walked to the farthest wall and began shifting things around,
making sure they weren't missing anything. As they worked, they chatted
about the jobs Holland Construction was working on and how demanding
her clients could sometimes be.

"Some of these people don't seem to understand that I can't simply make
the perfect house they want appear on the market. They seem to think it's
my job to find them a house that has absolutely everything on their wish
list. Which it is, I know. But I can't do it if it's not on the market."

"Tell them to build it then. That way they get everything they want."

"Oh, I do, believe me. Most of them don't want to wait that long."

"I get that. The businesses I work for always want everything done in
a ridiculous amount of time and they want it for half of what it would cost
me to do it and still pay my workers."

Pushing aside a piece of drywall, she placed her hands on her hips, pouting. "But you'll get my house done in a few weeks, right?"

"Sure, princess, whatever you want."

"Excellent." Her smile lit up the dim space even though she knew he was kidding. If he could build her a new house in a few weeks, he would.

"Have you been able to get replacements for the vital stuff yet? License, credit cards, Victoria's Secret lingerie?"

"Oh, you know I've got some of the lingerie. If I remember correctly you had no problem taking it off me the last few days."

His smirk couldn't be controlled. Not with those images in his mind. "And I enjoyed every second."

Heather stepped closer and wiped something off his face. "Some dirt. And I got the major things settled but there are so many things I never even realized I had in that house that suddenly I need."

Her sigh cut through his heart. If he could, he'd make everything better for her and give her the world. After hugging her, they got back to work moving more debris aside but still finding nothing worth killing for.

"You know if there's ever anything I can do for you, princess, all you need to do is ask. Right?"

She kicked at a box on the floor and nodded. "Actually, there is something you could do for me."

Walking closer, he pulled her into his arms and pressed a kiss to her forehead. "Name it."

"My family is having a big party tomorrow night. A fundraiser for one of my mother's favorite charities. I'm expected to be there."

"And what do you want me to do?"

Leaning her head against his chest, she whispered, "Would you come with me?"

Go to a big, fancy Silva shindig? Schmooze with the beautiful people, the rich and famous? Not his scene. But he nodded, saying, "If you want me there."

"Thank you," she squealed, attaching her lips to his. Giving in to the desire, he slid his hands down her back and cupped her sweet ass. Even in snug denim he could feel the amazing curves.

When she pulled back, her expression showed her delight. "It'll be great. I know a bunch of the people there might be willing to invest in our project."

"Are you talking about this place?"

She nodded.

"Why do we need investors?"

"These people know businesses in the state that might be looking to expand and locate here. We need to have some commitments to fill the first floor space."

"Aren't we getting ahead of ourselves a bit, princess? We have to figure out who wants to stop this project and why. I'm not sure anyone would want to invest in a place that has this much trouble attached to it."

Her excitement dimmed, and he hated being the cause of it. Although the frickin' person tormenting them was truly responsible.

"Then let's keep looking."

At least his wet blanket hadn't dimmed her spirit. He couldn't stand it if that happened. "All right then."

Hours later he was ready to give up. They'd moved every damn piece of wall board and debris in the place. Of course the basement was huge and ran the whole length of the building but only parts of it were filled. They'd checked out the other rooms as well.

"Maybe we should give up," he said as he leaned against the railing for the stairs on the west end of the mill. These would need fixing as well. The stairs themselves had fallen apart and the wood lay scattered all around nearby.

Wiping a strand of hair from her face, Heather sighed. She didn't want to stop, he could tell. And he'd keep going if she asked. He was beginning to think he'd do most anything for her. The last week had been the best time he'd ever spent with anyone. He hadn't even cared that her makeup littered his counter in the bathroom or that she had the habit of leaving half-empty water bottles all over the place. She was great company in all ways. And not only in bed, though that part had been fuckin' amazing. Conversation flowed easily between them, serious and humorous. Making fun of herself was something she did as much as teasing him.

"I hate to leave," she said as she shone the flashlight at him. "There's got to be something here. It doesn't make sense otherwise." The beam cut through the darkness in this part of the basement. Most of the lights here didn't work. It flickered behind him and she stepped closer, her head tilting. "What is that behind you?"

Scott turned around surveying the broken lumber. "All this debris?"

"No, there's something shiny under the wood."

Taking his own flashlight, he shined it on the trash and then pushed aside a few pieces to see what she was talking about. Under the stairs was a small trap door. He pulled on it, but it stuck. Then he saw the large lock holding the door in place. And the door wasn't made of the old timber much of the other doors were. It was steel and attached with sturdy hinges.

"Looks like we may have discovered what is so interesting about this place."

As she approached, Heather rested against his back, almost like she was using him as a shield. No problems there. He'd risk his life for hers. Of that he had no doubt.

"Can we open it?"

"Not with these tools. I'll need something stronger. Possibly even a power saw. Although a .45 might do it quickly enough."

"Do you have a .45?"

He nodded. "I think we can try bolt cutters first. The gun will be a last resort. There's always the chance of the bullet ricocheting around the room and hurting one of us."

"Can we go get the tools right now?" Her eyes almost glowed in the darkness.

Glancing at his watch, he said, "It's already seven. It'll take us a while to get them and return. I don't want to start messing around down there this late. Who knows what we'll find. We can come back during the day."

"Not tomorrow. We've got the party to go to."

"But that's not until night, correct?"

"Yeah, but I don't have a formal gown to wear so I need to go shopping. And there's no way you're going down there exploring without me."

Whatever was down there had been there for a while. It certainly wasn't going anywhere. It could wait.

"If you're not too hung over from this big soiree, we can come back Sunday."

"Oh, I won't be. I'll make sure to keep my eye on how much I drink."

Slipping his hand into her hair, he leaned in, whispering in her ear, "I don't know, I kind of like you drunk. That night at Chris and Meg's wedding is one I don't think I'll ever forget."

"Except I don't remember it, you ass."

"Get drunk again and I'll make sure you don't forget this one. I can go all night long until you remember every touch."

Chapter 19

Scott finished shaving and brushing his teeth then opened the bathroom door. Heather was in the bedroom getting her gown on for the big shindig tonight. She'd come back from running errands for most of the day with her hair and nails done. It looked like she had on more makeup than usual, also. Some combination that made her look more exotic.

He wasn't sure if he wanted to go or not. Being with Heather was always great but the rest of the rich and snobby, not a chance. Throwing the towel back into the bathroom, he entered his room and the air whooshed out of his lungs. Hot damn and holy hell. The gold-spangled fabric that draped across Heather's glorious body hugged her hips and was cut dramatically low on her back. Shit, another inch and you'd be able to see her ass crack.

"Um, I think they forgot the back of your dress, princess."

As she turned, his mouth dried up and his tongue didn't seem to work. The front of the dress was held up by a trio of straps on each shoulder, the lower one caressing her upper arm like a tiny sleeve. The V front dipped between her breasts, though nowhere near the amount of the back. But she couldn't possibly be wearing a bra underneath it. Besides the back being too low, her nipples poked through the alluring fabric.

"Glad to see me?"

Looking down, she frowned. "I thought that might be a problem. I got some special tape to fix it."

He watched mesmerized as she pulled open a box and removed what looked like flesh colored Band-Aids. She pressed them across her still erect nipples then flattened the dress down again. They might not be apparent to anyone else anymore, but he knew what was under there.

"Are you trying to make me walk around with a boner all night?"

She sashayed closer and ran her hand down his chest then lower, barely touching the front of his pants. The tenting grew more obvious and he bit back a groan.

"Do they make those Band-Aid things for men? I might need one with you walking around like that all night."

"You like the dress then."

Running his fingers down her back, he slid them inside the fabric and fingered between her butt cheeks. "I like the access it gives me, but I'm not sure I want anyone else having it. Or even seeing you like this."

She rolled her eyes and adjusted a wayward curl that had shifted from her fancy updo. "Believe me, Scott, this dress will be conservative compared to some of the people there tonight. You should see what Charlotte is wearing."

"I'm not sleeping with Charlotte, and I don't care if other men ogle her."

Sidling up to him and pressing her chest against his, she whispered, "I think I like your being jealous."

"Who said I was jealous?" Shit, he *was* jealous. When had that happened? "I just don't want guys picturing themselves fucking you up against a wall in a corner of the ballroom."

Shaking her head, she said, "No one's going to—"

"Oh, believe me, they will. They won't tell you though."

She straightened his collar and buttoned his top button. "Is that what you'll be picturing?"

"Me? No. I'll be imagining you and me out on the balcony again. I'll slide my hands in the sides of your dress then remove your little tit strips. After playing there for a bit, I'll bend you over the railing like before and push the fabric off this gorgeous ass. After a few minutes licking and nibbling on that, I'll plunge inside and screw you until you wake the neighbors with your screams."

A shiver ran through her and Scott felt a deep satisfaction at affecting her that way. "You like when I talk dirty to you, huh, princess?"

Resting her head on his chest, she nodded then eased away. "You need to stop. We'll be late for the party and my mother will nag all night to me about it. Here, I got you something."

As she walked toward the bag on the bed, he pulled on his suit jacket. She came back carrying a burgundy tie with a gold paisley print on it. "I thought you could wear this. It matches my dress."

"What, the ties I have aren't good enough?" he teased, putting the fabric around his neck and knotting it. He'd never been all that good at this and Heather pushed his hands away and helped him.

"Both of your ties are fine. I merely thought it would be nice to have a new one."

Was she emphasizing that he only had two? What the heck did he need with more? Although if they became a real couple, he'd most likely have to attend more fancy parties like this. That was a sobering thought. Would she be buying him a new suit...or two, also?

"There, all ready and handsome as ever." She reached up to comb her fingers through his hair, fluffing a bit here and moving a strand there.

"Did you want to check my teeth while you're at it?" He tried for a teasing tone, but in the back of his mind was the thought he hadn't quite come up to snuff on his own.

The look she threw him could have melted steel. "Let me grab my purse and we'll be all set."

The small gold clutch sat on the dresser and she picked it up, tossed in a lipstick and some other makeup thing, and then snapped it closed.

When he held his arm out, she slipped her hand through it and they set out. As they crossed the living room she stopped to grab some keys on the coffee table. "Here, I rented a car for tonight."

She'd rented a car. "Why?"

Her smile was huge and genuine so he tried not to take offense as she explained, "The cab of your truck is kind of high and this dress isn't all that easy to maneuver in. I thought it might be less difficult with a lower sedan."

"Sure, did you want to drive then?"

She handed him the keys and said, "No, you can. These four-inch heels aren't real conducive to manipulating a gas and brake pedal."

As they drove, they both took guesses as to what they'd find once they unlocked the trap door at the mill. Gold, more stolen goods, drugs, the Man in the Iron Mask.

"I hope it's not a dead body," Scott said. He'd seen enough of those in the sand box.

"Ooh, yuck. Wouldn't that smell and have flies everywhere?"

They pulled up and he avoided the question. She didn't need to know the details of dead bodies. Helping her out of the car, he handed the valet the keys and escorted her into the upscale hotel.

"My parents rented out the ballroom on the top floor."

"Of course they did," Scott muttered as they entered the elevator and he pushed the correct button. "I'm curious, this hotel must have cost a fortune to rent and you said there'd be food and drinks, so how do they actually raise funds for this worthy cause?"

Heather's eyes flicked away then moved back to him. "It's five hundred dollars for a ticket. Most people who are coming will be expected to donate as well."

"Five hundred bucks a person? Holy shit. Do they take credit cards because I left my checkbook at home?"

The elevator door opened and Heather slid her hand around his elbow. "This is my family's party and you're my date. You don't need to worry about it."

She never actually said she got free tickets. Did she pay for them? Or her parents? Great. He was mooching off the rich now. It wasn't just a tie.

"I need to let my mother know I'm here," she said, craning her neck to look through the room as it filled. "She'll already be upset I wasn't the first one here. I don't need to piss her off more."

They wended their way through the people and Heather grabbed two champagne flutes off a passing tray. Tipping her head back, she took a healthy swig.

"I thought you said you'd be staying sober tonight?" he teased, taking a smaller sip of his drink. "Didn't we have plans for creating some great memories tonight?"

Her eyes narrowed. "I simply needed a little bit of instant courage before I spoke to my mom. She's always a little high strung at these kinds of events."

"Then why does she do them?"

"She says they're expected of someone in her position. She's very into appearances if you hadn't noticed."

He had. He wouldn't say it out loud. *Never insult another person's mother.*

"Heather," Nicoletta Silva called out pleasantly as they approached. "It's so nice of you to be here."

Scott didn't know Heather's mom all that well, but even he could read the word she was leaving out. *Finally.*

"I would have been here earlier but with all my possessions gone..." She trailed off and kissed her mother's cheek.

"Mrs. Silva, it's nice to see you again."

"Thank you, Scott. You also." She presented her cheek for his soft kiss never even mentioning how he'd addressed her and that her husband had insisted he be less formal.

"The place looks amazing. Heather says you do all the organizing yourself." If he got her on another track, would she forget about chastising Heather for being late?

Kari Lemor

"Yes, I do. I keep asking Heather to assist me but she's always too busy with her little real estate business. And now this new building." Replace the late speech with one of guilt.

"You know, dear, Clifton is here tonight."

Who the hell was Clifton? Heather's eyes widened and her smile was forced.

"Wonderful. I'll have to make it a point to say hello."

"He's looking quite well, Heather. And from what I've heard he's being prepped to take over for when his father retires soon."

Heather's head tipped to the side bobbing up and down. "Fabulous. Mom, there's a crowd of people heading this way who, I'm sure, want to speak with the hostess. We'll let you get on with your duties."

Nicoletta's gaze swiveled and she pasted on what Scott assumed was her *good hostess* smile. Taking Heather's elbow, he steered her away into the throng of people then stopped.

"Is that Judge Barlow? Why would she be here?" His gut clenched at the memory of his arraignment.

Heather ran her hand down his arm. Was she trying to comfort him? "It's not unusual. Most of them have some sort of political agenda. And the people here can help them fulfill it."

"The rich people you mean."

Heather rolled her eyes and started walking. Judge Barlow caught sight of her and waylaid them. God, what did she want?

"Ms. Silva, Judge Mary Barlow." The woman held her hand out, introducing herself. Heather shook it, her smile serene and curious. He could barely keep from growling at her.

"My sister recently bought a house through you. Said you were fabulous at finding them exactly what they wanted."

Heather was all business. "I'm so glad they were satisfied. I do my best with what's on the market."

The judge made a little small talk but kept glancing at him while she did. *Yeah, you set my bail at half a million bucks, lady, and I was innocent.*

"I'm not sure if you remember my friend, Scott Holland," Heather interrupted their conversation. "He was in your court recently."

"Totally innocent, of course," Scott piped in, trying to keep his voice even. He'd have to get lessons from Heather and her mother. "Trumped-up charges by someone trying to put me out of business."

The woman looked uneasy and clasped her hands together. "Yes, I got word that the case had been dropped. I'm terribly sorry. I didn't realize the two of you were friends. The district attorney said she was looking into some new developments regarding this."

"Someone blew up my house. I'd say that was a new development." Heather's voice was still laced with syrup.

"Oh, you poor thing. May I call you Heather? I'll make sure this gets looked into further."

"Oh, the police are right on it," Scott said. "I'm sure you don't need to worry about a thing."

"Well, you know I'm running for Congress." She addressed this to Heather, barely looking in his direction. "One of my platforms is getting the crime rate down in Connecticut."

Heather nodded. "That's perfect. Perhaps you could start with the Prescott Street area in Menatuck. Scott and I have a building there we're renovating and we've had some problems."

"I can put that at the top of my priority list."

Why was this woman being so agreeable? Did everyone suck up to rich people like this?

"I'm wondering, Heather, if you could put in a good word for me with your father? He's very influential in the political arena. I certainly could use someone of his caliber giving me their support."

"I'd have to find the time first. This mill building problem we're having is keeping me quite busy."

"Oh, certainly. I understand. I'm in tight with the sheriff and will make sure to get him working on this right away."

Heather's smile was a mile wide. "I appreciate that. Now, if you'll excuse us, I see my father waving at me."

Heather propelled him to the other side of the room but they didn't see Domenic Silva along the way.

"That was smooth. You never actually promised to say anything to your dad. We'll see what kind of results we get in the neighborhood clean-up department."

"There's a lot of give and take that goes on in these fundraisers. You have to know how to play the game."

"Apparently you're very good at it."

"It's just—"

"Hey, Sugar Tush. You are looking sweet today."

Scott turned at the rich voice. An obvious playboy in a tux stood behind them, his eyes roaming Heather's figure in a far too familiar manner. Who the hell did he think he was?

Sighing, Heather faced the newcomer. "Hi, Clif."

* * * *

The last thing Heather wanted right now was to deal with Clif. The man was an obnoxious boor who thought everyone should fall at his feet. Unfortunately, he moved closer to give her a kiss. If she slapped him now it would cause a scene. Not that she cared, but her mother would have a fit and be embarrassed, especially since the woman apparently wanted to push her and Clif back together. Not in this lifetime.

Allowing the kiss, then pushing Clif's wandering hand off her ass, she stepped back.

"Clif, this is Scott Holland, my friend and business partner." She'd love to introduce him as more but they hadn't talked much about exactly what their relationship status was. Earlier he'd said something about them sleeping together. Was that all it was to him? It was beginning to feel like a whole lot more to her.

"Clifton Farthington, the third," Clif announced regally then held out his hand.

Scott shook it, his eyes assessing the newcomer. He didn't have anything to worry about. Clif was hardly competition. But the look on Scott's face had her wondering if he was jealous or feeling inferior. Which he definitely was not. Unfortunately, Clif always carried a larger-than-life air about him. His blond hair was styled perfectly in a slicked back wave and his facial hair was trimmed to look like casual stubble though, she knew for a fact he shaved every day.

"Business partner," Clif said, looking at her. "I didn't know you took on another real estate agent."

"I'm in the construction business," Scott said before she could correct Clif. "Heather and I are working on a project together."

"How lovely," Clif said drolly, then grinned as he glanced over her dress. "And I must say, you are looking ravishing as always. How about I go find you another drink then we can discuss renewing *our* partnership?" He took the empty glass from her hand and attempted to slide his arm around her. Quickly, she sidestepped and walked closer to Scott.

"Sorry, Clif, but Scott and I need to chat with a few people here. I'm sure you understand."

Clif sighed. "Sure, business first. I'll catch you later or call. Your mother seemed to think you'd be interested in getting together again."

Grabbing Scott's arm, she sauntered away muttering, "Yes, my mother always was delusional when it came to you." She honestly didn't care if he heard or not.

Scott stiffened. "If you want to reconnect with him, you only have to say the word. I'm sure I can find someone to chat with."

The jealous tone in Scott's voice sent thrills through her. Once they were far enough away from Clif and in a fairly empty part of the room, she turned and touched Scott's cheek.

"I have no desire whatsoever to reconnect or anything else with Clif. I dated him for a few years when we were younger and it was a few years too many. He doesn't care anything about me or what I want. His interest lies in merging our family fortunes together."

Although he was certainly interested enough in the sex they had too, but she wouldn't tell Scott that. Though he might like hearing he was far better in bed than anyone else she'd ever been with. Or maybe it was simply they had more chemistry together. But since she didn't want to hear about his ex-girlfriends, she figured he wouldn't want to hear about her past lovers.

"We'll forget about Clif then. Didn't you say there'd be food at this place? I'm kind of hungry."

"There is." She led him over to where waiters were setting up trays with fancy hors d'oeuvres. They grabbed a small plate and nibbled while discussing what other features she wanted in her new house.

Once done, she cleaned her hands on a napkin and placed the remnants on a side table.

"Shouldn't we throw this away somewhere?" Scott glanced around, probably looking for the trash barrel.

"That's what the waiters are here for." When Scott threw her a disgusted look, she ignored him. "Enjoy it while you can. You won't get it at home."

He placed his empty plate on the same table then scanned the room. His eyes narrowed. "Drew's here. Did you know he'd be here?"

Shrugging, she replied, "I asked my parents to invite him. There are people here who could help his career."

"And where'd he get the money for this? Prosecutors don't make millions."

"I sent him a ticket. I was hoping he and Charlotte might hit it off."

Scott looked around the room. "You know Charlotte is on one side of the room and Drew's on another. Do you plan on introducing them?"

"They've already met a few times, although I'm not sure if Charlotte remembers. She gets a little involved in her own world at times."

"Seriously? Drew and Charlotte? I'm not sure that's ever going to happen. Drew likes his women a bit more...substantial."

"Substantial?" How dare he insult her sister. "Are you saying Charlotte isn't good enough for him? I'll have you know Charlotte is extremely bright. She may not have finished a degree yet, mostly because she isn't sure what she wants to do, but she's not stupid."

"I never said she was." He caressed her shoulders then ran his hands down her arms. He could make her forget everything when he touched her like this. "I merely meant that Drew is the outdoorsy type. He likes to hike, fish, and play sports. Charlotte looks like she'd blow away in a stiff wind."

Rolling her eyes, she had to admit that was true. "That doesn't mean they wouldn't hit it off." Right now her sister was holding out her champagne flute to a waiter indicating she wanted another one. "She can be a little high maintenance though."

"I'm going to say hi to Drew. Did you want to come along?"

"I need to talk to Charlotte about a few things. And no, not about Drew. If they're going to hook up, I'd rather they figure it out on their own. I'll simply try and get them in the same place at the same time."

"You might want to do it when there aren't a few hundred other people around." He leaned down to kiss her cheek then drifted away.

Moving through the crowd, she stopped to acknowledge some of the people who might help with the mill project. She'd have to make sure to spend more time with them later. Charlotte stood holding court, her admirers stunned by the gossamer creation she wore.

Her sister sure knew how to emphasize her good assets while downplaying others. Her dress was a pale peach and the light fabric draped in two thin strips over her slim shoulders to dip almost to her navel in the front. Several long clunky necklaces dangled there. The dress was equally as low in the back. A light brown scarf wrapped around her tiny waist and draped down one hip, breaking up the pale color. A few pieces of ribbon crisscrossed around her torso; probably the only thing holding the dress in place. The full skirt flowed to the ground, but as Charlotte dismissed her crew and moved forward, her long trim leg poked out through the slit in the front.

"Sweetness," her sister greeted her. "That dress looks amazing on you. I knew it would."

Grabbing Charlotte's hands she pulled her in for a kiss. "Thanks for arranging for me to wear it. I hated the thought of forking out that kind of money for one night."

Charlotte rolled her eyes. "Mom would have bought it for you in a heartbeat. Half the guys here have been drooling over how you look."

"And I appreciate that I don't owe Mom any more than I already do. She'd have me marrying someone like Clif in no time." The shivers were automatic any time she thought of that man.

Charlotte had convinced their father to start a small gown rental business for occasions such as this. Many of the wealthy women had no problems spending thousands of dollars for a dress they'd only wear once. But a few of the more frugal ones preferred to simply borrow one and then give it back. Their dad had put Charlotte in charge of knowing who to offer the service to. Most of the customers wouldn't want anyone to know the dress was only on loan. Her sister was extremely discreet, and the gowns were housed in a back room at the largest Silvaggio's. Their father donated gowns that came in and had any kind of defect. The one she was wearing had a slight discoloration near the hem.

Charlotte's eyes sparkled. "What did Scott think of the dress?"

"He said they forgot the back of it. I told him yours was worse."

Looking down at the strips of exposed skin Charlotte shrugged. "It's not like I have a whole lot to show off. Some of the guys here tonight have bigger boobs than I do. I'd wear something skimpier but I only want to shock Mom, not send her into a coronary. I haven't heard a *word* from her about the dress but her eyes have said plenty."

"I'll bet. Hey, can you discreetly check my back? The beautician covered any of the remaining burn marks with airbrush makeup but I wasn't sure how it was lasting." Turning slowly, she pretended to search the room.

"Still looks great. How are the plans coming for the new house?"

Facing her sister again, she said, "I've picked out the plans and Scott has had me out a few times to see about cabinets and bathroom fixtures. The cops just released the property from their investigation so nothing's been done yet."

"What did they say?

Heather took a deep breath. "It looks like the gas line could have been tampered with."

Charlotte took her hand and squeezed. "I'm glad you're all right. Please, be careful. I don't want to lose you."

"You won't. Scott's being totally obnoxious about protecting me."

"I wouldn't mind him protecting me." Charlotte's eyes stared into the distance where Scott chatted with Drew.

"Eyes back in your head, Char. He's mine. You can have his friend, Drew. The one he's talking to."

Charlotte tipped her head as she glanced across the room. "Cute. He's the lawyer, right? That's too conventional and Mom might actually approve of him. I need someone who will shake her up a bit."

Jian came to Heather's mind but she quickly pushed it back. The guy had helped them out but a street gang leader was far too unconventional, even for her sister.

"That waiter who keeps offering me champagne is kind of adorable. I think I'll chat him up a bit more. See you later, sis."

Heather shook her head as Charlotte walked off and began flirting with the hired help. Scott was still talking with Drew and Judge Stokinger, the friend of Drew's who had offered to help when Scott was arrested. She'd let them have their time. She didn't want to relive any of that horror. The thought of Scott going to jail for something he didn't do, scared the crap out of her.

"Why does your sister do this to me?" Her mother's soft voice drifted into her musings.

"Do what?" Playing innocent always gained her a few minutes to get herself prepared to deal with her mother.

"Do what? Please, Heather, do you see what she's wearing, or should I say what she's almost wearing? And then flirting with the most inappropriate men."

"How is the waiter inappropriate?"

"He's being paid to work here tonight. Do I need to spell that out to you?"

"Scott's here as a guest. Does that make him appropriate?"

Her mother sighed heavily. "He's certainly better than a waiter, but not by much. You need someone who can give you what you want, dear. Not some construction worker."

He was much more than a construction worker, but Heather knew pointing that out to her mother would be a moot point.

"I saw you with Clif earlier and he seemed quite friendly. That's wonderful considering how you ended things with him. You should try and catch his attention again tonight. He might give you another chance."

"I don't want another chance with Clif, Mom. I broke up with him for a reason. You said I needed a man who could give me what I want. Well, I want a man who cares for me."

"I'm sure Clif cares for you. He's asked me several times about you."

"Clif is an arrogant jerk who doesn't care about pleasing me in any way. He likes the idea of merging our money."

"There's nothing wrong with that, Heather. And you need to make sure you please your man, not the other way around."

"That's so old-fashioned, Mom. Are you saying that Dad never pleased you? Never did anything because *you* wanted it? That you've done all the giving in your relationship?" She knew it wasn't true but needed her mother to realize it.

Her mother's eyes drifted off to the distance where her dad stood conversing with several other men. "No, your father is an amazing man, and I'm fortunate to have him. He always sees to my needs and is quite generous."

"Do you love him?" It wasn't something she'd heard much between her parents though she was fairly sure they did love each other.

"Of course I do, and he loves me. I don't know what I'd do without him."

"Then why can't I have someone who loves me and gives me what I want. Someone who I love."

"You can, Heather, but it's just as easy to fall in love with a wealthy, successful man as it is with a common laborer. I did."

"Well, don't hold your breath waiting for me to fall in love with Clif. That will never happen."

"It doesn't have to be Clif. There are many available men here tonight who are more suitable for you. Don't disregard them because you have a sudden itch for a man who works with his hands. I admit, those nice muscles under snug T-shirts can turn any woman's head, but you must think of the long term, your future."

That was the problem. Every time she did think of the future, it always involved a man with wavy dark hair, wearing Carhartts and smelling of sawdust.

Chapter 20

"How's that mill project you had me talk to ol' Florina Betts about? Is it well underway?" Judge Stokinger asked, after discussing one of Drew's recently finished cases.

"Not exactly. We've had a few more problems since I last saw you," Scott said, wishing he'd had better things to report. He appreciated the judge getting the Historical Society lady off their case.

"Anything I can help you with? I know plenty of people on different committees. All it would take is a word from me." Seems all these rich people loved helping others out. Made him wonder what he'd be expected to do in return.

"Thanks, though I don't think there's anything you can do. It has more to do with the history of the building and who owned it previously."

The judge looked up, stroking his jaw. "I'm not sure my history is up to date on that town. Long ago it was owned by a large fabric company."

"Well, recently it was owned by Victor Cabrini," Drew piped in.

"Oh, well, since he's recently deceased I'm not sure what the problem could be."

Scott shrugged. "Seems he might have hidden something in the sub-basement. I haven't had a chance to get down there yet, but probably next week."

The judge looked around, most likely bored since any action he could take was gone. He seemed like a man who wanted to be needed for who he knew.

"Probably some stolen goods. Let me know what you find," he said, patting Scott on the arm and gazing across the room. On to more important people. He'd had that impression since getting here. The few people he'd talked to weren't interested in hanging out when they discovered he wasn't worth millions.

"Where'd Heather get off to?" Drew asked once the judge was gone.

"Last I saw she was talking to her mother. I'm not getting anywhere near that."

"You don't like her mother?"

"It's more like I'm not good enough for her daughter. Not rich enough, not successful enough, and I don't have the right family name."

"Heather's not like that, is she?"

"I don't think so." Or he hadn't thought that recently. Perhaps in the past he'd believed she was a rich snob moving about her wealthy world, but the last few months he'd changed his opinion. But then he hadn't seen her in her element. For the past hour, while he'd been listening to the law talk between Drew and Judge Stokinger, he'd watched Heather work the room. She flitted from one person to the next, giving each of them her full attention. He couldn't hear what she was saying but if it was anything like the other conversations he'd overheard tonight, she was making deals and constructing bargains. And too many of these people loved touching her back or stroking her arm. He should be the only one doing that.

Possessive much, Holland?

This wasn't where he belonged. He didn't work on manipulations and back scratching. An honest day's work for an honest day's pay. Many of the people here tonight didn't know the meaning of the word honest.

"If you can manage without me, I want to go catch up with the district attorney. There's a big case coming up I need some info on."

"Go ahead." Scott waved his friend away. "I think I can be left alone for a few minutes without getting in trouble."

"I'm not so sure about that, Holland, but I'll do it anyway. I'll catch you before the night's over."

Scott's gaze roamed the room, narrowing in on Heather again. She was talking to an older couple, her face animated and excited. God, she was beautiful. What in hell did she see in him?

"Sugar Tush is just about to reel them in," Clif said from behind him. He did *not* want to have a conversation with the man. They had nothing in common. Except Heather. That fact cooled his desire.

"Nice nickname," he deadpanned. Could be one of the reasons Heather broke up with the guy.

"Let's face it, man, that woman has one fine ass. And let me tell you, it is so sweet. To touch and taste. Yum."

Scott wasn't sure if he wanted to throat-punch the guy or puke in his face. Perhaps he could do both. Clenching his fists by his side he called on all the control he'd needed while in the military to keep from following through.

"So, you two are partners, huh? In all ways, or business only?"

Scott glanced sideways at the arrogant jerk but remained silent. He wasn't about to discuss his intimate relationship with Heather. Unfortunately, Clif didn't have the same compulsion.

"She can be quite the tiger in bed, man. And shit, does she have the most gorgeous tits. I could play with those all day."

"You need to—"

"Construction, huh?" Clif interrupted as Scott was about to tell him to shut the fuck up. "Working with your hands, getting dirty. Chicks kind of dig that sometimes, don't they? Or so I'm told."

The rich bastard turned his back on Scott and perused the crowd. "I personally like to use my hands for better things. Like sliding it under Heather's dress and into her tight pussy. I'd even do her sister, though she's a bit skinny for my taste. If you haven't gotten into her pants yet, you should try soon. You know, while she's still in her slumming with the working class stage. She'll be upgrading soon enough. They always do."

"They?" Why did he even ask? He should be walking away from this piece of trash.

"The rich girls. They might dabble in the lower class for a bit of fun, but they won't ever stay there. Look at Charlotte, flirting with the waiter. She might fuck him a few times, mostly to piss off her mother, but when she gets married, it'll be to one of us."

"One of us?"

Clif rolled his eyes, tipping his head. "Well, one of my kind. Someone with a name and money. Old money."

Old money. He was doing well with his business and if this mill ever got renovated he'd be doing better, but he certainly could never compete with that kind of money.

"Great chatting with you, Heather's business partner. Sorry, not good with names. A little parting tip, she has this freckle on her inner thigh, if you nip a tiny bit up from that, she'll go nuts."

Heat permeated Scott as he watched Clif amble away and slide his arm around some other scantily clad debutante. Getting tips on how to sexually please the woman he was with wasn't why he'd come here. Or be reminded others had seen her naked and enjoyed her body.

Like the man who currently had his arms around her back in a fake hug, slipping his fingers into the side of her dress, hoping to cop a feel for those gorgeous tits Clif had talked about. Heather laughed and took a step away but continued the conversation. What happened to his warrior princess who would have slugged anyone else for doing that? Was this guy such an important contact that manhandling was allowed?

Grabbing another drink from a passing waiter, he turned to see if he could locate Drew. As much as he wanted to be with Heather, he wasn't enjoying this side of her. The rich girl side. He downed the drink and snagged another.

Nicoletta Silva appeared next to him and he almost turned to run in the other direction. Her smug grin let him know she wasn't coming over for a nice chat. Although she'd probably make it sound like one. She had that knack.

"Are you enjoying yourself, Scott?" Yes, pleasant and polite, as expected.

"I'm fine, thank you. The food and drink are wonderful. Congratulations. It looks like a big success."

"Yes," she said, her eyes drifting around the room. "Of course, we'll see how much of a success when all the donations are tallied. If my estimation is correct, we should be able to count on two million for charity."

Two million dollars. Holy shit. There couldn't be more than two hundred people here. He did the math and forced a smile. Hope she wasn't counting him in that donation.

"I'm so glad Heather was able to find something appropriate to wear for the party tonight at such short notice. Do you like her dress?"

"Absolutely." He wouldn't let her know what he wanted to do to Heather in that dress. Although Clif's words kept dulling his enthusiasm. The alcohol was dulling some things too.

"Typically she might get a dress custom made for her for an event like this. Luckily one of the stores had this in her size, and it works well, even if it was a less expensive dress. The tailor-made ones run far more than two thousand and also take a longer time to create."

"Two thousand? Dollars? For her dress?" Were his eyes bugging out of his head. Why the hell would anyone pay that much money for some stitched fabric? He took another swig.

"Yes." Nicoletta patted his arm. "Get used to that if you plan on sticking around. Heather is acquainted with this kind of life and she expects it. She may seem more down to earth when she's with her friend, Callie, but here is where she belongs. Look at her, she's in her element with these people. This environment."

"Certainly looks that way," he mumbled, still wondering how he'd ever afford to buy her clothes like that. The answer was, he wouldn't.

"Of course, if she had someone more in her league, she wouldn't have to lower her standards of clothing and accessories. She does love her Jimmy Choo's."

"Jimmy...?"

Brushing an invisible strand of hair off her cheek, she laughed. "Her shoes. She does love her shoes."

He loved them too, and the way they made her legs look when she had on a shorter skirt.

"Those were only five hundred because we carry them in the store and she gets a discount. Often she'll order Manolo Blahniks or Louboutins straight from Europe and they'll be a bit more."

Damn, you could barely see the shoes under the long train of the dress. Were they encrusted with diamonds?

"It was lovely chatting with you, Scott. Hopefully we'll see you around if you aren't busy on the construction site."

As she walked away he wanted to brush himself off and make sure he wasn't covered in sawdust and dirt. It was how she'd made him feel. Even though he owned a large construction company that was successful, he would always be a construction worker in the eyes of everyone here. For now, he needed some air. He finished off his drink, slapped the empty glass on a table, and stalked off.

The men's room was quiet and nicer than anything he'd ever seen. He splashed some water on his face then took a deep breath. What the fuck was he doing here? He was a blue-collar worker, an ex-military man, who worked with his hands and liked a cold beer when he watched sports on TV. This wasn't his idea of a good time.

When he went back into the large hall with the floor-to-ceiling windows overlooking downtown Waterbury, Heather stood gazing out, only a few other people milling around. The view of her gorgeous back was better than the one out the window. She'd come to mean a lot to him in the last few months. Heck, if he was being honest, the last few years as they'd been pretending to be together. But now he had to think about this.

Would she be happy with him? They seemed okay now, but what about if he wanted to get serious? Like marriage serious? He and Patrice had been going along well enough until he'd mentioned marriage. Then she'd ripped his heart out and left him bleeding all over the floor.

Would Heather do the same thing? Did he want to give her the opportunity? Watching her tonight, he'd realized she truly did belong in this world. She understood it, knew how to manipulate it. Thrived on the give and take, the back scratching and deal making. It wasn't his world.

It never would be. This type of environment would make him crazy in no time and he wasn't sure he'd be able to stomach it, even for her. Was it time to bow out gracefully? Before either one of them got hurt. Further.

As she turned around he almost lost his nerve. The smile she gave him lifted his heart, warming him all over. Until he thought of her insisting he wear suits and ties that she'd bought for him. Expensive ties that cost hundreds of dollars. Having her style his hair to her liking so he didn't embarrass her. Demanding he accompany her to these shindigs and kowtow to the high and mighty old money folks. Until she dismissed him from her life because he didn't fit in. That image stabbed through his lungs so much he couldn't breathe. But if he waited it out and stayed with her, loving her more, it would be far worse.

"I saw you leave and wanted to make sure you were all right." Her long manicured nails stroked up his arm. Swallowing the lump in his throat, he took a step back. Not a big one, but enough to put a little distance between them. Her smile faded.

"This place makes my skin crawl."

Looking around, she said, "Why? What happened?"

"Nothing specific. I came out here so I wouldn't embarrass you anymore."

The hurt expression that crossed her face dug into his soul and he faltered. He was doing this for her too, though.

"Embarrass me? What are you talking about? I'm not embarrassed by you."

"Maybe you should be. I'm hardly of the same quality as most of these other people."

"Listen, Scott, I don't give a shit what these people think. Of you or me. I brought you here because I wanted you here."

Lifting his hand, he caressed her soft cheek. He shouldn't since he didn't want to let go. "That's a great thought, princess, but let's face it, I don't fit in with these people. They're all a bunch of rich snobs, and I'm only a carpenter."

"Where is all this coming from?" The crack in her voice let him know she was getting upset.

"These people here, Heather, I'm nothing like them. They wheel and deal and backstab and manipulate. All in the name of business. As long as it's for a good cause, it's okay to do whatever it takes to get your way."

"They aren't all that bad."

"I've been listening to quite a few conversations tonight."

Glancing away, her shoulders rose and fell. Yeah, try and deny what he'd heard.

"And you introduced me as your *partner*."

Her head whipped around, her eyes glowing fiercely. "What did you want me to say? 'This is Scott Holland. He and I are having hot monkey sex in his kitchen.' Would that have been less embarrassing?"

"So, you are embarrassed that we're sleeping together?"

"Of course not, but it's hardly the place to announce it to the world." Her gaze flew around the hall, relief apparent when no one seemed to be focused on them.

"You're right. I'm sorry. Guess this is more proof I don't belong here with all of these beautiful people."

Tipping her head, she frowned. "I'm not like most of them." She stared at him as if looking for an answer. He didn't have one. "But you still think I am. Don't you?" Her voice squeaked at the last two words.

Eyeing her expensive dress, he let his mind wander to everything he'd seen and heard tonight. "Well, aren't you?"

"You can ask me that? Seriously?" The pain in her tone ripped him apart but this wasn't something that would go away. She'd always be the rich little girl of a megamillionaire and he'd always be the son of a carpenter.

"Letting that guy touch your ass as you got his business card, or the other one who tried to slip his fingers into your dress, that's all part of a normal world?"

Her lower lip trembled and she clamped her mouth together. Turning slightly away, she took a deep breath in. When it came out it shook. She took a few more breaths and he could see her trying to get her expression under control. Her profile was strong and her jaw tight then she faced him again. "I'll stay with my sister tonight," she whispered, "and send someone for my things in the morning."

Damn, he wanted to pull her close and kiss her sadness away, but it would only hurt worse for both of them if their feelings grew any stronger before they realized their relationship wouldn't work. Because it couldn't.

"Yeah, you...send someone. Can't break a nail doing it yourself." Leave her with him being a bastard. It might get some of that fight back into her. He loved that part of her. Damn, loved! It shouldn't be that far already.

As she turned to walk away, he pulled the keys out of his pocket and handed them to her. "Here, I'll grab a cab."

Confusion lit her face. "I don't have anywhere to put them and I don't have my license. Take the car and someone will pick it up later."

"I don't want it." He'd had too much to drink and he didn't want anyone coming over to remind him what a stupid thing he was doing by letting her go. He took her hand and shoved the keys into her palm, walking away as fast as he could. Not before he'd seen the sheen of moisture in her eyes.

The elevator would be too slow so he took the stairs. He might even skip the cab and walk back home. It was only about ten miles. He'd done that in full gear and a sixty-five pound pack on his back through the desert. This would be cake. It would give him time to cool down and get his emotions under control.

The image of her as he left wouldn't be dismissed. Her face had been like stone but her expressive eyes couldn't hide the fact she was close to tears. *Come on, warrior princess, buck up. You're stronger than that. Stronger than me. You'll survive this.* He wasn't sure he would.

As he started down the busy street he thought about their interaction. He'd been a jerk, but better to get rid of any thoughts of being together now than later when his feelings were already in too deep. Or maybe it was already too late.

* * * *

Heather clenched her jaw and pushed back her shoulders as Scott walked away. He was walking away. From her. Damn him. Didn't he realize how she felt about him? Of course not, because she'd never told him. Hadn't made it apparent to anyone here tonight that they were a couple. *Had* been a couple. Would it have mattered? Would he still have seen her as one of the spoiled, pampered guests who manipulated others to cater to their whim?

Something wet dropped onto the hand she held at her throat. Tears, shit, she never cried. Okay, maybe when her house had blown up but certainly never over a guy. Voices at her back had her rushing into the ladies' room and slipping into a stall. Leaning against the side, she let the pain come and the tears fall. Silently, though, because after all she was still Heather Silva and she had a reputation to uphold.

Damn Scott, he was right. She was a spoiled little princess who usually got what she wanted. And right now, she wanted him back here, telling her everything was fine and they'd make it all work. But all her Daddy's money couldn't buy someone's love. She'd learned that the hard way at twelve when she'd found out her Hollywood crush was already married and couldn't be bought to be her boyfriend.

A toilet flushed a few stalls over and she flinched. Had they heard her sniffling? Would they even now be bending over to see the bottom of her gown to surmise who was in here so they could go back out to spread some juicy gossip? Water in the sink ran then a few moments later the door sounded and a quiet greeting floated through the air. Damn, someone else had come in.

Her eyes and nose ran so she grabbed some toilet paper and tossed the keys, the damn keys to the rental car that Scott wouldn't take, onto the back of the toilet so she could blow her nose.

"Sweetness." Her sister's voice drifted through the door. "Is that you?"

"Char?" She couldn't stop the wobble in her voice. What the hell was wrong with her? Why was there this big empty hole in her chest? "Is anyone else out there?"

Charlotte moved closer to the door. "No, it's only us. Are you all right? I saw you run in here a few minutes ago."

Slowly easing the door open, she glanced out at her sister. Charlotte's eyes opened wide. "You're crying. What happened? My big sister never cries. Tell me who did this and I'll punch their lights out."

Heather laughed in a snorty, pathetic kind of way. It was the threat she'd always used whenever Charlotte cried. Now she took her hand and pulled.

"Let's get you cleaned up then you can tell me what's wrong. Where's your purse?"

"I left it on one of the tables when I was helping Mom with something."

"Good thing I have mine. Stand right there." Charlotte wet a wad of toilet paper, grabbing the keys she'd left in there, and gently dabbed at the skin under her eyes. Damn, her mascara trailed right down to her chin. After some concealer and a dash of powder, her sister dragged her into the other section of the powder room where there were upholstered chairs and benches. Heather sat near the corner so her back was to the door. She didn't need anyone coming in, seeing her looking such a mess. The tears weren't quite done yet.

"What happened?" Charlotte sat in a chair across from her, rubbing her thumbs over Heather's hands. "I thought I saw Scott leaving when I came out. Did something happen to Jack or Callie?"

"No." Oh God, that would be even more awkward now than after they'd slept together in Vermont.

Her sister didn't say anything more, simply stared at her. It was a trick their mother always used, but Heather would never tell Charlotte that she was copying their mom. She'd hate it.

After another minute of silence, she sighed. "I guess you could say Scott and I had a fight."

"Oh, honey, I'm sorry. But it'll be fine, you'll see. He couldn't keep his eyes off you tonight. He'll spend a little time by himself then realize he can't live without you. Back in no time."

Too bad she couldn't believe that. Shaking her head, more tears rushed to her eyes. Too bad he'd spent so much time watching her. Scott had seen

Walt Sorensen grope her backside. The poor guy was half-blind and was looking for his cane. Which his wife had but didn't want him using because it didn't look proper. Stupid woman. He'd immediately apologized to her and his face had turned beet red. Lawrence Dalton was another matter. He'd been rather blunt in what he was aiming to find when he slid his hand around her back and into the side of her dress. But the man was a distributor for their clothing line and she couldn't afford to piss him off. And his wife was a lovely person who didn't need reminders what a scum she'd married.

She couldn't even imagine the other things Scott had overheard or seen. It was what happened at these events. Women mingled and men made deals. Often women made deals too. But favors were exchanged for future favors. He wasn't wrong. Simply wrong for her.

But why did he feel so right when they were together? Why did his lips on her skin make her feel like she was free-falling? The sound of her name on his lips send chills running through her core? His presence beside her while watching TV or eating dinner give her the most content feeling she'd ever had?

"He won't be back." God, it hurt to admit that. "Can I stay with you tonight?"

"Of course you can, sweetness. I'll even let you have my bed. Or we can snuggle together like we did when we were little and eat popcorn and watch ridiculous movies."

"That'd be great." Stupid wobbly voice. Charlotte pulled out the extra toilet paper she'd snagged earlier and handed it to her. After blowing her nose she took a few deep breaths, thankful her sister wasn't prying too much into what happened. She deserved to know part of it.

"I think Mom got to him."

"Damn her. I wish she'd mind her own business. Me flirting with the waiter should have taken all the pressure off you and Scott."

"She did admit Scott was better than that, but only a tiny bit."

"What if I say something to Dad?" Charlotte offered. "I think he actually likes Scott."

"He does. But Char, I want a guy who'll stand up and fight for me. Who won't let what others think or say keep him from what he wants. I guess Scott isn't the one."

As Charlotte sat next to her, hugging her, her mind drifted to all their times together. Scott certainly felt like the one. The fact was he didn't want her badly enough. Or perhaps he simply didn't want her in any way except the physical, and that would never be enough for her. Not now.

* * * *

"What are you doing here today?"

Heather's voice was shrill but she had hoped not to see Scott in the building. She'd spent the last few days attempting to convince herself she didn't have strong feelings for him and she wasn't heartbroken over his actions at the party. Failure had been imminent.

The silence was more than awkward. Scott's Adam's apple bobbed up and down as he took deep breaths and tried to look anywhere but at her.

"I thought I'd check out what was here and why someone doesn't want us to know what's in there."

"I'm surprised you didn't come here Sunday or yesterday. It's not like you were following me around any longer." Sure, remind him of the fact he'd been chasing after her like a puppy the last few weeks.

"I have a company to run and I've been helping Jack with the addition for their house. I could say the same to you."

"Yeah, well, Charlotte kept me busy Sunday." Not that she'd tell him her sister had bugged her incessantly about trying to get back together with the gorgeous hunk while she'd cried her eyes out. "And I had a ton of clients that needed my attention and a closing that took far too long."

Looking around the space cluttered with debris, she flicked the switch on her flashlight. "And I had to find a tool that might work to get the lock off. I couldn't ask Jack because I figured he'd want to know what it was for and tell you."

"That's what you brought?" He indicated the small kitchen hammer in her other hand.

Shrugging she said, "I figured you'd have already broken in and I'd just come see what you found."

"I can handle this," Scott said and hefted a large cutting tool. "If you have better things to do with your time."

"I own half this place and have as much right to be here as you. Plus, it was my house they blew up, in case you'd forgotten."

"No, I haven't forgotten. Fine, use this flashlight and shine it over here." He handed her a much larger, industrial-strength flashlight to use.

The muscles in his arms and back flexed as he worked the large cutting tool. She wouldn't think about how she'd touched those muscles as they held her and... *No, mind on business.* It took a few minutes and some grunting but the lock snapped. Manipulating it off, Scott then took a crowbar and shoved it under the trap door. As he pushed, Heather moved closer to see what was under the metal panel.

The cover clanged and shook when Scott dropped it open. A dark hole greeted them, and when she flashed her light inside they saw a set of stairs leading down into a darker space.

"You up for this or do you want me to check it out?" His eyes sparkled with a dare and it was almost like old times.

"You aren't leaving me up here while you go and have all the fun."

"Suit yourself. Ladies first." He swept his hand still holding the crowbar in front of him, indicating the dark hole.

"I'm taking this, though," she said, indicating the huge flashlight shining in front of her. Damn her bravado and pride. It looked terrifying and someone didn't want them down there. All she could picture was some scary-ass clown jumping out with an ax or a chainsaw.

The stairs creaked as she pressed her feet onto them. Scott's presence behind her was the only thing helping her keep her shit together. Everything was black as pitch with the exception of where the beam flashed. A long narrow hallway spread out in front of her and she kept putting one foot in front of the other. It ended at a half wall, the space behind even darker than before and only about four feet wide.

"Do you want a chance to lead now?" Her voice quivered and she cleared her throat. The grin on Scott's face almost made her take back her offer. But she honestly wasn't sure she wanted to climb over that wall and into the space by herself.

Being a good half foot taller than her, he easily hopped onto the wall then reached down for the large flashlight. Trading with him, she took the smaller one and shined it behind her and around the area. Nothing but concrete walls all around. Soon he disappeared into the hole, so she hefted herself up onto the wall behind him.

Scooting her legs around, she let them dangle over the edge as she eyed the dim space. The small room was filled with long wooden boxes. Wooden boxes that looked exactly like…

"Shit," Scott swore, moving closer to one of them. "I was hoping this wasn't the case."

Dropping onto the floor, she took a tentative step toward him. "You know what those look like?"

"I'd say coffins, but I really want to be wrong about that. Could be automatic weapons." He narrowed his eyes, one side of his mouth curling up. "Cause that would be so much better. Only one way to find out," he said, slipping the end of the crowbar under the wooden top. Shifting his weight, he pushed down, and the wood creaked and lifted. He repeated that a few times then shoved aside the top.

Aah! She jumped back. A skeleton, totally emaciated and picked clean of any flesh, resided inside. Tiny pellets of rodent droppings littered the wooden bottom.

Moving up behind Scott, she shuddered and wrapped her arms around his waist. Right now she didn't care if they'd broken up. It wasn't every day you found a dead body in a building you owned.

Scott twisted, kissed her head, and then moved away to examine another one. She backed toward the half wall. As he lifted the crowbar, she said, "Do we have to? I'm gonna take a wild guess and say it's more of the same."

Scott cracked open the next one where another dead body rested inside. This one still had a little fabric covering part of it.

"We need to get out of here and tell the police," Scott said kneeling down near a third box.

Good idea.

"That won't be happening," a low voice sounded behind her. Before she could turn, everything went dark.

Chapter 21

Scott's head pounded as he opened his eyes. It took a few moments for them to adjust to the darkness. As details took shape, he rolled his shoulders, the ache unfamiliar. His arms were above his head and something kept them from moving. Pulling, he heard a metallic rattle. Chains. Pressing the fingers of one hand over the other, he felt a cuff around his wrist. What the fuck?

The voice behind them. *That won't be happening.* Who the hell had said it and what had he done to them? He didn't remember much after Heather's little moan of pain. He'd turned in her direction then wham. Shit, where was she?

"Heather?" His throat was dry, causing the word to barely come out.

"She's a little tied up right now, Mr. Holland. So sorry."

Who? He narrowed his eyes and focused on the dim light coming from the small opening into the chamber. The death chamber, if the number of wooden caskets was anything to go by. The voice was familiar, though. Where had he heard it?

And hadn't that area above the half wall been larger before? A face appeared in the opening and in the weak shadows Scott narrowed his eyes to try to make out who it was. He knew that shock of white hair and quickly attached it to the voice.

"Judge Stokinger? What the hell?"

"I'm sorry, Scott," the judge replied, his voice hardly repentant. "You should have taken the hint and sold the building when you first ran into problems. I had someone handy to scoop it up from you. They would have offered top dollar too."

"Where's Heather?" Had he hurt her?

"Oh, she's in there with you. She's chained to the wall on your left. I didn't want you to die alone."

"What the fuck are you doing? And why?"

"Blocking up this opening if you can't see well enough." Light flashed into the chamber and then a clink sounded as something dropped. The beam of a flashlight cut across the space then stopped, shooting light toward a corner.

"In case you're afraid of the dark." The man's vicious laugh floated through the still air.

A groan to his left snapped Scott's head in that direction. The flashlight had illuminated the small room a fraction. Heather stood to his left, her arms above her head clasped in chains attached to the wall.

"What...Scott? Oh, my God, Scott, my hands are...why are my hands like this?" The panic in her tone cut right to his gut.

"I'm right here, princess. Judge Stokinger was just about to tell me why he's doing this."

"I suppose it doesn't matter if I tell you. Neither one of you will be able to share the information with anyone."

"What information? Why is that hole smaller?" Her anxious voice rose higher and Scott pulled, testing the chains on his hands. Shit. The cuffs were attached to a bolt in the wall. One that was in tight.

"I'm sealing you in here, my dear. It's only for a short time really. Once the explosives go off I'm sure much of this new wall will come tumbling down."

"Explosives?" Scott's heart thudded in his chest.

"Yes. You see I can't have any evidence hanging around that leads to me."

"You mean these bodies?" Heather asked, anger echoing through the fear in her tone. Good girl. Get that warrior going strong. He had a feeling she'd need it.

"Yes, if the authorities were to identify them, they might be able to put two and two together. A few of them had found out about my dealings with certain individuals. Ones who I shouldn't have been dealing with."

"Criminals," Scott said.

"Let's just say they weren't up in the same social bracket as Miss Silva here. I couldn't very well have them tell anyone what they knew. My career would have been over."

"So you killed them?" Heather asked, her tone disgusted.

"Of course I didn't. But I had a nice association with Victor Cabrini and he was more than happy to assist me in eliminating the threat. Not that he ever got his hands dirty. No, he had a hit man on his payroll who was quite handy."

"Cabrini." Scott hated that name. Had it been the same hit man who'd been hunting Jack for years? Would Jack have ended up in here if Callie hadn't been able to get the needed information that brought down the mobster?

"Yes, see, I had a nice arrangement with Victor. I'd let him know when certain people had information that might harm him. He'd make sure that information never got out. I was paid well, and often he'd do favors for me."

"How is it you weren't on the list that Cabrini had of people who worked for him?" Scott knew Callie had found that list and the FBI had rounded up everyone on it.

"Plain luck. I'd retired a few years ago and was no longer any use to Cabrini."

A rustle in Heather's direction told him she was struggling to get free.

"You can't leave us in here," Heather shouted at him. Then she screamed.

Stokinger laughed. "I don't think anyone will hear you doing that. And if any of that sound manages to get up a few flights of stairs and through the concrete walls, I doubt it will be all that effective."

"Where are the explosives?" Scott asked. Best get as much information now while the judge seemed in a talkative mood.

"Oh, they're all over. I was an explosives expert in the war, you know. I've got quite a bit of C-4 sitting on the coffins and then even more planted on each floor of this building. I want the whole place to come down and I don't want more than shards of bone to be found. Certainly nothing that can be identified."

"You can't just leave us here to get blown up," Heather argued.

"And why even bother walling up that opening if the place is going to explode anyway?"

"Well, you see that's the great part of this plan. I'm leaving to go back to Florida this afternoon. The explosives aren't set to go off until tomorrow morning around four. I won't be anywhere near here, so I have a perfect alibi. Not that anyone would suspect me. You certainly didn't. Plus, that early, no one is likely to be around to get hurt. I wouldn't want to injure any innocent bystanders, you see."

"But it will kill *us*," Heather yelled.

"Yes, I'm very sorry about that, my dear. But you and Mr. Holland aren't innocent any longer. You are a threat to my retirement and must be removed."

"We'll get out of here and stop you." Oh, yeah, the warrior princess was back. She'd need that strong will.

"This is why I'm bricking the rest of this opening. Even if you somehow manage to get the manacles off, which is doubtful, there won't be any way to get through this wall."

A tiny whimper sounded to his left. Scott wanted to try and convince the man to let them go, but it wouldn't do any good. His mind whirred with ideas and ways to get them out of here. The opening was getting smaller as each brick was cemented into place. Could he get these cuffs off before the cement dried?

"Someone will come looking for us."

Heather wouldn't give up. He loved that about her.

"They might," Stokinger replied. "But they won't find you down here. And if they look around the building they won't see the explosives either. I've hidden them in the lumber and debris." One more brick went up and there was only a tiny space left.

"Enjoy your last day with each other. I'm sorry I couldn't have left you closer together."

"Nooooo!" Heather wailed as the last brick slid into place, shutting off any light from that avenue. The flashlight on the floor still shone bright, but how long would that last?

The sobs beside him tore at his soul. He should have insisted she stay upstairs while he came below. But would it have made a difference? Would Stokinger have knocked her out up there and dragged her down here? Or would she have heard him enter the basement and been able to hide then get help? Why would she have hidden from the judge, though? There was no reason to suspect him.

"Are you sure you didn't want to leave me to have all the fun?" he said, repeating the words she'd voiced earlier.

Chains clinked as she struggled and yelled, "Oh, you…are you seriously making jokes now?" A sniff echoed through the small chamber then another sob. "I should have stayed upstairs then I could have rescued you. I'm so stupid. I'm sorry, Scott. Sorry."

"Hey princess, no beating yourself up. We've got some time to figure this out." Glancing up at his hands, he pressed the button on his watch and the face lit up. It was nine twenty-eight. His mind ran through the math. "We've got about eighteen hours and thirty-two minutes before the explosives go off."

"Do you really think we can get out of here?" Her voice held hope and he couldn't squash that. He honestly had no idea if they'd be able to even get the manacles off never mind get through the wall, but he wouldn't share his fears.

"Sure, if I'm wrong, I'll do all the construction work on your house for free."

She snorted in a most unladylike way. "You're hysterical. You should go into comedy."

His eyes were starting to adjust to the darker environment and he could make things out a little better. Heather twisted and turned like she was trying to pull the bolt out of the wall. Wrapping his own hands around the metal, he pushed and pulled. Shit, it was in solid. Didn't mean it wouldn't eventually get loose, but would it take longer than eighteen hours and twenty-something minutes?

Time passed as they both struggled with their shackles. He didn't even know what to say to her. How did you apologize for putting someone's life in danger and getting them killed? Well, they weren't dead yet, but it seemed like a foregone conclusion if they couldn't get out of the chains or break through the wall. If his estimates were correct, they were well under the building, so there wasn't any chance of another way out except the way they came.

"Scott." Heather's tiny voice cut through him violently. "I wanted to say I'm sorry."

"Don't, princess. This certainly isn't your fault."

"I'm not talking about this. I'm sorry about the party. And not letting everyone know how much you meant to me. I'm sorry for being such a spoiled rotten brat and for anything else I did that made you hate me."

Her tears were apparent and her words made *his* clog in his throat. Clearing it, he said, "I don't hate you, princess. Far from it. I want you to be happy more than anything else in the world. I figured you wouldn't be with me."

"You do make me happy, Scott. More than I've ever been with anyone else. I wish I'd handled things differently that night, and we hadn't had that fight. I hate that our last thoughts of each other will be of anger."

"Nah, my last thought will be of how freakin' hot you look in those painted-on jeans. And that T-shirt seems like it was washed a few too many times."

Her chuckle had his muscles relaxing. Not much, but she wasn't sobbing at least.

"The shirt is Charlotte's. It's been around for a while."

"I wasn't knocking it. I wish I could see it a little better, though."

"Should I admit to how much I like seeing you in your work pants?"

"More than seeing me without them?" God, he wanted nothing more than to be with her without clothes right now. Someplace a bit more comfortable though.

"I like that too. We definitely need more light in here. Oh, wait, then I'd be reminded of the horrible situation we're in." Her voice was growing stronger, but there was still a catch every now and then.

"The shackles on your wrists aren't giving you enough of a reminder? Damn, I wish I could see what we've got to work with."

"More light, huh? Let me see. Can I…?" Her feet maneuvered closer to the flashlight and soon stopped. Moving one foot, she attempted to pull it closer. Slowly, slowly, it rolled an inch. Two inches. A few more and it rested in front of her.

"Can you push it so it shines in my direction?" It would be aimed at his feet, and he wanted to see the manacles but he couldn't ask for everything.

"Maybe I can do better than that."

Grabbing onto the bolt above her head, she kicked up. What was she doing? Her feet swung low again and this time she closed them around the flashlight. When her feet flew up this time, the light came with them. Her legs twisted right up in front of her and she grabbed the light with her hands.

"Shit, woman, that was amazing. Where did you learn to do that?"

"I took gymnastics growing up. I'm quite flexible."

That he knew from their short lived bedroom escapades. "I should have guessed."

"Where do you want me to shine this?" She sounded stronger, more confident, more like the warrior princess he knew her to be.

"Up here on my hands. I want to see what's on our wrists."

The light moved and he twisted checking out what he could of the metal surrounding his hands. Strong, unbending and far too small to even try and get out of.

"Heather, are your manacles tight? Any possibility you can wiggle your hand out?" Her hands were definitely smaller than his.

"I've been trying since I woke up. No good."

"Hmm, it looks like there's a lock holding it closed. If I had something to pick it with I might be able to open them."

"You know how to pick a lock?"

"They teach you all sorts of things in the military. You wouldn't happen to have a hairpin on you?"

"Even if I did, how the heck would I get it over to you? I certainly don't know how to pick a lock. And it's kind of hard to throw with your hands like this."

"Can you flash the light around the room? I want to see what's here."

The light bounced from surface to surface and froze when it landed on the stack of wooden boxes near the opposite wall.

"Hold it right there. I want to see where he's got the explosives."

"Is it that stuff? Looks like modeling clay."

The large blocks of claylike substance sat on and around the caskets. Shit, there was a lot. The detonators sat on top, shoved into the material. A slight glow showed the timer.

"I can't see the time on it. Can you?" His vision was getting used to the darker room and Heather was becoming clearer.

Shaking her head, she said, "No. It's facing the back wall."

"Shine the light near me again. On the wall and the floor."

The light bounced around and every now and then he'd ask her to hold it someplace so he could check something out. It never ended up being anything useful. Not that he could reach anything near him anyway.

"Stop, right there. To the right of my foot. What is that?"

Heather held the beam still and Scott squinted to make out a small piece of metal a few feet away. Could he do the acrobatics like she'd done? Doubtful, but he still might be able to get it.

"Keep holding it there. That's something metal, and I might be able to use it to get these cuffs off."

Sliding his feet away from the wall, he took little steps until he had them on both sides of the object. Pushing his feet closer together he clasped it and attempted to lift it, like Heather had done with the flashlight. It was thin and it took several tries before he could get it stuck between his boots. Grabbing hold of the bolt above his head, he raised his legs. Clink. It fell back to the ground.

"Damn." He tried again and again and his frustration level grew. Heather had remained quiet this whole time, holding the beam steady on the floor and the object he was trying to lift.

After what seemed like the four hundredth time, he let out a growl. "The treads of these boots are too thick. Fuck." Sweat trickled down his back and over his face.

Holding tight to the metal above him, he lifted and lowered his legs, needing to get some movement somehow so he didn't explode. There was a reason he liked to swing a hammer throughout the day.

The light switched off. Shit, had it died?

"I'll save the batteries for when we need them again. Are you all right?" Her concern flooded warmth back into him. But it brought back his determination to get them out of here.

His sigh echoed in the small chamber. "I promised to get you out of here. I'm not doing a very good job."

"Why don't you rest for a few minutes? You've been at this for a while."

Glancing at his watch, he saw it was almost noon. "Are you kidding me? How did that much time pass already?"

"You were busy."

"Busy accomplishing nothing." God, what a hero he was, getting them in this jam and not being prepared with a backup plan. Hadn't he learned anything in the military? He hadn't even mentioned where he was going to Jack. Stupid.

"Hey, princess, did you happen to tell anyone where you were going or what you were doing?"

"No," she wailed. "I told my secretary I was taking some time and Charlotte…well, she was more interested in how I was going to win you back. She thinks you're freakin' hot. Her words."

Chuckling, he said, "What do you think?"

"I think it's hot in here. How much air do you think we have left? Oh, my God, I never even thought of that. We could die from asphyxiation instead of blowing up. Hmm, that might be preferable. I hear it feels like you're sleepy. Asphyxiation, not getting blown up."

"Enough. We aren't going to die. I won't let us. How are you feeling?"

"I'm hungry." Her stomach took that moment to rumble. "See, right on cue. I only had a cup of coffee this morning."

He could use something to eat also but obviously that wasn't going to happen. He needed to pick up that damned metal strip on the floor. Could he get it with his toes? But that meant he'd have to take his boots off. No way he could kick them off. Not with how he usually tied them. But…

Grabbing hold of the bolt again, he reverse-crunched then frogged his legs so one boot came to his mouth. Grabbing the knot of the lace with his teeth, he tugged. His legs dropped but he'd felt it shift. Why the hell did he have to double knot them?

"Tell me what colors you want to paint each of the rooms in your new house."

"You want to discuss room color while we're hanging around here waiting to die."

"No, damn it, Heather, but I need something to distract me and keep my mind off the fact it's gonna take me another few hours to just get my fucking boot off. If I can even do it. Then it's back to trying to pick up that piece of metal. I don't even know if it's the right size to fit in the locks for these things."

He rattled the chains holding his hands. "It's the only chance we have unless you've got some trick up your sleeve to get these cuffs off I don't know about."

"No, no tricks. So, um, I was thinking of maybe a sage green in the kitchen."

Getting the knot out of his shoe wasn't the easiest thing, though he felt a bit more successful each time the lace shifted. As Heather rattled on about her new house and he kept pulling out the knot little by little, he gave some serious thought to dying. It wasn't anything new. When he'd been in Afghanistan he'd thought about it a lot. Like every time they lost one of their guys or even when someone was injured. Certainly, when he'd been in the rubble of the bombed-out building.

Closing his eyes and breathing deeply, he tried to keep the oppressive space from moving in on him. Ever since he'd been trapped for a few days, he had this thing about tight spaces. The room they were in wasn't all that small but the darkness somehow made it feel smaller and more cramped. And the fact he couldn't move or free himself exacerbated the claustrophobia more.

Resting for a few moments, he checked his watch again. Another few hours had passed. Holy shit, seriously, this was useless. Then Heather sighed a few feet from him and he knew he'd spend every last second they had in here trying to get her out and safe.

"So I told my mom I wasn't going to this latest party. To say she wasn't happy would be an understatement. I know she only wants to see me happily married and taken care of but I can't stand all the fakeness and snobbery. I want to puke on half these people."

Scott listened as she rattled on. She wasn't expecting any response from him, which was good, since he was using his teeth to untie the lace. But as she spoke, he got a better sense of who she was. Less the socialite and more the woman he'd fallen in love with. He could admit it now. It made perfect sense when he thought about his reactions to her. Maybe now wasn't the time to tell her. He'd keep an eye on the countdown, though. She deserved to know before it was too late.

"That's why I've been working so hard with my business and why I wanted this renovation project to be successful. If I can show my parents, especially my father, that I can earn money and take care of myself, then they might not push the whole marriage-to-a-billionaire thing."

"But your mom is the one who keeps pushing you to get married."

"Yeah, but my dad's opinion carries a lot of weight with her. She'd listen if he told her to stop."

Time after time, he lifted his boot to his face and attempted to loosen the tie. Monotonous and slow, it was frying his nerves, but the alternative wasn't acceptable. Finally, after what had to be a million times, his teeth grabbed the end of the shoe lace and it actually pulled all the way out. Fuck. About time.

Taking a few minutes to rest, he focused in on Heather. She was still talking though he hadn't been paying real close attention for a while. The sound of her voice had been soothing and helped keep him going. It didn't matter what she was saying. Something about volunteering at a veterans hospital and going with Charlotte to walk dogs at the pound. She was a good person. Why had he ever thought she was like those uptight snobs? Now she was back to the subject of her new house. The one he hoped he'd be able to build for her.

"I'm not sure about the two extra bedrooms upstairs. For now, I'll use one as an office but not sure what to do with the other. If I paint it a neutral color, will I have to repaint when I have a baby?"

A baby? Whoa, maybe he should have been listening a bit closer.

"Um, princess, is there something I need to know about? You said you'd been taking your pills."

"Nothing for you to worry about. If I'm going to daydream then I want to go all the way." Her little chuckle sounded whimsical. "I hadn't really thought about having kids, at least not yet. But someday. And now that I might not"—her voice had grown thick with tears—"I realize I want them. A little boy like Jonathan, or a little girl to dress up and fix her hair. Or one of each or a few of each."

The image of Heather all full and round with his child, his little boy or girl, slammed into his gut and shook him to his soul. Shit. He wanted that too.

Sticking the toe of one work boot against the back of the one with the loosened laces, he twisted his foot, pushing. The laces were still tight, but after a few minutes of wiggling and kicking at it, his foot slipped out of the boot. Immediately, he scraped his now-stockinged foot over the metal piece then slid it toward his other foot. Manipulating it with his toes, he was able to get it wedged between his feet. Now to lift and get it near his hand.

"Here's where I need your flexibility, princess."

Heather clicked the light back on and focused near the action. "This might help."

"Thanks." Grabbing the bolt in a secure grip, he slowly raised his legs, his ab muscles screaming at the continued torture. He wouldn't listen to them, though. If this fell and moved too far away, they were screwed. There wasn't any other way out of this that he could tell. Time was running out.

The muscles in his arms tightened and pulled as his legs got closer and closer. Another few inches. So close. A cramp in his thigh throbbed, almost making him drop his legs. No, damn it. He needed to do this. He wanted to look at Heather and get support from her but he didn't dare take his eyes off the piece of metal barely hanging on.

"You can do it, Scott. I know you can."

She believed in him. Glad someone did. He was having doubts personally. But his feet were getting closer, only another inch or so. Stretching his hand out as far as the manacle would let him he reached for the object. Almost. The tips of his fingers touched it. *Don't lose it now, Holland. You're almost there.*

Yes. He closed his hand around the metal and held tight. Dropping his legs to the floor he sagged against the wall and let out a huge sigh, his breathing rough.

"You did it. You did it."

His sweet little cheerleader.

"I'm going to need a minute to recover from that. Save the light for now."

The flashlight beam snapped off and silence permeated the chamber, the only sound his heavy breathing. Let's hope he didn't nod off and drop the damned piece of metal.

He took a few minutes to get his lungs working then glanced up. He'd been manipulating the metal between his hands and he had a bad feeling it wouldn't work. It felt too thick to fit into the lock.

"Can you flash that light over here now?"

The light flicked on and moved to his hands. It looked like part of a broken off hinge. Maybe from one of the caskets. Definitely too wide. Damn, shit, fuck.

"Is that going to fit?" God, he hated to tell her the truth.

"I may have to file it down a bit but I'll make it fit."

Then began the arduous task of scraping the metal against the stone behind him. Scrape a few minutes. Stop and check. Move the metal then scrape another part. Dust from the wall and the metal sprinkled down, getting in his eyes. The angle of the manacles caused his knuckles to be scraped as well. This was going to be a long process, but what choice did he have? The clock was ticking down.

Chapter 22

Heather didn't know how Scott was still moving. She didn't have a watch, but knew it had to have been hours since he'd started filing down the piece of metal in his hand. Every now and then he'd attempt to insert it in the lock of the cuff, but it wasn't the right size yet. And he wasn't saying it, but she had a feeling he wasn't even sure if it would ever be able to open the lock.

The chatter she'd been providing had dwindled as time moved on. Lack of food was making her weak, though the fact she was standing with her arms above her head for close to, what, maybe ten hours, might have something to do with it too. But damned if she'd complain. Scott had been doing far more.

They'd been using the flashlight on and off, trying to save the batteries. The light kept growing dimmer and dimmer, though. There was a perfectly good industrial-strength flashlight sitting in between them, but it wasn't close enough for either one of them to get.

"Do you need a break?"

His grunt let her know the metal wasn't the right size yet. "I need this fucking piece of shit to actually fit in the lock."

Before she could apologize, she bit her lip. It wasn't either of their faults, certainly not more so than the other. If only she could do more. Scott's hands were covered in blood and it wasn't difficult to figure out why. Every now and then he'd wince as he rubbed the metal, and his hands, against the wall. They must be scraped raw.

"When we get out of this, I want to take you to this amazing steak house in New York. My treat. The meat literally melts in your mouth and you can cut it with a butter knife."

"God, that sounds wonderful right about now. I'm going to hold you to that."

"Then it's a date." Didn't she wish it could be a date? Not some silly dream cooked up to keep their spirits from disintegrating.

"Holy shit, it fits," he yelled. She turned the light onto his hand. The sharpened piece of metal did indeed slide into the cuff lock. It had taken forever to get this to work.

"Now you simply need to pick the lock. You said you knew how."

"I do, but each lock is different and my hands are at a weird angle. It might take a while."

"I think we still have a few hours. No rush." She tried to sound casual, but the fact was even if they got the manacles off they still needed to get through the wall. How long did brick mortar take to dry? Where was Google when you needed it?

"Okay, yeah, I think I've...yes, I did it."

Scott's left hand suddenly swung free and he turned to face the wall. Shaking his arm, he clenched and unclenched his fist then dropped his forehead to the brick. "Give me a minute. My shoulder feels like it's been dislocated."

"I know the feeling," she whined, impatient to be out of these torture devices.

"Sorry, yeah, let me get this other one undone."

Luckily that took less than a minute. In another second he was in front of her and she could have kissed him. Desperately wanted to kiss him. And so many other things that couldn't be thought of while they were running down the clock.

Lifting his hands to hers, he suddenly stopped. She looked at him quizzically.

"You know I always had a fantasy of you chained to a wall and me having my way with you." A smirk grew on his face as his body pressed into hers and a hand skimmed her neck.

Grabbing the bolt, she hauled her legs up, wrapping them around his waist. His eyebrows went up and the grin grew larger.

"Guess now might not be the right time, huh?" Still he pushed closer, his growing erection apparent.

"Get us out of here and I promise you can chain me up and do whatever you want with me."

"Promise? I might need a kiss to seal the deal."

She pulled him closer with her legs, their mouths clinging to each other. Squeezing him tighter, she ordered, "Now get these undone."

Efficient as always, he had her hands free in no time and she practically fell into his arms. The strength in her legs had disappeared, so Scott held her and lowered to the ground with her. As they leaned against the wall, he kissed her hair.

"Thank you. I don't know what I would have done without you."

"Don't thank me yet," he said, skimming his lips over her cheek. "We still aren't out of the woods."

Resting against him, she felt safer than she had in a while. His heart beat quickly and she wondered if hers was matching his beat for beat. Because of their situation or because of their proximity to each other?

"Let's get a little more light in here," he said and reached shaky hands for the industrial flashlight then clicked it on.

"It was nice of Judge Stokinger to leave us that," she snapped, her sarcasm in overdrive. "Too bad he didn't leave my phone."

As she leaned closer, Scott shivered and his arms tightened.

"Are you all right? You've been going this whole time. You're allowed to take a break for a while."

His gaze wandered around the room, flitting from surface to surface, almost like he was afraid of something. Who wouldn't be with a bunch of dead people in boxes covered with explosives in a room you couldn't get out of?

"Tired." His muscles shook and she reached up to cup his face. The stubble on his cheeks had grown since this morning and scratched her fingers. It felt good. Her hands had been too immobile for too long.

"I guess you deserve to know."

"Know what?" Please don't let him tell her there was no way they'd get out. Hope was the only thing keeping her from a total freak-out.

"I have this little problem. I've been trying to hold it together all day, and with the frustration of trying to get my boot off and the metal filed down, it's been bearable."

"What problem? Anything I can help you with?"

"Claustrophobia. Never had it as a kid but something that happened in Afghanistan kind of brought it on. I can usually do elevators because it's only a short ride but any length of time and it starts sneaking in. Like when I was locked up at the county jail."

"What can I do to help?" Picking up his hand, she kissed the bloody, scraped knuckles.

"Just let me hold you right now. We'll get to working on that wall soon enough."

"Yeah, my legs need a break anyway."

With his arms around her and her head resting on his chest, she actually nodded off. Scott shifting under her woke her up.

"Oh, sorry. I guess I was tired."

"No worries. Gave me a little time to rest. I'm going to try and get through that wall. It's been a while but maybe that concrete hasn't solidified yet."

"How long does it usually take?

"Depends on what kind he used. If he used fast-setting we'll have our work cut out for us. It's already been…" He glanced at his watch. "Over thirteen hours."

"No wonder I nodded off. I didn't sleep well the last few days."

Getting to his feet, he mumbled, "Me neither."

As he flashed the light around and picked up the crowbar, she thought about why he hadn't slept. Could she surmise that it was their break-up or was she being self-centered? He could have been worried about getting the building renovations going again.

Scott moved to the offending wall and prodded in between the new bricks. The crowbar scratched the material, but it didn't look like it was easily scraping away.

"Must have used Quickrete. That sets pretty fast."

"So we can't get through?"

Lowering the crowbar, he touched her face and kissed her softly on the lips. She wanted to stay there forever.

"I never said that. It'll simply take us a bit longer to get through. We've still got five hours. Piece of cake."

"Cake, sure. I'll make you one of those too, when we get out of here. Notice I'm saying *when* not *if*."

"Good girl." He kissed her again then went back to the wall, this time jabbing the end of the tool harder into the wall.

"Can I do anything to help?"

Looking around, Scott focused on the piece of metal he'd used for the cuffs. "You can take that and run it back and forth over the brick seams. It might loosen the new mortar. And can you set up the large flashlight on one of the coffins so it shines over here?"

"Sure." Picking up the flashlight, she walked toward the coffins. She wasn't sure which was scarier, the bodies in them or the large amounts of explosives all around them.

"This isn't going to go off if I accidentally trip over it, is it?"

Scott stopped and stepped toward her, reaching for the clay. "No, C-4 is a stable explosive. It only goes off with extreme heat and a shock wave from a detonator." He pulled the mechanical device from the one on top of the wooden boxes and she covered her head then ducked.

Doing the same thing to the rest, he chuckled. "I'm disarming them. They can't go off if they don't have the detonator."

"That's all you need to do? Take that thing out?"

He nodded, set the flashlight so the beam was toward the wall, and walked back to attack it again.

Feeling foolish, she took up her metal piece and dug in. Her mind whirred with so many things. Didn't they say your life flashed before your eyes when you were about to die? It was all swirling past, the good and the bad.

"I know my mom said things to you at the party." She had to get this off her chest before they…got out. Yeah, got out. She wouldn't think it would end any other way.

"Your mom is always quite pleasant and the perfect hostess."

"Of course she is. That doesn't mean she didn't say anything that was cruel or inappropriate in a veiled sort of way. Right?"

The crowbar dug into the wall more viciously than before. Yup, Mom had said something to him. "What'd she say?"

Pausing for a moment, he glanced at her then went back to hacking. "She simply pointed out that you expected a certain quality of life, and that a mere carpenter would never be able to provide it for you. I could hardly disagree with her. Thousands of dollars for a dress or shoes is a little beyond my budget."

"That hag. She didn't tell you I borrowed the dress and shoes. Which I did because spending that kind of money is ridiculous when I'm trying to build a new house. And I sure as hell am not going to let *her* buy me anything. That would be selling my soul. It's not worth the price."

"What would she expect in return?"

"My complete obedience. Mostly in marrying someone of her choosing. She honestly means well and hopes I'll find someone like my Dad, but she doesn't understand that all of the guys she picks out are complete jerks."

"Like Clif?" The crowbar worked violently now.

"I told you Clif was an ass."

"Hm, yes, he certainly did like yours, Sugar Tush."

Brandishing the sharp metal close to his face, she shook her head. "Don't ever call me that. Or I will cut you."

"Welcome back, Xena."

"You have nothing to worry about with Clif. The whole time I dated him I was bored and annoyed. The man is so into himself it isn't funny."

"Apparently he's into the freckle you have on your inner thigh too. Gave me some good advice if I wanted to use it."

"You discussed having sex with Cliff?" How could he?

"No, I have no desire to have sex with Clif. But Clif still obviously thinks about having it with you." He tilted his head. "Or with your sister, even though she's skinny."

"Ew, Charlotte wouldn't touch him with a ten-foot pole."

"Charlotte has good taste." He went back to pounding on the wall.

"Charlotte can be a little snobby at times, like my mom. But she also means well. And she likes to buck authority, in this case what my mom wants. It takes a lot of the pressure off me."

"Your dad seems like a good guy."

"Yeah, he's awesome and he loves my mom, warts and all. He doesn't care how much money someone has or what their last name is. If a person has a good work ethic and integrity, he's okay. That's why he likes you."

Scott shook out his hand and looked at her. "He does, huh? Enough to go head to head with your mom?"

"Maybe."

The only sound out of his mouth was a slight hum as he hammered away at the wall. It didn't look like anything was happening. Of course it had taken hours to get out of the chains, but they had finally done it.

They stopped to rest alternately, each using the crowbar because it seemed to do a better job. At about two in the morning they'd managed to clear out a few of the new bricks. Still nowhere near large enough for either of them to fit through. And it had taken hours to get that far.

As Scott took his turn and she leaned against the wall, she blurted out, "I wanted you to fight for me."

"What? I'm fighting pretty darned hard right now, don't you think?"

She ran her hand down his arm as he stopped pummeling the wall. "I mean at the party. Or in general. It seems like you gave up too easily. I know Clif was an ass and my mom was hardly subtle in her thoughts on blue-collar workers, but I wanted to be wanted and fought for. I figured if you wanted me enough, you'd fight for me."

Gazing down at the floor, his shoulders rose and fell. When he looked up, his face held regret. "You're right, I should have. I was letting my experience with Patrice color this relationship. It hurt when she blew me off so easily and I didn't want to let it get that far so it would hurt even more when you finally left me."

"And what if I never did?"

"Good question. One I should have asked myself."

Lifting her hands to his shoulders, she said, "And I should have made it more apparent how I felt. That you were an important part of my life, and not only as a business partner or friend. I'm sorry if I made you feel that way."

He shrugged, sliding his thumb down the side of her face. "Maybe you didn't know how I felt. We both should have been more open. Talked about it."

"But our relationship is still fairly new, so I guess you were waiting to see how it panned out. Like I was."

Nodding, he kissed her. She wrapped her arms around his neck and gave back all he was giving her. This was what she needed. His touch, his desire, his imminent need for her.

"As much as I'd love to continue this, we've got a bit of a time crunch," he said, easing her back. One last quick kiss and he picked up the crowbar and began hacking away again.

"I didn't fight for you at the party, princess, but I'll do my damned best right now."

She rested a bit more then got back to scraping cement. When three-thirty rolled around, she dropped the metal she was working with and whimpered. "This is no use. We've only got a few more bricks out and there isn't much time left. It won't work."

"We've got half an hour. If we both keep at it we should be able to get a few more out. Enough to squeeze you through."

"Squeeze *me* through? Then what happens to you? I simply leave you here to blow up?"

His eyes clouded over and he grasped her arms. "You go and get help."

"And what if we only have a few minutes? I run for help and you blow up with the rest of the bodies."

"I already disarmed the C-4 down here. It won't explode."

"But the rest of the building will. Then it all rains down on you and it takes us three weeks to dig you out. Oh, but you'll be crushed by the building falling on top of you."

"I promised I'd get you out of here, princess. And I will." He went back to whacking away at the wall with a vengeance.

"I'm not leaving you here, Scott. I won't do it." Moving up behind him, she wrapped her arms around his waist and rested her head on his back. "Why don't we have some wild, amazing sex and then we can really go out with a bang?"

He chuckled and turned around.

After kissing him a few more times, she said, "Could you knock me over the head, though, so I don't actually feel the explosion?"

"You're too much. I love that about you."

How much should she read into that? He loved it about her. Did he love her? They hadn't ever said the words. Was it too early to say them? They'd known each other for years.

"You know once the explosion goes off, this wall will all come down. Too bad it'll blow us up."

Scott froze and stared at her. "Oh, God, you are brilliant."

His eyes darted around the room and he moved toward the wooden boxes.

"I'm glad you're finally acknowledging my brilliance, but what did I say to convince you of this?"

Picking up a block of the claylike substance he said, "Why didn't I think of this before? I can use this to blow a hole in the wall."

* * * *

Heather stared at him like he had six heads. "Won't that kill us too?"

Scott ripped the paper off the explosive and began to pull it apart. He needed the right amount.

"Not if I don't use the whole thing. A smaller amount might punch a hole in the wall large enough for both of us to get through."

"And the explosion won't hurt us?" Her expression was doubtful. She had a right to be concerned. He had doubts as well.

Moving toward the coffins, he began to shove them toward the back wall. Luckily, the judge had already stacked them into a few neat piles. Hoping to get the most bang for his buck?

"What are you doing?" she asked, but began helping him push anyway.

"Building a little wall to protect us when this stuff blows."

"We'll be safe behind these? They're only made of wood. And bones."

"If I use the right amount, sure, we should be." Once the coffins were in place, he ripped into the C-4, trying to remember blast waves and velocity and shit.

"And do you know the right amount?'

"Well, Keith was the explosives expert. He'd be able to get it right, no problem. I might not have paid as close attention to all that. My job was transportation. Confident I can blow a hole in that wall."

"So, too much, we still blow up. Or too little and the wall doesn't move."

"Yeah, that sums it up well enough. If I remember right, a block the size of a potato could bring down a typical house. And you'd be fine if you were standing fifty feet away."

"Um, Einstein, do I need to point out to you this room is barely twelve feet long?"

"I know, I know. If I place it on the outside of the wall we might not get hit with as much of the blast or shrapnel." Pulling more of the clay substance off, he stuck it through the small opening they'd managed. "Maybe."

Now to set the time correctly. Moving toward the flashlight they'd set up, he pressed the buttons and decided on one minute. It would give him enough time to get behind the caskets and cover Heather. He needed to protect her at all costs.

"I think I've got it. Get behind the boxes and crouch down in a ball with your back toward this wall."

"You're coming back here too, right?"

Turning his head, he raised an eyebrow. "No, I thought I'd stand in front of the blast wave. Of course I'm coming back there. Go."

She did as told and for once didn't argue. God, he hoped this worked.

"If anything happens to me but you're fine, you need to go get help. Don't sit around here trying to get me out. Do you understand?"

Her head poked up from behind the coffins. "What are you saying? Why would something happen to you and not me?"

"It won't. We'll both be fine. But if I set this thing wrong it could go off before I get back there. It won't, but it could."

"Scott." Her eyes filled with tears and her lower lip trembled as she took a step toward him.

Meeting her halfway, he kissed her beautiful lips. "I'll be fine. Just promise me."

"Okay. Leave you to rot and go get help."

Damn, she was something else. As soon as she was down, he set the timer, shoved it into the C-4 and hightailed it behind the boxes. Wrapping his body around hers, he waited. Had he used too much? Not enough? No, he definitely used enough. Only a few more seconds. Did he have any last things he wanted to say in case he didn't make it?

"Princess?"

"Mm," the sound came out muffled. Almost time.

"God, I love you."

"You—"

The explosion roared through the small space, the sound echoing in his ears. Debris rained down around them. Bits of wood and bone and probably parts of the wall filled the air, swirling and choking him with dust. He curled closer around Heather as his back was pummeled, protecting her from the backlash of the explosion. As the soot and grime settled, he slowly released his grip on her. They were still alive.

Easing back, he pulled Heather up. "Everything still attached?"

"I think so. You said—aah!" She pointed to a detached foot that rested near her thigh. A skeletal foot.

"Come on, let's check how we did." Kicking aside the debris, his breath released when he saw a much larger hole in the wall than had been there. Larger than when they'd first gotten here too. Perfect. Glancing at his watch, his heart tripped.

"Ten minutes until the rest of them go off. Let's get out of here." Grabbing her hand, he pulled her along and half-shoved her through the hole. He picked up the flashlight then followed.

"Up the stairs and outside. Get away from the building and see if you can find someone with a phone to call the cops."

As they got to the basement level, she whirled around. "Why are you telling me to do this? Where are you going to be?"

"I'm not letting this building go without a fight. I've got ten minutes and if I can disarm any of these bombs, then I plan to do that. Now go."

He ran along the basement flinging aside wood and soon found the first bomb. Ripping the detonator out and tossing it aside, he raced on. Heather blocked his way.

"Why the hell aren't you gone yet?"

"This is my building too. No way I'm letting you risk your life for it if I'm not willing to."

"I don't want you to risk your life, princess. I want you to be safe."

"Too bad. You pull out the detonator. That's all?"

God, this woman was insufferable and so damn stubborn. Wasn't that what he loved about her though?

"Holy shit. Fine."

They ran around the basement finding only three bombs then sprinted up to the first floor.

"I'll head up to three and four while you do one and two. But don't take too long. We only have a few minutes left."

Nodding, she sprinted off and he dashed up the stairs. He found three bombs on that floor, but the time was almost gone. His concern for Heather was far more than his concern for the building, so he rushed past the second floor, briefly checking if she was still there. Nothing. Not on the first either, and his glance out the window didn't show her out there. Damn, had she gone up to the fourth?

He sped back up the stairs, the two bombs on this floor sitting out in the open. There was nothing to hide them behind up here. Pulling out the first, he started for the second when flashing lights in the detonator caught his attention.

Shit. Out of time. He turned to run but the explosion threw him across the room and then everything went black.

Chapter 23

Pulling the last detonator out of the bomb on the second floor, Heather ran behind a pile of lumber checking if there was anything back there. Nothing. Hopefully she'd gotten them all.

Sound on the stairs told her Scott was probably on his way down. Good, maybe they'd have something left of this building after all. Once outside though, she didn't see him. Where the hell had he gotten to? Had he run off to find a phone?

Glancing around, her heart beat loudly in her chest. He hadn't gone back inside, had he?

"What happened?"

Heather whipped around to see Jian and a few of his men walking down the sidewalk toward her. "What are you doing here at this time?"

"Got word of something happening here. My men say it sounded like a small explosion. Holland charged me with keeping this place safe."

"We were locked in the sub-basement by the guy who's been sabotaging everything. He planted bombs all over, but I think we got most of them. I don't know where Scott is. I thought he came out."

Turning back to the building, she said, "I'm going back in to check."

Jian grabbed her arm but she pulled away. She had to find Scott. If they hadn't gotten all the bombs...

The windows above them shattered as a loud boom echoed through the early morning sky. Jian pulled her close to the building as shards of glass sprinkled down.

"Call nine-one-one and get them here," she yelled, jerking out of Jian's hands. No time to waste. If Scott had still been inside—she didn't even want to think of what might have happened.

The stairs behind her groaned as Jian followed her up.

"You should let one of us check this out first. There could be fire or more explosions. Holland will have my ass if you get hurt."

Not if he was already hurt. "The bombs were all set to go off at the same time. There shouldn't be anymore."

Her lungs burned as she raced up flight after flight. Rounding the top of the stairs, she cautiously approached the doorway. Windows and part of the roof had blown out or caved in. A small fire burned near the wall. Debris littered the floor, an arm sticking out from under one large pile.

"Scott." Her cries bounced around the room as she sprinted over to him. She pushed aside the broken timber and reached for his neck.

"Please be alive. Please." A deep sigh escaped as blood pulsed through his veins. Weakly, but there.

"Jian, he needs help. Now." Her voice trembled in fear and panic.

The gang leader and a few of his men were kicking aside the burning timbers trying to put them out. "We already called."

Not daring to move Scott, she simply hovered over him, caressing his face and whispering to him. "You need to be okay. Do you hear me? I promised you all sorts of things and I don't renege on stuff like that." She touched the cuts on his face, then kissed his cheek. "And you promised me you'd fight. Don't you break that promise."

God, how badly was he hurt? Just knocked out like they'd been after her house exploded? Or was it worse? Was she worrying for nothing and he'd wake up in a minute to say something snarky? Please, let it be that.

Sirens in the distance got louder, but she only looked at Jian, who nodded and sent one of his men to bring them up.

"Help is here. You'll be fine," she sobbed, anxious that Scott hadn't woken yet or even stirred. Why hadn't he woken up?

When the paramedics arrived, they tried to push her aside, asking if she was injured.

"I was outside when it exploded. He's fine, right?"

"Let us do our job and we'll know more in a few minutes."

Jian helped her up then led her toward two officers who tried to herd her downstairs.

"No, I'm not leaving him." Crossing her arms over her chest, she stood her ground, her eyes never leaving Scott. He still hadn't come to.

As the cops asked her questions and she filled them in on Stokinger and his connection to Victor Cabrini, she carefully watched what was happening with the paramedics. They'd started an IV and were strapping Scott onto a backboard.

"Are they involved with the judge?" one cop asked, indicating Jian and his men who stood on the perimeter of the large space.

Shaking her head, she said, "They keep an eye on this place for us. They're here because of the earlier explosion when we got out of the sub-basement."

The dubious expression made her want to defend the street gang members, but the paramedics lifted Scott up and began to leave. No way they were going without her.

Trotting down the stairs after them, she remembered her first time here when she'd tripped. Scott had picked her up and carried her. Made some silly comments and set her on fire with his touch. Now he was covered in blood and unconscious.

"Is he going to be okay?" she asked as they loaded him into the ambulance.

"We'll know more when we get to the hospital."

They started to close the door but she shook her head, desperate. "I need to go with him."

"Not in here," the paramedic answered. "If you don't have a ride, I'm sure one of the officers would be happy to drive you." He indicated the officer who had followed her down. The door closed and the vehicle took off, sirens blaring.

Go, yes, she had to go too. Her car was around here some place. Where the hell had she parked? Her mind was muddled and tears slipped down her face. She had to stay with Scott.

"Would you like a ride?" Jian said, taking her elbow and escorting her away from the building.

A ride, yes, she needed a ride. Her mind couldn't focus on anything more than that. Jian steered her toward an SUV and helped her get in. Why wasn't she able to function? She needed Scott.

"Is there anyone you should call? Holland's family?"

"Call? Yes, um, I should call Jack. That's his cousin." Looking around, she patted the seat next to her. "I don't have a phone." She knew that. Why was it such a surprise? God, she needed to get a grip.

"Use mine."

Taking the cell phone he handed her, she stared at it for a minute. Jack. Yes, she needed to call Jack. What the hell was Jack's number? Callie's house. She remembered that number. Her fingers moved automatically over the screen, and then she waited for the phone to connect.

"Hello?" Jack's deep voice sounded cautious. It was an unfamiliar number. And it was close to five in the morning.

"Jack, it's Heather."

"What's wrong and where have you been? Scott missed an appointment yesterday afternoon and Callie tried to call you all day."

"I'm on my way to the hospital."

"How bad are you hurt? Where's Scott?"

"I'm fine." Her tears made her a liar. "It's a long story but we found out who's been sabotaging the mill. There was an explosion…and Scott… he's in an ambulance, but he hasn't woken up yet and he was covered in blood. I've got someone driving me there. I thought you should know."

Jack confirmed which hospital and said he'd meet her there. Good, she'd need some support. Eventually, though it seemed like time had stood still, they arrived. Jian walked her in then went off to find her some coffee while she spoke to the people at the desk.

"The ambulance just brought my fiancé in. I need to know how he is. They wouldn't tell me anything." So she lied and they weren't engaged. But no way were they keeping her from Scott due to a technicality. She'd had that happen when Jonathan was hospitalized last year.

The woman at the desk took Scott's name and told her to sit while she got the information. Wandering to a vacant chair, she sat and pulled her knees to her chest. He had to be all right. Had to be. He'd said he loved her and then…boom. There hadn't been time to say it back. But she did love him. Had for some time.

It's why she'd been so afraid of him after their night in Vermont. He'd brought out too many deep feelings in her. Stupid fear. She could be independent and still be in love. They weren't mutually exclusive.

"Thought you could use this." Jian appeared in front of her and the scent of coffee filled her nose.

"You are a god. Thank you. And for bringing me here. And all you've done to help Scott. I know he'd appreciate it."

"No worries. Holland will be fine. He's made of strong stuff."

Yeah, she had to believe that. Jian sat next to her, silent but supportive as she pulled herself together and attempted to stop the flood of tears that insisted on falling. When she thought she had herself under control, Jack and Callie flew in, Callie scooping her close for a hug. Or as close as Callie could get in her condition.

"How is he?" Jack all but demanded.

The flood started again. "I don't know. No one's told me anything yet."

"I'll go get some answers." Callie sat next to her as Jack stormed off.

Jian stood, then bowed low. "You have family now. Here's my number if you need me." Handing her a card, he bowed again then left.

She was about to tell him she had his number in her phone, but then remembered Stokinger had taken it. Reaching for her hand, Callie moved closer and kissed her cheek.

"Do you want to talk about what happened?"

That was Callie. Always a good friend and supportive, but never overbearing. No wonder Jack loved her so much.

"Where's Jonathan?"

"Believe it or not," Callie said with a grin, "your sister came over to stay with him. He wasn't awake yet."

"Charlotte was up this early? My sister, Charlotte?"

"She was up once I called her. And she wants to know what's going on as soon as we know anything. She was worried when you didn't come home last night. She admitted she hoped it was because you were with Scott."

"I was." Her lip trembled and she bit it to keep it steady. "But we weren't doing what she thinks we were." Telling Callie about Stokinger and what had happened helped build her strength and keep her mind off the lack of information on Scott. Finally, Jack strode across the room, purpose in his step.

"They're prepping him for surgery. He's got some internal bleeding that needs to be stopped. They said there's a separate waiting room for that. Come on."

Helping Callie up first, Jack then held his hand out for her. She fell against him and his arms enveloped her. "He's tough. He'll make it, Heather."

She couldn't do more than nod as she followed him to the new waiting room. It was smaller and more comfortable than the big Emergency Room. One and only one other person sat there reading a book.

"Did they say how long it would take? What his chances were? Is he really going to be fine, or is he on the verge of death? I need to know so I can prepare myself." She glanced at Callie. "You know how I like things planned and organized."

Jack slipped his arm around her shoulder and pulled her close. Oh, so not good. He was preparing her for the "Scott's about to die" speech. She didn't want that one. She wanted the "it's just a routine procedure and won't take long at all" speech.

"The doctor said he wouldn't know until they got inside and took a look. He's got a few possible fractures and a concussion. But he's young and healthy and there isn't any reason he shouldn't pull through."

"You're quoting directly from the doctor, aren't you? Sounds too practiced."

"I'm not all that good with words. I need to borrow them occasionally."

They sat in companionable silence and she rested her head against the back of the chair, closing her eyes, but refusing to sleep. She needed to stay alert for when Scott came out of surgery.

The sound of deep voices woke her. Had she fallen asleep? How could she do that with Scott under the knife?

"Did Stokinger confess once they arrested him?" Jack was asking Drew. When had Drew gotten here? Glancing at the clock, she saw it was after eight. Damn, she'd been tired.

"You got the judge?" she questioned, her nerves shot to hell. That man could not be allowed to roam free. Not after what he'd done to them. Drew moved to sit next to her. Callie had disappeared.

"They picked him up in Florida about an hour ago. How are you feeling? That was quite an experience you had."

Ignoring his question, she faced Jack. "Any news on Scott?"

His negative shake had her curling in on herself, resting her head on her knees. Let them think she was still tired.

Drew patted her shoulder, then spoke to Jack. "Stokinger lawyered up once they got him. I still can't believe what he did. He was a good friend of my dad's."

"He pretended to help Scott so he could save his own skin."

"The bodies are being autopsied and they should have dental records to identify them soon."

"They didn't all explode? I definitely had a few skeleton parts fly on me when the bomb detonated." Shivering, she tried to get her mind off that gruesome detail.

"Most of the skulls were still intact."

"You must be starving, sweetie," Callie said, walking in with a bag in her hands and a tray of coffee. "I would have gotten you something as soon as we got here but you nodded off. I figured sleep was more important than food at that point."

Drew got up to make room for Callie and he and Jack drifted off to the other corner of the room. She wanted to know what they were discussing, but for the moment her stomach took precedence over her curiosity. It had been more than a day since she'd eaten.

"It's only bagels and an egg sandwich. You choose first and I'll take whatever you don't." Callie tipped her head to the side. "Unless you want them all. I can send Jack to get more."

The egg sandwich had more protein. She grabbed that and practically inhaled it. Between sips of coffee and bites of the egg and ham combination, she told her friend more details about what had happened while they'd been encased in the chamber.

"It's very Edgar Allan Poe and 'The Cask of Amontillado.' Remember we read that story in high school?"

Heather laughed. "Yeah, and I remember Kayla Reems saying she was going to do the same thing to Mr. Peabody."

A scrub covered man entered the room, stopping them in their memories. Jack turned swiftly and Heather jumped up, heading over.

"Mr. Holland."

Jack shook the man's hand. "Scott?"

At Heather and Callie's presence, the doctor introduced himself. "I'm Dr. Ruiz, the surgeon who worked on Mr. Holland. We managed to get the bleeding stopped but he had quite a bit of damage we had to fix. A ruptured spleen and a small puncture wound to his left lung were the worst."

"He'll be okay, though?" Heather needed to know.

"It'll be touch and go for the next few days. We'll keep him in the ICU so he'll be under constant care. But barring any unforeseen circumstances, in time, he should make a full recovery. We got to him fast enough and managed to do an arterial embolization. As long as there aren't complications with that, he should be fine."

"I'm not even going to ask what that is." Heather blinked a few times. "Can we see him?"

"He's still in recovery, but he'll be in ICU in about a half hour. It's only family and no more than two people at a time. He needs rest more than anything. Get something to eat and then you can head up."

As the doctor walked away Heather sank into one of the chairs. Jack settled beside her.

"Only family." Tears filled her eyes again. Damn, when would these stupid things stop?

Pulling her close to his shoulder he said, "You are family. His fiancé, according to the nurse at the desk."

Rolling her eyes, she smiled at him. If only that were true.

* * * *

Dull pain throbbed through Scott as he attempted to open his eyes. He'd been trying for some time. At least he thought it was a long time. He felt like he'd been drugged, or had a few too many shots. It had been college since he'd done any heavy drinking. Well, a few times when he'd first gotten home from Afghanistan, but not recently.

Medicinal smells set him on alert and he pushed his eyes open harder. Beeps from machines. Machines that seemed to be attached to him. An oxygen mask over his nose and mouth, IV jammed into his arm, and sticky things pulling at his chest hair. Definitely a hospital. Why was he here?

His foggy memory drifted back and it all fell into place. The mill. Being trapped in with the coffins. The explosion. Heather.

Struggling to sit up, he grunted at the pain in his abdomen. What the fuck had happened to him? Last he remembered they'd gotten out and were disarming the C-4. He hadn't gotten to one in time. But what had happened to Heather? Shit, he needed to know.

A nurse walked in, frowning when she saw him trying to sit up.

"Mr. Holland, you need to lie back down. You could reinjure yourself. You don't want to end up in surgery again, do you?"

He'd had surgery? Not important now. He needed to know.

"Heather." He slipped the mask off and grabbed the woman's arm, holding as tight as he could. Damn, he felt ridiculously weak. "What happened to Heather?"

"I'm sorry. I don't have any information on anyone named Heather. This is the Intensive Care Unit. She might have been sent to a regular floor."

"Has anyone been to see me? My cousin, Jack?" Jack was his emergency contact person and was listed in his wallet.

"I came on shift at three. The only person I saw was a tall, dark-haired man. Kind of intense."

"Jack." What about Heather? Had she gotten out of the building in time? Had she been near another bomb that had gone off? Closer than him. Close enough to—no, he couldn't think that way. But he needed to know.

"Can I get a phone? I need to find out what happened to the woman I was with. Please." He sounded desperate, but hell, he *was* desperate.

"I'll see what I can—oh, maybe this friend can help you."

When the nurse stepped aside, the air gushed out of his lungs. Heather stood there, her face beaming, eyes brimming with moisture. Relief, intense and strong, hit him, and he closed his eyes trying to catch his breath.

"Heather."

"I guess you have your answer," the nurse said as she left the room. "Try to keep him calm."

"I'll do my best." Walking over to the bed, she took his hand then bent over to kiss his forehead. "You scared the hell out of me."

"I scared...I didn't know if you were alive or..." He trailed off, not wanting to finish that sentence.

"Alive. And so are you. It's taken you a while to wake up though. I was worried sick." Her lower lip trembled so he pulled her closer until she rested on the edge of the mattress.

Squeezing her hand, he shut his eyes as he felt actual tears leak out of the corner. She was alive and so was he. They'd managed to escape from an almost impossible situation.

"I had surgery?" Now he was curious. Exactly how bad off was he? He felt like crap.

Nodding her head, Heather said, "Yes. Ruptured spleen and some other internal bleeding shit. You've got a few broken bones and another concussion. You're kind of a mess."

"Sorry."

"But you'll be good as new soon enough." The tears in her eyes and the anxious expression on her face made him believe otherwise.

"You're crying," he accused. "So you're upset about something. Did I make you miss a hair appointment?"

An unladylike snort erupted from her mouth, but he'd gotten the distraught expression off her face. Looking at her now, her hair was kind of a mess. Limp and tangled. She was still the most beautiful woman he'd ever seen.

"How are you feeling? Did you get injured, aside from the knock on your head from Stokinger?"

"No, and I've eaten now, so I'm not as grouchy either."

"Food, yeah, that would be nice." When he took stock of his stomach and the nausea that resided, he thought he might wait.

Heather leaned down and rested her elbows on either side of him, her face so close he could almost kiss her.

"The cops were amazed at how we managed to get out. Said it would make a great book."

"A book, huh? Are you getting into writing now?"

"No, we can hire someone to write it for us. Perhaps even get some movie rights."

Her expression was much better now. The inane chatter had brought her back to the beauty he loved.

"Who would they get to play you?"

Her eyes lit up and roamed the room in thought. "Not sure. Someone totally hot, of course."

"No one's as hot as you, princess. Especially not with your infamous gymnastic moves getting that flashlight up to your hands."

"You had the macho hero thing going on, picking up that metal and getting it to pick the lock."

Another reason his abs hurt, he was sure. "We're pretty badass, huh?"

"Totally badass. And Stokinger won't be doing that again anytime soon. Drew said they picked him up in Florida."

More tension left his body. "What happened to the building? How many bombs did we miss?"

"Only the one that got you." Her voice cracked so she cleared her throat. "Blew out a few windows and part of the roof. I thought we could do cathedral ceilings and skylights up there anyhow."

The laugh that escaped sent him into spasms of pain. Heather leaned closer and stroked his face, whispering, "Sorry, sorry. I promise no more jokes."

Her expression was one of remorse and he never wanted her to feel guilty for making him laugh. "No, it's fine. Good to know we've both still got a sense of humor."

"Then you'll really love this. My mom showed up here, mostly to give me a change of clothes and some *real* food. But she wanted to apologize for trying to run my social life. Since you rescued me—twice now—you're on her good list of guys I can get naked with."

"She what?"

"Well, that isn't exactly how she worded it, but she did say that anyone willing to risk his life for mine was on the top of the list in her book."

"Does she have an actual book?" From what he'd seen of Nicoletta Silva, she might.

"I'll never tell. But I will tell you something, something I should have said much sooner."

"I'm listening." Why was she nervous? This wasn't the big send-off, was it? No, she'd just made jokes about his being on her mother's list of good little boys.

"Right before you blew up the wall, you said something to me."

"I did." He'd said he loved her. But would she want that kind of declaration from him?

"Did you mean it? Or was it merely heat of the moment shit?"

Shifting, he grunted at the agony of movement. Taking her hand, he pressed it to his lips. "I meant it. Every word. Well, all three of them, anyway."

Her smile brightened up the drab room and warmed his heart. Please let it mean she felt the same. Or at least relatively close.

"Then I have a little secret to share with you."

"Do tell. I can hardly wait. Seriously, because I think these meds"—he pointed to the IV bags hanging beside the bed—"are putting me out again."

Leaning closer, she nibbled on his ear, whispering, "I love you, too, Scott Holland. And I promise I always will."

Her kiss was beautiful and gentle, but he couldn't wait to get out of here and show her what real love could be like.

"You know you also promised I could chain you up and have my way with you."

That smile again, the one that dug deep into his soul and brought peace, acceptance, bliss.

"You've got it, my hero. As soon as you think you can handle it."

"I think the better question is, can I handle *you*?"

Chapter 24

"I got you a beer," Drew said, handing Scott a long, tall bottle, then pulling it back. "Oh, wait, maybe I should check with your nurse first. Can you have alcohol yet?"

"It's been almost a month since the surgery. I think I can handle it." Scott grabbed the bottle before his friend could yank it back again. Taking a long swig, he surveyed the crowd. Even though Heather's house wasn't quite move-in ready, they'd decided to have a Labor Day weekend party here. She had a great yard, and the plumbing and electrical work had already been installed. Although the porta potty was still hanging out for use by the construction crew. Jonathan thought it was way cooler to use than the indoor bathroom.

Jack had been called on for that duty as Callie claimed, in her huge condition, she wouldn't be able to fit inside. As she waddled outside carrying a tray alongside Heather, he had to agree. His cousin didn't seem to mind her size, though, as indicated by his nibbling on her neck before he took the tray from her and placed it on the picnic table. Maybe he should go channel Jack and nibble on Heather's neck.

Turning his way, she smiled and his heart beat faster. He was totally and thoroughly whipped. And he'd admit it to anyone who would listen.

"Get a room," Keith mumbled, bumping into him from behind.

"I'm not even touching her," Scott objected.

"You've been eye-fucking her for the past half hour," Nick said, lifting his own beer to his lips. "Don't you get enough living with her?"

"Never enough." He meant that too. The past month with Heather at his place had been amazing. Yes, they'd had fights and intense discussions, but in the end they always made up before they went to bed. And the make-up sex was great too. He hadn't minded that Heather had needed to take the lead with his internal injuries. Watching her gyrate and get herself off always sent him over the edge. Shit, the woman was something else.

"How's the house coming along?" Chris asked. He and Meg had made it up for the long weekend.

"It's getting there," Scott replied. "After what happened with Heather's house blowing up and the judge almost killing us, everyone's pitched in to help. The permits all went through in record time and without a hitch."

"Unlike the mill building project," Heather piped in, coming to stand at his side. Lifting his free hand, he slid it around her shoulder and pulled her close.

"With that building still undergoing investigation by the police and FBI, who knows when it will be released back to us." Gritting his teeth, he took a deep breath, trying not to think about the fact he hadn't been able to move forward with the project.

"They promised us soon," Heather said. "But it gave us the opportunity to use those workers to finish my house."

"Anxious to get away from me?" he teased.

Pushing up on her toes, she kissed his cheek. "No, but I wouldn't mind having more than one bathroom."

"If it weren't for Heather," Jack explained, walking over to them, "this house wouldn't be anywhere near finished. All she has to do is flash the guys that big smile and they trip over themselves to get the work done."

"She's got that effect on lover-boy here, too," Keith drawled. "All of you are too sickly sweet for me. Nick, Drew, we should stand on the other side of the yard so we don't catch whatever they got infected with."

"You need to find the right woman, Keith, and it'll be all over. You wait," Chris said, pulling Meg to his side. "First time I met this one, she kissed the stuffing out of me, then pushed me in the pool."

Meg's eyes narrowed. "I didn't mean to push you in the pool. It just… kind of happened."

"You did mean to kiss me though." The grin on Chris's face grew.

"To keep from getting arrested, sure."

"I'm still waiting for some hot chick to walk up and kiss me," Nick said. "Hasn't happened yet."

"You're in the truck stop my mom works at often enough, Nick," Meg started. "She says you could have lots of the women there kissing you if you wanted."

Clutching his chest, Nick groaned. "I'm waiting for your mom to leave your dad and run away with me. No one else will do."

Meg laughed. "According to her, there's a shapely redhead you can't keep your eyes off."

"I think it's time for another beer," Nick said and marched off toward the cooler.

Keith's eyes followed his friend. "Maybe I need a road trip to check out this redhead."

"I'll go with you." Drew eyed the yard. "It's slim pickings around here."

Scott conceded they hadn't invited too many single women, though Charlotte was here. But she was rolling around on the ground with Jonathan and his new puppy. Jack had bought a German shepherd he was hoping to train to protect them. His few years on the run had made him severely neurotic when it came to the safety of his family. Scott couldn't blame him though. He'd do what he had to in order to keep Heather safe too.

Laughter and conversation floated around the yard all afternoon but Scott kept his eye on the time. There was something he wanted to do, and he wasn't sure when would be the best time.

"Are you happy with the work on the house so far?" he asked as he and Heather stood near the fence in her back yard.

"It's great. But I was wondering something and forgot to ask. A few days ago one of the men asked about pouring a concrete slab for a barbecue pit. I never asked for that."

Pushing her back against the fence, he caged her in with both hands. "Yeah, I wanted to ask you about that. You know I like barbecuing and I was hoping you'd let me set one up here."

"Because you can't at your place?"

He shrugged. "Once you move out, it'll be a little lonely. I was hoping I could spend more time at your place."

Reaching in his pocket he extracted a small box and popped the lid. "Or, I could make it my place too."

Her eyes opened wide and she chewed on her bottom lip. "You'd be okay moving into my house and not having a place that was yours?"

Lowering his head, he kissed her. "It would be *ours*. And if you're there, that's all I need."

Heather started to nod but a commotion near the house caught their attention. Jack held onto Callie, whose expression conveyed anxiety. They rushed over as Jack began to panic.

"She's in labor." His typically confident cousin looked lost.

"Today is Labor Day," Nick quipped and Keith slapped him on the side of the head.

"I'd suggest heading to the hospital," Drew said in his usual calm manner.

Charlotte looked at him with disgust. "Brilliant deduction."

"Jonathan..." Callie began, but Heather cut her off.

"We'll take Jonathan and the dog back to the house and stay with him as long as needed."

"Just go," Scott urged. He didn't want a baby being delivered here.

When the expectant parents left, the others began to tidy up and drift off. Scott remembered the ring he still clutched in his hand.

"Hey, you never quite answered me."

Heather sidled closer, Jonathan clinging to her leg. "I'm all you need, huh?"

Scott slid the ring onto her finger then bent to ruffle Jonathan's hair. "I might need one of these too. Would you be up for that challenge?"

Scooping the boy into her arms, she leaned against Scott. "I could be convinced. I hear it takes a lot of practice to get one, though."

He kissed her lips and rested his head against hers. "I think I'm up for it."

Her chuckle rumbled through the air. "You usually are."

Wild Card Undercover

Don't miss where the Love On the Line series began!

All that glitters in Miami is not gold . . .

Lured in by a bad ex-boyfriend and the moonlight of Miami, Meg O'Hara is trapped in a nightmare situation, waiting tables for a crime boss and fearing for her life. When undercover FBI agent Christopher Shaunessy offers her a way out, she seizes it. Getting the goods on Salazar Moreno might not be easy, but she'll do anything to be freed from her servitude and Moreno's sexual advances, even if it means moving in with the charismatic agent.

Chris Shaunessy pretends to be Meg's lover in order to keep her safe, but he steels his heart against further involvement. Passion has no place in the sordid world of organized crime. And yet, the closer they get to cracking the case, the stronger his feelings for the spirited waitress shine. It's a dangerous game he's playing, and taking Meg in his arms for real could prove a fatal misstep . . .

Chapter 1

"Does that man never have a day off?" Margaret Kathleen O'Hara grumbled, grabbing her tote bag and sarong to move surreptitiously along the chairs by the pool. If the hotel manager saw her here again she'd be toast. He'd more than toss her out. Threats to call the police had been thrown at her for months now. Although in her case, that might be a better deal.

With her eyes trained on his location and the Miami sun beating down on her exposed skin, Meg backed along the water's edge attempting to leave the area before he spotted her. She needed to shower the chlorine out of her tangled hair and change for work soon. He looked in her direction and she rushed behind the closest object. It was six-foot-plus of blond-haired gorgeousness. The man's eyes were glued to something on the upper deck. Her boss was sitting there with one of his expensive bimbos. Did Blondie like that type? Maybe he wouldn't notice her little game of Hide and Seek.

She leaned around him, ducking back when she saw the Pool Nazi still present. Getting caught was not an option. She already owed more than she could ever repay.

"Are you okay?" Forest green eyes stared down at her, puzzled. Would he buy that she was simply looking for shade? He was big enough to provide it.

With strong hands, he reached for her shoulders and Meg reflexively batted them away. She got enough of people groping her at work. Scorching curses froze before erupting from her mouth as the hotel manager moved, staring in their direction. Her mind kicked into overdrive, scrambling for a way to hide in plain sight.

"Sorry," she squeaked. Grabbing the man's head, she planted her mouth solidly on his. Short, thick strands of hair tickled her fingers. Firm lips yielded no resistance to the increased pressure of her mouth. Better make this look good.

An electric current skittered over her skin causing her heart to race. Maybe too good? Slowly he pulled her closer with his muscular arms. Her eyes flew open and she broke the connection. His hair-covered chest was too close for comfort. And much too tempting. Distance, she needed distance.

Her eyes darted around, seeing no signs of the manager. A sigh escaped. Time to make her exit as well.

"Sorry," she mumbled again, looking up. Big mistake. The stranger's curious eyes captivated her. They were soft and tender and filled with something she could...trust? If she still had any of that left in her. His hands were gentle as they held her. A tiny smile played about the full lips she'd brazenly kissed. She couldn't believe she'd done it. Her mother would be appalled. But it had worked.

The chlorine scent from the pool faded into the background as sweat and suntan lotion wafted off the man's damp skin. Her stomach did cartwheels followed by a few back flips. Dangerous.

"Let me go," she hissed as reality returned. She gave a swift shove at his well-defined pectorals, rushing to get past, to escape from this distraction and the possibility of being caught. Her head whipped around at the sound of a splash and water droplets from behind. Gorgeous was just breaking the surface of the pool. Had she pushed him that hard?

"Oops." No time for apologies. He looked like the forgiving type. She had to blow this joint before the Pool Nazi came back. Grabbing her fallen sarong, she ran across the deck to hustle inside the luxury hotel.

"Damn."

The manager stood sentry near the front door. A crowd appeared at her back making that way impossible. The stairwell to the left would have to do. She'd go up a few floors then down to the side entrance. She wrapped her sarong around her as she carried out her plan to avoid being seen...and caught.

Meg should stop coming here to use the pool: this proved it. Sneaking in was adding to her already hellish life but swimming always helped work out the stress and the pool here was more accessible than any other on the strip. Pretending she had money to stay in a place like this, rubbing elbows with all the beautiful people, yeah, that got her through too. She'd learned the best times to come and not be seen. Well, for the most part. It was well worth the risk to get away from her dump of a room and its enchanting neighborhood. She'd leave this all behind her soon. She kept telling herself that. Had to believe it for her own sanity.

Footsteps behind her pushed those thoughts away. Her bare feet padded silently along the lushly carpeted hallway. Heart racing, she ducked into the ice machine alcove, her sigh echoing in the silence. She glanced down. Her bag? She must have dropped it as she rushed off. How had she not realized? It couldn't have been the threat of being arrested. Or the crooked smile of the handsome stranger she'd kissed. The one with the kind eyes and gentle hands. No, she couldn't allow herself to be led astray by a pretty face. Not again.

She continued down the hall, her trip cut short when someone grabbed her by the arm and spun her around.

* * * *

Christopher Martin Shaunessy broke the surface of the pool and shook the water from his hair, spluttering, "What the hell...?"

The thin, shapely brunette sprinted out of the pool area, and he narrowed his eyes at her strange game of Peek-a-Boo. She'd kissed him passionately one second, yelled at him the next, then shoved him in the pool. The kissing part he'd liked, but he usually preferred to take a woman out on a date, or at the very least know her name, before he kissed her. Although technically she had kissed him.

Her bag floated nearby as he sloshed through the water to get out. Picking it up, he let it drip on the way to his deck chair. He dried himself off with a fluffy hotel towel then used it to prevent any more leakage from the bag. Now which way had she gone? Her room key was most likely in her bag so no need to hurry.

He glanced in the direction of Salazar Moreno, the reason he'd come to this hotel. It seemed Moreno had concluded his business. More reason to follow the brunette.

When he entered the lobby she was disappearing into the stairwell. Javier, the day manager was following, a frown on his face. What was his problem with the pretty lady? Had she pushed him in the pool, too?

The sound of the third floor door opening above him echoed through the stairwell. Nice. His suite was on that floor. She'd be a sweet-looking distraction while he was here...or would she? She'd almost made him forget his goal by the pool.

When shouts echoed down the hallway, he increased his pace. The little spitfire struggled against Javier's tight grip as he growled at her.

"That's it, young lady, you've been warned before. The pool and other amenities of this hotel are only for paying guests. This time I'm calling the police. You'll be charged with trespassing."

Long hair whipped around her head as she resisted. A look of panic crossed her face at the threat. "Let me go! Please." She yanked frantically, trying to break his hold on her as the manager dragged her down the hall away from Chris.

It wasn't any of his business, still curiosity gnawed at him. Manhandling women was high on his list of things he hated. He'd been raised to always respect and assist a lady, had it drilled into him. Plus, if she was taken away he might never find out why she kissed him. He never could resist a damsel in distress—and right now she looked quite distressed.

He picked up the pace, nearly reaching them as the woman gave one good yank, launching herself right into his path. He reached up to steady her shoulders.

"There you are, sweetheart," he crooned, noting the desperation in her eyes. "Did you forget your key again? You left your bag by the pool."

Javier's protest died when he noticed who was holding her.

"Oh, Mr. Martin, I didn't know...uh, didn't realize... This young lady... she's uh..."

Chris gently pulled her to his shoulder, smirking. "Yes, she is feisty. Thanks for bringing her back to our room."

"Of course, of course." The manager practically drooled, but his face tightened. He wouldn't argue with a VIP customer even if he didn't buy their act. "If there's anything else I can do for you, let me know."

"Sure thing." Chris guided the now grinning young lady the few steps to his door. She pulled back slightly, her eyes wide. When she glanced back at the glaring manager, who hadn't moved a foot, she threw him an innocent look, sighed then went in with Chris. As soon as the door closed behind them she pulled away.

Walking across the room, her eyes lit up. Yeah, this place rocked—no denying it. Top-dollar suite. Good thing he wasn't paying for it, especially for the amount of time he expected to stay here.

"Nice." She stuck her head past the sliding door to the living room balcony. "This must have cost a chunk of change."

He stared at her. His expression probably gave away his amusement as well as his confusion. She half rolled her eyes and said, "By the way, thanks."

He gave a small shrug. "You looked like a damsel in distress. Couldn't resist."

Her eyes rose as her lip curled up on one side. "I guess you're wondering what that was all about, huh?"

He nodded.

"Well." She moved around the room, running her hand over the expensive furniture, brazenly checking things out, checking him out. "I work around the corner, so sometimes I come by to use the pool. Unfortunately, management takes a dim view of freeloaders."

She passed through the kitchen area, opened the fridge, an expression of longing crossing her face. Reading the clock on the microwave she whipped around to face him again. "Damn, I didn't realize it was this late. There's no way I can get back, take a shower, and get to work on time. My boss is going to dock my pay for sure."

She picked up her drenched bag, peering inside. "And I don't even have anything to wear. I can hardly go prancing around the streets in just my bathing suit."

Chris didn't mind women prancing in bathing suits but now she was partially covered by some fabric thing. He recalled her suit was modest, boy-cut shorts and a tank-like top. A little of the stretchy blue fabric covering her nice figure peeked out. Conservative compared to some of the skimpy stuff he'd seen since he'd been here. Was she uncomfortable walking around with it on? He'd seen plenty of women in less material openly welcoming others to look. Was she like that? She had kissed him by the pool so she wasn't shy.

Her lips turned down as she pulled a pair of flip flops out of her soggy bag and tossed them on the floor. Sliding her feet inside, she slung her bag on her shoulder then walked toward the door. As she passed by the wall mirror she caught sight of herself in it and stopped. She raised a hand to her unruly, sun-kissed locks and gave a cry of horror.

"Oh, man, I'll be lucky if I get paid at all tonight with the way I look." She turned to face him. He'd never complain about her appearance. She was hot. Should he tell her she looked fine? He was about to when she gave him a genuine smile. "Thanks again. Sorry I bothered you."

"Hey," he called out as she approached the door to the hall. "Why don't you take a shower here, or at least straighten up in the bathroom? It would give more credit to our story."

He wasn't sure if he made the offer because she seemed lost or because there was something else, something about her that stirred his interest. He wanted to know more and if she walked out now, he never would. Never could resist a puzzle.

"He's going to know anyway with what I'm wearing." She glanced down at the thin sarong draped diagonally across her torso.

"Can you use that as a skirt? I can come up with something for a shirt. Why don't you head into the bathroom, and I'll see what I can find."

Her eyes were leery so he added, "It's the least I can do for a damsel. And you can lock yourself in."

She looked around the room, crossed to the door and checked through the peephole, sighing. Was Javier still hanging around out in the hallway? Her gaze darted around, flashed to the clock again, then she sized him up quite thoroughly. He threw her one of his most charming smiles. She placed her hand on her throat and lowered her eyes.

"My boss'll kill me if I get there late," she mumbled. Pressing her lips together she nodded. She grabbed a large brush from her bag and followed his finger pointing to the bathroom through the bedroom. Blushing, she dropped her sarong on the bed as she walked past. "It's still a little damp from being splashed by the pool."

She disappeared into the bathroom, the lock clicked then the sound of water started. He dug through his drawers coming up with a faded, red t-shirt he knew was snug on him. It might be big for her slim figure, but it wasn't something he had a deep attachment to.

He picked up the sarong and walked to the balcony to shake it out, hoping it would dry in the warm, Miami air. The crowded beach and the endless blue expanse of the Atlantic Ocean caught his attention. His time should be spent on the other balcony watching for Salazar Moreno.

Moreno was in charge of a lot in this city. High-priced prostitutes and drugs, even though he still gave the illusion of a successful businessman to the public eye. But new whispers suggested he was getting into guns as well. Guns that had been used to kill cops and federal agents. Chris's priority was to get close to Moreno, finagle his way into a business relationship and get more information on the man. Many of Moreno's business associates stayed at The Ocean Terrace Resort, so this is where Chris needed to be. And it was across the street from the strip where the glitziest nightclubs and restaurants were. Word was that Moreno had his finger in several of them. Clubbing and that crowd could be fun. Enjoy drinks, get his face seen and recognized, potentially have an in with Moreno.

Hearing the bathroom door open, he walked back into the bedroom and the woman poked her head out, chewing on her bottom lip. She looked younger, all cleaned and scrubbed with her hair brushed and secured in a ponytail, but she was hardly a teenager.

"Is that dry?" she asked pointing to the fabric in his hands.

"Yeah, just needed a few minutes in the sun. Here's a t-shirt for you. Hope that's good enough."

"Thank you."

Her small voice was surprising considering her brazen actions earlier with both him and the manager. Was she suspicious of him? Helping her was hardly a big deal. His army buddies loved to kid him about his hero complex. He'd admit he had a weakness for the underdog. Unfortunately it sometimes got him in trouble. Would she be trouble?

"I used one of the new hotel toothbrushes," she confessed. "I hope you don't mind." She reached for the two garments and moved back inside the bathroom door.

"Whatever you need."

As the door shut, he grabbed a pair of khaki pants, boxer briefs, and a button-down shirt to slide into while she was busy. It didn't take her long, and she exited the bathroom, the skirt and knotted t-shirt looking like a regular outfit. Her golden-streaked, chestnut hair slid like silk down her back almost to her waist, even in its upswept position.

"Thank you, again." She nodded shyly at him, moving to the door to leave. He quickly followed, stopping her, curious about her ping pong attitude; cheeky one minute, sweet the next?

"Wait. If we're living together, the least you can do is tell me your name," he teased.

She paused, appearing nervous. Did she have a reason to hide her name? Like he did.

Her answer took a moment. "Kate. Kate Harrington."

He stuck out his hand, enclosing hers inside. "Christopher Martin," he said using his alias. "You can call me Chris."

He opened the door catching her surprised look as he followed her into the hallway. "Thought I'd walk you to work. Make sure you don't get into any more trouble."

Her mouth opened and she shook her head. He cut her off before the words could come. "If we leave together, it'll seem like we're just going out for the night. The manager will buy it and you can get a few more free days in the pool."

"Okay." Her words were slow and drawn out. She'd been happy to use him earlier for her own needs but now couldn't wait to get rid of him. Really?

They took the elevator down, and as the doors opened, he slid his arm around her waist. She stiffened, her eyes shooting daggers at him. "Showtime," he whispered and her body relaxed.

The manager, strolling through the expansive lobby, paused and stared as they walked by. They kept their heads together, as if they were only interested in each other. Once outside, Chris was reluctant to let go.

Her soft body fit nicely next to his. It had been a while since he'd held something this sweet.

He still wasn't sure if she was sweet. Her behavior had been perplexing and controversial in the past hour. Good judgment about people was one of his better qualities. There was more to this one than the outer package showed. The scattering of freckles across her nose gave her an innocent look, but her flashing blue eyes contradicted that.

They walked a few blocks then she stopped mid-stride. "I work across the street. You don't have to walk me any farther. This damsel is fine." Her sassy, confident tone returned. "You have done your knightly duties. You're absolved of all obligations."

Standing on her toes, she touched her lips to his cheek with another whispered, "Thanks."

Her hips swayed as she walked away not looking back. Where did she work? She headed into a club and he smiled. Surf.

Surf was one of the high-end clubs Moreno used as a front. The place was a hot spot and the crowds helped hide any shady activities that happened there. Supposedly Moreno set up deals with business men for his top dollar escorts from this club. Was Kate one of them? She'd actually blushed at one point but that didn't necessarily mean she wasn't. Her kiss had been more than nice, and she also had the innocent look Moreno was famous for providing. The idea made him queasy, though he wasn't sure why.

Surf was high on his list to check out. It had a small room in the back for gambling and there were rumors it was used by Moreno to set up deals. The fact his little damsel worked there moved it a bit higher.

He walked back to his hotel room to get ready for the night. The first thing he'd do is run her fingerprints. She'd touched enough items in the suite there'd be no problem finding some. His curiosity was piqued at the thought of seeing her again. She could come in handy if she had knowledge of Moreno's dealings, but how loyal was she to him? Could he take a chance with this wild card? Using her could be dangerous to the task at hand. He couldn't allow that to happen.

Meet the Author

Kari Lemor was one of those children who read with a flashlight under the covers. Once she discovered her mom's stash of romance novels, there was no other genre to even consider. For years, she had stories stewing in her mind, stories of love and happily ever after. But writing wasn't something she ever liked in school. Of course, no one ever asked her to write a story about a couple falling in love. Now that her children are grown, she can concentrate on penning tales of dashing heroes who ride to the rescue and feisty heroines who have already saved themselves

Please visit her at karilemor.com and on Twitter and Facebook.

CPSIA information can be obtained
at www.ICGtesting.com
Printed in the USA
FFOW03n2031121017

9 781516 100774

TOMARE!

[STOP!]

You're going the wrong way!

Manga is a completely different type of reading experience.

To start at the *beginning*, go to the *end*!

That's right! Authentic manga is read the traditional Japanese way—from right to left. Exactly the opposite of how American books are read. It's easy to follow: Just go to the other end of the book, and read each page—and each panel—from right side to left side, starting at the top right. Now you're experiencing manga as it was meant to be!

KITCHEN PRINCESS

STORY BY MIYUKI KOBAYASHI
MANGA BY NATSUMI ANDO
CREATOR OF ZODIAC P.I.

HUNGRY HEART

Najika is a great cook and likes to make meals for the people she loves. But something is missing from her life. When she was a child, she met a boy who touched her heart— and now Najika is determined to find him. The only clue she has is a silver spoon that leads her to the prestigious Seika Academy.

Attending Seika will be a challenge. Every kid at the school has a special talent, and the girls in Najika's class think she doesn't deserve to be there. But Sora and Daichi, two popular brothers who barely speak to each other, recognize Najika's cooking for what it is—magical. Could one of the boys be Najika's mysterious prince?

Special extras in each volume! Read them all!

PEACH-PIT

Creators of *Dears* and *Rozen Maiden*

Everybody at Seiyo Elementary thinks that stylish and super-cool Amu has it all. But nobody knows the *real* Amu, a shy girl who wishes she had the courage to truly be herself. Changing Amu's life is going to take more than wishes and dreams—it's going to take a little magic! One morning, Amu finds a surprise in her bed: three strange little eggs. Each egg contains a Guardian Character, an angel-like being who can give her the power to be someone new. With the help of her Guardian Characters, Amu is about to discover that her true self is even more amazing than she ever dreamed.

Special extras in each volume! Read them all!

RATING T AGES 13+

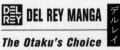

DEL REY MANGA デルレイ

The Otaku's Choice

You fed them crotchtent mushrooms, didn't you?

What will he think if he finds out that this happened?

And he doesn't seem to remember it.

I thought he was acting awfully strange at the banquet.

Eep!

Wh-

What are you talking about?

No, you don't have to be a maid.

You'll be the errand girl.

GRR

STARE

STARE

STARE

Fine. I just have to be a maid or whatever, right!?

Sigh...

If you don't want him to find out that it was your fault...

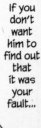

You stay here.

Then I'll go with you...

I'm going to go help with renovations!

EEEEEEEEK

Okay, next we're going to practice *Moe-moe* Homemade Rock-Paper-Scissors!

SOB SOB

フフフ

Scissors!

Moe-moe Rock, Paper!

Made

Home

Ho ho フォッ フッ

Eeeeehhh!?

Tell me when I've poured enough, please.

Would you like some milk in your tea, *Ojou-sama?*

Would you like some milk in your tea, *Ojou-sama?*

Do it like this! This!

The angle of your kitty pose is weak!

DOOOONG

DIIIIING

DEAD

Nothing...

You, too, Suzuki. Did something happen?

What on earth is the matter, Izumi?

Pardon me...

Sorry. Do what you can without me.

Hey, you're not coming to club today, either?

STAGGER...

High School Senior Izumi Oda-kun's Used Underwear (Sexy)

The used boxer-briefs of Izumi Oda-kun, a third year in the high school division at Meirinkan. As a bonus, we'll include a sexy undoctored photograph, taken just for this auction. We look forward to your bids.

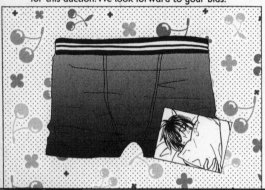

Product Information

Seller: lovery-kinoko2007

Current Price: 512,500 yen*

End time: 2 days

High bidder: kaorin24

Bids: 120

Number in stock: 1

Starting bid: 5,000 yen

Bid increment: 100 yen

Buy it now, 600,000 yen*

Complete

Bid

CLICK

CLICK

KATTA KATTA KATTA KATTA KATTA KATTA KATTA KATTA

Hmmm?

I-it's not what you think! There's a very good reason for this!

CLATTER

Itoigawa-sempai...!?

He's definitely hiding something.

He hasn't been coming to club, and he has been acting weird for a while now.

Why on earth would something like that be on the market?

And that photo was taken in Izumi's room, wasn't it?

What are all those people doing here?

Huh? The gate's open.

We're almost at Izumi's house.

What do you mean "really was"!?

But man, that was a shock. I thought Itoigawa-sempai really was into that stuff.

You're such an idiot.

So you finally noticed.

Being forced to do this is much more embarrassing anyway!

Sigh

I can't take it anymore! I quit!

If you're going to spread the photos, then just do it!

That's...

Izumi!

Izumi-samaaa!

Hey, did you hear? All of the Meirin hockey club is here!

Really!?

Ho ho ho. Delicious. Easy money.

To the second floor!

Next we'll have them go out on dates with customers.

One

Two

Three

*About ten dollars

Hana-chan, what photos is he talking about?

Photos? He can't mean...

I d-dunno...

W h a t !?

77

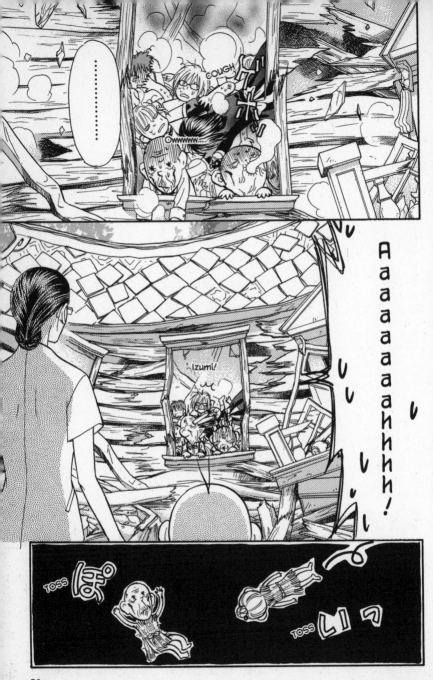

The End

Chapter 30:
Sonnet on a Quiet Lakeshore

It was quite a find.

Leave it to me. There was a nice place at Towada Lake, and we just bought it to use as a summer home.

Heh heh heh.

It must be nice to get good grades!

We are an escalator school, after all.

On the border between Aomori and Akita prefectures.

Where's Towada Lake again?

Towada Lake, huh? Sounds nice.

Eeeeeeeeek!

BRAAAAM!

If you go to Aomori, you just have to go to Mt. Osore!!

86

If you don't notice it, I'm sure it won't bother you.

What do you mean, "peculiar"?

Hey, guys! Help me out!

He's heavy!

We have a bed ready for him, so take him this way, please.

Ho-ho.

Hmmmm, it does look like he had quite an emotional shock.

Izumi-sempai's not waking up.

SNAP
パ
キ
ン

Hana-chan.

Butter sautée ♡ I wonder what sembei soup is!

Scallops, scallops

Aomori
Three Biggest Winter

Isn't it better for him to stay asleep? It's nice and peaceful that way.

....

Hana...

What was that sound?

Dunno.

Hana-san.

I've missed you...

Older Brother

OPEN は°

OPEN も っ

Ah!
He's
awake.

Izumi!

Are you
hurt
anywhere?

Are you
okay?

Izumi?

Aomori
2000

Aomori
Three
Biggest
Winter
Festi

Aomori
Three
Biggest
Win
Festi

What's the matter, Izumi?

Nothing.

What?

....

He's giving me the creeps.

Déjà vu*...

He's clearly possessed by something.

Older Brother

Younger Brother

*See volume 6

A young nobleman, huh? That explains the good manners.

Is this what that old lady was talking about?

We heard from the old gardener that this place is haunted

Hana-chan, do you think he's mistaken you for his lover or something?

Eeehh?
Popularity with ghosts...

by the spirit of a nobleman who died young at the beginning of the Showa Era.

SCRATCH

SCRATCH

Please, stop it. Just remembering gives me chills...

I think he's more likely to go on to heaven if Hana-chan talks to him than if we use a charm.

Oh yeah, where's Itoigawa-sempai?

Younger Brother

He went to buy some exorcism charms.

Roses really do suit you best, Hana-san.

Here, for you.

CHILL

Hana-san!

100

That's pretty Western for your era.

Did you have it often?

Apple pie, hm? This brings back memories.

It's home-made apple pie, made with locally grown apples.

Oooooohhh! It looks sooo good. ♡

Fresh pie!

It was Hana-san's only specialty.

Hana-san would bake apple pie,

Of all the servants who came here, she was the best at making apple pie.

Let's eat!

And make my favorite Darjeeling tea.

Stop, please! Don't you feel sorry for him?

Out of the way, Suzuki! What do you think you're doing!?

What *is* the "Kokkuri-san thing"!?

GULP

Izumi's the one I feel sorry for! Is this some grudge because of the Kokkuri-san thing!?

Liar! I know you're hiding something!!

SPIN

Nothing.

What happened with Kokkuri-san?

STARE

Uh, never mind.

Ah! Wait, I'm not through talking to him...!

Hana-chan, we'll be going on back.

Hey, I haven't exorcised him yet.

Guys!?

Stop, Itoigawa-sempai. People are watching.

Look me in the eye and say that!

I'm telling you I'm not hiding anything!

And hey, when did you all—!?

STARE STARE STARE

Older brother

STAMP STAMP

· · · · · · · · ·

Thank you, Hana-san.

Y-yes.

I was only a little startled, is all.

Are you okay?

111

I think I might like having Izumi-sempai like this...

Nn?

114

Weren't there any other choices...?

Even more so because he shut himself inside reading books all the time and didn't have any friends.

Sentarô was a huge geek.

CLAAAANG CLAAAANG

He died young, didn't he?

He... He was sick. I couldn't help it.

Well, I did keep him company during tea time.

Older Brother   Younger Brother

Trying to eat the whole thing at once. He was only in his 20th year.

He dropped dead when he choked on some apple pie on his birthday.

Sick?

Older Brother   Younger Brother

By the way, I'm the one next to him on the right. ♡

Eeeeeeehhh!!!??

What? You got a problem?

Time is a formidable opponent....!!

When we watched the video of our trip later, Izumi-sempai almost killed himself by hara-kiri.

Flowers may fade and fall,

But you will always be beautiful, Hana-san.

Let go, Takashi!

Cut it out, you guys!!

Ah ha ha ha ha

Ack! It itches!

♨ The End ♨

Chapter 31:
A Real Live Prince!?
Operation: Love Love Japan!

Hana-chan, if you don't slow down, you'll make yourself sick.

This is the first time I've ever had Densuke watermelon! Izumi-sempai's family gets the best Bon Festival gifts!!

oooohhh, I'm in heaven. ♡

The AC's on, the watermelon's delicious,

MUNCH

MUNCH

He said he'll be back the day after tomorrow.

Natsuki-sempai is in Kyoto for a memorial service, right?

If Natsuki-sempai and Itoigawa-sempai were here, they could have had some. I feel kind of bad for them.

But it's sooooo good. ♡

Oh, but then there'd be less for me!

Wait a minute! Don't eat it like that, Izumi-sempai! You're wasting it!

Ah!

あ

What about Itoigawa-sempai?

125

126

No, at one point when I was three, it was established that I'm not cut out for dancing.

Do you really dance, Itoigawa-sempai...?

What?

STARE

Traditional clothes...

What are you trying to say?

Oh, nothing.

I can tell by looking that you have no talent...

Oh, I knew it.

I have four brothers above me.

So you're not the designated heir.

It's so big...

129

No, this...

But this is unusual, you being in traditional clothes.

No kidding.

That's even more surprising!!

Eeehh!? You're the youngest, Itoigawa-sempai!?

Wha?

is because my family is having Japan Week.

My parents have known his family since they were invited to a Japan fair in their country.

He hates Japan?

I was told to do something about His Highness's hatred of Japan.

Hmmm. And if the heir hates Japan, that would cause some concern about the future.

They're putting a great deal of effort into attracting Japanese businesses.

The king and queen love Japan and are eager to have a cultural exchange.

Yummmmm!

Do they know why he hates us?

It's a small country, so even the king is the same class as a prefectural governor.

That could affect someone deeply...

Apparently it was caused by his first love, a Japanese girl, telling him *he's creepy* and dumping him.

When we serve him tea, he makes his own European tea, and he torments our Japanese cat. They told me to take care of him because I'm closest to his age, but...

Anyway, he says he doesn't want to take his shoes off, and he can't sleep on a futon, and he won't touch any Japanese food, and eats only imported junk food.

Begin Project: Make His Highness into a Japan-Lover!!

Of course! You're in the hockey club, aren't you!?

Ah, no, but...

Wait just one minute! *"We"*? You mean me, too!?

Mm!? Bentô!?

Box seats and *Maku-no-uchi bentô!* Good idea!

If we get *masuseki* box seats, we get a lunch!

How about *watching a sumo match?*

MUTTER MUTTER

We strike while the iron is hot.

What's something that would make a foreigner happy?

Mmgyaaaaaaaaaaaaaaaaahhh!

QUIVER

QUIVER

N-no, don't! We have to get him to *like* Japan!!

What was that!?

Karl, these people are from my club.

Um, I like your name. It sounds like "curry."

I'm Hana Suzuki.

I'm Kinta Ayuhara.

I'm Ginta Ayuhara.

I'm Izumi Oda. Nice to meet you.

I don't wanna watch fatties throw themselves at each other.

HUFF!

We were just talking,

and since you're here in Japan, we thought you'd like to see a sumo match.

I guess sumo is a little too cultured for a thirteen-year-old.

So *not* cute!

Something Japanese, something Japanese...

I know!

What a growing boy needs is *food*! *Food*!

Hmmm, food, huh? Good idea.

Like *shimofuri sukiyaki*, or *shabu-shabu*. Shabu-shabu!

If he eats delicious Japanese food, I think he'll stop being prejudiced. ♡

Traditional Japanese meals are good, too, but if you come to Japan, you just have to have Japanese beef!

This is shabu-shabu, made with the highest A5 ranking Matsusaka beef.

It reeks of the ocean.

Peh!

Even if you don't like Japanese food, you should like this.

Eat as much as you like.

Huff huff

Let me have it!

The seaweed?

Maybe it's the smell of the broth?

Eeeeeehhh!?

I'm going to the convenience store.

What did you come here for!!?

BELCH

I got extra meat!

Princes really are good, refreshing people. ♡

138

139

I-I know! Why don't we try *Akiba* next!?

Izumi-sempai! Izumi-sempai!

H-hey, let go!

All right, let's go! Electric Town, Otaku Town...

I have experience working at a maid cafe, so leave it to me!!

SUUULLLK

Akibahara

No!

Your Highness, is there somewhere you'd like to go?

Like a maid cafe?

I have maids at home. I'm not interested!

Right, Izumi-sempai?

Honey toast

Uhhh, but this could be pretty interesting, too.

Shut up!

The Japanese are all perverts.

Hey, are you listening!?

That maid-guided Akiba tour looks good, too ♡ ♡

I wanna eat canned *oden.* ♡

I don't know...

Me too, me too!

There's so much noise everywhere. It makes me tired.

I came here because my parents ordered me to, but I want to go home as soon as possible.

142

143

Eeeeehh?

The prince is still shut up in his room?

Of course I would!

You'd get mad if it happened to you.

That's fraud!

I was sure he'd like that. This is weird.

Yeah. And he won't answer when we call him.

What are you doing, making him hate Japan even more?

Hmmm.

152

You're such a good boy, Oscar.

Here, don't be scared.

This sure brings back memories...

If you're going to shoot Oscar, then shoot me!

They're showing *Oscar the Wild Bear.*

I learned that it was from Japan

and I thought it would be a good thing to talk to my first love Marié about.

I loved this when I was little. I watched it all the time.

In Japan, they call people like that *otaku*.

You're always just watching anime and drawing pictures, Karl.

For Marié?

CLAAAAAANG

Marié hates *otaku*. They're creepy.

PERK

KNOCK

KNOCK

SNIFFLE...

Don't *really* shoot!!

BLAM

I loved it so much.

But I haven't watched it since then.

Ah.

He opened the door.

KA-CHAK

Smells good...

Umm, I brought you something to eat.

You have to eat something.

but I thought if it was Western-style, you could eat it.

This is Japanese, too,

SILENCE

I think I made it pretty well.

Well?

156

Aaaaaaaaaaugh!

Ah! Why you—

See you again!

GARRRPE

H-hey, Hana!

My first kiss!

Eeeeeehh!!?

Now, now, he's only a boy.

Calm down, Izumi-sempai.

Don't ever come here again!!

🌀 The End 🌀   Look forward to Volume 9 ♪

Special Feature
Ai Morinaga's "Beautiful Online Shopping Life"

Your topic is *Ai Morinaga's "Beautiful Online Shopping Life"*

Since you're taking a break from Hockey Club, please write *eight pages* instead.

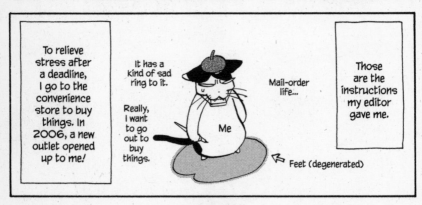

To relieve stress after a deadline, I go to the convenience store to buy things. In 2006, a new outlet opened up to me!

It has a kind of sad ring to it.

Really, I want to go out to buy things.

Mail-order life...

Me

← Feet (degenerated)

Those are the instructions my editor gave me.

I'd say whenever I found something yummy, and click away.

There are a lot of people here while I'm working. Somebody'll eat it!

But it's research for Hockey Club!

Just a little more and shipping's free!

Click! That looks good!

Ah! This, too!

CLICK

CLICK

Formidable child....!

The devil's box

This is one of the reasons I'm so generous even though I'm living alone, Captain. →

These days, they send cake, and *mentaiko*, and bread—everything frozen!!

Tee hee hee hee hee

ウフフフ

みっちり

PACKED

I imagine a dialect →

Dagnabit! The ice cream won't fit!!

And then I got yelled at.

Assistants ↓ ↓

Back from buying things →

Number 1: Pao's *kintoki* cream bread.

Fresh cream →

STUFFED

みっちり

Anko →

Pao's montblanc is delicious, too.

The things that I got addicted to through mail order.

It's delicious but it's *super* sweet. If I eat one before a deadline, it wakes me up in more ways than one.

But normally I'm satisfied after about half.

The blood to my brain...!!

When I'm tired, I can gulp one down whole.

The first time I ate it, I was deeply moved. I love cream and *anko*.

164

Japanese-grown fruits really are delicious.

Number 2: Various Japanese-grown fruits

I peel peaches all the way around and bite into them at the sink.

In Tokyo, white peaches are ridiculously expensive. I wanted to try an expensive peach just once, and they really are so good I cried.

White peaches from Shihoya

SLURP SLURP

Native of Okayama, who sold peaches and muscat grapes at a part-time job.

I forget where I ordered the best ones from!

I have to order some this year, too!

I ordered a whole kilo, but they were gone in an instant...

Yamagata cherries.

EMPTY

Big apple mangos are good, too, but I adore mini-mangos.

Slurp, slurp, aaaahh.

Fully ripe petite mangos from Okinawa Zanmai Tyanpuru Shop!?

I make it a lot thicker than the really thick Taiwanese version. It's a little slushy and oh so good.

I cut the frozen papaya and put it in a blender with milk and condensed milk.

This isn't related, but I also love papayas. Papaya milk is too delicious.

165

Number 3: Raw sea urchins from Rebun Island.

With the shell, packed in saltwater.

A bowl of sea urchins, salmon roe, crab legs, and scallops, yum yum!!

They don't smell at all, and they're sweet, and they melt in your mouth. They're super delicious. I could die.

I'm so glad I'm Japanese...!!

Ew... Friend

Mountain of innards

I wanted to try one that still had the shell. I split it, and it was pretty gross. Sea urchins are living things, too, after all...

Everyone, let's all make sure to not be rushing all the time. I mean, I was stupid.

This one's blank, too!

Gyaaaaaaa!

There's still background to draw here!?

Refrigerated goods

Frozen goods

And of course it only comes in large quantities at a time like this.

But I also have sad memories from some arriving when I was in a big pinch, and there was no time to put it in the freezer, and it was left out.

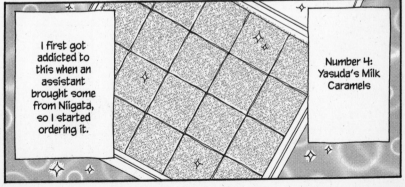

I first got addicted to this when an assistant brought some from Niigata, so I started ordering it.

Number 4: Yasuda's Milk Caramels

166

I don't normally like maccha things, but their New York cheesecake and unprocessed chocolate are seriously too delicious.

Number 3: Itoh Kyuemon *Uji maccha* New York Cheesecake and *Uji maccha* unprocessed chocolate.

I'm sitting all the time, so I'm clearly taking in too many calories. I wish I could draw manga while running.

YOINK YOINK YOINK
CHOMP CHOMP

Somebody stop me!

Shut up. Just take the box with you already.

Working by myself in my room

Refrigerator

The caramel and the chocolate are very sweet. They really are perfect for doping up before a deadline.

When I think meat bun, I think pork buns from Hôrai, but these meat buns are *steamy* and delicious.

The black pork something was good, too.

Pulling myself together, *Number 6: Meat Buns Ko-cho*

I'm good at imitating Ishizuka's face from Honjamaka.

When I go shopping normally, I almost never buy sweet or spicy snacks for myself. Online shopping really is formidable.

It's small, but full of meat soup.

And if it's in the house, I eat it...

I think I can eat them forever. It's scary.

Strongest Corps in the Galaxy

Galaxy Dream Team

It strums at my heart strings.

And it rains rubies.

Especially this part. Apparently it refers to them being the world champions of Chinese cooking.

Incidentally, I personally really like the Kouchou home page.

Anyway, has a weakness for steamy food found in town. Especially in winter.

Huff huff

ハアハ

World Champion Handmade Meat Bun

But these are fiercely good if you can get them fresh at the store instead of ordering them, so if you can, please, go to China Town in Yokohama and eat some.

I ordered almost all of them with a high level of optimism, and usually they don't let me down.

I only click when I'm backed into a corner and being escapist, so I don't have much time to look...

Bliss.... ♡

I also like Furano milk pudding, Sacher torte, apple pie, *gyūsuji nikomi*, and *gyūtan*.

is cat food.

Would eat anything when I first took him in, but recently is following Chibira's example.
⇩

Very picky and gets sick of things quickly
⇩

Food prescribed for allergies
⇩

But what I spend the most energy choosing and buying lots of

Tarezō   Chibira   Big Sister Fujio

GRR

SCRAAATCH SCRAAATCH SCRAAATCH SCRAAATCH SCRAAATCH SCRAAATCH

"It's yucky" pose

Now that I've kept him four years, he runs away at high speeds.

My assistants call him the "phantom cat" and "Kichijoji house cat"

Brings good luck to whoever sees it.

How will you like this one?

Chibiraaaa! Your new food came!

WHOOSH

Me-yow! Yummy Food

I never learn.

I always think I'm done trying new cat food, but I go right back to clicking.

You can't have any. You're allergic.

I'll eat it.

What'll I do with this...?

Tch. No good again?

I do my best and *click away* but with no luck.

It's heartbreaking just looking at *pictures* of local delicacies.

Apparently my assistants get hungry drawing it.

Here, this one. Draw it as if you're a gourmand assistant!

I wish I had a real one to draw from.

Katsudon with sauce. Huff, huff

Bururu Fukui

Speaking of no reward, because I'm drawing a gourmand traveling manga, I have mountains of guidebooks for reference. It's hard drawing up the manuscript.

I've been dreaming like that, but I don't think anything good would come of it, so I do without.

A dreaming maiden

Even just a freezer would be nice.

I wish I had a bigger refrigerator.

Now that I'm addicting to *clicking*

Cream cheese cake from Hakujuji

Xīao Yáng Shēng Jiān Guǎn

When I go back to Okayama, I always have some. Waffles are good, too. Yum yum.

And so, there are three things that would make me drool if I could order them online.

Steamed buns from Xīao Yáng Shēng Jiān Guǎn

When I go to Shanghai, I go get some. They're too good. Every time I go, the price goes up!...

Yaoiso* fruit sandwich

It's not yaoi. There's a "so." When I go to Kyoto, I always have one. I want to go now.

The information from this manga is from January 2007

*At Yaoiso, they handle deliveries over the phone.

Why don't you finish the manga early so you can go eat some?

They're super perishable...

Three whole things? Impossible.

DOKI DOKI

To those concerned, I hope to hear good news.

♨ The End ♨

Translation Notes

Japanese is a tricky language for most Westerners, and translation is often more art than science. For your edification and reading pleasure, here are notes on some of the places where we could have gone in a different direction with our translation of the work, or where a Japanese cultural reference is used.

Mame-daifuku, page 2
Mame-daifuku is a rice cake stuffed with bean jam, much like the one stuffed in Hana's mouth.

Kitakaro baumkuchen, page 6
Kitakaro is a famous confectionary in Hokkaido that makes all kinds of Western desserts, including the *baumkuchen*, a layered cake from Germany known as the "King of Cakes."

Grasshopper *tsukudani*, page 22
Tsukudani refers to food preserved by boiling it in soy sauce and sugar to give it a salty-sweet taste.

Kokkuri-san and Cupid-sama, pages 28 and 29

Kokkuri-san and Cupid-sama are Japanese variations of a Ouija board. For Kokkuri-san, because in Japanese tradition foxes, or *kitsune*, are thought to have supernatural powers, it is believed that the marker, often a coin, is moved not by a spirit of the dead, but by the spirit of a fox, called Kokkuri-san. In most legends, foxes are female. The board the hockey club used in their past Kokkuri-san adventure uses Japanese characters instead of the alphabet. Cupid-sama is very similar, only a pencil is used instead of a coin, and the board includes the special Japanese markings that change syllables' pronunciation for more accurate readings. So while Johnny Depp would be spelled "Shi-yo-ni Te-fu" on a Kokkuri-san board, the Cupid-sama board could change it to "Jiyonii Depu."

N vs ", page 31

On a Kokkuri-san board, Kinta and Ginta's names would be indicated exactly the same way, "Ki-N-Ta," but thanks to the new features on the Cupid-sama board, if the indicator goes to the " marks, the Ki changes to a Gi. So if the pencil goes straight to N, that means Yukio likes Kinta, but if it goes to the ", then she likes Ginta.

Kan ji zai bo satsu..., page 33

Fearing that Hana is possessed, Izumi's first reaction is to start a religious chant to repel the evil spirit. This particular chant is the Japanese version of the Buddhist Heart Sutra, commonly chanted in Zen Buddhist ceremonies.

Mushroom, Bombaye!!, page 43

"Bombaye" means "Kill him!" or "Beat him up!" in Lingala. It's popular as a chant at sporting events, particularly boxing matches.

Kinoko no Yama, page 44

Kinoko no Yama, meaning "mushroom mountain," is the name of a popular Japanese chocolate snack. As shown on the box, this snack is made to look like little mushrooms. The stems are made of little cookies, while the umbrella-like part is made of chocolate.

Well, actually, I prefer Takenoko no Sato!

GOBBLE

GOBBLE

Takenoko no Sato, page 45

Takenoko no Sato, meaning "bamboo shoot village," is like the brother candy of *Kinoko no Yama*. It's a little cookie surrounded in chocolate that's made to look like a little bamboo shoot.

Moe, page 61

Moe is a phrase used by fanboys and fangirls to describe the type of character from an anime or video game that they have a particular attraction to, and the strong feelings that those characters inspire. Such characters include, but are not limited to, maids and catgirls. Something like a Maid Café would take advantage of *moe* to attract customers.

Ojou-sama, page 64

Ojou-sama is a respectful way of addressing someone of a higher social status, but lower age, than your own, especially the daughter of a family where one works as a maid, butler, etc. Any girl going to a butler café can expect to be addressed in this manner, and would probably enjoy it as a compliment.

Salt, page 82

In the Shinto religion, it is believed that salt has the power to purify, so Takashi is throwing salt in order to banish the evil that has come before him and purify his home.

Salt

FLING

Escalator school, page 85

In Japan, students need to take entrance exams to get into most high schools and colleges, but an escalator school has middle school, high school, and even college divisions, so if someone is attending that school in high school, they can go on to college without having to work too hard.

Mt. Osore, *itako*, and *kuchiyose*, pages 85 and 86

As Mar-tan says, Mt. Osore, literally "Mt. Fear," is one of the three most haunted places in Japan. This would be a perfect place to have a special priestess called an *itako* perform a *kuchiyose*, a ritual in which she will summon the spirits of the dead and speak for them.

Meiji Era, page 88

The Meiji Era refers to the period of time in which the emperor of Japan was Emperor Meiji, from 1868 to 1912. This is the period when Japan opened up to the West and began a major period of modernization.

Wow. That looks like a manor with a respectable heritage.

It's a noble's mansion, built at the end of the Meiji Era.

WHACK

ビタン

Who are you calling a *yôkai*?

How rude.

Yôkai, page 89

Yôkai is a general term for all kinds of supernatural creatures found in Japan. Seeing this woman, Izumi assumes that she must be more monster than human.

Analog, page 95

Takashi calls Hana an "analog" for two reasons. First, in Japan, people who shy away from new technology, especially digital technology, are referred to as "analog people," and since Hana clearly doesn't know that you don't hit newer technology, she must be one of them. And second, he's saying that while Izumi is not an old, analog appliance, Hana is.

Sembei soup, page 91

To answer Hana's question, *sembei* soup is a kind of Japanese soup made by taking the broth from meat, fish, vegetables, etc. and breaking up *sembei*, rice crackers, into it.

Showa Era, page 97

The Showa Era refers to the period of time in which the emperor of Japan was Emperor Showa. His reign began in 1926 and ended in 1989. So the beginning of the Showa Era would be the late 1920s.

Rokkon Shôjô, page 108

Literally "six root purification," *rokkon shôjô* refers to the cleansing of the six roots of perception—eyes, ears, nose, tongue, body, and mind. Takashi uses this as a chant to cleanse Izumi of the spirit that is possessing him.

Densuke watermelon, page 125

Densuke watermelon are a special breed of watermelon with a hard black skin grown in Hokkaido. They're known for being very sweet.

The prince and his handkerchief, page 126

The famous Japanese baseball player Yuki Saito is also known in Japan as the Handkerchief Prince, because he wipes the sweat from his forehead with a handkerchief instead of with his sleeve. Because Hana doesn't see real princes very often, she assumes they're talking about him.

Futon, page 131

Unlike the futons we use in America, a Japanese futon has two parts. The thicker part is laid on the floor and used as a mattress, while the thinner part is used as a blanket. In the morning, it's all rolled up and put away. This kind of bedding is way too Japanese for the Japan-hating prince.

Masuseki and *Maku-no-uchi bentô*, page 133

Masuseki are special box seats where you sit on cushions to watch sumo tournaments. Paying for the special seating would also get the hockey club a special *maku-no-uchi bentô*, a boxed lunch named for the *maku-no-uchi* top division of professional sumo wrestlers.

Meat on the forehead, page 135

Karl may have gotten the idea of writing the Chinese character *niku*, meaning "meat" or "muscle," from the anime series *Kinnikuman*, or *Ultimate Muscle*, as it's known in America. The hero, Kinnikuman (or Suguru Muscle), has the character on his forehead because he is a muscle man. Translating it to "meat" can also mean that the cat is meat (or dead meat), or will be when the writing is completed. Because the character is unfinished, it looks like the character *uchi*, which means "inside."

Shimofuri sukiyaki and *shabu-shabu*, page 137

Sukiyaki and *shabu-shabu* are both kinds of Japanese stew in which the main ingredient is thin slices of beef. *Shimofuri*, meaning "frost," is fat-marbled beef—the best kind of beef to use for sukiyaki.

Electric Town and Otaku Town, page 140

Akihabara, or Akiba for short, is a district in Tokyo known for selling lots of computer and electronic goods, but also for selling a lot of anime and otaku, or anime geek, goods, so these would both be nicknames for the area.

Canned *oden*, page 141

Oden is another kind of Japanese stew with various ingredients, including eggs, tofu, daikon radish, etc. Pre-made, canned *oden* is one of the novelties you can find in Akihabara.

Raoh and the Zeon Army, page 142

Raoh is the villain of the famous manga/anime series, *Fist of the North Star*, and the Zeon Army is from the famed Gundam series. Since they're in Akihabara, the Ayuharas decide they might as well get some anime merchandise.

Bishôjo figures, page 144

Bishôjo means "beautiful young girl." A *bishôjo* figure would be a figurine of such a girl. These figures are sometimes just pretty statues, but often depict the girl in a very alluring position.

Natsu-yakko and Hana-yakko, page 146

Geisha often use stage names, so Natsuki and Hana are following their example. *Yakko*, meaning "person" (especially in reference to a servant), was a well-known geisha name ending.

Yakyûken, page 146

Yakyûken is the name of the game that Izumi describes to Prince Karl. It literally means "baseball fist," and started as a game between two company sports teams. The "fist" refers to "rock-paper-scissors," and originally the game involved singing and dancing to the song the hockey club sings, but no stripping.

Oscar the Wild Bear, page 154

This is a parody of the anime series *Rascal the Raccoon*. The term *araiguma* refers to a kind of raccoon, but can literally mean "wild bear."

Otaku, page 155

Japanese for geek or nerd, especially one who is obsessed with something, usually anime.

These days, they send cake, and *mentaiko*, and bread—everything frozen!!

Mentaiko, page 164

Mentaiko is a spicy dish made from the eggs of pollock or codfish and red pepper.

Uji maccha, page 167

Uji maccha is a very high quality brand of *maccha*, or Japanese green tea. Itoh Kyuemon sells all kinds of desserts made with *Uji maccha*, and they're all very green in color.

Sacher torte, *gyûsuji nikomi*, and *gyûtan*, page 168

Sacher torte is a kind of Austrian chocolate layer cake; *gyûsuji nikomi*, roughly "stewed beef dish," is a dish of beef and vegetables; and *gyûtan* is beef tongue.

Kintoki cream bread and *anko*, page 164

The Hockey Club ate this very treat at the beginning of volume six. *Kintoki* is a kind of red bean, and *anko* is the general term for red bean paste or jam. In other words, these treats are made with *anko* from *kintoki* beans.

Honjamaka, page 167

Honjamaka is the name of a Japanese comedy duo. Ishizuka plays the stooge to Megumi's straight man, and his face looks like the one Morinaga-sensei has drawn.

Number 3: Itoh Kyuemon *Uji maccha* New York Cheesecake and *Uji maccha* unprocessed chocolate.

Katsudon, page 169

Katsudon is breaded pork on rice.

Katsudon with sauce. Huff, huff

Bururu Fukui

Preview of Volume 9

We're pleased to present you a preview from volume 9. Please check our website (www.delreymanga.com) to see when this volume will be available in English. For now you'll have to make do with Japanese!

いいっスね——！

この部屋の露天広いし！

俺はいい

なに言ってんですか 一緒に入りましょう！

ぜひ鳥取の思い出に！！

む。

ハナちゃん ちょっとだけいいかな

2人っきり……

か

……まあいいか 寝てるし

どーぞどーぞ

男同士でみっちり

いってきま——す！

GULP

B-banquet?

Hana, do you remember the banquet at the Yama-no-Oku Inn...?

Izumi-sempai?

Ungh...

Eh? But!

I can't handle them alone!!

Never mind! Anyway, you're coming with me and taking care of things!

Moe ♡

Moe

62

And the fad doesn't just stop in Japan. Amazingly, it's spread to such places as France and Thailand!

These maids have become the face of Akihabara.

Wow, that's incredible.

Moe Moe

TWITCH

LEER

CLATTER

61

Certainly, Izumi-sama!

Don't let them lay a finger on Hanako or anyone else!

Take care of things while I'm gone! I'll come home as soon as school is over!

I'm hungry. Time for food.

It's too early in the morning to be wasting our efforts like this.

I want another cup of tea.

These scones are delicious. I want another.

Good work.

Yes, madam.

We finally have some capital. Isn't there some way we can strike it rich?

I thought it was a nice idea, but...

Oh, I've snatched another pair of undies.

Animals are no good. They're too much work.

Welcome home, Master. ♡

59

Fwip!

Should you really be talking to me like that?

Taking advantage of people's kindness.

Take it off the market and get out of here! Now!

They're pictures from our banquet.

Whoops!

SNATCH

Wha...

And such improper behavior.

What? Don't you remember?

What are those? When did you...?

56

What the hell is this!!?

Tch. He found us out.

If we're going to support ourselves, we'll need some capital.

If you want us out of here quickly, then you'll help us out *this* much at least.

Don't worry, don't worry. I'll make sure to use it first.

Don't make me smell old!!

I'm only 17!!!

Oh, goodness! They suit you, Grandpa! They'll never know.

Give me a break! First of all, that's *un*used underwear!

Sigh

?

It's a decent start.

Here we go!

Grandpa, we've already gotten a bid.

Ho ho! Next time, we'll raise the starting bid.

The undoctored photo is going up pretty fast, too.

...hoo Auction

Watch this item in My Auction...

...School Senior Izumi Oda-kun's Used Underwear (Sexy)

...ed boxer-briefs of Izumi Oda-kun, a third ...in the high school division at Meirinkan. ...t now, and we'll include a sexy undoctored ...otograph of Izumi-kun as an extra bonus.

Product Information

Seller: lovery-kinoko

Current bid: 5,000 yen*

End time: 5 days

High bidder: lem—

Bids: 1

Number in stock: ...

Starting bid: 5,00...

Bid increment

Buy it now

Aaaahhhh!

SNATCH

*About $50

53

And it'd leave a bad taste in your mouth if they collapsed and died once they're gone.

W-well, don't you kind of feel sorry for them?

Why do *we* need to look after them!?

Hana! They worked you to the bone, too, you know!

Erk...

Ghosts...

We'll curse you!

If we *will* die, we will come back to haunt you!

LEER

Fine! But only until you're healed!

Robbed of everything we had, Grandma and I were thrown out alone into the cold, cruel world.

Because our inn collapsed, we lost our land and the creditors took our pensions away.

Zoom! Accelerator!

加速装置！

Snatch!

Hello, police? We have an accident faker here.

STING STING TOUCHED

Grandpa, your elbow's bleeding.

A little

We can't find a new line of work at our age, so we've been forced to make a living faking car accidents.

GLANCE GLANCE

Sigh.

We could live in this car, Grandpa.

Don't!! Ho ho

This is a nice car you got here.

We're just gonna patch you up. That's all, okay!?

Yamano-Oku Inn...!

Y-y-y-you're...!

It collapsed because it was so run down. You brought it on yourselves.

?

How is it our fault?

Hate...!

It's your fault our inn with all its traditions was...!

What ill fate brings us together here?

You said it was your leg before!

Oooohhh, the paaain! My hand! My hand!

You're fine!

And, hey, what are you talking about? Broken bone?

Grandpa!

Right, Hana?

Y...

Yeah.

48

Truffles!?

But I like chocolate truffles.

Never heard of it.

That's un-Japanese!

Izumi-sempai! You've never heard of *Kinoko no Yama!*?

Well, actually, I prefer *Takenoko no Sato*.

Of course they are. Japanese chocolate snacks are the best in the world.

GOBBLE GOBBLE

Ah.

These are good.

. . . .

Buy your own!

Ugh.

Hana, want one more.

Ah!

Hey! Who said you could eat all of them!?

YANK

There's three left...

44

Chapter 29:
Burning Commercial Spirit!
Mushroom, Bombaye!!

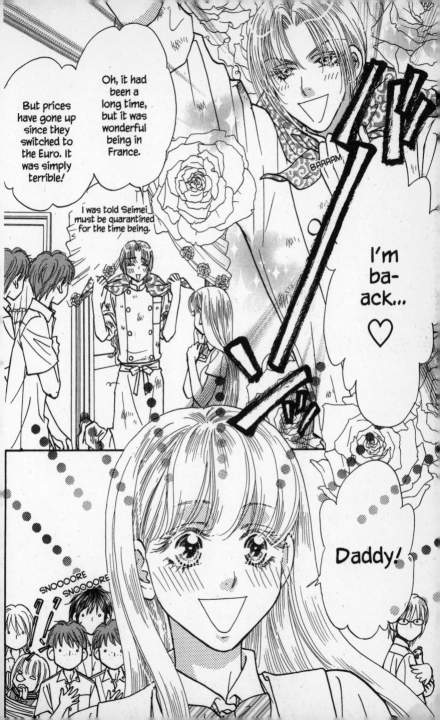

31

GLOOOOM

What's the matter? Kinta-san!? Ginta-san!?

Older twin! Younger twin! Hang in there! Here, have some water!

CRUNCH

CRUNCH

Urp!

I remembered...

...I'm fine. For Yukio-chan, one or two hundred grasshoppers is nothing...

You two okay?

YAAAAWN

It's Yukio's very favorite food.

It's not much as thanks, but this was sent to me from home.

Thank you, Yukio-chan!

Grasshopper *tsukudani* ♡

Eep!

18

BLUSH

SMILE

Y...

Pleased to meet you. I'm Yukio Satô.

Maybe she wants somebody specific.

DAAAAAAAZE

へ
ぼ

CHOMP CHOMP
ガッ ガッ

Ah.

They really do have the same taste in women.

They do.

Eh!?

She's here again.

So this time they both like the same girl?

Human-Faced Fish

You just told me to fatten up and get some flab!

Ah! Kinta! Don't take the bigger piece!

Now, now. Here, I've cut the baumkuchen.

What's that!?

If you hate it so much, then why don't you fatten up and add some extra flab to the soles of your feet and your scalp?

It'd make you a *little* taller.

Nothing.

Eh?

It's like there's three Hanas.

Ugh, that's so immature.

Don't be so spoiled! The older brother *always* gets priority!

The older brother always gives up the bigger piece for his younger brother!

I'd love to!!

Hana-chan!

Now's my chance!

Argh, I can't take this anymore! Let's take this outside!!

I'll go cut it. I'll only be a minute.

Hurry, hurry!

Huff huff

suuuuIIIIk

I'm not fighting!

What's with you guys? You fighting or something?

What are talking about? You cheated.

Really, I'm a millimeter taller!

Kinta's just sulking because I got taller than him.

Who knows?

I'm surprised he hasn't been fired.

We haven't seen Mar-tan since then. What's he doing?

Jingle

Contrite

Mar-tan and Seimei

Meanwhile, in Paris

Yaaaaay ♡

Our snack for today is Kitakaro baumkuchen.

Mom brought it home from Hokkaido.

Chapter 28:
Honey My Love ♥

Contents

My Heavenly Hockey Club

8

Ai Morinaga

Bozu: This is an informal way to refer to a boy, similar to the English terms "kid" and "squirt."

Sempai/Senpai: This title suggests that the addressee is one's senior in a group or organization. It is most often used in a school setting, where underclassmen refer to their upperclassmen as "sempai." It can also be used in the workplace, such as when a newer employee addresses an employee who has seniority in the company.

Kohai: This is the opposite of "sempai" and is used toward underclassmen in school or newcomers in the workplace. It connotes that the addressee is of a lower station.

Sensei: Literally meaning "one who has come before," this title is used for teachers, doctors, or masters of any profession or art.

-[blank]: This is usually forgotten in these lists, but it is perhaps the most significant difference between Japanese and English. The lack of honorific means that the speaker has permission to address the person in a very intimate way. Usually, only family, spouses, or very close friends have this kind of permission. Known as *yobisute*, it can be gratifying when someone who has earned the intimacy starts to call one by one's name without an honorific. But when that intimacy hasn't been earned, it can be very insulting.

Honorifics Explained

Throughout the Del Rey Manga books, you will find Japanese honorifics left intact in the translations. For those not familiar with how the Japanese use honorifics and, more important, how they differ from American honorifics, we present this brief overview.

Politeness has always been a critical facet of Japanese culture. Ever since the feudal era, when Japan was a highly stratified society, use of honorifics—which can be defined as polite speech that indicates relationship or status—has played an essential role in the Japanese language. When addressing someone in Japanese, an honorific usually takes the form of a suffix attached to one's name (example: "Asuna-san"), is used as a title at the end of one's name, or appears in place of the name itself (example: "Negi-sensei," or simply "Sensei!").

Honorifics can be expressions of respect or endearment. In the context of manga and anime, honorifics give insight into the nature of the relationship between characters. Many English translations leave out these important honorifics and therefore distort the feel of the original Japanese. Because Japanese honorifics contain nuances that English honorifics lack, it is our policy at Del Rey not to translate them. Here, instead, is a guide to some of the honorifics you may encounter in Del Rey Manga.

-san: This is the most common honorific and is equivalent to Mr., Miss, Ms., or Mrs. It is the all-purpose honorific and can be used in any situation where politeness is required.

-sama: This is one level higher than "-san" and is used to confer great respect.

-dono: This comes from the word "tono," which means "lord." It is an even higher level than "-sama" and confers utmost respect.

-kun: This suffix is used at the end of boys' names to express familiarity or endearment. It is also sometimes used by men among friends, or when addressing someone younger or of a lower station.

-chan: This is used to express endearment, mostly toward girls. It is also used for little boys, pets, and even among lovers. It gives a sense of childish cuteness.

Contents

A Del Rey Manga/Kodansha Trade Paperback Original

My Heavenly Hockey Club volume 8 copyright © 2007 by Ai Morinaga
English translation copyright © 2009 by Ai Morinaga

Published in the United States by Del Rey, an imprint of The Random House Publishing Group, a division of Random House, Inc., New York.

DEL REY is a registered trademark and the Del Rey colophon is a trademark of Random House, Inc.

Publication rights arranged through Kodansha Ltd.

First published in Japan in 2007 by Kodansha Ltd., Tokyo, as *Gokurako Seishun Hockeybu*.

ISBN 978-0-345-50674-0

Printed in the United States of America

www.delreymanga.com

9 8 7 6 5 4 3 2 1

Translators/Adapters—Athena Nibley and Alethea Nibley
Lettering—North Market Street Graphics

My Heavenly Hockey Club

8

Aɪ Morɪɴaɢa

Translated and adapted by Athena Nibley and Alethea Nibley

Lettered by North Market Street Graphics

BALLANTINE BOOKS • NEW YORK

7. Niall Ferguson, *Kissinger, 1923–1968: The Idealist* (London: Penguin, 2015); Winston Lord, *Kissinger on Kissinger: Reflections on Diplomacy, Grand Strategy, and Leadership* (New York: All Points Books, 2018); James K. Sebenius, *Kissinger the Negotiator: Lessons from Dealmaking at the Highest Level* (New York: Harper, 2019); Barry Gewen, *The Inevitability of Tragedy: Henry Kissinger and His World* (New York: Norton, 2020). For a more balanced historical assessment, David Greenberg, *Nixon's Shadow: The History of an Image* (New York: Norton, 2008).

8. Weldon Brown, *The Last Chopper: The Dénouement of the American Role in Vietnam, 1963–1975* (Port Washington: Kennikat Press, 1976); David Butler, *The Fall of Saigon* (New York: Simon & Schuster, 1985); Arnold Isaacs, *Without Honor: Defeat in Vietnam and Cambodia* (Baltimore: Johns Hopkins University Press, 1983).

9. Campbell Craig and Fredrik Logevall, *America's Cold War: The Politics of Insecurity* (Cambridge: Harvard University Press, 2009), pp. 273–8.

10. Ted Hopf, *Peripheral Visions: Deterrence Theory and American Foreign Policy in the Third World, 1965–1999* (Ann Arbor: University of Michigan Press, 1994); Richard Ned Lebow and Janice Gross Stein, *We All Lost the Cold War* (Princeton: Princeton University Press, 1994); Craig and Logevall, *America's Cold War*, pp. 239–40, 273–8.

11. Odd Arne Westad and Sophie Quinn-Judge, eds. *The Third Indochina War: Conflict between China, Vietnam and Cambodia, 1972–79* (London: Routledge, 2006); Qiang Zhai, *China and the Vietnam Wars, 1950–1975* (Chapel Hill: University of North Carolina Press, 2000); Xiaoming Zhang, *Deng Xiaoping's Long War: The Military Conflict Between China and Vietnam, 1979–1991* (Chapel Hill: University of North Carolina Press, 2018).

12. Valtin, "Obama administration embraces war criminal Henry Kissinger with Distinguished Public Servant Award," *Daily Kos*, May 10, 2015, www.dailykos.com/stories/2016/5/10/1525104/-Obama-administration-embraces-war-criminal-Henry-Kissinger-with-Distinguished-Public-Servant-Award; Zack Beauchamp, "The Obama administration is honoring Henry Kissinger today. It shouldn't be," *Vox*, May 9, 2016, www.vox.com/2016/5/9/11640562/kissinger-pentagon-award(both accessed November 27, 2019). Henry Kissinger, *Diplomacy* (New York: Simon & Schuster, 1994).

13. On this point, see Richard Ned Lebow, *A Democratic Foreign Policy: Regaining American Influence Abroad* (New York: Palgrave-Macmillan, 2019).

14. Richard Ned Lebow, *Between Peace and War: The Nature of International Crisis* (Baltimore: Johns Hopkins University Press, 1981)

and the forthcoming 40th anniversary revised edition (New York: Palgrave-Macmillan, 1981) and *The Tragic Vision of Politics: Ethics, Interests, and Orders* (Cambridge: Cambridge University Press, 2003).

15. For an elaboration of the uncertain relationship among material capabilities, power, and influence, see Simon Reich and Richard Ned Lebow, *Good-Bye Hegemony! Power and Influence in the Global System* (Princeton: Princeton University Press, 2014).

16. Hans J. Morgenthau, *Politics Among Nations* (New York: Knopf, 1948).

17. Hans J. Morgenthau, "The Purpose of Political Science," in James C. Charlesworth, ed., *A Design for Political Science: Scope, Objectives and Methods* (Philadelphia: American Academy of Political and Social Science, 1966), pp. 63–79; William E. Scheuerman, *Morgenthau* (London: Polity, 2009), pp. 165–95; Richard Ned Lebow, conversations with Hans Morgenthau, New York City, 1968–74, and David Bohmer Lebow and Richard Ned Lebow, "Weber's Tragic Legacy," in Richard Ned Lebow, ed., *Max Weber and International Relations* (Cambridge: Cambridge University Press, 2017), pp. 172–99.

1 | *Introduction*

There is a robust literature on ethics and IR, most of it concerned with how foreign policy ought to be formulated and implemented.[1] This project is in large part a reaction to the barbaric policies of the axis powers in the Second World War, the brutal suppression of states, ethnic groups, and freedom of expression by the Soviet Union, and the destructive excesses of US foreign policy in the Cold War and in its aftermath. The last includes military coups against popularly elected governments; military interventions, some of them resulting in long and costly wars; bombing and artillery barrages that produced high numbers of civilian casualties; support for right-wing dictators who behaved brutally toward their opposition, and the rendition and torture of captives, among them innocent noncombatants. Other states have behaved far worse in their treatment of their own and neighboring citizens. Brutal suppression of dissent, discrimination against minorities, ethnic cleansing, and attempted genocide are seemingly as prevalent in this century as they were in the last.

My approach to ethics differs substantially from other studies of the subject. I do not discuss principles of justice or international law or derive from them criteria for ethical policies or responsibilities. I rely more on induction than deduction. I make the case that ethical policies are more likely to succeed and unethical ones more likely to fail. My case for ethics is not deontological but empirical. It provides the basis for powerful arguments in support of ethics to audiences with no interest per se in the right or wrong of their behavior and are focused entirely on its success. My approach is in no way antagonistic or inimical to the dominant one to ethics, but rather complements it. It has the potential to create a productive dialogue between those who ask primarily "ought" questions and those who pose "is" ones.

The study of international relations reveals a deep divide between "ought" and "is" approaches, as does political science more generally. The former want to establish appropriate criteria for the behavior of state and non-state actors and the discourses that lead to their policy decisions.[2] Their research often focuses on rules, their appropriateness, and ethical and political consequences. Outstanding examples of this kind of inquiry include books by, among others, Reinhold Niebuhr, Michael Walzer, Chris Brown, Onora O'Neill, Mervyn Frost, and Toni Erskine.[3] All these works are characterized by a sophisticated understanding of international relations and the ways in which ethics is relevant to it.

Scholars who pose "is" questions are concerned with how political actors behave and the principles and assumptions that might explain their behavior. In political science, this distinction became formalized with the creation of the field of political theory to which "ought" questions were until recently unfortunately consigned. The "is" approach also became dominant in post-1945 international relations. The behavioral revolution encouraged the conceit that the "is" could be separated from the "ought," and had to be to do good "value-free" social "science." Political theory was marginalized, even done away with at some universities.[4]

In international relations, international law, associated with normative questions and projects, was subject to fierce attacks. Hans Morgenthau, who was extremely sympathetic to political theory, distinguished his version of realism from what he called "idealism."[5] He pilloried the latter, held it responsible in part for appeasement, and attributed it to the normative commitments of international lawyers who constructed "a dream world."[6] E. H. Carr made similar charges, depicting interwar "idealists" as a group of pacifists, moralists, and legalists who focused their attention on reforming, rather than analyzing, the harsh realities of international politics.[7] This binary was patently false because many of the so-called idealists were among the earliest opponents of Hitler's expansionism, and Morgenthau and Carr smuggle a fair degree of idealism into their accounts of international relations.[8] Morgenthau was a close friend and admired of the writings of Reinhold Niebuhr and wrote a book about Aristotle.[9] From its beginning, international relations theory was penetrated by analytical questions and normative concerns.[10]

Since the end of the Cold War, political theory has made a comeback, and within international relations, international political theory has emerged as an important subfield. Both are concerned with "ought" questions. Scholars in these traditions have engaged, among others, the writings of Habermas, poststructuralists, postcolonialists, and the liberal theories of John Rawls, Michael Walzer, and Michael Sandel.[11] It is hardly coincidental that most of the paradigms that have come to the fore since the end of the Cold War have normative agendas and recognize the importance of ethics for foreign policy. Here I am thinking of classical realism, constructivism, critical theory, feminism, post-colonialism, and many variants of poststructuralism. Each paradigm has foundational thinkers, who, in turn, are part of a larger intellectual tradition. Classical realism harks back to Thucydides. Constructivism looks to the linguistic turn, German historicists, Nietzsche, and Max Weber.[12] Critical theory is the product of the Frankfurt School, whose founders were influenced by Marx and Freud.[13]

I have always been sympathetic to the "ought" project but not surprised by its failure to gain wider traction. People are interested in results, and crude realists and their supporters in the media and the academy have succeeded in convincing many policymakers and much of the public that the *Realpolitik* policies they generally favor get results. Ethical constraints, they insist, would make good outcomes less likely. Every now and then is there a public outcry, as there was with rendition and waterboarding. Only rarely does it result in legislation or self-imposed ethically inspired limits on questionable policies. A recent example is the March 2019 termination by Congress of aid to Saudi Arabia for its war in Yemen. It was motivated in part by humanitarian concerns, but also by opposition to the current Saudi leader and Trump's support for him.[14] On 20 June 2019, Republicans joined Democrats in the Senate to extend the embargo and block Trump's arms sales to all the Gulf States.[15]

Demands to exclude ethics from foreign policy rest on the claim that the international arena is qualitatively different from its domestic counterparts. Many realists allege that it is populated by at least some very dangerous actors unconstrained by any principles. They point to "rogue states" such as North Korea, Iran, and before that, to Saddam Hussein's Iraq and "terrorist" non-state groups such as al-Qaeda and ISIS. To exercise self-restraint for ethical reasons would put one's nation at the mercy of these actors. Such arguments were routinely offered during the Cold War to justify American coup attempts and interventions. International relations theories that made another questionable binary between international anarchy and domestic order provided intellectual justification for these claims. This framing of international politics became a justification for behaving just as badly as one's adversaries and encouraged a race to the bottom. It has the potential to become self-fulfilling, as it did during the Cold War and has arguably again in the aftermath of the terrorist attacks of 9/11.

Equally damning is the total lack of evidence that policies that flaunt ethics are successful or necessary. This includes waterboarding and other forms of torture, extends to intervention in the domestic politics of other states, support for antidemocratic dictators, and the overthrow of unpalatable regimes by subversion, assassination, and outright invasion. There is little to no evidence these activities abetted American security or secured it more influence. Torture rarely results in useful information, support for right-wing dictators during the Cold War had damaging blowback, and subversion, assassination, and intervention more often than not proved costly and failed to produce any longer-term gains.[16] Such behavior is clearly at odds with the core values of democracy. This contradiction and the tensions to which it gives rise must ultimately be resolved, and from Athens on, history suggests it has invariably been at the expense of core values.[17] If so, unethical foreign policies subvert democracies at home as well as abroad.

International relations scholars have been sensitive to other ways in which realist and liberal theories have become handmaidens of American foreign policy. They have exposed the self-serving nature of the so-called neoliberal consensus and calls for adversity in times of economic downturn.[18] Realism and liberalism have been criticized as largely American paradigms that are used by scholars and policy-makers alike to justify Washington's claims to hegemony and the special privileges it claims as a result.[19] To be fair, we must acknowledge that nuclear weapons and the Cold War also inspired a kind of radical realism that considered the status quo destructive and sought to transcend sovereignty and transform international relations.[20]

"Is" and "ought" are different questions but they are co-constitutive at the most fundamental level. Much foreign policy is norm-based. Some norms are simply matters of convenience, like the separation of lanes of traffic moving in opposite directions. Most norms reflect some consensus about values. In international relations, they arise and gain acceptance to the degree that they are seen to bring the practice of international relations closer into compliance with what they consider proper and legitimate.[21] Human rights began as an "ought" and has increasingly become an "is." Richard Rorty describes human rights as "a fact of the world," and Charles Beitz as "an elaborate international practice."[22] They derive legitimacy from international law, find expression every day in foreign policy, and, to some degree, help shape the ways in which leaders and their advisors frame their interests and choose means to implement them. The right to intervene in other states to preserve the lives and well-being of populations is now widely accepted.[23] Human rights are nevertheless not supported by institutions that can adjudicate and enforce them in an authoritative manner. Neither is there anything approaching a universal consensus about what they are and where and how they apply.

The understandings that count in international relations are not those of philosophers but of political actors, which often extends beyond leaders to their wider publics. What philosophers, political theorists, and international political theorists write is generally read only by a narrow, academic audience. However, their views sometimes reach a wider public via the media or the classroom and there is, accordingly, some interplay between what they think and write and what political actors and ordinary people believe or come to believe. This is evident in the emergence of norms against slavery, conquest, imperialism, genocide, apartheid, and the first use of nuclear weapons.[24] Norms evolve, and arguably more rapidly in the last 100 years than ever before. As in the case of human rights, the "is" and the "ought" have become more tightly coupled, making it all the more important to study them in tandem, or at least to analyze the ways in which they influence one another. There interactions, moreover, are often complex and can produce consequences at odds with the intentions of actors. Power differentials among states have allowed some to exploit human rights as a vehicle to advance their interests at the expense of others. Charles Beitz worries that: "At the limit, human rights may appear to be a mechanism of domination rather than an instrument of emancipation."[25]

"Is" and "ought" are coupled epistemologically in the theory and practice of international relations. They cannot easily be separated once we reject the core positivist assumptions that facts can be separated from values and that truth claims can be assessed objectively. Exposure of these conceits compels us to acknowledge that our values and goals influence, often dictate, how we understand and evaluate the world. To act honestly and effectively – and here I follow Max Weber – we must interrogate these values and their associated projects, tease out the links connecting them, recognize how they commit us to certain pathways, and blind us to others.[26] In fundamental ways, our values shape our framing of interests, search for policies to defend or advance them, the kind of information we seek out or pay attention to, and often, the inferences we draw from it. Good policymaking is inescapably embedded in ethics because it reflects, or should reflect, our values.

This book bridges the gap between "is" and "ought" questions at least in part. I make an instrumental argument in favor of ethical foreign policy. I offer evidence that policies in accord with accepted domestic, regional, and international nomos are more likely to succeed than those that violate them. Some scholars who study war and terrorism, among them Michael Walzer, Stephen Garrett, and Gabriella Blum, have made similar, if narrower claims about the positive relationship between ethically defensible actions and their likelihood of success, most often in the context of just war.[27]

Nomos is a term I will unpack in due course. In brief, I use it to describe written law, accepted practices, and widely shared understandings of appropriate ways of behaving. Nomos is intended to guide, if not govern, the goals actors seek and the means they use to achieve them. It is equally relevant to how policy initiatives are formulated, presented, and support for them mobilized. As domestic societies are thicker than regional or international counterparts, nomos within states is thicker but it is also more varied and more subject to rapid change. In the USA, the witting use of untruths by leaders is considered unethical, as were the claims by Lyndon Johnson that North Vietnamese torpedo boats had attacked American destroyers and by the Bush administration that Saddam Hussein had, or would soon have, weapons of mass destruction.[28] In the Trump administration, lies and other formerly unacceptable forms of behavior became the norm and are made light of by his Republican supporters. It remains to be seen whether this is a short-lived aberration or the emergence of a new normal.

Ethics is equally relevant to the formulation of policy. Is it done behind closed doors or more transparently? If the former, is this secrecy justified by the circumstances? Is policy made with national goals in mind, for the benefit of special interests, or simply to advance the political or economic interests of leaders and elites? Are policymakers honest with themselves? Do they make serious efforts to explore multiple options and collect and assess information relevant to them before making a decision? Do they consider negative as well as positive outcomes and how they might respond to the former? A critical aspect of policymaking involves acknowledging and balancing risks against rewards, and recognizing whatever trade-offs must be made between or among important values. Do leaders face these responsibilities or evade them?

Nomos often instantiates ethical principles, but it can be at odds with what many consider to be just. Colonialism, slavery, occupation of debtor countries, and apartheid were once well-established norms. Some laws, understandings, and practices are openly contested, as all the above practices were. Norms can also undergo rapid reformulation, as sovereignty has in recent decades. We must be careful in our designation of nomos, using only those laws, understandings, and practices for which there is the widest consensus. We must also recognize that justice is a broader concept than nomos; the latter being only one way in which the former can find expression. Justice can prompt behavior that is at odds with or unrelated to existing nomos and can inspire challenges to existing practices and laws. Deviation from custom in the name of justice is courageous, especially when it is costly. It may be perceived as aggressive, foolhardy, or selfless, and other actors will respond based on their motives, values, and interests.

Motives are important in the first instance because they are critical to how people assess behavior. They respond differently to concessions or other actions they associate with generosity versus those they judge to be grudging or compelled by circumstance. These attributions prompt favorable and unfavorable assessments of character. Once formed, these judgments shape subsequent attributions of motive.[29] The belief in hostile intentions and opportunity-driven behavior encourages "worst-case" analysis, which we know exacerbates conflict and can encourage this kind of behavior. Belief in benign intentions has the potential to reduce or resolve conflict or to make a state's leadership more acceptable. Acting justly in the eyes of others may be the best way to encourage such a belief. I examine and document this process in Chapter 4.

Some religious traditions and philosophers emphasize the importance of acting for the right motives. I do not dispute the value of such behavior but think this too restrictive a definition of what ethical is.[30] I would also add that I consider it empirically questionable as people are poor judges of their motives and not always cognizant of the reasons why they act as they do.[31] What counts is that they are perceived as acting well and wisely. As Groucho Marx puts it: "[B]e sincere, whether you mean it or not." This maxim appears to validate hypocrisy, but as Immanuel Kant recognized, hypocrisy has the potential to sustain social order. People want to be respected by others in order to gain material and emotional rewards. To do so, they give the illusion of acting ethically and display modesty, affection, respect for others, even selflessness. Almost everybody understands the duplicity of this behavior, in large part because they are acting the same way and for much the same reasons.[32] "When human beings perform these roles," Kant suggests, "eventually the virtues, whose illusion they have merely affected for a considerable length of time, will gradually really be aroused and merge into the disposition."[33]

Ethical behavior commitment not infrequently requires psychological as well as political courage. Cognitive psychologists tell us that people are loath to admit that they must sacrifice one goal to achieve another. They are more likely to convince themselves that they can pursue multiple ends with equal chance of success.[34] American leaders have frequently ducked such trade-offs. They have deluded themselves into believing, among other things, that they could secretly intervene in other states and maintain their friendship, provide dictators with military and foreign aid without the money being diverted to their foreign bank accounts or the equipment used against their own people. More disturbing still, they have convinced themselves that they can undermine freely elected governments yet preserve democracy at home.

American leaders have no monopoly on self-delusion. As I write, the Brexit fiasco continues to consume the United Kingdom. Almost every one of the senior political leaders involved has behaved in partisan, self-serving, and myopic ways. Then Conservative Prime Minister David Cameron started the process by holding referendum in 2016 on European Union (EU) membership to head off a much-exaggerated threat from the right to the Conservative Party by Nigel Farrage's UKIP. He never even considered the possibility that a majority would vote to leave the EU. Theresa May, who succeeded him as Tory leader, put her own survival as leader above the national interest by allying with the Democratic Unionist Party of Northern Ireland to secure a majority in the House of Commons and then allowed herself to become hostage to right-wing Tories of the so-called European Research Group (ERG). She negotiated what was likely to be the best deal the UK could achieve but it was rejected out of hand by the DUP and the ERG. May was replaced by Boris Johnson, who had become a Brexiteer at the time of referendum and led the charge against May. Johnson and his supporters consistently lied about the economic consequences of a hard Brexit, arguing that its negative effects would be minor and short term.[35]

Jeremy Corbyn, then Labour leader, also put party politics above the national interest. For three years, he failed to commit himself either for or against Brexit. Like Johnson, he insisted that he would reopen negotiations and get a better deal than May, even though the EU had made it clear that any major changes were out of the question. The primacy of individual ambition and of party politics over the national interest combined with consistently bad political judgment on all sides infuriated voters. It led to an aporia in parliament and illegal behavior by the prime minister – for instance, in proroguing the House of Commons – that seriously threatened the stability of the British political system. So, too, does the rupture in the political culture brought about by demonization of opponents, the framing of the Brexit existential terms, and the rise of the nationalist right. The breakdown of tolerance and inclusiveness is manifest in a marked increase in violence against immigrants, minorities, and violent threats against officials of all kinds and political candidates, and rising concern for the survival of the United Kingdom as a political unit.[36]

Ethics involves owning up to one's failures, not just advertising one's successes. Policymakers are generally quick to do the latter, even when they have had little or no responsibility for the outcomes in question. Al Gore claims to have invented the Internet, Rudi Giuliani to have reduced crime in New York City and saved lives at 9/11. The opposite is closer to the truth in both cases.[37] Hardly anybody acknowledges failure, although it can pay political dividends as President Kennedy discovered when he accepted responsibility for the failure of the 1962 Bay of Pigs invasion.[38] Leaders must avoid hubris. Those who flatter themselves on their cleverness and successes, and suppress and deny their failures, are the most likely to make disastrous policy decisions. I will elaborate this pathway to disaster in subsequent chapters.

Leaders can also succumb to the fundamental attribution error. They attribute their behavior to the constraints acting on them but interpret the actions of adversaries as indicative of their character.[39] Here, too, tragic consequences can result. The fundamental attribution error provides an excuse – primarily to oneself – for explaining away unethical or confrontational policies and also a justification of applying worst-case analysis to the behavior of others. It is another form of self-delusion with a high potential for negative consequences because of how it ratchets up domestic or international conflict. I will analyze this pattern in Soviet-American and Chinese-American relations.

To probe the relationship between ethics and success I develop a complex definition of success based on political vs. military goals, short vs. longer-term temporal perspectives, and broad vs. narrow readings. I give more weight to political objectives as military action is not an end in itself but a means of achieving political goals. I emphasize longer- over shorter-term assessments to avoid the kind of opprobrium that landing on an aircraft carrier and proclaiming victory in Iraq shortly after Baghdad was occupied would later bring down on the head of President Bush.[40] Longer-term assessments offer better perspectives on both political and military consequences. I also privilege broad over narrower understandings of success, and measure the later in terms of influence. Influence is the ability to persuade others to do what you want, or refrain from doing what you do not want them to do. I consider it the principal goal of foreign policy

I reject using security – the definition preferred by realists – as my benchmark. It is too narrow because there is more to foreign policy than security; states seek status and wealth, and can at times value them over security.[41] Success in these other domains can enhance security, although their pursuit can at times be inimical to it.[42] Security, I will argue, depends as much on friendship as it does fear, and that persuasion is more effective and less costly than coercion in attaining it. Friendship can sustain cooperation in a way that coercion cannot. My definition of success arises from my empirical understanding of world politics, and it in turn reflects the benefits of behaving in accord with norms. Here, too, the "is" and "ought" are inseparable.

A brief elaboration of the above argument is in order. Coercion and bribery succeed when they frighten people or appeal to their greed. Compliance produced this way is always grudging because those coerced or bribed are not treated as equals and suffer a corresponding loss of self-esteem. They will do what is wanted as long as the coercing or bribing state has the power and resources to punish or reward them. Their compliance is nevertheless likely to be as minimal as possible and they will look for ways of avoiding what is expected of them. They are also likely to stop complying when the state in question can no longer punish or reward. Coercion and bribery are costly means of seeking influence. They consume resources, and often at a prodigious rate. Influence extracted by threats and bribes can create resentment and the desire to get even if and when the coercing and bribing state declines in power or wealth. So too can a change in government that builds legitimacy through its opposition to the coercing or bribing state.

Persuasion, by contrast, can have beneficial longer-term consequences. Working together successfully to advance common interests builds friendships across leaderships, and repeated cooperation builds some degree of shared identities. Friendships and overlapping identities promote future cooperation; they build trust and encourage similar framings of interest. Persuasion depends more on interpersonal and diplomatic skills than it does on raw power. It also requires self-restraint because it only succeeds when the subjects of these efforts see the ends being sought as in their interests as well. Leaders seeking to persuade must limit themselves to policies that can be sold to others as being in the common interest and must also be implemented by means acceptable to them. This involves consultation, compromise, and consensus.

Weak and strong states alike benefit from persuasion. For weak states, it is a means of gaining wider influence. Strong states gain by reducing resentment. Others are envious of their power, and all the more so if they have tried to impose their preferences on others. Leaders, elites, and the public are all angered when they must acknowledge publicly their subordinate status. As Hans Morgenthau recognized, power must be masked to be effective and this is another important reason why persuasion is the best route to influence.[43] Other actors are sometimes willing to pretend to themselves or their publics that they are acting on the basis of consensus. Their compliance might be gained by minimal or face-saving concessions, language that appeals to mutually shared values, and implementation through institutions in which they and others are represented and have some opportunity to influencing policy.

The starting point of my analysis is Greek tragedy. Tragedy is a description of the world and an abstract source of ethics. It combines the "is" and the "ought," although its two components can be disaggregated for purposes analysis. Tragedy is a vehicle for exploring ethical questions and dilemmas and teaching people to confront the uncertainty and risks of life, the value of self-restraint and tolerance, and the benefits of being honest with themselves and others. As Sophocles and Thucydides demonstrated it is a particularly apt framework for the conduct and the study of politics and foreign policy. I am also drawn to it because it is anchored in a sense of how to get on in the world, although admittedly in the premodern world. I nevertheless contend that many of tragedy's insights are just as relevant today as they were 2,500 years ago. It teaches us less about how to get ahead in the world than it does about reducing the likelihood of catastrophe. It nevertheless recognizes that catastrophe can strike the best of people. Tragedy is an art form, but it is one that is applicable to real life.[44] It is arguably the first sophisticated attempt to make the case that adherence to nomos has the potential to bring about personal and political benefits.

Chapter 2 elaborates the tragic vision of life and politics. It explores different kinds of tragedy, their causes, and relevance to foreign policy. It draws out some of the ethical lessons of tragedy for formulating and implementing foreign policy and illustrates them with present-day examples. I make than argument for the practical benefits of following nomos, but also for learning to live with others who understand nomos differently. I conclude with a discussion of the multiple methodological difficulties involved in establishing my claim and justification of the case study method on which I rely. I offer these case studies not in the form of a proof but as good illustrations not only of the greater success of ethical policies but of some of the reasons for this outcome.

Chapter 3 substantiates the first of my counterintuitive claims: that foreign policies that violate contemporary understandings of justice are less likely to succeed than those that conform to them. The most dramatic kinds of policy that violate nomos are war and military interventions. I turn to a data set of wars fought since 1945 that I assembled to show that the majority of wars fought since 1648 failed to achieve their political goals. Even when the armed forces achieved some military success these wars proved counterproductive to initiating leaders and their countries. This phenomenon is even more pronounced since 1945, where very few initiators of war have been able to achieve their political goals. They have also lost standing and influence by starting them. The clear policy lesson is that ethics does not stop at the water's edge but must become an integral component of foreign policy decisionmaking. Leaders need to ask themselves the extent to which their initiatives – and here I mean the ends sought and the means used – are acceptable to relevant foreign audiences.

Chapter 4 examines the other side of the equation: the association between successful policies and ethics. I open with a discussion of the methodological problems of distinguishing good from bad outcomes and of attributing them to the self-restraint encouraged, at times mandated, by international law, conventions, and accepted practices. I do this in the context of war and intervention and argue that those most likely to succeed are multilateral operations with the support of appropriate regional or international organizations. Multilateral coalitions almost invariably compel initiators to moderate their goals and pursue ends that other actors consider in their interest. Successful coalitions require a consensus on war aims and their justification on the basis of respected international norms.

In the second part of the chapter, I take a different approach to showing the nature and benefits of ethical foreign policy. I look at three sets of innovative policy initiatives that were rooted in widely shared conceptions of justice or that helped to pioneer them: US efforts to stimulate the economic reconstruction of Europe in the aftermath of the Second World War, China's efforts under Mao Zedong to settle territorial and border disputes with its neighbors, and postwar Germany's efforts to convince its neighbors that it was a peace-loving nation and reliable partner. All three initiatives were focused on accommodation, involved concessions of different kinds, relied on assurances rather than threats, and appealed to well-entrenched norms or understandings of justice. All three took several years or longer to implement and succeeded to varying degrees in building confidence across borders. In two of the three cases, they produced a high degree of cross-national solidarity.

Chapter 5 turns to the ethics of foreign policy decisionmaking. I open with a critique of the literature on this subject in political science and political psychology. I argue that it is unrealistic in a double sense: leaders are unlikely to adopt its recommendations, and even if they do, it does not necessarily lead to better policies. I then identify what I consider to be the most serious causes of bad policy decisions. At the top of the list are inappropriate assumptions, and ones moreover, that are rarely, if ever, interrogated. Then comes too narrow frames of reference. By this, I mean consideration of only one aspect of problem and best-case scenarios for responding to it. These two failings are related and reinforcing as is they blind policymakers to other ways of viewing or defining the problem, the possibility and consequences of the failure of their preferred, or of the possible negative follow-on consequences of short-term success.

I conclude by turning to tragedy as a framework for informing policy. I do not want to substitute it for modern approaches, but offer it as a much needed corrective. As with almost everything in life there needs to be a balance, in the case of foreign policy between self-interest and concern for others, risk taking and risk aversion, optimism and pessimism, overconfidence and unreasonable timidity, flying by the seat of one's pants versus acting on the basis of careful analysis and preparation, and a focus on the benefits of action versus those of inaction. At its core, decisonmaking is a question of ethics and tragedy is accordingly very germane to it.

Chapter 6 summarizes my argument and further explores the relationship between tragedy and foreign policy, and then between foreign policy and modernity. I make a different argument for ethical behavior. I review the trajectories of great powers that have jettisoned self-restraint and sought to expand their territory or influence by means of threats, bribes, and military intervention. Short-term successes encouraged further predation and were a cause of longer-term failure. This happened because leaders who succumb to hubris are increasingly unable to formulate their interests in a rational manner. It is only possible to do this as members of a community held together by common interests, bonds of friendship, and respect for nomos and justice. People outside of communities cannot realize their human potential. As the ancient Greeks understood, they are guided only by their raw appetites and instrumental reason and constitute a danger to themselves and all those around them.

Tragedy emphasizes self-awareness and with it the understanding that individuals and their political units are embedded in in communities from which they greatly benefit. Affection and reflection combine to make people construct collective as well as individual identities and to pursue community as well as personal interests. They come to see the two as at least in part reinforcing. The tragic understanding of the relationship of individuals to their societies is sharply at odds with post-Enlightenment liberalism that treats actors as autonomous, egoistic individuals. It offers a corrective to this unrealistic and dangerous understanding and holds out the potential to restore a healthy balance to understandings of self, interest, and interactions with others.

Notes

1. Charles Beitz, *Political Theory and International Relations* (Princeton: Princeton University Press, 1979); Chris Brown, *Sovereignty, Rights and Justice* (Cambridge: Polity Press, 2002); Michael Walzer, *Just and Unjust Wars: A Moral Argument with Historical Illustrations* (Harmondsworth: Penguin, 1980); Terry Nardin, *Law Morality and Relations of States* (Princeton: Princeton University Press, 1983); Michael Walzer, *Thick and Thin: Moral Argument at Home and Abroad* (Notre Dame: University of Notre Dame Press, 1994); Joel Rosenthal, *Ethics and International Affairs* (Washington: Georgetown University Press, 1999); Mervyn Frost, *Ethics in International Relations: A Constitutive Theory* (Cambridge: Cambridge University Press, 1996), *Global Ethics: Anarchy, Freedom and International Relations* (Routledge, 2008), and *Practice Theory and International Relations* (Cambridge University Press, 2018); Duncan Bell, *Ethics and Word Politics* (Oxford: Oxford University Press, 2010); Kimberly Hutchings, *Global Ethics: an introduction* (Cambridge: Polity, 2010); Richard Schapcott, *International Ethics: A Critical Introduction* (Cambridge: Polity, 2010).
2. Jürgen Habermas is generally considered the father of discourse ethics. See his *Discourse Ethics: Notes on a Program of Philosophical Justification* (Cambridge: MIT Press, 1990), *Moral Consciousness and Communicative Action* (Cambridge: MIT Press, 1991); and Craig Calhoun, ed., *Habermas and the Public Sphere* (Cambridge: MIT Press, 1992). Also, Seyla Benhabib and Fred Reinhard Dallmayr, eds., *The Communicative Ethics Controversy* (Cambridge: MIT Press, 1990).
3. Reinhold Niebuhr, *Christianity and Power Politics* (New York: Charles Scribner's Sons, 1940) and *The Structure of Nations and Empires* (New York: Charles Scribner's Sons, 1959); Michael Walzer, *Spheres of Justice: A Defense of Pluralism and Equality* (New York: Basic Books, 1983); Chris Brown, *Sovereignty, Rights and Justice: International Political Theory Today* (London: Polity, 2002); Mervyn Frost, *Global Ethics: Anarchy, Freedom and International Relations* (London: Routledge, 2008); Sylvia Lechner and Mervyn Frost, *Practice Theory and International Relations* (Cambridge: Cambridge University Press, 2018); Onora O'Neill, *Towards Justice and*

Virtue: A Constructive Account of Practical Reasoning (Cambridge: Cambridge University Press, 1996), *Acting on Principle: An Essay On Kantian Ethics* (Cambridge: Cambridge University Press, 2013), and *Justice Across Boundaries: Whose Obligations?* (Cambridge: Cambridge University Press, 2016); Toni Erskine, *Can Institutions Have Responsibilities?: Collective Moral Agency and International Relations* (London: Palgrave-Macmillan, 2003) and *Can Institutions Have Responsibilities?: Collective Moral Agency and International Relations* (Oxford: Oxford University Press, 2008).

4. Political theory quite self-consciously also moved away from political science. John G. Gunnell, *Between Philosophy and Politics: The Alienation of Political Theory* (Amherst: University of Massachusetts Press, 1986), chs. 8–9.

5. Hans J. Morgenthau, *Scientific Man vs. Power Politics* (Chicago: University of Chicago Press, 1956), pp. v–vi, 7.

6. Hans J. Morgenthau, *Politics Among Nations* (New York: Knopf, 1948), pp. 4–5, 43–45.

7. E. H. Carr, *The Twenty Years' Crisis, 1919–1939* (New York: Harper & Row, 1964 [1939]), p. 8.

8. Peter Wilson, "The Myth of the 'First Great Debate'," *Review of International Studies* 24 (1998), pp. 1–16; Lucian Ashworth, "Where Are the Idealists in Interwar International Relations?" *Review of International Studies* 32, 2 (2006): 291–308; Brian C. Schmidt ed., *International Relations and the First Great Debate* (London: Routledge, 2012); Richard Ned Lebow, *The Tragic Vision of Politics: Ethics, Interests Orders* (Cambridge: Cambridge University Press, 2003), ch. 4; Seán Molloy, "Pragmatism, Realism and the Ethics of Crisis and Transformation in International Relations," *International Theory* 6, 3 (2014), pp. 454–89.

9. Anthony F. Lang, Jr., *Hans J. Morgenthau on Aristotle's "The Politics"* (Westport: Praeger, 2004).

10. Morgenthau defends his theory on the grounds that it provides a better description of reality than the so-called idealist account he criticizes. But he acknowledges that powers sometimes fail to balance against serious threats, as Britain, France, and the USA failed to do in the 1930s. He holds out *Politics Among Nations* as a means of educating statesmen in the hope of improving the quality of policy in status quo powers. This is explicit statement of normative intent.

11. John Rawls, *A Theory of Justice*, rev. ed. (Cambridge: Harvard University Press, 1999), *The Law of Peoples* (Cambridge: Harvard University Press, 1999), and *Justice as Fairness*, ed. Erin Kelly (Cambridge: Harvard

University Press, 2001); Michael J. Sandel, *Liberalism and the Limits of Justice* (Cambridge: Cambridge University Press, 1982); Walzer, *Spheres of Justice*.

12. The founding constructivist works in international relations reveal engage seriously with political theory: Nicholas G. Onuf, *World of Our Making* (Columbia: University of South Carolina Press, 1989); Kratochwil, Friedrich V., *Rules, Norms, and Decisions: On the Conditions of Practical and Legal Reasoning in International Relations and Domestic Affairs* (Cambridge: Cambridge University Press, 1989).

13. Max Horkheimer, *Critical Theory* (New York, Continuum, 1982); Raymond Geuss, *The Idea of a Critical Theory. Habermas and the Frankfurt School* (Cambridge: Cambridge University Press, 1981).

14. Catie Edmondson, "Senate to Vote Again to End Aid Saudi War in Yemen," *New York Times*, March 12, 2019, www.nytimes.com/20 19/03/12/us/politics/senate-yemen-vote-saudi-arabia.html (accessed March 21, 2019).

15. Catie Edmondson, "Senate Votes to Block Trump's Arms Sales to Gulf Nations in Bipartisan Rebuke," *New York Times*, June 20, 2019, www .nytimes.com/2019/06/20/us/politics/saudi-arms-sales.html (accessed June 20, 2019).

16. Allison D. Redlich, Christopher E. Kelly, and Jeaneé C. Miller, "Interviewing High Value Detainees: Securing Cooperation and Disclosures." *Applied Cognitive Psychology* 28, 6 (2014): 883–97; Scott Shane, "Interrogations Effectiveness May Prove Elusive," *New York Times*, April 22, 2009, www.nytimes.com/2009/04/23/us/ politics/23detain.html; Jason Burke, "Does Torture Work – and Is It Worth the Cost?" *Guardian*, January 26, 2017, www .theguardian.com/law/2017/jan/26/does-torture-work-and-is-it-worth -the-cost-donald-trump (both accessed June 21, 2019); Mark A. Costanzo and Ellen Gerrity, "The Effects and Effectiveness of Using Torture as an Interrogation Device: Using Research to Inform the Policy Debate," *Social Issues and Policy Review* 3, 1 (2009): 179–210.

17. Thucydides account of the Peloponnesian War has long been read as making this point.

18. The most powerful accounts are S. M. Amadae, *Rationalizing Capitalist Democracy: The Cold War Origins of Rational Choice Liberalism* (Chicago: University of Chicago Press, 2003) and *Prisoners of Reason: Game Theory and Neoliberal Political Economy* (Cambridge: Cambridge University Press, 2016); Mark Blyth, *Austerity: The History of a Dangerous Idea* (Oxford: Oxford University Press, 2013);

Adam Tooze, *Crashed: How a Decade of Financial Crises Changed the World* (London: Allen Lane, 2018), esp. Part III.

19. Simon Reich and Richard Ned Lebow, *Good-Bye Hegemony! Power and Influence in the Global System* (Princeton: Princeton University Press, 2014); Richard Ned Lebow, *A Democratic Foreign Policy*, chs. 2 and 3.

20. This tradition may begin with E. H. Carr, *Twenty Year's Crisis* and finds resonance in the writings of Hans Morgenthau, Jon Herz, Frederick Shuman, Reinhold Niebuhr, Lewis Mumford, and C. Wright Mills. See Richard Ned Lebow, *Tragic Vision of Politics*, ch. 6; Duncan Bell, ed., *Political Thought and International Relations* (Oxford: Oxford University Press, 2008); William E. Scheuerman, *The Realist Case for Global Reform* (Cambridge: Polity, 2011); Rens van Munster and Caspar Sylvest, "The Thermonuclear Revolution and the Politics of Imagination: Realist Radicalism in Political Theory and IR," *International Organization* 32, 3 (2018): 255–74.

21. Ethan A. Nadelmann, "Global Prohibition Regimes: The Evolution of Norms in International Society," *International Organization* 44, 4 (1990): 479–526; Samuel Barkin and Bruce Cronin, "The State and the Nation: Changing Norms and the Rules of Sovereignty in International Relations," *International Organization* 48, 1 (1994): 107–30; Martha Finnemore, *National Interests in International Society* (Ithaca: Cornell University Press, 1996) and *The Purpose of Intervention: Changing Beliefs about the Use of Force* (Ithaca: Cornell University Press, 2003); Martha Finnemore and Kathryn Sikkink, "International Norm Dynamics and Political Change," *International Organization* 52, 4 (1998): 887–918; Peter J. Katzenstein, ed., *The Culture of National Security: Norms and Identity in World Politics* (New York: Columbia University Press, 1996); Margaret E. Keck and Kathryn Sikkink, *Activists Beyond Borders: Transnational Advocacy Networks in International Politics* (Ithaca: Cornell University Press, 1998); Amitav Acharya, "How Ideas Spread: Whose Norms Matter?" *International Organization* 58, 2 (2004): 239–75; Thomas Risse, Stephen C. Ropp, and Kathryn Sikkink, eds., *The Power of Human Rights: International Norms and Domestic Change* (Cambridge: Cambridge University Press, 1999) and *The Power of Human Rights: International Norms and Domestic Change* (Cambridge: Cambridge University Press, 2013); Markus Kornprobst, "Argumentation and Compromise: Ireland's Selection of the Territorial Status Quo Norm," *International Organization* 61, 1 (2007): 69–98 and *Co-Managing International Crises: Judgments and Justifications* (Cambridge: Cambridge University Press, 2019); Wayne Sandholtz, "Dynamics of

International Norm Change: Rules Against Wartime Plunder," *European Journal of International Relations* 14, 1 (2008): 101–31; Judith Kelley, "Assessing the Complex Evolution of Norms: The Rise of International Election Monitoring," *International Organization* 62, 2 (2008): 221–55.

22. Richard Rorty, "Human Rights, Rationality, and Sentimentality," in Stephen Shute and Susan Hurley, eds., *On Human Rights: The Oxford Amnesty Lectures 1993* (New York: Basic Books, 1993), pp. 111–34; Charles Beitz, *The Idea of Human Rights* (Oxford: Oxford University Press, 2009), pp. 1, 197.

23. Simon Chesterman, *Just War or Just Peace? Humanitarian Intervention and International Law* (Oxford: Oxford University Press, 2001), ch. 4; Taylor B. Seybolt, *Humanitarian Military Intervention: The Conditions for Success and Failure* (Oxford: Oxford University Press, 2007).

24. J. R. Oldfield, *Transatlantic Abolitionism in the Age of Revolution: An International History of Anti-Slavery, c.1787–1820* (Cambridge: Cambridge University Press, 2013); Richard Price, *The Chemical Weapons Taboo* (Ithaca: Cornell University Press, 1997); Nina Tannenwald, *The Nuclear Taboo: The United States and the Non-Use of Nuclear Weapons Since 1945* (New York: Cambridge University Press, 2007); T. V. Paul, *The Tradition of Non-Use of Nuclear Weapons* (Stanford: Stanford University Press, 2009); Gary Bass, *Freedom's Battle: The Origins of Humanitarian Intervention* (New York: Random House, 2008); Michael Barnett, *Empire of Humanity: A History of Humanitarianism* (Ithaca: Cornell University Press, 2013).

25. Beitz, *Idea of Human Rights*, p. 6.

26. Richard Ned Lebow, "Max Weber and International Relations" and "Max Weber's Search for Knowledge" in Richard Ned Lebow, ed., *Max Weber and International Relations* (Cambridge: Cambridge University Press, 2017), pp. 10–39, 40–78.

27. Michael Walzer, *Just and Unjust Wars*, rev. ed. (New York: Basic Books, 2015); Stephen Garrett, *Ethics and Airpower in World War II: British Bombing of German Cities* (London: Palgrave-Macmillan, 2007); Gabriella Blum and Philip Heymann, *Laws, Outlaws, and Terrorists* (Cambridge: MIT Press, 2010).

28. Edwin E. Moise, *Tonkin Gulf and the Escalation of the Vietnam War*, 2nd ed. (Annapolis: Naval Institute Press, 2019); Michael Isikoff and David Corn, *Hubris: The Inside Story of Spin, Scandal, and the Selling of the Iraq War* (New York: Broadway Books, 2007); Giovanni Coletta, "Politicising Intelligence: What Went Wrong with the UK and US Assessments on Iraqi WMD in 2002," *Journal of Intelligence History* 17, 1 (2018): 65–78.

29. Markus Kornprobst, Co-*Managing International Crises: Judgments and Justifications* (Cambridge: Cambridge University Press, 2019), for compelling evidence of the relationship between judgments and attributions in Britain, France, and Germany in three post-Cold War crises.

30. For a more critical view of this approach to policy, see Max Weber, "The Profession and Vocation of Politics," in Peter Lassman and Ronald Speirs, eds., *Weber: Political Writings* (Cambridge: Cambridge University Press, 2000), pp. 309–69.

31. Richard Ned Lebow, "Max Weber's Ethics," *International Political Theory* 13, 1 (2019): 37–58.

32. Immanuel Kant, "Perpetual Peace," in *Kant's Political Writings*, 2nd ed., ed., Hans Reiss, trans. H. B. Nisbet (Cambridge: Cambridge University Press, 1991), pp. 41–53 and *Anthropology from a Pragmatic Point of View*, ed. Robert Louden (Cambridge: Cambridge University Press, 2006); Seán Molloy, *Kant's International Relations: The Political Theology of Perpetual Peace* (Ann Arbor: University of Michigan Press, 2017), pp. 94–6, 100–111.

33. Kant, *Anthropology from a Pragmatic Point of View*, p. 32.

34. Robert Jervis, *Perception and Misperception in International Relations* (Princeton: Princeton University Press, 1976), pp. 128–42.

35. Tim Shipman, *All Out War: The Full Story of Brexit* (London: HarperCollins, 2017) and *Fallout: A Year of Political Mayhem* (London: Collins, 2018); Harold D. Clarke, Matthew Goodwin, and Paul Whiteley, *Brexit: Why Britain Voted to Leave the European Union* (Cambridge: Cambridge University Press, 2017); Geoffrey Evans and Anand Menon, *Brexit and British Politics* (Cambridge: Polity Press 2017); Sara B. Hobolt, "The Brexit Vote: A Divided Nation, A Divided Continent," *Journal of European Public Policy* 23, 9 (2016): 1259–77; Tim Oliver, *Understanding Brexit: A Concise Introduction* (Bristol: Policy Press, 2018); Kevin O'Rourke, *A Short History of Brexit: From Brentry to Backstop* (London: Pelican, 2019); Fintan O'Toole, *Heroic Failure: Brexit and the Politics of Pain* (London: Apollo, 2018); Ivan Rogers, *9 Lessons in Brexit* (London: Short Books, 2019); Jonathan Freedland, "How Brexit Is Causing the Strange Death of British Conservatism," *Guardian*, June 7, 2019, www.theguardian.com/commentisfree/2019/jun/07/brexit-strange-death-british-conservatism (accessed June 7, 2019).

36. Ibid; Jonathan Freedland, "This Political Crisis Now Goes Far Beyond Brexit – Our Very Democracy Is at Stake," *Guardian*, September 13, 2019, www.theguardian.com/commentisfree/2019/sep/13/brexit-boris-johnson-parliament-written-constitution; Nick Cohen, "Brexiters' Adoption of War Language Will Stop Britain from Finding Peace,"

Guardian, October 12, 2019, www.theguardian.com/commentisfree/20
19/oct/12/brexiters-adoption-war-language-will-stop-britain-finding-pea
ce; John Harris, "The Fantasy of Britain at War Could Be Nearing Its Last
Hurrah," *Guardian*, March 14, 2019, www.theguardian.com/commen
tisfree/2019/oct/14/fantasy-britain-war-last-hurrah-brexit-nostalgia.

37. Editorial, "Macho Mistakes at Ground Zero," *New York Times*,
May 22, 2007, www.nytimes.com/2007/05/22/opinion/22tue1.html
(accessed March 23, 2019). Wayne Barrett and Dan Collins, *Grand
Illusion: The Untold Story of Rudy Giuliani and 9/11* (New York:
Harper, 2006); Deborah Hart Strober and Gerald S. Strober, *Giuliani:
Flawed or Flawless? The Oral Biography* (New York: John Wiley &
Sons, 2007).

38. American Presidency Project, "139 – The President's News Conference
April 21, 1961," https://web.archive.org/web/20160506182204/http://
www.presidency.ucsb.edu/ws/index.php?pid=8077; National Security
Archive, "Interview with Robert McNamara," no date, https://nsarc
hive2.gwu.edu/coldwar/interviews/episode-10/mcnamara3.html (both
accessed March 23, 2019).

39. Edward E. Jones and Victor A. Harris, "The Attribution of Attitudes,"
Journal of Experimental Social Psychology 3, 1 (1967): 1–24; Lee Ross,
"The Intuitive Psychologist and His Shortcomings: Distortions in the
Attribution Process," in Leonard Berkowitz, *Advances in Experimental
Social Psychology*, no. 10 (New York: Academic Press, 1977), pp. 173–220.

40. Seth Cline, "The Other Symbol of George W. Bush's Legacy," *U.S. News*,
May 1, 2013, reflects the conventional wisdom when he suggests that "If
there's one day in particular Bush could choose to rewrite, it might be
May 1, 2003," www.usnews.com/news/blogs/press-past/2013/05/01/the-
other-symbol-of-george-w-bushs-legacy (accessed July 16, 2019).

41. On status, Richard Ned Lebow, *A Cultural Theory of International
Relations* (Cambridge: Cambridge University Press, 2008); Tudor Onea,
*US Foreign Policy in the Post-Cold War Era: Restraint versus Assertiveness
From George H. W. Bush to Barack Obama* (New York: Palgrave-
Macmillan, 2013); T. V. Paul, Deborah Welch Larson, and William
C. Wohlforth, eds. *Status in World Politics* (Cambridge: Cambridge
University Press, 2014); Joshua Renshon, *Fighting for Status: Hierarchy
and Conflict in World Politics* (Princeton: Princeton University Press, 2017).

42. Lebow, *Cultural Theory of International Relations*, for ancient,
medieval, and modern examples.

43. Morgenthau, *Scientific Man vs. Power Politics*, p. 145.

44. On this question, see the debate in Toni Erskine and Richard
Ned Lebow, eds., *Tragedy and International Relations* (London:
Palgrave-Macmillan, 2012).

2 | *Tragedy and Foreign Policy*

Developed by fifth-century BCE Athenian poets, tragedy is one of the oldest conceptual and ethical frameworks. It is no exaggeration to say that it is, at least in part, constitutive of Western culture. Writing in the aftermath of the Peloponnesian War, Thucydides thought it an appropriate lens through which to view international relations.[1] Following his example, I use tragedy to frame my analysis of catastrophic foreign policy decisions, including those leading up to the First World War and the Anglo-American invasion of Iraq.[2] Toni Erskine and I argued subsequently that international relations more generally could be understood in terms of tragedy.[3] In this chapter, I make the case for tragedy as a form of ethics particularly appropriate to the study and practice of contemporary foreign policy.

I open with a short account of the meaning and history of tragedy as a literary genre and how it is used to characterize contemporary events of all kinds that involve the possibility of substantial loss. I then turn to Aristotle's analysis of how and why people learn from tragedy. He emphasizes the structure of these plays and its emotional effect on audiences, but implicitly recognizes the importance of postperformance reflection and discussion. The tragic playwrights and Thucydides, who framed his account of the Peloponnesian War as a tragedy, left no testimony about the lessons – personal or political – they intended to impart. These must be inferred from their texts. Controversy surrounds these interpretations, although there is something of a consensus among classicists about the general orientation toward life that tragedy and other Greek writings appear to advocate.

The second part of the chapter describes four kinds of tragedy: those of unmerited suffering, character, hard choice, and moral dilemma. Each poses a different kind of ethical and political challenge and all four are common to international relations. I contend that an awareness of tragedy and the pathways to it has the potential to reduce its frequency. This is a controversial claim, but one I feel confident in making. But it does come with a caveat. Awareness can only succeed in reducing the likelihood of tragedy to the degree that policymakers put themselves in the plot. Instead of denying the possibility of catastrophe, they must recognize themselves as its possible victims and as actors who confront tragic choices. They must face up to these choices and their unpredictable consequences. This kind of intellectual and emotional openness is a form of courage, and a more important one for policymakers than that of steeling themselves to send others into battle.[4]

I conclude with a discussion of the broader lessons of tragedy for policymakers. Of the many insights this view of life and politics offers, two are particularly relevant to contemporary international relations: its clarion warning of the dangers of power and success, and its problematization of all conceptions of justice. Both realizations encourage self-restraint and tolerance as well temperance in the choice and pursuit of goals.

Before proceeding, I want to stress that although tragedy is a literature genre, it is also a form of political analysis. In his review of Hans Morgenthau's *Scientific Man Versus Power Politics*, Michael Oakeshott denied Morgenthau's contention that human life, and politics in particular, was tragic: "Tragedy belongs to art," he insisted, "not to life."[5] More recently, Nick Rengger made the same claim.[6] The Greek playwrights and Thucydides would strongly disagree. Aeschylus, Sophocles, and Euripides developed tragedy as a literary genre because they believed it captured fundamental attributes of human life and the human condition. Thucydides applied it to politics for the same reason.[7] These Athenians also believed that tragedy had practical as well as descriptive value. It encourages introspection, recognition of the limits of reason and power, empathy with others, and tolerance of competing conceptions of justice and of interest. They envisaged tragedy itself as a source of ethics, and I explore its implications for foreign policy in the course of this book.

Origins and Meaning

"Tragedy" and "tragic" are routinely used to describe instances of seemingly inexplicable suffering. These include earthquakes and floods, wars and famines, epidemics and environmental disasters.

The standard characterization of the 1994 genocide in which approximately 800,000 people were murdered is the "Rwanda tragedy," the 2010 Deepwater Horizon oil spill in the Gulf of Mexico was branded the "BP tragedy," and for Remainers and Leavers in the UK alike, the last two years have been labeled the "Brexit Tragedy." I use a more carefully defined and historical situated understanding of the term.

Tragedy can be traced back to plays the Athenian called *tragōidia*. It flourished in a short-lived moment – the second half of the fifth century BCE in Athens – when drama, politics, and philosophy were intimately connected. The venue was the Athenian Dionysia, a large festival held every year in late March in honor of the god Dionysus. Tragedies, comedies, and Satyr plays were performed in a large, open-air amphitheater on the southern slope of the Acropolis before an audience of citizens and noncitizens, foreigners, and people of all classes. The generals (*stratēgoi*) poured libations to open the festival. This was followed by a public display of allied tribute, an announcement of the names of benefactors – including those who underwrote the cost of producing the plays – and a parade of state-educated boys, now men, in full military panoply provided by the city. The plays themselves were organized as a contest (*agōn*) in which playwrights competed for public approval.

Aristotle famously described tragedy as a type of "imitation" (*mimesis*) that was distinct from other modes of imitation such as music, comedy, and epic poetry.[8] In his *Poetics*, he extols tragedy as "the imitation of an action that is serious, has magnitude, and is complete in itself . . . with incidents arousing pity and fear, that give rise to an emotional release (*katharsis*)." Aristotle maintained that only a particular kind of plot is capable of generating these emotions. It must be structured around some great miscalculation or error of judgment (*hamartia*) by the protagonist. This miscalculation sets in motion a chain of events that lead to a reversal of fortune (*peripeteia*) and recognition (*anagnorisis*) in the sense of a transformation from ignorance to knowledge as the protagonist realizes his error. Aristotle describes the protagonist as "a man like ourselves" – thereby eliciting fears of our vulnerability – but also someone of "great reputation and prosperity" who, in some respects, is "better than the average man" and therefore has further to fall.[9]

The tragic hero does make choices, but they are the wrong ones, and they lead ineluctably to disastrous outcomes. The hero is usually presented as someone with considerable free choice but who is also affected by forces beyond his control. A *hamartia* can be the product of hubris, as it arguably is for Ajax, but can also arise from a deep commitment to a laudable value such as honor, family or civil order, as it does for Antigone. Both causes appear responsible in the case of Oedipus. The pity and fear of audience members is a response to what they understand, at least in part, to be unmerited suffering by the protagonist. The fact that people of noble character can make profound and consequential mistakes drives home the realization that fortune is equally precarious for the mighty and powerless alike. We too can take wrong turns, antagonize the gods or our fellow human beings, and stumble into adversity.

Greek tragedies flourished for less than a century. Tragedy, however, was revived during the Renaissance, and the plays of William Shakespeare are thought to have reached an artistic level equal to those of ancient Athens. Shakespeare and Goethe successfully adapted the concept of tragedy to their eras and countries. One of the novel features of their plays is their foregrounding of the internal lives of key characters. Hamlet and Cordelia, and Faust and Gretchen have personalities and inner conflicts that drive the plot forward. This is in sharp contrast to Greek tragedies whose characters are, for the most part, archetypes. They are assemblages of different characteristics. These traits (i.e., courage, search for honor, curiosity, intelligence, commitment to family and religion), not inner conflicts, are generally admirable but are also responsible for catastrophic choices and outcomes. The tragic genre attracted the attention of a number of prominent eighteenth- and nineteenth-century European philosophers, David Hume, G. W. F. Hegel, Karl Marx, and Friedrich Nietzsche among them. Hegel and Nietzsche were two of a long line of German writers and philosophers who mobilized tragedy to understand modernity or use it as a template for German identity.[10]

Many classicists regard tragedy as a culturally specific phenomenon and a vehicle for studying fifth-century Athens. I respect their concern for context but insist that just as texts take on meanings beyond those intended by their authors, as do genres. Tragedy speaks to us today and is relevant to our lives. We can ask questions about it that could not have been imagined by our fifth-century counterparts.

Four Kinds of Tragedy

Aristotle emphasizes one kind of tragic plot line but Greek tragedies unfold in different ways due to different causes. Catherine Lu identifies four kinds of tragedy: those of unmerited suffering, character, hard choice, and moral dilemma. Each poses a different kind of ethical and political challenge.[11]

Tragedies of suffering drive home the lesson that "bad things happen to good people." Greek plays are replete with stories of virtuous people who suffer. Agamemnon's daughter Iphigenia is sacrificed like a goat so the Greek fleet can receive the winds it needs to sail to Troy. The Trojan women suffer as slaves after the fall of their city. In Thucydides' account of the Archidamian and Peloponnesian Wars, Athenians die in large numbers from the plague, the Plataean democrats are slaughtered by the Spartans and the Melians by the Athenians. Modern tragedies of this kind abound. Some of them preventable, as were the Rwanda genocide and the BP oil spill. Others are more difficult to predict or prevent, including tsunamis, monsoon-fueled floods, Ebola outbreaks, and some refugee crises. And we must remember that interventions intended to reduce suffering may increase it, as NATO's in Libya in 2011 arguably did.

Tragedies of character are the focus of many Greek plays. As Aristotle notes, they are often the product of hubris, as is true of Sophocles' Oedipus. He is overly confident about his powers of reasoning and his ability to deal with any threat facing him and Thebes. Earlier in life, he left his parents and home city of Corinth to avoid any chance of fulfilling the prophecy that he would kill his father and have sex with his mother. Oedipus kills his biological father at a crossroads when attacked by him and his servants. He becomes King of Thebes after he solves the riddle of the Sphinx. He marries the widow queen who turns out to be his birth mother. Oedipus's exercise of agency, much of it intended to avoid his fate, ends up fulfilling it.

Some suspect that Oedipus was a personification of Athens. The play was first performed in 429 BCE, two years into the Peloponnesian War. Like Oedipus, Athens was supremely confident and would act in ways that hastened its loss of empire and ultimate defeat. Thucydides wrote a famous account of this war and its immediate predecessor, which is generally considered to have invented the genre of history. He structures it as a tragedy. His Athens commits a *hamartia* by allying with Corcyra and then another one when it votes to send an expedition to Sicily. Readers of Thucydides' narrative, like the audience at a Sophocles Tragedy, know before the characters do that a dramatic reversal is about to occur. Readers may experience a *katharis* and learn something from Athens' fate that is applicable to their lives. Sophocles and Thucydides are telling us that great men and great powers are their own worst enemies.[12]

Tragedies of character are endemic to international relations. The First World War can readily be described as one because of the miscalculations of Austrian and German leaders. They counted on fighting a limited war in the Balkans but Russian support for Serbia began a chain reaction that transformed a local war into, first, a European war and, then, a world war. In an attempt to strengthen their empires, Vienna and Berlin set in motion a chain of events that destroyed them and created the conditions for an even more destructive war a generation later. Like Oedipus, their leaders sought to escape an imagined fate – the weakening of their empires – and their responses made their worst fears self-fulfilling. More recently, the Anglo-American invasion of Iraq offers another example of the Oedipus effect. Well-intentioned people – if woefully misinformed, arrogant, and deluded – brought about the very outcome they tried to avoid: destabilization of the Middle East.

Tragedies of hard choice arise from scare financial or human resources. Governments and nongovernmental organizations (NGOs) must constantly make all kinds of difficult choice. In the medical realm, these concern such things as what research to fund, which drugs and treatments to pay for, what populations to prioritize, and how much money should go to healthcare as opposed to other research and services. Deserving people are bound to suffer, if not entire categories of them. Some of these difficult choices might to some degree be finessed or mitigated in part by more astute political skill and moral courage. Other tragedies could only be avoided by broad structural changes and financial redistributions that require a far-seeing population and favorable political conditions.

Tragedies of moral dilemma derive from conflicting ethical imperatives. In the *Oresteia*, Aeschylus has Orestes kill his mother to revenge her murder of his father. He is then pursued by the Erinyes, a trio of goddesses who enforce traditional understandings of justice, especially those centered on the family. Orestes had been encouraged to seek revenge by Apollo and is later defended by Athena. The conflict between Orestes and the Erinyes is really one between two largely irreconcilable forms of traditional justice. Clytemnestra's murder of Agamemnon, her husband and Orestes' father, was also an act of revenge for his sacrifice of their daughter Iphigenia. The Trojan War was, in turn, retribution for Paris absconding with Helen, wife of Agamemnon's brother Menelaus. Homer and Aeschylus are telling us that attempts to implement justice can involve injustices and set in motion an escalating spiral of violence.

The other classic representation of conflicting ethical imperatives is Sophocles' *Antigone*, first performed in 441 BCE. Thebes has overcome a revolt, one of whose leaders was Polyneices, the sister of Antigone. She is engaged to Haemon, son of the ruler Creon. Creon, intent on demonstrating his authority, decrees that none of the rebels is to be buried but their corpses are to be left to rot outside the city or be eaten by dogs. Antigone, committed to her family and Greek customs, ignores his dictate and buries her brother. An enraged Creon walls her up and leaves her to starve. Antigone hangs herself and Haemon – Creon's son and her betrothed – discovers her body and stabs himself in grief. Creon's extreme and unflinching commitment to civil order, and Antigone's to family and religion, lead to an intense, escalating conflict that is destructive to family and city alike.

We can find similar conflicts in contemporary international relations. They arise in the first instance from the diversity of values and beliefs and the different goals and commitments to which they lead. Western commitments to democracy and equality, and tolerance of difference dissent – admittedly, often honored more in the breech than in practice – are strikingly at odds with beliefs and practices in most other parts of the world. Conflict is inevitable if any culture attempts to impose its beliefs and practice on the other. Framing these differences and conflicts they generate as "clashes of civilization," as Samuel Huntington famously did, put him and those who adopt this perspective into the role of Creon.[13] In practice, the most serious conflicts are within cultures, not between them. Consider, for example, the Shia-Sunni division in the Muslim world, the dispute between India and Pakistan, or the rising conflict between right-wing, anti-immigration, nationalists in the West and their liberal, cosmopolitan, prodemocracy rivals.[14]

A second source of conflict is unwillingness to compromise when conflicts arise. Disputes about money or property, or other substantive issues, lend themselves to compromise solutions. They are not either-or in nature. Compromise, even splitting the difference, only means that one side or the other gets a little more or less of whatever is at stake. This is more difficult, and sometimes impossible, if fundamental values are perceived to be at stake. When people do this, and frame conflicts in terms of justice, they are correspondingly reluctant to compromise. Being a little honest, observing a commitment only in part, tolerating only some kinds of speech or religion is difficult, perhaps contradictory, and certainly more difficult to defend logically and politically to oneself and others.

Transforming differences over interests into conflicts over principles is all too frequent a phenomenon in international relations. It encourages maximalist demands, refusal to compromise, and greater willingness to resort to force to achieve one's goals. Consider the conflict between Israelis and Palestinians, one of the most intractable of disputes associated with partitioned countries.[15] Israelis frame their relations with the Palestinians as largely one of security. The Palestinians understand it more in terms of self-esteem. They define themselves as an oppressed group in search of recognition and physical control of a homeland. Almost everything the Israelis do to enhance their security threatens Palestinian self-esteem, and much of what Palestinians do to buttress their self-esteem threatens Israel's security. Until these two goals can be disaggregated and to some degree satisfied there is no chance of compromise and an agreed political solution. These two peoples are Antigone and Creon writ large.

Can We Learn from Tragedy?

Greeks believed that tragedy was a source of political education. According to Peter Euben, it was intended to teach citizens that words, and the ideas and practices they instantiate, have multiple and often irreconcilable meanings.[16] This reality is not only acceptable but perhaps beneficial to the degree that people learn to accept it. How does such insight and acceptance come about?

Tragedies generally present only a small slice of their heroes' lives and often end with their deaths at a young age. The Oedipus cycle is unique in that we encounter the eponymous hero as a youth and later in his old age. The Oedipus we meet in *Oedipus at Colonus* has reflected on his fate and become wise. Wisdom (*sophia*) for the Greeks, and for the lame, blind, and aging Oedipus, consists of a holistic understanding of the world and one's place in it. It is a source, not only of prudential behavior, but of the happiness and fulfillment that comes from being at one with nature and human society.

Real-life tragic figures are rarely blessed with this kind of insight. Pericles died before the tragic consequences of his hubris became apparent. The Kaiser, along with many other Germans, denied any responsibility for the continental tragedy they brought about; they convinced themselves that they were victims of British perfidy or socialist and Jewish treachery. It seems unlikely that George Bush and his advisors will ever reflect and learn the way Oedipus did. Like Greek audiences, we can learn something from these tragedies even if we cannot achieve the kind of wisdom that Oedipus ultimately gained. We can progress far enough to become more empathetic, prudential, insightful, less arrogant, and reasonable in our goals and expectations.

For fifth-century Athenians tragedies were the principal means of social knowledge. In today's world, social science claims this authority. Many mainstream social scientists search for the kind of regularities they believe will allow prediction and make their research indispensable to investors, corporations, local, and national governments. They are quintessential products of the Enlightenment in their optimism about the ability of reason to understand, control, and reshape the physical and social worlds. Tragedy dramatizes the consequences of hubris, and social science is a modern exemplar.

I find tragedy appealing because it alerts us to the parochial nature of our beliefs, especially of our conceptions of justice, and, in part because of this, the uncertainty of even the most carefully planned courses of action. These reinforcing recognitions can make us more, tolerant, cautious, respectful of uncertainty, and humbler. A tragic view of life and politics also has the potential, I believe, to reduce the frequency of tragedy. I advanced this argument in *Tragic Vision of Politics* and then in a debate that spanned several issues of *International Relations*. These articles and commentaries on them came out as an edited volume: *Tragedy and International Relations*.[17] Contributors took a range of positions. Mervyn Frost was sympathetic to my argument but warned that most tragic figures in Greek plays would have acted just as they did in full knowledge of any consequences. Agamemnon,

Orestes, Oedipus, and Hamlet would have considered themselves ethically bound to follow their courses of action. Frost poses an interesting, but ultimately unanswerable counterfactual because one of the defining features of life is our inability to predict the consequences of our own and others' actions. This, of course, encourages us to act in ways that appear to advance our interests or honor our commitments.[18] Kamila Stullerova contends that the tragic vision of life rests in part on this realization.[19]

If foreknowledge would not sway the decisions of tragic heroes how can the sensitivity to catastrophe that tragedy provides possibly influence us? After all, we are notorious for deluding ourselves that all will work out for the best. Psychological research demonstrates that actors committing themselves to risky initiatives routinely deny the possibility that their actions will result in disaster by distorting, rejecting, and explaining away threatening information and punishing, marginalizing, or isolating themselves from those who warn they are heading for disaster. Motivated bias of this kind is most likely in situations in which any choice brings a high probability of loss, although it is certainly not limited to it.[20] Frost suggests that tragedy can help us identify ethical problems and face up to difficult choices. He offers the example of political change in South Africa that indicates that ethical questioning of even deeply embedded political practices can provide the catalyst for transformation.[21] James Mayall challenges Frost's optimism but is willing to concede that awareness of tragedy can serve as an antidote to the hubris of progressive thought and the constant temptation to avoid accepting responsibility for well-intentioned actions that go awry.[22]

There appears to be no consensus on this question among the tragic playwrights themselves. Aeschylus is by far the most optimistic. His *Oresteia* tells the tragic tale of the house of Atreus, in which one violent deed breeds another, all conceived and carried out in the name of justice. The cycle of revenge, which pits Orestes against his mother and the Furies (*Erinyes*) against Orestes, is finally ended by a court established by Athena. The twelve Athenians of the jury are deadlocked and Athena intervenes to cast the deciding vote for Orestes. She convinces the Furies to accept an honored home beneath the city and henceforth to become the well-wishers (*Eumenides*). Justice, which takes the form of revenge in the *Oresteia* and in Athens, is transformed from a private to a public responsibility, and argument replaces

violence as the means by which justice is pursued. The potential for
feuding is accordingly much reduced but that of violence remains. The
supposedly now benign *Eumenides* can be understood as repressed
urges ready to reemerge when conditions are ripe.

Sophocles is less sanguine about the ability of human beings to
overcome the worst attributes of their nature through civic life and
the education and solidarity its institutions provide. He nevertheless
authored one optimistic play – *Philoctetes* – in which friendship and
persuasion, represented by Neoptolemus, triumph over force and chi-
canery, as personified by Odysseus. Euripides's plays are bloody and
pessimistic and treat learning as instrumental and destructive in its
consequences. Thucydides was a contemporary of Sophocles and
Euripides but lived long enough to witness the final defeat of Athens,
the civil unrest that followed, and the restoration of democracy in 404
BCE. His account of the Peloponnesian War is generally read as
a fatalistic take on power and its exercise, presented most dramatically
in the famous Melian Dialogue.[23] Thucydides can also be interpreted as
a complex and nuanced thinker who thought learning and order possible and fragile.[24]

I contend that Thucydides would not have spent decades researching
and writing his account and labeling it at the outset "a possession for all
time" unless he thought people could learn from the past and had some
ability to alter their destinies. I draw a parallel here: psychotherapy.
Freudians assumes that people will continue to act out self-destructive
scripts until they become aware of what they are doing, and the
destructive consequences of it, and come to terms with the traumas
that compel them to act this way. This recognition is to be achieved
through regression; people must allow themselves to relive painful
experiences they have repressed in order to understand how they
shape their present behavior. Thucydides' account encourages
Athenians and others to revisit the pain and trauma of the
Peloponnesian War in the most vivid way and work through its meaning for their lives and society.[25]

Chris Brown and Peter Euben make more cautious claims. Brown
agrees that awareness of tragedy "ought to cause us to act more
modestly, to be aware of our limitations and to be suspicious of
grand narratives of salvation which pretend that there are no tragic
choices to be made."[26] Euben applauds my efforts to warn against the
self-fulfilling nature of pessimism, but chides me for attempting to

square tragedy with rational analysis and faith in progress. He nevertheless acknowledges that Greek drama was conceived with educational purposes in mind and that tragedy can stimulate learning, but only if you allow it to master you before you master it.

Euben's critique is slightly off the mark because I do not attempt to square tragedy and its stress on the unpredictable but inescapable vicissitudes of life with reason and its commitment to transparency, planning, and progress. I accept that they are polar opposite understandings of existence. In contrast to modernity's optimistic view of the power of reason, tragedy minimizes the capability of individuals and emphasizes the often counterproductive consequences of their efforts to influence others and their environment. The Enlightenment spawned utopias, while tragedy offers corrective dystopias. What I am suggesting is that both views of life capture essential truths.[27] There can be little doubt that the application of reason has transformed the world – for better and worse. We benefit from Science and technology in myriad ways, but they are also responsible, directly and indirectly, for climate change. If humanity does not address the problem of carbon and methane emissions, the climate will change in ways that make the planet increasingly inhospitable to human life. From this longer-term perspective, the trajectory of modernity could turn into a tragedy akin to Oedipus where the application of reason once again produces consequences the reverse of those intended.

Understanding life and politics in the twenty-first century requires both perspectives. I do not argue that they can be combined, and certainly not that one can be subsumed to the other, but rather that they are parallel, clashing visions of the world and our relationship to it. We need to think and operate in terms of both as each is a partial corrective to the other. This is not easy to do and requires the kind of personality and mind that accepts uncertainty, copes with, rather than suppresses, the tensions associated with opposing world views, and works through the implications of both when making important decisions. I follow ancient Greeks in believing that balance between extremes made for a happier and more successful life, and the kind of balance I am arguing for may be among the most important in this regard.

By framing tragedy as a corrective, I am not arguing that it can overcome or circumvent the limitations or drawbacks of reason. They are insurmountable. Tragedy can alert us to the limitations and dangers of reason and make us more cautious and more sensitive to information that suggests that our choices and policies are not working out as intended. Freudians maintain that analysands must recognize the counterproductive nature of scripts they enact and develop the will to alter them. Tragedy is a vehicle for the same end, and one, as Aristotle recognized, does so by a clever combination of emotional arousal and subsequent reflection. I believe Thucydides framed his account of the Peloponnesian War as a tragedy to serve this end. If readers – and leaders in particular – could feel the suffering of those they read about and see the parallel between Athens and their own political units they might develop the will to escape the destructive nature of such scripts.

Insights for Foreign Policy

Tragedy teaches us that single-minded efforts to enhance security are likely to increase disorder and undermine security. Societies must accordingly find a place for the passions that are foundational to politics, even if they are volatile and dangerous when expressed. Reason is part of the solution, but also part of the problem when it rides roughshod over emotions, or thinks it can.

More fundamentally, tragedy encourages us to confront our limits. It reveals human fallibility and vulnerability, illustrates the complexities of our existence, and highlights the contradictions and uncertain consequences of our beliefs and behavior. It teaches us that we not infrequently initiate courses of action without being able to understand or control them, let alone calculate accurately their consequences. It suggests that wisdom and self-awareness might emerge out of adversity and despair. Tragedy cautions against assuming that our own conceptions of justice are universally applicable and should be enforced as such. It warns of the dangers that accompany overconfidence and perceived invincibility. If an appreciation of tragedy can foster a deeper, more sophisticated understanding of ourselves and of international relations how should it influence our choice of goals and means to achieve them? How can such understandings guide our behavior as citizens or policymakers?

Of the many insights revealed by tragedy, two seem particularly relevant to contemporary international relations: its enduring capacity to warn us of the dangers of power and success, and its problematization of all conceptions of justice. The first of these has to do with hubris and its likely consequences. The more powerful and successful an actor becomes the greater the temptation to overreach in the unreasonable expectation that it is possible to predict, influence or control the actions of others and by doing so gain more honor, wealth, or power. Hubris for the Greeks is a category error; powerful people make the mistake of comparing themselves to the gods, who have the ability to foresee and control the future. This arrogance and overconfidence leads them to embrace complex and risky initiatives that frequently have outcomes diametrically opposed to those they seek.

In Greek tragedy, hubris leads to self-seduction (*atē*), serious miscalculation (*hamartia*), and, finally, revenge of the gods (*nemesis*). Oedipus brings his fate on himself by a double act of hubris: he refuses to back off at the crossroads when confronted with a stranger's road rage, and he trusts "blindly" in his ability to reason his way to a solution of the city's infertility, in spite of multiple warnings to the contrary. In *Antigone*, Creon's actions were intended to save the city but brought disorder and the downfall of his house. We all harbor a dangerous propensity for overestimating our capacities and the favorable, even benign, consequences of our actions. By making us confront our limits and recognize that chaos lurks just beyond the fragile barriers we erect to keep it at bay, tragedy can help keep our conceptions of ourselves, and our societies, from becoming infused with hubris.

The 2003 Anglo-American invasion of Iraq revealed all the hallmarks of hubris and total lack of ethical reflexivity. The invasion of Iraq was expected to be a short-term, low-cost operation that would replace Saddam Hussein's regime with a pro-American one and make Iran, North Korea, and the Palestinians more compliant.[28] It turned into a costly, open-ended commitment that undermined British and American prestige and may have encouraged Iran and North Korea to accelerate their nuclear programs. Leaders of both countries were frightened by the Iraq invasion but also convinced that, for the time being at least, there would be less pressure on them. The hubris of the Bush administration, which led its senior officials to assume the presence of weapons of mass destruction, a quick victory with minimal forces, a joyous welcome by "liberated" Iraqis and, given their power and popularity, no need to plan their occupation of the country beyond occupation of the oil ministry.[29]

Foreign policy goals must be carefully evaluated – and not on the basis of cherry-picked intelligence of questionable provenance. They must be assessed for their feasibility, the risks they involve, and possible gains and losses carefully weighed. The Bush administration considered only the rosiest of scenarios when formulating its invasion policy. Good policymakers also imagine what might go wrong and devise worst-case scenarios, not only best-case ones. They also consider what comes next. Here, too, the Bush administration erred; it had no plans for the Iraq occupation and proceeded to blunder in ways that inspired and strengthened resistance to them, triggering off a war that continues with no end in sight as this book goes to press.

The Iraq case may be extreme but it is not unique. The drug war and policy toward Mexico; the Libyan intervention; military aid and sales to Egypt, Israel, and Saudi Arabia; Trump's embrace of dictators and his trade war with China, are all pertinent examples. There are multiple reasons for this kind of hubris. Sophocles and Thucydides tell the same story of past successes and how they go to the heads of people and convince them of their superiority, invulnerability, and ability to manipulate others to serve their ends. America as a whole has suffered from hubris since 1945 and seems not to have learned from its many postwar failures. Each is explained away, as revisionists have attempted to do with the catastrophic intervention in Indochina.[30] Its leaders focus instead on their successes and exaggerate their ability to lead and the desire of others to have them do so. Their analysis of international affairs has become increasingly self-referential. The belief in American hegemony is a quintessential expression of hubris and has already led to some of its negative consequences.

The second tragic insight for contemporary international relations has to do with our conceptions of justice. Tragedies often present the audience with contrasting and equally valid conceptions of justice, as *Antigone* does. In Aeschylus' *Oresteia*, which tells the tragic tale of the house of Atreus, the audience confronts the moral dilemma caused by Orestes' murder of his mother, Clytemnestra. The Furies, who pursue him, insist that it is wrong to murder a parent, while Orestes maintains that he was fulfilling his duty as a son by avenging his father's murder at the hands of his mother and her lover. Orestes' murder is only the last of a series in his family and the trilogy. Each murder is conceived as necessary, just even, and each provokes more violence – violence carried out, as was Orestes's murder of his mother and her lover, in the name of justice. There is no clear villain and no discernible or "just" solution. This is reflected in the deadlocked jury when Orestes is brought to trial. Tragedies thereby demonstrate that our conceptions of justice are parochial, not universal, and are readily undermined by too unwavering a commitment to them.

An appreciation of tragedy can sensitize us to the downside of our views of the world and ethical commitments. It can make us wary of arguments that there is an obvious and legitimate course of action – indeed, only one legitimate course of action – and it should be patently obvious all what that is. The lack of readily discernible external evaluative criteria to adjudicate between competing conceptions of what is morally permissible, or indeed required, means that our conviction in the justness of our cause needs to be tempered with and the scope and depth of our tolerance expanded.

There is a crucial distinction to be made between denying the existence of standards of good and evil and right and acknowledging our limits and difficulties in discerning what these are. Tragedy teaches the latter without rejecting the former. It warns us that the unremitting pursuit of any one conception of justice is self-defeating. This insight has the potential to foster a more sophisticated treatment of international conflict. It might also help us better to understand why certain conflicts appear intractable, the dynamics by which they escalate, and the relative unwillingness of adversaries to compromise or at least act with restraint.

Tragedy is a vehicle to develop and teach ethics and to promote discussion about how they have the potential to foster a happier life. For the tragic poets, and for Plato, the first requirement of a happy life was to avoid becoming a slave of one's appetites or craving for recognition and status. Tragedy teaches the counterintuitive lesson that less is often more. At first blush, it seems illsuited for an age in which excess of every kind has become the norm. Rich people in rich Western societies give evidence of being happier than those of poor, non-Western ones, but wealth alone does not appear to produce that happiness.[31] When people measure their self-esteem by comparing what they have or have achieved to what others have or have done, they discover there are always people who have more and deserve it less. For this reason alone, the unrestrained pursuit of wealth, power, or status can be selfdefeating, as tragedy illustrates so effectively.

Notes

1. Thucydides, *The Landmark Thucydides: A Comprehensive Guide to the Peloponnesian War*, ed. Robert B. Strassler (New York: Free Press, 1996).

2. Richard Ned Lebow, *The Tragic Vision of Politics: Ethics, Interests, and Orders* (Cambridge: Cambridge University Press, 2003) and *A Cultural Theory of International Relations* (Cambridge: Cambridge University Press, 2008).

3. Toni Erskine and Richard Ned Lebow, "Understanding Tragedy and Understanding International Relations" and "Learning from Tragedy and Refocusing International Relations," in Erskine and Lebow, eds., *Tragedy and International Relations* (London: Palgrave-Macmillan, 2012), pp. 1–18, 195–217; Richard Ned Lebow, "Tragedy, Politics and Political Science," in Erskine and Lebow, *Tragedy and International Relations*, pp. 63–71.

4. Max Weber, "The Profession and Vocation of Politics," in Peter Lassman and Ronald Speirs, eds., *Weber: Political Writings* (Cambridge: Cambridge University Press, 1994), pp. 309–69, makes a similar plea.

5. Michael Oakeshott, *Religion, Politics, and the Moral Life*, ed. Tim Fuller (New Haven: Yale University Press, 1996), pp. 107–108.

6. Nicholas Rengger, "Tragedy or Skepticism? Defending the Anti-Pelagian Mind in World Politics," in Erskine and Lebow, *Tragedy and International Relations*, pp. 53–62, critiquing Mervyn Frost, "Tragedy, Ethics and International Relations," in Erskine and Lebow, eds., *Tragedy and International Relations*, pp. 21–43.

7. Lebow, "Tragedy, Politics, and Political Science."

8. Aristotle, *Poetics*, 1447a, in Jonathan Barnes, ed., *The Complete Works of Aristotle* (Princeton: Princeton University Press, 1984), 2 vols.

9. Ibid, 1453a.

10. Dennis J. Schmidt, *On Germans and Other Greeks: Tragedy and Ethical Life* (Bloomington: Indiana University Press, 2001), pp. 122–64; Frederick C. Beiser, *German Idealism: The Struggle Against Subjectivism, 1781–1801* (Cambridge: Harvard University Press, 2002), pp. 391–6; Richard Ned Lebow, *The Politics and Ethics of Identity* (Cambridge: Cambridge University Press, 2012), ch. 5.

11. Catherine Lu, "Tragedies and International Relations, in Erskine and Lebow," in Erskine and Lebow, eds., *Tragedy and International Relations*, pp. 158–71.

12. For a fuller elaboration of this argument, see Lebow, *Tragic Vision of Politics*, chs. 3–4 and *Reason and Cause* (Cambridge: Cambridge University Press, 2020), chs. 2–3.

13. Samuel Huntington, *The Clash of Civilizations and the Remaking of World Order* (New York: Simon & Schuster, 1996).
14. Salim Rashid, *The Clash of Civilizations? Asian Responses* (New York: Oxford University Press, 1997); Chiara Bottici and Benoît Challand, *The Myth of the Clash of Civilisations* (New York: Routledge, 2010); Tzvetan Todorov, *The Fear of Barbarians: Beyond the Clash of Civilizations* (Chicago: University of Chicago Press, 2010).
15. On the origins of this kind of conflict, see Gregory Henderson, Richard Ned Lebow, and John G. Stoessinger, *Divided Nations in a Divided World* (New York: David McKay, 1974).
16. Peter Euben, "The Tragedy of Tragedy," in Erskine and Lebow, *Tragedy and International Relations*, pp. 86–96.
17. Lebow, *Tragic Vision of Politics*; Erskine and Lebow, *Tragedy and International Relations*.
18. Frost, "Tragedy, Ethics, and International Relations."
19. Hans J. Morgenthau, *Scientific Man versus Power Politics* (Chicago: University of Chicago Press, 1965 [1946]), pp. 189, 209; Kamila Stullerova, "Tragedy and Political Theory: Progressivism Without an Ideal," in Erskine and Lebow, *Tragedy and International Relations*, pp. 112–28.
20. Irving L. Janis and Leon Mann, *Decision Making: A Psychological Analysis of Conflict, Choice, and Commitment* (New York: Free Press, 1977); Richard Ned Lebow, *Between Peace and War: The Nature of International Crisis* (Baltimore: Johns Hopkins University Press, 1981), chs. 4–5.
21. Frost, "Tragedy, Ethics, and International Relations."
22. James Mayall, "Tragedy, Progress and the International Order," in Erskine and Lebow, *Tragedy and International Relations*, pp. 44–52.
23. Thucydides, 5.85–113.
24. Lebow, *Tragic Vision of Politics*, ch. 3–4.
25. Lebow, "Tragedy, Politics and Political Science."
26. Chris Brown, "Tragic Choices and Contemporary International Political Theory," in Erskine and Lebow, *Tragedy and International Relations*, pp. 75–85.
27. See also Mayall, "Tragedy, Progress, and the International Order"; Richard Beardswotth, "Tragedy, World Politics, and Ethical Community," and Tracy Strong, "Nietzsche and Questions of Tragedy, Tyranny and International Relations," in Erskine and Lebow, *Tragedy and International Relations*, pp. 97–11, 144–57.
28. Richard Ned Lebow, *A Cultural Theory of International Relations* (Cambridge: Cambridge University Press, 2008), ch. 9, for an analysis of the Bush administration's motives.

29. Bob Woodward, *Plan of Attack* (New York: Simon & Schuster, 2004); Michael R. Gordon and Bernard E. Trainor, *Cobra II: The Inside Story of the Invasion and Occupation of Iraq* (New York: Pantheon, 2006); Michael Isakoff and David Corn, *Hubris: The Inside Story of Spin, Scandal, and the Selling of the Iraq War* (New York: Crown, 2006); Thomas E. Ricks, *Fiasco: The American Military Adventure in Iraq* (New York: Penguin, 2006).

30. Norman Podhoretz, *Why We are in Vietnam* (New York: Simon & Schuster, 1982); Harry G. Summers, Jr., *On Strategy: A Critical Analysis of the Vietnam War* (New York: Random House, 1982); Michael Lind, *Vietnam; The Necessary War* (New York: Free Press, 1999); Lewis Sorley, *The Unexamined Victories and the Tragedy of America's Final Years in Vietnam* (New York: Harcourt, 1999); Mark Moyer, *Triumph Forsaken: The Vietnam War, 1954–65* (New York: Cambridge University Press, 2006) argue that intervention was necessary and proper or that with different strategies the USA could have prevailed. Guenther Lewy, *America in Vietnam* (Oxford: Oxford University Press, 1980) maintains that we should feel no residual guilt about the war that we could have won.

31. Ronald F. Inglehart, *Cultural Evolution: People's Motivations Are Changing and Reshaping the World* (Cambridge: Cambridge University Press, 2018).

3 | *Crime and Punishment*

This chapter explores foreign policies that are unethical because they violate nomos. The most dramatic violations are wars of aggression, military interventions unauthorized by appropriate regional or international organizations, ethnic cleansing, and genocide. I devote my attention to wars and intervention since they are unambiguously international in character. For war, I rely in the first instance on a data set I put together of all wars since 1648 involving a great or rising power on both sides. I also use a second data set that Benjamin Valentino and I constructed of all wars since 1945. Interventions vary sufficiently in scope and transparency that it is difficult to put together a comprehensive data set around which any consensus will form. Many involve direct military action and are difficult to distinguish from wars.[1] Other interventions are on a small scale and difficult to trace and attribute. I accordingly reject any attempt at quantitative analysis and rely on a few case studies to make my point. Such an approach is of no use in attempting to establish the claim that policies in violation of accepted nomos are less successful than those that conform to it. But is does let me explore some of the reasons why this may be so.

My data set of twenty-six post-1945 wars indicates that the overwhelming majority of them failed to achieve their political goals. Those that did in the short-term (e.g., Soviet intervention in Afghanistan, the Anglo-American invasion of Iraq) were often counterproductive in the longer-term. In both these cases, and in others, foreign occupation was increasingly contested and costly and resulted in a loss of standing and influence for intervening states. In the few successful wars in the data set, initiators had the backing of appropriate regional or international organizations and were led multinational coalitions, as in the Persian Gulf War of 1991. Regional and international authorization and multilateral coalitions almost invariably compel initiators to moderate their goals to gain the support of other actors. This generally requires them to frame and justify their war aims with respect to respected international norms. One of the most important of those norms is that intervention be carried out for humanitarian reasons, not self-interested ones.[2]

The core claim of this chapter is that foreign policies that violate contemporary understandings of justice are less likely to succeed than those that do conform to them. The unambiguous policy lesson is that ethics does not stop at the water's edge but must become an integral component of foreign policy. Leaders need to ask themselves the extent to which their initiatives – and here I mean the ends that are sought as well as the means used to achieve them – are consistent with the understandings relevant foreign audiences have of acceptable international practices. Although this is a book about ethics and international relations the former makes only a shadow appearance in this chapter. Its focus is on violations of ethics and they remain in the background as the template against which this behavior is assessed.

Wars

Intimidation, coercion, and violence are ancient practices. Evidence of them precedes the beginning of historical records.[3] All empires and most states were constructed and maintained by multiple acts of violence, and many were deconstructed by the same means. Wars fought for purposes of expansion failed at least as often as they succeeded but winners nevertheless emerged. In many cases (e.g., Assyria, Babylon, the Moghuls, Spain), they, in turn, suffered the fate they had inflicted on others.

Modern warriors have a bad success rate. I constructed a data set of all wars fought since 1648 – the conventional starting date of the modern state system – in which at least one great or rising power fought on opposite sides.[4] The initiators of these wars lost slightly more than half of them. A fifty-fifty success rate is worse than it sounds because in almost all cases initiators had a choice of whether or not to initiate hostilities. If leaders were rational and conducted any kind of reasonable assessment of the risks involved in drawing their swords, we would expect a much higher rate of success. Even in a world of incomplete information, rational leaders ought to have a better-than-even chance of getting it right if they gather pertinent information, assess its implications, and preemption aside, only start wars only when they consider the likelihood of success to be high. The empirical record tells a different story.

Even more revealing are so-called "systemic" wars, conflicts that bring most or all of the great powers into conflict. There have been nine of these wars since 1672 (see Figure 3.1). Three of them were initiated by a dominant power, that is, by a great power that was generally recognized as more powerful than others. France was a dominant power from the mid-seventeenth century until the end of the Napoleonic Wars, and the United States has been the dominant power since 1918. Four wars were started by great powers, two in alliance with rising powers, and one by a rising power acting alone. Dominant and great powers are more powerful than other states and should have a greater chance of winning the wars that they start. However, all but one initiator of any of these systemic wars ended up the loser.

Since the Second World War, when the norm against territorial conquest has become increasingly robust, initiators of wars have been markedly less successful . Benjamin Valentino and I assembled a second data set, of all wars fought since 1945 (see Figure 3.2). We identified thirty-one interstate wars fought since 1945 that involved a minimum of 1,000 casualties. We found that only eight initiators (26 percent) achieved their wartime goals. If we relax our criterion for success and make it simply the defeat of their adversaries' armed forces the number of successful initiators rises to only ten (32 percent).[5]

WAR	INITIATOR	RESULT	CAUSE
Franco-Dutch (1672–1679)	D	I loses	ME
Grand Alliance (1688–97)	D	I loses	ME
Spanish Succession (1701–14)	D	I loses	ME
Austrian Succession (1740–48)	R	R wins	E
Seven Year's (1756–63)	R/D	I's lose	ME
French Revolutionary (1792–1815)	G/D	I's lose	multiple MFs
Crimean (1853–56)	G	I loses	ME
World War I (1914–18)	R/G	I's lose	ME/MF
World War II (1939–45)	G	I's lose	MF

D = dominant power; R = rising power; G = great power; I = initiator; ME = miscalculated escalation; E = escalation; MF = military failure; PF = erroneous calculations of adversarial resolve and domestic support

Figure 3.1 Systemic wars

WAR NAME	DATES	MILITARY VICTORY	ACHIEVES WAR AIMS
India-Pakistan (First Kashmir) SIDE A: India SIDE B: Pakistan	1947–1949	NO	NO
War of Israeli Independence (Israel vs. Palestine/Arab coalition) SIDE A: COALITION: Egypt (A1), Iraq (A2), Jordan (A3), Syria (A4) SIDE B: Israel	1948–1949	NO	NO
China-Tibet I SIDE A: China SIDE B: Tibet	1950	YES	YES
Korean SIDE A: COALITION: China (A1), North Korea (A2) SIDE B: USA	1949–1953	NO	NO
Russo-Hungarian SIDE A: Hungary SIDE B: Russia (Soviet Union)	1956	YES	YES
Sinai/Suez SIDE A: Egypt SIDE B: COALITION: Israel (B1), France (B2), UK (B3)	1956	YES	YES
Vietnam SIDE A: North Vietnam SIDE B: USA	1959–1975	NO	NO
Indo-Chinese SIDE A: China SIDE B: India	1962	YES	YES
Second Kashmir SIDE A: India SIDE B: Pakistan	1965	NO	NO
Six Day War SIDE A: COALITION:	1967	NO	NO

Figure 3.2 Post-1945 wars[7]

Egypt (A1), Iraq (A2), Syria (A3) SIDE B: Israel			
US vs. Cambodia	1971	NO	NO
Israeli-Egyptian (War of Attrition) SIDE A: Egypt SIDE B: Israel	1969–1970	NO	NO
Football (El Salvador vs. Honduras) SIDE A: El Salvador SIDE B: Honduras	1969	YES	YES
India-Pakistan (Bangladesh) SIDE A: India SIDE B: Pakistan	1971	YES	YES
Yom Kippur SIDE A: COALITION: Egypt (A1), Syria (A2) SIDE B: Israel	1973	NO	NO
Cyprus SIDE A: Greece SIDE B: Turkey	1974	YES	YES
Vietnamese-Cambodian SIDE A: Cambodia SIDE B: Vietnam	1977–79	YES	NO
Ethiopia-Somalia (Ogaden) SIDE A: COALITION: Cuba (A1), Ethiopia (A2) SIDE B: Somalia	1977–78	NO	NO
Ugandan-Tanzanian SIDE A: Tanzania SIDE B: Uganda	1978–79	NO	NO
First Sino-Vietnamese SIDE A: China SIDE B: Vietnam	1979	NO	NO
Iran-Iraq SIDE A: Iran SIDE B: Iraq	1980–88	NO	NO
Falklands/Malvinas War (UK vs. Argentina) SIDE A: Argentina SIDE B: UK	1982	NO	NO

Figure 3.2 (cont.)

Israel-Syria (Lebanon) SIDE A: Israel SIDE B: Syria	1982	NO	NO
Second Sino-Vietnamese SIDE A: China SIDE B: Vietnam	1987	NO	NO
Iraq-Kuwait War SIDE A: Iraq SIDE B: Kuwait/USA	1990	NO	NO
Democratic Republic of Congo vs. Rwanda/Uganda SIDE A: Democratic Republic of Congo SIDE B: COALITION: Rwanda (B1) and Uganda (B2)	1998–2003	YES	NO
Ethiopia-Eritrea SIDE A: Eritrea SIDE B: Ethiopia	1998–2000	NO	NO
Afghanistan (Taliban)-USA (Northern Alliance) SIDE A: Afghanistan SIDE B: USA	2001	YES	NO
Anglo-American Invasion of Iraq SIDE A: Iraq SIDE B: USA	2003	YES	NO
Russian incursion Into Georgia	2008	YES	YES
NATO Intervention in Libya	2011	YES	PARTIAL

Figure 3.2 (cont.)

"Win" generally has two accepted meanings. The first is military victory, which involves a corresponding defeat of the adversary. This outcome may be obvious in some situations but not in every case. Which side, if any, "won" the 1950–53 Chinese-American conflict in Korean or the 1969–70 War of Attrition between Egypt and Israel? The second, Clausewitzian understanding of victory, is determined with reference to the goals for which initiators resorted to force. Have they been achieved? Often, this requires some kind of military success, but not always. Egypt lost the 1973 October War against Israel but the costly nature of Israel's victory paved the way for a peace treaty and return of the Sinai Peninsula to Egypt. The war helped Egyptian president Anwar el-Sadat to achieve his overall strategic goal.[6] On other occasions, victory fails to attain the political goals for which the war was fought, as was the case with Israel's 1978 and 1982 invasions of Lebanon. There can also be a disconnect between the objectives of war and the underlying concerns that motivated it. In 2003, the USA invaded Iraq and overthrew Saddam Hussein, achieving its proclaimed political goal. However, the Bush administration then confronted an insurgency, growing military causalities, and loss of support at home and abroad. In retrospect, military victory appears to have undermined, not advanced, the security and material interests of the USA and its international standing. To avoid the problem of interpretation at multiple layers of analysis, I have chosen to use the most superficial definition of victory, the military one. Even with this relaxed criterion of success, initiators won less than one-third of the wars they began.

What explains this low rate of success? Case studies point to several generic causes, two of them having to do with policymaking. The first is motivated bias. Leaders facing a combination of strategic and domestic threats they believe can only be surmounted by war, or a challenge of adversary that raises the prospect of war, recognize that such challenges involve the risk of serious loss. To move confidently toward a decision to use force they must reduce this anxiety and most commonly do so by bolstering. They minimize or deny the risk associated with their policies, solicit supporting information and confirming judgments from subordinates. They may even rig intelligence agencies or reject out of hand warnings and other threatening information that their policies may, or are likely to, lead to disaster.[8]

Janice Stein, Jack Snyder and I documented this kind of motivated bias in a number of crisis decisions, including Germany, Austria-Hungary, and Russia in 1914; the US decision to cross the

38th parallel in Korea in 1950; India's "Forward Policy" that provoked its 1962 border war with China; Khrushchev's 1962 decision to deploy missiles in Cuba secretly; Israel's intelligence failure in October 1973; and Argentina's invasion of the Falklands/Malvinas in 1982.[9]

Minimal or self-serving risk assessment is also typical of actors seeking honor or standing, traditionally won by starting and winning wars. Rising powers have been especially risk accepting because they were so intent on increasing their standing. This was true of France under Louis XIV, Sweden under Charles XII, Prussia under its several eighteenth-century rulers, Russia under Peter and Catherine, and Germany in the late-nineteenth and early-twentieth century[10] Indeed, whenever honor and standing become central concerns, leaders are willing to accept considerable risks to avoid losses or make gains. Italy and Japan in the 1930s offer more evidence in support of this proposition. Hitler, Mussolini, and the Japanese military were willing to take the most extraordinary gambles. Hitler may have been idiosyncratic; he had the authority to impose his preferences on a military elite that wanted to act more cautiously. Mussolini lacked Hitler's authority, and his policies were more reflective of elite preferences.[11] In the Japanese case, Hideki Tojo, a general and prime minister during the Second World War was one of the key military leaders behind Japan's decision to attack Pearl Harbor in December 1941.[12] Tojo brushed aside objections with the insouciant but revealing remark that: "Sometimes people have to shut their eyes and take the plunge."[13]

Anger can have the same effect. It enters the picture when leaders believe they or their state has been slighted. Elsewhere, I document decisions for war (e.g., Germany and Austria in 1914, the Anglo-American invasion of Iraq in 2004) where anger, and a related a concern for honor, combined to produce rash and ill-considered initiatives.[14] Historical accounts indicate evidence for this phenomenon in Louis XIV's wars against the Netherlands and the Rhineland-Palatinate, the Wars of the Second and Third Coalitions and the Crimean War. Anger and the quest for honor or standing can combine to bring about decisions to use force with only minimal evaluation of the risks. Regardless of the possible causes of superficial risk assessment, the demonstrable fact that it is widespread helps explain some of the otherwise anomalous outcomes we observe. It also raises serious problems for rational theories of war.

Even good and careful policymaking can lead to catastrophe. As the ancient Greeks understood, human action can produce results diametrically opposed to those intended. One of the most famous oracular statements from Delphi was a typically ambiguous response to Croesus, King of Lydia, who was told that if he attacked the Persians, he would destroy a great empire. Buoyed up with this prophecy, he launched his campaign in 547 BCE and was defeated and dethroned by Cyrus of Persia.[15] Oedipus was also misled by a prophecy. Both these stories tap into fundamental and reinforcing insights about the social world. It is complex and opaque, making efforts to manipulate others in complex scenarios very risk exercises, but, for the same reason, make it easier to those who would do so to delude themselves about their likely success. Nowhere are both phenomena more evident than in the use of violence on a large scale.

There is another, equally fundamental explanation for the failure of war, and one that also applies to interventions. It has to do with justice and the expression it finds in norms.[16] As noted in the introduction, justice is a broader concept than norms. It can describe acts for which there are no norms or violate existing ones. Norms, and more generally speaking, nomos, in turn do not coincide perfectly with justice. There have always been norms that are considered unjust by many actors. Empire, conquest, slavery, racism, and special privileges for great powers were all deeply embedded practices that were enacted in accord with existing Western norms and justified by them. They offended many people – especially the conquered, but also citizens in metropoles – and, ultimately, there are enough of them to create new norms against slavery, colonialism, and conquest.[17] These practices are now considered unacceptable.

Consider the concept of hegemony, which is still contested. By hegemony, I mean the conquest and domination of enough other units to bring all the units under the direct or indirect rule of the conquering unit. Even before the beginning of the modern state system, efforts by any political unit to establish control over all the others were certain to meet some form of collective resistance.

Conquest was legitimate for many centuries, but not the kind of conquest that would end the de jure or de facto independence of other actors. This helps to explain the high failure rate of initiators of systemic wars. Deterrence and alliances did not prevent these wars for beginning – although they may have forestalled others that never happened – but they did prevent any political unit from achieving hegemony. Spain under Philip II, France under Louis XIV and Napoleon, and Germany under Kaiser Wilhelm and Adolf Hitler tried and failed. Failure resulted not only in defeat but in serious losses of territory and status.[18]

The problem of nomos is complicated by the existence of multiple norms, some resting on different principles of justice. The principle of equality would require equal representation and distribution of whatever actors considered important. The principle of fairness justifies giving more authority and rewards to those who do the most for the community. In domestic and foreign affairs these principles are frequently in competition and one or the other is invoked by actors in defense, or in challenge, of the status quo.[19] Occasionally, institutions or procedures are designed to take account of both principles, as is the United Nations. The General Assembly is based on the principle of equality with each member having one vote. The Security Council is constituted on the principal of fairness with only the great powers having permanent seats and the right of veto. The twentieth century witnessed a global shift in which equality gained appeal at the expense of fairness. Some existing practices lost their legitimacy and new ones arose.[20] For this and other reasons, norms are never stable, constantly open to challenge, and not infrequently violated by actors seeking to advance their power, wealth, and standing at the expense of others, or of the community as a whole.

Violations of justice at the expense of other actors are certain to raise hackles. Their anger reflects not only the judgment that this behavior is wrong but that they are threatened by it. People – and leaders of states – are sensitive to three kinds of threat: those affecting their security, material wellbeing, and honor and status. They value their independence and freedom of action as ends in their own right. Conquest or de facto domination clearly constitutes all these threats, and bids for hegemony have historically been perceived as such.

Norms change, but there is usually a lag time between shifts of opinion about what is right and wrong and the norm change. Sometimes, this involved the delegitimization of existing norms and the emergence of new ones, as it did with empire, conquest, slavery, racism. These changes are invariably contested, and often hotly. Such contestation is a sign that the regional or international community is divided. This division is likely to be mirrored within countries as well.[21] Norm evolution can undergo a phase transition when support reaches a certain level. This happened with slavery and decolonization, and also with the exchange or sale of territories and their peoples from one state to another. The strength of the last norm is evident in the nearly universal outrage at Donald Trump's suggestion in August 2019 that Denmark sell him Greenland.[22] Perhaps the most dramatic example is a domestic one: decriminalization and legal and social acceptance of homosexuality in Western countries, a transformation that occurred in record time.[23]

Change in norms helps to account for the astoundingly high failure rate of twentieth-century wars, especially in the post-1945 period (see Figure 3.2). In the course of the last century, conquest became unacceptable, both as a matter of public opinion and international law.[24] This shift in opinion hastened decolonization and brought opprobrium on states that conquered other ones or their territory. China successfully conquered Tibet but its occupation of that country is widely regarded as illegitimate. So too is Israel's occupation of the West Bank, even though it was the outcome of a war of aggression waged against it by its Arab neighbors. Russia successfully intervened in Hungary and Czechoslovakia to suppress non-communist regimes, but the governments it imposed never gained legitimacy, and communism in Eastern Europe collapsed like a pack of cards when Soviet General Secretary Mikhail Gorbachev announced he would no longer intervene to protect satellite governments.[25] Other wars of conquest failed, among them Egypt and Syria's attack on Israel, Uganda's attack on Tanzania, Argentina's invasion of the Falkland Islands, and Iraq's invasions of Iran and Kuwait. More recently, Russia occupied Crimea and other parts of Ukraine. It has been condemned by the USA and the European Union and made the object of costly sanctions.[26]

Conquest was traditionally how rising powers became accepted as great powers. Today, conquest – if it succeeds – makes states something of pariahs. The use of force without appropriate international support and authorization by regional organizations or the United Nations Security Council will lead to a precipitous decline in standing. This happened to the USA in the aftermath of its invasion of Iraq. Public opinion in Europe, extremely sympathetic to the USA after 9/11, reversed itself and came to consider it a greater threat to world peace than North Korea.[27] In Britain, the number of those with favorable opinions of the USA dropped from 83 percent in 2000 to 56 percent in 2006. In other countries, the USA underwent an even steeper decline.[28] In 2007, an opinion poll carried out for the BBC World Service in twenty-seven countries found that 51 percent of respondents regarded the USA negatively, a figure surpassed only by their negative evaluations of Iran (54) and Israel (56). North Korea was regarded negatively by 48 percent of the respondents.[29] This and later surveys indicate that the USA is perceived as acting against, not for, the interests of the international community. Whatever legitimacy its leadership once had has significantly eroded as publics around the world are particularly worried about the way in which the USA uses its military power.[30] Since the Iraq War, the USA has, in effect, undergone a shift in its international profile from a status quo to that of a revisionist power.[31]

Delegitimization of war, occupation, and conquest has important practical effects, the most significant of which is to encourage and legitimize local opposition. Palestinians have benefitted enormously from their exploitation of the norm against conquest, but so too, to varying degrees, did Afghanis, Iraqis, Muslim Kashmiris, and Tibetans. It is easier to start and maintain an insurgency when those involved believe they are doing the right thing, acting in a just way, and are supported by unbiased outsiders. This perception can, of course, can be as much a self-serving delusion as the belief by invaders that they were acting justly and in the name of international order.

Intervention

Intervention is a broader category than war, although almost invariably it also involves the use of force. Martha Finnemore describes intervention at the boundary between peace and war. It is a term used to describe infringements on the sovereignty of states "that are exceptional in some way."[32] James Rosenau suggests intervention seeks to change a country's "political authority structure" and by military means.[33] Finnemore dissents from efforts to impose a uniform definition on the grounds that understandings of intervention have changed significantly in the last 100 years. Intervention was not a term used in the nineteenth century. Force was used to change governments, sometimes without altering state boundaries, but it was called "war." What we label intervention was, nevertheless, common in the nineteenth century and often used to collect debts owned by individuals or states.[34] It decoupled the use of force from territorial conquest. Finnemore further notes that the focus of intervention has changed. Humanitarian intervention was formerly restricted to protecting white Christians. Now it is more likely to be to help nonwhite, non-Christian, minorities. States now also claim to be intervening to uphold regional or international orders, and according to "the Right to Protect," have a moral, if not legal responsibility to do so.[35]

Since 1945, there have been many more interventions than wars – if we use Rosenau's working definition of the use of force to bring about political but not territorial change. There are only twenty-six wars in my data set of post-1945 wars. However, the International Military Intervention data set identifies 1,114 cases for the years 1946 to 2005.[36] They include outright military intervention, peacekeeping, border and other territorial conflicts, cross-border rocket firing and shelling, air raids, naval and air bombardments and incursions, troop deployments, military and cross-border raids. Some of these categories overlap, and many of the cases stretch the meaning of intervention, in my opinion. It is nevertheless evident that many events that indisputably qualify as interventions cannot be considered wars. Examples include the 2005 collaborative peacekeeping effort of Australia, New Zealand, Papua New Guinea, Fiji, and Tonga in the Solomon Islands, NATO support for anti-Qaddafi forces in Libya in 2011, and the 2013 intervention of Rwandan forces in the Democratic Republic of the Congo in 2013 to put down local rebels.

The most prominent recent example of intervention is that of the Soviet Union in Ukraine, first to repatriate Crimea, and then to support pro-Russian rebels in territories bordering on Russia. The Crimean intervention was supported by 70 percent of Russians and a majority of the local population who self-identified as Russian.[37] It pitted two accepted international principles against one another: national self-determination and sovereignty. Nationalities have a recognized right to live under governments of their choosing but sovereignty generally trumps nationalism. The latter principle is dominant and almost inviolate. It may be breeched only in self-defense – and then in only limited circumstances – or for humanitarian reasons with the support of appropriate regional or international organizations.

Vladimir Putin and his supporters seek to restore Russia as a great power as far as possible. Toward this end, they have looked for opportunities to annex territories populated largely by Russians and expand their influence in the near abroad. They are willing to use force to do this, as they did in Georgia (2007–08), Crimea (2014), and Ukraine (2014–). These interventions appear to have had significant popular support and rebounded to Putin's domestic advantage.[38] The annexation of Crimea in February–March 2014 was facilitated by the Ukrainian revolution and the internal turmoil that followed. On February 27, Russian troops wearing masks and in uniforms with no identifying insignia occupied the Crimea parliament and other strategic sites across the region. They installed a pro-Russian government, which conducted referendum on the region's status, followed by a declaration of independence and incorporation into the Russian Federation, effective as of March 18, 2014.[39]

Non-Russian minorities – most notably Ukrainians and Tatars – opposed annexation and were quickly repressed. In March 2014, Human Rights Watch reported that pro-Ukrainian activists and journalists had been attacked, abducted, and tortured.[40] In May 2014, an "anti-extremist" amendment to Russia's criminal code made any call for the secession of Crimea a criminal offense punishable by a fine of 300,000 roubles or imprisonment of up to three years.[41]

International condemnation followed quickly. The G8 suspended Russia, cancelled its planned summit in Sochi, and imposed economic sanctions. The United Nations General Assembly rejected the Crimean annexation and adopted a nonbinding resolution affirming the "territorial integrity of Ukraine within its internationally recognised border." The United States announced sanctions against persons they deem to have assisted in the violation of Ukraine's sovereignty. The European Union suspended talks with Russia on economic and visa-related matters and imposed asset freezes, as did Japan. The Council of Europe expressed its full support for the territorial integrity and national unity of Ukraine.[42]

Western sanctions were quickly extended and seriously damaged the business interests of some of Russia's richest people. The Americans focused on freezing assets of the Russian political and economic leadership and Fitch and Standard & Poor downgraded Russia's credit standing. Russian banks warned of a sanctions-induced recession, capital outflows increased dramatically, and the value of Russian government-bond issues plummeted. Within six months of sanctions, Novatek, Russia's second-largest gas producer, lost $2.5 billion in market value, reducing the wealth of investors. Among them was Putin's close friend Gennady Timchenko, who had a 23 percent stake in the company. More severe sanctions were imposed after Russia's intervention in Ukraine.[43]

Russia also lost on the propaganda front. The country's standing dropped precipitously in the eyes of world public opinion. A 2017 BBC World Service Poll found that in the seventeen countries it surveyed, 49 percent of respondents held negative views of Russia. It is almost as unpopular as the USA, North Korea, Iran, and Israel.[44] All of these countries are perceived to have violated international norms. The Crimean annexation and subsequent support for insurgents in Ukraine arguably worsened its strategic position because NATO increased its spending and planning for possible defense of the Baltic countries and Poland.[45]

These examples offer evidence of the extent to which the concept of intervention has developed and undergone a normative evolution. In the imperial age, the term was hardly ever used but has since come to assume the meaning of the violation of a political unit's sovereignty. Most of the territories into which Europeans expanded were not recognized by them as sovereign states. There was a consensus among colonial powers that expansion of this kind was an entirely legitimate activity and even in the interest of "the natives." Between the wars intervention and conquest lost their legitimacy.[46] They acquired more odium in the post-Second

World War era as former colonies achieved their independence and came to constitute a majority of the members of the United Nations.

Those intervening always claimed to be acting selflessly, and occasionally were when great powers interceded in efforts to protect minority populations.[47] In the last decades of the twentieth century, building on the Genocide Convention and other developments in international law, intervention gained a new legitimacy and even legal standing. It came to be seen as upholding homos in certain circumstances, provided it was carried out for humanitarian ends and sanctioned by appropriate regional and international organizations.[48]

Andrea Talentino observes that "a permissive environment now seems to exist that legitimates intervention on normative grounds." This normative shift is significant enough that military intervention for humanitarian reasons might be considered "a defining characteristic of the modern international system."[49] It is most evident in the Responsibility to Protect (R2P), a global political commitment endorsed by member states of the United Nations at the 2005 World Summit. It authorizes intervention to prevent genocide, war crimes, ethnic cleansing and crimes against humanity.[50] Alex Bellamy, who has written extensively in support of R2P, makes the case that military intervention has the potential to end genocide.[51] He nevertheless acknowledges that states intervene only infrequently for this and other humanitarian goals despite their rhetorical and legal commitments. The overwhelming majority of interventions are still carried out for self-serving purposes and generally in violation of international norms and law.[52] Considerable opposition to humanitarian intervention continues to be voiced by conservatives and many realists.[53]

The overall success rate of intervention is much harder to assess than in the case of war. How do we measure the military or political success of a bombardment? Equally problematic are full-scale interventions. Immediate failures, including the US 1962 Bay of Pigs invasion of Cuba, or the 1992–95 UN intervention in Somalia, are relatively easy to assess. So, too, are some successes, such as the Turkish intervention in Cyprus in 1974 achieved its goal of preventing further ethnic cleansing of Turks by Greek Cypriot forces. Other interventions, perhaps most, lend themselves to divergent interpretations. Almost invariably, those in favor of intervention were likely to judge it successful, and those opposed to consider it a failure. The two sides start with different benchmarks and may turn to different evidence for support. US intervention in Chile is a case in point.

The Nixon administration denied any intervention in Chile but the 1975 Church Commission Report documents extensive and continuous covert American involvement between 1963 and 1973. The USA tried to influence the outcome of every election in this historically democratic country and was particularly opposed to socialist Salvador Allende, who won a narrow victory in the 1970 presidential election. President Nixon feared – quite unreasonably – that Chile could become "another Cuba," terminated most aid to the country, and then ordered the CIA to have its leader overthrown.[54] The CIA collaborated with Chilean generals toward this end, Allende was killed, and a military junta came to power. For the next seventeen years, they suppressed democracy and trade unions, ruled with an iron thumb, tortured and killed dissidents almost at random, and committed numerous other atrocities.[55] There are, nevertheless, those who defend both the coup and US policy. Jeanne Kirkpatrick argued at the time that it prevented communists from coming to power, and Milton Friedman would later contend that the generals – whose were advised by Chicago School economists – were to be applauded for ushering in an economic growth miracle.[56] Assessment is inescapably political and ideological.

Another source of differing assessments is the periodization that is used. A better case can sometimes be made by restricting evaluation to short-term consequences. A recent RAND study of American intervention is illustrative.[57] The researchers involved identified 492 objectives for 145 military interventions carried out from 1898 to 2016. They coded 63 percent of political objectives as meeting full success, and only 8 percent as having been unsuccessful. The study recognizes that intervention is becoming more difficult, although never considers the nomos- and justice-based explanation I posit for this change. Rather, it attributes it to expanding the political objectives of interveners. When it comes to individual cases, assessment is largely based on narrow technical criteria like military tactics and coordination.

The RAND study examines three cases in detail: the American occupation of Japan, the Cuban missile crisis, and the Iraq War.[58] The first two are prominent successes and reasonably coded as such. There is no recognition in the case of Cuba that hardline deterrence policies, attempts to assassinate Castro, and nuclear threats against the Soviet Union provided strong incentives to Khrushchev to secretly deploy the missiles that provoked the crisis.[59] In their magisterial study of the Cold War, Campbell Craig and Fredrik Logevall offer a parallel argument of the Berlin crisis of 1948–49. This crisis "was laid at the feet of the Soviet Union, even though it had been quietly triggered by American actions."[60] The coding of Iraq is nothing short of bizarre: three successes, four partial successes, and two no successes. It is worth examining in detail (see Figure 3.3).

Saddam was indeed removed from power, which was the principal objective of the invasion. The authors claim the WMD programs were neutralized, when, in fact, no such programs or weapons were ever found. They give a partial success to ending Iraq's support of terrorism. There is no evidence that Saddam ever supported terrorism; the claim that he did was an undocumented assertion of Vice President Dick Cheney made to mobilize public support for the

Remove Saddam Hussein from power	Success
Neutralize WMD Programs	Success
End alleged support for terrorism	Some success
Create a prosperous free Iraq	No success
Create a united, secure Iraq	No success
Build Iraqi Institutions	Some success
Make full partner in War on Terror	Some success
Make Iraq at peace with neighbors	Some success
Integrate Iraq into world community	Some success[61]

Figure 3.3 Operation Iraqi Freedom 2003–

invasion.[62] The authors admit that years of occupation have not produced a free or secure Iraq. They nevertheless contend that the Americans and their supporters have had some success in building Iraqi institutions, making the country a full partner in the War on Terror, bringing peace with neighbors, and integrating it into the world community. These judgments fly in the face of considerable empirical evidence and neutral judgments. Iraq remains fragmented, makes no contribution to fighting terrorism in the region, is hardly at peace with its neighbors, and is in no way integrated into the world community. The authors acknowledge problems with the intervention, attributing the only partial successes they describe to lack of host nation support, sectarian conflict, inadequate Congressional funding, poor interagency coordination, interference by Iran, and failures in US decisionmaking and planning.

There is absolutely no mention in the study of just how much the wars in Iraq and Afghanistan have cost taxpayers. By 2017, this came to a total of $2.4 trillion, and expenditure continue with no cutoff in sight. The actual costs are higher because some of these expenses were financed with borrowed money. Neither is there any consideration of all the destabilizing consequences of American intervention in Afghanistan and Iraq for these countries and the Middle East as a whole. Arguably, the Iraq insurrection, the rise and temporary spread of ISIS, the extension of Iranian influence into Iraq, the increase of terrorism directed against the USA and other Western countries, and growing US military involvement in Yemen and elsewhere would not have happened in the absence of these interventions. Finally, there is no accounting of the loss of lives – local and American – due to this US intervention. The Brown University Costs of War Project estimated that by November 2018 that there were 7,000 US military deaths, 788 contractor deaths, 1,464 allied troop deaths, 363 journalists, and 566 NGO and humanitarian aid worker deaths.[63] The Iraq Body Count project documents 288,000 violent Iraqi deaths through February 2019.[64] The 2007 Opinion Research Business survey estimated as many as 1.2 million violent deaths as of August 2007.[65] It is not known how many more people died, were wounded, or raped in follow-on conflicts.

What is so striking about this study is its narrow framework of analysis. It is not idiosyncratic but reflects, I believe, a wider understanding within the American national security establishment. It encourages the illusion that intervention is militarily and politically productive. It is only possible to come to this conclusion by refusing to engage its human and economic costs, wider and longer-term political consequences, and the security implications for the USA and countries in the targeted region.

The most obvious costs are to local people. Some interventions are close to bloodless, as were the American intervention in Grenada and the Soviet intervention in Czechoslovakia. Many lead to death and destruction on a large scale. This was true of American interventions in Indochina, Afghanistan, and Iraq, of the Soviet Union in Afghanistan, and Russia in Chechnya, and Syria. As I write, the Saudi intervention in Yemen, furtively but extensively backed by the USA is wreaking havoc in that country.[66]

Foreign interventions, and especially those that impose severe human costs on the local population, arouse deep resentment. They provoke the kind of hatred that makes people willing to risk their lives to oppose foreign occupations. This was evident in Vietnam and Iraq, among other places. Foreign intervention destabilizes local politics making it difficult to sustain or put in place a government responsive to the wishes of the occupier. Americans and Soviets confronted this problem in Vietnam, Laos, Cambodia, Afghanistan, Chechnya, and Iraq. Insurrections increase the human and economic costs of occupation and can result in stalemates – Iraq and Afghanistan for the Americans – or ultimate defeat, as it did for the Soviet Union in Afghanistan and the Americans in Indochina.

None of these interventions achieved its political goals, and in most cases they were seriously damaging to the intervener for reasons that its leaders never considered at the time. Defeat in Indochina led to a serious loss of American prestige and influence in the region, if not globally. It transformed a largely positive image of the USA in many parts of the world, but especially in Europe, into a largely negative one. The Anglo-French intervention in Egypt in 1956 resulted in a humiliating withdrawal, collapse of both governments, and a sharp decline in their influence in the Middle East. Egyptian reoccupation of the Sinai in 1967 triggered off the Six Day War, resulting in a catastrophic military defeat for Egypt. Israel's partial occupation of Lebanon in 1978 further destabilized that country, strengthened extremist elements within it, thereby creating a more serious threat to Israel's northern border. China's invasion of Vietnam demonstrated that the Soviet Union could not protect its ally, but poisoned relations with its neighbor.

Several of these interventions had serious negative consequences at home. The Suez intervention has already been mentioned. The stalemate and withdrawal from Afghanistan contributed to the loss of legitimacy of the communist regime in the Soviet Union, and the Soviet withdrawal was the first step toward the collapse of the regime and breakup of the country. The prolonged American intervention in Indochina produced great domestic unrest, leading to the resignation of President Lyndon Johnson and defeat of Democratic candidate Hubert Humphrey by Republican Richard Nixon. Opposition to Vietnam and the civil rights movement were catalysts for a social revolution that had far-reaching consequences that were anathema to those in power.[67]

Interventions may also have follow-on effects for the region that work against the interests of the intervening state or states. Nowhere is this clearer than in the Anglo-American invasion of Iraq. It resulted in greater Iranian influence, the rise of ISIS, and was a catalyst for the Syrian civil war. The net effect has been to reduce significantly American influence in the region while giving rise to new threats to American security. The most dramatic of these was the rise of ISIS, but there is also the rise of Islamic militancy elsewhere in the Middle East and further afield.[68]

In this day and age, when the horrors of interventions are immediately filmed and photographed, posted on social media, broadcast on television, and published in newspapers, there is no hiding them from public gaze. Consider the political and reputational effects of the Serbian siege of Sarajevo, pictures of torture and humiliation of insurgents in the Abu Ghraib by American soldiers, or the barrel bombing of civilians in Syria. Daily news coverage of the slaughter of civilians in Sarajevo by shelling and snipers generated enormous public pressure in the USA and Western Europe for intervention in the Yugoslav civil war.[69] NATO intervention, although half-hearted at best, compelled a Serbian retreat from the territory it sought to incorporate. Pictures of Abu Ghraib and those of American soldiers burning a copy of the Koran went viral and damaged American standing while providing incentives for Iraqis to join or support the resistance.[70] It provided Islamic fundamentalists with seeming evidence in support of their attempt to define the interventions in Afghanistan and Iraq as anti-Muslim crusades. And, ultimately, it helped to create ISIS.[71]

Abu Ghraib and civilian casualties from drone attacks were self-inflicted damage. Adversaries – states and non-state actors alike – can set what Mervyn Frost and I call ethical traps. They also involve military action, or at least, violence in some form. Their goal is not to defeat the other's side's military but to secure political advantages and leverage. By goading an adversary into overreacting and acting in a manner inconsistent with the foundational or proclaimed values those who set these traps attempt in the first instance to undermine domestic support for the perpetrator. They may also garner the support of third parties, putting more pressure on the target actor to back off or reach, some kind of accommodation, or at the very least, suffer a loss in standing.[72] State that fall into ethical traps can lose legitimacy, influence, and power,

Ethical traps are a particularly salient component of asymmetrical warfare, but this has not been satisfactorily illustrated in the literature. Frost and I document four examples of successful ethical trapping: in the American colonies, Spain, Northern Ireland, and, more recently, Hamas in Gaza. We explore two ethical traps that were set, but not sprung: the 2008 terrorist attacks in Mumbai and efforts by ISIS to use beheadings and other atrocities to entice the USA and other Western powers to commit ground forces to the conflict in Syria. We contend that ethical traps are more likely in the future because the evolution of international norms over the course of the postwar era has held states accountable to a higher standard of conduct than before. The spread of media and social media has also facilitated documentation and publicity of violations.[73]

My analysis is not complete without considering opportunity costs. What if the USA had not intervened in Indochina, Afghanistan, and Iraq? How else might this vast sum of money have been spent? How could it have benefitted the economy in a productive way and perhaps have improved internal security by encouraging employment and reducing drug dependency, crime, and other social problems? Consider a second counterfactual: suppose that the USA had followed its European allies in cutting back on military spending in the post-Cold War era, rather than dramatically increasing it? What if it had used this money to fund education, scientific research, the creation and maintenance of infrastructure, and the beefing up and enforcement of rules governing banking, investment, and tax collection? This kind of outlay would almost certainly would have promoted a more robust and innovative economy, avoided the banking crisis and, with it, the most recent recession. It would also reduce the federal deficit and avoided costly loans from China. A stronger and more independent American economy would have made the USA a more powerful arbiter of international economic issues and made others more willing to accept its leadership. So, too, would have restraint in dealing with Afghanistan and Iraq.

Similar counterfactual arguments can be made about 1978 and 1982 Israeli interventions in Lebanon, Soviet intervention in Afghanistan, and NATO intervention in Libya. Israel responded to repeated cross-border attacks by the Palestine Liberation Organization (PLO) against civilian settlements in the north. Outrage following Israel's role in the Christian Lebanese Phalangist militia's massacres of Shi'a Muslims at the Sabra and Shatila refugee camps. Israeli disillusionment with the war would compel a gradual and costly withdrawal from Beirut to the areas claimed by the self-proclaimed Free Lebanon State in southern Lebanon. After Israeli forces withdrew from most of Lebanon, the War of the Camps broke out between different Lebanese factions. Shi'a militant groups began a low-intensity guerrilla war over the Israeli occupation of southern Lebanon, leading to fifteen years of low-scale armed conflict. The Lebanese Civil War would continue until 1990, when Syria established its dominance in the country. Heavy Israeli casualties, alleged disinformation propagated by the Israeli government and military, and lack of clear goals led to increasing disenchantment among Israelis. Israel's northern border ended up even less secure.[74] Non-intervention in Lebanon would like have proved more beneficial to Israeli security.

NATO's intervention in Libya was conceived as a humanitarian operation that would remove an oppressive dictator from power, free the Libyan people from his grip, and enhance security in the southern Mediterranean. In practice, it accomplished only the first objective. Qaddafi was thought to be on the verge of committing massive violence against civilians in the Libyan city of Benghazi where the uprising against him had begun. President Obama insisted that: "We knew that if we waited one more day, Benghazi – a city nearly the size of Charlotte – could suffer a massacre that would have reverberated across the region and stained the conscience of the world,"[75] On March 21, 2011, with the backing of the UN Security Council, the United States and other NATO countries established a no-fly zone over Libya and started bombing Qaddafi's forces. Seven months later, in after an extended military campaign, rebel forces, with extensive NATO support, were in control of the country and had killed Qaddafi.[76]

The Libyan intervention was initially hailed as a huge success by President Obama and representatives of the national security establishment.[77] In retrospect, it is actually more accurately characterized as a disaster. Libya did not evolve into a democracy, but has become a failed state. Violent deaths and other human rights abuses are arguably greater than they were under Qaddafi. Libya is a safe haven for militias affiliated with both al-Qaeda and the Islamic State of Iraq and al-Sham (ISIS). Libyan refugees, and those from Syria, created a political crisis in Europe something close to an existential threat for the EU. Some people think the Libyan uprising was a model for its Syrian counterpart, and, if so, then the refugee crisis and its successful exploitation by the right in Europe are ultimately traceable to intervention in Libya. The civil war in Libya had negative repercussions elsewhere in Africa, most notably in Mali. Developments in Libya since the intervention have also done much to discredit the concept of the "responsibility to protect." It will be correspondingly harder in the future to mobilize great power support for humanitarian intervention.[78]

Some of the ex post facto analysis of what went wrong is ideologically driven. Those who favor humanitarian intervention point to bad intelligence to explain interventions that did not work out as planned. Gareth Evans, Chief Executive Officer of the Brussels-based International Crisis Group from 2000 to 2009, asserts:

The problem with the Libyan case was not the original decision by the Security Council in March 2011 to authorize coercive military force, made in the context of almost universally held fears of an imminent massacre by Gaddafi forces marching on Benghazi: there was no opposition to that resolution, it was immediately successfully implemented, and it was widely hailed at the time – including by me – as the coming of age of R2P, demonstrating that with quick and robust collective action, the horrors of Rwanda and Srebrenica could indeed be made a thing of the past.[79]

In the United Kingdom, the House of Commons' Foreign Affairs Committee concluded that the government "failed to identify that the threat to civilians was overstated and that the rebels included a significant Islamist element." They found no evidence that Qaddafi was planning to massacre civilians, and that reports to the contrary had been propagated by rebels and believed by Western governments.[80]

Opponents of humanitarian intervention usually self-identify as realists and argue that it is not only risky but has little or nothing to do with national interests. The more extreme adherents of this position deny that non-intervention involves any trade-offs by downplaying or dismissing claims of humanitarian emergency. Alan J. Kuperman offers a rosy scenario of this kind about Libya, insisting that: "[T]here was a better policy available – not intervening at all, because peaceful Libyan civilians were not actually being targeted. Had the United States and its allies followed that course, they could have spared Libya from the resulting chaos and given it a chance of progress under Qaddafi's chosen successor: his relatively liberal, Western-educated son Saif al-Islam." There may or may not have been a humanitarian emergency, but it is simply untrue that Saif al-Islam was a liberal or would have been any less cruel and authoritarian than his father once in power.

Richard K. Betts offers a more nuanced argument. He is properly critical of the deeply entrenched belief that intervention should be limited and impartial in the belief that support for any contestants in a local struggle undermines the legitimacy and effectiveness of outside involvement. This belief originates with humanitarian organizations such as the Red Cross. An Olympian perspective like this "has the ring of prudence, fairness, and restraint." It makes sense in some UN peacekeeping operations where foreign forces are not to make peace but to monitor and perhaps enforce a ceasefire accepted by warring parties. It is "a destructive misconception" when it guides entry into a territory where competing forces are still at war and believe they have more to gain by continuing fighting. Impartial intervention can only promote civil or interstate war when the outside forces intervene on a massive scale, outgun and overawe warring parties and impose a peace settlement. Limited intervention can only end wars if outside forces takes sides, shift the local balance of power, and enable one side to gain victory. NATO intervention was enough to keep any of the warring local factions from defeating the others, but not enough to make them stop trying to become dominant. The attempt to intervene on the cheap has been responsible for the failures of the UN and the US in Bosnia, Somalia, and Haiti.[81]

Lessons

Unfortunately, the Libyan experience appears to have taught many leaders that humanitarian intervention is a trap to be avoided. The more justifiable lesson should be that it is only possible in some contexts and is rarely successful on the cheap. Ironically, repeated failures of more self-interested interventions give no evidence of making leaders more cautious. The wrong lessons have been learned, and this is largely because of the worldviews of the "learners."

There has nevertheless been change of a positive kind. Conquest and other uses of force not sanctioned by international organizations now have the opposite effect. Their initiators lose status internationally rather than gaining it.[82] Countries claiming higher status now do so on the basis of wealth, economic equality, and high levels of foreign aid, as do the Scandinavian countries, Canada, the European Community, Japan, and South Korea. Canada and Scandinavia also claim status on the basis of the efforts to reduce conflict through mediation, go-between diplomacy, sponsorship of agreements and treaties, like those to ban landmines, as well as participation in peacekeeping missions. The UN Charter recognized the USA, the Soviet Union, China, France, and the United Kingdom as permanent members of the Security Council. Brazil, Germany, India, and Japan have sought membership in recent years on the basis of their wealth, support for the

UN – indeed, Japan and Germany are two of the top three funders of the organization – and the need to have representatives from different regions of the world.[83] Success in becoming a great power depends on fulfilling the conditions other great powers consider essential. These markers have changed over the centuries, and those states seeking permanent Security Council seats have attempted to redefine them in ways supportive of their respective claims. The five great powers have shown no willingness to enlarge their circle, so much of the effort of would-be great powers is directed at third parties in an effort to bring indirect pressure on the Security Council and mobilize necessary backing in the General Assembly.

For almost thirty years the BBC World Service has been conducting an annual country ratings poll in which people around the world are asked their impressions of sixteen countries and the European Union. Canada, Japan, Germany, and the European Union consistently receive the highest rankings as the most respected and admired countries, with between 54 and 60 percent of respondents evaluating them positively.[84] The USA, North Korea, Iran, Israel, and, more recently, Russia, are consistently the most unpopular countries[85]

Negative views of the USA have steadily increased in the majority of countries surveyed in the latest global country poll for the BBC World Service. The Country Ratings Poll was conducted by GlobeScan/PPC among 18,000 people in nineteen countries between December 2016 and April 2017. It asked respondents to evaluate sixteen countries and the EU on whether their influence in the world is "mostly positive" or "mostly negative." In the course of three decades of polling, the biggest drops were in the Bush administration following the invasions of Afghanistan and Iraq and in the Trump administration. Since Trump took office there were double-digit increases in negative views of the USA, rising to majorities among NATO allies: the UK (up from 42 to 64 percent), Spain (44 to 67 percent), France (41 to 56 percent), and Turkey (36 to 64 percent). Negative opinion also rose sharply in Latin American and Russia. In the last, negative views of the USA increased from 55 to 64 percent. Between 2014 and 2017, negative views of USA influence in the world rose by six points to nearly half (49 percent), while positive views dropped by five points to about one- third (34 percent). The USA showed the most substantial decline in ratings out of all the countries polled in 2017.[86]

In the ranking of favorably viewed nations, Canada and Germany are followed by Japan and France. On average, Canada is now ranked first in terms of the perceived positive influence, ahead of Germany (which stands at 59 percent, up by one point).[87] Positive public opinion rankings are not the same thing as influence but they are related, albeit in complicated ways. My goal here is not to elaborate this connection but to illustrate the nature of the reversal that has occurred in international relations. This is attributable to a fundamental shift in values, most markedly affecting the use of force and conquest. They have both lost their legitimacy and are now considered unethical behaviors. Powerful states can still occupy other states or disputed territories but the imposition and maintenance of their rule has become increasingly difficult. It is not only nationalism that is responsible for this situation but loss of legitimacy. It inspires anger and local opposition, which often gains at least moral support from outside parties. States that intervene without the support of appropriate regional and international organizations can now suffer two kinds of cost: opposition on the ground and international sanctions. Whatever they gain in the short term may be offset in the longer term.

The core claim of this chapter is that foreign policies that violate contemporary understandings of justice are less likely to succeed than those that conform to them. I have attempted to support my argument with evidence of just how unsuccessful war and intervention have become in the postwar world. I have also offered reasons for why this is so. The clear policy lesson is that ethics does not stop at the water's edge but must become an integral component of foreign policy decisionmaking. Leaders need to ask themselves the extent to which their initiatives – and here I mean the ends sought and the means used – are in accord with the understandings of justice and accepted practices of relevant foreign audiences. I am not suggesting that all policy should by fiat conform to these understandings. They are sometimes ambiguous or controversial, as certain liberal Western values are in Africa, the Middle East, and Asia. Leaders nevertheless need to take them into account and recognize the likely costs of ignoring or violating them.

Notes

1. Martha Finnemore, *The Purpose of Intervention: Changing Beliefs About the Use of Force* (Ithaca: Cornell University Press, 2003), pp. 7–11, for a good discussion of how difficult it is to define intervention and how this category bleeds into that of war.
2. Ibid, pp. 53–84.
3. Lawrence H. Keeley, *War Before Civilization: the Myth of the Peaceful Savage* (Oxford: Oxford University Press, 1996).
4. Richard Ned Lebow, *Why Nations Fight: The Past and Future of War* (Cambridge: Cambridge University Press, 2010), ch. 4 and Appendix.
5. Ibid, ch. 4.
6. Janice Gross Stein, "Calculation, Miscalculation, and Conventional Deterrence 1: The View from Cairo," in Robert Jervis, Richard Ned Lebow and Janice Gross Stein, *Psychology and Deterrence* (Baltimore: Johns Hopkins University Press, 1984), pp. 34–59.
7. Prepared by Benjamin Valentino and the author, 2012.
8. Irving L. Janis and Leon Mann, *Decision-Making: A Psychological Model of Conflict, Choice, and Commitment.* New York: Free Press, 1977), pp. 57–8, 197–233.
9. Richard Ned Lebow, *Between Peace and War: The Nature of International Crisis* (Baltimore: Johns Hopkins University Press, 1981); Jervis, Lebow, and Stein, *Psychology and Deterrence*; Richard Ned Lebow and Janice Gross Stein, *We All Lost the Cold War* (Princeton: Princeton University Press, 1994).
10. Lebow, *Cultural Theory of International Relations*, chs. 6–8.
11. Ibid, ch. 8 for discussion and citations.
12. Ian Nish, *Japan's Struggle with Internationalism* (London: Athlone, 1992); Gilbert Rozman, "Japan's Quest for Great Power Identity," *Orbis*, 46, 1 (2002): 73–91; Richard Storry, *Double Patriots: A Study of Japanese Nationalism* (Boston: Houghton- Mifflin, 1957); Dorothy Borg and Shumpei Okamoto, eds., *Pearl Harbor as History* (New York: Columbia University Press, 1973); Toshio Shiratori, *Kokusai Nihon no chii* [The Status of Japan in the World], quoted in Chihiro Hosoya, "Retrogression in Japan's Foreign Policy Decision-Making Process," in James W. Morley, ed., *Dilemma of Growth in Prewar Japan* (Princeton: Princeton University Press, 1971), pp. 81–105.
13. Konoe Fumumaro, *Ushinawareshi Seiji*, p. 131, quoted in Masao Maruyama, *Thought and Behavior in Modern Japanese Politics* (New York: Oxford University Press, 1966), p. 85.
14. Richard Ned Lebow, *A Cultural Theory of International Relations* (Cambridge: Cambridge University Press, 2008), chs. 7 and 9.

15. Herodotus, *The Histories*, rev. ed. (London: Penguin, 2003), 1.53–77.

16. Thomas Risse, Stephen C. Ropp, and Kathryn Sikkink, eds., *The Power of Human Rights: International Norms and Domestic Change* (Cambridge: Cambridge University Press, 1999) and *The Persistent Power of Human Rights: From Commitment to Compliance* (Cambridge: Cambridge University Press, 2013).

17. J. R. Oldfield, *Transatlantic Abolitionism in the Age of Revolution: An International History of Anti-Slavery, c.1787–1820* (Cambridge: Cambridge University Press, 2013); Richard Price, *The Chemical Weapons Taboo* (Ithaca: Cornell University Press, 1997); Nina Tannenwald, *The Nuclear Taboo: The United States and the Non-Use of Nuclear Weapons Since 1945* (New York: Cambridge University Press, 2007); T. V. Paul, *The Tradition of Non-Use of Nuclear Weapons* (Stanford: Stanford University Press, 2009); Bass, *Freedom's Battle*; Barnett, *Empire of Humanity: A History of Humanitarianism* (Ithaca: Cornell University Press, 2013); Leslie Bethell, *The Abolition of the Brazilian Slave Trade* (Cambridge: Cambridge University Press, 1970).

18. Lebow, *Why Nations Fight*, ch. 4, for more evidence and discussion.

19. Richard Ned Lebow, *The Rise and Fall of Political Orders* (Cambridge: Cambridge University Press, 2018), ch. 3, for further elaboration of these principles.

20. Richard Ned Lebow, *National Identifications and International Relations* (Cambridge: Cambridge University Press, 2016), ch. 4, for more analysis.

21. For the example of apartheid, see Audie Klotz, *Norms in International Regimes: The Struggle Against Apartheid* (Ithaca: Cornell University Press, 1995).

22. Editorial Board, "Trump, Greenland, Denmark. Is This Real Life?," *New York Times*, August 21, 2019, www.nytimes.com/2019/08/21/opinion/trump-greenland.html?searchResultPosition=1; Martin Selsoe Sorensen, "In Denmark, Bewilderment and Anger Over Trump's Canceled Visit," *New York Times*, August 21, 2019, www.nytimes.com/2019/08/21/world/europe/greenland-denmark-trump.html?searchResultPosition=1 (accessed August 22, 2019).

23. Linda Hirschman, *Victory: The Triumphant Gay Revolution* (New York: HarperCollins, 2012); Lilian Faderman, *The Gay Revolution: The Story of the Struggle* (New York: Simon & Schuster, 2015).

24. Mark W. Zacher, "The Territorial Integrity Norm: International Boundaries and the Use of Force," *International Organization* 55, 2 (2001): 215–250; Dan Altman, "The Evolution of Territorial Conquest,"

paper presented at the annual meeting of the International Studies Association, San Francisco, April 2018; Sharon Korman, *The Right of Conquest: The Acquisition of Territory by Force in International Law and Practice* (New York: Oxford University Press, 1996).

25. Jacques Lévesque, *The Enigma of 1989: The USSR and the Liberation of Eastern Europe*, trans. K. Martin (Berkeley: University of California Press, 1997).

26. See references on Crimea in discussion below on intervention.

27. BBC News, March 18, 2003, http://news.bbc.co.uk/2/hi/americas/286 2343.stm (accessed May 20, 2013).

28. The Pew Global Attitudes Project, "15-Nation Pew Global Attitudes Survey," release date June 13, 2006. A series of subsequent Pew surveys reflect this view as a continuing theme.

29. *The Age* (Melbourne), March 6, 2007, p. 7.

30. Pew Survey, "Obama More Popular Abroad Than At Home, Global Image of US Continues to Benefit," June 17, 2011, www.pewglobal. org/2010/06/17/obama-more-popular-abroad-than-at-home/ (accessed September 26, 2011); Pew Research Global Attitudes Project, "Global Opinion of Obama Slips, International Policies Faulted," June 13, 2012, www.pewglobal.org/2012/06/13/global-opi nion-of-obama-slips-international-policies-faulted/ (accessed January 28, 2013).

31. Pew Research Global Attitudes Project, "Global Public Opinion in the Bush Year (2001–2008), December 18, 2008, www.pewglobal.org/20 08/12/18/global-public-opinion-in-the-bush-years-2001-2008/ (accessed November 7, 2013).

32. Finnemore, *The Purpose of Intervention*, pp. 7–9. Also, Cynthia Weber, *Simulating Sovereignty: Intervention, the State, and Symbolic Exchange* (New York: Cambridge University Press, 1995).

33. James Rosenau, "The Concept of Intervention," *Journal of International Affairs*, 22, 2 (1968), pp. 165–76.

34. Finnemore, The Purpose of Intervention, pp. 1–5, 24–51; Chris Reus-Smit, *Moral Purpose of the State: Culture, Social Identity, and Institutional Rationality in International Relations* (Princeton: Princeton University Press, 1999), pp. 140–45, attributes the delegitimization to the Hague Peace Conference of 1899 and the legalization of the problem of debt collection.

35. Finnemore, *The Purpose of Intervention*, pp. 8–11, 52–84. Gareth Evans and Mohamed Sahnoun, "The Responsibility to Protect," *Foreign Affairs* 81 (November/December 2002): 99–110; David Luban, "Just War and Human Rights," *Philosophy and Public Affairs*, 9, 2 (1980), pp. 160–81; Terry Nardin, "The Moral Basis of Humanitarian Intervention," *Ethics*

and International Affairs, 16, 1 (2002), pp. 1–20; Rajan Menon, *The Conceit of Humanitarian Intervention* (New York: Oxford University Press, 2016) and "R2P: It's Fatally Flawed," *American Interest*, 8, 6 (2013), pp. 6–16.

36. Department of Political Science, Kansas State University, *The International Military Intervention DataCollection, 2010*, www.k-state .edu/polsci/intervention/ (accessed April 2, 2019).

37. Mike Eckel, "Poll: Majority of Russians Support Crimea Annexation, But Worry About Economic Effects," *Radio Free Europe*, April 3, 2019, www.rferl.org/a/poll-majority-of-russians-su pport-crimea-annexation-but-worry-about-economic-effects/298595 70.html; Steve Pifer, "Five years after Crimea's illegal annexation, the issue is no closer to resolution," *Brookings*, March 18, 2019, www.brookings.edu/blog/order-from-chaos/2019/03/18/five-years-af ter-crimeas-illegal-annexation-the-issue-is-no-closer-to-resolution/ (both accessed June 28, 2019). According to Pifer, referendum unsurprisingly produced a Soviet-style result: 97 percent allegedly voted to join Russia with a turnout of 83 percent. True referendum, fairly conducted, might have shown a significant number of Crimean voters in favor of joining Russia. Some 60 percent were ethnic Russians, and many might have concluded their economic situation would be better as a part Russia.

38. Angela Stent, *Putin's World: Russia Against the West and with the Rest* (New York: Twelve, 2019); Andrew Bowen, "Coercive Diplomacy and the Donbas: Explaining Russian Strategy in Eastern Ukraine," *Journal of Strategic Studies* 42, 3–4 (2017), pp. 312–43; Gerard Toal *Near Abroad: Russia, the West, and the Contest over the Caucasus* (Oxford: Oxford University Press, 2017); Robert Legvold, *Russian Foreign Policy in the Twenty-First Century and the Shadow of the Past* (New York: Columbia University Press, 2013).

39. Alissa de Carbonnel, "RPT Insight – How the Separatists Delivered Crimea to Moscow," *Reuters*, March 18, 2014, https://in.reuters.c om/article/ukraine-crisis-russia-aksyonov-idINL6N0M93A H20140313; Ilya Somin, "Russian Government Agency Reveals Fraudulent Nature of the Crimean Referendum Results," *Washington Post*, May 6, 2014, p. 1. Fred Dews, "NATO Secretary-General: Russia's Annexation of Crime," *Brookings Now*, March 19, 2014, www.brookings.edu/blog/brookings-now/2 014/03/19/nato-secretary-general-russias-annexation-of-crimea-is-ill egal-and-illegitimate/ (both accessed April 20, 2019); Katri Pynnöniemi and András Rácz, eds., *Fog of Falsehood: Russian*

Strategy of Deception and the Conflict in Ukraine. FIIA Report, 45 (Helsinki: Finnish Institute of International Affairs, 2016).

40. "Crimea: Attacks, 'Disappearances' by Illegal Forces," *Human Rights Watch*, March 14, 2014, www.hrw.org/news/2014/03/14/crimea-att acks-disappearances-illegal-forces; Sarah Rainsford, "Ukraine Crisis: Crimean Tatars Uneasy under Russia Rule," BBC News, August 25, 2015, www.bbc.com/news/world-europe-34042938; Katherine Hille, "History Repeats itself as Moscow Cracks Down on Crimea's Tatars," *Financial Times*, November 4, 2014, www.ft.com/content/ 0fb85596-636c-11e4-8a63-00144feabdc0 (all accessed April 20, 2019).

41. Evgeny Kalyukov, Maria Makutina, Farida Rustamova, and Tatyana Klenova, "Подробнее на За призывы вернуть Крым Украине можно будет лишиться свободы сроком до пяти лет" [Deputies Introduced a Criminal Punishment for Appeals to Return Crimea], *РБК Daily*, July 4, 2014, www.rbc.ru/politics/04/07/2014/57041ef99a794760d3 d3fc92 (accessed April 20, 2019).

42. Louis Charbonneau, Mirjam Donath, "U.N. General Assembly Declares Crimea Secession Vote Invalid," *Reuters*, March 27, 2014, www.reuters.com/article/us-ukraine-crisis-un/u-n-general-assembly-declares-crimea-secession-vote-invalid-idUSBREA2Q1G A20140327; U.S. Department of State, "Ukraine and Russia Sanctions," www.state.gov/e/eb/tfs/spi/ukrainerussia/; European Council, Council of the European Union, "EU restrictive measures in response to the crisis in Ukraine," www.consilium.europa.eu/en/ policies/sanctions/ukraine-crisis/; Jim Acosta, "U.S., other powers kick Russia out of G8," CNN Politics, March 25, 2014, https://edi tion.cnn.com/2014/03/24/politics/obama-europe-trip/index.html (all accessed April 20, 2019).

43. Neil Buckley, "Putin Feels the Heat as Sanctions Target President's Inner Circle," *Financial Times*, March 21, 2014, www.ft.com/con tent/c8859528-b11c-11e3-bbd4-00144feab7de; Ian Traynor, "European Union Prepares for Trade War with Russia over Crimea," *Guardian*, January 2, 2016, www.theguardian.com/worl d/2014/mar/21/eu-mobilises-trade-war-russia-crimea-ukraine; Olga Tanas, "Russia's Credit Outlook Cut as U.S., EU Widen Sanction Lists," *Bloomberg*, March 21, 2014, www.bloomberg.com/news/ar ticles/2014-03-20/russia-outlook-cut-to-negative-by-s-p-as-obama-widens-sanctions; Andra Timu, Henry Meyer and Olga Tanas, "Russia Staring at Recession on Sanctions That Could Get Tougher," *Bloomberg*, March 24, 2014, www.bloomberg.com/new s/articles/2014-03-23/russia-staring-at-recession-on-sanctions-that-c

ould-get-tougher; Courtney Weaver and Jack Farchy, "Funds Cut Russian Holdings after Sanctions," *Financial Times*, March 25, 2014, www.ft.com/content/b67f8da4-b3f4-11e3-a102-00144feabd c0; Jack Farchy and Martin Arnold, "Banks Retreat from Moscow Deals." *Financial Times*, April 18, 2014, www.ft.com/content/36e9 88ea-c576-11e3-89a9-00144feabdc0; Alan Rappeport and Neil MacFarquhar, "Trump Imposes New Sanctions on Russia Over Ukraine Incursion," *New York Times*, June 20, 2017, www.nytime s.com/2017/06/20/world/europe/united-states-sanctions-russia-ukrai ne.html (all accessed April 21, 2019); For an account that finds sanctions less effective than supposed, Steven Rosefielde, *The Kremlin Strikes Back: Russia and the West after Crimea's Annexation* (Cambridge: Cambridge University Press, 2017), pp. 61–117.

44. BBC Poll, Globe Scan, "BBC World Service Poll," July 4, 2017, https://globescan.com/images/.../bbc2017.../BBC2017_Country_Ratings_Po ll.pdf (accessed April 1, 2019).

45. Paul Belkin, Derek E. Mix and Steven Woehrel, "NATO: Response to the Crisis in Ukraine and Security Concerns in Central and Eastern Europe," Congressional Research Service, July 31, 2014; Jonathan Marcus, "Ukraine-Russia Clash: NATO's Dilemma in the Black Sea," BBC News, December 4, 2018, www.bbc.com/news/world-europe-46 425777 (accessed June 13, 2019).

46. Zacher, "Territorial Integrity Norm"; Altman, "Evolution of Territorial Conquest"; Finnemore, *Purpose of Intervention*, pp. 52–84; Neta Crawford, "Decolonization and as International Norm: The Evolution of Practices, Arguments, and Beliefs," in Laura Reed and Carl Kaysen, *Emerging Norms of Justified Intervention* (Cambridge: American Academy of Arts and Sciences, 1993), pp. 37–61.

47. Reinhold Niebuhr, *Moral Man and Immoral Society*, in *Reinhold Niebuhr: Major Works on Religion and Politics* (New York: Library of America, 2015), pp. 135–350, for some wonderful examples of self-serving rhetoric associated with British and American colonial expansion

48. Geoffrey Best, *War and Law Since 1945* (Oxford: Oxford University Press, 1994); Andrea Kathryn Talentino, "Intervention as Nation-Building: Illusion or Possibility? *Security Dialogue* 33, 1 (2002), pp. 27–43. Gary J. Bass, *Freedom's Battle: The Origins of Humanitarian Intervention* (New York: Knopf, 2008); Barnett, *Empire of Humanity*.

49. James Mayall, *The New Interventionism, 1991–1994* (Cambridge: Cambridge University Press, 1996).

50. Alex J. Bellamy, *Responsibility to Protect* (London: Polity, 2009); Alex J. Bellamy, ed., *The Oxford Handbook of the Responsibility to Protect* (Oxford: Oxford University Press, 2016); Alex J. Bellamy and Edward Luck, *The Responsibility to Protect: From Promise to Practice* (New York: Wiley, 2018).

51. Alex J. Bellamy, "Military Intervention," *The Oxford Handbook of Genocide Studies* (Oxford: Oxford University Press, 2010), ch. 30.

52. Beitz, *Idea of Human Rights*, p. 6.

53. Bass, *Freedom's Battle*, pp. 11–24.

54. Peter Kornbluh, *Chile and the United States: Declassified Documents Relating to the Military Coup, September 11, 1973*, National Security Archive, 11 September 1973, https://nsarchive2.gwu.edu//NSAEBB/NSAEBB8/nsaebb8.htm; CIA Reports: Hinchey Report: CIA Activities in Chile, *Homeland Security Digital Archive*, 18 September 2000, www.hsdl.org/?abstract&did=438476 (both accessed June 29, 2019); Peter Kornbluh, *The Pinochet File: A Declassified Dossier on Atrocity and Accountability* (New York: The New Press, 2003); Morton Halperin, Jerry Berman, Robert Borosage, and Christine Marwick, *The CIA's Campaign Against Salvador Allende* (New York: Penguin, 1976); Kristian Gustafson, *Hostile Intent: U.S. Covert Operations in Chile, 1964–1974* (Dulles: Potomac Books, 2007); Tanya Harmer, *Allende's Chile and the Inter-American Cold War* (Chapel Hill: University of North Carolina Press, 2011); Jonathan Haslam, *Nixon Administration and the Death of Allende's Chile: A Case of Assisted Suicide* (London: Verso, 2005); Lubna Z. Qureshi, *Nixon, Kissinger, and Allende: U.S. Involvement in the 1973 Coup in Chile* (Lanham: Lexington Books, 2009); Zakia Shiraz, "CIA Intervention in Chile and the Fall of the Allende Government in 1973," *Journal of American Studies* 45, 3 (2011), pp. 603–13.

55. Pamela Constable and Arturo Valenzuela, *A Nation of Enemies: Chile Under Pinochet* (New York: Norton, 1993); Kornbluh, *Pinochet File*; John Dinges, *The Condor Years: How Pinochet and His Allies Brought Terrorism to Three Continents* (New York: New Press, 2005); John H. Bawden, *The Pinochet Generation: The Chilean Military in the Twentieth Century* (Tuscaloosa: University of Alabama Press, 2016), for a more sympathetic portrayal of the junta.

56. Jeanne Kirkpatrick, "Dictatorships and Double Standards," *Commentary*, November 1979, pp. 34–45; Commanding Heights, "Interview with Milton Friedman," October 1, 2000, www.pbs.org/wgbh/commandingheights/shared/minitext/int_miltonfriedman.html (accessed June 29, 2019).

57. Jennifer Kavanagh, Bryan Frederick, Alexandra Stark, Nathan Chandler, Meagan L. Smith, Matthew Povlock, Lynn E. Davis, and Edward Geist, *Characteristics of Successful U.S. Military Interventions* (Santa Monica: Rand, 2019).

58. Ibid.

59. Richard Ned Lebow and Janice Gross Stein, *We All Lost the Cold War* (Princeton: Princeton University Press, 1994), ch. 3; Raymond L., *Reflections on the Cuban Missile Crisis*, 2nd ed. Rev (Washington: Brookings, 1989).

60. Campbell Craig and Fredrik Logevall, *America's Cold War: The Politics of Insecurity* (Cambridge: Harvard University Press, 2009), p. 93.

61. Lebow and Stein, *We All Lost the Cold War*, p. 78.

62. Ibid, p. 234, acknowledges the lack of any evidence connecting Saddam to terrorism.

63. Brown University Costs of War Project, reported by Daniel Brown, "Here's How Many People Have Died in the Wars in Afghanistan And Iraq," *Task & Purpose*, November 9, 2018, https://taskandpur pose.com/afghanistan-iraq-death-toll (accessed April 5, 2019).

64. Iraq Body Count Project, "Iraq Body Count," February 28, 2019, www .iraqbodycount.org/ (accessed April 5, 2019).

65. Opinion Research Bureau, "Survey of Iraq War Casualties," September 2007, Wikipedia, https://en.wikipedia.org/wiki/ORB_surve y_of_Iraq_War_casualties#cite_note-ORB-1 (accessed April 5, 2019).

66. Hannah Summers, "Yemen on Brink of 'World's Worst Famine in 100 Years' if War Continues," *Guardian*, October 15, 2018, www.theguar dian.com/global-development/2018/oct/15/yemen-on-brink-worst-fam ine-100-years-un (accessed October 26, 2018); Catie Edmondson and Charlie Savage, "House Votes to Halt Aid for Saudi Arabia's War in Yemen," *New York Times*, February 13, 2019, www.nytimes.com/20 19/02/13/us/politics/yemen-war-saudi-arabia.html (accessed April 22, 2019).

67. Harrison Salisbury, *The Shook-Up Generation* (New York: Harper & Row, 1958); Grace Palladino, *Teenagers: An American History* (New York: Basic Books, 1996); Glenn C. Altschuler, *All Shook Up: How Rock 'n' Roll Changed America* (New York: Oxford University Press, 2003); Arthur Marwick, *The Sixties: Cultural Revolution in Britain, France, Italy, and the United States, c.1958–c.1974* (Oxford: Oxford University Press, 1998); Christopher B. Strain, *The Long Sixties: America, 1955–1973* (New York: Wiley, 2017).

68. Gywnne Dyer, *After Iraq: Anarchy and Renewal in the Middle East* (London: Thomas Dunne, 2008); Frederic Wehrey Dalia Dassa Kaye Jessica Watkins Jeffrey Martini Robert A. Guffey, *The Iraq Effect: The*

Middle East After the Iraq War (Santa Monica: Rand, 2010); Christopher Davidson, *Shadow Wars: The Secret Struggle for the Middle East* (London: One World, 2017); Christopher Philips, *The Battle for Syria: International Rivalry in the New Middle East* (New Haven: Yale University Press, 2018).

69. Dana H. Allin, *Nato's Balkan Interventions* (London: Routledge, 2005); Richard Holbrooke, *How to End a War: Sarajevo to Dayton: The Inside Story* (New York: Random House, 1998).

70. Michael Otterman, *American Torture: From the Cold War to Abu Ghraib and Beyond* (Melbourne: Melbourne University Press, 2007); Seymour M. Hersh, *Chain of Command: The Road from 9/11 to Abu Ghraib* (New York: Harper, 2009); Mark Bowden, Lessons of Abu Ghraib," *Atlantic*, July-August 2004, www.theatlantic.com/magazine/archive/200 4/07/lessons-of-abu-ghraib/302980/ (accessed December 3, 2019).

71. Simon Mable and Stephen Roykle, *The Origins of ISIS: The Collapse of Nations and Revolution in the Middle East* (London: I. B. Tauris, 2016); Michael Weiss and Hassan Hassan, *ISIS: Inside the Army of Terror*, rev. ed. (New York: Regan Arts, 2015); Fawaz Gerges, *ISIS: A History* (Princeton: Princeton University Press, 2017).

72. Richard Ned Lebow and Mervyn Frost, "Ethical Traps," *International Relations* 33, 2 (2019), pp. 1–20.

73. Ibid.

74. Ahron Bregman, *Israel's Wars: A History Since 1947*, 3rd ed. (London: Routledge, 2002), pp. 252–92; Ze'ev Schiff and Ehud Ya'ari, *Israel's Lebanon War* (New York: Simon & Schuster, 1984); Robert Fisk, *Pity the Nation: Lebanon at War* (Oxford: Oxford University Press, 2001); Zeev Maoz, *Defending the Holy Land: A Critical Analysis of Israel's Security and Foreign Policy* (Ann Arbor: University of Michigan Press, 2006).

75. White House, Office of the Press Secretary, "Remarks by the President in Address to the Nation on Libya," Washington DC, March 28, 2011, https://obamawhitehouse.archives.gov/the-press-office/2011/03/28/remarks-president-address-nation-libya (accessed April 24, 2019).

76. "Security Council Approves 'No-Fly Zone' over Libya, Authorizing 'All Necessary Measures' To Protect Civilians in Libya, by a Vote of Ten For, None Against, with Five Abstentions," United Nations, March 17, 2011; Lindsey Hilsum, *Sandstorm: Libya in the Time of Revolution* (London: Faber & Faber, 2012); Heba Morayef, *Truth and Justice Can't Wait: Human Rights Developments in Libya Amid Institutional Obstacles* (New York: Human Rights Watch, 2009); Jason Pack, ed., *The 2011 Libyan Uprisings and the Struggle for the Post-Qadhafi*

Future (London: Palgrave-Macmillan, pp. 2013); Hugh Roberts, "Who Said Gaddafi Had to Go?" *London Review of Books* 33, 22 (2011): 8–18; Ronald Bruce St. John, *Libya: Continuity and Change* (New York: Routledge, 2011); Arash Heydarian Pashakhanlou, "Decapitation in Libya: Winning the Conflict and Losing the Peace," *Washington Quarterly* 40, 4 (2017), pp. 135–49.

77. White House, Office of the Press Secretary, "Remarks by the President on the Death of Muammar Qaddafi," October 20, 2011, https://obama whitehouse.archives.gov/the-press-office/2011/10/20/remarks-presiden t-death-muammar-qaddafi (accessed October 12, 2019); Ivo H. Daalder and James G. Stavridis, "NATO's Victory in Libya: The Right Way to Run an Intervention," *Foreign Affairs* 91, 2 (2012), pp. 2–7.

78. Richard K. Betts, "The Delusion of Impartial Intervention," *Foreign Affairs* 73, 6 (1994), pp. 20–33; Simon Chesterman, "'Leading from Behind': The Responsibility to Protect, the Obama Doctrine, and Humanitarian Intervention After Libya," *Ethics & International Affairs*, August 12, 2011, www.cambridge.org/core/journals/ethics-an d-international-affairs/article/leading-from-behind-the-responsibility-t o-protect-the-obama-doctrine-and-humanitarian-intervention-after-lib ya/147948891E63A065C42823AB8D1A5BA5 (accessed April 24, 2019); Arash Heydarian Pashakhanlou, "Decapitation in Libya: Winning the Conflict and Losing the Peace," *Washington Quarterly* 40, 4 (2017), pp. 135–49; Timothy W. Crawford and Alan J. Kuperman, eds. *Gambling on Humanitarian Intervention: Moral Hazard, Rebellion, and Civil War* (New York: Routledge, 2006); Alan J. Kuperman, "The Moral Hazard of Humanitarian Intervention: Lessons from the Balkans," *International Studies Quarterly* 52, 1 (2008), pp. 49–80; Roberts, "Who Said Gaddafi Had to Go?"; United Nations Human Rights Council, Nineteenth Session, "Report of the International Commission of Inquiry on Libya," advance unedited version, March 8, 2012, www.google.com/search?client=firefox-b -d&q=United+Nations+Human+Rights+Council%2C+nineteenth+ses sion%2C+%E2%80%9CReport+of+the+International+Commission+ of+Inquiry+on+Libya%2C%22%E2%80%9D (accessed April 24, 2019); Partrick C. R. Terry, "The Libya Intervention (2011): Neither Lawful, Nor Successful," *Comparative and International Law Journal of Southern Africa* 48, 2 (2015), pp. 162–82.

79. Gareth Evans, "Responsibility to Protect: Ten Years On," Address to the South African Institute of International Affairs, Pretoria, December 7, 2015 and Cape Town, December 9, 2015, evans_- _responsibility_to_protect_-_ten_years_on.pdf (accessed April 23, 2019); Jennifer M. Welsh, "Humanitarian Intervention After

September 11," in Jennifer M. Welsh, ed., *Humanitarian Intervention and International Relations* (Oxford: Oxford University Press, 2004), ch. 10; Antonios Tzanakopoulos, *Disobeying the Security Council: Countermeasures Against Wrongful Sanctions* (Oxford: Oxford University Press, 2011).

80. House of Commons, Foreign Affairs Committee, *Libya: Examination of intervention and collapse and the UK's future policy options*, Third Report of Session 2016–2017, September 14, 2016, www.google.com/search?clie nt=firefox-b-d&q=Libya%3A+Examination+of+intervention+and+col lapse+and+the+UK%27s+future+policy+options%22+%28PDF%29.+H ouse+of+Commons%27+Foreign+Affairs+Committee; Alan J. Kuperman, "Obama's Libya Debacle; How a Well-Meaning Intervention Ended in Failure." *Foreign Affairs*, March-April 2015, www.foreignaffairs.com/arti cles/libya/2019-02-18/obamas-libya-debacle (both accessed April 24, 2019).

81. Betts, "The Delusion of Impartial Intervention."

82. Richard Ned Lebow, *National Identifications and International Relations* (Cambridge: Cambridge University Press, 2016), ch. 4.

83. Amrita Narilkar, "Introduction: Negotiating the Rise of New Powers," *International Affairs* 89, 3 (2013), pp. 561–76; Sean W. Burgess, "Brazil as a Bridge Between Old and New Powers?" *International Affairs* 89, 3 (2013), pp. 577–94: Mile Kahler, "Rising Power and Global Governance: Negotiating Change in a Resilient Status Quo," *International Affairs* 89, 3 (2013), pp. 711–29.

84. BBC News, "BBC Poll: Germany Most Popular Country in the World," May 23, 2013, www.bbc BBC News,.co.uk/news/world-europe-22624 104 (accessed April 1, 2019).

85. Nick Childs, "Israel, Iran Top 'Negative List'," BBC News, March 6, 2007, http://news.bbc.co.uk/1/hi/world/middle_east/6421597.stm (accessed April 1, 2019).

86. BBC Poll, Globe Scan, "BBC World Service Poll," July 4, 2017, https:// globescan.com/images/ ... /bbc2017 ... /BBC2017_Country_Ratings_ Poll.pdf (accessed April 1, 2019).

87. Ibid.

4 | *Successful Foreign Policies*

This chapter explores the flipside of ethics and foreign policy and makes the case that policies in accord with accepted practices are more likely to succeed and more likely to confer longer-term advantages. The term "accepted practices" generally refers to norms, but justice encompasses more than adherence to norms, and can sometimes be attributed to behavior that violates norms or for which there are no norms. I will explore this relationship as well as norm-adhering and norm-creating initiatives in this chapter.

I open with a discussion of the methodological problems of distinguishing good from bad outcomes and of attributing good ones to international law, conventions, accepted practices or other understandings of justice or simply self-interest. I make an important distinction between what analysts think and what relevant actors believe. The latter is what counts for the purpose of my argument, but the former may also have substantive impact.

The second part of the chapter is empirical and returns to my data set to compare and contrast wars that succeeded with those that failed. I argue that the wars most likely to succeed are multilateral operations with the support of appropriate regional or international organizations. The principal reason for their success, I surmise, is that coalitions require consensus and it can rarely be achieved by states that pursue maximalist goals. They are generally compelled to limit their objectives, and to those for which there are good legal and political arguments.

A third section offers short case studies of three foreign policy initiatives that I consider extremely successful because they were consistent with shared understandings of justice. They are US policy toward Europe in the immediate aftermath of the Second World War, China's efforts to resolve territorial disputes with its neighbors under Mao Zedong, and the Federal Republic of Germany's efforts to restructure its relations with its neighbors. The first sought to strengthen the economies and political systems of European allies, the last two to reach accommodations and transform relations with neighbors, initially, through border settlements. The Marshall Plan and related initiatives involved the transfer of considerable resources, the other two initiatives were built around concessions and assurances. They involved multiple, major diplomatic and other efforts that took several years at least to implement. All three were nested in well-entrenched norms and helped to create new ones. They fostered belief in the benign intentions of the leaders and states responsible for these initiatives. They built trust across borders, and in two of the three initiatives, among peoples.

Ethics and Outcomes

It is difficult to document the claim that foreign policy initiatives perceived as appropriate, and even more, as just are more likely to succeed than those that violate norms or are considered unjust. Just how do we determine which norms are widely shared, which ones are considered just, and by whom? We might seek an answer to the first question by identifying those norms we consider robust and then determining the extent to which they are followed by regional and international actors. We could also look at how actors respond to their violation. Do they comment publicly when these norms are violated? What do they say? Do they describe these violations as unjust and unjustified? How much consensus do these comments reveal? What, if anything, is done to punish violators? We are almost certain to find that some norms are robust, others weak, and some flashpoints. By flashpoint, I mean that some actors defend these norms while others criticize or even condemn them.

A good example of a contested norm involves the treatment of migrants and refugees. Immanuel Kant described *xenia* (guest friendship) as the oldest and most universal of norms.[1] Political asylum is governed by convention once people enter a state's territory. Since experiencing a flood of refugees from Libya, Syria, and north and sub-Saharan Africa into Europe, public opinion there – both within and across states – has become deeply divided on the question of refugees. Nationalist parties almost everywhere in Europe have made considerable gains by opposing immigration. Frontline countries including

Spain, Italy, and Greece, which have borne the brunt of the immigration, complain that other countries have not taken their fair share.
Italy, now governed by an anti-establishment coalition is using its
navy to keep unwanted migrants at an arm's length, even though rescue
at sea is a longstanding international norm.

The divisions in Europe came to a head in June 2019 when the *Sea-
Watch-3*, a Dutch ship with a German captain, rescued migrants off the
coast of Libya. The Italian coastguard stopped the rescue boat, making
it anchor just off the coast. The captain of the ship broke free after
seventeen days and forced her way into the Italian port of Lampedusa.
"The situation was desperate," she reported. The boat's forty migrants
were allowed to disembark, taken to a reception center, and made
ready to travel on to France, Germany, Finland, Luxembourg, and
Portugal. Captain Rackete was placed under house arrest and charged
with abetting illegal immigration and forcing her way past a military
vessel that tried to block her entry into port. This last crime is punishable by three to ten years in jail.[2] Rackete became a leftwing hero in
Italy for challenging the "closed-ports" policy of the far-right interior
minister, Matteo Salvini, who welcomed her arrest. In Germany, her
treatment prompted a fundraising appeal launched by two prominent
German TV stars and a condemnation of Italy's behavior by the head of
the Green Party.[3]

Equally problematic are the criteria for determining success or failure of a foreign policy. Should analysts stipulate these criteria or should
we follow the assessment of leaders? Initiatives that leaders and analysts consider successful because they achieve their immediate goals can
create greater problems in the longer term. Consider the Soviet annexation of the Baltic countries in 1940 in the aftermath of the 1939 Stalin-
Hitler Pact. Stalin thought it a big win as it extended the Soviet defense
perimeter further west. However, it made Hitler more intent on attacking the Soviet Union and easier to do because much of the Soviet army
and air force were now in more exposed forward positions.

The Truman administration transported American-equipped French
troops to Indochina to combat local nationalist movements. The
French were decisively defeated at Dien Bien Phu in 1954 and
Vietnam, Cambodia, and Laos gained independence as a result of the
1954 Geneva Treaty. In the negotiations, Secretary of State John Foster
Dulles insisted that Vietnam be temporarily divided into northern and
southern parts. The latter was ruled by a procolonial emperor and

prime minister. South Korea's refusal, with Dulles's support, to hold free elections and reunify Vietnam prompted an insurgency supported by the communist government in North Korea. The regime in the south was never seen as legitimate and became increasingly dependent on American military and economic aid. In 1964, hoping to preserve South Vietnam's independence and American influence in Southeast Asia, President Lyndon Johnson intervened on a massive scale. By 1970, there were 475,000 American troops in the country. When the USA withdrew ignominiously from Saigon in 1975, it had lost 47,000 combat personnel.[4] Ironically, intervention from the very beginning was promoted by the perceived need to oppose communism and display resolve.[5] Communism became more attractive *because* of American intervention, and American leaders felt even greater need to display resolve in the aftermath of their withdrawal from Indochina. Initial American successes paved the way for subsequent defeats.

In 1953, the CIA helped to overthrow the democratically elected prime minister Mohammad Mosaddegh and install Mohammad Reza Pahlavi in power. It was the first postwar peacetime covert action by Washington to overthrow a foreign government.[6] The Eisenhower administration considered the coup a big win because it removed a leftist from power who, they worried, would be receptive to Soviet influence. Over the course of the next two decades, the USA became a major prop of the increasingly authoritarian and brutal Pahlevi regime. Iranians on both sides of the political spectrum who opposed to the regime developed hostility to the USA. The 1979 revolution brought to power religious fundamentalists who established an Islamic republic under the leadership of the Grand Ayatollah Ruhollah Khomeini.[7] The government readily mobilized support against the United States, whom it branded as "the Great Satan."[8] Ever since, the USA and Iran have been adversaries, to the detriments of the long-term interests of both states. A short-term perceived gain became a long-term loss.

Evaluating outcomes depends on one's frame of reference. As these examples illustrate, short- versus longer-term perspectives can lead to diametrically opposed assessments.

Comparison and assessment is further complicated by the fact that foreign policy initiatives vary enormously in intent, scope, feasibility, and dependence on third parties. The most reasonable procedure for evaluating my claim about the practical benefits of ethical policies is within multiple categories of comparison, each of them describing a roughly comparable type of initiative. This avoids the notorious apples vs. oranges problem. Focused comparisons of this kind may also tell us more about the mechanisms and processes responsible for the outcomes we observe. Within this end in mind, I offer what is an initial probe in the category of intervention. I take a longer- rather short-term perspective on evaluating success, although with the understanding that this is difficult to impossible when assessing the most recent initiatives. I rely on my judgment of success and failure, not that of policymakers, and then make explicit the reasons for my judgment.

Wars

War is a risky activity even in the best of circumstances. Multilateral interventions against weak foes can have undesirable outcomes, as, arguably, did the 2011 intervention in Libya.[9] Nevertheless, the evidence suggests that multilateral interventions with the backing of regional and international organizations are more likely to succeed than unilateral ones without such sanction. I discuss and compare two sets of paired cases: Korea, June and September 1950, and Iraq, 1990 and 2003.

The initial response to the North Korean invasion of the South in June 1950 was multilateral and successful; North Korean forces were expelled within months and South Korea liberated. So too was the Gulf War of 1990 brief and successful; Iraqi forces were expelled from Kuwait with great losses at little human cost to the allies. Both operations had clearly specified and limited aims. The invasion of North Korea that followed the retreating North Korean army was unilateral, based on faulty intelligence, poorly executed, and led to disaster in the form of a Chinese attack that compelled an American retreat deep into South Korea. The war resulted in 34,000 American combat deaths and ended in a stalemate in 1953 after long drawn-out negotiations.[10]

Let us revisit my list of 1945 wars (Figure 4.1) to which I have added two new columns to code for unilateral action versus multilateral coalition, and authorization or not by regional or international organizations. There are seven coalitional wars on the initiator side: the 1948–49 Arab war against Israel; the Anglo-French-Israeli attack on Egypt in 1956; the 1973 Middle East War in which Egypt and Syria attacked Israel; the Gulf War of 1990 in

WAR NAME	DATE	MILITARY VICTORY	ACHIEVES WAR AIMS
India-Pakistan (First Kashmir) SIDE A: India SIDE B: Pakistan	1947–1949	NO	NO
War of Israeli Independence (Israel vs. Palestine/Arab coalition) SIDE A: COALITION: Egypt (A1), Iraq (A2), Jordan (A3), Syria (A4) SIDE B: Israel	1948–1949	NO	NO
China-Tibet I SIDE A: China SIDE B: Tibet	1950	YES	YES
Korean SIDE A: COALITION: China (A1), North Korea (A2) SIDE B: USA + NATO	1949–1953	NO	NO
Soviet-Hungarian SIDE A: Hungary SIDE B: (Soviet Union)	1956	YES	YES
Sinai/Suez SIDE A: Egypt SIDE B: COALITION: Israel (B1), France (B2), UK (B3)	1956	YES	YES
Vietnam SIDE A: USA SIDE B: North Vietnam	1959–1975	NO	NO

Figure 4.1 Post-1945 wars[11]

Indo-Chinese **SIDE A: China** **SIDE B: India**	1962	YES	YES
Second Kashmir **SIDE A: India** **SIDE B: Pakistan**	1965	NO	NO
Six Day War **SIDE A:** **COALITION: Egypt** **(A1), Iraq (A2), Syria** **(A3)** **SIDE B: Israel**	1967	NO	NO
US vs. Cambodia	1971	NO	NO
Israeli-Egyptian **(War of Attrition)** **SIDE A: Egypt** **SIDE B: Israel**	1969– 1970	NO	NO
Football (El Salvador **vs. Honduras)** **SIDE A: El Salvador** **SIDE B: Honduras**	1969	YES	YES
India-Pakistan **(Bangladesh)** **SIDE A: India** **SIDE B: Pakistan**	1971	YES	YES
Yom Kippur **SIDE A:** **COALITION: Egypt** **(A1), Syria (A2)** **SIDE B: Israel**	1973	NO	NO
Cyprus **SIDE A:Greece** **SIDE B: Turkey**	1974	YES	YES
Vietnamese- **Cambodian** **SIDE A: Cambodia** **SIDE B: Vietnam**	1977– 79	YES	NO

Figure **4.1** (cont.)

Ethiopia-Somalia (Ogaden) SIDE A: COALITION: Cuba (A1), Ethiopia (A2) SIDE B: Somalia	1977–78	NO	NO
Ugandan-Tanzanian SIDE A: Tanzania SIDE B: Uganda	1978–79	NO	NO
First Sino-Vietnamese SIDE A: China SIDE B: Vietnam	1979	NO	NO
Iran-Iraq SIDE A: Iran SIDE B: Iraq	1980–88	NO	NO
Falklands/Malvinas War (UK vs. Argentina) SIDE A: Argentina SIDE B: UK	1982	NO	NO
Israel-Syria (Lebanon) SIDE A: Israel SIDE B: Syria	1982	NO	NO
Second Sino-Vietnamese SIDE A: China SIDE B: Vietnam	1987	NO	NO
Iraq-Kuwait War SIDE A: Iraq SIDE B: Kuwait/USA	1990	NO	NO
Democratic Republic of Congo vs. Rwanda/Uganda SIDE A: Democratic Republic of Congo SIDE B: COALITION: Rwanda (B1) and Uganda (B2)	1998–2003	YES	PARTIAL

Figure 4.1 (cont.)

Ethiopia-Eritrea SIDE A: Eritrea SIDE B: Ethiopia	1998–2000	NO	NO
Afghanistan (Taliban) -USA (Northern Alliance) SIDE A: Afghanistan SIDE B: USA	2001	YES	NO
Anglo-American Invasion of Iraq SIDE A: Iraq SIDE B: USA	2003	YES	NO
Russian incursion into Georgia	2008	YES	YES
NATO Intervention in Libya	2011	YES	PARTIAL

Figure 4.1 (cont.)

which a large coalition led by the USA went to war, or supported the war, against Iraq; the 1998–2003 Second Congo War in which nine African countries participated; the 2003 Anglo-American invasion of Iraq; and the 2011 NATO intervention in Libya. On the defensive side, there are two wars: the Korean War involved a defensive coalition drawn from NATO in its first phase and in its second phase when China entered the conflict in support of North Korea when the USA was on the verge of conquering the country. Initiators won four of these wars in a military sense (1956, 1990, and 2003) but only one (1990) achieved its political goal. The two military victories resulted in political defeats. France, Britain, and Israel were forced to withdraw by the USA, and the Iraq invasion led to a continuing and costly occupation and insurgency. Defensive coalitions fared better. NATO achieved a low cost political-military victory in South Korea and China preserved North Korean independence, which was its political goal, even though the actual fighting ended in something close to a draw.

"Coalition" is a loose term that refers to coordinated military action by multiple states. Coalitions may be voluntary and form because leaders – and possibly, peoples – of participating states regard it to be in their national interest. They can also form when a powerful state coerces or bribes others into joining it. The Warsaw Pact intervention in Czechoslovakia in 1968 is an example of the latter. The so-called "Coalition of the Willing" assembled by the Bush administration in its 2003 Iraq invasion relied on both voluntary participation and bribery; and an element of coercion. One journalist called it the "Coalition of the Billing."[12] Coalitions can act to uphold international law and norms or pursue goals in violation of them. Three of the seven coalition wars – the Gulf War of 1990, the 1998–2003 Second Congo War, the 2011 NATO intervention in Libya – were intended to uphold international law or protect civilian lives. One achieved it political goals, the other two did so only in part. The other four coalitional wars on the initiator side – the 1948–49 and 1973 Arab wars against Israel; the Anglo-French-Israeli attack on Egypt in 1956; and the Anglo-American invasion of Iraq were failures. The two Arab attacks against Israel failed military, and the other two coalitions succeeded militarily but failed politically.

Of the six coalitional initiators of wars three had the backing of regional and international organizations: the nine African states that intervened in the Democratic Republic of the Congo were authorized to do so by the Organization of African States; the coalition what waged the Gulf War against Iraq in 1990 had authorization from NATO and the United Nations; the Libyan intervention was also under the auspices of NATO. The Gulf War was the only intervention that that achieved its military and political aims.

In this admittedly small sample, coalitional warfare appears to fare better than unilateral action, and more so when it is intended to protect lives or expel invasions in accord with international law and with the backing of regional or international organizations. The international community rarely, if ever, regards wars of conquest as legitimate, even when they are initially justified as defensive. At best they achieve some degree of partisan support. If successful in a military sense – as the Soviets initially were in Afghanistan and the Americans in Iraq – they are almost certain to provoke internal resistance. Israel's occupation of the West Bank – which was the unanticipated consequences of a Jordanian attempt to invade Israel – is another case in point. Israel has had to face a long smouldering local opposition that has periodically become violent.

Coalitions that are freely entered into compacts are more likely to have limited goals, and goals in accord with international law and norms. This was true of NATO in the Korean War, the USA and its allies in the Gulf War, and NATO in Libya.[13] There are, of course, exceptions: in 1948, a voluntary Arab coalition had a maximal goal of snuffing out the state of Israel and expelling its Jewish inhabitants.

Coalitions that are consensual are usually organized by a dominant power or group of powers that persuade others to join them. Persuasion involves convincing others that joint military action is in their interest. This means advocating goals that other leaders regard as beneficial. It often requires initiators to bargain with would-be coalition partners. Such bargaining can lead to maximalist or minimalist wars aims. In the former, this often involves territorial promises to new partners. France and Britain offered such concessions to Italy and Romania to bring them into their side of the First World War. The Arab coalitions against Israel in 1948 and 1973 were also wars of conquest.

In minimalist coalitions bargaining works to limit war aims. This was the pattern in the first phase of the Korean War where the USA was anxious not to alienate its allies in light of their fear that intervention could lead to a wider war with China or Russia. General Omar Bradley, Chairman of the Joint Chiefs of Staff, agreed with Secretary of State Marshall that the USA should stay within the limits laid down by the UN "even if going along with the United Nations meant some difficult problems for us."[14] In the Gulf War, the George H. W. Bush administration agreed to limit its objectives to the expulsion of Iraqi forces from Kuwait. Both wars were successful. Some Americans chafed under these restrictions, and when South Korea was liberated, President Truman was all but compelled to invade North Korea or face the prospect of political defeat at home.[15] NATO intervention in Libya also had limited and negotiated goals, although NATO states were reluctantly drawn into ground operations due to the deteriorating situation in the country.[16] President George Bush, by contrast, was persuaded by officials around him to seek the maximalist goal of regime change in Iraq. For this reason, he was unable to gain United Nations' support and the only ally to participate in the attack was the United Kingdom.[17] The Iraq invasion was a tragedy brought about by hubris, a concept to which I will return in the conclusion.

Successful Foreign Policies

Successful foreign policies avoid hubris, pursue goals that are acceptable to others, do so by consent, and are often multilateral in their
implementation. At the very least, they require the uncoerced acquies-
cence of other actors. In the second section of this chapter, I provide
overviews of three such policies initiated by three different actors. First
is the response by the USA to postwar Europe, to countries whose
industry was in ruins, whose businesses had insufficient access to
capital, and whose peoples were pessimistic about their futures.
Second is the German project to restructure relations with its neighbors
by accepting responsibility for its past crimes and demonstrating that
its leaders and people had become good Europeans. Third is the efforts
made by Maoist China to reach an accommodation with its neighbors
and put relations with them on a peaceful and more cooperative
footing.

All three initiatives qualify as ethical and successful. The Marshall
Plan and NATO helped to rebuild and protect Europe and create
a strong sense of community among the Western powers. German
efforts to acknowledge past wrongs, accept the postwar territorial
status quo, and become good neighbors provided material and psychological benefits to Germans and made them and their country more
acceptable to their neighbors. In the long term, it greatly enhanced
German influence in Europe. China's extension of the olive branch to
its neighbors resolved outstanding territorial disputes and normalized
relations with many of them. It was a major step toward China's
acceptance by the non-communist world. All three initiatives broke
with past practices in important ways and in doing so demonstrated the
bona fides of those responsible for these initiatives. They succeeded as
much because of the respect and trust they promoted as for the ways in
which they served state interests. Two of the three initiatives set in
motion a process of collaboration that led to the construction of new
common identities. They transformed relations among the participating states and peoples.

The USA and Europe

The story of US aid to postwar Europe and the extension of a security
umbrella via the Truman Doctrine and NATO has been told many

times.[18] The briefest recap will suffice. The Marshall Plan (known officially as the European Recovery Program) was passed by Congress in 1948 to aid Western Europe. It was offered to Western and Eastern Europe and the Soviet Union.[19] Moscow rejected the offer of aid and made certain that other Eastern European countries did so as well.

The USA gave over $12 billion in economic assistance to help rebuild Western European economies. The plan had bipartisan support in Washington from a Republican-controlled Congress and Democratic White House. It was largely the brainchild of State Department officials, especially William L. Clayton and George F. Kennan, responding to a request from Senator Arthur H. Vandenberg, chairman of the Foreign Relations Committee. American goals were to rebuild and modernize industry, remove trade barriers, and prevent the spread of communism. The Marshall Plan required a reduction of European interstate barriers, the dropping of many regulations, and adoption of modern business procedures.[20] Eighteen European countries received Plan aid. In principle, it was distributed on a per capita basis. However, disproportionate sums were given to the major industrial powers, as they were regarded as critical to European revival. The largest recipient was the United Kingdom, which received 26 percent of the total, followed by 18 percent for France and 11 percent for West Germany.

Early American scholarship on the Cold War heaped praise on the "far-seeing" statesmen responsible for the institutions set up at Dumbarton Oaks and the policy initiatives that followed.[21] The Marshall Plan, in particular, was regarded as an altruistic and far-sighted measure intended to strengthen Europe and build lasting ties with its democracies. This interpretation begins with George Kennan and George Marshall, with the latter describing it as "the ultimate act of good will."[22] In 2000, members of the American Historical Association voted the Marshall Plan by a large margin as the country's supreme legislative accomplishment. Foreign Secretary Ernest Bevin called it "a lifeline to sinking men."[23] The West German Vice Chancellor described it as "the first fact by which Germany was reintroduced into the family of nations .... Without the Marshall Plan we wouldn't have been able to survive."[24]

Revisionist interpretations began to appear in the 1960s and stressed the economic benefits of the Marshall Plan for American corporations.[25] The April 1947 report of the Coordinating Committee of State, War, and Navy Departments attributed the Plan to a mix of motives, including national economic aims, security interests, and humanitarian concerns.[26] US GNP had fallen 11.6 percent in 1946 due to the sharp decline in government spending after the war. Government spending in the form of aid credits, it was hoped, would avoid a further recession. Walter LaFeber attributed a more nefarious purpose to the Plan: he insists that it was a blatant attempt to gain control over Western Europe that paralleled, albeit by peaceful means, what the Soviets did in Eastern Europe.[27] Michael Cox and Caroline Kennedy-Pipe describe the Plan as being, at least in part, responsible for the division of Europe and the Cold War. They reject the claim that the Marshall Plan was defensive in character, insisting that its goal from the outset was to undermine Soviet control of Eastern Europe.[28] Revisionist scholarship also questioned the economic benefits of the plan for recipients. British historian Alan S. Milward attributed European economic revival more to local initiatives, most of them already underway.[29] Subsequent research indicates that Marshall Plan aid accounted for less than 3 percent of recipients' national income and less than one-fifth of their total investment.[30]

Beginning in the 1970s, post-revisionist scholarship has tried to strike a balance between orthodox Cold War interpretations and revisionists. John Lewis Gaddis and Vojtech Mastny, and later, Robert Pollard and Marc Trachtenberg, described the Marshall Plan as having multiple goals, some of them self-serving, and others more in the interest of other Western democracies. They stressed the political and strategic concerns that underlay the Plan, not only the economic ones.[31] Corporatist scholarship recast the Plan as a wider initiative in which nongovernmental actors – business, agriculture, organized labor – played a major role.[32] Michael Hogan argues that the Marshall Plan imposed on Western Europe the politico-economic compromise of the American New Deal. The growing collaboration between business and government in Europe, and the closer alignment of both with their American counterparts, he contends, was a fundamental cause of prosperity and political stability.[33]

It is hardly a discovery that the Marshall Plan was motivated by self-interest; all foreign policies are. The important question is how self-interest is conceived and how policies based on it are implemented.

President Truman and his advisors responsible for the Plan, and later for NATO, had a sophisticated understanding of the national interest. The Great Depression and the Second World War taught them that even the most powerful state cannot survive and prosper in isolation. Other countries and peoples must also do so, too – and feel secure. They framed material wellbeing and security as common goals, best achieved in cooperation with trading and political partners. The USA had the resources to take the lead. It devised and sought European support for institutions and practices it thought best suited to this end.

Self-congratulatory treatments of the Marshall and the postwar order created by the USA can still be found. The most influential has undoubtedly been that of John Ikenberry. He argues that the United States was successful in the postwar era because it combined a realist-inspired containment of the Soviet Union with liberal internationalist construction of "a democratic club."[34] Unlike previous victors who sought to impose an imperium, the USA practiced "strategic restraint." The postwar strategic and economic orders it designed served the weak as well as the powerful. They did so because it exercised influence through institutions – most notably, the Marshall Plan, IMF, NATO, and the World Bank – that created a "constitutional order" with agreed on rules that extended but also channeled and restrained American power. These institutions guaranteed the survival of liberal democratic orders and encouraged their spread. Ikenberry attributes these American strategies to its liberalism and hegemony. Only a hegemon, he maintains, has the resources and incentives to establish binding multilateral institutions that lower the enforcement costs of maintaining a favorable order.

Ikenberry overstates an important truth. Washington did exercise some degree of constraint, and was at times compelled – as in the first stage of the Korean War – to moderate its aims to maintain allied support. On other occasions, however, it coerced recalcitrant allies, intervened in their domestic affairs, and sought to impose its preferences. It exercised considerably less restraint after the Cold War and the collapse of the Soviet Union, when some American realists insisted the world had become "unipolar."[35]

As for hegemony, its existence, let alone its allegedly benign effects, is dubious. Simon Reich and I have tried to demonstrate that at best the USA had a limited hegemony in the Western hemisphere. It was never powerful enough to impose its preferences across the board on other actors, although it has certainly not hesitated in attempting to do so. We further contend that hegemony is a threat to order, not its essential pillar, and that America's pursuit of it has made it one of the principal threats to economic and political stability since the end of the Cold War.[36] It is simply wrong to contend, as Ikenberry does, that the institutions the USA established lead to the near-global spread of liberalism and democracy. These institutions might just as reasonably be held responsible for globalization and the wave of anti-liberal and antidemocratic protests it has inspired. Ikenberry greatly overstates the case of the USA as a benign dominant power. He has had some second thoughts about the claim in his 2001 book but still adheres to his belief in the value of hegemony, the USA as a hegemon, and the enduring value of the institutions it brought into being.[37] I will return to this question at the end of the chapter, where I argue that theses of the kind Ikenberry advances are intended to justify as ethical policies that are patently self-serving and counterproductive to their proclaimed goals.

China and Its Neighbors

In 1949 China had more neighbors than any other country; it shared frontiers with twelve states.[38] That number rose to fourteen after the dissolution of the Soviet Union.[39] Along its land and maritime frontiers it confronted, then as now, extremely complicated geopolitical environments.

Republican China had never signed a comprehensive border treaty with any of its neighbors. Most of its frontiers were little more than lines drawn on maps. Some of them had been drawn by imperialist powers and conformed only in part to actual practice. These frontiers reflected the rise and fall of Chinese political authority. During the nineteenth century, the territory of the Qing dynasty shrank by almost one-quarter and its authority diminished over much of the territory it still controlled.[40] Even where there was agreement in principle with a neighboring state about a mutual frontier borders were often undemarcated and problems arose. Maps and surveys, if any, were often inaccurate or incomplete; boundary markers, where they existed, had sometimes been moved and local populations had little interest or regard for boundaries. The territory controlled by China and its neighbors often had only a casual resemblance to any agreed on frontiers.

In the 1960s, China took the lead in attempting to settle border disputes with its twelve neighbors.[41] By 2006, it had negotiated boundaries along 90 percent of its land frontiers.[42] Not all border disputes were peacefully resolved. Territorial disputes led to wars with India in 1962 and Vietnam in 1979, and, currently, China is involved in escalating maritime disputes with its East and South China Sea neighbors.[43]

Analysts of China's border problem offer a range of explanations for its responses to different neighbors. Nie Hongyi maintains that China took a hard line toward states such as India that it considered expansionist, but was willing to make concessions to neighbors it believed were committed to the status quo. Toward the latter, it emphasized mutual understanding, tolerance, and beneficial arrangements that improved bilateral relations and enhanced regional stability.[44]

Taylor Fravel asserts that China's approach to territorial disputes was primarily a function of leadership perceptions of regime stability. When leaders considered China's domestic politics to be fragile, and this fragility became exacerbated by external threats, they adopt a concessionary approach. They offered concessions in exchange for cooperation to end isolation or buy time for domestic reforms. Chinese leaders sought border agreements in the hope of shoring up the political power base and regime stability. Between 1960 and 1964, China negotiated compromise solutions to eight border disputes, and between 1990 and 1999, reached agreements in another nine. These efforts coincided with periods of peak domestic insecurity: the former following the 1959 revolt in Tibet and the failure of the Great Leap Forward, and the latter in the aftermath of the 1989 Tiananmen Square demonstrations and their suppression.[45]

A third view, advanced by Shena and Lovell, is that Chinese efforts to resolve border disputes were motivated by foreign policy considerations. They offered territorial concessions as means of achieving broader and more important foreign policy objectives. Chief among these was breaking out of American-imposed isolation.[46]

There are problems with all these accounts. Nie Hongyi assumes that Chinese perceptions of whether a state was expansionist or status quo was the result of some wider Chinese assessment. In reality, it seems to have depended largely on their leaders' responses to Chinese initiatives for border settlements. In the case of India, China continued to pursue a conciliatory policy after repeated Indian efforts to build up its military forces in disputed territory – denounced by China as incursions – stalemated diplomacy, and escalating rhetoric from New Delhi. Beijing moved to a more confrontational policy toward Indian only very late in the process, and even then it was gradually.[47] It is also difficult to document and theorize the correlation between Chinese perceptions of the Soviet Union and Chinese border policy. The Chinese were most accommodating when Stalin ruled in the Kremlin but Mao Zedong and Zhou Enlai regarded him as expansionist. Their border conflict with the Soviet Union reached its peak intensity in 1969, when Khrushchev was in power; he was not perceived as expansionist, although he *was* seen as a dangerous revisionist. The waxing and waning of this conflict appears to reflect the relative power balance between the countries and their degree of ideological unity or confrontation. The 1969 border incidents coincided with the Sino-Soviet split, provoked by ideological and substantive policy differences.

Fravel contends that China's approach to border conflicts reflects the perceived stability of its domestic order. However, case studies indicate that China pursued opposing strategies at the same time toward different neighbors. Beijing adopted a conciliatory, even concessionary, approach to resolving boundary issues with Myanmar, Nepal, Mongolia, Pakistan, and Afghanistan when it initiated a border war with India. These differences suggest that leadership understandings of domestic stability are only one factor influencing border policies. As Fravel acknowledges, a third period of internal turmoil, during the early stage of the Cultural Revolution, from 1966 to 1969, did not prompt any effort at compromise in border disputes. He explains this away by arguing that this disruption was of Mao's own making, but the Great Leap Forward was also a Maoist initiative.[48]

Shena and Lovell's claim that the Chinese communists had a poorly developed sense of sovereignty ignores the longstanding history of border relations going back to the Ming period. During the era of colonial humiliation, Chinese had the concept of sovereignty used against them and had no choice but to develop a sophisticated understanding its meaning and political implications. Their second claim makes more sense. Chinese leaders undeniably conducted border negotiations within a broader framework that took into account both domestic and foreign considerations. Border disputes did not dictate China's policy toward a neighbor, but, rather, policy toward that neighbor determined how its leaders treated border disputes.

The twelve states sharing land borders with the newly proclaimed People's Republic were politically diverse. Four of them were socialist and generally sided with China on Cold War issues. The remaining eight had capitalist economies, and at least two of them – Taiwan and Thailand – welcomed, and even supported, American attempts to restrain or weaken China. Chinese leaders faced fundamental choices about how to respond to these political units. Should they regard them as enemies in the Cold War or neighbors with whom friendly relations might bring positive rewards?

This was not strictly a conflict between ideology and interests, as the two were perceived by Chinese leaders to be closely related. In the 1950s and early 1960s, Mao Zedong was exporting revolution, regionally and globally. This was an end in itself, but as with Lenin's commitment to worldwide revolution following the Bolshevik coup in Russia, reflected the belief that a communist regime could not survive for long in a world dominated by capitalist enemies. Security was also a concern with regard to neighboring countries that harbored nationalist forces and allowed their incursion into Chinese territory. Border agreements with these states were regarded as a means of reducing this threat. Well-defined and secured borders that eliminated these kinds of incursion and strengthened Chinese control over its own territory would also make it appear more robust in the eyes of its adversaries.

Chinese leaders opted for an accommodative over a confrontational strategy based on a longer-term and broadly conceived understanding of their regime and national interests. Central to this formulation was the understanding that China needed to escape isolation and that the best way to do this was through friendly relations with its neighbors. Improved relations would also make them less likely to serve as staging bases for the Americans. By the mid-1950s, China had adopted a foreign policy of "peaceful coexistence" with its neighbors. Such a policy also served to create a more stable regional environment, which was also good for economic development. These goals were sufficiently important to make Chinese leaders will to make territorial concessions and to accept frontiers initially imposed by imperialists.

Chinese border policy was generally successful. The most notable exception was India. Initially, there were grounds for optimism. India appeared to want good relations and China hoped this might help reconcile Tibetans to Chinese rule. Sino-Indian tensions nevertheless intensified after China's suppression of the 1959 Tibetan uprising. India, in turn, adopted an aggressive, forward policy, sending what military forces it could into disputed mountainous terrain in Ladakh in the west and the Northeast Frontier Agency in the east. Nehru rejected out of hand Chinese demands that both sides maintain the territorial status quo. By 1962, when China attacked and quickly overwhelmed forward-deployed Indian forces, the border dispute had been raging for a decade. In retrospect, it is apparent that Nehru and his advisors greatly underestimated Chinese resolve and military capability. At the same time, they tied their own hands by stoking nationalist opinion by making maximalist claims in the parliament and the press.[49]

India and Vietnam aside, China's policy of accommodation succeeded because it was sensitive to the diverse needs of its many neighbors. To the extent that they reciprocated, agreements were reached and that were mutually beneficial as they resolved outstanding issues that might easily have been exploited to poison relations. To varying degrees, these agreements and the negotiations that led up to them established China's reputation as a reliable and moderate interlocutor and paved the way for closer trade and political relations. It is no exaggeration to claim that this, China's first diplomatic initiatives in the region, set a pattern that paid handsome dividends in later decades and contributed significantly to regional security.

Germany and Its Neighbors

Germany's accommodation with its neighbors was based on a radical and entirely unexpected shift in German policy. Following the First World War, Germans across almost the entire political spectrum resented their loss of territory, especially in East Germany. Irredentism stoked nationalism during the Weimar era and galvanized support behind Hitler when he regained the Sudetenland without having to go to war. Germany lost more territory after the Second World War and similar irredentist sympathies found roots. In early postwar decades, Western maps of the country described East Germany (the DDR) as "central Germany," and organizations of refugees from the former eastern lands had significant political influence. Chancellor Konrad Adenauer, head of a CDU-CSU coalition, treaded softly around this question.[50]

The Treaty of Versailles, which held Germany responsible for the war initiated the so-called *Kriegsschuldfrage* (the war guilt question). Foreign offices of the major powers published collections of diplomatic documents intended to establish their innocence for the Great War. It was much more difficult for Germans to deny responsibility for the Second World War, and many Germans did the next best thing: they pretended they had nothing to do with the Nazis and their aggressive wars of conquest and genocidal policies toward Jews, Roma, and homosexuals. This denial was abetted by the USA, whose leaders sought to mobilize the *Bundesrepublik* (Federal Republic of Germany) as an ally in the Cold War. Washington ended de-Nazification, provided Marshall Plan aid, and turned a blind eye to the many ex-Nazis who resumed their political and professional life. Under pressure from the USA, Konrad Adenauer negotiated a reparations agreement with Israel in 1952.[51] Germany provided money for Jewish Holocaust survivors and ultimately three billion Deutschmark to Israel.[52] The year before Adenauer made a typically elliptical acknowledgement to the German parliament, saying that: "[U]nspeakable crimes have been committed in the name of the German people, calling for moral and material indemnity."[53] Adenauer, nevertheless, was committed to overcoming Franco-German antagonism as an essential step to his country's rehabilitation and European security.[54]

Anenauer's government propagated the myth of "good" and "bad" Germans. It condemned the Nazi past but denied any collective responsibility for it. He portrayed the majority of Germans as victims of the Nazis and attributed their crimes to a small number of "corrupt" Nazi leaders and officials. He exonerated the army and spoke of former *Wehrmacht* soldiers as "honorable men," totally ignoring their role in the Holocaust and other atrocities. Adenauer favored forgetting and forgiveness rather than exposure and punishment and sponsored legislation that rehabilitated former Nazi officials.[55] War memorials financed by the federal government conveyed the message that Germans were the victims of war, not its perpetrators. Textbooks conveyed the same message, all but ignored the Holocaust, and portrayed Eastern Europeans, and, more particularly the Poles, much as they had in the Nazi era, as inferior and backward people.[56]

Meaningful political and foreign policy change began in the late 1960s. Willy Brandt, head of the Social Democratic Party (SPD) and seemed easy to achieve because the USA, China, and Germany were offering their neighbors something they very much wanted: reconstruction aid or territorial concessions. Some degree of persuasion was still required, and collaboration beyond these immediate objectives was necessary to achieve the larger objectives sought by those three countries.

Common interest was not enough in itself to bring about the initial collaboration or accommodation. In two of the three cases, the initiatives originated from states – Germany and communist China – that were not trusted by their neighbors and regarded with some hostility. To reduce suspicion and convince would-be partners that their initiatives were serious and well-intentioned German and Chinese leaders had to break through imposing cognitive barriers. German chancellor, Willy Brandt, did so by a dramatic gesture and a bargaining position that created a sharp caesura with the past by means of unilateral concessions. Chinese foreign minister, Zhou Enlai, achieved the same end by pragmatic, low-key, and non-ideological negotiations with his neighbors and the generous terms he offered to them. Sadat and Gorbachev are later examples of leaders who used this strategy successfully.[69]

American, German, and Chinese leaders established a requisite degree of trust with their respective interlocutors, but also with wider public opinion in their countries. They succeeded in doing so in the first instance because of their probity and follow-through on their commitments and obligations. Of equal importance, they came across as ethical, admirable figures, as statesmen of high caliber acting in pursuit of goals that were not only legitimate but in some ways transcended narrow formulations of national self-interest. This imparted a special ethical character to them and their goals.

People respond differently to concessions they associate with generosity versus those they consider to be grudging and compelled by circumstance. These attributions prompt different judgments of character. They, in turn, encourage different attributions of motive. The negative side of this relationship has been more extensively explored; the belief in hostile intentions and opportunity-driven behavior encourages "worst-case" analyses, and they exacerbate conflict. Belief in benign intentions has the potential to reduce or resolve conflict, and acting justly in the eyes of others may be the best way to encourage such a belief. Some religious traditions and philosophers emphasize the

chancellor from 1969 to 1974, initiated what became known as *Ostpolitik*. Its goal was normalization of relations between the Federal Republic and the countries of Eastern Europe, particularly the German Democratic Republic (East Germany). In 1970, Brandt signed the Treaty of Moscow, renouncing the first use of force and recognizing the current European borders. Later that year, Brandt signed the Treaty of Warsaw, formally recognizing the People's Republic of Poland and the Oder–Neisse line as the de facto and de jure border with Poland. Treaties with other Eastern European countries quickly followed.[57] Germany gave up all claims to territories taken from it at the end of the war. The Treaties met with significant conservative opposition at home, although they did achieve majority support as German public opinion had undergone significant change. Back in 1952 only 3 percent of Germans were willing to renounce lost territories in the east to achieve reunification.[58]

Even more controversial was the Basic Treaty of 1972 that established formal relations between the two German states. It superseded the Hallstein Doctrine that had sought to isolate and undermine East Germany.[59] Conservative groups and Germans displaced from eastern territories accused Brandt of high treason. His policies were welcomed by many on the left as a means of reducing the "siege mentality" of East Germany and bringing about better living conditions for East Germans.[60]

On his trip to Poland in December 1970, Brandt made an important symbolic gesture: what became known in Germany as the *Warschauer Kniefall* (literally, "Warsaw knee fall"). He spontaneously knelt down after laying a wreath at the monument to victims of the Warsaw Ghetto Uprising: Jews who fought against their liquidation by the Nazis. Brandt's *Kniefall* was an unambiguous act of contrition, the first by a German chancellor ever.[61]

Brandt's *Ostpolitik* and symbolic gestures were part and parcel of a broader political and cultural movement in Germany known as *Vergangenheitsbewältigung* (struggle to overcome the past). The past is understood as the legal obligations of the German state and the moral obligations of individual Germans to accept responsibility for the crimes committed by their country in the Second World War. These include the invasion and occupation of other states, the use of slave labor, and above all, the Holocaust and related efforts to murder entire categories of people. Under Brandt, trials began of Nazi war criminals.

Vergangenheitsbewältigung also involves learning from the past; remembering and commemorating its victims; adopting liberal, democratic values; teaching these values and the horrors of the past to the young; and becoming good Europeans. The movement led to revision of school textbooks and curricula, efforts by local communities to reestablish contact with families of Jews who had fled or were murdered, erection of monuments to Holocaust victims, and museums that attempt to be honest about the German past. It also found further expression in the cinema, novels, and television programs.[62]

Germany's acceptance of postwar borders, renunciation of irredenta, treaties with its neighbors, and, of equal importance, internal efforts to confront and accept responsibility for its past, had a profound effect on its neighbors. So too did official and informal interactions with Germans over the next several decades. These included organized activities such as joint military exercises and, later, academies, rewriting of school textbooks to informal citizen-to-citizen visits and exchanges. A consensus developed in France, the Low Countries, Scandinavia, and Eastern Europe that leopards really could change their spots. By 1998, the Polish public regarded Germany as its closest military partner, second only to the USA.[63] In 2004, at the sixtieth anniversary of D-Day, the German foreign minister was invited to attend for the first time, and public opinion polls revealed that the French public considered Germany their closest ally.[64] President Jacques Chirac of France told those assembled: "I wanted Germany to remember with us those hours when the ideal of freedom returned to our continent . . . . We hold up the example of Franco-German reconciliation to show the world that hatred has no future, that the path to peace is always possible."[65]

Germans and Germany became trusted collaborators in the European project.[66] In the absence of *Ostpolitik* and *Vergangenheitsbewältigung*, this would not have happened. Germany's neighbors would have remained suspicious, even hostile, and the European project would have been severely limited in scope. One of its original institutions, the European Coal and Steel Community, established in 1951, had as an overriding goal supranational oversight of coal and iron the aim of preventing a revanchist Germany, if it developed, from diverting these resources for rearmament. NATO, founded in 1949, was directed against the Soviet Union but also intended to exercise oversight over German rearmament.[67]

Cold War exigencies made American leaders more recepti German efforts to end the occupation and allow German rearma but Germany's immediate neighbors remained wary, espe France.[68] As these suspicions waned and the Federal Republic be accepted as a responsible nation, its influence increased. Togethe France, it became the dominant political force in Europe. P perceptions of Germans and their country were also critical to r cation. Britain's prime minister, Margaret Thatcher, was not p by the prospect, but other Europeans were supportive. Germa war foreign policy demonstrates the validity of the claim tha often more. By renouncing irredentist territorial claims in the strong domestic opposition, recognizing the DDR (East Ge exercising restraint on a range of issues, and largely equa national interests with the wider interests of Europe, German respect and influence that paid off handsomely at the end of t War.

As in the USA and China, Germany's *Ostpolitik* was moti self-interest, but conceptions of self-interest that were a sophisticated understanding that German security, affluenc ing, and influence required first acceptance of, and then colla with neighbors toward mutual security and economic gro Federal Republic wisely renounced some sovereign rights ir supranational ones and in the process overcame the remai tions imposed on it by the allied victors and gained a voice in economic and strategic decisions. One again, ethical formi interest that stressed the connection between actors and the nities paid a handsome dividend. Critical, too, in the case o was *Vergangenheitsbewältigung*. It was not policy but an e mitment by Germans, individually and collectively, to acc sibility for their country's past and distant themselves adopting and practicing the defining democratic values of others and the law, tolerance of differences among people sion of all citizens in civic and political life. Foreign poli restructuring were synergistic in their beneficial consequer

Lessons

These several foreign policy initiatives succeeded beca willing international partners. At least superficially this

importance of acting for the right motives. I do not dispute this ideal but suggest that, in international relations at least, what counts is that others *perceive* you as acting for the right motives.

Justice and self-interest can be difficult to distinguish in theory and practice, but this does not discourage others from doing so. Analysts may see an overlap between the two motives or both at play for different actors supporting the same initiatives. But those who are the objects of these initiatives may often reduce them to binaries when make attributions about other's motives. If so, this may be one reason why these attributions are so important in interpersonal relations and foreign policy.

Ethical standing is not by any means critical to international agreements. They can be based on pure self-interest and conducted by people who detest one another, as was the infamous 1939 pact Ribbentrop and Molotov negotiated for Hitler and Stalin to divide Eastern Europe between them. More often, international agreements are concluded by leaders who admire one another, if for nothing else, their hard-nosed commitment to their national interests and skill at advancing or defending them. This kind of respect arose in the negotiations between Henry Kissinger and Zhou Enlai that led to Sino-American rapprochement.[70] It does not lead to the same kind of trust and rethinking that occurred in the three initiatives analyzed in this chapter.

Ethical commitments are generally not at odds with national interests but rather represent a different framing of them. They encourage, indeed require, a broad perspective that centers on mutual as opposed to unilateral gain. This starts from the assumption that security, material prosperity, and status are best achieved through cooperation rather than cutthroat competition with other states. Political and economic goals and projects that recognize and advance the interests of other states as well as one's own have multiple advantages. Collaboration based on persuasion rules out unilateral initiatives that fly in the face of what others understand as their won and community interests. Collaborative initiatives that succeed have positive follow-on effects. They can build friendship and solidarity that constructs partially shared identities. Interests are always subjectively defined, so overlapping or congruent self-identifications are an important generator of common interests. They consume fewer resources because other actors are more willing to contribute at least some of what is required.

Ethical strategies have the potential to set in motion a reinforcing process of cooperation, shared identities, and common interests. They enable further cooperation by building trust, creating networks, and enhancing mutual empathy.[71] Common interests arising from successful joint ventures can also make others more likely to accept the leadership of the state or states that originated and coordinated these initiatives. For these reasons, leadership is best achieved and sustained through common projects. The construction of a North Atlantic Community via the Marshall Plan and NATO, Germany's rapprochement with its neighbors, and the broader European integration project are cases in point. They built cross-national friendship among peoples, served as catalysts for further common efforts, built common identities, and made the leadership of the USA in NATO and Germany and France in Europe more acceptable.

Ethical strategies rely on sophisticated psychological mechanisms that may or may not be understood explicitly by leaders committed to them. They appeal to peoples and leaders by conferring practical rewards but also by making people part of communities that enhance their security, material and status. Communities and their common projects are more highly valued by relevant audiences if they are seen to serve a higher purpose. NATO and the European project benefitted greatly from the ability of those in positions of authority them to cast them in this light. NATO was sold as a form of collective security that would transcend past national rivalries. So, too, was the European project.

NATO and the EU are no more immune to conflicts and use of power to advance national and personal political goals than nation states and traditional alliances. But there is a powerful norm that distinguishes this kind of competition from that might have led to civil or interstate wars in the past. Swords must stay sheathed and rhetoric restrained in conflicts among members. Power is still very much in evidence but it is used in more subtle ways, channeled down pathways members regard as acceptable, and legitimated by institutional procedures and ceremonies. These norms and procedures are intended to preclude – and usually manage to do so – the imposition of outcomes by single, powerful states, or even a coalition of powerful states. NATO and the EU operate largely by consensus, which requires compromise regardless of the power balance. These procedures and the restraint they enforce make outcomes about more acceptable to members. Of course, they also make it more difficult to respond rapidly and effectively to crises.

The Marshall Plan and NATO were government initiatives but they succeeded because they involved participation well beyond the upper levels of governments or the armed forces. The Marshall Plan required active participation of European governments, but also of businesses, banks, and labor unions in both Europe and the US.[72] NATO began as an agreement among governments but required collaboration across national armed forces, at times down to the platoon level. German reconciliation with its neighbors was only possible because the actions of Germans from every walk of life – not just government initiatives – were able to persuade other Europeans that they had become good Europeans committed to democracy, the rule of law, and building peaceful relations with their neighbors.

These initiatives succeeded because they were ethical in conception and execution and understood as such by actors who became willing collaborators. They were consistent with accepted international laws and practices but went beyond them. Sharing resources and extending credits were not the norm in international practice. Generally, states offered loans, although Britain had financed military operations on the continent in the Seven Years' War and the Napoleonic conflicts.[73] Lend-lease during the Second World War did this on a massive scale and the Marshall Plan built on this precedent. The Common Market, and subsequently, the European Union, followed suit by extending development aid to poorer regions of Europe. This redistribution of resources was not entirely selfless as the donors also expected to gain. Lend-lease was motivated by the recognition that American security would be seriously threatened by Britain and Russia's defeat. The Marshall Plan was intended to help rebuild Europe, but also to strengthen pro-American governments against the Soviet Union and indigenous communist parties. It was also expected to provide markets for American goods and help stave off any postwar depression. Both projects, and European aid to poorer regions of Europe, fired the imagination of many people, especially the younger ones, and stretched their identifications to include a new supranational one. So, too, did the introduction of a common currency and open borders under the Schengen Agreement.

Unraveling

My three cases drive home the importance and value of ethical and imaginative foreign policies. Mutual initiatives that succeed generally have positive follow-on effects. They can build friendship and solidarity across borders that in turn structure shared identities. Shared identities lead to framing of more interests in common and thus create the conditions for further collaboration. When such a process binds together multiple states and peoples it leaves behind the anarchy, fear of violence, suspicion of others, and worst-case analysis that can otherwise poison interstate relations. Unethical policies are almost certain to do the reverse. They are the root cause of negative spirals of suspicion, hostility, and conflict. Such processes have been well-documented in pre-1914 Anglo-German relations, European relations in the 1930s, Japanese-American relations before Pearl Harbor, Soviet-American relations before and during the Cold War, and Sino-American relations in the current century.

Ethical policies can be self-sustaining but this requires self-restraint, patience, positive networking, and belief by peoples as well as by governments in the rewards of collaboration. In 1955, at the height of the Cold War, Reinhold Niebuhr observed that these qualities conferred prestige and made leadership more acceptable: "[P]ower ... cannot maintain itself very long if prestige is not added as a source of authority. When prestige is lacking, the addition of power does not remedy the defect. In ... communities, an increase of power without prestige merely changes implicit consent to sullen fear; this is the mark of despotism."[74] My three cases provide sobering confirmations. Ethical policies have to varying degrees given way to less ethical ones, and longer-term, more inclusive framings of interest to short-term and narrower ones. Leaders with vision and the courage have been replaced in many countries by those focused on electoral politics and personal political gain.

Why does this happen? Visionary leaders with good political skills are unusual beasts and there is usually a regression to the mean when they leave office. Collective memory loss also features prominently. Commitments to collaborate foreign policies and self-restraint often arise in association with titanic struggles, as they did with Americans and Europeans in the course and immediate aftermath of the Second World War. When the generation who lived through these traumatic events passes, their place is taken by those with no personal memories of these events. They and their successors may take peace and stability for granted and lose the commitments that made them possible. This phenomenon is evident across Europe, from Brexiteers in Britain to racists and nationalists in Central and Eastern Europe. And not to be forgotten is the fact that in the realm of foreign policy, we are not dealing with individual but social units. To quote Reinhold Niebuhr again: "In every human group there is less reason to guide and check impulse, less capacity for self-transcendence, less ability to comprehend the needs of others and therefore more unrestrained egoism than the individuals, who compose the group, reveal in their personal relationships."[75]

The USA increasingly moved away from multilateralism toward unilateralism, a process that accelerated when the Cold War ended and the Soviet Union collapsed.[76] A big giant step in this direction was taken by Donald Trump, showed little to no regard for longstanding allies, international norms, or laws. He and his closest advisors framed international relations as something close to a cutthroat zero-sum game in which all that mattered was naked power. He consistently put his own economic and political interests over those of the nation. He represented the very opposite of the generation responsible for embedding the USA in a set of international institutions that exercised power for common ends – for the most part – and generally by means of painstakingly negotiated understandings.[77] Trump and Turkey's President, Recep Erdoğan, turned the December 2019 NATO seventieth anniversary summit into a near shambles. Turkey and France went at each other over Turkey's attack on the Kurds. Trump repeated Erdoğan's rude characterization of French President Emmanuel Macron as "brain dead," described NATO countries as "delinquent" in their defense spending, described Canada's President Justin Trudeau as "two-faced, and "envisaged France" as "breaking away" from NATO even though, he insisted, it was the country that was most in need of its protection. When Trump was accused of being bad-mouthed by other leaders at a reception at Buckingham Palace, he was enraged, cancelled a closing press conference, and left the summit early.[78]

China has also reversed course in recent years. Its power has encouraged its leaders to deal with its neighbors in a more confident and assertive manner. It can more forcefully assert its interests in areas where it previously lacked leverage, such as American arms sales to Taiwan. Chinese leaders no longer believe it necessary to accord the United States the same degree of respect and deference.[79] Triumphalist nationalism is much more pronounced at the elite than at the mass level.[80] It has been at least partially responsible for what Thomas Christensen describes as China's more recent "ideological and acerbic" foreign policy.[81] In the East and South China Seas, China has been increasingly assertive, and is often criticized for acting as a bully.[82] To be fair, Japan, the Philippines, and Vietnam are also guilty of unilateral and provocative behavior with respect to disputed islands and islets.

The situation along the Pacific Rim is further complicated by the so-called American "pivot" to Asia and its balancing against China by supporting the countries with which it has territorial disputes. China has been constructed as a threat to American self-esteem. The American national security establishment portrays that country's rise as a threat to American security and its alleged hegemony. This concern for self-esteem resonates with the population at large. Many Americans also see China as an economic threat and bully. Chinese purchase of numerous flagship enterprises also threatens American self-esteem. For all these reasons, the population generally backs confrontational measures toward China – although they were divided on Trump's imposition of import duties.[83] The Trump administration announced publicly that that it would come to the aid of Japan in the event of a conflict with China over the territorial disputes in the East China Sea. We currently confront a situation where two major world powers, previously committed to more cautious and multilateral policies, are confronting one another over issues that have more symbolic than substantive importance.

American truculence is likely to encourage China to behave in more confrontational ways, pushing the USA, in turn, toward a more open containment policy and closer military collaboration with allies in the region. Feng Zhang rightly notes that such policies have the potential to shift the balance of power in both countries away from moderate-accommodationists toward hardline confrontationists.[84]

Germany continues to be a good European. Soon to retire Chancellor Angela Merkel was outspoken at the 2019 Harvard University commencement in her commitment to multilateralism, rejection of isolationism and nationalism, and the fight against climate change. She insisted on the need to see the world through the eyes of others and never "to describe lies as truth and truth as lies." The audience broke into sustained and spontaneous applause on multiple occasions.[85]

Even Germany and its much admired former Chancellor show signs of slipping away from their ethical commitments. In 2013, Germany was the most popular country in the world.[86] In southern Europe, Germany and Merkel are now widely despised because of their patently self-serving approach to the economic crises experienced by Greece, Cyprus, Italy, Spain, and Portugal.[87] Since 2009, these countries have been unable to repay their debts. European nations implemented a series of financial support measures to solve the crisis by lowering interest rates and providing loans of more than one trillion euros to maintain money flows among European banks. These banks, especially German banks, own a significant percentage of this debt and many of these loans were made in an irresponsible way. The European bailouts were largely about shifting exposure from northern European banks to citizens of southern European indebted countries through foreign-imposed policies of austerity. These policies had significant adverse economic effects, especially in labour market effects, with unemployment rates in Greece and Spain reaching 27 percent.[88]

Austerity was imposed by *diktat*. Germany threatened to cut Greece loose from the euro and let it go bankrupt. Germany and France conspired to remove Greece and Italian prime ministers who stood in the way and replace them with more pliant leaders.[89] One senior German official boasted that: "We do regime change better than the Americans."[90] Philosopher Jürgen Habermas expressed his concern that "the German government, including its Social Democratic faction, have gambled away in one night all the political capital that a better Germany had accumulated in a half century."[91]

The refugee crisis, greatly accelerated by the Libyan and Syrian civil wars, offers another example of selfish policymaking by members of the European Community. Beginning in 2015, there was a substantial increase in the numbers of refugees seeking entry into Europe, many arriving overland through southeastern Europe or via hazardous journeys across the Mediterranean in unseaworthy vessels. Angela Merkel's approach was highly ethical. She insisted from the outset that Germany could and would accommodate a large number of refugees. She told a crowd in Dresden in August 2015: "*Wir schaffen das*" (we can do this).[92] Her policy was highly controversial. Many liberal Germans supported her and welcomed the opportunity to demonstrate their humanitarianism. Others were hostile, a sentiment effectively adopted by Alternative für Deutschland (Alternative for Germany) a right-wing nationalist political party founded in 2013. Four years later, it became the largest opposition party in the Bundestag. The European Commission updated its Common European Asylum System intended to manage the crisis and distribute refugees among member states. In 2015, the Visegrád Group (Czech Republic, Hungary, Poland, Slovakia) rejected any compulsory long-term quota on the redistribution of immigrants.[93]

Some European countries pursued a de facto "hot potato" policy of taking as few asylum seekers as possible or passing them on to their neighbors. The United Kingdom's failure to honor its commitments is particularly glaring. The government of Theresa May committed itself to relocate there some of the most vulnerable refugee children in Europe. Yet in the six months between the passage of the Dubs Amendment to the 2016 Immigration Act and the demolition of the refugee "jungle" in Calais, in northern France, the Home Office failed to transfer a single child under the scheme. As of 2019, only some 1,500 children had been admitted.[94] This kind of resistance to immigration means that frontline countries such as Greece, Italy, and Spain have been compelled to cope with the lion's share of refugees. To the degree that solidarity has developed, it is among the right-wing opponents of the EU and immigration.

The European project is at risk.[95] In part, this is a function of external pressures such as immigration. But it is also due to short-term, self-seeking responses by national leaders or would-be leaders to a number of economic and political issues. In Eastern Europe, right-wing leaders in Poland and Hungary have fanned nationalism and eroded the rule of law. Germany responded in self-serving and destructive ways to southern Europe's economic crisis, leading to support for anti-European nationalists in Greece and Italy. Following referendum in the United Kingdom on June 23, 2016 in which 51.9 percent of those voting supported leaving the EU, the government of Theresa May invoked Article 50 of the Treaty on European Union. These individual challenges to European cohesion have had a synergistic effect and, for the first time in its history, scholars and pundits worry about the survival of the EU.[96]

My cases indicate that ethical policies do not prevent conflicts; neither do they prevent wars. But ethical policies pursued by multiple actors succeed in doing both. These kinds of commitment are fragile, even in liberal, democratic orders. They unravel when leaders feel threatened at home and make choices that some of them realize are not in the national interest but may be in their political interest. Sometimes, as in the case of Brexit, they are not even in the interests of the politicians. Moral qualities are critical in foreign and domestic politics, and their absence is a major source of tragedy.

My analysis differs in fundamental ways from rationalist accounts that stress constant evaluation of the costs and gains of any collaborative independent of any commitment to collaboration as an end in itself. Rationalist models assume that people make decisions on the basis of their interest but say nothing about how these interests arise or evolve. Their authors simply assume that people are utility maximizers when it comes to economic decisions and some form of realists – often offensive realists – when it comes to security. These crude formulations bear little relationship to how people and leaders conceive of their interests. They rule out any kind of deeper framing of interests or recognition of the ways in which short-term losses might be seen to confer longer-term gains. They also ignore the ways conceptions of interest can change in the course of interactions with other leaders and states.

Interests take shape in context. People and states alike are socialized into certain roles and with them taught to aspire to certain goals. Their past successes and failures are equally important for their current framings of interests and assessments of the policy options open to them. More fundamentally, they determine the options that are considered, their relative appeal, and assessments of their feasibility. Maintaining friendships and the solidarity they encourage can become important ends in themselves regardless of the benefits and costs of particular projects in which they are involved. So, too, do commitments to institutions, the rule of law, and other political values. Instrumentally rational people and states not infrequently accept, even actively participate in, decisions, policies, and projects they do not consider to benefit them directly – and may even involve real costs – because they sustain friendships, institutions, procedures, laws, or values. They and their countries are embedded in relationships that encourage interests to be formulated with other states in mind.[97]

Rationalist models all but exclude process from consideration. At best, they model interactions as sequences of moves, which is simple framing that makes possible their analysis but bears little relationship to what happens in the real world.[98] Ethical choices are guided by longer- vs. shorter-term interests and the recognition that individual actors benefit from being part of a community. Leaders with this understanding and a vision of a collaborative and cooperative future were responsible for the several successful initiatives I discussed in this chapter. Their success does not mean that other leaders will follow their example. Their successors may not be as capable of or committed to long-range thinking, lack their understanding of the national interest, and their savvy. Different leaders, changing domestic and foreign circumstances, and above all, those who prioritize their political advancement over the national interest, can halt and reverse the development of collaboration and community.

Notes

1. Immanuel Kant, "Perpetual Peace," in Hans Reiss ed., trans. H. B. Nisbet, *Kant's Political Writings* (Cambridge: Cambridge University Press, 1991), pp. 41–53.
2. Lorenzo Tondo, "Rescue Ship Captain Arrested for Breaking Italian Blockade," *Guardian*, June 29, 2019, www.theguardian.com/world/20 19/jun/29/sea-watch-captain-carola-rackete-arrested-italian-blockade; Agence France-Presse in Rome, "Captain Defends her Decision to Force Rescue Boat into Italian Port," *Guardian*, June 30, 2019, www .theguardian.com/world/2019/jun/30/italy-refugee-rescue-boat-captain -carola-rackete-defends-decision (both accessed June 30, 2019).
3. Ibid.
4. American War Library, "Vietnam War Allied Troop Levels 1960–73," drawing on Department of Defense Manpower Center, December 6, 2008, www.americanwarlibrary.com/vietnam/vwatl.htm; Nese F. DeBruyne, "American War and Military Operations Casualties: Lists and Statistics," Congressional Research Service, September 2018, https://fas.o rg/sgp/crs/natsec/RL32492.pdf (accessed May 18, 2019), pp. 35–6.
5. For the US fixation on resolve in general, Ted Hopf, *Peripheral Visions: Deterrence Theory and American Foreign Policy in the Third World, 1965–1990* (Ann Arbor: University of Michigan Press, 1994). For Vietnam, Fredrik Logevall, *Choosing War: The Lost Chance for Peace*

and the Escalation of War in Vietnam (Berkeley: University of California Press, 2001); Pat Proctor, *Containment and Credibility: The Ideology and Deception that Plunged America into the Vietnam War* (New York: Carrel Books, 2016).

6. James Risen, "SECRETS OF HISTORY: The C.I.A. in Iran – A Special Report: How a Plot Convulsed Iran in '53 (and in '79)," *New York Times*, April 16, 2000, www.nytimes.com/2000/04/16/world/secrets-history-cia-iran-special-report-plot-convulsed-iran-53–79.html (accessed May 19, 2019); Stephen Kinzer, *All the Shah's Men: An American Coup and the Roots of Middle East Terror* (New York: Wiley, 2008).

7. Ervand Abrahamian, *Iran Between Two Revolutions* (Princeton: Princeton University Press, 1982); Saïd Amir Arjomand, *Turban for the Crown: The Islamic Revolution in Iran* (Oxford: Oxford University Press, 1988); Misagh Parsa, *Social Origins of the Iranian Revolution* (New Brunswick: Rutgers University Press, 1989); Nikki Keddie, *Modern Iran: Roots and Results of Revolution* (New Haven: Yale University Press, 2003); Charles Kurzman, *The Unthinkable Revolution in Iran* (Cambridge: Harvard University Press, 2004).

8. Henry Munson, Jr., *Islam and Revolution in the Middle East* (New Haven: Yale University Press, 1988); William Shawcross, *The Shah's Last Ride: The Death of an Ally* (New York: Touchstone, 1989); Gary Sick, *All Fall Down: America's Tragic Encounter with Iran* (New York: Penguin Books, 1986).

9. Hugh Roberts, "Who Said Gaddafi Had to Go?" *London Review of Books* 33, 22 (November 2011): 8–18; Patrick C. R. Terry, "The Libya Intervention (2011): Neither Lawful, Nor Successful," *Comparative and International Law Journal of Southern Africa* 48, 2 (2015), pp. 162–82; Jennifer M. Welsh, "Humanitarian Intervention After September 11," in Jennifer M. Welsh, ed., *Humanitarian Intervention and International Relations* (Oxford: Oxford University Press, 2004), ch. 10; House of Commons, Foreign Affairs Committee, *Libya: Examination of intervention and collapse and the UK's future policy options*, Third Report of Session 2016–2017, September 14, 2016, www.google.com/search?client=firefox-b-d&q=Libya%3A+Examination+of+intervention+and+collapse+and+the+UK%27s+future+policy+options%22+%28PDF%29.+House+of+Commons%27+Foreign+Affairs+Committee; Alan J. Kuperman, "Obama's Libya Debacle; How a Well-Meaning Intervention Ended in Failure." *Foreign Affairs*, March-April 2015, www.foreignaffairs.com/articles/libya/2019–02-18/obamas-libya-debacle (both accessed April 24, 2019).

10. DeBruyne, "American War and Military Operations Casualties: Lists and Statistics," pp. 37–9; William Stueck, *The Korean War: An International History* (Princeton: Princeton University Press, 1995).

11. Prepared by Benjamin Valentino and the author.

12. Laura McClure, "Coalition of the Billing – or Unwilling?" *Salon*, March 13, 2003, www.salon.com/2003/03/12/foreign_aid/ (accessed July 2, 2019).

13. Timothy Andrews Sayle, *Enduring Alliance: A History of NATO and the Postwar Global Order* (Ithaca: Cornell University Press, 2019).

14. David S. McClellan, *Dean Acheson: The State Department Year* (New York: Dodd, Mead, 1976), pp. 295–6; William Stueck, *Rethinking the Korea War: A New Diplomatic and Strategic History* (Princeton: Princeton University Press, 2002), pp. 99, 125–6.

15. Larry Blomstedt, *Truman, Congress, and Korea: The Politics of America's First Undeclared War* (Lexington: University of Kentucky Press, 2016), on Truman, Congress, and public opinion during the Korean War.

16. House of Commons, *Libya*; Kuperman, "Obama's Libya Debacle"; Peter Cole, ed., *The Libyan Revolution and its Aftermath* (Oxford: Oxford University Press, 2015), especially the chapter by Frederic Wehrey, "NATO's Intervention," pp. 105–26.

17. David Coates and Joel Krieger, *Blair's War* (London: Polity, 2014); John Chilcot, Lawrence Freedman, Usha Kumari Prashar, Roderic Lyne, and Martin Gilbert, *Chilcot Report: Report of the Iraq Inquiry: Executive Summary* (London: Canbury Press, 2019).

18. On NATO, Lawrence Kaplan, *A Community of Interests: NATO and the Military Assistance Program, 1948–1951* (Washington: Office of the Secretary of Defense, 1980) and *The United States and NATO: The Formative Years* (Lexington: University Press of Kentucky, 1984).

19. George Marshall, "Speech to the Harvard Alumni, 5 June 1947 in Larry L. Bland and Mark Stoler, eds., *The Papers of George Catlett Marshall*, 6 (Baltimore: Johns Hopkins University Press, 2013), pp. 146–8; Michael Holm, *The Marshall Plan: A New Deal for Europe* (New York: Routledge, 2017), p. xvi.

20. John Gimbel, *The Origins of the Marshall Plan* (Stanford: Stanford University Press, 1976); Michael J. Hogan, *The Marshall Plan: America, Britain, and the Reconstruction of Western Europe, 1947–1952* (Cambridge: Cambridge University Press, 1987); Alan S. Milward, *The Reconstruction of Western Europe 1945–51* (Berkeley: University of California Press, 2006); Jeffry M. Diefendorf, Axel Frohn, and Hermann-Josef Rupieper, eds., *American Policy and*

the *Reconstruction of Western Germany, 1945–1955* (Cambridge: Cambridge University Press, 1993); Hans-Herbert Holzamer and Marc Hoch, eds., *Der Marshall-Plan: Geschichte und Zukunft* (Landsberg/Lech: Olzog, 1997); Richard N. Gardner, *Sterling-Dollar Diplomacy in Current Perspective: The Origins and Prospects of Our International Economic Order, 3rd Edition* (New York: Columbia University Press, 1980); Geir Lundestad, *The American Non-Policy Towards Eastern Europe, 1943–1947: Universalism in an Area Not of Essential Interest to the United States* (New York: Humanities, 1975) and "Empire by Invitation? The United States and Western Europe, 1945–1952" *Journal of Peace Research* 23, 6 (1986), pp. 262–78.

21. Joseph M. Jones, *The Fifteen Weeks* (New York: Viking Press, 1955); Walter Isaacson and Evan Thomas, *The Wise Men: Six Friends and the World They Made: Acheson, Bohlen, Harriman, Kennan, Lovett, McCloy* (New York: Simon & Schuster, 1986); John Lewis Gaddis, *Strategies of Containment: A Critical Appraisal of Postwar American National Security Policy* (Oxford: Oxford University Press, 1982), particularly on George Kennan; Gregory A Fossedal, *Our Finest Hour: Will Clayton, The Marshall Plan, and the Triumph Of Democracy* (Stanford: Hoover Institution Press,1993).

22. Holm, *The Marshall Plan*, p. xvi.

23. Alan Bullock, *Ernest Bevin: Foreign Secretary, 1945–1951* (Oxford: Oxford University Press, 1983), p. 405. More recently, Campbell Craig and Fredrik Logevall, *America's Cold War: The Politics of Insecurity* (Cambridge: Harvard University Press, 2009), p. 91, describe it "as perhaps the most successful single foreign policy ever undertaken by the United States."

24. Greg Behrman, *The Most Noble Adventure: The Marshall Plan and the Time When America Helped Save Europe* (New York: Free Press, 2007), p. 334.

25. William Appleman Williams, *The Tragedy of American Foreign Policy* (New York: Norton, 1972), p. 239; Gabriel Kolko, *The Roots of American Foreign Policy: An Analysis of Power and Purpose* (1969); Walter LaFeber, *America, Russia, and the Cold War, 1945–2006, 10th Edition* (New York: McGraw-Hill, 2007); Carolyn Eisenberg, *Drawing the Line: The American Decision to Divide Germany* (New York: Cambridge University Press, 1998).

26. Benn Steil, *The Marshall Plan: Dawn of the Cold War* (New York: Simon & Schuster, 2018), pp. 86–7.

27. Walter LaFeber, *America, Russia, and the Cold War, 1945–1984, 5th Edition* (New York: Knopf, 1985); Joyce Kolko and Gabriel Kolko, *The Limits of Power: The World and United States Foreign Policy,*

1945–1954 (New York: Harper & Row, 1972); Hadley Arkes, *Bureaucracy, the Marshall Plan, and the National Interest* (Princeton: Princeton University Press, 1972); Melvyn Leffler, "The United States and the Strategic Dimensions of the Marshall Plan" *Diplomatic History* 12, 3 (1988), pp. 277–306; Robert A. Pollard, *Economic Security and the Origins of the Cold War, 1945–1950* (New York: Columbia University Press, 1985); David Elwood, "Was the Marshall Plan Necessary?" in Fernando Guirao, Frances M. B. Lynch, and Sigfrido M. Ramírez Pérez, eds., *Alan S. Milward and a Century of European Change* (London: Routledge, 2012), pp. 240–54.

28. Michael Cox and Caroline Kennedy-Pipe, "The Tragedy of American Diplomacy? Rethinking the Marshall Plan," *Journal of Cold War Studies* 7, 1 (2005), pp. 97–134; Marc Trachtenberg, "Response: The Marshall Plan as Tragedy,' *Journal of Cold War Studies*, 7, 1 (2005), pp. 135–40.

29. Alan S. Milward, *The Reconstruction of Western Europe, 1945–1951* (London: Methuen, 1984) and "Review: Was the Marshall Plan Necessary?" *Diplomatic History* 13, 2 (1989), pp. 231–53.

30. Robert C. Grogin, *Natural Enemies: The United States and the Soviet Union in the Cold War, 1917–1991* (Lanham: Lexington Books, 2001), p. 118; Bradford J. DeLong and Barry Eichengreen, "The Marshall Plan: History's Most Successful Structural Adjustment Program," in Rudiger Dornbusch, Wilhelm Nolling and Richard Layard, eds., *Postwar Economic Reconstruction and Lessons for the East Today* (Cambridge: MIT Press, 1993), pp. 189–230; William Diebold, "The Marshall Plan in Retrospect: A Review of Recent Scholarship," *Journal of International Affairs* 41, 2 (1988), pp. 421–35; Martin Schain, ed. *The Marshall Plan: Fifty Years After* (New York: Palgrave, 2001); Kathleen Burk, "The Marshall Plan: Filling in Some of the Blanks," *Contemporary European History* 10, 2 (2001), pp. 267–94.

31. John Lewis Gaddis, *The United States and the End of the Cold War, 1941–1947* (New York: Columbia University Press, 1972); Vojtech Mastny, *Russia's Road to the Cold War: Diplomacy, Warfare, and the Politics of Communism* (New York: Columbia University Press, 1979); Robert A. Pollard, *Economic Security and the Origins of the Cold War* (New York: Columbia University Press, 1985); Marc Trachtrenberg, *A Constructed Peace: The Making of the European Settlement, 1945–1963* (Princeton: Princeton University Press, 1999).

32. Thomas J. McCormik, "Drift or Mastery? A Corporatist Synthesis for American Diplomatic History," *Reviews in American History* 10, 4 (1982), pp. 323–29; Michael J. Hogan, *Marshall Plan*; Emily

S. Rosenberg, *Spreading the American Dream: American Economic and Cultural Expansion* (New York: Hill & Wang, 1982). Also Melvyn Leffler, *A Preponderance of Power: National Security, the Truman Administration, and the Cold War* (Stanford: Stanford University Press, 1993), pp. 182–237; Charles S. Maier, "The Politics of Productivity: Foundations of American Economic Policy after World War II," *International Organization* 31, 4 (1977), pp. 607–33.

33. Hogan, *Marshall Plan*.
34. G. John Ikenberry, *After Victory: Institutions, Strategic Restraint, and The Rebuilding of Order After Major Wars* (Princeton: Princeton University Press, 2001) and *The Liberal Leviathan* (Princeton: Princeton University Press, 2011).
35. Charles Krauthammer, "The Unipolar Moment: America and the World, 1990," *Foreign Affairs* 70, 1 (1990/1991), pp. 23–33; G. John Ikenberry, Michael Mastanduno, and William C. Wohlforth, eds., *Unipolarity and International Relations Theory* (New York: Cambridge University Press, 2011); William C. Wohlforth, "The Stability of a Unipolar World," *International Security*, 24, 1 (1999), pp. 5–41 and "U.S. Strategy in a Unipolar World," in G. John Ikenberry, ed., *America Unrivaled: The Future of the Balance of Power* (Ithaca: Cornell University Press, 2002), pp. 98–120.
36. Simon Reich and Richard Ned Lebow, *Good-Bye Hegemony! Power and Influence in the Global System* (Princeton: Princeton University Press, 2014), ch. 2.
37. G. John Ikenberry, Reflections on After Victory," *British Journal of Politics and International Relations*, August 10, 2018, https://journals.sagepub.com/doi/abs/10.1177/1369148118791402 (accessed May 28, 2019).
38. North Korea, the USSR, Mongolia, Afghanistan, Pakistan, India, Sikkim, Bhutan, Nepal, Burma, Laos, and Vietnam.
39. Russia replaced the Soviet Union. The new post-Soviet states are Kazakhstan, Kyrgyzstan, and Tajikistan.
40. Owen Lattimore, *Inner Asian Frontiers of China* (New York: American Geographical Society, 1940); Gerald Segal, *China Changes Shape: Regionalism and Foreign Policy*, Adelphi Paper 287 (London: International Institute of Strategic Studies, 1994).
41. M. Taylor Fravel, *Strong Borders, Secure Nation: Cooperation and Conflict in China's Territorial Disputes* (Princeton: Princeton University Press, 2008; Chien-peng Chung, Domestic Politics: International Bargaining, and China's Territorial Disputes," *Chinese Journal of International Politics*, 2 (2009), pp. 487–523; Nie Hongy, "Explaining Chinese Solutions to Territorial Disputes with Neighbor

States," *Chinese Journal of International Politics*, 2 (2009), pp. 487–523; Zhang Yungling, "China and Its Neighbourhood: Transformation, Challenges and Grand Strategy," *International Affairs* 92, 4 (2016), pp. 835–48; Zhihua Shena and Julia Lovell, "Undesired Outcomes: China's Approach to Border Disputes during the Early Cold War," *Cold War History* 15, 1 (2015), pp. 89–111; Feng Zhang, "Chinese Thinking on the South China Sea and the Future of Regional Security," *Political Science Quarterly* 132, 3 (2017), pp. 435–66.

42. Nie Hongy, "Explaining Chinese Solutions to Territorial Disputes with Neighbour States," for this list of disputes.

43. Robert S. Ross, *The Indochina Tangle: China's Vietnam Policy, 1975–1979* (New York: Columbia University Press, 1988); Zhang Xiaoming, "China 1979 Border War with Vietnam: A Reassessment," *China Quarterly* 84 (2005), pp. 851–74; King V. Chen, *China's War With Việt Nam, 1979* (Stanford: Hoover Institution Press, 1987); Fravel, *Strong Borders*, pp. 280–87.

44. Nie Hongyi, "Explaining Chinese Solutions to Territorial Disputes with Neighbour States."

45. Fravel, *Strong Borders*.

46. Shena and Lovell, "Undesired Outcomes."

47. On India, Neville Maxwell, *India's China War* (New York: Pantheon Books, 1970); Steven A. Hoffman, *India and the China Crisis* (Berkeley: University of California Press, 1990). On China, Allen S, Whiting, *The Chinese Calculus of Deterrence: India and Indochina* (Ann Arbor: University of Michigan Press, 1975); Melvin Gurtov and Byong-Moo Hwang, *China Under Threat: The Politics of Strategy and Diplomacy* (Baltimore: Johns Hopkins University Press, 1980), pp. 99–154; John W. Garver, "China's Decision for War with India in 1962," in Alastair Ian Johnson and Robert S. Ross, eds., *New Directions in the Study of China's Foreign Policy* (Stanford: Stanford University Press, 2006), pp. 86–130; Fravel, *Strong Borders*, pp. 174–83.

48. Fravel, *Strong Borders*, p. 60.

49. Maxwell, *India's China War*; Hoffman, *India and the China Crisis*; Whiting, *Chinese Calculus of Deterrence*; Gurtov and Hwang, *China Under Threat*), pp. 99–154; Garver, "China's Decision for War with India in 1962"; Fravel, *Strong Borders, Secure Nation*, pp. 174–83.

50. Jeffrey Herf, *Divided Memory: The Nazi Past in the Two Germanys* (Cambridge: Harvard University Press, 1997); Norbert Frei, *Adenauer's Germany and the Nazi Past: The Politics of Amnesty and Integration* (New York: Columbia University Press, 2002), pp. 212–21; Yinan He, *The Search for Reconciliation: Sino-Japanese and German-Polish*

Relations since World War II (Cambridge: Cambridge University Press, 2009), pp. 57–61.

51. Norbert Frei, *Adenauer's Germany and the Nazi Past*; Robert G. Moeller, ed., *West Germany Under Construction: Politics, Society and Culture in the Adenauer Era* (Ann Arbor: University of Michigan Press, 1997); Helga Haftendorn, *Coming of Age: German Foreign Policy Since 1945* (Lanham: Rowman & Littlefield, 2006), pp. 83–120; Peter Hoeres, *Außenpolitik und Öffentlichkeit. Massenmedien, Meinungsforschung und Arkanpolitik in den deutsch-amerikanischen Beziehungen von Erhard bis Brandt* (Munich: Oldenbourg, 2013).

52. Lily Gardner Feldman, *The Special Relationship Between Germany and Israel* (London: Allen & Unwin, 1984); Nana Sagi, *German Reparations: A History of the Negotiations* (London: Palgrave-Macmillan, 1986); Ronald W. Zweig, *German Reparations and the Jewish World: A History of the Claims Conference* (Boulder: Westview Press, 1987); Christian Pross, *Paying for the Past: The Struggle over Reparations for Surviving Victims of the Nazi Terror* (Baltimore: Johns Hopkins University Press, 1998).

53. Konrad Adenauer, Speech to the Bundestag, September 27, 1951, in Rolf Vogel, ed. , *Deutschlands Weg nach Israel: Eine Dokumentation mit einem Geleitwort von Konrad Adenauer* (Stuttgart, Seewald Verlag, 1967), p. 36.

54. Haftendorn, *Coming of Age*, p. 17.

55. Herf, *Divided Memory*, p. 212; Frei, *Adenauer's Germany*, pp. 229–30; He, *Search for Reconciliation*, pp. 58–9.

56. Herf, *Divided Memory*, pp. 287–8; Stephen A. Pagaard, "German Schools and the Holocaust: A Focus on the Secondary Schools of Nordrhein-Westfalen" *History Teacher* 28, 4 (1995), pp. 541–4; Mark M. Krug, "The Teaching of History at the Center of the Cold War: History Textbooks in East and West Germany," *School Review* 69, 4 (1961), pp. 461–87; Jeffrey K. Olick and Daniel Levy, "Collective Memory and Cultural Constraint: Holocaust Myth and Reality in German Politics," *American Sociology Review* 62, 6 (1997), pp. 921–36; He, *Search for Reconciliation*, pp. 57–61.

57. Haftendorn, Coming of Age, pp. 157–96; W. W. Kulski, Germany and Poland: From War to Peaceful Relations (Syracuse: Syracuse University Press, 1976); Marcin Zaborowski, *Germany, Poland, and Europe: Conflict, Cooperation, and Europeanisation* (Manchester: Manchester University Press, 2004; He, *Search for Reconciliation*, pp. 67–70.

58. Elisabeth Noelle and Erik Peter Neumann, eds., *The Germans: Public Opinion Polls 1947–1956* (Allensbach: Verlag für Demoskopie, 1967), p. 470, cited in He, *Search for Reconciliation*, p. 67.

59. Hans-Joachim Noack and Willy Brandt, *Ein Leben, Ein Jahrhunde. Lars Brandt: Andenken* (München: Carl-Hanser-Verlag, 2006); Helga Grebing, *Willy Brandt. Der andere Deutsche* (Paderborn: Wilhelm-Fink-Verlag, 2008).

60. Haftendorn, *Coming of Age*, pp. 170–73; Pertii Ahonen, *After the Expulsion: West Germany and Eastern Europe, 1945–1990* (Oxford: Oxford University Press, 2003), pp. 119–202.

61. Spiegel On Line, "Kniefall vor der Geschichte," www.spiegel.de/eines tages/willy-brandt-in-warschau-a-946886.html (accessed June 5, 2019); Wily Brandt, "Der Kniefall von Warschau," in Friedbert Pflüger and Winfried Lipscher, eds., *Feinde werden Freunde* (Bonn: Bouvier, 1993), pp. 51–60.

62. Charles S. Maier, *The Unmasterable Past: History, Holocaust, and German National Identity* (Cambridge: Harvard University Press, 1988); Herf, *Divided Memory*; Robert G. Moeller, *War Stories: The Search for a Usable Past in the Federal Republic of Germany* (Berkeley: University of California Press, 2001); Jay Howard Geller, *Jews in Post-Holocaust Germany* (Cambridge: Cambridge University Press, 2005); Wulf Kansteiner, *In Pursuit of German Memory: History, Television, and Politics after Auschwitz* (Athens: Ohio University Press, 2006); Richard Ned Lebow, Wulf Kansteiner, and Claudio Fogu, eds., *The Politics of Memory in Postwar Europe* (Durham: Duke University Press, 2006); Mark Wolfgram, *Getting History Right: East And West German Collective Memories of the Holocaust and War* (Lewisburg: Bucknell University Press, 2011).

63. CBOS, *Polish Public Opinion* (Bulletin), July/August 1998. Cited in He, *Search for Reconciliation*, p. 98.

64. Henry Samuel and Caroline Davies, "Germans Invited to D-Day Anniversary Ceremonies for First Time," *Telegraph*, January 2, 2004, www.telegraph.co.uk/news/worldnews/europe/germany/14507 65/Germans-invited-to-D-Day-anniversary-ceremonies-for-first-time .html; Thomas Fuller and Katrin Bennhold, "D-DAY/60 Years Later: 60th Anniversary of D-Day: Leaders Stress Friendship," *International Herald Tribune*, June 7, 2004, www.nytimes.com/2004/06/07/news/ dday-60-years-later-60th-anniversary-of-ddayleaders-stress-friend ship.html (both accessed January 4, 2018).

65. Fuller and Katrin Bennhold, "D-DAY/60 Years Later."

66. Kornprobst, Markus, *Co-Managing International Crises: Judgments and Justifications* (Cambridge: Cambridge University Press, 2019) on the growth of European trust and collaboration in crisis management.

67. Kaplan, *N.A.T.O. 1948*, p. 12; William Park, *Defending the West: A History of NATO* (Boulder: Westview, 1986), p. 4; Simon

J. Bulmer, "Shaping the Rules? The Constitutive Politics of the European Union and German Power," in Peter J. Katzenstein, ed., *Tamed Power: Germany in Europe* (Ithaca: Cornell University Press, 1997), pp. 1–48.

68. Haftendorn, *Coming of Age*, pp. 83–120.

69. For a comparative analysis, Richard Ned Lebow, "Transitions and Transformations: Building International Cooperation," *Security Studies* 6, 1 (Spring 1997), pp. 154–79.

70. Henry Kissinger, *White House Years* (New York: Little, Brown, 1979), pp. 733–87; Raymond L. Garthoff, *Détente and Confrontation: American-Soviet Relations from Nixon to Reagan*, rev. ed. (Washington: Brookings, 1994), pp. 227–8, for the substance of these negotiations.

71. See Andrew H. *Kydd, Trust and Mistrust in International Relations* (Princeton: Princeton University Press, 2005); Brian C. Rathbun, *Trust in International Cooperation: International Security Institutions, Domestic Politics and American Multilateralism* (Cambridge: Cambridge University Press, 2011); Hiski Haukkala, *Carina van de Wetering, Johanna Vuorelma, Trust in International Relations: Rationalist, Constructivist, and Psychological Approaches* (London: Routledge, 2016); Christopher Rathbun, Trust in International Relations (Oxford: Oxford University Press, 2018).

72. Hogan, *Marshall Plan*, provides good documentation of nongovernmental collaboration.

73. John M. Sherwig, *Guineas and Gunpowder: British Foreign Aid in the Wars Against France: 1793–1815* (Cambridge: Harvard University Press, 1969); Dominic Lieven, *Russia Against Napoleon: The Battle for Europe, 1807–14* (London: Penguin, 2009), p. 337; Roger Knight, *Britain Against Napoleon: The Organization of Victory 1793–1815* (London: Allen Lane, 2013), pp. 421–2.

74. Reinhold Niebuhr, 'The Sources of American Prestige," in Elisabeth Sifton, ed., *Reinhold Niebuhr: Major Works on Religion and Politics* (New York: Library of America, 2015), pp. 666–70.

75. Reinhold Niebuhr, *Moral Man and Immoral Society* [1932], in Sifton, *Reinhold Niebuhr*, p. 139.

76. Reich and Lebow, *Good-Bye Hegemony*, for documentation.

77. Hal Brands, *American Grand Strategy in the Age of Trump* (Washington: Brookings, 2018); Howard A. Dewitt, *Trump Against The World: Foreign Policy Bully, Russian Collusion* (New York: Horizon, 2018); John Glaser, Christopher A. Preble, and A. Trevor, *Thrall Fuel to the Fire: How Trump Made America's Broken Foreign Policy Even Worse (and How We Can Recover)* (Washington: Cato Institute, 2019).

78. Katie Rogers et al., "Tensions Overshadow NATO Meeting Intended as Show of Unity," *New York Times*, December 4, 2019, www.nyti mes.com/2019/12/04/world/europe/nato-live-updates-trump-mac ron.html; *Economist*, "NATO Marks its 70th Anniversary in Typically Chaotic Fashion," December 4, 2009, www.economist.co m/europe/2019/12/04/nato-marks-its-70th-anniversary-in-typically -chaotic-fashion?cid1=cust/dailypicks1/n/bl/n/2019124n/owned/n/n/ dailypicks1/n/n/na/354622/n; (both accessed December 5, 2019); Patrick Wintour and Rowena Mason, "Trump Leaves Nato Talks after Ridicule from Allies," *Guardian*, December 5, 2009, pp. 1 and 4; Patrick Wintour, "Leaders Agree to Review Bid to Heal Bitter Divisions," *Guardian*, December 5, 2009, p. 6; Dan Sabbagh, "Split Loyalties in Alliance Raise Doubts over Its Effectiveness," *Guardian*, December 5, 2009, p. 6.

79. Thomas J. Christensen, "Obama and Asia: Confronting the China Challenge," *Foreign Affairs* 94, 5 (2015), pp. 28–36, quote at p. 28; Zhang Yunling, "China and Its Neighbourhood."

80. Alastair Iain Johnston, "Is Chinese Nationalism Rising? Evidence from Beijing," *International Security* 41, 3 (2016/2017), pp. 7–43.

81. Christensen, *The China Challenge*, p. 255. Also, Zhang and Lebow, *Taming Sino-American Rivalry*, chs. 3 and 7.

82. Katherine Morton, "China's Ambition in the South China Sea: Is a Legitimate Maritime Order Possible?" *International Affairs* 92, 4 (2016), pp. 909–40.

83. Anthony Salvato, "CBS News Poll on Trade and Tariffs: Americans Want China to Change Policies; They're Wary of Short-term Tariff Impact," CBS News, May 16, 2019, www.cbsnews.com/news/cbs-ne ws-poll-on-trade-and-tariffs-americans-want-china-to-change-poli cies-wary-of-short-term-tariff-impact/ (accessed July 5, 2019).

84. Feng Zhang, "Chinese Thinking on the South China Sea and the Future of Regional Security"; Feng Zheng and Richard Ned Lebow, *Taming Sino-American Rivalry*, ch. 4.

85. Rick Gladstone, "In Harvard Speech, Merkel Rebukes Trump's Worldview in All but Name," *New Times*, May 30, 2019, www .nytimes.com/2019/05/30/world/europe/merkel-harvard-speech.html (accessed June 6, 2019).

86. BBC News, "BBC Poll: Germany Most Popular Country in the World," May 23, 2013, www.bbc.com/news/world-europe-22624104 (accessed July 5, 2019).

87. Adam Tooze, *Crashed: How a Decade of Financial Crises Changed the World* (London: Allen Lane, 2018), Part III; Amie Ferris-Rotman, "Nazi Jokes, Wrath at Germans Highlight Greek Despair," *Reuters*,

October 26, 2017, www.reuters.com/article/us-greece-germany-rela tions/nazi-jokes-wrath-at-germans-highlight-greek-despair-idUSTR E79P3LN20111026; Patrick Kingsley and Josie Le Blond, "Tourists in Greece: 'Don't Tell the Cook We're German'," *Guardian*, July 17, 2015, www.theguardian.com/world/2015/jul/17/tourists-in-greece-dont-tell-the-cook-were-german; Bruce Stokes, Richard Wike, and Dorothy Maleviuch, "Favorable Views of Germany Don't Erase Concerns about its Influence within EU," *Pew Research Center*, June 15, 2017, www.pewresearch.org/global/2017/06/15/favorable-views-of-germany-dont-erase-concerns-about-its-influence-within-eu/ (all accessed July 5, 2019). According to Pew, only 21 percent of Europeans hold a negative view of Germany, but 48 percent think it wields too much power in the EU. Greeks are outliers with 79 percent having a negative opinion of Germany, followed by Italy at 42 percent.

88. Paul Belkin, Martin A. Weiss, Rebecca M. Nelson, and Darek E. Mix, "The Eurozone Crisis: Overview and Issues For Congress," Congressional Research Service, Report R42377, February 29, 2012; Peter Nedergaard, Henrik Bang, and Mads Dagnis Jensen, "'We the People' versus 'We the Heads of States': the Debate on the Democratic Deficit of the European Union," *Policy Studies* 36, 2 (2015), pp. 196–216; Mark Blyth, *Austerity* (Oxford: Oxford University Press, 2013).

89. Tooze, *Crashed*, pp. 404–21.

90. Ibid. Adam Tooze interview with Hans Knundani, September 2017, p. 412.

91. Philip Otterman, "Merkel "Gambling Away' Germany's Reputation Over Greece, Says Habermas," *Guardian*, July 16, 2015, www.the guardian.com/business/2015/jul/16/merkel-gambling-away-germa nys-reputation-over-greece-says-habermas (accessed August 21, 2019).

92. The full sentence, at a speech in August 2015 in Dresden, was: "*Wir haben so vieles geschafft – wir schaffen das*" (We've accomplished so many things, we can do this). Janosch Delker, "The Phrase that Haunts Angela Merkel," *Politico*, August 19, 2016, www.politico.eu/article/th e-phrase-that-haunts-angela-merkel/ (accessed July 5, 2019).

93. Antoine Pécoud, *Depoliticising Migration: Global Governance and International Migration Narratives* (London: Palgrave-Macmillan, 2015); Ettore Recchi, *Mobile Europe: The Theory and Practice of Free Movement in the EU* (London: Palgrave-Macmillan, 2015); Gabriella Lazaridis and Khursheed Wadia, eds., *The Securitisation of Migration in the EU: Debates since 9/11* (London: Palgrave-Macmillan, 2015); Gabriella Lazaridis, *International Migration into Europe: From Subjects to Abjects* (London: Palgrave-Macmillan, 2015);

Pontus Odmalm, *The Party Politics of the EU and Immigration* (London: Palgrave-Macmillan, 2014); Hans Andersson, "Liberal Intergovernmentalism, Spillover and Supranational Immigration Policy," *Cooperation and Conflict*, 1 (2016), pp. 8–54; Hannes Weber, "National and Regional Proportion of Immigrants and Perceived Threat of Immigration: A Three-Level Analysis in Western Europe," *International Journal of Comparative Sociology* 56, 2 (2015), pp. 116–40; A. A. Lozano, et al., "Revisiting the European Union Framework on Immigrant Integration: The European Integration Forum as a Technology of Agency," *Ethnicities* 14, 4 (2014), pp. 556–76.

94. May Bulman, "Government's Treatment of Child Refugees under Dubs Scheme Broke Law, Court of Appeal Rules," *Independent*, October 3, 2018, www.independent.co.uk/news/uk/home-news/dubs-child-refugees-home-office-immigration-home-office-supreme-court-a8566191.html; Stella Creasy, "Britain Willfully Ignored its Promise to Child Refugees. That Shame Has to End," *Guardian*, October 5, 2018, www.theguardian.com/commentisfree/2018/oct/05/britain-ignored-promise-child-refugees-dubs-amendment (both accessed June 7, 2019).

95. For the most thoughtful analysis, see Douglas Webber, *European Disintegration? The Politics of Crisis in the European Union* (London: Red Globe Press, 2019).

96. Tim Shipman, *All Out War: The Full Story of Brexit* (London: Collins, 2017) and *Fall Out: A Year of Political Mayhem* (London: Collins, 2018); Anthony Seldon, *May at 10* (London: Biteback, 2019); Harold D. Clarke, Matthew Goodwin, and Paul Whiteley, *Brexit: Why Britain Voted to Leave the European Union* (Cambridge: Cambridge University Press, 2017); Geoffrey Evans and Anand Menon, *Brexit and British Politics* (Cambridge: Polity Press, 2017); Sara B. Hobolt, "The Brexit Vote: A Divided Nation, A Divided Continent," *Journal of European Public Policy* 23, 9 (2016), pp. 1259–77; Tim Oliver, *Understanding Brexit: A Concise Introduction* (Bristol: Policy Press, 2018); Kevin O'Rourke, *A Short History of Brexit: From Brentry to Backstop* (London: Pelican, 2019); Fintan O'Toole, *Heroic Failure: Brexit and the Politics of Pain* (London: Apollo, 2018); Ivan Rogers, *9 Lessons in Brexit* (London: Short Books, 2019); Jonathan Freedland, "How Brexit Is Causing the Strange Death of British Conservatism," *Guardian*, June 7, 2019, www.theguardian.com/commentisfree/2019/jun/07/brexit-strange-death-british-conservatism (accessed June 7, 2019).

97. Karl W. Deutsch, *Nationalism and Social Communication* (Cambridge: MIT Press, 1953), described the "we" feeling that arises in such relationships. For case studies, Patrick T. Jackson, *Civilizing the Enemy: German Reconstruction and the Invention of the West* (Ann

Arbor: University of Michigan Press, 2006); Ulrich Krotz and Joachim Schild, *Shaping Europe: France, Germany, and Embedded Bilateralism from the Élysee Treaty to Twenty-First Century Politics* (Oxford: Oxford University Press, 2013).

98. Richard Ned Lebow, "Reason Divorced from Reality: Thomas Schelling and Strategic Bargaining," *International Politics* 43, 4 (2006), pp. 429–52 and "Beyond Parsimony: Rethinking Theories of Coercive Bargaining," *European Journal of International Relations* 4, 1 (1998), pp. 31–66.

5 | Policymaking

A dominant propensity of American culture is the belief that most problems have solutions and that they are technical in nature. This belief has probably contributed as much to American prosperity as the country's natural resources and hard-working population. The belief that progress is paved by technical solutions also has a downside, however. There are problems that do not lend themselves readily to solutions, and, even if they do, the keys to their resolution may have nothing to do with technology.

Belief in progress and technology are products of modernity. They may be more pronounced in America but are shared to some degree by leaders and peoples of other developed countries. They are part and parcel of the optimism to which the Enlightenment gave rise to which there was later a pessimistic pushback. Beginning in the nineteenth century, philosophers, writers, and sociologists worried that technological progress, industrialization, and bureaucracy had begun to enslave people in new and terrifying ways.[1] Matthew Arnold, Friedrich Nietzsche, and Max Weber are well-known exemplars.[2] Their concerns find resonance today in fears about the consequences of globalization, artificial intelligence, robotics, and surveillance technologies. Historically, these fears have been exaggerated in the sense that none of the worst case scenarios has come to pass, and some of their early, horrifying consequences of urbanization and industrialization were subsequently corrected. The Internet is the hottest current focus of debate. Some argue for its potential to enlighten and liberate people and others for the ease with which it can propagate falsehoods, shutdown dialogue, spread fear and anger, and arouse hostility and violence.[3]

The tragic view of life offers an alternative to this kind of binary thinking. It encourages people to accept, even attempt to transcend the contradictory consequences of individual and social behavior and the forces that shape them. It offers a strategy for coping with an unsettling and threatening status quo: be like blades of grass that survive by not

128

resisting the wind. It values the present over any imagined future, caution over risk, passivity over activity, and acceptance over rebellion. It is appropriate to worlds in which actors have little to no control over their environments. It is not in and of itself an appropriate guide to today's world. My claim, rather, is that it is a necessary corrective to the naïve optimism about progress, agency, and the efficacy of power that is so prevalent today, and especially so in foreign policy. A tragic understanding of life and politics can go a long way in restraining the excesses of modernism by making people painfully aware of the extent to which efforts to control the physical or social environment are at least as likely to backfire as they are to succeed. At the same time, we need to engage the world in ways that were impossible and unnecessary before the advent of modern technology.

In this chapter, I apply the above insight to policymaking. It is an arena that has received increasing attention in business and politics. Not surprisingly, organizational theorists, political scientists, and international relations scholars have looked for technical fixes. I will review and critique some of these efforts and show why they are misdirected. I do not deny that many, if not most, of the recommendations that derive from organizational and psychological studies are reasonable. However, I do contend they are only likely to bring about marginal improvements in policy. This is because bad decisions are not only, or even primarily, the product of sloppy or flawed decisionmaking processes. Catastrophic decisions more often have deeper causes. They are most often the result of inappropriate assumptions about the nature of the problem or the best way of coping with it. More rigorous decisionmaking procedures are unlikely to bring these misconceptions to light. It is well-known that leaders confronted with high-risk decisions surround themselves with people with whom they feel comfortable, and these are people who share their assumptions. Bad decisions are also due to the refusal of leaders to make trade-offs among competing goals or take seriously information that suggests their preferred policy is likely to lead to disaster. These are motivated errors, often brought about by the anxiety associated with the fear of possible loss. They also make leaders unwilling to engage in the kind of decisionmaking process that might expose their bias.

There is a deeper link between inappropriate assumptions and modernity. The belief in progress, technical fixes, and the efficacy of power encourages unrealistic expectations about our species ability to manipulate physical and social environments toward desired ends. It makes people more insensitive to evidence about past failures and more receptive to information in support of future successes. To the extent that modernity breeds overconfidence of this kind, it is a source of wishful thinking and a barrier to caution and due diligence.

Ethics enters the picture because a tragic conception of life and politics is very germane to policymaking. It encourages reflection, caution, respect for others, and careful assessment of risks, but with recognition that they will not necessarily prevent disaster. A tragic perspective encourages making decisions that pay as much attention to what can go wrong as they do to what leaders hope to achieve. It insists that people accept responsibility for their choices. This perspective is only likely to appeal to leaders with the courage to face that truth that we are, to a large degree, at the mercy of our physical, biological, political, economic, and social environments.

Of equal importance, a tragic view of life and politics encourages policymakers to consider the ethical implications of the goals they seek and the means by which they pursue them. Policymakers must expand their horizons beyond a narrow focus of the goal in question. Critiquing bureaucracy from a tragic perspective, Max Weber predicted that it threatened to reorient people's loyalties by narrowing their ethical horizons to those of their institution. In the absence of deeper ethical commitments, bureaucracy would impose its own values on people. The *Kulturmensch* (person of culture) would give way to the *Fachmensch* (occupational specialist). For the latter, the only ethical yardstick would be the interests and power of the organization. Quoting Nietzsche, Weber predicted "the 'last men'" would be "specialists without spirit [and] sensualists without heart."[4] Tragic, too, would be the longer-term consequences: institutions established to liberate people and improve their lives would only succeed in narrowing their perspectives and further enslaving them.

The 2003 Iraq invasion, which I will discuss in the pages that follow, is one of many events that offers frightening proof of the validity of Weber's concerns. Let me highlight here that American policymaking represented a low point in ethical reflexivity. President Bush and his advisors focused entirely on the military campaign that would lead to the overthrow of Saddam Hussein. There is no evidence that they ever considered the human costs of air strikes and an invasion. To the extent that they contemplated the consequences of their invasion beyond the removal of Saddam, they imagined and took refuge in only the rosiest of scenarios. They expected to be welcomed as liberators, have their puppet regime command the support of the Iraqi people, and their military campaign of "shock and awe" to make Iran and North Korea more compliant. Their hopes were based on thoroughly faulty assumptions, most significantly the related beliefs that military power could substitute for political influence and that an impressive display of military power would intimidate friend and foe alike.

The American approach to decisionmaking was not responsible for the Iraq War fiasco. But neither did it create any kind of impediment to it. By excluding ethics from the picture, focusing on power rather than influence and procedures rather than substance, and evaluating policy choices in terms of narrow goals that could be quantitatively measured, it encouraged the kind of military planning and decisionmaking that set in motion this tragedy. Tragedy, by contrast, encourages a holistic view of people, the contexts in which they operate, and they ways in which they are likely to respond to one's initiatives. It emphasizes the extent to which individuals and their political units are embedded in communities. They make people human and life worthwhile by providing affiliations and roles and some degree of security, affluence, and standing. People outside communities, or acting at odds with them, are guided only by their raw appetites and instrumental reason and constitute a danger to themselves and all those around them.

Guided by a tragic view of life, ancient Greeks rightly regarded the community as the source of wisdom, respect and sympathy for others, and self-restraint. They would have regarded the autonomous, egoistic actor – the goal of much modern philosophy and the starting point for the realist, liberal, and rationalist paradigms – as dangerous to themselves and everyone around them. The Bush administration became an autonomous actor by all but removing itself from the community of nations by disregarding nomos, attacking another political unit without the support of the United Nations Security Council, and in the face of opposition from most of its closest allies. It is hardly surprising from a tragic perspective that its leaders could not calculate the national interest, or even their own political interests, in any kind of rational manner.

I begin this chapter with a critique of the literature on foreign policy decisionmaking in political science and political psychology. I argue that it is unrealistic in a double sense: leaders are unlikely to adopt its most significant recommendations, and, if they did, they would not make a crucial difference in most policy decisions. The second and third parts address what I consider to be the most serious decision-related causes of bad and catastrophic policy decisions. These are inappropriate assumptions, and ones moreover, that are rarely, if ever, interrogated. Next come narrow frames of reference for policy formulation. These two failings are related, as is the general failure to give appropriate attention to negative outcomes and the pathways that might lead to them.

I conclude by making the case for a more tragic and less technical approach to decisionmaking. I repeat that I am not offering a tragic framework as a substitute for modern ways of addressing problems, but as a much needed corrective. As in everything else in life, there needs to be a balance, in this instance between self-interest and concern for others, risk taking and risk aversion, optimism and pessimism, overconfidence and timidity, flying by the seat of the pants and acting on the basis of careful analysis and preparation, and a focus on the benefits of action versus those of inaction. People and leaders alike must overcome the propensity to think in black-and-white terms and accept the need for larger perspectives that incorporate tensions, contradictions, uncertainties, incorporate an ethical dimension, and the need to accept responsibility for one's actions.

Technical Fixes

The Cuban missile crisis was the catalyst for studies of foreign policy decisionmaking. It spawned a large literature, much of it about why deterrence failed to prevent the crisis and how compellence resolved it.[5] These analyses focused on the substance of policy, almost entirely on the American side as there was no information available about what went on inside the Kremlin. Some scholars argued for a strong link between process and outcome, suggesting that good policy was the result of good decisionmaking, and vice versa. President Kennedy and his ExComm – an informal group of officials who met regularly with him throughout the crisis – were given credit for their policy of a naval quarantine of Cuba. It avoided simple diplomacy, which critics contended would only have given the Soviets time to complete their missile deployment, making any air attacks and invasion a much costlier proposition for the USA. It also postponed the taking off the table the possibility of an invasion and airstrikes, thus avoiding direct hostilities. The "Goldilocks" choice as a naval blockade was not obvious at the outset and much discussion took place in the Ex Comm and outside before it became the President's preferred option. For this and other reasons, Kennedy's handling of the missile crisis became the template for good decisionmaking.[6]

On the eve of the missile crisis, Barbara Tuchman published a best-selling study of the origins of the First World War. She described it as an unwanted war caused by the faulty policymaking of the major powers.[7] Post-Cuba interest in crisis management kindled renewed interest in 1914 – and all the more so because Kennedy told reporters that he had read Tuchman's book and had it very much in mind during the missile crisis. Follow-on analyses of the July 1914 crisis emphasized mistakes of judgment, attributed to problems of information, coordination, and control. In the 1970s and early 1980s, the literature on decisionmaking was enriched by additional case studies ranging from the Fashoda crisis of 1898 to the 1962 Bay of Pigs invasion.[8]

The growing interest in crisis decisionmaking among international relations scholars promoted a dialogue with diplomatic historians. New scholarship on the First World War, made possible by access to hitherto unavailable primary sources, called into question the extent to which that conflict was in any way accidental in its origins.[9] The centennial of the July crisis revealed something of a consensus that German and Austrian leaders had wanted at least a limited war.[10] This research raised a host of new questions relevant to crisis management and decisionmaking. Revisionist work on Cuba challenged traditional understandings of the origins and outcome of that crisis. The evidence is now clear that it was Khrushchev, not Kennedy, whose miscalculation was responsible for the crisis, that the outcome was closer to a compromise than a Soviet capitulation, and brought about as much by reassurance as by compellence.[11] These interpretations encourage a different set of lessons about crisis management and decisionmaking.

A wide gap opened in the literature between scholars who emphasize the independent role of decisionmaking in crisis resolution – and foreign policy more generally – and those who give primary importance to so-called structural features of context. The latter found early expression in the writings of present or former RAND analysts who attributed the American "victory" in the Cuban missile crisis to the military balance, the level of interests at stake, and the value of defending versus challenging the status quo.[12] The emphasis on so-called structural features of context would find their fullest expression Ken Waltz's 1979 *Theory of International Politics* and his acolyte John Mearsheimer's *The Tragedy of Great Power Politics*, published in 2001.[13] Constructivist scholars, who opt for bottom-up versus top-down approaches to foreign policy, argue that all features of context are all subjective in nature; they are understood differently by different actors, often within the same policymaking elite. They may also evaluate their importance and policy implications differently.[14]

The most notable early works on decisionmaking in international relations were rooted in different intellectual traditions. Robert Jervis's impressive study of perception and misperception in international relations introduced scholars in his field to recent work in cognitive psychology and the ways in which cognitive biases and heuristics could prompt assessments at odds with rational decisionmaking.[15] He described numerous instances where this appeared to have happened and inspired a number of studies that explore biases and heuristics in foreign policy decisionmaking.[16]

Jervis drew attention to the well-documented finding that people often learn inappropriate lessons because they attribute outcomes to superficial causes. They also make facile and misleading comparisons between past and present situations. This can result in the application of questionable policy lessons to inappropriate situations. A case in point is appeasement of Hitler. There were many political pressures and strategic reasons why French and British leaders sought to buy off the German dictator to preserve the peace. They convinced themselves they could do this because revisionist studies of the First World War held that military buildups, alliances, and bellicose rhetoric were more likely to provoke war than to prevent it.[17] The failure of appeasement in the 1930s encouraged the reverse lesson: that aggressive leaders needed to be opposed, and early on. Hardline deterrence policies were accordingly thought necessary, especially in the USA, to constrain Stalin once the Cold War began.[18] In the 1930s and the Cold War, historical "learning" was out of synch with the needs of the day.

Alexander L. George approached the problem of decisionmaking from a more political and organizational perspective. He associated high-quality policymaking with access to good information and its careful and open analysis. He identified a number of constraints on the ability of presidents to obtain useful information and evaluate it properly. Among the most prominent are the need for consensus or support, time constraints, inadequate decisionmaking resources, and the political risks of what might be the best policy options.[19]

Working within the motivational psychology research program, Irving Janis analyzed the ways in which stress-avoidance encourages behavioral pathologies.[20] Like George, he recognized the problem as complex as its causes and argued that there were no panaceas. Good decisionmaking sometimes lead to bad outcomes and vice versa as luck and factors outside the control of leaders entered into the picture. Janis nevertheless argued that "the quality of the procedures used to arrive at fundamental policy decisions is one of the major determinants of a successful outcome."[21] He identified three generic kinds of problem. Chief among them are defective pathways that "fail to correct *avoidable* errors – rectifiable misperceptions, refutable false assumptions, resolvable ignorance, and remediable lapses in judgment concerning the probability or magnitude of expected costs and benefits."[22] Janis thought leaders capable of overcoming these impediments, and all the more so when they regarded the decision in question a critical one.[23]

Cognitive Psychology

The cognitive critique of decisionmaking builds on research in psychology that suggests human beings are "hardwired" to make a series of shortcuts in information processing. Richard Nisbett and Lee Ross characterize heuristics as relatively simple judgment strategies. They are not irrational and probably lead to "vastly more correct or partially correct inferences than erroneous one, and they do so with great speed and little effort."[24] They speculate that heuristics and biases may have conferred important evolutionary advantages as they permitted rapid and largely effective decisionmaking. They can nevertheless be damaging if used to make important and complex life or policy decisions.

Arguably the most important bias for international relations is what Baruch Fischoff called the "certainty of hindsight." It refers to the common tendency to perceive events that have already occurred as more determined than they actually were. In the aftermath of an event, people often believe that it could have been predicted with a high degree of certainty. Hindsight bias distorts memories of what we thought beforehand and is a significant source of overconfidence in our ability to predict future events. It has been well-documented in historical and theoretical explanations of wars and depressions, physician recall of clinical trials, and judicial attribution of responsibility for accidents.[25] There is evidence that the hindsight bias is mediated by vividness; the more vivid an event appears to us, the more determined we believe it to be.[26] For this reason, counterfactual experiments that evoke vividness can be used to combat the hindsight bias and make people recognize that the past was as unpredictable as the future.[27]

Much of the cognitive research in international relations has built on prospect theory. Developed by Daniel Kahneman and Amos Tversky, it builds on earlier work that shows how poor people are at estimating probabilities because of the biases and heuristics. Prospect theory describes the way people choose between probabilistic alternatives that involve risk, where the probabilities of outcomes are uncertain. The theory states that people make decisions based on the perceived losses and gains and are more concerned with avoiding loss than making gains. Their assessments of losses and gains are often based on widely used heuristics and their benchmark for determining what constitutes a loss or gain is highly subjective. If a couple has bought a house for $200,000 and it rises in value to $600,000 over several decades but then drops to $500,000 and they sell at this price they are likely to consider their investment a loss.[28] International relations scholars have used prospect theory as an alternative to rational choice to explain a wide range of important foreign policy outcomes.[29] I respect this research, but contend that prospect theory depends on the motives of actors. When people or leaders are concerned with material gains or losses prospect theory provides a good account of risk taking. When they are focused on security or standing, my historical case studies indicate that they will be equally risk prone when it comes to averting losses or making gains.[30]

The cognitive revolution has been very important for our understanding of individual behavior. It is germane to foreign policy but difficult in its application. Cognitive psychologists have been interested in documenting these biases and heuristics and have done so by means of experiments that rely on large samples. Their studies tell us little to nothing about who will make use of biases and heuristics or the circumstances when this is most likely to happen. Neither cognitive psychologists nor political scientists have been able to identify a set of triggering conditions. Sometimes, decisionmaking is free of cognitive bias and other times, people and political leaders give evidence of using them. Both outcomes are observed in situations that appear similar and many important respects. Cognitive approaches identify real problems but do not have solutions to offer. The best they appear to offer is the hope that sensitivity to the existence and effects of biases and heuristics will somehow improve the likelihood that people or policymakers will not succumb to them.

Motivational Psychology

Motivational approaches assume that decisionmaking involves the emotions. It is about making difficult choices, which almost invariably arouse anxiety if it means giving up something valued to secure something else. Choice is more difficult still when it involves serious risk of loss, as is often true of investments, medical procedures, and military interventions. It is even more difficult if the risk is unknowable. Those of open heart surgery are known, but there is still uncertainty for the individual because base rates are statistical averages that say nothing about single cases. When it comes to investments in new technologies or military interventions there are no base rates and uncertainty prevails.[31]

Janis and Mann reason that people do their best to avoid or reduce anxiety and develop a theory of decisionmaking based on this fundamental premise. They may defer or refuse to commit themselves to a decision or pass responsibility for it on to someone else. If compelled to decide and commit, they may engage in bolstering and defensive avoidance. The former involves convincing oneself that what looked like a 51–49 percent choice is now closer to a 90–10 in the aftermath of commitment. Bolstering involves a range of tactics that are designed to protect decisionmakers from threatening information. They include isolation, silencing, and disparagement of critics; rigging feedback networks so they provide only favorable information and interpretations; and denial, reinterpretation, and distortion of information suggestion that the current course of action will not achieve its intended goals.[32]

Janis and Mann identify four generic situations policymakers routinely confront, two of which arouse anxiety and prompt psychological defenses that degrade the quality of decision making:[33]

1 *Unconflicted inertia* occurs when information suggests the existing policy is succeeding or, at least, will not lead to serious loss.

Policymakers follow the "if it's ain't broke, don't fix it rule" and do nothing, or make only minor adjustments to the current policy.

2 *Unconflicted change* occurs when information indicates that policy is not succeeding, an alternative is available, and there are no strong warnings that it too might fail. In this circumstance, policymakers may welcome the "nutshell briefing," in which their advisers or experts suggest change to the alternative without further search or evaluation.

3 *Defensive avoidance* is a response to impressive warnings of serious loss if the present policy is continued, but there are no more promising alternatives available. Policymakers are likely to respond by not "beating their heads against the wall." They stop thinking about the problem, remain committed to the current course of action, and hope it will succeed.

4 *Hypervigilance* is characterized by impulsive action to escape from a dilemma as quickly as possible. Decisionmakers resort to this coping strategy when they believe they may be a better policy available to them but lack the time to identify or implement it.

I documented defensive avoidance and bolstering in the American decisions that provoked Chinese intervention in the Korean War and Indian decisionmaking that provoked Chinese intervention in 1962. Jack Snyder and Janice Gross Stein have done the same with Russian decisionmaking in 1914 and Israeli decisionmaking in 1973.[34] It was also evident in American decisionmaking in Vietnam. President Johnson dismissed such critics as George Kennan, General James Gavin, and Hans J. Morgenthau as "nervous nellies ... who become frustrated and break ranks under the strain and turn on their leaders, their own country and their fighting men."[35]

Hypervigilance, the other anxiety-provoking situation, is relevant to crisis situations, civil disturbances, and wars. Events in East Germany in November 1989 offer a good illustration. In September of that year, Hungary opened its borders, allowing thousands of East Germans to flee to the West. Other East Germans who had found refuge in West German embassies were allowed to transit East Germany by train to West Germany. Their passage provoked huge public demonstrations in East German cities. The East German police chief prepared for a Tiananmen Square showdown but the leadership lost its nerve. Events followed in quick succession: hardliner Erich Honecker was replaced by more reform-inclined Egon Krenz, schools closed, services began to fail as so many people were on the streets protesting, a Politburo member made a public announcement that people would be free to leave the country, thousands gathered at the Berlin Wall, guards unable to contact their superiors, opened the gates. During the course of events, the communist party flitted from one course of action to another and quickly lost control of the situation, and of the country.[36] A series of rapid decisions, each designed to address an immediate threat, exacerbated the political situation to the point where the government lost control and the regime collapsed.

Motivational models of decisionmaking have an advantage over their cognitive counterparts because they identify the contextual triggering conditions of defensive avoidance and hypervigilance. There is nevertheless a problem with the Janis and Mann formulation because it verges on circularity. The effects of defensive avoidance and hypervigilance are used to identify the presence of high anxiety that is theorized as responsible for them. This is a surmountable obstacle as recent work by Noel Sawatzky demonstrates. He devised estimates of anxiety independent from the effects stipulated by Janis and Mann that rely instead on measurements of cognitive complexity.[37] Sawatzy reasons that higher anxiety should lead to a decline in cognitive complexity and tests this proposition by quantitative and qualitative analyses of speeches and other statements of American policymakers in the Berlin and Cuban missile crises. A decline in cognitive complexity correlates with defensive avoidance.

Janis is also well known for his concept of "groupthink," another pathology arising from efforts to avoid or reduce anxiety when confronting risky decisions and their consequences.[38] It builds on his and others' research on group cohesiveness and its consequences.[39] Groupthink is a psychological phenomenon that occurs within a moderately or highly cohesive group of people in which the desire for harmony or conformity results in an irrational or dysfunctional decisionmaking outcome. Group members try to minimize conflict and reach a consensus decision. Once a decision is made, groupthink discourages criticism of the policy and avoidance of any serious evaluation of alternatives. Cohesive groups can actively suppress dissenting viewpoints and isolate themselves from outside influences. They use their collective resources to develop rationalizations to support a successful outcome, often by invoking shared illusions about the invulnerability of their organization or nation. They are also likely to display hostility to anyone outside the group who challenge their decisions or the logic that led to them.

Once a decision has been made dysfunctional group dynamics produce an "illusion of invulnerability." Janis attempted to document groupthink in five major American foreign policy initiatives or crises: Pearl Harbor, crossing the 38th parallel in Korea, the Bay of Pigs, and escalation in Vietnam. He offers the Marshall Plan and the Cuban missile crisis as counterpoints in which groupthink was avoided and good outcomes achieved. Janis attributed these outcomes to reliance on superior decisionmaking procedures by Presidents Truman and Kennedy. Other scholars identified groupthink in more recent foreign policy failures, including the 2003 invasion of Iraq. Some sought to reformulate the Janis model on the basis of experimental research.[40]

Motivational analyses confront a problem that cognitive approaches do not. Cognitive biases and heuristics are not motivated. People are not assumed to have strong emotional commitment to particular interpretations of information or the inferences that might be drawn from them. Pointing out conceptual errors they have made, or are about to make, might be sufficient to correct or prevent them. This is not true for motivated biases where there is strong resistance to information that challenges the likelihood of success of policies to which leaders are committed. Advisors who bring such information to the attention of leaders are likely to be ignored, reprimanded or even dismissed. In a follow-on book on better decisionmaking, Janis also recognizes cognitive, affiliative, and egocentric limitations or commitments that interfere with the careful search for and evaluation of relevant information.[41] Cognitive constraints include the usual biases and heuristics but also lack of knowledge, the likely consequences of different choices, and inability to devote necessary organization resources to the problem. Affiliative impediments arise from policymaker commitments to particular policies or values, diverse social constraints and demands, and the need to avoid any policy that would disrupt the organization. Egocentric problems arise from personal ambitions, self-esteem, and commitments and antipathies that might come into play.[42]

Writing well before the presidencies of George Bush and Donald Trump, Janis believed that important institutional safeguards were already in place. They included the need of presidents to justify and legitimate their policies to their advisors, Congress, and public opinion with reference to the national interest. Organizational, procedural, and staff arrangements also provided "structure and discipline" to presidential choices, and "reduce though certainly they do not eliminate" the potential for "personal motives and interests" to intrude and distort judgment.[43] Janis remained optimistic that political and business leaders could be persuaded to adopt better decisional procedures in situations they recognized, or could be made to recognize, were critical to their nation, business, or careers.

Building on his own research, and earlier work by others, most notably Amitai Etzioni and Herbert Simon, Janis developed procedures for what he describes as "vigilant decisionmaking."[44] Policymakers and policymaking groups should meet seven conditions designed to overcome what Janis believes are the most common and important failures in the decisionmaking process:

1 survey a wide range of objectives and the multiple values that they represent;
2 canvas a wide range of possible courses of action;
3 search intensively for new information relevant to assessing these courses of action;
4 correctly assimilate and take into account new information and expert judgments, especially when it does not support the course of action initially preferred;
5 reconsider the positive and negative consequences of courses of action initially judged unacceptable;
6 carefully assess the costs and risks of possible negative consequences of any policy, not just the positive ones;
7 make detailed provision for implementing and monitoring the chosen course of action, with special attention to contingency plans that might be enacted.[45]

Janis maintains that if these procedures are followed the problems to which they respond can be avoided. Leaders confronting what he calls "fundamental decisions" will not make rapid-fire decisions, satisfice, or succumb to bolstering. They will also be wary of "nutshell briefings": quick summaries of the supposed benefits and downsides of options. Like satisficing and incrementalism, nutshell briefings are another simple decision rule that allow leaders to avoid engaging problems and move toward decisions with confidence by relying on the judgment of experts. These so-called experts often have strong vested interests in the outcome and leaders who listen to their advice in lieu than immersing themselves in the details of what is at stake unwittingly allow themselves to be captured by them.[46] Janis acknowledges that his checklist of good procedures is not "a cure-all" that will eliminate all decisionmaking problems. Lack of information, even after extensive search, may lead to faulty inferences and unsuccessful policies.[47] But Janis still believes that adherence to the procedures he outlines will make a big difference and increase the likelihood, not only of better decisionmaking, but of better policy. He devotes a chapter to offering evidence from international crises to this effect.[48]

Janis was less sanguine about groupthink. In most cohesive groups, he reasoned, "concurrence seeking tendencies are probably much too powerful to be subdued by administrative changes." At best, they "might somewhat decrease" this tendency "thereby reducing the frequency of error.[49] Janis nevertheless makes a series of procedural recommendations, not dissimilar from those he would later propose in *Crucial Decisions*. He wants the group leader to communicate his or her openness to criticism and assign each member the task of critical evaluation; group and organizational leaders should refrain from stating their preferences at the outset of deliberations; set up several planning groups to consider independently the problem and options for addressing it; the dominant policymaking group should from time to time divide into subgroups to consider the problem; group members should have independent conversations with advisors they trust; outside experts or colleagues should periodically be involved in group deliberations; and at every meeting at least one member should be assigned the role of devil's advocate.[50]

Such checklists of procedures are valuable in situations where people are motivated to get things right. In the days when I piloted aircraft, I never failed to perform the preflight checklist with diligence to make certain that engine, controls, instruments, and the fuselage and wings were ready to fly and, of course, that there was adequate fuel and oil. I wanted a safe journey and was primed to take seriously and respond to the slightest hint that something might be amiss. The checklist helped me to reduce stress when it indicated that all was well. This is the situation that Janis and Mann call unconflicted inertia. Policymakers are no different from pilots in this regard. Problems arise when they are committed, for whatever reason, to particular policies and see no acceptable alternatives to them. They must accordingly succeed. An airplane equivalent might be the need to evacuate an island because it is in the path of a powerful typhoon. In this circumstance, pilots want to believe that they can reach safe destinations and are strongly motivated to reject calculations that they do not quite have enough fuel. If policymakers count on their persuasive skills, luck, or some unknown factor to bring about a favorable outcome, pilots might convince themselves that favorable headwinds, a recently tuned engine, or their ability to cruise at just the right speed will give the plane the necessary extended range.

Janis nevertheless seems to acknowledge that policymakers may confront serious impediments to implementing the procedures he considers essential. He cites Anthony Downs to the effect that officials everywhere want to suppress information inimical to their goals or interests while foregrounding that which is favorable. He also cites Ole Holsti and Alexander George on the almost universal demands of bureaucracies to bypass, ignore, or discredit, other channels of information.[51] Summarizing the findings of numerous studies, Susan Fiske and Shelley Taylor conclude that "people tend to make the data fit the schema, rather than vice versa."[52] Although some experiments suggest that contrary data may make them somewhat less confident about their beliefs."[53] These reinforcing tendencies can make it difficult for even the most committed leaders to obtain unbiased and relevant information.

Multiple Advocacy

Alexander George builds on research in psychology and is sensitive to the range of political and organization constraints that presidents confront. He foregrounds the tendency of leaders to interpret information in accord with their expectations or needs, assimilate new information to existing beliefs, refuse to make trade-offs among important values, failure to perform well under extreme stress, and avoid the anxiety associated with risk and possible political and personal loss. He is sensitive to different president styles of management and the ways in which small groups can both facilitate and interfere with good decisionmaking.

George's writings focus on the USA and its president although they have implications for other leaders and countries. His primary concern is providing more and better information to the president to permit "high-quality" decisions. These are defined as those in which the president "correctly weighs the national interest in a particular situation and chooses a policy or option that is most likely to achieve the national interest at acceptable cost and risk."[54]

George identifies a number of generic problems that stand in the way of good decisionmaking and how they might be overcome. He wants to prevent "satisficing" – going with the first option that appear to work – in situations where "optimizing" should be the decision rule; incrementalism, often a means of deferring critical decisions; consensus politics, by which he means choosing options with the most support as opposed to the best ones; use of inappropriate or superficial historical analogies; reliance on ideologies or general principles as unquestioned guides to action; and a focus on strategies and tactics at the expense of goals and their feasibility.[55]

George elaborates three institutional mechanisms he believes could play an important role in this regard: appointing a devil's advocate, what he calls the formal options system, and multiple advocacy.[56] All three innovations are intended to stimulate open debate about policy alternatives. They do so by building on and adapting the opposing advocates principle of the Anglo-American justice system. George wants to ensure that there are advocates for a range of relevant policy options, equalize or compensate for disparities in their relative authority, and identify and correct possible "malfunctions" in the policymaking process before they can have a harmful effect on the executive's choice of policy. In all, he identifies nine types of malfunction that these procedures have the potential to overcome. He is nevertheless cautious as these procedures depend on bureaucratic and analytical resources, capable leaders, and willing subordinates. Like Janis, he insists that his procedures "cannot be regarded as a panacea."[57]

Following the Bay of Pigs fiasco, Bobby Kennedy suggested that if there were no dissenting opinions in a policy debate someone should be appointed a devil's advocate to make certain the other options were introduced and criticisms of the favored policy voiced.[58] Joseph De Rivera and Irving Janis offered lengthy arguments in support.[59] George sees good reasons for institutionalizing the practice but also great difficulties that stand in the way of doing so. He also worries about its effectiveness.[60]

A devil's advocate, he warns, is not the same thing as a real advocate. People assigned this role are not real dissenters, must couch their objections in moderate ways, may not pursue them beyond a certain point, and certainly may not attempt to build coalitions of support for any alternative policy. Being too critical and outspoken of a favored option can be damaging to one's career, while merely going through the motions of presenting another point of view can make any criticism meaningless. It takes a person with considerable interpersonal skills to perform the role well and a secure leader to allow a subordinate to do so.[61]

Devil's advocacy is a double-edged sword. Leaders can use the procedure to marginalize dissent, and dissenters and to reassure themselves they have been suitably diligent. President Lyndon Johnson appears to have used a devil's advocate this way in the run-up to military intervention in Vietnam. Undersecretary of State George Ball, who opposed escalation, was given an afternoon to make his case and was then refuted by Defense Secretary Robert McNamara and National Security Advisor McGeorge Bundy. Johnson had begun calling Ball his "devil's advocate" early on in the Vietnam debate as a means of defanging his opposition. After listening to his presentation and all counterarguments, Johnson convinced himself that he had been fair and open in his policymaking and moved more confidently toward a decision for intervention. Citing this example, George warns that devil's advocates can be "domesticated."[62]

George believes that a devil's advocate is nevertheless a useful innovation. By convincing the president and his advisors that they have thrashed through the pros and contras of different options, it may allow them to move more confidently to a decision that involves considerable risk. Listening and responding to a devil's advocate compels them to develop counterarguments and prepares them for the kind of criticism they may encounter from Congressional and other critics. The process of challenge and response can heighten group solidarity and hold it together, which may be important in the face of opposition or failure. Finally, doubters in private deliberations may be more likely to be mobilized as defenders in public presentations and debates about the policy in question.[63]

The formal options system is another institutional procedure that might facilitate better information gathering and more open discussion of its implications. It is a response to the need to coordinate the activities of diverse bureaucracies involved in the formulation and implementation of foreign policy. Lateral coordination through committees, conferences, and clearances "cannot be counted on to produce the caliber of policy analysis, the level of consensus, and the procedures for implementation" of an effective foreign policy.[64] Presidents have, accordingly, sought to impose a degree of hierarchical control and the nature and extent of these controls have varied across administrations.

George focuses his attention on the centralized and formal system of control imposed by President Richard Nixon and his national security advisor, then Secretary of State, Henry Kissinger. Kissinger's chairmanship of the National Security Council greatly enhanced presidential control over foreign policy and correspondingly weakened that of agencies and departments. It came closer than any of its predecessor in imposing a model of "unitary and rational policymaker" on an otherwise loosely structured and pluralistic system. In effect, it separated information gathering and policy analysis from policymaking, the last being almost entirely the preserve of the president and his national security advisor.

George is obviously impressed by what Nixon and Kissinger did, and he does not say so, but his judgment appears to be a response to his belief that their foreign policies were, on the whole, successful. He nevertheless sees problems with rigid hierarchies, among them the dangers of "solo decisionmaking" by the president, restriction of the options available to him, overload of responsibilities at the apex of the hierarchy, multiple and conflicting roles of the national security advisor, selective use of formal options by the president allowing him to bypass the system when it suits his convenience, and a reduced role for Congress in foreign policymaking. He comes down in favor of a mixed system that allows more central control than has historically been the case but enough latitude and pluralism to avoid the disadvantages of absolute hierarchy.[65]

Multiple advocacy is the third option George explores and the one he finds most compelling. It is a means of making sure that the president is presented with opposing policy options and arguments and information in their support. It is the embodiment of the mixed system he thinks likely to be most successful. The procedure requires "executive initiative and controlled coordination" of some of the process and participants in decisionmaking, but also accepts and welcomes the inevitability of conflicts over relative authority and the substance of policy.[66] For multiple advocacy to function there can be no major power imbalances among participating actors in their intellectual and bureaucratic resources, their access to the oval office, or the time available to them for presentation and debate. A president cannot be expected to arrange for these conditions so the task must be delegated to the special assistant for national security affairs. This person must become a "custodian-manager" and have responsibility for managing multiple advocacy identifying and correcting any possible imbalances.[67]

George is clear that multiple advocacy does not attempt to eliminate different viewpoints or partisanship. Rather, it seeks to exploit them to elaborate and develop their analytical component and to make it serve the needs of the president. He proposes selective rather than universal use of the procedure and hopes that it might be used to prevent premature commitment by president to a favored policy before it is openly debated. Its success will depend above all else on a president's openness to the procedure; George recognizes that it would have been anathema to Nixon. He acknowledges that it can fail when policy differences expose and reflect deeper differences about values. And even a willing president can find it difficult to implement in practice.[68]

The suggestions of Janis and George are only appropriate in a world populated with responsible, diligent, and intelligent politicians. They presuppose a high level of ethical standards and commitments. They require leaders who are, above all else, committed to doing the right thing for their country and not simply using high office as a means of personal aggrandizement or ego satisfaction. Janis and George are the first to recognize that the procedures they propose make big demands on leaders. These leaders must possess the necessary political, management, and interpersonal skills, and a personality that can tolerate uncertainty, relaxed hierarchy, open debate, challenges to their preferences, and the anxiety that can be aroused by threatening information.[69] They must also have the political nous to look for ways around the pressures they face in pursuit of reasonable goals while adhering to the law and informal constitutional constraints.

Both scholars produced their major works on decisionmaking in the 1970s and 1980s, in a very different America, if not a different political world. It is difficult to imagine a George Bush, Donald Trump, Theresa May, or Boris Johnson having any interest in Janis' checklists or George's procedural safeguards. They surrounded themselves with people who were and are quick to agree with them regardless of what they actually believe, or, alternatively, became unwitting accomplices, if not prisoners, of advisors with strong views. Former President Barrack Obama stands out as an exception, but even he seems to have been coopted, like Lyndon Johnson before him, into supporting questionable military ventures.

President Donald Trump's decisionmaking bears little relationship to anything George and Janis recommend. He acted instinctively, often without much deliberation or consultation with officials. They are frequently left in the dark about his decisions, only learning about them from a tweet or newspaper, as they did when he decided to ban transgender people from military service.[70] Trump held summits with North Korean leader Kim Jong-un without extensive prior briefings or consultations with Korean experts or other key national security officials.[71] He judged North Korea and other countries on the basis of their leaders. In the case of Kim Jong-un, Trump believed that he had developed a close personal relationship that would overcome the obstacles that stood in the way of prior efforts to convince the to give up his nuclear weapons.[72]

Trump has little time for those who urge caution or disagree with him on this or other foreign policy matters. In domestic affairs, he was even more authoritarian and adverse to information or opinions he finds unpleasant or threatening. This began from the moment he took office, where he insisted against all evidence that his inauguration crowd had been the largest in history. He continued to issue known falsehoods, doing so at a record pace that outstrips by far any previous president. Trump told so many falsehoods that CNN appointed a correspondent whose chief task was to tally them.[73] In contrast to the openness urged by Janis and George, Trump consistently sought to protect himself from threatening information. In June 2019, he dismissed as meaningless a public opinion poll that showed him trailing all possible Democratic challengers, and when press coverage continued, fired the pollsters who had conducted the survey.[74]

Trump's decisionmaking process was noticeably different that of his predecessors. Even when considering the use of force, he trusted his own judgment, was willing to defy officials and advisors, and reached out to unconventional sources of guidance. He appeared untroubled by unfilled positions at the highest level; when considering an attack against Iran in June 2019 he had not had a Senate-confirmed defense secretary for almost six months, and his acting secretary resigned in the course of the deliberations. Trump gave every appearance of enjoying the attention and flattery he from officials and advisers who did not hide their efforts to outmaneuver him and one other.[75]

Trump's reliance on instinct rather than so-called expert advice occasionally served him well. In June 2019, Iran shot down an American drone, which the US military insisted was flying over international waters in the Persian Gulf and the Iranians maintained had entered its air space. As rhetoric escalated, Trump ordered the military to prepare a proportional response. Their plan, "Cocked and Ready," consisted of limited strikes against Iranian military sites. Trump called off the operation at the last moment, when strike aircraft were already airborne on the grounds that perhaps the Iranians had made a mistake and that the strike would kill at least 150 people, a death toll he considered disproportionate.[76] Trump had initially been guided by his hawkish generals, national security advisor John Bolton, Secretary of State Mike Pompeo, and CIA director Gina Haspel, but allowed others to express contrary opinions. Most decisive in this regard was one of his lawyers who came up with the figure of 150 dead. He appeared to have pulled this figure out of the air, as it was not based on any military information or input. Trump also found persuasive the comments by Fox News talking head Tucker Carlson, one of his favorite tele-journalists. Carlson had advised him that responding to Tehran's provocations with force was crazy and if he got into a war with Iran, he could kiss his chances of reelection goodbye.[77]

Trump had pulled back on previous occasion from the use of force, convinced that America has wasted too many lives and too much money in pointless Middle East wars and wary of repeating what he considers the mistakes of his predecessors. His instinct was a good one. On NBC News's "Meet the Press," he told a reporter: "And I didn't like it . . . . I didn't think it was proportionate." Although he later added that if war were to come there would be "total obliteration."[78] Also important was Trump's apparent concern with reelection. Lyndon Johnson had similar "gut feelings" on the eve of his escalation in Vietnam, into which he was pushed by his hawkish civilian and military advisors. Had he followed his own instincts, and his desire for reelection, as Trump did in Iran, history would have taken a very different, and arguably, better pathway for both the USA and Southeast Asia.

This comparison is revealing for purposes of my argument. Johnson relied on a more formal set of decisionmaking procedures, one that incorporated a devil's advocate. He had ample time to revisit the policy of military escalation in Vietnam on multiple occasions. He also put what he thought was the national interest about his personal political interest or ego needs, which Trump rarely, if ever, did. President Johnson made a bad decision – a catastrophically bad one that led to creeping escalations and a long, costly, and unsuccessful war. Trump appears to have made the right decision, as a military strike might easily have provoked further escalation by both sides that would have been in the interest of neither country. What counted in both cases had little to do with decisionmaking procedures. The most chaotic of procedures promoted a good decision and outcome for Trump. Crispin Blunt, a Tory MP and former head of the House of Commons Foreign Affairs Committee, thought that "Trump's rather unconventional decision-making style may have saved the day."[79] What counted was the personalities of the presidents, the assumptions they brought to the problem, and how willing they were to oppose the nearly unanimous advice of the officials who surrounded them. The inevitable conclusion is that there is a certain randomness to both good and bad policy decisions.

Constraints and Assumptions

The character of democratic politics in the West has been changing and there are fewer and fewer leaders who are willing to expose themselves to the level of openness, criticism, and uncertainty that Janis and George stipulate as essential to good policymaking. Today's leaders are more likely to perceive these recommendations as threats to their authority. They are also likely to ignore or design around existing procedural safeguards to advance preselected policies and reduce anxiety associated with their perceived risks. Cognitive and motivational biases combine to work against openness to implications of information at odds with one's expectations or needs.

Even committed leaders face serious obstacles. There are domestic, organizational, and other constraints that seriously constrain policymaking. They are not going to be mitigated by better decisionmaking procedures. If anything, it may be necessary or useful to resort to secrecy, limit consultation to a few advisors to avoid leaks, even rush to judgment to circumvent or finesse these restraints or avoid losing control to the media. There is a large literature on domestic and foreign policy constraints, which I will not engage in this chapter. I will note only that in countries such as the USA and the UK, where deep political divisions are pronounced, and responsible treatment of opponents a practice of the past, domestic constraints have become considerably more formidable.

Analyses of the 2016 American presidential election have identified a number of factors that appear to have contributed to Trump's victory. They include popular disenchantment with immigration and international trade, a high degree of alienation from the political system, and hostility to women, African-Americans, and other minorities by White Protestants.[80] According to exit polls, 61 percent of non-college-educated white voters cast their ballots for Republicans while just 45 percent of college-educated white voters did so. Meanwhile, 53 percent of college-educated white voters cast their votes for Democrats compared to 37 percent of those without a degree. During Trump's time in office, polarization increased dramatically. Donald Trump's job approval ratings were the most polarized of any first-term president dating back to Dwight D. Eisenhower in 1953.[81] Cross-party cooperation in Congress is also at an all-time low, as are violations of long-standing governing norms, almost all by the Republican Party.[82]

In the UK, public opinion polls and focus groups indicate a deeply polarized and highly pessimistic populace. A 2019 survey by Britain Thinks reveals an astonishing lack of faith in the political system, with fewer than 6 percent of people believing that their politicians understand them or their interests. Some 75 percent say that UK politics is not fit for its purpose. In light of a shambolic Brexit, 86 percent think the country needs a strong leader but only 21 percent think the next prime minister will be up to the job. People say Brexit has made them more politically engaged; 40 percent claim to pay more attention to politics since the 2016 referendum, rising to 50 percent in the 18 to 24 age group. This involvement appears to have had negative consequences as it has helped to destroy trust in how the nation is governed.[83] Enormous disenchantment with both major political parties has led to a sharp rise in support for a new, if short-lived, right-wing party that was pro-Brexit and anti-establishment.[84] In both the USA and UK, this kind of polarization not only constrains top officials but encourages the emergence of the kind of leaders that are much more likely to give priority to their political interests over national needs and interests.

Times change and more responsible leaders may come to power. There are still reasons to question the claim made by Janis and Georg, that is, that the principal reason for bad policy is bad decision-making. I believe bad policy has more substantive causes and that they are unlikely to be overcome by adopting any of the recommendations of these two thoughtful scholars.

I offer three reasons for this judgment. The first has to do with the domestic political constraints and pressures that leaders face. The kinds of people who come to office in democracies are sensitive to them. They are predisposed to respond to important constituencies and avoiding doing anything likely to antagonize them. With rare and notable exceptions, politicians everywhere are likely to exaggerate the extent to which they are victims of external pressures and constraints and correspondingly minimize their freedom to finesse or reshape them. Harry Truman crossed the 38th parallel in 1950 because he feared the political consequences of not doing so.[85] Similar claims were made about Lyndon Johnson's response to Vietnam: that the President felt that he had little choice to escalate or face serious domestic punishment.[86] Johnson nevertheless had foreign policy concerns and few illusions that a war in Vietnam could be won easily or quickly.[87] Brexit offers a third example, with both Conservative and Labour leaders advocating policies they knew were unrealistic but were responsive to their respective domestic bases. As I was writing this book, Labour leader Jeremy Corbyn was committed to the patently contradictory positions of campaigning against Brexit if were a second referendum but opposing a second referendum. If he had become prime minister, he promised to negotiate a better Brexit deal than his predecessors even though the EU had made it clear in January 2019, and repeatedly thereafter, that there would be no new negotiations.[88] While politicians played games, the British economy began to shrink as investors worried about the future and banks and business sought safe havens in the EU. In 2018, the economic costs of Brexit were estimated at 2.5 percent of GDP, and the figure is expected to be considerably higher for 2019.[89] In July 2019, sterling hit a two-year low.[90]

The second impediment to good foreign policy is motivated bias. Irving Janis was the first to alert us to this phenomenon of motivated bias and its damaging effects on policymaking. When leaders have made up their mind to pursue a policy that involves high risk and could lead to significant loss, or are moving toward commitment to it, they become increasingly insensitive to evidence and arguments suggesting that they are heading toward disaster. The last thing they are likely to do is to embrace procedures that expose their views and the information on which it is based to serious, sustained, and open criticism. The very circumstances in which the procedures that Janis and George recommend are most needed may be those where they are least likely to be applied. Risk and possible loss are inescapable features of the most important foreign policy decisions, especially those involving the use of force or other kinds of sanction. There is powerful evidence for motivated bias in decisions of this kind. They include Austrian, German, and Russian policy in 1914, the German decision to invade the Soviet Union in 1941, the American invasion of North Korea in 1950, Khrushchev's 1962 missile deployment in Cuba, Nehru's disastrous "forward policy" against China that provoked the 1962 Sino-Indian War, American intervention in Vietnam and Cambodia, Israel's 1978 invasion of Lebanon Argentine invasion of the Falklands in 1982, and the Anglo-American invasion of Iraq in 2003.[91] Presumably, if, and when, more archives open and documents and memoirs become available, we will be able to document motivated bias in more recent uses of force.

The final problem, and it is of equal magnitude to the other two, has to do with the assumptions that drive policy analysis and decisionmaking. Janis has no doubts that assumptions act as filters "that exclude certain alternatives from consideration" but make others more "acceptable."[92] He nevertheless believes that policymakers "are capable of changing their faulty initial assumptions or misleading stereotypes when they are exposed to corrective information in the course of working on a policy decision."[93] Yet, a few pages earlier he admits that he has "rarely found instances of policymakers changing any of their fundamental assumptions in response to new information they had gathered."[94] He thinks that assumptions have the best chance of being identified and interrogated in a group with "*a moderate degree of heterogeneity* in basic attitudes among the members of the policymaking group."[95] This requires members of the group "to be dubious about one another's key presumptions, particularly those affecting the way the problem is formulated."[96]

Janis' supposition makes more sense intellectually than it does politically. Groups with moderate degrees of heterogeneity are certainly like to be more open in discussion and less likely to succumb to group-think than groups with higher solidarity. Unusual circumstances aside, they are also less likely to be involved in deliberations involving critical foreign policy decisions.[97] Political leaders only infrequently used the group format for policy deliberations. Kennedy's ExComm, which Janis so admires, is the exception, not the norm. Subsequent presidents have rarely used group formats. More frequently, they have consulted other officials and advisors on an individual basis. When they meet with larger groups, such as the cabinet or the National Security Council, they rarely, if ever, encourage officials to speak independently and criticize preferred policy options. To the extent that they work with a few officials in a group setting, they almost always surround them-selves with people with whom they feel comfortable, personally and politically. It goes without saying that these are people who share their assumptions. A case in point is the Bush administration's deliberations leading up to the invasion of Iraq in 2003. President Bush met indivi-dually and collectively with Vice President Dick Cheney, Secretary of Defense Donald Rumsfeld, and National Security Advisor Condoleeza Rice, all of whom were committed from the outset of the new admin-istration to an invasion of Iraq and overthrow of Saddam Hussein. Secretary of State Colin Powell, who had serious doubts about the need and wisdom of this policy, was excluded from the inner councils of policymaking.[98]

Faulty assumptions are largely beyond the reach of checklists and decisionmaking procedures. They reflect views of the world, of adver-saries and allies, and of the best way of responding to problems. They may be very deeply held as they are in the case of deterrence and shows of force. The former, I argued, helped to provoke the Cuban missile crisis and prolong the Cold War, and the latter was responsible for the surge in Iraq. Other examples abound. In 1914, Germany's leaders were convinced that Austria, with their support, could fight a limited war in the Balkans against Serbia. Russia would stand aside, as it had in 1909 when threatened with war by Germany, and, even if Russia intervened, France would remain neutral. If worse came to worst and Germany had to fight a two-front war, Great Britain was expected to remain neutral. Prince Lichnowsky, the German minister in Britain, made no headway in his efforts to warn against the illusion of British neutrality and was made a pariah afterwards for having been correct.[99] The debate in Germany in July 1914 was more over timing and tactics that it was about goals. At no point did anyone in the leadership circle, Lichnowsky aside, question the need for an offensive strategy, the incentive it created to go to war sooner rather than later, or the belief that war was inevitable.

Assumptions of this kind are rarely challenged because they are often shared within a decisionmaking elite. This is true is the case of the American national security establishment's beliefs in the importance of hegemony, military spending, the need to oppose China, and American world leadership. Challenges to these assumptions are dismissed as coming from people who know nothing about foreign affairs. In 2015, at the University of Cambridge, I debated then head of the Council on Foreign Relations, Richard Haas. He was close to Hilary Clinton and many expected him to be given a high post in the new administration had she won the election. Haas gave the audience an intelligent Cook's Tour of the world's trouble spots and problems that any new administration would confront. I suggested that he had omitted one of the bigger problems the world faced: American arrogance, sense of entitlement, confrontational policy toward China, and an itchy trigger finger that prompted interventions including those in Afghanistan and Iraq. He looked at me uncomprehendingly and would not respond to my argument. Instead, he told the audience that he did not know what planet "this fellow" came from. The crowd, being for the most part English, smiled politely.

Flawed assumptions not only lead to policy failures, the failures frequently confirm them in the eyes of believers. This is because the failures are assimilated to existing assumptions rather than seen as an incentive to interrogate them. Consider the American "surge" in Iraq in 2007. President Bush ordered the deployment of more than 20,000 soldiers into Iraq and extended the tour of most of the Army and many Marine troops already in the country.[100] The goal was to establish a "unified, democratic federal Iraq that can govern itself, defend itself, and sustain itself, and is an ally in the War on Terror."[101] The President declared that the surge would also serve to reconcile warring ethnic communities.[102] One White House staffer explained the political rationale succinctly: "If you're going to be a bear, be a grizzly."[103] Barrack Obama and Hilary Clinton opposed the surge, but supported its underlying goals. Clinton, in particular, was hawkish, favoring intervention in Libya, Pakistan, Afghanistan, Iraq, and Syria.[104] Advocates and opponents shared unrealistic assumptions about what military force could accomplish in Iraq, assumptions that were unquestioned by policymakers during the debate. Or afterwards. Senator John McCain, a leading proponent of the surge, and many other supporters, insisted, *in spite of the accumulating evidence*, that it had been a success.[105]

This kind of tautological confirmation is another feature of policymaking in which underlying assumptions are neither discussed nor debated. It happened repeatedly with deterrence. Each time it failed, American policymakers and academic advocates refused to consider the possibility that the strategy was provocative or failed because of motivated bias on the part of the challenger. They concluded, as in the case of Cuba, that it had not been practiced forcefully enough.[106]

Even when assumptions are questioned by people with perceived legitimacy in foreign affairs, leaders are likely to ignore their views if they are seen as constraining. It is notorious in Washington that regardless of which party is in the White House, county experts are routinely excluded from policy deliberations. I have already mentioned Iraq in this connection. Not only were known or perceived dissenters kept away from the decisionmaking circle, those on the inside did their best to only look at, even generate, information and opinions that supported their policy preferences. Intelligence was cherry-picked, the wrong sources were listened to, inferences were drawn on the basis of uncertain even questionable information, and people in the know were excluded from the deliberations. The scope of discussion was severely constrained. No serious consideration was given to what to do in Iraq after the invasion, and the briefing book that Secretary of State Colin Powell had prepared on the subject was ordered destroyed by Secretary of Defense Donald Rumsfeld because it suggested that the occupation would be difficult.[107] Many of these decisional pathologies resulted from the desire to invade Iraq and to isolate and marginalize anyone opposed to this course of action.

The Iraq war decision is not unique in demonstrating that leaders facing risk surround themselves with people who share their assumptions and goals. The riskier the decision is perceived to be the more likely this is to happen. The preexisting bonds among these people and their shared viewpoints makes it much more likely that something like groupthink will develop if these individuals take on a group identity in the course of their deliberations.

Faulty assumptions and motivated bias often combine to produce overconfidence. It is also attributable to personality. Some leaders are born risk takers, although most, as I have argued, are risk averse. Some welcome other viewpoints and suggestions from subordinates, others expect unquestioned support; some need the backing of others to make decisions, still others are self-confident to an extreme; some try to defer decisions as long as possible, others like to "clear the deck" as quickly as possible. These differences matter. Brian Rathbun makes an important distinction between realist and romantic leaders. Realists, whom he thinks are uncommon, have clearly formulated out and feasible goals, and are rational in their assessment of information and risk. Romantics are, in many ways, the opposite. They have great belief in their agency. They pursue idealistic goals, and believe themselves capable of overcoming what others might see as daunting odds by the power of resolve, charisma, and commitment. Romantics have goals but do not pursue them in a particularly deliberate fashion. Rathbun offers Winston Churchill and Ronald Reagan as examples.[108] Mikhail Gorbachev, Ronald Reagan, and Boris Johnson could convincingly be added to his list of romantics.

Those who espouse far-reaching reforms are almost invariably attempting something extremely difficult, in part because they are challenging the status quo. The likelihood of success is not high, which is one reason why such reform programs are only infrequently undertaken. Given the odds of success, they require the kind of leaders whom Rathbun characterizes as romantic. They must believe in both the justness and necessity of their cause, and convince themselves that their charisma, and their commitment, will overcome whatever obstacles stand in their way. Examples include Anwar el-Sadat and Mikhail Gorbachev, and, arguably, Turgot, the Young Turks, and Mustafa Kemal Atatürk. Gorbachev convinced himself *glasnost* and *perestroika* would succeed, just as he persuaded himself that he could make the West his willing partner to end the Cold War. He succeeded in overcoming Western suspicions and hostility by committing himself and his country to multiple acts of reassurance: withdrawal from Afghanistan, arms control, allowing Eastern Europe to choose its own political systems, and, finally, the reunification of Germany. The last was the final step in ending the Cold War and a powerful symbol of East–West collaboration.[109]

Gorbachev was clever and very lucky – up to a point. He exploited a series of unexpected events early in his secretary generalship – the 1986 nuclear power plant disaster at Chernobyl and the 1987 surprise landing in Red Square of Matthias Rust's Cessna – to purge the military and civilian *nomenklatura* of hundreds of hardline officials who opposed his reforms.[110] Anwar el-Sadat is another example. He was committed to transforming Egypt by ending its decades' long conflict with Israel and jettisoning ties with the Soviet Union in favor of links with the United States. He hoped this would bring peace, American aid and investments, and create the conditions for economic growth. Sadat's reforms were cut short by his assassination.[111]

Gorbachev thought – unrealistically, as it turned out – that he could use reforms to put pressure from below on recalcitrant bureaucrats and party officials. He further deluded himself into believing he could turn the tap of reform off when it threatened to carry the country in directions he did not wish to go. Instead, he provoked a coup against him that failed but quickly led to the unraveling of the Soviet Union.[112] One of the ironies of the Soviet system is that centralization gave the general secretary power to initiate the kind of sweeping changes that could not be made by a democratic leader, but that efforts to decentralize authority and increase political participation undermined the authority, not only of the leader, but of the political system.

Overconfidence is often an expression of hubris. For the ancient Greeks, hubris is a category error. People mistake themselves for gods and believe that they can manipulate the physical and social worlds to serve their own ends. Anyone can succumb to hubris but it is most likely to be people who are successful, or believe they have been. Success can easily go to the head, leading people to believe that they are better, smarter, more persuasive, or simply luckier than others, and, accordingly, more likely to succeed in elaborate ventures. They downplay risks, convinced of their golden touch. Thucydides portrays Pericles and Athens as hubristic, setting in motion schemes that produce the opposite of their intended goals.[113] Sophocles does the same with Oedipus.

The most recent exemplar is Donald Trump, whose hubris spans business and politics. He believes he has superior genes that are responsible for his business and political success and has no hesitation in tweeting his alleged accomplishments to the world.[114] The self-proclaimed king of deal making turns out to have made one bad deal after another, losing $1.7 billion in the 1980s alone and making him the biggest loser in America. He would have lost considerably more had he repaid his debts rather than stonewalling them and legally harassing contractors and others to whom he owed money. He remained personally solvent because much of the money he lost was borrowed in the first place.[115] As President, he made up his own truths; in his first two years in office Trump has made 7,645 false or misleading claims according to the Fact Checker database. He has lied about everything from immigration figures to the number of burgers he served to the Clemson football team at the White House.[116] His foreign policies were shoot-from-the-hip stuff, intended to garner publicity, appeal to his base, and place him front-and-center at all times. For all these reasons, they (generally) failed. Trump nevertheless convinced himself that he is one of the all-time great presidents, when historians are likely to judge him the worst. In 2018, a poll of nearly 200 political scientists, which has routinely placed Republicans higher than Democrats, ranked Trump 44th out of the forty-four men who have occupied the Oval Office.[117]

Ethics and Policymaking

I do not believe that we can find technical, procedural fixes to decision-making pathologies. Procedure is important – and bad procedures can lead result in bad decisions. But it is not demonstrably true that good procedures will promote good policies. The belief in procedure is not a solution but may be part and parcel of the problem. To improve policy, we need to engage its substance, and, above all else, the beliefs – most of them unspoken and unquestioned – that policymakers bring to the table.

This is where ethics enters the picture. It is relevant to three levels of faulty assumptions. The first pertains to specific initiatives. One of the most common errors is unwarranted expectations about how other actors will respond to your policies. In 1914, Berlin and Vienna misjudged the likely Russian response to the Austrian ultimatum to Serbia. In 1941, the Japanese misjudged how the American would react to their attack on Pearl Harbor. In 1962, Khrushchev misjudged Kennedy's response to his secret deployment of missiles in Cuba. In 1982, the Argentine junta was convinced that the British would not contest their occupation of the Falkland-Malvinas Islands. In 2003, the Bush administration believed that they could easily topple Saddam and replace him with a pliant client who could govern with the consent of the local population.

Most of these miscalculations were the result of motivated bias. The policymakers in question believed that they needed to act as they did to overcome domestic and strategy problems. They accordingly convinced themselves that other parties would understand the constraints under which they operated or not respond forcefully for reasons of their own. They were resistant to information and advice to the contrary.[118] Iraq is an exception and indicates the extent to which motivated bias is also associated with hubris. The only pressure President Bush was under to invade Iraq came from within his administration and had little or nothing to do with any strategic, economic, or domestic political concerns.[119]

Motivated bias in decisionmaking is difficult to overcome because leaders will do their best to insulate themselves from information and advice warning of the dangers of their initiatives. Once they commit to questionable and risky policies, it becomes that much more difficult to open their eyes to the dangers involved. Policymakers must inoculate themselves against motivated bias so they do not succumb to this decisional pathology. The best way to do this is through ethical engagement. Policymakers commit themselves to responsible decisionmaking in the understanding that it is not only appropriate but likely to lead to better outcomes for their countries and themselves. They must do their best to avoid easy ways out, represented by postponement in lieu of timely decisionmaking, foisting off responsibility on to someone else, and defensive avoidance. Such a commitment is, of course, never absolute. There will be occasions where leaders find it advisable, necessary even, for a range of reasons to defer judgment or shift responsibility for it. They should always be alert to the dangers of defensive avoidance and hypervigilance, with the former posing the most serious problem.

This recommendation is hardly a solution. Leaders who commit themselves to ethical policymaking may be an endangered species. But such a commitment may nevertheless be the only way – luck aside – in which they are likely to confront, rather than hide from, the kinds of trade-offs policy choices often entail, face up to the likely risks of favored policies, and monitor their progress in lieu of rigging the feedback networks to provide only reassuring information and assessments. At the height of the Cold War, Hans Morgenthau recognized that nuclear weapons and bipolarity had created a novel international situation. In contrast to theorists who sought to derive

We All Lost the Cold War (Princeton: Princeton University Press, 1994); Sheldon M. Stern, *John F. Kennedy and the Secret Missile Crisis Meetings* (Stanford: Stanford University Press, 2003).

12. Horelick and Rush, *Strategic Power and Soviet Foreign Policy*; Schelling, *Arms and Influence*; Abel, *Missile Crisis*.

13. Kenneth N. Waltz, *Theory of International Politics* (Boston: McGraw-Hill, 1979); John Mearsheimer, *The Tragedy of Great Power Politics* (New York: Norton, 2001).

14. Richard Ned Lebow, "Beyond Parsimony: Rethinking Theories of Coercive Bargaining," *European Journal of International Relations* 4, 1 (1998), pp. 31–66.

15. Robert Jervis, *Perception and Misperception in International Relations* (Princeton: Princeton University Press, 1976). A second edition with a new foreword was published by Princeton in 2016.

16. They are discussed later in this chapter.

17. On appeasement, Martin Gilbert, *The Roots of Appeasement* (London: Weidenfeld & Nicolson, 1966); Frank McDonaugh, *Hitler, Chamberlain and Appeasement* (Cambridge: Cambridge University Press, 2002); R. J. Q. Adams, *British Politics and Foreign Policy in the Age of Appeasement, 1935–39* (Stanford: Stanford University Press, 1993); Norrin M. Ripsman and Jack S. Levy, "Wishful Thinking of Buying Time? The Logic of British Appeasement in the 1930s," *International Security* 33, 2 (2008), pp. 148–81.

18. Richard Ned Lebow, "Generational Learning and Foreign Policy," *International Journal* 40 (Autumn 1985), pp. 556–85.

19. Alexander L. George, "The Case for Multiple Advocacy in Making Foreign Policy," *American Political Science Review* 66, 3 (1972): 751–85 and *Presidential Decisionmaking in Foreign Policy: The Effective Use of Information and Advice* (Boulder: Westview, 1980), pp. 1–2.

20. Irving L. Janis, Victims of Groupthink: A Psychological Study of Foreign-Policy Decisions and Fiascoes (Boston: Houghton-Mifflin, 1972), rev. 1982, Crucial Decisions; Irving L. Janis and Leon Mann, *Decision Making: A Psychological Analysis of Conflict, Choice, and Commitment* (New York: Free Press, 1977).

21. Janis, *Crucial Decisions*, p. 20.

22. Ibid, p. 5.

23. Ibid, p. 20.

24. Robert Nisbet and Lee Ross, *Human Inference: Strategies and Shortcomings of Social Judgment* (Englewood Cliffs: Prentice-Hall, 1980), p. 18.

25. Baruch Fischhoff, "Hindsight ≠ Foresight: The Effect of Outcome Knowledge on Judgment Under Uncertainty," *Journal of Experimental Psychology: Human Perception and Performance* 1, 3 (1975), pp. 288–99 and "An Early History of Hindsight Research," *Social Cognition* 25, 1 (2007), pp. 10–13; Neal J. Roese and K. D. Vohs, "Hindsight Bias," *Perspectives on Psychological Science* 7, 5 (1975), pp. 411–26; Ulrich Hoffrage and Rüdiger Pohl, "Research on Hindsight Bias: A Rich Past, a Productive Present, and a Challenging Future," *Memory* 11, 4–5 (2003), pp. 329–35; H Arkes, D. Faust, T. J. Guilmette, and K. Hart, "Eliminating the Hindsight Bias," *Journal of Applied Psychology* 73, 2 (1998), pp. 305–7; H. Blank, S. Nestler, G. von Collani, and V. Fischer, "How Many Hindsight Biases Are There? *Cognition* 106, 3 (2008), pp. 1408–40; Robyn M. Dawes, "A Note on Base Rates and Psychometric Efficiency, *Journal of Consulting Psychology* 26, 5 (1962), pp. 422–4; Robyn M. Dawes, D. Faust, D., and P. E. Meehl, "Clinical Versus Actuarial Judgment," *Science* 243, 4899 (1989), pp. 1668–74; Robyn M. Dawes, *House of Cards: Psychology and Psychotherapy Built on Myth* (New York: Free Press, 1994).
26. L. Ross, M. R. Lepper, F. Strack, and J. Steinmetz, "Social Explanation and Social Expectation: Effects of Real and Hypothetical Explanations on Subjective Likelihood," *Journal of Personality and Social Psychology* 35 (1977), pp. 817–29; Amos Tversky and Daniel Kahneman, "Extensional versus Intuitive Reason: The Conjunction Fallacy as Probability Judgment," *Psychological Review* 90, 2 (1983), pp. 292–315.
27. Scott Hawkins and Reid Hastie, "Hindsight: Biased Judgement of Past Events after the Outcomes Are Known," *Psychological Bulletin* 107, 21 (1990), pp. 311–27; Philip E. Tetlock and Richard Ned Lebow, "Poking Counterfactual Holes in Covering Laws: Cognitive Styles and Historical Reasoning," *American Political Science Review* 95, 4 (2001), pp. 829–43.
28. Daniel Kahneman and Amos Tversky, "Prospect Theory: An Analysis of Decision under Risk," *Econometrica* 47, 2 (1979), pp. 263–91; Amos Tversky and Daniel Kahneman, "Rational Choice and the Framing of Decisions," *Journal of Business* 59, 4 (1986), pp. 251–78; Amos Tversky and Daniel Kahneman, "Advances in Prospect Theory: Cumulative Representation of Uncertainty," *Journal of Risk and Uncertainty* 5, 4 (1992), pp. 297–323; Daniel Kahneman, Paul Slovic, and Amos Tversky, *Judgment Under Uncertainty: Heuristics and Biases* (New York: Cambridge University Press, 1982); Robert H. Frank, "The Frame of Reference as a Public Good," *Economic Journal* 107, 445 (1997), pp. 1832–47. For a popular treatment,

Daniel Kahneman, *Thinking, Fast and Slow* (New York: Farrar, Straus, & Giroux, 2011).

29. Jack S. Levy, "Prospect Theory, Rational Choice, and International Relations," *International Studies Quarterly* 41, 1 (1997), pp. 87–112; Rose McDermott, ed., Special Issue: "Prospect Theory and Political Science," *Political Psychology* 25, 2 (2004); Rose McDermott, James H. Fowler, and Oleg Smirnov, "On the Evolutionary Origin of Prospect Theory Preferences," *Journal of Politics* 70, 2 (2008), pp. 335–50; Janice Gross Stein, "Prospect Theory in International Relations," *Oxford Research Encyclopedia: Politics,* September 2017, 10.1093/acrefore/9780190228637.013.531 (accessed May 10, 2019).

30. Lebow, *Cultural Theory of International Relations*, pp. 365–8.

31. On the difference between risk and uncertainty, Frank H. Knight, *Risk, Uncertainty, and Profit* (Boston: Houghton-Mifflin, 1921); G. L. S. Shackle, *Expectations, Investment and Income* (Oxford: Oxford University Press, 1968); Julia Köhn, *Uncertainty in Economics: A New Approach* (London: Springer, 2017).

32. Janis and Mann, *Decision Making*, pp. 82–5, 91–4.

33. Ibid, pp. 45–80; Janis, *Crucial Decisions*, pp. 79–81.

34. Lebow, *Between Peace and War*; Snyder, *Ideology of the Offensive*; Jervis, Lebow, and Stein, *Psychology of Deterrence*.

35. Robert D,. Schulzinger, *U.S. Diplomacy since 1900, 6th Edition* (New York: Oxford University Press, 2008), pp. 239–40; Joseph A. Fry, *Debating Vietnam: Fulbright, Stennis, and Their Senate Hearings* (Lanham: Rowman & Littlefield, 2006), pp. 34–44; Campbell Craig and Fredrik Logevall, *America's Cold War: The Politics of Insecurity* (Cambridge: Harvard University Press, 2009), p. 242.

36. Mary Elise Sarotte, *The Collapse: The Accidental Opening of the Berlin Wall* (New York: Basic Books, 2014).

37. Noel Sawatzky, "Understanding the Impact of Emotional Stress on Crisis Decision Making," PhD Dissertation, King's College London, December 2019.

38. Irving L. Janis, *Groupthink, 2nd Edition* (Boston: Houghton-Mifflin, 1982); Janis, *Crucial Decisions*, pp. 56–63.

39. Kurt Lewin, *Field Theory in Social Science* (London: Tavistock, 1952); Leon Festinger, ed., *Conflict, Decision, and Dissonance* (Palo Alto: Stanford University Press, 1954); John W. Thibault, and Harold H. Kelley, *The Social Psychology of Groups* (New York: Wiley, 1959); Stanley Schachter, *The Psychology of Affiliation* (Palo Alto: Stanford University Press, 1959).

40. Paul Kowert, *Groupthink or Deadlock: When Do Leaders Learn from Their Advisors?* (Albany: State University of New York Press, 2002); Mark Schafer and Scott Crichlow, *Groupthink versus High-Quality Decision Making in International Relations* (New York: Columbia University Press, 2010); Cass R. Sunstein and Reid Hastie, *Wiser: Getting Beyond Groupthink to Make Groups Smarter* (Cambridge: Harvard Business Review Press, 2014); Paul 't Hart, Erik K. Stern, and Bengt Sundelius, *Beyond Groupthink: Political Group Dynamics and Foreign Policy-Making* (Ann Arbor: University of Michigan Press, 1997); B. H. Raven, "Groupthink: Bay of Pigs and Watergate Reconsidered," *Organizational Behavior and Human Decision Processes* 73, 2–3 (1998), pp. 352–61; Dina Badie, "Groupthink, Iraq, and the War on Terror: Explaining US Policy Shift Toward Iraq," *Foreign Policy Analysis* 6, 4 (2010), pp. 277–96; R. S. Baron, "So Right It's Wrong: Groupthink and the Ubiquitous Nature of Polarized Group Decision Making," *Advances in Experimental Social Psychology* 37 (2005), pp. 219–53; James K. Esser, "Alive and Well After 25 Years: A Review of Groupthink Research," *Organizational Behavior and Human Decision Processes* 73, 2–3 (1998), pp. 116–41; M. A. Hogg and S. C. Hains, "Friendship and Group Identification: A New Look at the Role of Cohesiveness in Groupthink," *European Journal of Social Psychology* 28, 3 (1998), pp. 323–41; B. Mullen, T. Anthony, E. Salas, and J. E. Driskell, "Group Cohesiveness and Quality of Decision Making: An Integration of Tests of the Groupthink Hypothesis," *Small Group Research* 25, 2 (1994), pp. 189–204; G. Moorhead, R. Ference, and C. P. Neck, "Group Decision Fiascoes Continue: Space Shuttle Challenger and a Revised Groupthink Framework," *Human Relations* 44, 6 (1991), pp. 539–50; D. J. Packer, "Avoiding Groupthink: Whereas Weakly Identified Members Remain Silent, Strongly Identified Members Dissent about Collective Problems," *Psychological Science* 20, 5 (2009), pp. 546–8; Philip E. Tetlock, "Identifying Victims of Groupthink from Public Statements of Decision Makers," *Journal of Personality and Social Psychology* 37, 8 (1979), pp. 1314–24; Philip E. Tetlock, R. S. Peterson, C. McGuire, S. J. Chang, and P. Feld, "Assessing Political Group Dynamics: A Test of the Groupthink Model," *Journal of Personality and Social Psychology* 63, 3 (1992), pp. 403–25; M. E. Turner, A. R Pratkanis, P. Probasco, and C. Leve, "Threat, Cohesion, and Group Effectiveness: Testing a Social Identity Maintenance Perspective on Groupthink," *Journal of Personality and Social Psychology* 63, 5 (1992), pp. 781–96.

41. Janis, *Crucial Decisions*, pp. 16–18.

42. On egocentric constraints, Janis quotes George, *Presidential Decision Making in Foreign Policy*, p. 4.
43. Janis, *Crucial Decisions*, pp. 18–19.
44. Ibid, pp. 89–117; Amitai Etzioni, *The Active Society* (New York: Free Press, 1968); Herbert A. Simon, *Administrative Behavior: A Study of Decision-Making Processes in Administrative Organizations*, 2nd Edition (New York: Free Press, 1957); Daniel Katz and Robert L. Kahn, *The Social Psychology of Organizations* (New York: Wiley, 1966); Norman R. Maier, "Group Problem Solving," *Psychological Review* 74, 4 (1967), pp. 239–49; D. W. Miller and M. K. Starr, *The Structure of Human Decisions* (Englewood Cliffs: Prentice-Hall, 1967); D. W. Taylor, "Decision Making and Problem Solving," in James March, ed. *Handbook of Organizations* (Chicago: Rand McNally, 1965), pp. 48–86; V. H. Vroom and P. W. Yetton, *Leadership and Decision-Making* (Pittsburgh: University of Pittsburgh Press, 1973); Harold L. Wilensky, *Organizational Intelligence* (New York: Basic Books, 1967); Stanley Young, *Management: A Systems Analysis* (Glenview: Scott Foresman, 1966).
45. Ibid, pp. 30–33.
46. Ibid, pp. 34–42. Other constraints are addressed on pp. 148–53. So, too, is the personality of decisionmakers, pp. 203–30.
47. Ibid, p. 96.
48. Ibid, pp. 98, 119–35.
49. Janis, *Victims of Groupthink*, p. 262.
50. Ibid, pp. 260–71.
51. Anthony Downs, *Inside Bureaucracy* (Boston: Little, Brown, 1967), pp. 265–6, 282; Ole Holsti and Alexander L. George, "The Effects of Stress on the Performance of Foreign Policy Makers," *Political Science Annual* 6 (1975), pp. 255–319.
52. Susan E. Fiske and Shelley E. Taylor, *Social Cognition* (Reading: Addison-Wesley, 1984), pp. 177–8.
53. Ibid.
54. George, *Presidential Decisionmaking*, pp. 1–3.
55. Ibid, p. 19, and elaborated in detail in Part I of his book.
56. George, "Case for Multiple Advocacy in Making Foreign Policy."
57. George, *Presidential Decisionmaking*, p. 140 for disclaimers.
58. Robert F. Kennedy, *Thirteen Days: A Memoir of the Cuban Missile Crisis* (New York: Norton, 1969), p. 90.
59. Joseph de Rivera, *The Psychological Dimension of Foreign Policy* (Columbus: Charles E. Merrill, 1968), pp. 61–4, 209–11; Janis, *Victims of Groupthink*, pp. 215–16.
60. George, *Presidential Decisionmaking*, pp. 169–74.

61. Ibid, pp. 170–71; George E. Reedy, *The Twilight of the Presidency* (New York: World, 1970), p. 11.

62. George, *Presidential Decisionmaking*, pp. 171–75.

63. Ibid, pp. 172–3.

64. Ibid, pp. 175–6.

65. Ibid, pp. 181–5.

66. Ibid, pp. 191–3.

67. Ibid, pp. 193–4.

68. Ibid, pp. 202–6.

69. Ibid, pp. 4–9.

70. Julie Hirschfeld Davis and Helene Cooper, "Trump Says Transgender People Will Not Be Allowed in the Military," *New York Times*, July 26, 2017, www.nytimes.com/2017/07/26/us/politics/trump-transgender-military.html (accessed June 21, 2019)

71. Victor Cha, "Will Trump Take Us Back to 'Fire and Fury'?," *New York Times*, February 28, 2019, www.nytimes.com/2019/02/28 /opinion/north-korea-summit-trump.html; Editorial Board, "What Trump Got Wrong, and Right, on North Korea," *New York Times*, February 28, 2019, www.nytimes.com/2019/02/28/opinion/trump-kim-vietnam-summit.html (accessed February 29, 2019).

72. Robbie Gramer and Michael Hirsch, "It's Not Personal. It's Just Diplomacy," *Foreign Policy*, March 15, 2019, https://foreignpolicy.com/2019/03/15/its-not-personal-just-diplomacy-trump-kim-jong-un-north-korea-negotiations-history-diplomatic/; Christopher Green, "Trump and Kim Need to Go Small," *Foreign Policy*, March 27, 2019, https://foreignpolicy.com/2019/03/27/trump-and-kim-need-to-go-small/; Jennifer Rubin, "Trump's Personality-driven Foreign Policy Must End," *Washington Post*, October 26, 2018, www.washingtonpost.com/ … /trumps-personality-driven-foreign-policy-must-end/ (all accessed June 21, 2019).

73. Julie Hirschfeld and Matthew Rosenberg, "With False Claims, Trump Attacks Media on Turnout and Intelligence Rift," *New York Times*, January 21, 2017, www.nytimes.com/2017/01/21/us/politics/trump-white-house-briefing-inauguration-crowd-size.html; David Leonhardt and Stuart A. Thompson, "Trump's Lies," *New York Times*, December 14, 2017, www.nytimes.com/interactive/2017/06/23/opinion/trumps-lies.html (both accessed June 21, 2019).

74. Peter Baker and Maggie Haberman, "Trump Campaign to Purge Pollsters After Leak of Dismal Results," *New York Times*, June 16, 2019, www.nytimes.com/2019/06/16/us/politics/trump-polls.html (accessed June 20, 2019).

75. Bob Woodward, *Fear: Trump in the White House, 2nd Edition* (New York: Simon & Schuster, 2018) for examples.

76. Toluse Olorunnipa, Josh Dawsey, Karoun Demirjian, and Dan Lamothe, "'I Stopped It': Inside Trump's Last-minute Reversal on Striking Iran," *Washington Post*, June 21, 2019, www.washington post.com/politics/i-stopped-it-inside-trumps-last-minute-reversal-o n-striking-iran/2019/06/21/e016effe-9431-11e9-b570-6416efd c0803_story.html?utm_term=.cd204983c414; Peter Baker, Maggie Haberman, and Thomas Gibbons-Neff, "Urged to Launch an Attack, Trump Listened to the Skeptics Who Said It Would Be a Costly Mistake," *New York Times*, June 22, 2019, www .nytimes.com/2019/06/21/us/politics/trump-iran-strike.html. (both accessed June 21, 2019).

77. Ibid; Edward Wong and Michael Crowley, "Pompeo, a Steadfast Hawk, Coaxes a Hesitant Trump on Iran," *New York Times*, June 22, 2019, www.nytimes.com/2019/06/22/world/middleeast/tru mp-pompeo-iran.html?action=click&module=Top%20Stories&pgty pe=Homepage (accessed June 22, 2019).

78. Daniela Silva, "Trump Says He Doesn't Want War with Iran, but There Will Be 'Obliteration' if It Comes," *NBC News*, June 21, 2019, www.nbcnews.com/politics/politics-news/trump-says-he-did-not-given-final-approval-iran-strikes-n1020386 (accessed June 21, 2019).

79. Patrick Kingsley, "Trump's Iran Reversal Raises Allies' Doubts Over His Tactics, and U.S. Power," *New York Times*, June 23, 2019, www.nytimes.com/2019/06/23/world/europe/trump-iran-us a.html?action=click&module=Top%20Stories&pgtype=Homepage (accessed June 23, 2019).

80. Andrew J. Gaughan, "Five Things that Explain Donald Trump's Stunning Presidential Election Victory," *Conversation*, November 9, 2016, https://theconversation.com/five-things-that-explain-donald-trumps-stunning-presidential-election-victory-66891; Niraj Chokshi, "Trump Voters Driven by Fear of Losing Status, Not Economic Anxiety, New Study Finds," *New York Times*, April 24, 2018, reporting on a study by Diane Mutz for the National Academy of Sciences, www.nytimes.com/2018/04/24/us/politics/trump-economic-anxiety.html (all accessed June 16, 2019); John Sides Lynn Vavreck, and Michael Tesler, "The 2016 U.S. Election: How Trump Lost and Won," *Journal of Democracy*, 28, 2 (2018), pp. 34–44.

81. Adam Harris, "America Is Divided by Education," *Atlantic*, November 7, 2018, www.theatlantic.com/education/archive/2018/11/education-gap-e xplains-american-politics/575113/; Carroll Doherty, "Key Takeaways

on Americans' Growing Partisan Divide over Political Values," *Pew Research Center*, October 5, 2017, www.pewresearch.org/fact-tank/201 7/10/05/takeaways-on-americans-growing-partisan-divide-over-political-values/ (both accessed January 21, 2019).

82. Julian E. Zelizer and Morton Keller, "What Would It Take for Democrats and Republicans to Work Together?" *Atlantic*, August 27, 2017, www.theatlantic.com/politics/archive/2017/08/rep ublicans-democrats-bipartisanship-trump/538029/; E. J. Dionne, Jr., Norm Ornstein, and Thomas E. Mann, "How the GOP Prompted the Decay of Political Norms," *Atlantic*, September 19, 2017, www.thea tlantic.com/politics/archive/2017/09/gop-decay-of-political-norms/54 0165/; Anita Kumar and Andrew Desiderio, "Trump Showdown with House Democrats Ignites into All-out War," *Politico*, April 23, 2019, www.politico.com/story/2019/04/23/trump-investigators-congress-1 288795 (accessed June 16, 2019).

83. Nosheen Iqbal, "Divided, Pessimistic, Angry: Survey Reveals Bleak Mood of Pre-Brexit UK," *Sunday Observer*, June 16, 2019, www.the guardian.com/politics/2019/jun/15/divided-pessimistic-angry-survey-re veals-bleak-mood-of-pre-brexit-uk (accessed June 16, 2019).

84. Toby Helm and Michael Savage, "Tories Hit by New Defections and Slump in Opinion Polls as Party Divide Widens," April 14, 2019, www.theguardian.com/politics/2019/apr/14/stephen-dorrell-defec tion-change-uk-tory-poll-five-year-low; Toby Helm, "Grassroots and Shadow Cabinet Add to Pressure on Corbyn over Brexit," *Guardian*, June 16, 2019, www.theguardian.com/politics/2019/jun/16/jeremy-corbyn-faces-revolt-second-eu-referendum; Toby Helm and Michael Savage, "Poll Surge for Brexit Party Sparks Panic Among Tories and Labour," *Guardian*, May 12, 2019, www.theguardian.com/politics/2 019/may/11/poll-surge-for-farage-panic-conservatives-and-labour (all accessed June 16, 2019).

85. The strongest argument for the determining role of domestic politics is Richard E. Neustadt, *Presidential Power: The Politics of Leadership* (New York: Signet, 1964).

86. Leslie H. Gelb and Richard K. Betts, *The Irony of Vietnam: The System Worked* (Washington: Brookings, 1979).

87. The Joint Chiefs of Staff estimated five years and 500,000 troops for a victory. Campbell Craig and Fredrik Logevall, *America's Cold War: The Politics of Insecurity* (Cambridge: Harvard University Press, 2009), pp. 232–3, 236–40.

88. Jessica Elgot, "Unions Agree Labour Should Back Remain in Referendum on Tory Deal," *Guardian*, July 8, 2009, www.theguardian.com/politics/ 2019/jul/08/unions-agree-labour-should-back-remain-second-referen

dum-brexit; Gaby Hinsliff, "Labour Is Finally Backing a Second Referendum. Is it too Little, too Late?," *Guardian*, July 9, 2019, www .theguardian.com/commentisfree/2019/jul/09/labour-second-referen dum-jeremy-corbyn-brexit; Heather Stewart, "Corbyn Says Labour Would Back Remain in Brexit Referendum," *Guardian*, July 9, 2019, www.theguardian.com/politics/2019/jul/09/corbyn-says-labour-would-b ack-remain-in-brexit-referendum; Daniel Boffey and Jennifer Rankin, "No Renegotiation, Says EU after MPs Back Plan to Replace Backstop," *Guardian*, January 29, 2019, www.theguardian.com/poli tics/2019/jan/29/eu-rule-out-brexit-renegotiation-brady-amendment-pas s; Ursula von der Leyen, "Ursula von der Leyen Signals she Will not Reopen Brexit Talks," *Guardian*, July 9, 2019, www.theguardian.com/ world/2019/jul/10/ursula-von-der-leyen-signals-not-reopen-brexit-talks-backstop (all accessed July 9, 2019).
89. Wiki, "Economic Effects of Brexit," June 27, 2019, https://en .wikipedia.org/wiki/Economic_effects_of_Brexit (accessed July 8, 2019).
90. Kevin Granville and Amie Tsang, "British Pound Falls to Two-Year Low Amid U.K. Economic Worries," *New York Times*, July 10, 2019, www.nytimes.com/2019/07/09/business/uk-pound-dollar.html?t e=1&nl=morning-briefing&emc=edit_MBE_p_20190710&section=t opNews?campaign_id=51&instance_id=10802&segment_i d=15061&user_id=bab57aa60273e9188d1cc67a153af862&regi_i d=6995046 5tion=topNews (accessed July 10, 2019).
91. Richard Ned Lebow, *Between Peace and War: The Nature of International Crisis* (Baltimore: Johns Hopkins University Press, 1981); Jack Snyder, *Ideology of the Offensive; Military Decision Making and the Disasters of 1914* (Ithaca: Cornell University Press, 1984); Jervis, Lebow, and Stein, *Psychology of Deterrence*; Lebow and Stein, *We All Lost the Cold War*; Steven A. Hoffmann, *India and the China Crisis* (Berkeley: University of California Press, 1990): Fredrik Logevall, *Choosing War: The Lost Chance for Peace and the Escalation of War in Vietnam* (Berkeley: University of California Press, 2001); Woodward, *Plan of Attack*; Gordon and Trainor, *Cobra II*; Isakoff and Corn, Hubris; Ricks, *Fiasco*.
92. Janis, *Crucial Decisions*, p. 98.
93. Ibid, p. 103.
94. Ibid, p. 99.
95. Ibid.
96. Ibid.
97. Lebow, *Between Peace and War*, pp. 302–5, for a discussion of these conditions and identification of three decisionmaking groups that met this criterion and performed well.

98. Woodward, *Plan of Attack*; Gordon and Trainor, *Cobra II*; Isakoff and Corn, *Hubris*; Ricks, *Fiasco*.

99. Lebow, *Between Peace and War*, ch. 5.

100. President George W. Bush, "President's Address to the Nation," January 10, 2007, The White House, https://georgewbush-white house.archives.gov/news/releases/2007/01/20070110-7.html (accessed June 12, 2019).

101. The White House, "Fact Sheet: The New Way Forward in Iraq," Office of the Press Secretary, January 10, 2007, https://georgewbush- white house.archives.gov/news/releases/2007/01/20070110-3.html (accessed May 13, 2019).

102. Ibid.

103. Fred Barnes, "Conversations with Bill Kristol," https://conversa tionswithbillkristol.org/video/fred-barnes/n (accessed June 17, 2019).

104. Micah Zenko, "Hillary the Hawk: A History," *Foreign Policy*, July 27, 2016, https://foreignpolicy.com/2016/07/27/hillary-the-ha wk-a-history-clinton-2016-military-intervention-libya-iraq-syria/ (accessed May 7, 2019).

105. Fox News, "Senator John McCain Defends Iraq War, Bush's Troop Surge Plan," April 11, 2007, www.foxnews.com/story/senator-john-mccain-defends-iraq-war-bushs-troop-surge-plan; James A. Baker, III, and Lee H. Hamilton, *Iraq Study Group Report,* December 6, 2006, https://web.archive.org/web/20090601191410/http://www.usip.org/i sg/iraq_study_group_report/report/1206/iraq_study_group_report.p df (both accessed May 7, 2019); Bruce R. Pirnie and Edward O' Connell, *Counterinsurgency in Iraq: 2003–2006* (Santa Monica: RAND, 2008).

106. Richard Ned Lebow, *Avoiding War, Making Peace* (London: Palgrave-Macmillan, 2017), ch. 3 and *A Democratic Foreign Policy: Regaining American Influence Abroad* (New York: Palgrave-Macmillan, 2019), ch. 4.

107. Bob Woodward, *Plan of Attack* (New York: Simon & Schuster, 2004); Michael R. Gordon and Bernard E. Trainor, *Cobra II: The Inside Story of the Invasion and Occupation of Iraq* (New York: Pantheon, 2006); Michael Isakoff and David Corn, *Hubris: The Inside Story of Spin, Scandal, and the Selling of the Iraq War* (New York: Crown, 2006); Thomas E. Ricks, *Fiasco: The American Military Adventure in Iraq* (New York: Penguin, 2006).

108. Brian C. Rathbun, *Reasoning of State: Realists, Romantics and Rationality in International Relations* (Cambridge: Cambridge University Press, 2019).

109. Richard K. Herrmann and Richard Ned Lebow, eds., *Ending the Cold War* (New York: Palgrave-Macmillan, 2003), for analyses of these five turning points and of Gorbachev's motivated bias.

110. Vladimir Krychkov, transcripts of tapes of Moscow Cold War Conference, June 1999; Richard Ned Lebow and Janice Gross Stein, "Understanding the End of the Cold War as a Non-Linear Confluence," in Richard K. Herrmann and Richard Ned Lebow, eds., *Ending the Cold War: Interpretations, Causation, and the Study of International Relations* (New York: Palgrave-Macmillan, 2004), pp. 189–218.

111. Richard Ned Lebow, "Transitions and Transformations: Building International Cooperation," *Security Studies* 6, 3 (1997): 154–79.

112. Archie Brown, *The Rise and Fall of Communism* (London: Ecco, 2011), chs. 25, 27, 29; William Taubman, *Gorbachev: His Life and Times* (New York: Norton, 2017), chs. 14–17.

113. Robert B. Strassler, ed., *The Landmark Thucydides: A Comprehensive Guide to the Peloponnesian War* (New York: Free Press, 1996).

114. *Huffington Post* "This May Be the Most Dangerous Thing Donald Trump Believes," 25 April 2017, www.huffpost.com/entry/donald-tr ump-genes-eugenics_n_58ffd428e4b0af6d71898737?guccounte r=1&guce_referrer=aHR0cHM6Ly93d3cuZ29vZ2xlLmNvbS8&guc e_referrer_sig=AQAAALEnhjIRjcx3pb1SRbGaqKDEitiqA6RteZCo8 W_yTVgmoEdNV70Aj_IDwxIhsvgKfFGt9pTXfujTvrMQUgugMK-t 6XDaTfQ_JgAnBJzijiLx_Sp2iprPEoaE6LerTTiHEzhd8PJ7Ad5YEB Xvj9MRzwMSy-fU4F2e_qNehLrxU6Vv (accessed May 9, 2019).

115. Russ Buettner and Susanne Craig, "Decade in the Red: Trump Tax Figures Show Over $1 Billion in Business Losses," *New York Times*, May 8, 2019, www.nytimes.com/interactive/2019/05/07/us/politics/ donald-trump-taxes.html (accessed May 9, 2019).

116. Adam Gabbatt, "The 'Exhausting' Work of Factcheckers Who Track Trump's Barrage of Lies," *Guardian*, January 21, 2019, www.theguardian.com/us-news/2019/jan/21/donald-trump-lies-fac tcheckers; Maggie Haberman of the *New York Times* suggests that Trump "tries to escape or win a particular transactional exchange with no regard to what he said in the past, no regard to what he might have to say ten seconds or ten minutes in the future. He's just trying to get out of the moment." Quoted in Benjamin Hart, "Daniel Dale on Whether President Trump Believes His Own Lies," *Intelligencer*, April 17, 2019, http://nym ag.com/intelligencer/2019/04/daniel-dale-president-trump-lies.html (both accessed May 9, 2019).

117. For a riff on Trump's claim, Dana Millbank, "Let's Impeach Trump for Being Such a Great President," *Washington Post*, April 29, 2019, www.washingtonpost.com/opinions/lets-impeach-trump-fo r-being-a-great-president/2019/04/29/67d0a720-6ac3-11e9-8f44- e8d8bb1df986_story.html?noredirect=on&utm_term=.697 c0efc07cf; Nick Bryant, "How Will History Judge President Trump?," *BBC News*, January 17, 2019, www.bbc.com/news/wor ld-us-canada-46895634 (both accessed May 9, 2019).

118. For individual cases, Lebow, *Between Peace and War*, chs. 4–6; Jervis, Lebow and Stein, *Psychology and Deterrence*, chs. 3–5, 7; Lebow and Stein, *We All Lost the Cold War*, chs. 2–4.

119. Lebow, *Cultural Theory of International Relations*, ch. 9.

120. Hans Morgenthau, "World Politics in the Mid-Twentieth Century," *Review of Politics* 19 (April 1948) 154–73 and *Politics Among Nations* (New York: Knopf, 1948), p. 172.

121. Wikipedia, "List of Trump Administration Dismissals and Resignations," July 9, 2019, https://en.wikipedia.org/wiki/List_of_Tr ump_administration_dismissals_and_resignations; Michael Tomasky, "The Steady Bedlam of the Trump Administration," *New York Times*, December 24, 2018, www.nytimes.com/2018/12/24/opinion/trump- mattis-turnover.html (both accessed July 9, 2019).

122. James Mann, "The Adults in the Room, *New York Review of Books*, October 26, 2017, www.nybooks.com/articles/2017/10/26/trump- adult-supervision/ (accessed July 9, 2019).

123. Tim Shipman, *All Out War: The Full Story of Brexit* (London: Collins, 2017) and *Fall Out: A Year of Political Mayhem* (London: Collins, 2018); Fintan O'Toole, *Heroic Failure: Brexit and the Politics of Pain* (London: Apollo, 2018).

124. Andrew Rawnsley, "Where Are the Politicians with Principles They Would Stand Down For?" *Guardian*, July 14, 2019, www.theguar dian.com/commentisfree/2019/jul/14/where-are-the-uk-politicians-wi th-principles-they-would-stand-down-for (accessed July 14, 2019).

6 | *Conclusions*

In this book, I offer an alternative vision of foreign policy, one based on an understanding of life and politics as tragedy. It is significantly at odds with realist approaches to politics that emphasize power, dominance, and pursuit of self-interest independently of other actors. In keeping with modernity's emphasis on the individual realists and liberals conceive of states as autonomous and egoistic actors. Tragedy teaches us people and political units only function effectively as members of communities. Communities constitute individuals and their collectives by conferring recognition, assigning or confirming roles, and enabling affiliations. Neither people nor states can formulate interests intelligently outside of them. Their first commitment is to uphold their community and its values because they make possible security, wealth, and status.

The kind of realism that is routinely espoused by American academics and talking heads, and practiced by US presidents has encouraged repeated military interventions, political subversion, and other violations of what is considered acceptable practice in international affairs. In contrast to realist claims that domestic politics and ethics should stop, so to speak, at the water's edge, I contend that they should inform foreign policy. In an earlier book, I argued that any meaningful construction of the national interest must be based on our values and adopt means as well as ends that do not violate them.[1] In this study, I offer evidence in support of my claim that such policies are more likely to succeed than those that violate them.

This is a difficult proposition to substantiate for conceptual and empirical reasons. There is the double challenge of distinguishing success from failure, and behavior that is considered acceptable from that which is not. Assessments of success and failure – and anything in between – depend very much on the benchmarks used. Military vs. political outcomes, short- versus longer-term perspectives, specific goals vs. wider implications can lead to diametrically opposed assessments. In evaluating outcomes I rely on political outcomes, longer-term perspectives, and their wider domestic and foreign policy implications on the grounds that they are the most compelling metrics.

Equally problematic is the determination of ethical and non-ethical behavior. Regional societies vary in their thickness and international society is also lumpy and thinner overall. Relative thickness and thinness reflects in part the degree of consensus among actors with regard to fundamental values and practices. Agreement often finds expression in norms and even laws. Norms are constantly evolving, as they have, for example, regarding sovereignty, unilateral use of force, the sale of territories and their peoples, restrictions – or their absence – of the mobility of people, money, and goods. This makes the substance and robustness of norms difficult to assess and comparisons across decades deeply problematic. So too does the variation in the robustness – even the existence – of norms – across regions. Different norms can also clash, making it possible for actors to choose between them. Certain norms have nevertheless become nearly universal. This does not mean that they are always honored. Only that those who violate them almost invariably feel the need to justify their behavior with reference to some other norm. As François de La Rochefoucauld astutely observed: "Hypocrisy is the tribute that vice pays to virtue."[2] I limited myself more or less to such "high-end" norms, the best example being that against territorial conquest.

In Chapter 3, the first of my empirical chapters, I used two original data sets to show how unsuccessful initiators of war have been, especially in the post-1945 world where conquest and other uses of force unauthorized by international authorities have become all but unacceptable. My data set of twenty-six post-1945 wars indicates that very few wars fought since 1945 achieved their political goals. Those that did in the short term (the Soviet intervention in Afghanistan, the Anglo-American invasion of Iraq, for example) were often counterproductive in the longer term in the sense that occupation was increasingly contested and costly and resulted in a loss standing and influence for intervening states. The most successful wars had the backing of appropriate regional or international organizations and were fought by multinational coalitions, as was the Persian Gulf War of 1991.

The core claim of this chapter is that foreign policies that violate contemporary understandings of justice are less likely to succeed than those that conform to them. The unambiguous policy lesson is that ethics must become an integral component of foreign policy. Leaders need to ask themselves the extent to which their initiatives – and here I mean the ends that are sought and the means used to achieve them – are consistent with the understandings by relevant foreign audiences of what constitute acceptable practices.

Chapter 4 looks at the opposite side of the coin. It explores the consequences of initiatives in accord with accepted norms and under-standings of justice and argues that they are more likely to succeed and more likely to confer longer-term advantages. Wars rarely achieve their political goals but have a better chance of doing so when there are multilateral operations that have the backing of appropriate regional or international organizations. The principal reason for this, in my opinion, is that coalitions require consensus and that minimizes the ability of initiating powers to pursue maximalist goals. Rather, they are often compelled to limit their objectives to those for which there is wider political support, and these are almost invariably objectives that can convincingly be portrayed as upholding international law and norms.

I follow with short case studies of three dramatically successful foreign policy initiatives. They are US policy toward Europe in the immediate aftermath of the Second World War, China's attempts under Mao Zedong, to resolve territorial disputes with its neighbors, and the Federal Republic of Germany's efforts to restructure its rela-tions with its neighbors. The first sought to strengthen the economies and political systems of European allies, the last two to reach accom-modations and transform relations with neighbors, initially through border settlements. The American Marshall Plan involved the transfer of considerable resources, the Chinese and German initiatives conces-sions and assurances. All three appealed to well-entrenched norms or created new ones. They involved multiple, major proposals or pro-grams that took several years at least to negotiate or implement. They succeeded in varying degrees in building trust across borders – and, in two of the three cases, across peoples. They encouraged belief in the benign intentions of the leaders and states involved. In all three cases, territorial or financial sacrifices brought longer-term political and eco-nomic benefits. The American and German initiatives helped to build a degree of "we" feeling among leaders and peoples, bringing their interests into closer harmony. They created more influence for the USA and Germany respectively, but also more influence for them indirectly by strengthening the communities to which they belonged.

Chapter 5 addresses policymaking. This is an arena that has received increasing attention in both business and politics. Organizational theorists, political scientists, and international relations scholars have looked for technical fixes. I have no objection to efforts to improve decisionmaking but argue that checklists, procedures, and other initiatives and safeguards, will not necessarily lead to better policy. This is because bad policies are more often attributable to deeper causes than mere sloppy decisionmaking. They are the result of unrealistic goals, which, in turn, often arise from inappropriate assumptions of all kinds. Postwar American leaders, for example, routinely exaggerated the ability of military force to achieve political goals, the degree to which allies and adversaries alike questioned their resolve, and that others looked to them to play world policeman. More rigorous decisionmaking procedures are unlikely to bring these misconceptions to light. It is well-known that leaders confronted with high-risk decisions surround themselves with people with whom they feel comfortable, and these are usually people who share their assumptions. Bad decisions also arise from the refusal of leaders to make trade-offs among competing goals or take seriously information that suggests their preferred policy is likely to lead to disaster. These are motivated errors, brought about by the anxiety associated with the fear of possible loss. They tend to make leaders unwilling to engage in the kind of decisionmaking process that might expose their bias.

There is a relationship between ethics and good policies. Policymakers who resist being stampeded into action in response to domestic pressures or threats, learn to live with the anxiety generated with uncertainty and risk, recognize the need to gather good intelligence and engage in careful assessment before acting, are likely to make better policy decisions. So, too, are those who seek and respond to new information as their policy unfolds rather than hiding ostrich-like from danger. They will be more willing to change if their policy is not succeeding and to accept responsibility for their failures. These qualities do not arise from decisionmaking courses, multiple briefings, or institutional procedures designed to compel consideration of different policy recommendations. Rather, they come from within. They are associated with people with sufficient courage and intelligence to accept the duties of office and carry them out in a responsible manner.

Ethics enters the picture in a second way. To the degree that leaders appreciate the longer-term benefits of behaving in accord with domestic law, conventions, and international norms and practices, they will be less likely to engage in a range of activities, including resorts to force in the absence of authorization by relevant international organizations. For ethical – but also purely instrumental reasons – policymaking should take place within a framework that respects national and international law and eschew any policies (including illegal military action, torture of prisoners, support for corrupt, authoritarian regimes) that are at odds with the law and the values on which democracy rests. Some kinds of behavior should be considered unacceptable regardless of their perceived benefit to the state. Postwar history also teaches us that their putative benefits rarely, if ever, materialize. This is true of torture, the necessity of which is routinely touted by the ill-informed.[3]

There is a deeper link between inappropriate assumptions and modernity. Belief in progress, technical fixes, the all empowering role of reason, and the efficacy of power encourages highly unrealistic expectations about one's ability to manipulate physical and social environments toward desired ends. It also makes people more insensitive to evidence about past failures of such efforts and overly receptive to information in support of future successes.

Tragedy offers a possible antidote to some of the most dangerous conceits of modernity. It makes people more humble and cautious and encourages decisionmaking that pay as much attention to what can go wrong as they do to what leaders hope will go right. However, tragic understanding of politics will appeal only to leaders with the courage to face that truth that we are, to a large degree, at the mercy of our physical and social environments. It is less a substitute for modern ways of addressing problems as it is a much needed corrective. As with everything else in life, there should be a balance, in case of foreign policy, between self-interest and concern for others, risk taking and risk aversion, optimism and pessimism, overconfidence and lack of confidence, flying by the seat of the pants and acting on the basis of careful analysis and preparation, and focus on the benefits of action versus those of inaction. A tragic perspective also gives people a useful outside vantage point on their behavior and a focus on its longer-term consequences, even if they are ultimately unknowable. It compels policymakers to recognize and accept uncertainty and responsibility in lieu of denying them.

Tragedy

The tragic view of life is rooted in an understanding that the world is, to a significant degree, opaque. We have at best a limited ability to control and manipulate it and our best efforts to do so often backfire. We are acted on at least as often as we are responsible agents, and efforts to enhance our agency and power can just as readily reduce them. Tragedy encourages us to confront our limits. It emphasizes human fallibility and vulnerability and the contradictions and ambiguities of agency. It shows us that we not infrequently initiate courses of action without being able to control them or calculate beforehand their consequences. It cautions against assuming that our own conceptions of justice are universally applicable and should be imposed on others. It warns of the dangers of overconfidence and perceived invincibility. It teaches us that wisdom and self-awareness can emerge from adversity and despair.

In Chapter 2, I describe four kinds of tragedy: those of unmerited suffering, of character, of hard choice, and of moral dilemma. Each has a different source and poses a different kind of ethical and political challenge. All four are regularly apparent in international relations. Awareness of them, I argue, has the potential to reduce their frequency. But knowledge of tragedy is only useful if policy-makers take these lessons to their heart. Rather than distancing themselves from tragedy, they need to see themselves as tragic actors who must sometimes make unpalatable choices on the basis of incomplete information. This kind of intellectual and emotional openness is a form of courage, and a more important one for policy-makers than that of sending others into battle.

Tragedy offers not only general lessons about life but also more specific policy guidance. It warns us against hubris. The more powerful and successful actors are the more arrogant and overconfident they are likely to become. In the pursuit of honor, wealth, or power they may embrace complex and risky initiatives without openly facing up to their risks, how other actors are likely to respond to them, or making back-up plans in case they run into trouble. Not surprisingly, these initiatives not infrequently produce outcomes diametrically opposed to those sought. Arrogance encourages overvaluation of the self and under-valuation of others. It makes leaders insensitive to others' needs, beliefs, and agency, and makes it difficult to impossible, to put oneself in their place to understand how they might respond.

In international relations the riskiest policies of all are unilateral uses of force that violate law, conventions, or widely shared understandings of what is acceptable. Lesser powers not infrequently behave this way, as have Iraq under Saddam, Syria, Israel, Iran, and North Korea. They become something of a pariah and not infrequently the object of sanctions.[4] Great powers are even more likely to go down this path. Their leaders are convinced that they are powerful enough to ignore the constraints that other actors must accept. Realists not infrequently cite with seeming approval the famous line that Thucydides puts in the mouth of an Athenian general in the Melian Dialogue. In urging the Melians to submit he proclaims: "[T]he powerful do what they want, the weak what they must."[5] Thucydides intends the substitution of power for justice as a pathology and a demonstration of how far the Athenians have taken themselves outside the community of Greek city states because they believed they could gain more by escaping the restraints imposed by the web of reciprocal obligations in which they and other city states were embedded and rely more on force than persuasion.[6]

Thucydides' narrative makes clear just how catastrophic this super-ficially appealing strategy is in the longer term. Empires – or hegemo-nies – rely on bribes and coercion to keep others in line and succeed only last as long as they are needy and cowed. This kind of domination consumes resources at a prodigious rate. It also encourages – actually requires – further expansion to convince others of one's power and resolve. Overextension, resentful allies, opposing coalitions, declining resources, and ever more risky strategies for coping with these pro-blems, inevitably leads to defeat, if not collapse.[7]

Throughout history, great powers have behaved this way and have lost power and status in the process. Philip II of Spain, Louis XIV and Napoleon of France, Kaiser Wilhelm and Hitler in Nazi Germany all sought to conquer Europe. More recently, the Soviet Union and the United States behaved in an aggressive, albeit a more restrained way. The Soviet collapse did not come about through military defeat but through overextension and its political and economic costs. Soviet leaders engaged in a level of military spending the economy could not sustain and their Russification efforts further alienated restive popula-tions along their peripheries. Rebellion came from without and within; the countries of Eastern Europe overthrew their communist regimes and deserted the Warsaw Pact. In a parallel to Athens, a foreign military expedition – the invasion and occupation of Afghanistan – was the catalyst for the chain of events that led to implosion.

The United States has avoided catastrophe but has suffered a series of self-inflicted foreign policy defeats, most dramatically in Indochina and Iraq, but elsewhere as well. The USA has also squandered resources at a prodigious rate in its never-ending and inevitably unsuccessful search for hegemony and the license to police the world to enforce its interests and values. It is big enough and rich enough to have avoided the fate of Athens and the Soviet Union but has paid a vast economic price for doing so. Beyond the resources wasted, the armed force and defense industry draw large numbers of highly qualified and talented personnel away from economically productive activities. Even before Trump entered the White House, the USA was a living illustration of how interests cannot be formulated intelligently outside of a language of justice.

This self-destructive pattern is, of course, the classic narrative of hubris. It prompts leaders to embark on risky or even unrealistic ventures. Their miscalculations set in motion a chain of events that lead them to disaster. They often help to bring about this outcome by additional misjudgments. In the Melian Dialogue, the Athenians argue that restraint toward weaker actors will be seen as weakness by allies and encourage rebellion. This was a misplaced fear. The destruction of Melos appears to have made allies and neutral parties more resentful of Athens and more favorable to Sparta.

Since the beginning of the Cold War, the Americans have had a similar fixation on resolve. Thomas Schelling, author of one of the most influential studies of deterrence, emphasized the interdependent nature of commitments; failure to defend one of them, he insisted, will make willingness to defend any of the others questionable in the eyes of an adversary. "We tell the Soviets," a prominent deterrence theorist wrote in 1966, "that we have to react here because, if we did not, they would not believe us when we said that we will react there."[8] Such fears were greatly exaggerated, if not entirely misplaced. Ted Hopf examined Soviet reactions to thirty-eight cases of American intervention over a twenty-five year period of the Cold War and could not discover a single Soviet document that drew negative inferences about American resolve in Europe or northeast Asia. Janice Stein and I demonstrated that neither Khrushchev and his advisors nor Brezhnev and his ever doubted American credibility but rather considered the Americans rash, unpredictable, and aggressive. Khrushchev deployed missiles in Cuba secretly, even though Fidel Castro pleaded for a public deployment, because he was convinced that Kennedy would send out his navy to intercept or even sink the ships transporting the missiles to Cuba.[9]

Thucydides and the tragic playwrights hold that people or political units can only formulated interests intelligently as members of a community. Society makes life meaningful for them enabling affiliations, providing roles, and conferring status and authorizing pathways by which they can be achieved. Affiliations, roles, and statuses also provide identities. They, in turn, make possible the intelligent formulation of interests. People outside communities cannot realize their human potential. They are guided by their raw appetites and instrumental reason and constitute a danger to themselves and all those around them. In Thucydides' narrative, this is evident in the Athenian decision to invade Sicily. It is a foolhardy bid for domination of a distant island with at least one very powerful polis, motivated by greed, unchecked by any rational assessment of risk, and initiated while still at war with Sparta and its allies.

Tragedy emphasizes the extent to which individuals and their political units benefit from being embedded in communities. Affection and reflection combine to make them construct collective identities in addition to individual ones, and to pursue community as well as personal interests. They come to understand the two as at least in part coconstitutive and mutually reinforcing. The tragic understanding of the relationship of individuals to their societies is sharply at odds with post-Enlightenment liberalism that treats actors as autonomous, egoistic individuals. Ancient Greeks guided by a tragic view of life would rightly regard the concept of the autonomous, egoistic individual as a starting point for ethical consideration (for instance, rational choice, John Rawls) as an oxymoron, and a dangerous one at that.

Policymaking must accordingly take place in a broader setting. Leaders should consider the interests of their political unit or its leader in terms of the broader concerns, goals, and survival of the community that enables and sustains units or leaders and confers standing on them. For communities to prosper there must be opportunities for all members to satisfy to some degree their appetites and *thumos*. This all but rules out personal or foreign policy goals pursued at the expense of the community. To survive and prosper, communities foster rules and procedures from which they benefit and socialize actors to behave in accord with them. Those who do gain respect and others are more willing to follow their leadership. This by no means rules out attempting to change them, but by rule-based appeals rooted in shared understandings of justice.

Ancient Greeks wrote about the polis. Most of the city states about which we have evidence had thick civic cultures, although their norms sometimes broke down and conflicts between aristocrats and democrats could lead to civil war. In today's world, equal diversity exists when it comes to the political structure and culture of units, and, once again, regional and international societies are thinner than their domestic counterparts. The balance between narrow self-interest and community interests shifts toward the former in the absence of any meaningful regional community. However, pursuit of narrow interests is what keeps such regions from developing communities. Escaping this dilemma is one of the most difficult of all international problems.

Tragedy teaches us that conflict is inevitable because of clashing value systems and interests. Too firm a commitment to these values and interests and corresponding unwillingness to compromise or exercise restraint is almost certain to intensify conflict. The same is true with regard to conceptions of justice. The tragic view of life sensitizes us to the downside of our views of the world and ethical commitments. It makes us wary of arguments that there is an obvious and legitimate course of action, even only one legitimate course of action. The lack of readily discernible criteria to adjudicate competing conceptions of ethics and interests means that our convictions must be tempered with the recognition that others may reach different, equally defensible conclusions. Recognition of this truth might foster an understanding of why certain conflicts appear intractable, the dynamics by which they escalate, and the importance of self-restraint. To the extent that political actors come to see it as an appropriate frame of reference, it has the potential to foster a better understanding of the means by which the frequency and intensity of conflicts might be reduced.

Tragedy is a vehicle to develop and teach ethics and to promote discussion about what leads to a happier life. For the tragic poets, and for Plato, too, the first requirement of such a life was to avoid becoming a slave to one's appetites or craving for honor and status. For the poets, this is to be achieved by respecting nomos and imposing limits on one's ambitions. For Plato, it is the ability of reason to constrain and then educate appetite and *thumos* alike. Tragedy teaches the counterintuitive lesson that less is often more. At first blush, it seems ill-suited for an age in which excess of every kind has become the norm. Rich people in rich Western societies give evidence of being happier than those of poor, non-Western ones, but wealth alone does not appear to produce happiness.[10] People who attain wealth, power, or status often discover that they are no happier than before. This will almost certainly be the case when they measure their wealth or standing in relative terms, as there are always people who have more and deserve it less. The unrestrained pursuit of wealth, power, and status is not only self-defeating but may, in the end, prove pointless.

Tragedy is not all doom and gloom. It has a positive side, although that might strike some readers as something of a contradiction. Friedrich Nietzsche, the most interesting modern advocate of tragedy, thought we might turn the chaotic, unpredictable, and often tragic world to our advantage by embracing its instability. We should start with ourselves and the recognition that our so-called identities are a fiction. We are unstable because we are constantly in the process of becoming; the present is accordingly always being reborn.[11] Nietzsche insists that a tragic vision of life is a precondition of progress. As tragedy disappears from society, people became less capable of adjusting to change, recognizing their dependence on others, and of acting intentionally and ethically.[12]

Modernity

Modernity is a catchall phrase for a variety of developments that collectively have brought about a monumental change in the way in which people think about themselves and their relations to society.[13] Modernity created the individual and sought to free "him" – and belatedly, "her" – from all kinds of traditional constraint that were considered unreasonable barriers to freedom of choice. Neoliberalism is the latest and by far the most extreme version of this ideology. Especially in the West, people have increasingly come to mistake the ideology of the autonomous, egoistic actor for a reality. In economics and politics, they are taught to think this way by economics, public policy, political science, and international relations courses that take rational choice and game theory as their foundations. These approaches substitute a simple fiction for a complex reality and disregard the critical limitations imposed on self-interest by traditional liberal theories.[14] In the words of Sonia Amadae:

The no harm principle at the root of classical liberalism no longer, either in theory or practice, animates the action of rational actors who instead seek gain despite others. The concept of mutual benefit has yielded to the inevitability of winners and losers. Norm bound negotiation has given way to coercive bargaining. Financialization, risk management and algorithmic control replace the functional use of resources and technological innovations as the major engines of profit. Freedom, once rooted in self-determination and equality before the law, is reduced to individual choice as defined by one's willingness and ability to pay for a product or service.[15]

The legitimatization of narrowly formulated self-interest predisposes actors to formulate maximalist aims and take a confrontational – even a "take no prisoners" – attitude toward others. Such an approach maximizes conflict because it treats victory as an important end in its own right. Needless to say, it minimizes the value of rewarding "opponents" in any way that is not absolutely necessary, and by doing so destroys whatever comity exists and generates hostility. Rational choice and neoliberalism have the potential to make their atomized and conflictual view of social interactions self-fulfilling. So, too, does *Realpolitik*, its equivalent in foreign affairs.

These two ethical dimensions of policymaking are captured by Max Weber's famous distinction between the ethics of conviction (*Gesinnungsethik*) and that of responsibility (*Verantwortungsethik*). The former requires people to act in accord with their principles, regardless of the expected outcome. Weber disparages this ethic as an unaffordable luxury in a world in which force must sometimes be used for survival or important policy ends. "No ethics in the world," he reasons, "can get round the fact that the achievement of 'good' ends is in many cases tied to the necessity of employing morally dangerous means, and that one must reckon with the possibility or even likelihood of evil side-effects."[16] The ethic of responsibility, which directs attention to the consequences of one's behavior, is more appropriate to politics. Anybody who fails to recognize this truth, he asserts, "is indeed a child in political matters."[17]

Toward the end of his essay, Weber recognizes that both ethics are essential; that there are some actions that should be proscribed regardless of their perceived benefits. The two ethics are also inseparable in the sense that any evaluation of the consequences is a normative one and must be derived from the same values that would proscribe certain kinds of behavior. They are also linked in a second sense. The outcomes of policies are very hard to predict, and all the more so when they involve the use of violence. To the extent that they are unknown, there is good reason to fall back on the ethics of conviction.[18]

Many decisions based on the ethic of responsibility that led policymakers down catastrophic pathways share a common feature. The distinguishing feature of the German blank check to Austria, the German invasion of Belgium and unrestricted submarine warfare in the First World War, the Nazi attempt to conquer Europe and then the world, the Argentine invasion of the Falkland-Malvinas, Soviet intervention in Afghanistan, and the American invasions of Afghanistan and Iraq was the failure by initiators to develop a reasonable understanding of how those who were the targets of their policies were likely to respond.[19] These failures are ethical failures. They arise from a single-minded, egoistic, and counterproductive focus on one's self and country and its political problems and needs. Reasonable guesses about the likely outcomes of foreign policy initiatives require openness to others and their needs and problems and recognition that policy, whether domestic or foreign, occurs within a social setting whose rules and practices create a set of expectations. Ethics, and by extension, the ethics of conviction, lie at the core of the successful application of the ethics of responsibility.

I am not arguing that the ethics of conviction be given priority over the ethics of responsibility. Both ethics rest on considerations that are absolutely fundamental to good policymaking. They should be combined as stages of decisionmaking. The ethics of conviction should prompt leaders to reject outright certain goals and means as unacceptable for both moral and practical reasons. They contradict, even undermine, democratic and other values that they are trying to preserve or advance. Alternatively, because these goals or means violate nomos, laws, and national self-images, they provide openings for opponents to mobilize support by exposing the contradictions and hypocrisy of their adversary's foreign policy. Along these lines, Mervyn Frost and I have explored "ethical traps" that weaker parties set to entrap more powerful adversaries, often with telling effect.[20]

When leaders have settled on ethically acceptable goals and means they must evaluate their likely effectiveness. This assessment is not merely a practical one, guided by "efficiency," as most economists and public choice social scientists would insist. Efficient smuggles in a particular value: economic cost, or loss of life on your side in the case of war. These are only one kind of cost and, while always relevant, are not necessarily the most important. Here too, values are as central to the ethics of responsibility as they are to that of conviction. We must recognize that some values can only be defended or upheld at the cost of others. We need to identify and consider possible trade-offs before we defend or reject a policy on ethical or responsible grounds. With regard to goals, we must ask if they are realistic, necessary or merely advantageous, and the challenges and cost to which they attainment might lead. All aspects of this assessment process involve crystal ball gazing, and failure to get any one of them right can negate the value of the action. Failure makes whatever ethical costs were involved all the more unpalatable.

Difficult and costly choices are a defining feature of tragedy. Do we, for example, allocate money to combatting breast cancer or prostate cancer? If we have a finite sum to allocate and it cannot adequately support both kinds of research, some people will inevitably suffer. There are many tragic choices to be confronted in political and foreign policy, some of them obvious advances and others much less so. They often involve a trade-off between different ethical end and between ethical standards and policy objectives. These trade-offs are most challenging when we are trying to safeguard ourselves against loss; in this context, we are most likely to consider policies at odds with our ethics. These are the very situations in which any trade-offs are likely to be biased in favor of downgrading ethical costs and upgrading the benefits of policies. As rigorous and effective assessments are difficult, even impossible to make, due to the inability to see into the future, we cannot rely on them to act as any kind of meaningful restraint. This makes the ethics of conviction all the more appropriate and important.

This discussion of Weber, and my book as a whole, leads me to close on a sobering note. The commitment to ethical policymaking and foreign policy is emotionally and intellectual challenging. It requires courage, a willingness to reconsider positions to which you may be committed, and recognition that even the most carefully considered policies can leave to undesired and costly outcomes. The challenging nature of ethical policymaking and foreign policy discourages many leaders from behaving this way. So does its potential to unsettle us in the most fundamental ways by demanding that we question what we take to be our firmest personal and political anchors. These difficulties do not detract from the fact that ethical policies are more likely to be successful policies and provide early warning about those that are not working out as planned.

Can we and our leaders rise to the challenge?

Notes

1. Richard Ned Lebow, *A Democratic Foreign Policy* (New York: Palgrave-Macmillan, 2019) for the strongest statement of this position.
2. François de la La Rochefoucauld, *The Maxims,* trans. Louis Kronenberger (New York: Stackpole, 1936), no. 218.
3. Committee on Intelligence, US Senate, *Report of the Senate Select Committee on Senate Select Committee on Intelligence Committee Study of the Central Intelligence Agency's Detention and Interrogation Program,* December 9, 2014, www.intelligence.senate.gov/sites/default/f iles/publications/CRPT-113srpt288.pdf (accessed December 7, 2019); John W. Schiemann, *Does torture Work?* (New York: Oxford University Press, 2015); Shane O'Mara, *Why Torture Doesn't Work: The Neuroscience of Interrogation* (Cambridge: Harvard University Press, 2015).
4. T. D. Allman, *Rogue State: America at War with the World* (New York: Nation Books, 2004); Robert Litwak, *Rogue States and U.S. Foreign Policy: Containment after the Cold War* (Washington: Woodrow Wilson Center Press, 2000); Robert I. Rotberg, *Worst of the Worst: Dealing with Repressive and Rogue Nations* (Washington: World Peace Foundation, 2007); Richard Ned Lebow, *National Identifications and International Relations* (Cambridge: Cambridge University Press, 2016), ch. 6.
5. Robert B. Strassler, ed., *The Landmark Thucydides: A Comprehensive Guide to the Peloponnesian War* (New York: Free Press, 1996), Book 5, pp. 84–116.
6. Richard Ned Lebow, *The Tragic Vision of Politics: Ethics, Interests, and Orders* (Cambridge: Cambridge University Press, 2003), chs. 3–4.
7. Ibid.
8. Thomas Schelling, *Arms and Influence* (New Haven: Yale University Press, 1966), p. 55.
9. Ted Hopf, *Deterrence Theory and American Foreign Policy in the Third World, 1965–1990* (Ann Arbor: University of Michigan Press, 1994); Daryl G. Press, *Calculating Credibility: How Leaders Assess Military*

Threats (Ithaca: Cornell University Press, 2007); Richard Ned Lebow and Janice Gross Stein, *We All Lost the Cold War* (Princeton: Princeton University Press, 1994), pp. 10–11.

10. Ronald F. Inglehart, *Cultural Evolution: People's Motivations Are Changing and Reshaping the World* (Cambridge: Cambridge University Press, 2018).

11. Friedrich Nietzsche, *The Will to Power*, trans. Walter Kaufmann and R. J. Hollindale (New York: Random House, 1967), p. 417.

12. Friedrich Nietzsche, *The Birth of Tragedy* and *the Case of Wagner*, trans. Walter Kaufmann (New York: Random House, 1967), pp. 17–18, 59–60, 84, 96–8.

13. Bernard Yack, *The Fetishism of Modernities: Epochal Self-Consciousness in Contemporary Social and Political Thought* (Notre Dame: University of Notre Dame Press, 1997).

14. S. M. Amadae, *Rationalizing Capitalist Democracy: The Cold War Origins of Rational Choice Liberalism* (Chicago: University of Chicago Press, 2003) and *Prisoners of Reason: Game Theory and Neoliberal Political Economy* (Cambridge: Cambridge University Press, 2016).

15. Amadae, *Prisoners of Reason*, p. xvi.

16. Weber, "Profession and Vocation of Politics," in Peter Lassman and Ronald Speirs, *Weber: Political Writings* (Cambridge: Cambridge University Press, 2000), pp. 309–69.

17. Ibid.

18. For an analysis and critique of Weber's essay, Richard Ned Lebow, "Max Weber's Ethics," *International Political Theory*, web version published in July 2019, https://doi.org/10.1177/1755088219854780.

19. In some instances (for instance, the carpet bombing of Dresden, firebombing of Tokyo, nuclear bombing of Hiroshima and Nagasaki), target actors were too weak to resist or retaliate.

20. Mervyn Frost and Richard Ned Lebow, "Ethical Traps," *International Relations* 33, 2 (2019), pp. 1–20.

Index